# STAR TREK®
## THE ORIGINAL SERIES

## THE JANUS GATE

# STAR TREK®
## THE ORIGINAL SERIES

## THE JANUS GATE

PRESENT TENSE

FUTURE IMPERFECT

PAST PROLOGUE

# L.A. GRAF

SF BC®

SCIENCE FICTION

PRESENT TENSE  Copyright © 2002 by Paramount Pictures.
All Rights Reserved.
Printing History: Pocket Books paperback June 2002

FUTURE IMPERFECT  Copyright © 2002 by Paramount Pictures.
All Rights Reserved.
Printing History: Pocket Books paperback June 2002

PAST PROLOGUE Copyright © 2002 by Paramount Pictures.
All Rights Reserved.
Printing History: Pocket Books paperback July 2002

First SFBC Science Fiction Printing: September 2002

Published by arrangement with:
Pocket Books
A division of
Simon & Schuster Inc.
1230 Avenue of the Americas
New York, New York 10020

ISBN 0-7394-2854-3

Visit our website at *http://www.sfbc.com*

Visit Pocket Books's website at *http://www.simonsays.com/startrek/*

PRINTED IN THE UNITED STATES OF AMERICA.

# Contents

# THE JANUS GATE

## PRESENT TENSE

# Chapter One

THE GREAT STARSHIP TREMBLED, frame and struts wailing in distress as she careened into her own attenuated warp field. Behind her, the ice-blue sphere of Psi 2000 shattered like a bursting bubble, filling the *Enterprise*'s main viewscreen with glittering fragments that evaporated almost as soon as they were made. A planet in its death throes, chasing after a starship who just might be dying herself.

James Kirk gripped the arms of his command chair so hard his hands hurt. He'd never heard a ship howl like this before. As many times as he'd pushed this girl to her limits—and sometimes beyond—he'd never truly, in his heart, believed for a moment that she could fail him. But he'd also never imploded a small universe inside her belly, never sling-shotted all hundred tons of her through a dying planet's gravity well and flung her back out into space. Never felt her surge so convulsively ahead of herself as the fabric of space all around her thinned, stretched, twisted into a bright spinning whiteness that teetered just on the edge of comprehension—

Then, just that suddenly, it was over.

Kirk felt as though he bolted awake from a dream. Solidity returned with an almost audible *pop!,* and all around him his bridge crew stirred at their stations, casting half-glances at each other and touching the edges of panels and screens to make sure they were really still there.

Kirk forced himself to uncurl his grip on the command chair and straighten his shoulders. No matter how distracted the crew might seem by their duties, they would be aware of their captain's mood, just as he was always aware of theirs. They didn't need to sense any uncertainty in their commander after the chaos they'd all suffered these last few days. The movement made his upper arm throb where McCoy had only moments ago injected him with a dose of antiviral serum as he came aboard the bridge. Not for the first time, he wished the doctor hadn't ripped open his uniform sleeve to administer the injection. Sitting bare-shouldered in front of the crew made him feel ill-kempt and undignified.

"Are you all right, Jim?"

Kirk glanced aside at Spock, worried for just an instant that the Vulcan had somehow sensed his spasm of insecurity. He sketched a self-conscious nod as his first officer stepped up to the arm of the command chair. "You?"

The Vulcan paused a moment, as if it had only occurred to him to consider his condition because his captain asked. Then he nodded as well. A blur of surreal light still throbbed at the center of the viewscreen, and the ship beneath them thrummed in dangerous sympathy.

"We found a cure." McCoy, out of Kirk's view behind the shoulder of the command chair, sounded definitive but grim. As though his intellect knew this to be true, but his emotions weren't quite so sure despite the empty hypospray in his hands. "We're over that part of it."

It was the only part McCoy could influence, not to mention the part that had first gotten them into this mess. Kirk didn't have the heart to tell the doctor that developing an antiviral inoculation to counteract the infection they'd brought up from Psi 2000 was probably the least of their worries now. He still hadn't moved his eyes from the viewscreen, where blurred light had replaced the usual streaming view of stars, almost as if they had somehow all congealed into that formless glow. At first, Kirk thought the viewscreen had sustained some unspecific damage in their flight from the dying planet, ruining its ability to show them the space outside. Then a single spinning star, coiled almost like a tiny galaxy, peeled away from the mass and slid swiftly underneath their bow. That was when Kirk realized he *was* seeing the space outside, twisted until it was unrecognizable.

"Obviously, we were successful." Spock no doubt read Kirk's thoughts on the captain's all-too-expressive human face. His own face was impassive, dark eyes flicking over the maelstrom outside as though counting every misplaced star. "The engines imploded."

*Unless what we're racing toward is the afterlife.* Only minutes before, they'd been screaming through Psi 2000's upper atmosphere, plummeting toward the planet's disintegrating surface with half the ship's crew incapacitated by a neurogenic virus for which they hadn't yet devised a cure. One of those infected crewmen had shut down the ship's main reactor hours before, for reasons known only to his own fevered imaginings. The engines had been left powerless, her matter/antimatter cores too cold to ignite by the time Chief Engineer Scott discovered the full extent of what had been done. If they didn't want to end up just another cloud of detritus amid the planetary rubble, they had to be willing to dare a drastic gamble.

Theory said they could throw matter and antimatter together without the usual quantum physics introductions, so long as there existed a magnetic bottle of such perfect mathematical shape that the resultant explosion could be turned back in upon itself, collapsed into a microsecond's singularity, and all of its raging energy channeled into a reactor ready to cast it back out again in an instananeous leap to light speed.

"It's never been done," Spock had objected when Kirk explained the plan to him.

As far as Kirk knew, no one had ever pulled a 190,000-ton starship out of a planetary nosedive before, either, but that wouldn't stop him from trying. "We might go up in the biggest ball of fire since the last sun in these parts exploded, but we've got to take that one in ten thousand chance that we'll succeed."

And taking that minuscule chance had flung them here. Wherever "here" was.

"Captain!" Sulu twisted around at the helm, straining to look at Kirk and his panel all at the same time. His face was still drawn and pale in the aftermath of viral infection. "My velocity gauge is off the scale!"

Kirk leaned forward, hands clenched, and flashed keen eyes across Sulu's console. He couldn't see the numbers, but the play of lights across the panel told their own story.

"Engine power went off the scale, as well," Spock told the captain as the readouts began to fall into some kind of strange sense in Kirk's mind. "We are now traveling faster than is possible for normal space."

Faster than Kirk had dreamed possible, even at warp speeds. Middle-school conundrums inspired by Einstein, Hawking, and Cochrane came rushing back like a badly distorted echo, and he heard himself saying, "Check elapsed time, Mr. Sulu," before his conscious mind even realized why he wanted to know.

Yet, somehow, he wasn't entirely surprised by the shock in his young helmsman's face when Sulu complied. "My chronometer's running... *backwards,* sir..."

Of course it was. Kirk settled back into his command chair with a slow nod. They'd performed the impossible intermix, flooded the engines with nearly infinite power, and roared away from Psi 2000 in full reverse. Back the way they'd come. "A time warp. We're going backward in time." Kirk's agile mind was already racing through the implications, rehearsing how he would word his report to Starfleet Command, worrying about just how much he should tell them, then feeling guilty when his first instinct was to withhold as much of the details of how they accomplished this as he could. Starfleet itself could be trusted with the knowledge, of course, but if anyone else ever found out about it and gained the ability to travel through time, changing the past and destroying the future, there was no telling where the havoc would end.

Kirk dragged himself back to the moment. He wouldn't have to worry about explaining anything to Starfleet if they didn't first shake loose from their accidental time slip. He thought about the trajectory Spock and Scotty had so carefully planned for their slingshot around Psi 2000, and about the surge in engine power *Enterprise* had experienced just following her warp core implosion. "Helm, begin reversing power." Sometimes, the most obvious course of action looked that way for a reason.

Sulu's nimble hands flew across his panel. Kirk understood the basics of the language his pilot used to coax the ship to his bidding, but had never met anyone who employed it so instinctively and well. A dim sense of movement, so ghostly it was almost a sound, slid along the length of the vessel in response to Sulu's commands. The distorted image on the main screen bled a few microns closer to resolution; the moment felt suddenly less attenuated, tasted faintly of metal and ozone. When Kirk felt some unexpected resistance buck through the ship's frame, he startled more sharply than he intended. "Slowly," he reminded Sulu through clenched teeth.

The helmsman had the grace not to glance away from his work. "Helm answering, sir," he reported in his usual steady, professional tone. "Power reversing."

The blurry corona on the forward screen seemed to throb, draw inward like the fiery heart of an event horizon, then folded so swiftly in on itself that its brightness snuffed into black like a candle flame in the fist of a god. With an almost bashful slowness, individual stars blossomed one-by-one across the fresh darkness. Tiny diamonds in red, blue, and yellow, washed over by the familiar gauzy veil of the Milky Way.

Spock had gone back to his science station, and was bending intently over his viewer. Kirk heard McCoy release an unsteady breath from behind him, and wondered how long the doctor had been holding it.

"We're back to normal time, Captain," Spock announced, somewhat unnecessarily.

Kirk nodded absently. The stars were too comforting to turn away from just now. "Engines ahead." He was a little surprised at how relaxed he sounded. As though he accidentally hurled his ship backward in time every day. "Warp one."

"Warp one, sir," Sulu echoed.

And just that simply, they were back to business as usual. Kirk almost thought he *could* take the ship through time every day, and his crew would follow without question as long as their captain said everything would be okay. It was a frightening power to hold over them all, but a reassuring one, as well.

"Mr. Spock..." He finally pulled his gaze away from the viewscreen, knowing that its return to a familiar starscape didn't solve the problem of where—and when—they were.

"Yes, sir."

"The time warp—" Kirk swivelled the command chair to face Spock as the science officer descended the steps from his station. "What did it do to us?"

"We've regressed in time seventy-one hours." Then he elaborated, as though the humans listening to him might not appreciate the full impact of what they'd done. "It is now three days ago, Captain. We have three days to live over again."

Thinking about the mental and physical anguish Scott's engine implosion had only barely wrenched them free of, Kirk had to suppress a sudden urge to laugh. "Not those *last* three days." Why was it that you were never given the opportunity to relive your three best days of shore leave? Was that part of the price Fate extracted for letting humans pull off such outrageous feats as time travel to begin with?

"This does open some intriguing prospects, Captain." Spock's brows knit into what would have been a worried frown for anyone else. "Since the formula worked, we can go back in time. To any planet, any era." Apparently, his own imagination had finally begun to catch up to Kirk's.

"We may risk it some day, Mr. Spock." Kirk hadn't forgotten the misgivings that had swept over him when they first realized what they'd done. "Resume course to our next destination, Mr. Sulu."

"Course laid in, sir."

"Steady as she goes."

Lingering beside Kirk's command chair, Spock stirred. "Captain, if I may..."

"Is there a problem, Mr. Spock?"

Spock seemed to seriously consider his captain's question before answering, even though his hesitation lasted barely a heartbeat. "Potential complications," he finally said. Another brief pause that Kirk suspected no one but he actually noticed. "Given our current situation, continuing on to our next destination may be ill advised."

McCoy gave a little snort from behind Kirk. "You've got something against arriving early?"

Spock lifted his eyebrows in a semblance of Vulcan surprise. "Indeed, Doctor, arriving early is precisely the problem." He turned his attention back toward Kirk, tacitly more concerned with his captain's understanding than with the doctor's. "We are presently at stardate 1704. Again. According to Starfleet—according to history—the *Enterprise*'s next scheduled destination is Psi 2000 for the retrieval of the geological survey team."

"So if we show up three days early for our rendezvous with the *Antares,* there will be questions about why we aren't where we're supposed to be." Just as it had when he first realized what they'd done, Kirk's agile mind immediately leapt through the tangle of implications.

"Questions," Spock stressed, "which would be received—and answered—by two separate *Enterprise*s, the first with no knowledge of the second."

McCoy shrugged, twisting the empty serum vial off the hypospray in his hands. "So we explain the situation, tell Starfleet what happened." He fitted the vial back into the medikit at his hip.

"Except we didn't." Kirk waited while McCoy frowned, then stilled as the doctor began to realize where the conversation was going. "We went to Psi 2000, Bones. We stayed there through the destruction of the planet, and we never once heard from Starfleet. Not about *Enterprise* being out of position, not about anything. Which means either something happens to us now, and we never make the early rendezvous with the *Antares*—"

"Or we never tried to make the early rendezvous in the first place." McCoy rubbed his mouth thoughtfully.

Kirk clapped him on the shoulder in an effort to lighten the mood. "I know which of those two options I'd prefer." But he was serious about his concern, despite his wry smile.

"So we do what?" The doctor looked between Kirk and Spock with a scowl the captain recognized as being worried frustration rather than the irritation it resembled. "Hang out in deep space and hope nobody stumbles across us?" He gave an almost petulant grunt. "Seems like an awful waste of three perfectly good days."

"I don't see why being displaced in time should mean we have to waste any." Kirk stood to lean over the railing between his command chair and Spock's station. "Mr. Spock, we left a planetary survey team back in the Tlaoli system, in sector alpha nineteen."

Spock nodded slowly. "They are scheduled for retrieval immediately after our rendezvous with the *Antares.*" Kirk had a feeling his first officer already knew where he was heading.

"I'm sure they'll be delighted to have a little company for the next three days. And limiting ourselves to planetside research on a previously uncharted planet—" Not to mention a little judicious shore leave.

"—ought to minimize our potential impact on the timestream. Wouldn't you say?"

Spock crossed his arms in what might have been Vulcan displeasure, but the curious arch of his eyebrows made his expression hard to quantify. "It could be argued that our very existence at this moment in time has already altered history in ways we cannot yet recognize. Therefore, any action we take—even inaction—unavoidably impacts the current timestream."

McCoy made a wry face. "And if a butterfly flaps its wings in Tibet?"

Spock frowned and cocked his head, obviously ready to address the doctor's apparent non sequitur, but Kirk stepped between them to head the discussion off. "Unfortunately, we can't go back and take ourselves out of this timestream," he said to Spock, "so we have to work with what we've got."

"True," his first officer conceded. "Then no doubt sequestering ourselves on Tlaoli 4 is our most . . . productive option." He said "productive" as though congenitally incapable of understanding the human need for almost constant activity.

Kirk had a feeling he'd have no choice but to get used to it if he planned on staying with Kirk for the next five years. "Mr. Sulu, set course for Tlaoli, warp four."

"Aye, aye, sir."

Kirk settled back into his command chair as the ship beneath him began the purring hum up to warp speed. He could feel something subtly amiss, a deep trembling in her bowels that hadn't been there three days ago . . . three days from now. . . . Something else for Scott to work on while they bided their time at Tlaoli, and while Kirk assessed the rest of their damage, physical and otherwise.

"I don't see what he's so worried about," McCoy grumbled, coming to lean his elbows on the back of Kirk's chair as the ship got under way. "How much damage can we possibly do to history in just three days?"

Kirk gave a dark little laugh and rubbed at the knot in his shoulder where the antiviral shot still stung. "I think that's exactly what he's worried about, Bones."

"*Enterprise* to Tlaoli Base One. Come in, Base One."

Only silence answered Uhura's standard hail. She frowned, then got a firm grip on her overactive imagination and reminded herself that they were no longer at Psi 2000. The bridge crew behind her wasn't giggling or ranting or threatening to commit suicide—they had all been inoculated against the alien virus, and the ones most affected, such as Sulu and Riley, had been sent down to sickbay for an in-depth toxin screen and some much-needed rest. Even with second-shift officers such as Stiles and Leslie at navigation and helm, the ship's command center had regained its usual quiet efficiency. And for further reassurance, all Uhura had to do was glance sideways at the viewscreen.

The sunlit planet that the *Enterprise* had just swung into orbit around wasn't silver-blue and quivering with tectonic instability. It was old and brown and done with life, worn down to nothing but dusty grasslands and rocky karst plains and thick rims of saltwater swamp around its drying oceans. It revolved around an ordinary yellow star and was accompanied by an ordinary natural satellite about half the size of Earth's moon. The only thing unusual about Tlaoli 4 was the rose-quartz tinge of its atmosphere, caused by the high load of windblown iron oxides and garnet dust. The planetary assessment team had assured them there was nothing strange or dangerous about that. It just meant that the landing parties would see some spectacular sunsets.

Uhura knew perfectly well that this placid little planet had been given the highest safety rating possible, which was why the *Enterprise* had left its landing teams behind while it had gone on to its rendezvous with Psi 2000. There was no hint of peril in the humming silence of her open communicator channel, either, she told herself bracingly. With only a few scientists assigned to each of the three planetary survey teams—and only a few days available for them to describe and catalog as much as they could of an entire planet—the probability of someone sitting at the main communications panel when she hailed was pretty remote. She closed the first base camp's channel and instead scanned through the frequency distributions of the communicators she'd assigned to the fifteen members of the landing party. She had bracketed the ranges so that each team overlapped only with its own members. That made it a fairly easy task to select multiple communicator addresses for her next hail.

"*Enterprise* to Tlaoli Survey Team One." She watched rainbows of subspace frequencies replicate across her board as the communications computer automatically generated the multiple hail. "Come in, Technician Fisher, Lieutenants Boma, Kulessa, and Kelowitz."

The reply came back so fast that Uhura thought she could still hear the hiss of the hand communicator being snapped open. "Fisher here," said a startled voice. "*Enterprise,* are you in system?"

"Yes, we arrived early. Captain Kirk thought—"

"Is the captain on the bridge?" Fisher cut across her explanation with much more urgency than politeness.

"Affirmative." Uhura swung away from her panel and caught the bright hazel glance that immediately darted her way. In the months she'd served under James T. Kirk, Uhura had come to depend on her captain's attentiveness to his bridge crew so much that she had internalized it into her own actions. A slight turn of her head and shoulder would get her noticed in a moment or two, whenever Kirk finished signing orders or conferring with his line officers. A more complete swing got her a quicker look, and a rapid pivot always got his full, focused attention. "Captain, Geological Technician Fisher of Survey Team One needs to speak with you."

"Put him through," Kirk said, and Uhura toggled the open communicator channel into the main bridge speaker. "Report, Mr. Fisher."

"We've got a problem, Captain." One thing Kirk had successfully pounded into his crew over the past year was to waste no time with regulation greetings in times of crisis. "Actually, we have several problems, sir, but the most urgent one is that we've lost touch with Survey Team Three."

Kirk frowned across the bridge at Spock. "Where was Team Three assigned?"

The Vulcan Science Officer opened his mouth, then clamped it shut again and tapped a query into his science panel. The chaotic frenzy of their visit to Psi 2000 had apparently erased even his supernaturally good memory of what the different Tlaoli landing parties had been sent down to do.

Before he could respond, Fisher answered for him through the com channel. "That was the cave exploration team, Captain. They were originally set down on that big karst plateau in the southern continent, but yesterday we flew them up to check on a smaller karst terrain in the northern continent, due west of where the wetland team is stationed."

Kirk's frown deepened. "Why did you reassign Team Three's location, Mr. Fisher? I believe your standing orders were to stay near your base camps until the *Enterprise* returned."

"Yes, sir, I know." There was a pause and a mutter of inaudible conversation in the background behind Fisher, as if his fellow scientists were suggesting things for him to say. Uhura could hear the geologist take a deep breath and plunge back into speech as if speed could somehow make his confession less painful. "Captain, we did disobey our standing orders. But it was because of what we found down here after the *Enterprise* left the system. We were afraid there might be a safety risk, sir, to the ship."

"A safety risk to the research shuttle you took down to the planet's surface, Mr. Fisher?"

"No, sir," the geologist said firmly. "A safety risk to the *Enterprise*."

Uhura glanced over her shoulder in surprise at the drab brown planet on the viewscreen, but saw nothing more threatening on its ancient and worn surface than she had a few minutes ago. She noticed Captain Kirk gazing up at Tlaoli with a similar look of incomprehension. When he spoke, however, his voice held none of the doubt that was so clearly expressed on his face. A good commander like Kirk never passed premature judgement on his crew's decisions, especially when they were on the surface and he was still on board.

"What made you think the *Enterprise* might be in danger, Mr. Fisher?"

The geologist paused to listen to another advisory murmur of voices behind him. "Sir, we think you and Mr. Spock should see this for yourselves. Request permission to uplink our visual tricorder's data buffer through my communicator to the main viewscreen."

Kirk lifted an eyebrow at Uhura, and she nodded back at him while her fingers danced across the communications panel, widening the bandwidth she'd assigned to Fisher's handheld communicator so it wouldn't choke on the much thicker flow of a visual record. "Permission granted. Spock, make sure we get this in the main computer log."

The Vulcan science officer gave his captain the kind of austere look that said the command had been unnecessary, but all he replied was, "Aye, sir."

There was a pause as the data stream from the planet spooled itself into the viewscreen's buffer, then the dusty little planet abruptly vanished. It was replaced by a much more grainy image of sand dunes rippling into the horizon. The image panned slowly to the right, over a long, pale scar where a lake or sea had dried up into what looked like endless salt flats, then paused a moment before zooming in to focus on an anomalous patch of darkness in the midst of all that white. The tricorder continued to increase its magnification until each pixel of the image covered a hand's width of the viewscreen. Even with that lack of resolution, Uhura could clearly see the intricate lines and curves of something unnatural, some shape that had been constructed rather than deposited or eroded.

"Alien ruins?" Kirk said to Spock.

The science officer lifted an eyebrow at the confusing angles and lines now frozen on the screen, waiting for the next spool of data to be received. "That would not be impossible, Captain, but I admit that it would surprise me. Our initial long-range surveys of Tlaoli indicated that its ecosystems have been incapable of sustaining animal life for several millions of years. Very few structures, whether natural or constructed, can withstand surface erosion for that long."

"So we don't know if the planet was ever occupied?"

"On the contrary," Spock said, with the sidelong look of reproof he saved for what he considered particularly egregious leaps of illogic. "Our preliminary studies detected an anomalous lack of near-surface metal deposits, and absolutely no trace of fossil fuels or enriched nuclear isotopes anywhere in the upper crust. Based on that, we assumed that an alien race did indeed occupy Tlaoli once, millions of years ago, but left when its resources became exhausted and its ecosystems began to collapse."

"Or went extinct," Kirk said wryly. "So what the hell is *that?*"

Uhura glanced over her shoulder again. The still image on the screen rippled and was replaced by another, sharper image obviously taken at much closer range. She could clearly make out the smooth curves of the main hemispherical structure rising from the salt deposits of the former lake. Whatever it was, it looked to Uhura as if the lake had actually dried up around it, embedding the lower parts completely in its evaporated deposits. The tricorder image scanned a little further along, then paused to focus in on two dark towers rising from the salt flats in the background. It took her a minute to recognize them as the ends of pointed fins that looked unmistakably like shorter and bulkier versions of the *Enterprise*'s warp nacelles.

"Captain, that's a ship!" said Lieutenant Leslie from the helm, startled out of his usual phlegmatic silence.

"And it's not an atmospheric shuttle, either," Kirk agreed grimly. "It looks like a deep space vessel. Spock, can the computer identify its origin based on the design?"

The science officer tapped a quick inquiry into his computer monitor and watched the results flicker across his screen at rates faster than any human could have absorbed. "It appears similar to the starships constructed by ancient civilizations we know from the galactic core, Captain, but it cannot be assigned to any known race or planet."

"Hmm." Kirk watched the image until it flickered and disappeared, replaced once again by the undistinguished brown disk that was Tlaoli 4. "Was that the end of the tricorder transmission, Lieutenant Uhura?"

"Aye, sir." She shrank the communicator's data feed back down to the optimum range for voice transmission. "Survey Team One should be back on line now, Captain."

"Mr. Fisher," said Kirk crisply. "Where and when did you find that ship?"

"About fifty kilometers from our base camp, sir, two days after you left the system. It *is* a starship, isn't it?"

"We think so," Kirk agreed. "But starships have been known to crash on planets for lots of reasons, Mr. Fisher. It might have been shot down in some kind of war, or been forced to land by a mechanical systems failure. It doesn't necessarily mean the planet it landed on is dangerous."

The geologist's answer came back so readily that Uhura knew he must have anticipated Kirk's remark. "That's what we thought, too, sir, when we first saw it. We didn't even go any closer to look at it, we just marked it on our survey sheets for a later archeological survey to examine. But after we found the other remains, we started to wonder—"

"Other remains?" Kirk demanded. "Of other starships?"

"Yes, sir." Fisher paused, and this time there wasn't so much as a whisper of voices to be heard in the background. The explanation for the Survey Team's violated orders had obviously reached a crucial stage. "We were doing a geophysical survey of the salt flats, Captain, when we first spotted that thing, so we knew what its electromagnetic signature looked like. And for the next two days, we kept seeing what looked like that same signature over and over again, but it was always deep below ground so we couldn't be sure. Then we started surveying the smaller karst plateau on the northern continent, and we could actually see down to where the signature was coming from, at the bottom of a couple sinkholes. A lot of them weren't very well preserved, and none of them looked the same as any of the others, but they were all definitely spaceships." Fisher paused to take a deep breath. "Sir, I know it sounds unbelievable...but including the signatures we detected under the salt deposits, we think at least nineteen different starships have crashed down here on Tlaoli."

# Chapter Two

THE BRIDGE OF THE *Enterprise* was never truly silent, with the white background noise of the ship's life-support systems overlain by the clicks and taps of crew members interacting with their various data stations. But there were times, like now, when the bridge crew seemed to take a collective breath in such unison that Kirk felt as if silence had abruptly descended.

*Spock was right,* he thought, a bit wearily. *We should have hidden out in deep space and just waited for the rest of the universe to catch up to our timeline.* But even as he thought it, he knew that a three-day delay in arriving at Tlaoli wouldn't have helped the situation. If the *Enterprise* had arrived three days from now to find the landing parties so distressed and the cave survey team missing for nearly a week, Kirk would never have forgiven himself for twiddling his thumbs in safety only a few light-years away.

Still, the thought of plunging back into danger only a few hours after their escape from Psi 2000 was more than Kirk had hoped to ask from his crew.

But the *Enterprise* was on a deep-space mission, and everyone on board her had been forced to learn how to weather one crisis after another without losing focus or succumbing to fear. After only a moment of dismayed silence, the bridge crew went back steadfastly to their monitors and station displays. Kirk saw Uhura run what she probably meant to be a discreet safety check on her station, even as she filtered a faint hiss of encroaching static from Fisher's signal.

"Very well, Mr. Fisher." It was the standard acknowledgment to a subordinate's report, but Kirk tried to make it sound no more formal or full of tension than a simple "so far, so good." "I see why you thought there might be a problem. But I still don't understand why you moved Team Three to a new location."

"Our spatial analysis showed an unusual concentration of wrecks in and around the northern karst terrain, Captain." Fisher launched into his explanation with an ease that made Kirk suspect he appreciated his captain's calm reaction to the news. "Lieutenant Boma's wetland survey team had noticed a lot of subspace static interfering with their tricorder readings whenever they got close to that same area, so we suspected that the karst dissolution had allowed some kind of late-stage ore deposit to form there. That could have concentrated enough transperiodic elements like dilithium or trifluorine to generate a natural subspace aperture." The geologist's voice had taken on the slightly pedantic rhythm of a researcher who was already forming his hypothesis into a potential scientific paper. "A natural subspace anomaly like that was found on the dilithium-enriched asteroid that started the prospecting rush in Beta Carinae back in 2204. It's been suggested by several recent studies that the same kinds of deposits might explain places where things have mysteriously disappeared through time, like the Bermuda Triangle back on Earth—"

"We observed no evidence of either transperiodic elements or subspace radiation in our preliminary surveys of this planet, Mr. Fisher." Spock cut across the scientist's theorizing with the relentless cool only Vulcans could manage. "In fact, Tlaoli 4 was determined by the planetary assessment team to be singularly lacking in anything resembling either an ore deposit or a power source."

The pedantry in Fisher's voice vanished, replaced by a more apologetic tone. "I realize that, Mr. Spock. But it was the only thing we could think of to explain how an uninhabited planet could knock a starship out of orbit. According to the Rogers-Kline-Roth hypothesis, a transperiodic ore deposit *could* interfere with sensor readings enough to explain why it often goes undetected."

Spock lifted a disdainful eyebrow, glancing toward Kirk as though assuming the captain shared his assessment of Fisher's hypothesis. "I do not believe that either Professor Rogers-Kline or Professor Roth understands the physics of six-dimensional space sufficiently well to make any prediction about possible sensor interference, much less one that so conveniently explains away their lack of evidence—"

Kirk did his best to smother a tired grin. "Gentlemen." The situation wasn't particularly funny—nothing about the prospect of losing an entire survey team, not to mention his starship, struck Kirk as something to laugh about. Yet he could never help being at least a little amused by the deadly seriousness with which scientists could debate the least important details of any crisis. "I suggest you continue this academic discussion after we've made sure that Survey Team Three is safely accounted for." Spock closed his mouth obediently, no doubt bookmarking the next sentence in his argument for later retrieval. Kirk turned his attention back to the now-silent geologist on the other end of the com channel. "Mr. Fisher, I'm still waiting to hear why you disobeyed orders and moved Team Three."

"Yes, sir." Fisher paused to clear his throat uncertainly. "We did try hailing the *Enterprise* at Psi 2000, Captain, to tell you about what we'd found and to get updated orders, but no one answered. Since we didn't really have a ranking officer on Tlaoli, we got all the lieutenants together by communicator and took a vote on what to do. It was unanimous, sir. We decided to move the six members of the karst team up to the northern continent and have them explore the cave closest to most of the wrecks, to see if they could verify whether there was a large transperiodic ore deposit there."

Kirk glanced over at his science officer, whose narrow Vulcan face had been growing steadily more somber as he listened to the geologist's report. "What's the matter, Spock?"

The Vulcan's eyes snapped back into focus from their pensive stare. "I have been scanning the entire northern karst terrain with long-range sensors since Mr. Fisher first reported that Survey Team Three had been sent there, Captain," he said quietly. "I have not detected any trace of life, either on or beneath the surface."

"That's exactly the problem, Mr. Spock." Fisher spoke a bit more loudly, as though taking the volume of Spock's voice to mean the science officer had moved farther away from the com station. "None of our scanners have been able to see anything under that karst terrain, either, not since about four hours ago."

Kirk nodded, starting to do the math in his head. "Was that when you last made contact with the cave team, Mr. Fisher?"

"Yes, sir. They entered the caves seven hours ago, and were reporting on their progress hourly. The last time we talked to them, they mentioned having some problems with their tricorders, so when we didn't hear from them an hour later we figured maybe they were having communicator problems as well."

"That's something we should be able to verify." Kirk caught up Uhura's gaze with his own. "Lieutenant, try to punch through to Survey Team Three's communicators. With the power of the *Enterprise*'s signal generator and receiver, we might be able to pick up something Mr. Fisher's handheld communicator couldn't."

"I'll try, sir." Uhura turned to skim her fingers over the panel. Kirk watched without interrupting as she opened a second channel, then jacked the narrow-beam power setting up to its fullest. They could have sent a shout all the way to Sigma Draconis at that power.

"*Enterprise* to Tlaoli Survey Team Three. Come in, please." She cocked her head in her slight pause, as though listening to sounds no one else around her could hear. Another slight adjustment to her controls, then, "*Enterprise* to Survey Team Three, please respond."

Still nothing. Uhura looked back over her shoulder at the captain, shaking her head almost apologetically. "Nothing, sir. If I had to guess, I'd say that Survey Team Three's communicators just weren't working."

Which fit with Fisher's earlier assumptions. "So you were right about their communicators not working, Mr. Fisher. What did you do next?"

"We tried to fly over in the research shuttle and scan for them, but as soon as we got close to the cave area, all of our geophysical sensors started to malfunction. And then—" The geologist's voice tightened. "—then the shuttle started to lose power, too, sir, for no apparent reason. We managed to get out of the karst area and back to the wetlands base camp before we had to set down, but now the shuttle doesn't even have enough power to charge the ionization rings on the impulse engines."

"How far away are you from the cave site?"

"Thirty kilometers, sir. Since we didn't know you'd be coming back early, we put a rescue team together and started hiking from the wetlands back into the karst terrain. Best estimate of our arrival time at the cave is—" Fisher paused to exchange murmurs with someone in the background "—sometime tomorrow evening, sir."

"Thirty hours from now?" Kirk frowned up at the image of Tlaoli 4 on the viewscreen, trying to imagine how any part of its worn and ancient surface could be so difficult to travel. "Mr. Fisher, do you know how far Survey Team Three penetrated into that cave system before you lost contact?"

"At least two kilometers, sir. They started in at local sunrise, which would be about six hundred hours ship time."

Kirk twisted a quick look over his shoulder to glance at the chronometer on the arm of his command chair. "It's thirteen hundred hours now." *God, only thirteen hundred?* "If Team Three had turned around and started back out of the cave four hours ago, when we know their equipment began to malfunction, they should have reached the surface about ship's noon." He paced over to the viewscreen again, peering up at the dots on it thoughtfully. "When you brought Team Three up to the northern continent, Mr. Fisher, did you leave their equipment behind?"

"No, sir. Lieutenant Jaeger thought it might take several days to explore the caves thoroughly enough to find the source of the shipwrecks, so we brought all of their supplies and tents up with them."

"Good." That simplified one thing, at least. Kirk swung back to Uhura. "Lieutenant, see if you can make contact with Survey Team Three's base communicator unit."

Uhura addressed her panel again, repeating her formal hail. Despite the lack of response, even Kirk could hear the faint buzzing that burned across the open channel. "That's the sound of an open subspace channel, sir," Uhura told him, correctly reading the intent look on his face. "I think the main communicator at their base camp is operational; there's just no one there to answer it."

Kirk rapped his fingers thoughtfully on the edge of her panel, his thoughts leaping ahead of him now that his suspicion was verified. "No sane geologist would stay inside a cave if their equipment wasn't working, especially if they knew there was some kind of dangerous transperiodic ore deposit down there." He didn't mean to step through his reasoning out loud, but didn't dare stop once he noticed Uhura and the others staring at him. It wouldn't do to have them see he was sometimes caught off guard by his own impulses that way. "The fact that Survey Team Three hasn't left means they probably *can't* leave." He nodded, certain now. "They're trapped down there."

A worried crease furrowed Uhura's brow. "Captain, do you think their lights have malfunctioned in addition to their tricorders and communicators?" She seemed to hesitate before going on to suggest, "It wouldn't be safe for them to move in total darkness, would it?"

"No, it wouldn't." He didn't even like the image of the survey team trying. "They could also be trapped by a roof collapse, or flooded out by a surge in water levels." He frowned a threat up at the planet on the viewscreen. "A lot of things can go wrong in a cave."

"That's what we thought, sir." He'd almost forgotten about Fisher down on the surface. "What do you want us to do?"

Kirk shook off the parade of unpleasant images Uhura's question had set loose in his head. "All I need right now, Mr. Fisher, is the coordinates of the cave where you lost Team Three, and the location of their base camp. From here on in, the cave rescue will be our responsibility. You head back to the wetlands base camp and start packing your samples. We'll evacuate you and the other survey crews by transporter as soon as you're ready." He barely waited for the geologist to acknowledge his orders before nodding at Uhura to cut the channel. "Mr. Spock, we did a preliminary assessment before we sent the landing party down to that planet. Bring up the surface scans—I want to see what that northern karst terrain looks like."

"Aye, sir." A few brisk taps on his science controls overlaid the small brown planet on the viewscreen with a detailed grid depicting its surface. "This is the topographic data gathered by our long-range scans. I had the computer convert it into three dimensions and zoom to a low-elevation viewpoint to better illustrate the terrain."

Kirk moved down to reclaim his command chair as the network of growing lines slowly enlarged on the screen and rotated on the main screen. What had initially looked like a gently rumpled rock plateau resolved on closer inspection into a jagged nightmare of steep monolithic mounds, knife-sharp ridges and jumbled boulder fields pocked with sinkholes so deep that their bases were lost in shadow. "Where the hell is all that vertical relief coming from? I thought this planet was ancient."

"Twelve billion years old," Spock clarified. "Approximately four times the age of Vulcan. Most of Tlaoli's surface is eroded down to a peneplain, Captain, but in the karst areas, the erosion is occurring underground in the form of caves. When those caves collapse, they form this kind of surface landscape."

Kirk could suddenly understand why it would take more than thirty hours to cross less than thirty kilometers. "Do we have those coordinates yet from Fisher? I want to see where that cave is."

No one said anything in acknowledgment, but Kirk heard the gentle sounds of data transfer behind him as Uhura and Spock combined their information. A red dot appeared near the center of the crazy-quilt terrain. "That is the cave Survey Team Three entered, Captain," Spock said. A smaller blue dot appeared a short distance to the north on the barren gray plateau. "And that is the new location of their base camp."

"Which we know still has power, even if the people in the cave don't." Still half-lost in thought, Kirk bounced the side of his hand against the com button on the arm of his command chair. "Bridge to engineering. Mr. Scott, are you down there?"

"Aye, Captain, but I can't give you any warp drive right now." The chief engineer sounded particularly gloomy, and more than just a little harassed. "I've just taken the warp nacelles offline to clean out the thrusters and recalibrate the field angles. It'll take a half hour to get them put back together again, much less up and running."

Kirk smiled at Scott's attempt at clairvoyance. "Thanks for the heads-up, Scotty, but I don't need the warp drive just yet. What I do need is for your engineers to manufacture some equipment for me so I can outfit a landing party for an emergency cave rescue."

"Aye, sir." Kirk could almost picture the way Montgomery Scott's face crinkled doubtfully as he answered; Scotty had quite the knack for acknowledging an order while still managing to convey his complete incomprehension of it at the same time. "And what kind of equipment might you need that's not already in our stores?"

"Primitive equipment. The kind that doesn't depend on dilithium power cells or permanent magnetic batteries." Kirk paused a moment to mentally outfit a cave party in his head, then translate all the necessary equipment into its old-fashioned counterparts. "I'll need chemical batteries that can run our communicators and tricorders, and headlamps that use carbide fuel illumination."

"You want *combustion* lamps?" The chief engineer sounded scandalized, as if he were being asked to equip the *Enterprise* with a hitch for a team of draft horses. "And just how many of these will you be needing, Captain?"

"Five or six, for sure—twice that many if you have time." Kirk glanced around the bridge, his gaze skipping past the tall figures of Spock, Stiles, and Leslie almost without seeing them, until finally coming to rest on Uhura's far more petite form. "Lieutenant Uhura, you're the smallest communications officer aboard, aren't you?"

Her eyes widened in apparent surprise. "Yes, sir."

"Then you'll be coming with me." He angled his voice back down toward the com. "Mr. Scott, I want that equipment within an hour." The plan became more clear by the moment. Kirk already knew what he had to do for every step before leaving the ship, and was already impatient at having to slow down and actually issue the orders. "Yeoman Rand," he summoned, almost before he'd finished switching channels on the com. "I need you to locate our ship's smallest medic, our smallest power supply expert, and our smallest geologist. And the smallest person on board who's had some recent orienteering experience, say within the last four months."

If his assistant was startled by the strange request, nothing in her composed voice gave the emotion away. "Smallest by weight or by height, sir?" was all she asked.

"By height. We may be crawling through some narrow cave passages, so make sure none of them are claustrophobic. I'll give you a list of the equipment they'll each need. Tell them all to meet me in the main transporter room by fourteen hundred."

"Aye-aye, sir. Rand out."

"Spock, you have the conn." Kirk pushed to his feet, energized at the prospect of taking action. "Keep the ship in the highest orbit that's gravitationally stable, just in case that planet really does throw some kind of subspace aperture at us. And make sure Scotty gets those warp nacelles back online as soon as he can. We might need to evacuate quickly." He vaulted up the steps to the turbolift, but couldn't resist pausing at the threshold to toss a grin back at the silent Vulcan. "It's a good thing we opted for coming here instead of meeting the *Antares*. If we'd waited until after our rendezvous, we might have arrived too late."

Spock arched one eyebrow in an eloquent remark Kirk wasn't sure how to interpret. "Indeed, Captain," was all he said, "that is the aspect of our situation that troubles me the most."

"Listen up, all you scuts! You're not going to be doing anything in there that a well-trained monkey couldn't do just as well or better. Unfortunately, we used up our last trained monkey cold-starting the engines, so you guys are all we have left."

Ensign Pavel Chekov lingered just inside the engine room's main doorway, delaying his departure long enough to eavesdrop on First Technician Singh's welcome to the department's new temporary workers. There were three of them this time, their races and genders obscured by bulky radiation suits, clustered together like mutant goslings as they scurried across the huge bay behind Singh.

"In-and-out in fifteen-minute shifts. I don't want you formulating opinions about the new magnetic bottle, trying to figure out how we pulled off such a nifty ignition feat, or analyzing the engines' function. Your job is to scour subspace residue out of the interior thruster compartments. You've got your scrubbers, you've got your rad monitors. If anything blinks or turns red, get out. We'll have a medic outside with a tasty antiradiation cocktail waiting for you. But if you do everything the way you're told, you'll be eating supper tonight instead of a fistful of meds. Any questions?"

A suited arm waggled above the clutter of helmets, only to sink out of sight again when its owner finally realized that Singh's offer had been largely rhetorical. *Get used to it,* Chekov wanted to tell the new arrival. Because no matter who you were back home, or how brilliant you were at the academy, once you got to a starship you were assumed to be about as useful as a Belgian chocolate until you proved yourself otherwise. Here, you were just the latest batch of scuts.

Sighing, Chekov slipped out into the corridor without waiting to see when Singh would deign to acknowledge the nervous faces and waving arms (he always did eventually; he just liked to make sure that the recent arrivals knew they were at his mercy first). At least this temporary work crew got to do something interesting. Chekov had spent three and a half weeks in engineering, and the most exciting thing he'd done had entailed being locked out of the department while a member of the bridge crew powered down the engines and sang very badly for eighteen hours. Now that there was real, hard work to be done beyond calibrating sensors and counting surplus hand tools, he was off to spend fourteen days in astrophysics. While the ship was in orbit around an M-Class planet. While no one needed stellar analyses, pulsar identifications, or even the most simple navigation equations. As if a month in Planetary Sciences while the ship was in deep space hadn't been irony enough.

How all this leaping from department to department was supposed to help him become the perfect starship commander made less sense to Chekov every day. He still couldn't remember the operational tolerances of a theta-class warp shield, could remember only half of the fifty or so points used to determine the environmental class of a planet (although, thank God, retaining the meanings of the various classifications themselves proved anomalously easy), and he had yet to figure out how to tell which deck he was on without stealing surreptitious peeks at the bulkhead markings. I'm *the future commander of a starship?* he would think with something approaching horror while wandering aimlessly in search of a turbolift shaft that wasn't where he remembered. *What was Starfleet thinking?*

It wasn't much consolation to realize there was apparently no one here from his academy class with any hope of a career beyond polishing laboratory glassware or mopping up coolant spills. Or so Singh and all the other noncom supervisors before him had assured Chekov from almost his first day on the job. This was apparently not the most promising collection of new crewmen to have ever graced the *Enterprise*'s hallways.

*But I just want to fly the ship,* Chekov could have told them. *I want to be on the bridge, and see the planets when we first come into orbit, and watch the stars drift by while everyone from the daylight shift is at home in bed.* He'd figured out, just from what he'd overheard at mealtimes or in the gym, that the *Enterprise* already had a helmsman so good that the man would have to go blind and lose the use of one hand before Kirk would consider replacing him. That meant the chances of Chekov working on the bridge during first shift were so small he couldn't have found them with an electron microscope. *I don't care where we're going, or who's giving the orders, or what we have to do to get there, just please, please, please! don't leave me down in the lower decks!*

He'd already walked several sections too far forward before realizing he'd completely bypassed the proper turboshaft to take him up to crew's quarters. Maintenance teams had apparently begun the chore of removing graffiti from the starship's bulkheads, thus eradicating the obscene line-drawing Chekov had been using to identify his turbolift for the last day or so. He tried again (unsuccessfully, he was certain) to lock some distinctive image from this junction in his memory, then ducked into the car and sent it racing up toward Deck Six. He could just imagine himself explaining to the captain, "No, sir, I cannot find my own quarters, but I can pilot a starship anywhere in the galaxy without getting lost, I promise."

So while he wasn't exactly *expecting* to walk into someone else's cabin while meaning to enter his own, it wasn't as though he hadn't already had nightmares about this very moment that differed only in the details.

The woman standing beside the room's only desk jerked around with a gasp when the door hissed open. Chekov barely had time to register the hand which flew to her mouth and the shocked embarrassment in her blue eyes before he'd jumped backward through the closing hatch and into the corridor again. That was as long as it took him to realize that it was *his* desk she was standing over, *his* books and disks stacked on top of it, and *his* quarters in which she was doing it. All the same, he spared one extra moment to verify the cabin number and the name stenciled on the door before striding boldly back inside to confront her. "Excuse me—"

She seemed to have recovered herself by this time, and interrupted as though their first compromising encounter had never happened. "There you are! You're late."

It wasn't the painfully abashed apology he'd expected. Blinking, he found himself suddenly unable to think past where he'd already started. "Excuse me?"

"Engineering told me you left twenty minutes ago." She had to be someone's yeoman—probably some high-ranking officer's, judging from her elaborate blonde coif and stiffly superior attitude. No yeoman who worked for anyone below a commander would have had the time to maintain such a hairstyle, much less the gall to speak so disdainfully to someone who was technically her superior. "I didn't expect it would take you half the afternoon to get back to your own quarters."

Chekov decided not to comment on that. Before he could inject something different, she swept up a bundle of clothing and equipment from the top of his desk and shoveled it into his arms as though glad to be rid of it.

Before Chekov could protest, she asked brusquely, "You don't have any mental problems, do you?"

"What?"

The blonde yeoman twirled a finger alongside elaborate tresses, as if he needed to be shown where mental problems came from. "You know— fear of heights, paranoia, claustrophobia. Anything like that?"

*What about fear of surreal visits from unfamiliar yeomen?* "No."

"Then report to Transporter Room 4. They're probably waiting on you, too."

This, at least, he knew how to respond to. "There must be some mistake."

"You're Ensign Pavel Chekov?" When he didn't answer during her nonexistent pause, she planted her fists impatiently on her hips. "Command track cadet? Just released from a temporary tour in engineering services?"

"Yes," he finally blurted. "But I'm scheduled to report to astrophysics at fourteen hundred hours." He'd estimated that he only barely had enough time to clear out of engineering and visit his quarters to collect his reference books before reporting in—and that was before his twenty minute detour and this ridiculous delay. "I can show you my orders if you don't believe me."

If the yeoman was at all impressed with his version of his schedule, she gave no sign. "It doesn't matter what you were told before. You've been called up to assist on a planetary rescue mission."

*"What?"* He hurried to intercept her as she whisked past him on her way to the door. The bundle in his arms threatened to tumble apart at the sudden movement, and he struggled to tame it so he wouldn't have to gather up the pieces just to give them all back to her. "What possible use can I be to a rescue mission?"

"How am I supposed to know? I'd think you'd be thrilled to get off the ship for a change." She shooed him toward the door with the same prissy fluttering of hands that old women in the Moscow suburbs used to chase sled dogs out of their kitchens. "Now get going! If you think I'm irritable when you're twenty minutes late, wait until you meet Captain Kirk."

# Chapter Three

WHY, oh *why*, did it have to be D'Artagnan?

The teasing didn't start right away, of course. Sulu hadn't heard a single comment when he'd reported to the bridge after McCoy's prototype antiviral vaccine had yanked him screaming back to sanity. The urgent need to escape from Psi 2000's death spasms had dominated the first hour of that watch, followed by the sudden shock of finding out that they'd hurled themselves three days into the past. While the other bridge officers were still discussing the ramifications of time travel, Sulu had been called down to Sickbay where Dr. McCoy had ordered another round of detoxification for him and Kevin Riley, "just in case."

It wasn't until Riley accused the doctor of trying to shield them from unkind comments that Sulu started to wonder exactly what it was that he'd done. His last clear memory of their stay at Psi 2000 was trying to keep a despondent Joe Tormolen from doing away with himself. After that came a blur of running, laughing, and fencing, laced through with the indistinct feeling that he'd made a total ass of himself. McCoy had gruffly denied Riley's charge and told them both to rest while the last viral toxins that his prototype antidote had missed were screened out of their blood.

Exhausted from what felt like hours of fencing practice, and still depressed about the loss of Joe Tormolen, Sulu would probably have obeyed the doctor readily enough. But Kevin Riley in the next medical bed over had been more determined and more creative. As soon as McCoy left them alone, Riley squirmed out of his bed long enough to activate their room's link to the ship's main computer. At his request, the computer had shown them the visual logs it had recorded over the past two days, complete with Riley's tuneless serenades from engineering and Sulu's irrational dueling escapades. Sulu had spent the rest of his medical treatment wondering if Uhura would ever speak to him again, while Riley bemoaned his own stupidity and lack of musical taste.

An hour later, Sulu got a glimpse of things to come.

Nurse Christine Chapel began it, when she stopped by to check his blood counts and clear him for return to duty. "So, how is it with this madman?" she asked in her best professional nurse's voice. Sulu shot her a quick look, startled by the not-very-professional question. The nurse's face looked innocent enough, but the dancing glint in her eyes and the finger she had stuck into an antique paper book with worn gilt letters spelling "Dumas," gave her away. Sulu groaned.

"I read it when I was a teenager," he pleaded. "It had a big impact on me...."

The nurse opened her dog-eared book and read aloud, " 'Never fear quarrels, but seek adventures. Fight on all occasions. Fight the more for duels being forbidden, since consequently there is twice as much courage in fighting.' " She waggled her forefinger at him as if it were a fencing foil. "Was that the part that made such a big impact?"

Her voice held a lilting mix of mockery, laughter, and feminine admiration. Sulu felt his cheeks tighten and he hurried to drag his tunic over his head so she couldn't see what color his face had turned. He muttered something about being due on the bridge and bolted for the turbolift, not even waiting for Riley to join him. As the deck lights flashed by, however, Sulu faced the unpleasant fact that he would soon be stepping onto a bridge filled with people who had watched him swing shirtless down out of a hatchway, like a maniacal cross between a French musketeer and Tarzan.

He got a temporary reprieve when the turbolift whistled to a stop a few decks below the bridge to pick up another crewmate, but his sense of relief was very short-lived.

"All for one and one for all," chanted John Russ, the engineering tech who usually worked the morning shift with him. His tone was insufferably cheerful. "The bridge crew has sworn to stick with you, buddy, even if you get arrested by Cardinal Richelieu—I mean Captain Kirk."

Sulu was saved from needing to reply by the hiss of the turbolift doors. He headed for the pilot's console with the sound of the engineer's laughter chasing him. Fortunately, Mr. Spock had the conn and merely gave Sulu an impassive glance as the pilot seated himself. But because Riley hadn't reported for duty yet, Sulu had to share the helm with Lieutenant Stiles for now. The second-shift navigator gave him a wicked smile.

" 'Why, this fellow must be the devil in person!' " Stiles said to the departing pilot, Ed Leslie. Evidently, Leslie hadn't decided to take part in the shipwide joke, because he merely gave his fellow pilot a sympathetic look and a clap on the shoulder as he left. " 'Don Quixote took windmills for giants, and sheep for armies,' " Stiles continued smoothly. He must have spent the last few hours memorizing passages from the ship's library. " 'D'Artagnan took every smile for an insult, and every look as a provocation.' "

"Then you'd better stop smiling, hadn't you?" Sulu snapped at him.

Stiles's obnoxious grin merely widened. " 'And for the first time in his life D'Artagnan, who had till that day entertained a very good opinion of himself, felt ridiculous.' "

That, unfortunately, was all too true. Sulu gritted his teeth and gazed down at his helm monitors, checking the orbital equations as carefully as if the *Enterprise* had been circling a complex triplicate moon instead of a normal terrestrial planet. He didn't even look up when the bridge doors swished open again, and knew it was Riley only when Lieutenant Stiles started to hum a familiar Irish tune under his breath.

"Stop it," Riley snapped as he came to a stop beside the helm. "I don't ever want to hear that song again!"

Stiles snorted with laughter. "Gee, that's a shame. You were *so* good at singing it—"

Sulu reached out and caught Riley's fist before it could connect with Stiles's jaw. He succeeded, but there was no way he could disguise his movement to make it look like anything other than the interception of a punch. He heard Commander Spock clear his throat meaningfully behind them.

"Gentlemen, some of you may not be aware of it, but we are in the midst of an emergency operation. In a few moments, we will begin beaming down a party to rescue one of the survey teams on Tlaoli. And because of a possible danger to the *Enterprise* itself, we are maintaining a heightened state of alert on the bridge." The tone of the science officer's voice was so cold and steely that it sounded almost—but not quite—like irritation. "All departing shift members should clear the bridge immediately, and all arriving ones should review the ship's logs to acquaint themselves with the situation."

Given that direct order from a senior officer, even a troublemaker like Stiles couldn't find an excuse to linger and torment them further. Sulu sighed in relief when the turbolift doors slid shut behind him.

"Get used to it," he advised Riley quietly as the navigator dropped into the seat beside him. "Neither of us is going to live this down for a while."

Riley shot him a sour look. "Easy for you to say, D'Artagnan. *You're* not the one who almost got the ship blown up the other day."

Sulu gritted his teeth and began reviewing the helm records to find out what had happened while he was gone. If even fellow victims of the Psi 2000 virus couldn't resist teasing him, he knew the next few days weren't going to be fun. Maybe he'd use his spare time on this shift to figure out exactly how they'd managed to slingshot themselves back in time. If he could fling the *Enterprise* even farther into the past, he just might be able to steal every copy of *The Three Musketeers* from the San Francisco public library before a certain impressionable young fencing student ever read one.

Chekov was on deck three of the primary hull, halfway down the corridor to Transporter Room 4, when he finally decided this had to be some kind of elaborate joke. It had taken him that long to verify what combination of turbolifts and corridors would take him to his destination, and it was only just before exiting the last lift car that he'd finally taken a moment to paw through the bundle that had been thrust upon him by the prickly yeoman.

The coverall wasn't all that different from the jumpers they'd sometimes worn in engineering, except this one was gold and it carried the command division star over the left breast instead of the twisted engineering lightning bolt. A lumpy plastic pouch with a loop of black nylon cord contained everything else, and it was dumping out this miscellany that finally convinced him he'd been targeted as just another scut on someone's humor radar.

A manual tape measure and compass. A smaller pouch-within-a-pouch of reflective directional markers. A bound booklet of blank waterproof plastisheets, a plastic-and-graphite mechanical pencil to go with it. And a metal whistle. It reminded him of the paraphernalia they were issued at the beginning of the Academy's orienteering course. And it was all ridiculously redundant and useless on any kind of planetary mission he could think of. Tricorders and communicators did these jobs now, and did them better than humans. Issuing these sorts of materials to a new crew member could only be some kind of statement on his lack of usefulness, a joking implication that he might be left behind on some planet and have to find his own way home.

Indignation stopped Chekov just outside the transporter room door. He didn't want to go in blushing with anger, but didn't want to walk in as though he was too stupid to have figured out what was happening. Truth be told, he didn't want to go in at all. He just couldn't figure out what was worse—facing and identifying his tormentor, or slinking away to be laughed at behind his back for the rest of his term on this ship.

*Of course, there's always the possibility that a landing party really is waiting for you in there.*

The thought of walking away from an actual duty summons was more frightening than any of the other prospects. He took a deep breath and straightened. If he were about to become the butt of some junior officer's underdeveloped sense of humor, at least he could console himself with the knowledge that he'd let it happen rather than risk disobeying a direct command.

Lifting his chin, he stepped boldly forward through the sliding doors.

All but one of the six people who turned to look at him were sealed into jumpsuits just like the one he now hugged against his chest. Three women in a rainbow of Services red, Command gold, and Science blue; a stocky man maybe twice Chekov's age wearing a blue jumper that had seen better decades; the indifferent transporter tech in his unremarkable duty uniform; and the only other man in command gold, pale eyes irritable with waiting and a metal whistle bouncing impatiently in one hand.

"Ensign Chekov." It wasn't a question or a guess, even though Chekov knew he'd never met the captain face-to-face before. Kirk's eyes flicked over him. "You're not dressed."

The blush Chekov had tried so hard to leave outside the door roared over him again. "Uh, no, sir. I assumed there must—"

"Let me worry about the assumptions, Ensign. Get dressed."

"Yes, sir." He willed himself not to stammer, but only partially succeeded.

Kirk turned to collect the rest of the room with his gaze while Chekov hastily shook out his jumper and began stepping into it. "All right, everyone, listen up. We'll be beaming down to the survey team's base camp, because we know it hasn't been affected by whatever on this planet drains power and pulls ships out of orbit. That will give us a one-kilometer hike to the cave entrance itself. The terrain is wicked, so I want us to stay close together, both on the surface and once we get inside the cave." His gaze swept across them and, to Chekov's relief, snagged up on the woman in the gold jumper instead of him. "Ensign Martine, I'll want our power supplies kept close to Lieutenant Uhura so we can maintain contact with the ship as we travel."

The pretty, dark-haired woman nodded, reaching back to touch the bulky pack across her shoulders as though to make sure it was still there.

"Lieutenant Wright, I'm going to ask you to stay in the middle of the group until we locate the missing survey team." A surprisingly boyish smile flashed across Kirk's face. "If anyone is going to run into trouble, I'd rather it wasn't our only medic."

"I understand, sir." The blue-clad medic passed a hand through her close-cropped blonde hair. "To tell you the truth, I'd rather it wasn't anyone."

Kirk grinned again. "Point taken." Then he waved forward the last figure in Science Division blue, catching the abbreviated helmet the other man tossed to him. "Equipment orientation now. Mr. Sanner, if you please."

Sanner worked down the line of them, pushing a helmet toward each of them and barely pausing long enough to make sure each one was taken. "I know they're uncomfortable and they look stupid," he said, with that complete lack of formality only research scientists could get away with in Starfleet, "but wear 'em anyway. You'd be amazed what you'll find to bump your head on inside a cave." He thumped a lumpy structure on the top of the helmet he was handing Martine, and it rattled as though filled with small marbles. "Once we get underground, you're going to need to light your carbide lamp. There's water in the reservoir here, carbide rocks down below. This little knob controls the drip. The more water you add to the carbide, the more gas it lets off, which means you can turn up the flow if you need a bright light, but you're gonna be using up your light faster that way. I've got extra carbide with my gear, in case one of you decides he has to go wild and light up an entire chamber." This time he paused in front of Chekov, quickly demonstrated how to start the water drip again, and triggered a small ignitor with his thumb. A neat feather of blue-and-gold flame sprang to life just in front of the lamp's brightly polished reflector. "Don't blow it out," he instructed, "or you'll waste gas. Just turn off the water." Which he did, and the little flame guttered and died.

Turning the helmet over to Chekov, Sanner wandered back toward his place near the base of the transporter. "I've got a rope ladder, if we need it, and plenty of pitons. You've all got whistles—make as much noise as you can if we get separated in the cave, and we'll find you. Otherwise..." Sanner shrugged, seating himself on the transporter's steps. "Don't step anyplace where you can't see the bottom."

Kirk gave a businesslike nod, tucking his own helmet under one arm. "All right, then. Any questions?"

Chekov raised his hand tentatively, more convinced than ever that some horrible mistake had been made. At Kirk's sharp glance of acknowledgment, he admitted, as evenly as possible, "Sir, I don't understand why I'm here."

"You took the orienteering course at Starfleet Academy."

The answer was so close to his earlier thoughts that Chekov wasn't sure at first what to say. "Yes, sir." It seemed a safe enough option.

To his even greater surprise, Kirk smiled, a little gently. "We're going into an uncharted cave to retrieve a lost survey team, and there's a very good chance we won't be able to use tricorders to map our way in and out. I need someone who can accurately record the route we take into this cave, and read his own map well enough to get us all home again." Kirk clapped a hand to his shoulder. "Can you do that, Ensign?"

The course had, indeed, covered the basics of mapmaking and surveying. But Chekov had always viewed it as an interesting introduction to the science of navigating, not to mention a complementary elective to go with his other mathematics courses. It had never occurred to him that the primitive marriage of compass and measuring stick would have any practical use once he got to outer space.

There was a lot about serving on a starship that he hadn't expected.

"Yes, sir. I can do that, sir."

Kirk gave a satisfied nod. "Then let's head into the abyss."

There was something wrong with the *Enterprise*'s orbit.

Sulu wasn't sure when he first became aware of the problem. Despite McCoy's viral detoxification, he'd spent the morning trying to ignore sporadic attacks of hand tremors and the unpleasant feeling that a layer of cotton wool had been inserted between his brain and his sensory nerves. From the sidelong glimpses he'd caught of Kevin Riley clenching his jaw or pinching at the bridge of his nose, he suspected the navigator was feeling much the same. Fortunately, with the *Enterprise* parked in slow, stable orbit around Tlaoli's Earth-sized mass, Sulu didn't think his muzziness posed too much danger to the ship.

Until he noticed that their orbital altitude had decayed by almost twelve percent.

"Mr. Spock, permission to adjust orbit," he said at once.

Commander Spock glanced down at him from the engineering station, where he was working with Crewman Russ and Commander Scott to finish bringing their warp nacelles into alignment. "Why should our orbit require correction, Mr. Sulu? I do not recall ordering any course changes."

"You didn't, sir." Sulu scanned his monitors with a frown, wondering if his tremors had jerked his hands into doing something his brain had never ordered. But all of his controls insisted that no helm changes had occurred since Stiles and Leslie had first laid in their course several hours ago. Which made their current position even more of a mystery. "According to my logs, sir, we didn't change course. But somehow, we're fifty kilometers closer to the planet now than we were an hour ago."

"Due to a helm malfunction?" Spock crossed the bridge with strides that looked calm and unhurried but still brought him to Sulu's side within seconds. "Run a systems check, Lieutenant."

Sulu programed it in with a quick stab, aware of Riley doing the same thing on his side of the console. In a moment, green monitor lights flashed across both their panels, as one by one the ship's internal systems were checked and verified. None showed anomalies, but the gap between the perfect yellow circle that should have marked their orbit around Tlaoli and the blue spiral that was their actual position continued to widen. Spock lifted an eyebrow when he saw it.

"Correct our heading, Mr. Sulu."

"Aye, sir." Sulu lifted the ship's nose and nudged it gently to starboard. With a kick of impulse acceleration so subtle that he wondered if anyone besides him even noticed it, the *Enterprise* slid back onto the plane of her stable orbit, and the blue and yellow lines merged into a smooth white curve.

"Interesting," Mr. Spock murmured. "As well as disturbing."

From across the bridge, Montgomery Scott made the deep rumbling noise that was his version of clearing his throat. "It didn't look as if the ship had any trouble regaining altitude, Mr. Spock."

"No," the Vulcan agreed. "But given the record of previous starships that have crashed on this planet, Mr. Scott, I fail to find that entirely reassuring. Please continue to observe our position, Lieutenant. If this discrepancy occurs again, I want to—"

"Hail coming in from the captain!"

The loud declaration from the communications station sliced through whatever Spock had been going to say. As a second-shift bridge officer, Lieutenant Palmer was perfectly competent, but she didn't have Lieutenant Uhura's deft ability to announce a hail without disrupting the flow of normal ship business. Sulu could have sworn Spock let out a tiny sigh behind him, but all the Vulcan first officer said out loud was, "Put it through, Ensign."

A burst of static followed his words, intense enough to make Sulu's teeth hurt. After a moment, it subsided to a low-pitched drone, and he could hear Kirk's voice. It seemed to be haloed in echoes, as if the captain were standing in a large empty room.

"We're about one hundred meters inside the cave system, Mr. Spock." Kirk sounded as calm and composed as if he were seated on his own bridge. "It's really cold in here, and we're already seeing some instability in our tricorder readings, even though we've got it rigged to battery power. Any suggestions for shielding it from whatever disruption we're running into?"

"I believe it may be counterproductive to protect the tricorder's scanners, Captain." Spock's voice held the carefully neutral note that he usually employed to disagree with his captain. "Any shielding device you installed would prevent the tricorder from detecting the source of whatever is affecting it, perhaps leading you into greater danger than if you left it unshielded."

"Good point, Spock." One of the things Sulu liked most about his captain was Kirk's ability to accept criticism and modify his plans accordingly. "Is there anything else we can do?"

"I would suggest, Captain, that you program the tricorder to take an average of several readings and report the error function along with the median value."

"Did you get that, Mr. Sanner?" Kirk's voice faded as if he had turned away from his communicator's voice detection panel.

From farther away in the echoing cave passage, Sulu could hear a muffled male voice saying, "Yeah, but what do we do if the error function is larger than the reading?"

"We'll worry about that when it happens," Kirk told him, then his voice strengthened again. "Spock, I'm going to have Lieutenant Uhura begin reporting in every fifteen minutes as we proceed through the cave. If you stop getting reports, try to lock in on our communicator signals with the transporter and follow us from that point. Is that clear?"

Spock exchanged doubtful glances with Chief Engineer Scott, and his voice dropped into careful neutrality again. "Your instructions are clear, Captain. However, given our previous failure to locate the lost survey team on long-range scanners, I estimate the probability of our being able to carry them out to be less than thirty-five percent."

"Understood," Kirk said calmly. Sulu just hoped the other members of the rescue party shared their leader's love of a challenge. "Do the best you can, Mr. Spock. Kirk out."

Scotty was already closing up the warp control panel on the engineering station. "I'll get down to the main transporter room, Mr. Spock, and start tracking them now, while we still have a good connection to their communicator signals. We can finish the warp alignment later. It's good enough now for anything you'll need to do inside the system."

"Very well, Mr. Scott." Spock returned to the command chair, although, as usual, he stood near it rather than occupy it in Kirk's absence. "Lieutenant Palmer, please inform Mr. Boma's base camp that we are going to interrupt the transport of their rock samples back to the ship. I want the transporter free to evacuate the rescue team on a moment's notice."

"Aye-aye, sir." Palmer relayed the Vulcan's message. A few moments later, she turned from the communications desk again. "Mr. Spock, Geologic Technician Kulessa wants to know if we can beam him and Mr. Fisher over to Team One's original base camp so they can begin packing up the samples there. He says they left some important fossiliferous specimens behind when they went to move Survey Team Three to the northern karst region."

The Vulcan tilted his head to one side as he considered the request. Instead of answering directly, he touched the intraship communicator controls. "Spock to main transporter room. Commander Scott, are you there?"

"Just arrived," said the engineer's dour voice. "Don't tell me you need to beam the captain out already?"

"No, but we have a request for a cross-surface transport. Can you lock onto Mr. Fisher and Mr. Kulessa's communicator signals in the wetlands region and transport them to the coordinates of Base Camp One?"

"That I can," Scotty replied. "Locked on and beaming now."

And that was when it happened. With a deflection so swift and small that it barely escaped the automatic suppression of the inertial dampeners, the *Enterprise* broke out of orbit and began to slowly spiral down toward the planet again. Sulu activated the systems monitor as soon as he felt the change, and a moment later it confirmed what he already knew. He turned around to report his discovery to Spock, but two other voices overrode him.

"Transporter room to bridge," said Montgomery Scott's voice. It sounded even more somber than it had before. "We got those geologists to their destination, Mr. Spock, but just barely. The transporter beam hit some kind of energy field down on that planet, and now our long-range sensors aren't working at all. I can't focus in on the cave party's communicators."

"Neither can I, sir," said Lieutenant Palmer. "There's a burst of subspace static coming from the cave region. I'm barely maintaining contact with Lieutenant Uhura's narrow-beam communicator."

Despite the competing claims on his attention, Spock's keen Vulcan gaze focused directly on Sulu. "Have we experienced another helm change, Lieutenant?"

"Yes, sir. Thirty seconds ago, the *Enterprise* veered two degrees to port and five degrees off vertical." Sulu tightened his grip on his helm controls to still another spasm of tremors. "Permission to correct our course heading, sir."

"Granted." Spock came forward to the helm again, stooping to watch the piloting monitor. "Computer, run the helm log buffer backward for the last ninety seconds."

The monitor obediently flashed an inset miniature of its usual display, one in which the course curves contracted back on themselves instead of extending forward. Sulu glanced from the real-time orbital path which he had just adjusted back to a stable white line, to the data buffer which was replaying the previous ninety seconds of helm control. Two discrepant blue and yellow lines raced each other backward for fifty seconds, then suddenly jogged back into a single white line. None of the engine or helm displays showed so much as a whisker of movement when they did.

"It's not a ship malfunction, sir," Sulu said.

"No," Spock agreed. "Nor does it resemble the kind of natural subspace aperture Mr. Fisher suspected. Nevertheless, I believe we may be seeing what caused the crash of nineteen other spaceships." His dark gaze lifted to the nondescript, sunlit curve of Tlaoli which filled half the viewscreen. "Some unknown force on that planet is beginning to pull the *Enterprise* down toward it."

# Chapter Four

THE LAST TIME Uhura had been inside a cave, she had been twelve, and there had been handrails to help you through passages like these.

She edged her way along a sinuous vertical cavern, the glow of her carbide lamp inching forward with each cautious step. Where the light touched the wet cave walls, it made the translucent flowstone shine like polished marble. Occasional cascades of runoff splattered down to pool on the narrow ledge where she walked before they spilled over into the darkness below. Smaller trickles fell from the travertine draperies and stalagmites that filled the passage above her head. Uhura had learned the hard way to be wary of them. Her sturdy cave helmet protected her from bumps, but it also had an unfortunate tendency to divert trickles of water right down the back of her neck. The nano-woven fabric of her cave jumper wicked away the moisture, but it couldn't protect her from the shiver of cold that came with each unexpected drip.

"You know what I'd like to see?" asked a voice from the darkness ahead of Uhura.

She thought for a moment, then suggested, "A concession stand?"

"Hey, good idea!" The pleasant tenor could have belonged to any of the three men on the rescue team, but only caving expert Zap Sanner could sound so nonchalant after the hours they'd spent threading through this cold, wet maze. Uhura saw the misty glow of his carbide lamp appear around the shoulder of rock in front of her, followed a moment later by his scratched and dented caving helmet. "How about one with a transporter pad built in, for all us wimps who don't want to finish the all-day tour?"

"I'd settle for one with a restroom." Uhura shifted back a step along the ledge, to where the footing was a little flatter and drier. If Sanner was backtracking, that meant he intended to confer with the rest of the rescue team and perhaps make them retrace their steps. Again.

The geologist confirmed her guess by hunkering down on the edge of the bedrock ledge they'd been following, his muddy arms folded across his knees. "I'd settle for a tape measure, to see just how far down this solution fracture goes."

"Why? So you could figure out how long it would take you to fall if you slipped?" The caustic female voice was followed by a third halo of light inching its way forward beneath the overhanging flowstone. Medic Diana Wright was even shorter than Uhura, but built along sturdier lines. She had to be careful to keep her shoulders parallel to the rock face so as not to overbalance and tip backward into the open chasm, which made the tartness of her voice a little more understandable. "Maybe you could take a tricorder reading while you were going down."

Fortunately, Sanner was as good-natured as he was oblivious to cold and damp. "You'd probably get a better measurement by counting how many seconds it took before you heard me hit the bottom." He gave his geologic tricorder an exasperated look. "Even using Mr. Spock's error-averaging technique, I'm pretty sure I can spit farther than this thing can scan right now."

"Want to try another chemical battery?" Angela Martine came around the curving passage in Wright's wake. Even after two hours of cave exploration, the weapons officer looked barely encumbered by her pack-load of power sources. Uhura felt almost guilty about carrying a light day pack with only rations and water and a narrow-beam communicator inside. She had offered to share Martine's load, and had been politely but firmly turned down. All she could do now was squeeze a little closer to Sanner, to make more room in the curving passage for the arriving members of the team.

"It's not the battery," Sanner was saying. "It's the weird subspace interference that comes out of the rocks down here. It's like it reaches out and grabs whatever power is flowing through the electronic circuits, so no matter how much the battery generates, it's never enough. All my data looks wacky now, even the stuff I collected before when Mr. Spock's averaging program was working." He glanced up at the rest of the team. "Are your instruments working any better?"

Uhura carefully wriggled out of her backpack and slid the narrow-beam communicator out of its waterproof case. The last time she'd used it, it had been able to open a subspace channel to the *Enterprise,* but the internal amplifier hadn't been able to separate words from the fierce crackle of static. She hoped the computers on the ship had been able to process her status report out of the subspace background noise. Whether the source of the problem was a transperiodic ore deposit or not, there was no doubt they were drawing closer to it. When Uhura toggled the communicator this time, the dim glow of the wavelength monitor didn't show a single frequency open for hailing.

"We've got no subspace reception," she reported. "The ship may be able to track our signal with its sensors, but we can't hear them and we can't hail them."

Diana Wright freed her medical tricorder from where she had slung it beneath one arm and bent her carbide light directly on it. The tricorder came to life with a chirp that sounded odd even to Uhura. After a moment, Wright looked up at them with a wry smile.

"Here's how well my instrument is working. According to it, we all have Andorian distemper."

Martine snorted, dropping her pack beside her and hunkering down on her heels to sort through it. "Is that fatal?"

"Only if you're an Andorian camel. Which, apparently, is what we now are." The medic snapped her instrument shut and stowed it back under her arm. "What about your phasers, Martine?"

"Their circuits are working," said the weapons officer, lifting one up to carbide lamp level to run an internal check. "But if you keep them fully charged, they lose power at a ridiculous rate. I have them all drained and disconnected now, so we'll have to snap in new charge units if we need them. And I'm not sure how long they'll hold out."

"Then let's hope we don't need them." James Kirk came through the curve of passage behind them, as surefooted and secure as if the wet ledge of bedrock were his own bridge deck. He was shadowed by the smaller and stockier figure of the young command-track ensign he'd brought along to carry the rescue gear and map the cave the old-fashioned way, drawing all of its twists and turns in a waterproof plastisheet notebook. Uhura hadn't quite caught the ensign's name when he'd first been introduced, and all she remembered now was that it was something Slavic.

"Do we have a problem, Mr. Sanner?" The glow from Kirk's carbide lamp brightened as he turned up his water drip, then swung around until it faced the cave specialist. Still, it barely made enough of a dent in the darkness around them to reveal the frown on Sanner's mud-streaked face. "Have we lost the trail of Survey Team Three?"

"Not exactly," said the geologist.

"Then what exactly have we done?" Kirk inquired. It was hard to see his expression beneath the glare of the carbide lamp, but Uhura knew that tone well enough to straighten up automatically, even in the darkness.

"We ran out of cave," Sanner said baldly. "This passage ends around the corner."

The silence that followed his remark was the thudding kind Uhura usually associated with stand-offs between groups of armed men. Oddly enough, it was the quiet young ensign who broke it. "So we're on another sidetrack?" he asked stoically, pulling out his notebook and flipping through to find the most recent page.

"No." Sanner took off his helmet and turned it around in his hands, slanting it down along the wall of the vertical fracture. About a meter in front of Uhura, the unmistakable print of a human hand gleamed on the rock face, outlined by diverted runnels of cave water. "Survey Team Three came through here. They left prints on the travertine all the way to the end." He put his helmet back on with a snort. "I thought Jaeger knew better than to let them touch flowstone with their bare hands like that. It poisons the crystal growth faces and kills the formation."

"Maybe they'd lost their lights by the time they got here," Angela Martine said quietly. "Holding onto the wall might have been their only way to keep from falling."

"But if they came this way, where are they now?" Wright asked. "We went down every cave passage that looked like it might be worth following. Every time, we either came to a dead end or saw no evidence that Survey Team Three had gone any farther than we did."

"So they're not behind us," Uhura said. "And if they can't be ahead of us, either—"

"—then there's only one place they can be." The geologist leaned out over the chasm, angling his carbide lamp to catch the narrow ribbons of water that spilled off the ledge, disappearing into glitter and dark. "Which is why I wish I could see how far down this goes."

Kirk leaned over, too, adding his carbide glow to Sanner's. The mist-filled depths stayed obstinately dark. "Why would they have climbed down there?"

"To see if it goes," Sanner said, as if that explained everything. Their silence must have told him that it didn't. "There's lots of times like this when you're exploring caves and it looks like you've come to a dead end. But if you just keep poking around in the little cracks and roof holes and pinches, you can get through to whole new sections of the cave."

"This," said Kirk wryly, "is not what I'd call a little crack."

"No," Sanner admitted. "If there was any other hole that looked more promising, I'd be squirming through it now. But we didn't see any good side passages coming here, and there's no use going up a vertical solution fracture. It always just narrows upward, and it hardly ever leads to another section of the cave." He jerked a thumb at the water cascading from their rock ledge. "The real cave development is always down where that stuff goes. That's where rocks get dissolved the most."

"And you think Lieutenant Jaeger would have known that?" Kirk asked.

"We've gone caving together on at least a dozen planets, sir. I know if I'd gotten to this point and still had my lights, I'd be trying to get a little farther through." Sanner sighed and wriggled out of his backpack. "I hate to throw our one rope ladder down there when we don't know how deep it is or how jagged the rocks are at the bottom, but the damn tricorder can't scan past the end of my arm. We'll have to hope this is close to where those guys went down—"

"Wait, Mr. Sanner." Kirk sounded thoughtful. "You say you've caved with Jaeger. If he had any inkling that his lights and survey instruments were on the verge of losing power, would he have still gone down into this fracture?"

"No, sir," Sanner said emphatically. "No way. The first rule of cave exploration is to head back out at the first sign of anything going wrong."

"So if we're sure Survey Team Three went down this crack, that means they still had full power for their lights." Kirk reached up to tap the lamp on his helmet, making some of the rocks inside rattle and hiss out more of their flammable gas. "Our carbide lamps are probably one-tenth as strong as the photon lanterns the survey team carried. They must have been able to see much further down, maybe even spotted an opening..."

"Possibly, sir," Sanner agreed. "But we can't see what they saw. Our best bet is to go down right here, so we don't miss their trail."

"You're assuming the bottom is accessible everywhere." Kirk glanced along the narrow rock ledge they stood on, then moved to stamp his foot down hard on an out-thrust part of the rim. A large section of rock broke off and plummeted into the crevice below. It vanished into the mist and darkness, but they clearly heard the splash that echoed up after it. It sounded as if had hit fairly deep water. "I'd rather not have to swim once we got down there, Mr. Sanner."

"Me, either." Sanner scrubbed thoughtfully at his chin, leaving mud streaks from his caving gloves. "Maybe we could lower the rope with someone on it in a couple places, to see how accessible the bottom is."

"I've got a better idea." Kirk held out a hand to Martine and she gave him the phaser she was still holding. "Let's charge up three or four of the weapons and fire some wide-angle sprays at low power into the crevice. They should be able to light the place up so we can see what Survey Team Three saw." He handed the weapon he was holding back to the young ensign. "Lieutenant Uhura, you take one, too. I want you and Mr. Chekov to concentrate your firing on the upper parts of the fracture. Ensign Martine and I will aim for the lower, narrow parts."

"Aye sir." Uhura took the phaser and charge unit Martine had handed to Wright. She started to insert the charge unit into the butt of the weapon, then paused. "Power up now, or on your signal, Captain?"

"On my signal, for maximum illumination," Kirk said. Out of the corner of her eye, Uhura saw the young command-track ensign hurriedly eject his charge unit, then stand with his shoulders a little hunched, as if he expected to be called on his mistake. She wished she had a chance to tell him that on a real landing mission like this, he wasn't being graded on his performance.

Martine handed the captain a phaser, then extracted a fourth one for herself. "We could spread out a little farther, sir, and still overlap our light on wide-spray," she suggested to Kirk.

The captain nodded. "Mr. Chekov, go a few meters back down the passage. Lieutenant Uhura, follow Mr. Sanner a few meters further ahead. Fire on my signal."

Uhura moved along the ledge toward the shoulder of wet rock at its end, leaving just enough room for Sanner to stand and watch the light show. She turned and adjusted the phaser, then aimed it toward the upper parts of the chasm. "Ready, sir," she said, and heard a Russian-accented voice echo hers from further down the passage.

"On my mark," said Kirk. "Fire."

The wide-spray beam of the phasers dazzled Uhura's sight for a moment. Her eyes quickly adjusted to the brighter light, but all she could see inside the chasm was a chandelier glitter of falling water drops and the mirror-sharp reflection of standing water below. The walls on both sides of the vertical cavern looked as smooth and opaque as poured milk.

"Nothing here, or around the corner," reported Sanner.

"Cease fire," Kirk ordered. It took Uhura's eyes longer to adjust back down to the warm carbide glow of their helmet lamps. She glanced at her phaser's charge readout and could barely believe what it told her.

"Captain, my power unit is nearly drained!"

"Mine, too." Kirk unclipped the power cell from his phaser, frowning. "We must be close to whatever is leaching power out of them. How many more cells do we have, Ensign Martine?"

"Fifteen, sir."

"Then from now on, we'd better fire only two at a time." Kirk turned to retrace their steps. The glow of his carbide lamp sketched a glittering path along the wet walls, then snagged on the motionless figure at the end of the line. "Is something wrong, Mr. Chekov?"

"No, sir." The young man hurriedly turned to go, then glanced over his shoulder with the tentative look that ensigns often got when they weren't sure they had the right to state their own opinions. "Begging the captain's pardon—is it my imagination, sir, or has it gotten colder in here since we fired the phasers?"

"Colder?" Kirk repeated. "Why would it get colder?"

Uhura paused to let Wright take her time on a particularly wet and treacherous part of the ledge. As soon as she stopped moving, she felt it, too—a chilly bite in the dank air that hadn't been there before. "I think Mr. Chekov's right, Captain," she said, and got a grateful look from the young ensign. "I feel colder, too."

"We might be passing an opening to another cave passage. Sometimes, the first clue is that you feel a draft." Sanner peeled off one of his caving gloves and waved his bare hand through the air as they continued along the ledge. "It does feel like it's getting colder along here. Captain, could we fire the phasers again?"

Kirk took the power cell Martine held out to him, and passed it along to Chekov. "Mr. Chekov, you aim high. Ensign Martine, you'll fire with him. Lieutenant Uhura and I will wait for the next section of cave. Ready?"

"Aye, sir," said Martine and Chekov in unison.

"Fire."

Once again, the brilliant white of phaser light flashed out in the cavern, chasing all the shadows out of the dangling stalactites and turning the blackness below them into a glittering fountain of white falling water. Uhura scanned the rock walls on either side of the cascade, and saw only long spans of travertine laced with occasional balconies of thicker flowstone. She craned her head to see if there was a pool of water in the bottom of this section, too, but before she could even catch a glimpse of mirrored reflection, the phaser light flickered and died.

"The power cells drained faster this time, Captain," Martine reported grimly.

"I noticed. Mr. Sanner, any sign of a passage?"

"No." The geologist motioned them to continue onward. "But there's got to be one around here somewhere, sir. Feel how cold it's getting?"

No one answered him, because no one needed to. The cave air, formerly cool and soft with underground humidity, now held an almost wintry bite. Uhura shivered, chilled for a moment before the temperature-sensing fibers of her cave jumper measured the change and adjusted their insulating capacity upward.

"I know it wasn't this cold the first time we came through here, because I'm not sweating at all this time." Wright glanced down into the chasm beneath their feet and grimaced. "And I'm just as scared now as I was then."

Angela Martine cleared her throat. "Could we be affecting the temperature by firing the phasers? Maybe we're helping to open the cave up further every time we fire."

"Or maybe the phasers are catalyzing some kind of reaction in the transperiodic ore deposit," Sanner suggested. "If it's undergoing some kind of chemical change, that could explain the weird subspace static and power fluxes that we're seeing down here."

"Be that as it may," Kirk said crisply. "It doesn't alter the fact that some of my crewmen are trapped somewhere inside this cave, and we have to find out where they are. We need to keep firing the phasers, even if it does make us a little colder than we were before." They rounded another curving twist in the passage, and the sound of falling water grew fainter below. "This seems like a good spot to check. Lieutenant Uhura, are you ready?"

Uhura slid the new power cell Martine handed her into her phaser, leaving it just short of making contact. "Ready, sir."

"Fire on my mark." Kirk lifted his own phaser, then slapped the power cell into it in one smooth motion. "Fire!"

Uhura tamped the power cell down and triggered the wide-angle phaser spray. Her eyes seemed to adapt faster this time to the white dazzle of light—or was that dazzle a little less white than it had been before? It was certainly shorter. Before Uhura even had time to glance away from the phaser's rapidly falling power indicator, the bright light flickered and faded away. As it did, a distinct arctic chill swept through the cave, accompanied by an almost subliminal crackling. Uhura could feel her cave jumper hum with the effort to tighten its weave even further and maintain her body heat against the sapping cold.

"I think I saw something," Sanner said urgently. He leaned out over the chasm and angled his carbide reflector downward, but the hazy light made no headway against the darkness below. "There's still water down there, but there seemed to be some kind of opening along the side wall, just a little further down the way we came."

"Let's see if we can get one more good look at it." Kirk held out his hand to Martine for another power cell, then fired his phaser in the direction Sanner pointed. The flash was fierce but swift, more like the glare of a bursting photon torpedo than a weapon designed for hours of steady use. In that burst of light, however, even Uhura caught a glimpse of the shadowy arch of something that looked almost like a window set into the travertine walls of the fracture.

"That's it." Sanner's breath misted in the frigid air, frosting immediately into tiny ice crystals. He seemed too excited to care. "I know Jaeger would climb down to look at that, if he still had lots of power."

"Then that's where we're going." Kirk pocketed his phaser, and swung around on the ledge, gesturing Chekov to begin moving again. Their carbide lights seemed to Uhura to spark an unusually bright glitter off the cave walls near them. She froze abruptly, her muscles locking up before her brain had even finished putting together bits and pieces of what she'd glimpsed.

"Careful!" she called out, when she finally realized what she had seen. "The run-off is starting to freeze—"

Her warning came too late. She saw one of Kirk's boots slip out from under him, but the captain's quick reflexes let him grab onto the travertine wall and pull himself back to safety. The young ensign named Chekov wasn't so lucky. Both feet slipped out from under him on the ice-slicked ledge and his grab at the wall caught only air. With a sound more like a gasp than a yell, he went plunging down into darkness.

Kirk crooked his fingers into the wall's irregularities, suspended his breathing, and willed his weight to drift forward over his toes instead of backward into the abyss. He hovered with his cheek not quite touching the slick travertine only because the alignment of muscles and bones had accidentally placed him here. As if to punctuate the delicacy of his position, he heard the fragile shattering of the water's surface somewhere behind him and unknowably far below. He intuited what had happened even though he didn't dare crane his head around to see. "Sanner!"

He didn't have to ask the question outright—the geologist wasted neither words nor time. "The kid's down." The scrape and clatter of boots and equipment belts as Sanner scrambled to some new position. "I can't see his light." Another moment's pause, this time filled with a brisk ripping sound as Sanner tore open his pack. "It'll take me a minute to tie off the ladder—"

Then there was no point spending even longer discussing it. "Do it. Meet us down there as close to Jaeger's exit as you can."

"Captain, I wouldn't—!" One of the women. Kirk assumed it was Wright. It didn't matter—before she'd finished her warning, he'd let his balance deviate the necessary hair's breadth. He was already so close to falling that the mere thought of doing it made it so.

The moment's free fall rushed past more quickly than Kirk expected. He had time for one instant of surreal panic as the total darkness swallowed his lantern flame in the wind of his fall, then razor-bright cold crashed around him and sucked him into silence.

His whole body seized once, violently, in reaction. He'd clenched his teeth before impact with the water, so was only able to take in an agonizing noseful when his lungs tried to gasp. He thought about Chekov, unprepared for both the drop and the landing, and felt a pulse of adrenaline bring his body back under his control. He tried to remember how long someone could go without breathing while immersed in frigid water—he knew it was longer than under normal circumstances, but the exact figure wasn't the sort of detail he'd thought to memorize in his capacity as a starship commander. His lack of foresight irritated him now.

The smooth irregularity of flowstone bumped against his hip. Twisting to find the solid bottom with one hand, Kirk brought his feet under him and pushed off. But instead of breaking into air, he glided a too-long distance only to fumble headfirst into another expanse of rock. He felt his way in the direction all his instincts said was upward, found himself jammed shoulder-to-shoulder between two equally impenetrable surfaces, surged away from that confinement into limbo again. Why hadn't he anticipated this disorienting darkness? *Too used to waterproof lights.* It hadn't even occurred to him that carbide would be useless underwater. The edge of panic he'd tasted earlier flooded his mouth, threatened to ambush his common sense and leave him flailing. Kirk fought the animal impulse to gasp for air—any air!—and concentrated instead on stilling his thoughts and calming down his pounding heart.

Common sense. He couldn't see, he couldn't hear, he couldn't breathe, but gravity still functioned. Kirk's body and his equipment pack were both heavier than water, which meant they would sink straight down, given half a chance. Expelling the stale air he'd been hoarding, Kirk tried to notice the feel of the bubbles as they rolled past his face, tried to sense toward which direction they were rising. He couldn't. So he slipped his pack off his back and dangled it from one hand, barely maintaining a hold on its strap so that gravity could take it from him and draw it away. If this didn't work, there were no other options. He'd blown away any second chances with his last lungful of air.

Kirk didn't feel the pack try to sink, only a vague tension in his arm in response to its heaviness. He counted his heartbeats to keep from focusing on the deepening burn in his airless lungs. *One. Two. Three.* The pack's weight seemed to abate slightly, his floating body equalizing with its new lack of movement. *Four. Five.* Still gripping its strap in his fist, Kirk carefully brought his feet down to find the stone on either side of the sunken pack. This was bottom. This was *down.* He tipped his head back to face the darkness beyond his head. So this direction could only be *up.* Had to be up, or he and Chekov would drown down here forever and the ship would never recover their bodies.

*Sixseveneight!*

His heels struck hard into the rock, pistoning him toward air. Kirk thought he felt himself move upward, then jolted painfully as instead the pack was ripped from his grasp and his legs, shoulder, torso tangled sideways into rock that was both there and too rapidly falling away. A rumble like dull thunder, or distant rapids, exploded suddenly into the crash of water onto open stone as frigid air replaced freezing water. Kirk gulped in a breath so cold and desperate it hurt, even as he realized that he was not only free of the water, he was falling.

Then he hit bottom for a second time, this time with all the force of gravitational acceleration. He tried to roll with the landing, but couldn't time himself without being able to see the ground. The rock floor smashed away the breath he'd just taken, cracking against his helmet like a thrown boulder and battering him with a heavy curtain of water. He dragged himself over onto his belly and buried his face against his arms. He still couldn't breathe, but at least he could avoid the irony of drowning while stretched out in the open air.

Faint movement, barely loud enough to hear over the cascading water, caught his attention from what seemed only a short distance away. Kirk pushed up on his elbows and turned to look out of instinct. Nothing. Only the same unyielding black that had enveloped him since his carbide snuffed out on the way down.

But he wasn't underwater anymore. Or, at least, he didn't have to be. Pulling himself up onto hands and knees, he crawled forward, away from the already-weakening torrent. High above him, the birdlike shrilling of whistles danced off the cave walls, punctuated by the occasional bellow of a masculine voice. *As soon as I get my wind back, I'll answer you,* Kirk promised Sanner and the others. Although they sounded impossibly farther away now. Whatever he and Chekov had fallen through—however they had fallen through it—they were now several meters further down in a cave that had already swallowed one landing party.

Nano-weave hugged him more tightly as he finally dragged himself completely free of the waterfall. It sounded like little more than a bathtub faucet turned up to maximum now, still rumbling and threatening, but rapidly losing the ability to damage anything. Or so Kirk hoped. Clawing loose the chin strap, he rolled onto his knees and leveled the helmet across his lap. Cold fingers found the lumpy outlines of his carbide lantern, traced it until he found the round reflector and its attached striking mechanism. A quick sniff verified that the distinctively acid smell of acetylene still hissed from the pilot hole, but he had to thumb the striking wheel five or six times before the waterlogged apparatus finally rewarded him with a spark. Light shattered the darkness with a tiny *puff!,* and a flame no longer than the end of Kirk's thumb pirouetted in front of the shiny reflector like a vain ballerina. The illumination was so welcome, he didn't even resent the pain it drove through his dark-adapted eyes.

After long moments of darkness, the tiny shred of fire might have been a supernova. Kirk spotted Chekov immediately, barely raised up on his elbows not far from where a steady rivulet of water still drizzled from the ceiling. At least he was breathing, Kirk thought with almost dizzying relief. At least he didn't have to write a letter home to the boy's poor mother, explaining how he'd dragged her son halfway across the galaxy just to drown him on the very first planet he visited.

"Mr. Chekov?" Kirk didn't really expect a reply. The boy was busy coughing out all the water he'd taken in, and was having trouble enough breathing between spasms to try and make conversation. But Kirk wanted him to know he wasn't down here alone. "Sorry if dropping us from a great height wasn't very graceful. I'm a little rusty on my lifeguard technique."

Chekov, still coughing, nodded as though his captain had offered the most reasonable explanation in the world. It occurred to Kirk that Chekov was either too busy trying to breathe to pay him much attention, or the boy didn't have a sense of humor. The latter possibility reminded Kirk of Spock, and made him smile a little. He tried to hide the expression by turning away to blow a quick blast on his whistle. Up above, Sanner's whistle answered in frantic staccato, then fell silent.

"Well, let's have a look at where we are." Pushing to his feet, Kirk dialed the flame on his helmet light to maximum before holding it out at arm's length and turning in a slow circle. The tunnel surrounding them was maybe twice as wide as one of the *Enterprise*'s corridors, and taller again by half. A surprisingly regular hole—and the clutter of rocks beneath it—marked where Kirk had kicked through the smooth, domed ceiling in an effort to find the water's surface. So the roof of the tunnel was the bottom of the lake. Or what used to be the lake—icicles were already accreting around the edges of the hole as the last of the trapped water dribbled down to join the stream now slithering off away from them across the floor. But it wasn't the water, or the rapidly crystalizing ice, that riveted Kirk's attention near where the dark, corrugated walls met the ceiling. He took a slow step closer, lifting the helmet light higher over his head to illuminate the uppermost corners.

"I don't understand...." He heard Chekov climb shakily to his feet, following a few steps behind. His voice still sounded thick with inhaled water. "How did we get here? Where are the others?"

"On their way down to join us, no doubt." A strip of what might have been wainscoting ribbonned the upper wall, obviously a refined metal for all that time and water had frosted it as dark as tarnished silver. Rusty streaks wept down its rippled surface, neatly tracing the spidery-thin etchings that decorated its surface like scattered grains of rice. "I have a feeling this isn't flowstone."

Chekov moved up next to him, just into his line of sight, and squinted upward toward where Kirk aimed the light. The blue chill to his lips worried Kirk a little, but he was reassured by the keen intensity with which the boy studied the rows of alien markings. "It's writing," Chekov said at last, with a sort of dull certainty that caught Kirk by surprise.

The captain nodded slowly. "Possibly. It's certainly not anything natural." Then he smiled down at this new member of his crew as the thought suddenly occurred to him. "Congratulations, Ensign Chekov. You've just discovered your first alien artifact."

# Chapter Five

"WATCH THE LAST FEW STEPS," Sanner yelled up through the rush and pour of falling water. "They're icy!"

*Great,* Uhura thought, tightening her grip on the rungs of the rope ladder. *It's not bad enough that I'm climbing down through a waterfall. It has to be a* freezing *waterfall.*

She wished she could take a deep breath to ease the tightness in her chest, but at the moment there was too much water splashing around her to make that safe. The chasm above her drained itself in fits and starts into this new lower level of the cave system. When she had started down the ladder, the rush of water had been a mere trickle, but another section of ponded cave runoff must have broken through and was now pouring itself down this new drain. The icy water had drenched her so thoroughly that her carbide lamp had gone out and the wicking fibers of her jumper had expanded like foam in a vain effort to keep her dry. Uhura ducked her head below one shielding arm to take a breath, and still got enough water mixed with her air to make her cough as she took another step down the ladder.

There was no time to stop and clear her throat. Uhura felt the polymer strands jerk and twist as Martine swung onto the rope ladder from the cave ledge above her. The fear of getting her hands stepped on sent her down the next few rungs a little faster than she'd intended. When she hit the strand of rope that was slick with ice, her boot sole skidded off so violently that it took her other foothold with it. Uhura was left dangling from gloved hands, swinging her feet through buffeting water as she tried to find ladder rungs she couldn't see.

"You're almost down!" Sanner's voice barely cut through the clatter of water hitting the jagged edges of travertine through which Kirk and Chekov had fallen. "You can slide from there!"

Uhura tried to cast a glance down to make sure he was right, but all she could make out were watery shadows silhouetted against a dim carbide glow. She swung her gloved hands around to the outside of the rope ladder and tightened her grip as much as she could, then deliberately let herself drop. It wasn't until after she began sliding that she felt the icy slickness of the rope ladder's sides as well as its rungs. Her pace downward quickened alarmingly, despite her fierce grip.

"Got you," said a calm tenor voice, and Uhura felt herself plucked from the ladder and swung out of the rush of water in one smooth movement.

"Thanks—I think!" Uhura swiped the water from her face and scowled upward, intending to give Sanner a piece of her mind about his advice to slide. To her surprise, the face that gazed down at her was youthful, and lit with amused hazel eyes.

"Yes, Lieutenant?" Kirk asked blandly.

"Nothing, sir."

He smiled and turned away, ducking back out under the icy waterfall to join Sanner at the base of the rope ladder. The light went with him, and Uhura hurriedly took off her helmet to fumble with its extinguished carbide light. It ignited on the second try, its glow reaching out until it touched the rounded surfaces of a conduit ten feet in diameter and as smooth as the inside of a pipe. The passage sloped slightly, making a gradient that pulled the cave runoff down into darkness on the far side of its new plunge pool. Thin veils of mist shredded off the waterfall as it slowed back to a trickle again, making Uhura wish she'd waited just a few minutes more before she'd made her descent. The mist turned instantly to ice in the frigid air, some of it clinging like hoarfrost to the shards of rusty metal and shattered travertine that littered the conduit floor. The rest swirled in the drafty breeze, forming a fog of tiny ice crystals that made breathing unpleasant and visibility poor.

Uhura picked her way carefully up the sloping conduit, heading for a vague clot of lamplight she could see through the murk. Her movement sent water trickling down her cave jumper in thick runnels as its nanofibers wrung themselves dry, wicking off the water she'd absorbed on her way down the waterfall. Unfortunately, since her hair wasn't made of microscopically engineered polymers, it remained completely sodden. Uhura just hoped it wouldn't freeze to her helmet. The cave air felt even more glacial down here than it had in the vertical chasm above.

As she came closer to the carbide light, she could see Diana Wright crouched near the huddled figure of Ensign Chekov. The young Russian was shivering despite his cave jumper's insulation, and breathing so harshly that at times it almost sounded as if he were strangling.

"Hang on, kid." Wright loaded medicine from a vial into the tube of her hypospray, then pressed it to Chekov's throat above the collar of his cave jumper. "That should help you breathe a little better. Can you stand up and move around? You need to generate some kinetic energy so your jumper can pump all that absorbed water out. That's why you feel so cold."

"I don't—" Chekov broke off with a grimace, pushing himself halfway to his feet. Uhura hurried forward and helped Wright haul him the rest of the way up and then push him gently into motion. He walked between them obediently enough, his breath easing to a rasp as the medication took hold, but shivers still racked his body. A wet sheen began to coat his jumper as the polymer expelled its absorbed water.

"I'm not sure how I got here," the young man blurted after a moment, as if it were a shameful confession he had to make. "I told the captain, but he didn't say anything."

Uhura and Wright exchanged speculative looks behind his back. "You don't remember falling into the cave?" the medic asked. She began to examine his skull under his hair, dark and slick as a seal's coat with the water it had absorbed. "You might have gotten a concussion after you lost your helmet. Does your head hurt anywhere?"

"No," Chekov said. "And I do remember falling. There was ice on the ledge, right after we fired the phasers." He shivered again, strongly enough that Uhura almost lost her grip on his shoulder. "It just seems like that was a long while ago. Didn't something else happen after that?"

"Captain Kirk jumped in after you," Uhura told him. "You broke through the bottom of the cave into this level, and then he whistled so we knew you were here. Maybe that's what you're remembering."

"It must be." Despite his words, the young man didn't sound entirely convinced. He glanced at the conduit around them as they moved further up its gentle slope. The double glow of Uhura's and Wright's carbide lamps clearly showed its artificial curvature, unbroken here by jagged rents or waterfalls. "The first thing I remember clearly is lying on my back and coughing while the captain lit his carbide light. Then he found some kind of alien artifact..."

"You can take the credit for that discovery, Mr. Chekov." Captain Kirk materialized out of the chilly mist as if he'd just transported in. Sanner and Martine followed him, their cave jumpers and backpacks glistening with extruded water in the gathered light. "We never would have seen it if you hadn't fallen in where you did. It's on the wall over here." He stepped past Chekov and Wright, crossing the conduit until his carbide light finally drove the darkness back from the far side. "Any idea what it might be, Lieutenant Uhura?"

Chekov seemed a little steadier on his feet now that his cave jumper had drained out most of its water. Uhura released him and went to add her light to the captain's. Several rows of rice-like markings jumped into high relief under the double illumination. It looked as if they'd been engraved into the rust-streaked metal of the passage wall, rather than being painted on it. Perhaps that was why they'd survived as long as the cave itself.

"It's definitely an alien script, Captain. The breaks and repetitions make it look like a series of phonemes, but I've never seen any alphabet quite like it before." Uhura glanced over her shoulder at Sanner. "I don't suppose we can take a visual recording?"

"With this thing?" The cave specialist hefted his tricorder with a snort. "Only if you draw on the screen with a real sharp rock."

"You could make a copy by hand, in Mr. Chekov's map book," Martine suggested. She was peering at the writing and didn't see the effect of her words, but Uhura was still looking back at the rest of the group. She saw the young ensign slide his hand automatically into the chest pocket of his cave jumper, then jerk in dismay when it came out empty.

"Captain, the map—" Chekov stopped and swallowed when Kirk turned to face him. The light of the captain's carbide lamp showed them all the young ensign's stricken expression. "Sir, I don't have it anymore."

"Commander Spock, I'm adjusting orbit again."

Sulu didn't wait for a response from the first officer. This was the third time he'd had to correct the ship's heading in the past hour, and the procedure had become almost routine. Almost. Despite Spock's intensive use of the ship's scanners and sensors, they still had no idea where these inexplicable losses of altitude were coming from. That uncertainty bothered Sulu more than he cared to admit.

It was true that whatever force Tlaoli was exerting on them was trivial compared to the power of the *Enterprise*'s warp drive. Even their sublight impulse engines barely needed to be pulsed in order to bump the ship back up into stable orbit. Chief Engineer Scott thought they were encountering a subspace anomaly in Tlaoli's gravity well, and had suggested programming an automatic correction into the impulse engines. But something in Sulu balked at the idea of not knowing exactly when and how the orbital changes were occurring. He had an uncomfortable image of all the ships now rotting on the planet's surface having made just such an automatic adjustment right before they fell out of the sky. Besides, whatever was affecting the ship didn't feel like gravity fluctuations to Sulu; they felt like the tug of a more purposeful force. And the only clues to what that force might be were the timing and magnitude of the shifts themselves.

"Was the adjustment within the usual parameters?" Spock inquired without looking up from the communications station. He had temporarily evicted Lieutenant Palmer from her post in an attempt to augment the ship's signal discrimination amplifiers. Tantalizing flashes of contact had been coming in from the surface of Tlaoli, brief bursts of unusual sub-space static from the vicinity of the caves. Only the timing of the bursts, received at precise fifteen-minute intervals, marked them as attempts at communication. No actual message could be filtered out of the snarl of subspace noise.

Sulu checked the helm records to verify his manual adjustment. "Yes, sir. Six percent decay, initiated thirteen minutes after the previous shift."

The science officer made a noise that was almost, but not quite, a sigh of frustration. "Unfortunately, I do not believe the addition of that data point will allow the computer to identify the origin of these anomalies. Until we see a shift large enough to extrapolate a vector of interaction, we will remain ignorant of the root cause of these diversions."

"Spock, why don't you just come out and say that you don't know what the hell is going on?" Leonard McCoy had come up onto the bridge half an hour ago, ostensibly to check on Sulu's and Kevin Riley's vital signs, but more likely to keep a watchful eye on their efforts to contact the captain's rescue team. Sulu wasn't sure if McCoy actually doubted the first officer's leadership, or if he just didn't trust the junior bridge officers to ask the kind of blunt and probing questions he did. "Anyway, isn't our real problem that we can't contact the rescue team?"

"No, Doctor," Spock said evenly. "That is our *immediate* problem. Given the evidence of the previous starships which have crashed on this planet, I suspect the real problem is something much larger and more fundamental, which is causing both our loss of altitude and the captain's loss of contact."

McCoy groaned. "Please don't tell me we've got another planet getting ready to blow up on us. I don't think I could deal with that."

Spock lifted an unsympathetic eyebrow. "Your emotional condition is irrelevant to the discussion, Doctor. At the moment, all the evidence suggests that Tlaoli is stable but generating some kind of anomalous force whose interactions with us cannot be predicted. Whether or not that force derives from a natural transperiodic ore deposit—which seems doubtful—it certainly does appear to coincide with the region of caves

Survey Team Three was exploring. If we could determine the nature of that anomaly, we might be able to neutralize it sufficiently to keep the *Enterprise* safe, and to rescue the lost survey team and the captain's party."

"And if we can't determine its nature?" McCoy demanded.

The Vulcan lowered his voice, but Sulu was still close enough to the command console to hear his grave reply. "Then, Doctor, there is a statistically significant chance that we will become the twentieth starship to crash on this planet."

There was a moment of tense silence inside the fog-shrouded darkness of the alien cave. Then Captain James T. Kirk did the kind of thing that made his crewmen willing to follow him into Hell. He didn't swear, exclaim in surprise, or even ask young Ensign Chekov how he could have possibly lost the only map of their escape route. Instead, Kirk said matter-of-factly, "After the dunking you got, Mr. Chekov, that's no surprise. We'll just have to reconstruct it as we go along."

He made the missing map sound like a minor inconvenience, a problem they could rectify with just a little hard work. And Captain Kirk's gift for command, Uhura thought, was that he brought out so much of the best in his crew that he really could turn catastrophes like this into minor inconveniences. She saw the young ensign's shoulders straighten with fierce determination. "Aye-aye, sir." He reached into his backpack for his spare notebook. "I'll start on it right away."

"Good." Kirk swung around and eyed the dark length of passage that ran uphill, away from the trickling waterfall and their dangling rope ladder. "We'll explore this side of the passage first. That should give the cave runoff enough time to finish draining before we go down the other way."

"Let's just hope the survey team isn't down where the water's draining to," Wright said. Uhura flinched, and wished the medic hadn't put that particular fear into words. It was all too easy for her to visualize the landing party trapped without lights in the underground darkness, hearing the rush and spill of oncoming water but unable to get out of its way—

Wright's comment must have had the same effect on the rest of the rescue team. An appalled hush fell over them, made even more intense by the quiet trickle of the plunge pool in the background. Uhura could see Kirk frown and glance back in the direction of the waning waterfall, as if he was reconsidering his decision. Before he could break the silence, however, Angela Martine spoke in an urgent whisper.

"Voices! I hear voices!"

Sanner frowned and opened his mouth, but Kirk gestured him back into silence. "Women hear better than men," he reminded the cave expert, in an almost soundless whisper. "Everyone quiet."

Uhura stiffened, trying to calm her own breathing enough to let her hear past it. At first, all she could sense was the soft drip and splash of water behind them, then above that came an almost inaudible murmur, the distorted and wordless slush that words turned into when they echoed down long stretches of empty space. "I hear them, too," she said. "They're coming from uphill."

Kirk's breath misted out in a small but intense sound of relief. "Start walking—and whistling." He set off at a brisk pace with his own whistle clenched between his teeth. He blew a loud clarion blast, then paused to see if there was a response before he blew again. One by one, all of them joined in until the conduit echoed with the pulse of whistle blast and pause. All except Chekov, that is. The young ensign was intent on sketching a memorized version of his cave map into his plastisheet notebook as they walked, using the borrowed light of Diana Wright's carbide.

The murmur of echoed voices grew to a distant clamor as their conduit joined up with another. They had to pause for a moment to make sure which branch the echo sounded loudest in, but both Uhura and Martine agreed on the steeper of the two paths. After that, the response to their whistles had slowly resolved into a muffled chorus of male and female voices, while the passage curved up into a distinctly engineered spiral. As soon as the word "Help!" resolved from the din, Kirk dropped his whistle and ordered the rest of them to do the same. "This is Captain Kirk, and we're coming to get you," he shouted back. "One person keep shouting, to make sure we don't lose the way."

*"Captain!"* That was a strong male voice, suddenly sounding energized despite its hoarseness. "We weren't expecting a rescue team from the ship! What are you doing back at Tlaoli so soon?"

"We—" Kirk paused, then apparently decided it would be better not to try and explain the events of the last few days. "We got a little ahead of schedule at Psi 2000."

"That's great!" The voice grew more faint, as if its owner had turned to shout in a different direction. "Hey, guys! It's Captain Kirk!"

There was a pause, then a distant burst of laughter from the lost survey team. "Very funny, Mr. Tomlinson!" This was a different male voice, a little lower-pitched and a lot more exhausted. "So which survey team finally found us, hm? Mr. Fisher's or Mr. Boma's?"

"I'm telling you, it's the captain, with a team from the *Enterprise*!"

"Of course it is. And I am telling you that you don't want to admit you have lost our bet. That would mean that it's Mr. Fisher. Hello, Edward!"

The voices grew clearer as they hiked up the last steep curve of the spiral. "We've got to be getting awfully close to the surface, Captain," Sanner commented. He peeled off one glove and licked his finger, then held it up above his head. "I can feel a draft of warmer air coming through here. We may not need to backtrack all the way through the cave to get out."

Kirk glanced over his shoulder at Chekov, still sketching furiously in his notebook. "Let's not make any assumptions until we know what's going on," he said quietly, then raised his voice. "Survey Team Three, you still there?"

"Nowhere much else to go, Captain," said the first hoarse voice, at surprisingly close range. The conduit suddenly straightened again, and the glow of Kirk's carbide light caught on a mud-sodden figure in a gold jumper standing at the end of it. The young man blinked furiously at what must have seemed to him like a fierce glare of light, but he managed to smile despite that. "With the captain's permission, sir, allow me to say that you are a sight for sore eyes. Er, literally."

"It's good to see you, too, Lieutenant Tomlinson." Kirk was already reaching up to adjust the water flow on his carbide lamp, dampening the rush of acetylene gas. The glow around them dimmed to a softer gold halo as Uhura and the others did the same. "What's the status of your party?"

"Holding up pretty well, sir, after four hours of digging in the dark," said the young weapons officer. He waited for them to reach him, then turned to walk beside Kirk as they climbed up another tight spiral of conduit. "We were pretty sure one of the other survey teams would come looking for us after a few hours. In the meantime we've been trying to clear a path through a pile of cave breakdown that Mr. Jaeger thinks is blocking a natural exit from this upper cavern. Crewman Davis, our surveyor, got hit by some falling rock and has a pretty bad concussion. We've been taking turns watching to make sure she doesn't lose consciousness. Lieutenant Jaeger has done most of the crawling through the rubble pile, and he's a little banged up. The rest of us are okay."

"You have blood on your hands," Martine noted softly.

Tomlinson glanced over at his fellow weapons officer, and his smile warmed a little at the look of concern he saw on her face. "Yeah, well . . . caving gloves only last so long when you're trying to dig through rock with your fingers. We were almost getting ready to give up when we heard your whistles, way off in the distance."

"For that you can thank Ensign Chekov—" Kirk's voice broke off abruptly as Tomlinson led them around a final curve of conduit and, without warning, into a space that looked like an underground cathedral. Huge columns of travertine ran from floor to arching ceiling, frosted and laced with flowstone until they looked like tall, thin wedding cakes. A giant rubble pile spilled down the back of the space, and hanging draperies of travertine above it showed where the mineral-laden cave runoff had come from to decorate this space. Above the rubble, the room's smooth, constructed roof had cracked and split upward into a darkness so high that their dimmed carbide lights couldn't chase away all its shadows.

"Wow." Tomlinson paused to regard the jagged spill of boulders. "That looks a lot worse than I remembered from when our lights went out. No wonder we were having so much trouble getting to the top."

"I'd think getting down again would be even worse." Kirk followed the young weapons officer out into the echoing space of the chamber, to where four other survey team members waited around a jumble of packs that had been heaped up to make a bed for the fifth member of the party. They were all blinking like owls at the approach of light, although not as painfully as Tomlinson had done. Their eyes must have had a chance to get accustomed more gradually as the carbide glow of the rescue party spilled through into their cavern.

"Is it really the captain?" asked the woman on the bed, turning to squint in their direction.

"Yes, it is." Kirk headed over to the injured crewman, with Diana Wright nearly treading on his heels. "How are you feeling, Davis?"

"Like someone fired a photon torpedo through my head, sir." The dark-haired woman began to sit up, but Wright was already beside her and had lowered her back down before she could do more than grimace in pain. The medic began unwinding the clumsy blood-stained bandage on the surveyor's head. "Sorry, sir. I really can stand up and walk, if you need me to."

"With any luck, we won't." Kirk glanced around at the other members of the survey team, all mud-stained and exhausted but beaming with the unexpected relief of being rescued by the man they trusted more than anyone else aboard the *Enterprise*. One of them, a stocky young Asian woman in security red, had as many bloody scrapes on her hands as Tomlinson did, although it didn't affect her cheerfully crooked smile. Another, a middle-aged man whom Uhura vaguely remembered from a previous landing party, had a badly swollen eye and a reddish gray bruise spilling down one cheek to meet a fresh cut on the edge of his mouth. His blue cave jumper had long gashes across the shoulders despite its toughly woven nanofibers. Although his facial injuries kept him from smiling, the look he threw at Sanner was definitely amused.

"Carbide lamps, eh, Zap?" The slight trace of a German accent told Uhura this must be Karl Jaeger, the survey team's cave specialist. "Wait until the Society of Interstellar Speleologists hears about that."

Sanner scrubbed at his chin, looking embarrassed. "It was Captain Kirk's idea. When Fisher told us about the power problems you guys were having down here, the captain figured you might have lost your lights. He decided to use something that didn't run on electricity."

"Mr. Fisher had power problems, too?" Jaeger exchanged worried glances with Tomlinson. "He didn't try to bring the research shuttle here to look for us, then, did he?"

"Yes, he did," Kirk said. "And nearly crashed when it lost power, although he didn't say that in quite so many words. But he made it back to the wetland base camp. In fact, he's probably been beamed back aboard ship by now." He glanced around at the members of the lost survey team, clearly noticing the exhaustion on their faces now that the initial excitement of being rescued had faded. "When did you start losing your power?"

"Not for a long while into the trip," said one of the blue-clad women in the party. She lifted a surveying tricorder from the ground beside him and gave it an exasperated look. "Crewman Davis says she got the whole upper level and most of the lower level of the cave mapped into her tricorder before it crashed and lost all the data. That took us almost three hours, didn't it, Lieutenant D'Amato?"

The other male scientist, as muddy and tired as Jaeger, nodded. "But I noticed the first fluctuations in my tricorder when I started to analyze the rocks around the ice cave. That was about half an hour earlier."

"Ice cave?" Kirk demanded.

"A large chamber similar to this one, but at the lower end of the conduit system," Jaeger explained. "It was much colder than the rest of the cave when we first entered it. I initially thought it might be the location of the natural transperiodic ore deposit we were looking for, but that was before we realized this whole structure was an alien installation." He glanced up at his darker-haired colleague. "Lieutenant D'Amato still thinks the power drain is coming from somewhere near that chamber, which was another reason we decided to stay at this end of the caves. We didn't want the other survey teams to run into the same problem we did."

"We thought maybe they would hear us digging and help clear the cave exit from the surface," said Tomlinson. "That way, we could just climb out here instead of retracing the whole trip in."

"With any luck, we won't need to do either of those things now." Kirk glanced around until his gaze found and snagged on Uhura. "Lieutenant, I think it's time to contact the ship."

She blinked, then pulled her narrow-beam communicator out of her pack, seeing from its lack of monitor lights that its chemical battery had died since the last time she'd used it. Martine was already extracting another battery from her backpack. "I can try to hail them, sir." Uhura attached the new power supply, although she left in the inert spacer that kept the chemicals separate until electrical power was required to flow. "But there's so much subspace static on the channel that I'm not sure they can hear anything I'm saying."

"Can they detect that we're hailing them?"

"Yes, sir. As long as Lieutenant Palmer keeps this frequency centered on her receivers, she'll know when it's active. She probably gets a burst of static whenever I call."

"Well, that should work," said Kirk. It was hard to see his expression in the dimmed glow of their lamps, but Uhura thought he was gazing at her impatiently. "Shouldn't it, Lieutenant?"

Uhura felt a small burst of sympathy for Chekov, who must have spent much of his time on this planet feeling as unsure and bewildered as she did now. "Work for what, sir?"

"For sending a message up to the ship." Kirk reached up to tap on his helmet. At first, Uhura thought he was rattling his carbide rocks to make them burn brighter. Then she heard the rhythm he was making, and her eyes widened in comprehension. "We're going to do it just like we're doing everything else on this rescue mission, Lieutenant. The old-fashioned way."

"Commander Spock!" Lieutenant Palmer swung around from the communications panel, her voice loud and excited enough to cut through all the other conversations on the bridge. "I'm getting a signal from the planet!"

Spock's eyebrows lifted abruptly, the closest he ever came to showing surprise. "Put it through, Lieutenant."

"Aye, sir." Palmer swung back to her panel and punched a control there. Sulu grimaced as a burst of static assaulted the bridge of the *Enterprise,* followed by a few seconds of silence, then by an even longer salvo of static. Another silence, another short burst—

"It's Starfleet code!" Palmer said. "Lieutenant Uhura must have guessed that we weren't able to deconvolve her signal, so she's turning her communicator off and on to contact us."

"N," recited Spock, as he listened to the static. "S, P."

"That's not the beginning of the message, sir." Palmer bent over her communications panel, scrolling back the buffer to the beginning of Uhura's coded communication. "It started with T, R and A."

"Transport," Sulu said softly.

He saw Spock nod confirmation as the long-short-long code for the letter "O" crackled through the bridge, followed by the two short bursts that were "R". The static paused for an unusually long time after the final "T", then began the pattern all over again. "She's just repeating that word, sir," Palmer said unnecessarily.

"Then we shall presume that Captain Kirk wishes to be transported back to the ship." Spock leaned over the arm of the command console and activated the ship's intercom. "Bridge to Mr. Scott."

"Scott here."

"Commander, how wide an area can we encompass with the ship's cargo transporter?"

"Depends on how careful you need to be with the cargo," the chief engineer responded. "If you want it beamed in molecule for molecule, then I'd say about four cubic meters."

"Spock!" McCoy took a step closer to where the Vulcan first officer stood near the empty command chair. The doctor's forehead rumpled with the intensity of his scowl. "You're not going to beam up the captain and his team like a pile of packing boxes, are you?"

"I have no choice, Doctor," said Spock patiently. "None of our long-range sensors can focus on the karst terrain, and the landing party's communicators no longer appear to function. Our only solid connection is through Lieutenant Uhura's narrow-beam communicator, and that gives us only a single point coordinate."

"Which is *exactly* why you shouldn't be transporting anyone based on that," McCoy snapped. "If the edge of the transporter beam happens to land halfway through someone's skull, you're going to kill them by beaming them up!"

"I am aware of that, Doctor." Spock templed his fingers and rested his chin against them, a pose that usually meant he was sorting through a complex sequence of logical deductions. "We can presume that the captain is aware of it, too, since he knows we cannot lock on to their communicator signals. If he still wants to be transported out of the cave system, then either he has managed to gather his team into a tight group around Lieutenant Uhura's communicator or—"

He fell silent, as if he didn't think the doctor would appreciate where his logic had led. McCoy's frown deepened, and after a moment he jabbed a finger toward the Vulcan, although Sulu noticed that he didn't quite poke him. "Or *what,* Spock?"

"Or the captain is in such dire straits that the risks of an incomplete transport are outweighed by their need to escape." The Vulcan turned away without waiting for McCoy's response. "Lieutenant Palmer, transfer the frequency of Lieutenant Uhura's narrow-beam signal down to the main cargo transporter, so that Mr. Scott can use it to center the beam."

"Sir, he'd better hurry," said the junior communications officer urgently. "The signal's fading fast."

"I'm on it," said Scotty's voice from the open intraship channel. "I've already got the cargo controls linked through to my console here, and as soon as we get that frequency—aah, there it is. I've got the beam centered, Mr. Spock. On your orders."

Sulu glanced up at the haggard brown crescent that hung in their mostly dark viewscreen. Tlaoli's day side was slowly withering as the system's pale yellow sun swung out of view, in what looked like the most pedestrian of sunsets. What was going on under the surface of that seemingly innocuous planet? he wondered. Had the captain found the survey team in need of immediate evacuation, or was the rescue team itself in such danger that they were willing to risk an unlocked transport?

"Spock," McCoy warned. "Think about what you're going to do here."

"I always do, Doctor." Like Sulu, Spock gazed up at the viewscreen as if he could somehow see the effects of his decision there. "Proceed with transport, Mr. Scott."

"Transport initiated—no, shut down, shut down *now!*"

Sulu had less than a second to wonder what the chief engineer's outburst meant. An eerie shudder ran through the bridge, so strong and deep that he knew it must have shaken the entire ship. He shot a glance down at his helm controls and saw their smooth white orbital curve spiral off into multicolored chaos as the ship slewed into an insane and unplotted deceleration curve. The unknown force that had previously flirted with them, gently tugging them toward the surface, had in the space of an instant become a full-fledged roaring pull, like a tractor beam operating on a monstrous and inhuman scale.

Sulu reached for the impulse controls before he was even aware of conscious thought, jamming them to full starboard thrust to compensate for the ship's sudden curl toward the planet. For an instant, he felt the sublight engines hurl themselves into the effort to turn the ship, then their power indicators abruptly fell to zero on his screens. An instant later, the screens themselves went dead, the lights on the bridge snuffed out, and Sulu heard the eerie silence as the life support systems stopped functioning. He grabbed onto the helm as hard as he could, knowing what was coming next. But the ship was wheeling too sharply to port. When the inertial dampeners gave way, the centrifugal force they'd been holding back slammed across the bridge like a tidal wave.

# Chapter Six

*THERE SHOULD HAVE BEEN SIRENS,* Sulu thought dazedly. He reached out for something to hang onto, trying to brace himself against the persistent pull of centrifugal force. His hand slid helplessly across a smooth surface that could only be the main viewscreen. *Where are the sirens and flashing red lights? If this isn't an emergency, I don't know what is.*

But the bridge of the *Enterprise* remained eerily silent, and the only light came from the fluorescent glow of the evacuation lights, triggered by the dark and lack of power. Sulu glanced around and saw fallen figures everywhere. Only Spock was still on his feet, fighting the ship's dizzying spin with that superhuman resilience Vulcans could summon in emergencies. The first officer had just finished lifting Dr. McCoy into the command chair, and was flipping open his personal communicator. Sulu spared a moment to admire Spock's quick thinking. With no power, the ship's internal communications system would be as useless as its inertial dampeners.

"Spock to engineering. We need auxiliary power on the bridge."

Sulu levered himself up to hands and knees, and took advantage of an aft plunge to slide toward the helm. He caught it just as the ship rolled to starboard, and cursed as his own chair banged him smartly in the back. At least he was now close enough to grab onto it and pull himself up into his seat. He hit the emergency belt release, hoping it would still work. Fortunately, the ship's designers must have made it internally powered, and it sprang out to encircle his waist with a reassuring click. He saw other members of the bridge crew doing the same thing, one by one struggling back into position. Unfortunately, their stations remained dark and lifeless, so there was nothing any of them could do once they got there except wait.

Except for Spock. He headed over to join John Russ at the engineering panel, somehow managing to keep his balance despite the ship's severe roll and pitch. He looked like a man walking through an invisible windstorm. "Commander Scott, can you hear me? We need auxiliary power on the bridge."

"I hear you, Mr. Spock." The chief engineer sounded as close to frantic as Sulu had ever heard him. "But I'm stuck here in the transporter room with none of the turbolifts working. I've got my crew down in engineering working on the auxiliary generators, but we lost every shred of backup power we had stored in our batteries. It'll take us a minute or two just to prime them. As soon as I've got any power at all, I'll be routing it up to you. I'll warn you, though, that it won't be enough to run all the bridge stations."

Spock was already hauling panels out of the engineering station. From somewhere in his engineer's tool kit, Russ had found a stronger emergency light and was slanting it down onto the intricate boards. Sulu could see the Vulcan's slender fingers flash across the controls, rearranging the flow of nonexistent power. "I am giving priority to helm controls and sensors," Spock said into the communicator that he had given Russ to hold. "Send the rest to the impulse engines, Mr. Scott."

"Can't we fire the impulse engines manually?" Sulu asked. Without a working viewscreen or helm monitor, he couldn't be sure where the *Enterprise* was heading, but his pilot's instincts told him that it was down toward the planet again. "If we continued on the heading we had just before we lost power, we've got to be deep into the gravity well by now."

"A distinct possibility," admitted Spock. "But without enough power to charge the ionization rings, there is no way to activate or aim the impulse engines."

"How about the warp drive?" Russ asked.

"Bollixed." Even heard secondhand and distantly through Spock's communicator, Scott's voice sounded very grim. "That was the first place the power drain headed for after it knocked out the main transporter. I had to cut every circuit between the core and the drive nacelles or the electromagnetic surge would have blasted our dilithium crystals to smithereens. I think I managed to save the core, but it's not connected to anything now."

"Did you let the rest of our power just get drained?" McCoy demanded.

"Aye, Doctor," said Scotty. "I don't know what kind of energy field that transporter beam activated, but it overrode every safety switch I threw. There was no stopping it without destroying all the power circuits in the ship, like I did in the warp core. I thought it would be better to just let it run its course and power the ship back up when it was gone."

"A logical prediction, Mr. Scott," said Spock. A dim flicker of light appeared on the main viewscreen, but Sulu ignored it to focus on his pi-loting monitor instead. Light began to pulse on the helm as it got a wash of power from the auxiliary generators. Sulu hurriedly punched through the helm's initial start-up sequence, canceling most of its safety checks and tests in order to get it up and running sooner. "Let us hope that the *Enterprise* manages to stay aloft long enough for it to come true."

Sulu glanced up from his coalescing orbital curves just in time to see the night-dark surface of Tlaoli rising toward them on the viewscreen.

A wave of frigid air rolled across the underground chamber, cleaving itself on the narrow flowstone columns until it seemed to come at them from all directions with hurricane force. Kirk ducked his head to avoid the bite of blowing ice, realized even as he did that the gesture was point-less. There was no wind. The flames on the rescue team's carbide lamps never so much as flickered, and Chekov—still engrossed in his map re-construction—made no subconscious move to protect his thin plastisheet pages from fluttering about. It was just another temperature drop, Kirk re-alized. As sudden and profound as all the rest.

An eerie hiss filled the chamber as a new skin of ice adhered to the travertine walls. Kirk had clustered both parties into a single tight group as far from any nonliving structure as he could, offering as clean a lift as possible on the assumption Scott would opt to pick them up with the cargo transporter. He'd placed Uhura with her open communicator chan-nel at the center of the group, letting the others fit in where they would. Right now, he was just relieved that no one was touching the flowstone during this latest quick freeze.

"This is getting ridiculous." Sanner bumped shoulders with Kirk as he batted fresh frost off the front of his jumper. "Does anybody know the minimum temperature these cave suits are rated for?"

No one did.

"I would give my eye teeth to know what is causing this effect." Jaeger, close on Kirk's other side, heaved a frustrated sigh that material-ized in front of his face as a tattered curtain of steam. He looked across Kirk toward Sanner, one frustrated scientist appealing to another. "I don't care what Fisher says, there's no way this can be due to transperiodic ore deposits. They generate heat and create energy, not the other way around! This negative gradient that we're seeing in both power and heat...that energy has to be going somewhere."

"Into the latent heat of crystallization," his fellow geologist said cryptically.

"But that wouldn't be enough to explain..." Jaeger's unswollen eye narrowed in a way that gave him a slightly piratical look. "Not unless there was some trace contaminant in the cave runoff that inhibited freezing and allowed the crystals to absorb far more than the usual amount of energy."

"Something like dilithium?" Kirk inquired wryly.

"We analyzed for dissolved dilithium, Captain, back when we first entered the cave." That was the third and quietest geologist, D'Amato. "The levels were always below detection limits."

"Then maybe there's some other element or compound here, something we don't even know about yet," Sanner said excitedly. "I've seen papers proposing the existence of ultra-transperiodic quadra-hydrogen—"

"And I've seen papers that say Zephram Cochrane had outside help in designing the first warp drive," retorted Jaeger. "That doesn't make it true! It's more likely we're seeing an exaggerated version of evaporative cooling due to subsurface airflow through the caves."

Sanner let out an explosive snort. "Yeah, that would be reasonable— if the air in here were moving at about a thousand kilometers an hour!"

"Do you think the cold is why the aliens built this place?" Tomlinson asked from the other side of their huddle. He stood just behind Ensign Martine, a little closer than Kirk suspected was strictly necessary for transporting purposes. Tomlinson's fellow weapons officer did not appear to mind the proximity. "To take advantage of the refrigerating effect?"

Jaeger was busy scowling at Sanner and merely made a curt, dismissive gesture with his hand. It was the other geologist, D'Amato, who answered. "The structure we're inside—" He motioned vaguely at the huge chamber around them, "—the conduits, these larger chambers—those are all millions of years older than the cave system above us. I'm not even sure this structure was originally underground when the aliens built it." His hands played restlessly with the cover on his tricorder, as though wishing he could snap it open and access the information trapped inside. "The limestone was probably deposited over the structure, then began dissolving millions of years later, probably because the original conduits and rooms provided large, natural permeability contrasts. The only reason we see flowstone decorations inside the man-made—well, alien-made—parts is because of cracks that formed in the ceiling a few millennia ago, like the break at the back of this room."

"You're assuming this travertine formed the same way it would in a natural cave," Sanner objected. "But what if it was the cold that made it precipitate out in the first place?"

Jaeger heaved an exaggerated sigh. "Zap, please recall that most carbonate minerals have retrograde solubility—"

Kirk restrained his own sigh, all too aware how obvious even the most quiet expression of frustration would be right now. While in one regard he appreciated the way scientists could generate a speculative debate out of anything, right now it was the conspicuous absence of the transporter beam, rather than the presence of the cold or the relative age of caverns versus ruins, that bothered him the most. He caught Uhura's eye while Sanner and Jaeger began to vigorously debate the pros and cons of freeze-drying versus evaporation as an explanation for the various travertine formations they had seen. "Anything yet?" he asked quietly.

The communications officer looked as though she'd been waiting for his question. "I'm sorry, Captain. I signaled until I ran out of power, and I didn't get any indication that the ship was attempting to respond."

"But you're sure the signal got through?"

She shrugged a little. "As sure as I can be, sir." Half-turning, she reached toward Martine for another chemical battery. "Would you like me to try again?"

Kirk shook his head and waved Martine to stop digging about in her pack. "No, Lieutenant, thank you." He caught himself sighing anyway. "Either the *Enterprise* wasn't able to receive our message, or they weren't able to comply. In any case, wasting another battery isn't going to get us out of here any faster." He noticed abruptly that the rest of the group had fallen silent, listening to his conversation with Uhura while at the same time trying to seem as though they weren't technically eavesdropping. "At ease, everyone," he ordered, a little brusquely.

The team broke obediently apart, heading to different quarters of the chamber in groups of two and three in what was no doubt their effort to give Kirk some privacy to sort out where they'd go from here. He wasn't sure whether or not he fully appreciated the gesture. Only Ensign Chekov stayed within an arm's length of his commander—he simply sat down where he stood and continued working on his map. Uhura stooped to quietly leave her helmet on the ground next to him before following Martine and Tomlinson. Kirk wasn't certain the boy had consciously heard the dismissal, much less noticed the lieutenant's simple kindness. *He's either very good at concentrating, or just old-fashioned anal.* Both of which traits had their uses.

Kirk waited until Wright had finished settling Davis back on her makeshift futon of packs with D'Amato and Palamas sitting on either side to keep her warm, then summoned the medic over with a flick of his hand. He met her halfway, letting her fall in beside him as they walked a little distance away from the others. "I need a report on Chekov and Davis," he said quietly. "Are they able to walk out of here?"

Wright tossed a look back over her shoulder, taking in both patients with that single quick glance. "Ensign Chekov's fine," she said, turning back to Kirk. "His breathing's clear now, he's alert. I'm not so sure about

Davis. She's in a lot of pain, and while she hasn't suffered a loss of consciousness, I'm not convinced she's entirely stable."

Kirk nodded his understanding. "But can she walk?"

"If she can't, I'll carry her." At first, Kirk thought she'd meant the remark as a joke. Then he saw the serious crease between her dark blue eyes. "Captain, until I can do a proper medical scan, I can't tell how badly she's injured. That bump on her head could just mean a killer headache, or it could mean she's bleeding into her brain. It's important that we get her out of here as soon as possible."

*It's important to get us all out of here.* No matter what kind of temperatures their cave jumpers were designed to withstand, Kirk knew that none of them would survive the night if the cold continued to deepen. He thanked Wright, trying to seem calm and confident about their chances, and started back across the chamber to check on the other two parts of his plan.

Chekov still sat where Kirk had left him, cross-legged with his compass and map notebook balanced in his lap. Kirk paused just behind him to steal a look at what might be their only roadmap home. "I'm impressed."

Chekov jerked in surprise, instinctively clapping one hand down on top of his notebook as though hiding illicit notes from a prowling teacher. But not before Kirk glimpsed a nearly complete rendering of the cave system's upper level, with remembered measurements appended to the main passage and many of the dead ends and side tunnels simply not filled in.

The captain tried on a fatherly smile; he hadn't intended to startle the boy, and now felt slightly guilty for appearing to sneak up on him. "You have a good memory, Ensign. That map's going to help us a lot."

"Thank you, sir...." Chekov looked back down at his work, then glanced abruptly at the helmet next to him as though equally startled to find it there. Kirk couldn't tell for sure in the dark, but he thought the boy was blushing. "I'm sure it's only because we were over the territory so many times, sir."

Not that many. But maybe it felt like more when you were the one who had to first walk it, then measure it, then draw it and walk it again. "Put your finishing touches on," Kirk warned him. "We're going to be heading out soon."

"Aye-aye, sir."

Which left only one element of their escape still open to question. "Mr. Sanner—How confident are you that you can climb back up that crack we all came down half an hour ago?"

Sanner paused to balance himself halfway up the pile of rubble Jaeger's team had tried to clear a way through. "With the ladder all frozen to the walls?" He gave a crooked grin and hopped a few levels closer to the floor. "Do I have to promise not to fall?"

Kirk wasn't in the mood for the geologist's humor. "That would be preferred, yes."

Picking up on his captain's tone, Sanner finished his climb to the floor. "I can do it if I have to, sir," he said, more seriously. Then he tossed a concerned look toward Davis on her makeshift infirmary. "But even if we make it up the ladder, I'm not sure everybody else is going to be able to walk that ledge back to the cave entrance. Not with all the ice that's going to be there. I don't have enough crampons for all of us."

And trying to pass one or two pairs back and forth down a line of inexperienced cavers was a disaster just waiting to happen.

"Captain . . ." Jaeger sat on one of the larger travertine boulders, collecting samples of stone and ice into slides and tiny jars. "Am I correct in assuming that we won't be transporting out of here?"

"It's beginning to look that way, Mr. Jaeger."

"Then might I suggest an alternative?" He answered Kirk's nod with one of his own, then carefully snapped shut the last of his little jars. "There is another cavern similar to this one at the other end of the conduit system."

"I remember," Kirk said. "You called it 'the ice cave.' "

"Because that was where we first noticed the chilling anomaly, yes." Jaeger made a little face, as though he regretted that particular misnomer now that every surface in the cave system was covered in ice. "According to our tricorders, that chamber was only a few dozen meters below the natural cave's main entrance. There were breaks in the ceiling's integrity that I think correspond to a cluster of vertical pipes just inside the mouth of the cave." His hands outlined what he was trying to describe, and Sanner nodded enthusiastically.

"I remember those! I wanted to drop a light down to see how far they went, but we didn't have time." He turned to Kirk with renewed intensity. "Even if I have to rock climb up those pipes, I'm pretty sure I could get back up there and drop a rope for the rest of you."

With any three of the men up above, they could simply tie the rope around Davis and haul her up manually if she couldn't make the climb on her own. A fist of dread that Kirk hadn't even fully acknowledged began to loosen its grip on his heart, but a thought occurred to him that made it vise-tight again.

"Didn't you say that was where you thought the transperiodic ore deposit was?" Kirk jerked his head back toward D'Amato, tinkering with his tricorder even as he wedged himself tighter up against a shivering Davis. "Where Lieutenant D'Amato thought the power drain was coming from?"

"True," Jaeger admitted. "But a lot of that was based on the unusual chilliness we noticed in that room. Now that the cold has spread through the entire cavern system, I'm not sure that going through the ice cave would necessarily be any more—or any less—dangerous than any other route we could take."

"And if those solution pipes lead us straight up to the cave entrance," Sanner pointed out, "we can get out of here a hell of a lot faster than if we went back along the ledge through that vertical chasm."

If for no other reason than that, Kirk was willing to investigate this alternate route. No matter what strange phenomenon was causing the increasing cold in these caves, so far all it had done was get progressively worse. It would be worth taking a calculated risk as long as it paid off in a quicker escape.

"All right, gentlemen, we'll try your way first." He helped Sanner collect up the rest of Jaeger's gear. "Maybe while we're hiking, the *Enterprise* will have a chance to fix whatever problems she's having topside and we can try hailing her again."

"That would be an even better solution," Jaeger agreed. He sounded weary with the cold and the long hours spent waiting in the dark. "It seems almost unbelievable that the ship should be having mechanical problems right at the moment when we needed her to retrieve us."

Kirk considered the events of the past few days and found an unexpected smile tugging at his mouth. He hoped it didn't look as sardonic as it felt. "Not really, Lieutenant. Not if you knew what the ship's been through since we left you here."

"Well, there is one thing we know for sure." Sanner swung a pack over his shoulder and straightened his carbide light on his head. "Whatever's going on up there, it can't possibly be as bad as what's going on down here."

Sulu had a hard time tearing his gaze away from the ominous planetary shadow that was Tlaoli. He knew that staring at its looming bulk wouldn't do anything but deepen the icy spike of adrenaline in his bloodstream, but there was something hypnotic, almost majestic, about the way the planet swirled closer and closer on their visual scanners. It might almost have been beautiful if he hadn't been sickly aware that it was actually the *Enterprise* doing the spinning as she was dragged down the curve of Tlaoli's gravity well by the strange forces emanating from this malevolent alien planet.

"Helm, report!" Spock said sharply.

Sulu glanced down at his monitors and discovered that his hands had somehow punched in the appropriate course analysis commands while his brain was transfixed with the unexpected beauty of disaster. "Five minutes to terminal atmospheric impact," he said. "We need full thrust from the auxiliary engines in two minutes or less, sir, or we won't be able to change course in time to avoid it."

"Mr. Scott, did you hear that?" Spock asked through his personal communicator. He had handed it to McCoy to hold for him now, and the doctor had thoughtfully dialed its amplifier to maximum levels. Right now, that only made it easier to hear the bleakness of the chief engineer's voice.

"I can't give you impulse power that fast, Mr. Spock. The ionization rings have just started charging. Three minutes is the soonest I can give you even partial thrust."

Sulu punched the estimate into his projected course curves. "That will put us through the thermosphere and several kilometers into the mesosphere before we change course," he warned. "Without shields, the ship could burn up or break apart completely."

"And we cannot power the shields without creating further delay in the ignition of the impulse engines. Hmmm." Spock's tone was deliberative rather than despairing, as if he'd just been given a complicated intellectual puzzle to solve. Sulu heard an indignant snort from McCoy, still strapped into the command chair.

"Don't just stand there thinking about how ironic it all is, Spock. Do something!"

The Vulcan turned, swaying just a little as the ship plummeted into another series of spins. "Do you have a suggestion, Doctor?"

McCoy glared at him. "No. But if the captain were here, I know he wouldn't just be standing around thinking! He'd be—hell, I don't know—throwing rocks out the hatches to lighten the load or something!"

Spock's voice turned very dry. "Dr. McCoy, we are not a hot air balloon."

"But we could throw out photon torpedoes!" said Sulu. "If we could manage to get the shields up in time—"

At first, he wasn't sure Spock understood what he meant. Before he could open his mouth to explain further, however, the Vulcan first officer swung around so abruptly that for the first time, he lost his balance and slid across the plunging bridge. McCoy shot out his free hand to steady him, but instead of grabbing hold, Spock simply plucked the communicator out of the doctor's hand and let his momentum carry him across to the unmanned weapons station. "Mr. Scott! Stop charging the impulse engines and divert that power to shields and torpedo bays. I repeat, divert impulse power to shields and torpedo bays!" He glanced over his shoulder at the engineering station. "Mr. Russ, reroute the power circuits from helm to weapons control—"

"I can do it quicker from here, Commander." Sulu punched in a command he had only ever used in battle simulations, usually ones in which the ship ended up being destroyed. It was designed to shunt all helm power temporarily to weapons, so the ship could fire one last-ditch salvo at an overwhelming enemy. An ordinary planetary gravity well probably wasn't the sort of enemy the ship's designers had foreseen when they built in that emergency override, but otherwise this was exactly the kind of desperate situation it was designed for. Sulu just hoped the final outcome would be better.

His helm panel abruptly went dark, and Sulu glanced over in time to see a flicker of lights spring up on the weapons panel instead. "Torpedo bays at full power!" said Scotty's tense voice. Sulu wondered if he, like Spock, had understood the plan without being told, or if he was loyally obeying orders that must have seemed suicidal on their face. "It's going to take a few minutes for the shields to reach full strength—"

"We don't have a few minutes." Sulu had glanced at the countdown clock on his monitor, just before the screen went black again. The neon shriek of auroral discharge across the viewscreen confirmed his memory of where the orbital curves intersected the planet's atmospheric layers. "We're already into the thermosphere. If we don't change the ship's course in the next thirty seconds, we won't be able to avoid terminal impact."

"Launching torpedoes now," was the first officer's terse reply.

There was a brief pause, just long enough for the silence on the bridge to become almost suffocating in its intensity. In that hush, Sulu could hear the hissing of Tlaoli's uppermost atmosphere across the *Enterprise*'s unprotected hull. Then a streak of silver knifed across the spinning night sky, the glow of gases scorched to phosphorescence by the force of an unseen object tearing through them at tremendous speed. In another minute, that same glow would envelop the *Enterprise* and all hope of avoiding destruction would be gone. "Torpedo detonation in five seconds," Spock said calmly. "Four, three, two, one—"

Photon torpedoes made impressive light displays when they exploded in deep space. In the plasmalike thermosphere of a terrestrial planet, however, they were nothing short of spectacular. The initial burst of light was only a little larger than normal, but its afterglow seemed to expand and brighten rather than fade. It flared from white to blue, from blue to nearly ultraviolet. For a moment the glow almost vanished, but then it burst out again as a series of auroras that streamed and rippled and dripped down the sky like liquid ribbons.

The atmospheric shock wave hit the ship three seconds later, slamming it so fiercely back toward empty space that sparks flew out from the weapons station and Mr. Spock finally staggered and fell. Sulu felt more than heard the deep groaning thunder of the ship's tough duranium hull as it absorbed the force of the impact through the incomplete shields, and heard the distant shriek of hull breach alarms. After a moment, he realized they were coming from Spock's open communicator, which had fetched up against the helm console.

"Rerouting power to helm control," Sulu said, although he wasn't sure if anyone was listening to him. He reversed the emergency override and ran through another abbreviated start-up sequence, then waited impatiently for the helm's internal gyroscopes to detect the speed and direction of the ship's unpowered motion. His instinct told him the *Enterprise* had reversed her course, but she was now surging in an unknown direction, helpless as flotsam carried on the expanding tide of the torpedo blast. He waited while the helm curves built up on his screen, and was relieved to see that although they were an unstable pulsing green, they were at least no longer spinning in multicolored chaos.

"We've been thrown out of planetary orbit and are headed for the outer edge of the solar system on vector nine-one-seven, speed seventeen hundred kilometers per second and stable." He glanced over his shoulder, searching for Spock's tall figure. It was nowhere to be seen, and the empty command chair told him that McCoy must have gone in search of the fallen Vulcan. "Commander Spock?"

"Helm report acknowledged," said a tight Vulcan voice. Sulu heard a grunt from McCoy, then saw the doctor lever Spock carefully to his feet near the viewscreen. The Vulcan stood with one shoulder hunched so awkwardly that the joint must have been knocked out of place. "Are any planets or asteroids known to intersect this heading, Lieutenant?"

"Nothing closer than the system's cometary cloud, sir," Riley reported as his own navigation boards came to life. Despite the continuing wail of alarms from the fallen communicator, power was starting to flow back into all of the bridge stations. Sulu could hear the life-support ventilators reactivate, filling the bridge with their familiar white noise. "And we should have several hours to adjust our course before we get there."

"Very good, Mr. Riley." Spock shrugged off McCoy's supporting arm and walked up the inertially generated tilt of the bridge deck toward the command chair. For once, the Vulcan actually sat down in it, releasing his breath with a small hiss although no expression of pain touched his narrow face. His intraship communicator whistled to life and he began to reach toward it, but froze in midmotion. "Doctor, if you would—" he said between his teeth.

McCoy snorted and came over to depress the button for him. "That's what you get for disobeying safety protocols, Mr. Spock. The regs clearly state that when inertial dampeners aren't working—"

"All sectors, damage reports," Spock said into the intercom, effectively cutting off the physician's lecture.

"Scott here," said the main intercom. Behind the sound of the chief engineer's voice, Sulu could hear purposeful shouting and the sound of running feet as the lower decks crew scrambled to cope with the breach in the *Enterprise*'s hull. "Since the ship isn't tearing herself entirely to pieces, Mr. Spock, I'm assuming we managed to blast ourselves back out of the planet's gravity well."

"You are correct, Commander. How much damage did we sustain in the explosion?"

"Enough to keep me busy for the rest of our three-day visit here," Montgomery Scott said. "We didn't lose anyone in the hull breach, thank God, but it did wipe out our entire sensor array. If you want to do anything that involves scanning, beaming, or even communicating with that planet down there, Mr. Spock, you'll have to wait at least six hours to do it."

"That is—unfortunate," Spock said after a moment. His voice held a deepening timbre that might, in a human, have signified either sadness or regret. Sulu glanced over his shoulder in surprise, and saw Dr. McCoy giving the Vulcan an even more astonished look. Spock gazed back at them with a hint of reproach in his eyes, as if he found it hard to believe that the recent crisis could have erased their memories of what had taken place just before it. "I assume you recall our previous discussion, gentlemen, about why the captain might have called for immediate transport back to the ship. If any of our inferences were correct, six hours may be far too long a time for the cave rescue team to survive."

# Chapter Seven

THERE WAS A STRANGE kind of time dilation that occurred during times of crisis, Sulu had noticed. The rush of adrenaline triggered when your life hung in the balance stretched each individual second out like a bead of molten glass, drawn and twisted to an unbearably fragile thread. Once the instant had been endured, however, it melted back into transparency and was gone, leaving no trace of its passage in your mind. More than once when he'd piloted the *Enterprise* during long frantic chases or escapes, Sulu had glanced down at his helm chronometer and been astounded to see just how long he'd actually been on duty.

But time also took its revenge. The stretch of duty that followed right after a serious crisis moved as slowly and ponderously as geologic time, each minute weighted with the leaden aftermath of too much adrenaline and too much stress. It made some officers talk more than usual and others fall silent; some reluctant to leave their posts even when their shifts had ended and others anxious for release. In Sulu's case, the aftermath of tension always left him restless and bored and itching for more work. He could usually quench his unrest with a fierce session at the gym and a good night's sleep, but he did occasionally wonder if it meant he found the rush of making life-and-death decisions addictive. He wasn't sure that was a good trait to have when you were climbing Starfleet's command ladder . . . although he privately suspected that it was a trait he shared with James Kirk.

"Stop fidgeting!" Riley grumbled at him from down the helm. The navigator was usually one of those crewmen who got light-hearted and garrulous after a crisis, but Sulu suspected he was restraining his natural reaction so as not to remind anyone about his recent antics back at Psi 2000. "You're driving me and the computer both nuts."

Sulu glanced down at the stylus he had been tapping absently against his helm monitor, and was abashed to see that he had left a trail of thousands of little points dotted along their new orbital curves, as the computer obediently recorded each of his mindless marks. "Sorry," he said, erasing the electronic litter with a brush of his hand across the screen. "I was thinking."

"About changing the orbit again?" Riley asked. "Sir," he added as a hasty afterthought. With Spock currently down in sickbay to have his shoulder put back in place, and Scotty deeply absorbed in trying to repair the damaged sections of the ship, command of the *Enterprise* had unexpectedly defaulted to Sulu. He hadn't bothered to call Rhada or Hansen to the bridge to replace him at the helm, since he knew Spock wouldn't let McCoy keep him out of commission for very long. But Sulu had never missed fourth-in-command Uhura more than right now.

"I think the orbit's fine just the way Mr. Spock approved it," Sulu told his navigator, and wished he could believe that as firmly as he could say it. When they had first gotten impulse power back and swung the *Enterprise* away from her unplanned trip to the cometary cloud, he and Riley had laid in a course that kept them safely distant from Tlaoli and its starship-snagging power surges. It wasn't common for a ship to maintain a cruising level that far away from the planet, because when gravity could no longer be balanced against the ship's momentum to create a stable orbit, constant monitoring was required of the ship's pilot and navigator. But since Tlaoli's gravity well was no longer safe to orbit in, and neither the ship's scanners nor her transporters needed to be in range of the planet's surface until they had been repaired, Sulu hadn't expected any objections when he'd asked the ship's commanding officer to approve the course change.

But to his surprise, Commander Spock had vetoed the new course that had been presented to him. Instead, he'd ordered Sulu to resume cruising at their previous orbital level, at the far end of gravitational stability but well inside the planet's gravitational field. The Vulcan's rationale was, as usual, chillingly logical: To study the forces generated by this seemingly mundane planet, they had to activate it by staying within its reach. Of course, as Riley had sourly pointed out after Spock had left the bridge, the counterargument to that was pretty much the exact same statement.

"So what *were* you thinking about?" Riley inquired, and once again only tacked on the obligatory "Sir?" afterward.

"Warp cores," said Sulu absently, then took in a deep breath as he realized what he'd said. The restlessness plaguing him had been so bone deep that his surface thoughts had seemed trivial in comparison, idle speculations on the various salvage operations going on around the ship at that moment. *I should tell the commanding officer about what I just realized,* Sulu thought, then remembered that the commanding officer right now was himself. He sat indecisive for a moment, before it occurred to him to consider what Captain Kirk would do if he'd been the one to think of this. That made it easy.

"Riley, take the helm." The simple act of leaving his seat released so much of Sulu's restlessness that he suddenly understood why the captain tended to roam the bridge whenever things got tense. "I'm going to go check on something. Rhada will be coming on duty soon. Call her to the bridge early if anything strange starts happening."

"But you can't—" Riley closed his mouth on that protest, apparently realizing that, as the ship's current commanding officer, Sulu could in fact do anything he wanted. Even though he was technically Sulu's subordinate at this moment, however, they were still junior officers together, and junior officers looked after each other. "You sure you know what you're doing here, D'Artagnan?" the navigator asked in an undertone of real concern.

"Yes," Sulu said. And then, in a burst of honesty, "Pretty sure."

Riley snorted. "Well, get going, then. I'll try to remember the difference between forward and reverse while you're gone."

He was joking, of course. Like all starship navigators, Kevin Riley had trained as an emergency pilot and was perfectly capable of watching over the *Enterprise* as she orbited Tlaoli's modest disk. Unless the planet began tugging them down toward it again. That thought didn't stop Sulu, but it did lend some extra speed to his leap up the bridge steps and into the turbolift.

The lift seemed sluggish, and it jerked rather than slid through the transfer to the secondary hull. The auxiliary power generators were strong enough to run the ship's essential systems, but that didn't mean they all ran as smoothly as usual. Sulu caught himself drumming his fingers impatiently on the side of the lift chamber and forced himself to wrap them into fists instead. The trip to the main shuttlebay always took longer than he thought it should, he reminded himself. For all its deceptive nimbleness in battle, the *Enterprise* was an immense ship of the line, after all.

The turbolift finally slowed to a halt, its final jerk strong enough to make Sulu sway on his feet. The door didn't even try to slide open, however, and after a moment it occurred to Sulu that the force of the photon shock wave might also have breached the shuttle bay. A slow, underpowered hiss built up in the lift chamber and, with another little jerk, the doors grudgingly slid open on the vast coldness of the main shuttle bay.

It was entirely dark.

It was a good thing, Sulu thought in exasperation, that he was fifth in line of command among the primary bridge crew. Of course the shuttle bay would be dark. Hadn't he just been thinking about how only the ship's essential systems would be powered up to minimize the strain on the auxiliary generators? If he had been Captain Kirk, he'd have already thought of that and brought along a portable light for his inspection. As it was, he either had to face a long turbolift ride back up to the bridge—and possibly an interrogation from Mr. Spock once he got there—or take his chances bumping around in the dark looking for shuttles.

This time, Sulu's moment of indecision paid off. The longer he stood in the open doorway, the more his eyes adjusted to the dark, until eventually he could see the vague firefly glow that marked the cockpit windows of each shuttle nose. All the controls inside were alight and flashing, ready as usual for instant deployment should the need arise. The refracted glimmer of multicolored lights not only reassured Sulu that he could locate the shuttles in the darkness, it also told him that his original speculation about them had been correct.

He strode out into the shuttle bay with confidence, not even faltering when the turbolift door hissed shut and made the immense dark space even darker. He ducked under the first shuttle's landing gear with only the slightest brush of his head against the hull, and fumbled along the side until he found the touch panel that activated its hatch. It folded itself open with the powerful hum of a vessel whose warp core was functioning and fully connected. Brightness cascaded down around him as the internal lights sprang on in the shuttle's hold.

"Yes!" breathed Sulu in satisfaction. He vaulted into the hold and hurried forward to the cockpit. The shuttle's communicator was as alive and glowing as the rest of it, and he tuned it easily to the internal *Enterprise* frequency.

"Lieutenant Sulu to Commander Spock."

There was a pause, as if the ship's communications systems were having a little trouble with the automatic channel connection back to this unexpected source. Then he heard an imperturbable voice reply, "Spock here." From the background roar and shriek of ventilators and welding torches, Sulu guessed the first officer had already left the confines of Sickbay and was supervising the repairs to the hull and sensor array.

"Commander Spock, I'm down in the main shuttlebay—"

"And who has the conn, Lieutenant?"

Sulu swallowed. It had not occurred to him that he had to delegate command of anything but the ship's helm when he'd left the bridge, and none of the other junior officers there had thought to remind him. "Umm—Lieutenant Riley, sir."

"May the saints preserve us all." That was Montgomery Scott's distant but heartfelt voice through the din. Sulu winced, remembering that only twenty-four hours ago, the young man he'd just left in charge of the ship had been holed up in the engine room, blithely consigning them all to total destruction.

"Yes, well—it occurred to me, Mr. Spock, that the shuttles weren't connected to any of the *Enterprise*'s power circuits when the transporter beam hit that energy field. I came down to see if their internal warp cores were still functioning. And they are, sir."

"You're a remarkably bright lad, Mr. Sulu." Scott's voice held nothing but admiration now. Even alone in the darkened shuttle bay, Sulu felt his cheeks tighten a little with embarrassment. "We can hook one or two of those little warp cores into the main circuits and punch ourselves back up to full power before you can say whist."

"I actually wasn't thinking of that, sir," Sulu admitted. "I was thinking that we could take a shuttle down to the planet right now, without waiting for the transporters to be fixed."

For a while, there was only forbidding silence on the other end of the communicator channel. "An interesting suggestion, Lieutenant," Spock said at last. "But allow me to point out that the research shuttle originally sent down to the planet lost its power when it flew over the caves where Captain Kirk is now trapped. What makes you think that any other shuttle would be safe to fly?"

"Nothing, sir. But if I stayed away from the cave region, I could at least evacuate the members of the landing party that didn't get transported back to the ship." Sulu took a deep breath, gazing down at the reassuring lights that flashed up from the piloting boards. "And after that...you were the one, Mr. Spock, who said we needed to activate Tlaoli's energy field again in order to study it."

"Indeed," Spock said. "However, it would be preferable, Lieutenant, not to be in danger of falling out of the sky when you did so."

"If you don't mind me interrupting, Mr. Spock," said Montgomery Scott's voice in the background. "Now that I've seen how well our warp core's magnetic shielding stood up to that planet's power drain, I'm thinking that I could manage to install a similar shield around the shuttle's core and engines together, so they couldn't be made to lose power. Mr. Sulu might lose his communicator and his sensors, but if he can fly by sight he at least won't fall out of the sky."

"I can fly by sight," Sulu assured them both. "During the day for certain, and maybe even at night once I've found my way around the area once or twice."

"There should be several hours of daylight remaining on the side of Tlaoli where the remaining survey crews are." Spock's voice had lost its repressive edge and now sounded merely thoughtful. "How soon will you be able to divert a crew of engineers to the task of shielding one of the shuttles, Mr. Scott?"

"If it means getting the captain back and evicting that young idiot Riley from the conn?" Sulu could practically feel the gust of the Chief Engineer's snort. "Immediately!"

"You've got ice in your hair."

Chekov combed a hand back through his hair without actually looking up from the map he had wedged against the conduit wall. Bits of half-frozen water spattered the surface of his notebook, deflating on impact into regular liquid drops, only to begin freezing again almost immediately. He'd given up being irritated by them. Swiping them off his workspace with the side of his hand, he then had to pull his glove off with his teeth to keep from smearing wet nano-weave all over the map. At least he knew the glove would dry. It had managed to do so the dozen other times he'd paused with it suspended in his mouth while he finished updating his measurements.

By now the ice was everywhere. It had coated the travertine flowstone like poured polyurethane, sharpening the delicate oranges, greens and reds of the original mineral salts into a crystalline riot of color. The omnipresent shush and drip of water that had accompanied their descent into the caves was now silenced. In its place, expanding ice ticked an irregular rhythm, sometimes firing off a deep-voiced cannon shot to catch everyone by surprise and make them jump. It reminded Chekov of how the lake at the heart of Gorky Park grudgingly gave itself over to autumn's advance every year. You could hear the battle raging several blocks away for weeks at a time, until winter finally swept in one long bitter night and put an end to all of it. The next morning, the lake lay still and silent, as smooth and tame as if it had been paved over by glass.

Tlaoli's caves were not so simple a matter. Chekov had long ago given up trying to represent the true shape of their passages on his map. Ice had reduced them all to narrowed, glass tubes, with less floor exposed every meter they traveled, and only faint hints of the surfaces beneath. If the landing party somehow passed from these artificially straight and regular conduits into more wild and undirected natural cave at this point, Chekov almost doubted any of them would be able to tell until they caught themselves straddling another abyss. Which made the compass readings and measurements he recorded on this new map even more important than the ones he'd had to recall from his memory of the trip in. At least up top they would have the fallback of the spot markers they'd left propped on little ledges and piles of stones, pointing back the way they'd come in. Down here, they had only Jaeger's memory and Chekov's maps to tell them where they stood in relation to the surface world. A discrepancy of five or ten meters could mean the difference between finding the topside entrance, or wandering about down here until their carbide ran out.

A little laugh from the other end of his old-fashioned tape measure brought part of his attention back to the security guard Kirk had assigned to assist him. "I don't know how you can work in this cold without gloves." Crewman Yuki Smith switched the metal roll from one hand to the other, careful not to move it from the spot where Chekov had instructed her to hold it, but obviously eager to alternate her gloved hands in her pockets in an effort to keep herself warm. "They're gonna have to cut off half my fingers by the time we get home."

Chekov flexed his own fingers, noted that they were pink with cold but only a little stiff. He shrugged and went back to writing. "It's not so bad."

Smith fidgeted foot-to-foot for another long moment, then guessed, "You're Russian, aren't you?"

The question, so apparently unrelated to anything else they were doing, surprised him almost to the point of embarrassment. He looked up for the first time, and found Smith's round Asian face split by a delighted smile.

"I thought you might be," she explained cheerfully. "I could kind of tell by your name, and your accent. But mostly it was just by how the cold doesn't seem to bother you while I'm *dying!*" Then, when it seemed to occur to her that even further explanation might be required, "I lived in Moscow for four years." She sounded quite proud of this feat. "My dad's a history professor—he had a temporary position at the University of Moscow when I was six." Just as quickly, she colored self-consciously and dipped an awkward little shrug. "Everybody at the University knew English, though, so I never did learn how to speak Russian."

As near as Chekov had been able to tell, no one else on board the ship knew how to speak Russian, either. "You pronounce *Moscow* correctly," he told her. Partly because it was true, and partly because it seemed like the sort of thing she would be glad to know.

He was right. Her smile exploded into full brightness again, as though he's just paid her the most wonderful compliment. "I do?"

"You do." He released his end of the tape measure and let it go skittering back toward her across the icy floor.

Smith caught the slithering tape in a smooth, athletic gesture, arcing the metal holding reel over to her other hand as she again switched pockets. "You must be really good at this." It seemed an odd compliment to pay someone who was only doing what he'd been told, but became odder still when she continued, "You haven't had to ask me even once for the measurement. I can never estimate distances like that."

Ice as cold and killing as anything the cave had yet produced curdled inside his stomach. "Of course I've asked. I must have asked!" Every passage they'd traversed had its length marked in meters on his map, every minute angle or turn they'd made had its own compass reading carefully noted alongside. And yet even as he protested, he realized that he couldn't specifically remember asking Smith to read off any values. Ever. Not even when they first left the big column-crowded upper chamber where Smith's party had waited for so long. Chekov tried to swallow with a throat suddenly clogged with panic. "What was the last measurement?" he asked, as evenly as he could manage.

Even though she'd already dropped the reel back into one pocket, she came up with the number quickly enough. "Seven point nine meters."

Which was exactly what he had written within that narrow stretch of tunnel. He hadn't thought he was that good at visually measuring anything, not even a nearly straight line. But at the same time, he hadn't thought he could reconstruct his original map in the kind of detail he'd finally managed. Once he'd gotten started, though, it had all seemed very straightforward and obvious—as though he were sketching streets that he knew well, even if he'd never drawn them before.

While anyone else might have given himself credit for simply discovering skills he hadn't known he possessed, Chekov found himself struggling with the urge to retrace their entire route through these lower tunnels, checking each value he'd already committed to his map but apparently never measured. It was bad enough that he'd had to make the reconstruction at all—he didn't want to find out how Captain Kirk would react to finding out that the new maps they had might be completely untrustworthy.

"We should catch up with the others." He tried to mask his unease by hastily gathering up the rest of the gear. Chiseling a little shelf in the ice for one of the spot markers, he arranged it extra carefully, as if that could make up for everything else he'd done wrong today.

They measured the next two segments—both of them straight and purely line-of-sight—with maximum care and minimum conversation.

Chekov made a point of verifying each compass reading before writing it down, and of asking Smith (sometimes twice) for each linear value before letting her roll up the tape measure. In every case, he knew what the answer would be as soon as he thought to look for it. Even so, the thought of backtracking gnawed at him as they approached the entrance to the final chamber. *What kind of an officer am I?* he thought angrily. *If I'm not sure about the accuracy of my work, I should say something!* Yet another part of him *was* sure. He knew without being able to defend his conviction that the numbers as they stood were correct—that backtracking would only waste time without supplying them with the slightest bit of useful information. His certainty about that scared him a little.

*It seems like you're scared of everything.* And he realized that fear was what lay at the heart of his frantic need to be right about this. Not just fear of being wrong, or fear of being reprimanded. Fear in general, and the fact that it churned in his belly like an out of control fire while being apparently absent in everyone else.

Chekov caught himself slowing as they reached the archway leading into Jaeger's "ice cave." Human voices floated out to meet them on the soft glow of a half-dozen carbide lamps. Sanner had produced a few extra of the primitive devices, although the earlier landing party's helmets had no place to mount them. Chekov and Smith had one of the unmounted lamps, dangling from a piece of rope in the security guard's hand when it wasn't waiting equidistant between them while they measured out some distance for the map. Chekov used adjusting the flame on the clunky device as an excuse to pause while they were still out in the ice-bound conduit.

"Crewman Smith—"

"You can call me Yuki."

He nodded absently, not wanting to lose his momentum now that he'd gotten started. "Yuki... When you're down on planetary missions, do you..." He looked squarely at her, committed himself to the question. "Are you ever afraid?"

She lifted her eyebrows in surprise, as though the thought had never occurred to her. "Nah. Why should I be?"

Why indeed. Although she wasn't quite as tall as Chekov, she was powerfully built and possessed of the reflexes and easy coordination that Chekov had always envied in natural athletes. In addition, she was a security specialist. Unlike the command cadets, who were expected to know a little bit about almost everything, trained security personnel focused only on the skills required to protect a starship and her crew from every imaginable danger. If someone like Smith didn't feel one hundred percent capable and safe while doing her job, who on board could?

He nodded slowly, handing back the unmounted lamp and holding out his hand for the tape measure in return. He realized now that he should have expected as much from an experienced crewman. He should have known when he first came to, vomiting up what felt like ten liters of water after tripping stupidly on an icy rock ledge, to find Captain Kirk kneeling beside him and joking about their predicament. Joking. They'd gone down the same chasm, nearly drowned in the same freezing water, and Chekov had been so scared he felt like crying. More than ever, he found it very hard to believe that there was anything resembling command potential hiding anywhere inside him.

Smith caught his elbow when he turned to escape into the final chamber. "Hey, wait a sec...."

He stopped, but couldn't bring himself to turn and face her. *Cowardice has many forms.*

"I lied a little." She said it very quietly. Chekov couldn't tell whose dignity she was hoping to preserve, his or her own. "The first time I went down—maybe the first two or three—I was really scared." Her hand fell away, and she moved around in front of him to sit on a boulder just outside the entrance arch. "I know that probably sounds stupid. But I've been out of Security Academy for almost a year, and it seems like we lose somebody from the division every month. There are so many guys that I helped pack up to go down...only to have them not come back. When Chief Giotto first told me I was going on a landing party, I almost called in sick." She tried on a little smile that came nowhere near its earlier brightness.

"But you don't get scared anymore?"

She shrugged, seemed to reconsider giving him another too-easy answer. "Just nervous now, I guess. I mean, I still feel something, but so far this is the first excitement I've ever seen on a planet, and it hasn't been so bad." She aimed a playful punch at his shoulder. "And I got to meet you, didn't I?"

Right now, Chekov wasn't sure how much value she ought to place on that.

"Don't worry—you'll get used to it. After you've been down two or three times, you'll get so psyched about seeing all the new stuff and learning all the new things, you won't even think about being scared. I promise."

Somehow, that completely sincere assertion charmed him most of all. He smiled. "Two or three," he echoed, trying for a touch of humor. "I'll start keeping count, then, so I don't miss the one where it gets easy."

She laughed, a full-bodied, brazen peal that echoed marvelously off the frozen walls. Chekov was beginning to suspect that Smith did very few things by half-measures.

"Do me a favor—" She bumped close to him as they passed through the entrance, grabbing his arm again to whisper in his ear. "—don't tell anybody what we talked about. Security guards aren't supposed to get scared, you know."

Neither were future commanders. He gave her hand a single solemn shake. "You have my word as an officer."

Her return grip was a good deal stronger than he expected. "I'm not an officer, so all I can do is promise."

"That's good enough for me."

The ice chamber seemed to swarm into existence from the darkness as they made their way inside. Flows and curtains of ice, as intricate as any travertine, glowed as their light swept across them, and Chekov could just pick out the positions of the other party members by the auroras haloing their helmet lamps. The ceiling overhead soared higher than the reach of the dim carbides, but its surface twinkled like the stars outside where ice had clustered in the crevices. Mist swirled in gentle eddies, tiny frost-like crystals coalesced out of the chamber's ambient humidity. Chekov had no idea if this chamber was any colder than the one they'd left behind, but the twisted columns of ice staggered across its expanse leant a unique sense of chill to its murky air.

"Stop here." He pushed the tape measure back into Smith's hand, and backed away from her toward the nearest column. She clapped her end to the edge of the doorway without having to ask what he was doing.

Already their cave jumpers had dulled to a soft pastel, furred over with frost as though they were grains of sand in an oyster's maw. It occurred to Chekov that these pillars of ice must have formed in the same way the flowstone structures had in the previous chamber—built up by dripping water leaking in from overhead. While their spacing wasn't strictly regular, they occurred often enough across the expanse of room that Chekov suspected they corresponded to the breaches in the ceiling Jaeger had described earlier. That meant matching them precisely to the details of the upstairs map would go a long way toward guaranteeing their safe exit from this place.

Apparently, he wasn't the only one to have considered that possibility.

"Heads up, Rand McNally!" Sanner appeared as if out of nowhere, sliding down the pillar behind Chekov in a shower of dislodged frost. He pushed himself neatly off the column just in time to hit the frozen floor flat-footed. "Sorry about that—" The geologist tousled Chekov's hair in a gesture the young ensign assumed was meant to be friendly. New bits of ice went flying everywhere. "I didn't want you to end up with a crampon in your head."

"I appreciate your dedication to team safety, Mr. Sanner." Kirk's voice preceded the captain out of the darkness. He'd apparently left his helmet and its attached light with one of the other groups, and joined them now bareheaded in the circle of Sanner's carbide. "How do our chances of making the top look?" the captain asked Sanner. Chekov started to excuse himself, but stopped when Kirk lifted a stilling hand.

Sanner grinned as he picked ice off of one boot. "Good! This one doesn't go through, but I'm sure a lot of these must." He twisted loose a piton with some effort. "Once we locate the right one, I shouldn't have any trouble getting up there and securing a rope."

"Then our only question is how to locate the right one." Kirk turned to Chekov. "Have you got those maps handy, Ensign?"

"Yes, sir." Chekov handed Kirk the notebook without thinking, then realized the captain might not immediately follow how he'd tried to over-lay the various pages of mapping one on top the other. Feeling his face heat up with discomfort, he moved awkwardly alongside Kirk to flip through several of the sheets. "I didn't map all of the holes in the floor when we passed them inside the first entrance, sir," he explained, hurry-ing to find that sheet to illustrate his explanation. "But as long as we know for certain *where* this room is below that entrance—" He flipped back several pages to the newest maps. "—we should be able to identify which of these columns corresponds to the holes I did record."

Kirk studied the maps for a moment, turning back and forth through the pages himself as if committing them to memory. "All right, then, Mr. Chekov—which pillar is your first choice?"

Chekov opened his mouth to stammer an answer, then shut it again abruptly. *This is when you should tell him! This is when you should admit that you don't know how you made this map!* But he couldn't. Everything inside him insisted the map was correct—as correct as he could make it— and he couldn't pretend it wasn't just because fear made him insecure. He waved Smith over, took the lamp from her hand and positioned her with the tape measure against the side of the frozen column. Then, consulting the earliest of the maps he had redrawn, he said to her, "Tell me when I've gone almost seventy-five meters."

He flipped open the compass, rotated it carefully to place himself just a few degrees shy of Tlaoli's magnetic south, and began pacing off the distance to the closest hole he was sure of. Behind him, he could hear Kirk's steady footsteps, and the arrhythmic *clank, clank* of Sanner wrestling the last of his pitons out of the pillar before following a few me-ters farther back. *Please, let this be right,* Chekov prayed. He didn't think he could stand to fail Kirk another time.

He didn't know how far they'd gone—he had his end of the tape held near his hip, and Smith had the end with the readings that counted. But he knew they must be almost to the pass-through he was looking for when Kirk's hand suddenly seized on his shoulder. "Do you hear that?" the captain asked with frightening urgency.

Chekov tried to listen, tried to turn and face his commander before asking what he was supposed to be listening for. Instead, his feet seemed to drop out from under him, and the cold crashed in with a force so powerful, he felt his whole body go numb with shock and terror. Then water flooded into his lungs and he was drowning. And he had no idea or memory of how he came to be here.

# Chapter Eight

LATER, what Uhura would remember about that moment wasn't the shock of the event itself or the sudden awareness of danger that prickled in the cavern's frigid air. It was her own sickening plummet from hope to unexpected horror. She had let herself be lulled into premature confidence, watching Sanner clamber so easily up the icy staircase that could be their ladder out of darkness. She'd even smiled a little, hearing Tomlinson tease Martine about finally giving up the responsibility of her pack full of power supplies. There had been a warmth in the young weapons officer's voice that implied a little more than camaraderie, although not yet quite affection. Uhura was just romantic enough to appreciate that delicate transition in a man's voice, and just old enough not to wish she had been its recipient. So she had smiled and remained discreetly silent, listening to Martine gently refuse to ever surrender her burden to a man who'd spent ten hours trying to dig his way out of a cave with his bare hands. There would be small notes and flowers appearing on the weapons deck as soon as they were back on the ship, Uhura thought in amusement. And it was then, in that moment of relaxation, that instant of certainty that there *would* be a "back-on-the-ship" in the very near future, that she had heard Sanner's fierce bellow of alarm.

"They're *gone!*"

The cave geologist stood frozen in the circle of his own carbide glow, particles of frost kicked up into a swirl around him from his sudden plunging stop. Beyond him, where Uhura's subconscious mind had a moment before recorded an impression of light and activity and human presence, there was now only darkness.

"What happened? Did someone fall into a crevasse?" The other cave specialist, Jaeger, swung around and began to cross from the far side of the ice-filled chamber. The urgency of Sanner's outflung arm stopped him in his tracks. "A hidden one, covered with a crust of ice?"

"No, nothing like that!" Sanner turned to face them with an exaggerated care that revealed even more so than his strained voice just how apprehensive he was. "They were standing on solid rock, I could see it sticking out through the ice. There was some kind of funny rushing noise, almost like a vacuum chamber opening. And now the rock's still there, but they're gone!" His voice rose as if it needed to cut through something besides the appalled silence. Perhaps it was their stunned disbelief he was trying to pierce. "The captain and Ensign Chekov just disappeared into thin air!"

That was it. In that moment, Uhura felt her easy end-of-mission confidence crash down into something that might almost have been despair. Her first instinct was one of pure denial—Sanner couldn't possibly be right, his story was just too ludicrous to believe. She opened her mouth, but before she could speak, Tomlinson voiced the thought for her.

"Are you sure of that, Sanner?"

"No, Lieutenant, he's right." Yuki Smith's voice held such an unhappy mixture of shock and sadness that Uhura's doubts were shriveling even before the security guard went on to explain. "I was watching Ensign Chekov the whole time he walked the tape out. At sixty meters, he and the captain stopped for a moment, and then they just vanished. The light went away with them—blown out, just like a candle flame."

"You're sure of that?" Jaeger demanded. "They didn't take a step forward or fall down—they were standing absolutely still when it happened?"

"Yes, sir."

Sanner craned his head around, and the appalled look on his face told Uhura he had already come to the same conclusion she had. The mysterious force that had once brought ancient starships crashing down on Tlaoli had just proved that it was still in existence... and that it could make individual people vanish completely. Uhura opened her mouth, unsure of what she meant to say until it emerged.

"Mr. Sanner, I want you to back away very slowly from where you're standing."

He blinked at her, looking a little startled by the sternness of her order. Uhura gulped in an ice-cold breath, feeling a little startled herself. If anyone had asked her a moment ago who among this group was Kirk's second-in-command, she would have been hard pressed to remember that it was her. But now that Kirk was gone and a crisis had engulfed them, the realization that she was in charge and responsible for the safety of this small, stranded group unexpectedly steadied her topsy-turvy emotions and gave her voice an edge it usually lacked.

"How do I know where it's safe to step?" Sanner demanded. Uhura lost a little more of her own hopelessness as she heard the need for reassurance in his voice. She glanced around the ice cave in search of justification for him.

"The tape measure that Ensign Chekov dropped is lying on the ground behind you. If you follow it straight back, you won't hit whatever—whatever took them away." Uhura wasn't really sure about that, but she *was* sure that Sanner needed to move. Whatever alien force had swallowed Kirk and Chekov had swept over them while they were standing still. That implied it could sweep over other members of the party, and Sanner was in the most dangerous spot, only a few meters away from the point where the other two had vanished.

"Move, Mr. Sanner. *Now!*" Uhura put all the force she could muster into that final command, and to her surprise it came out sounding remarkably like something Kirk would say. Sanner gulped, but inched three careful backward steps along the tape measure before turning and covering the rest of the distance in an undignified rush.

"Now, I want everyone else to make their way back here toward the entrance, one at a time. Mr. Jaeger, you're the closest to that side of the cave. Please move first."

The older geologist nodded and came toward her at a less hurried pace. He looked more baffled than worried, and kept peering down at the ground as if he was still sure that a natural cave phenomenon could explain what had just happened. "D'Amato next," said Uhura and watched the other geologist cross back safely from the ice column he'd been examining. Something in Uhura wanted to relax and let them all come back at once, now that three had made it across the ice-sheathed room safely, but she remembered all too clearly her recent brush with overconfidence.

"Palamas next," she ordered, ignoring the impatient way Sanner shifted from boot to boot in the entranceway. Since Yuki Smith had never left the threshold, and Davis and Wright were standing right next to it, the number of carbide lights in the chamber had dwindled down to two by now, and the primeval darkness they had chased out of the ice cave was starting to surge back in from its corners. Since Tomlinson wore no light, his shadow stretched out away from Uhura and Martine to join the darkness at the cave edges, like a stream going back to the sea. It wavered a little, either from the carbide flicker or the weapons officer's own weariness. Or maybe—

"Tomlinson next," Uhura said, but before the young man could move, Martine screamed and threw out a hand to stop him.

"There's something there, right beside you—Robbie, hold still!"

"What is it?" Sanner was almost leaping up and down in the threshold in an attempt to get a better view inside the darkened cave. "I can't see anything!"

"I saw something waver in the air," Martine said, her voice tense. "It almost looked like heat shimmers, like the afterglow you get right after a torpedo goes out the bay. It's just to Lieutenant Tomlinson's right."

"I see it." Tomlinson craned his head across one shoulder. He took a sideways step toward Martine, then froze abruptly. "Is it following me? I think I saw it move, and I don't want—"

"Lieutenant Uhura." That was Yuki Smith's diffident voice from the entrance. "We might be able to see it better if it were darker in here."

Uhura took a breath that was a little too fast and deep. She paid the price when cold air burned down the inside of her throat, but right now that was the least of her worries. "Everyone adjust your lights down," she ordered, but that wasn't the hard part. The hard part was what came next. "Martine, you and I will shut our lights off entirely."

"Aye, sir," said the female weapons officer, as if it was a perfectly normal command to be given when you were inside a cave with a completely unknown hazard on the loose. She reached up to her helmet quickly enough to make Uhura a little ashamed about her own hesitation, and her light was the first to wink out. Uhura's went a second later, then the glow from the threshold dimmed to orange-gold. The darkness inside the ice cave congealed down to a nearly solid black. Uhura closed her eyes and counted to twenty to help them adjust, then opened them again.

A veil of phosphorescence, the clear burning blue of a flame's heart, hung in the air about ten meters away from her. It rippled and swirled and billowed, sometimes drifting a little further away, sometimes curling a little closer. There didn't seem to be any particular purpose in its movement, but it was eddying perilously close to the darker shadows that were the two weapons officers.

"Crewmen, fall back to your left!" Uhura didn't wait to watch them obey. She could see that she was blocking their only safe line of retreat, and she scrambled to clear it without even looking behind her. A jagged block of ice caught at her heels and nearly spun her to the ground, but Uhura felt a gloved hand catch her and steady her back to balance before she could fall. She glanced up and saw Sanner's face peering down at her worriedly.

"Thanks, Zap." It didn't seem like the right moment to chastise him for leaving the safety of the threshold. "Did Martine and Tomlinson get away safely?"

"Yes, sir." Their joined voices came from so nearly the same place in the darkness beside her that Uhura suspected they were clutching at each other's hands.

"Good." She kept her gaze fixed on the fire-colored phosphorescence that hung across the room from them. "It didn't follow us, did it?"

"No, but it's not exactly staying put, either," Sanner said frankly. "I'd feel a lot better, Lieutenant, if we were as far away from that thing as we could possibly get."

"Me, too." Uhura reached up to reignite her carbide lamp and brightened it to a fierce white glow that made the ominous phosphorescent curtain disappear. Then she headed back to the entrance of the ice cave, thinking out her orders as she went. "We're going to head back down the conduits. Jaeger and Sanner, you're in the lead. Smith, follow them and make sure you find the spot markers Mr. Chekov left along the way. Wright, you go next with Palamas and D'Amato to help you—" She had been about to say, "carry Davis," but that determined young woman was already making her way unsteadily toward the exit. "—with anything," Uhura finished lamely, but Wright gave her a somber nod before she turned to go, as if she'd heard the thought that had been left unspoken.

That left her with Martine and Tomlinson. Uhura turned to face them, wondering if the two young weapons officers were up to the task she was about to assign. The glare of her carbide light showed her two tired but steadfast faces, as well as a pair of unabashedly clasped hands.

"We're going to be the rear guard," she told them quietly. "That means one of us has to wait in the dark while the rest of the team goes on, to make sure that blue glow isn't coming after us."

Tomlinson reached up ruefully to touch the useless photon lamp on his caving helmet. "I guess that would be me."

"That helmet's not glued to your head," Angela Martine told him tartly. "And neither is mine. We can take turns."

"We'll all three take turns," Uhura said. "Staring at nothing for too long makes you start to think you're seeing things whether they're there or not." She pulled out her whistle and swung it between her fingers. "We'll leave one lookout on guard for five minutes, then whistle them up the right path to join us and leave a new one behind. Understood, gentlemen?"

"Aye, sir!" said Tomlinson, but it was Martine who asked, "What should we do if we see the blue glow coming behind us?"

"Whistle the Starfleet emergency signal," Uhura said. "Three short, three long, three short."

"Then run like hell," Tomlinson added grimly. "Before you find out the hard way where the captain and Mr. Chekov went."

She had started to measure the trip in watches, Uhura realized. Two more until she had to be the one left behind, then one more, then the ice-cold moment when Martine and Tomlinson tramped away after the rest of the cave party and left her standing alone with her helmet in her hands, watching the twirl of fire die in front of the reflector as a final drip of water sizzled on the reactive carbide rocks inside. By the time her eyes adjusted enough to see the departing glow of Martine's helmet, it was nearly gone. The sound of Tomlinson's voice lingered a little longer, rising once to a crack of laughter at something Martine said. Then the noise faded under the ubiquitous pop and crack of ice crystallizing inside the alien conduits, and Uhura was truly alone in the darkness.

It had gotten even colder than when they first tramped down this way, cold enough that the engineered fibers of her cave jumper couldn't tighten enough to insulate her body against it anymore. While she'd been walking, Uhura barely noticed the minute heat loss, but as soon as she began standing watch, she could feel a slow, inexorable chill seeping through to her skin. Her first instinct was to start pacing and generate more heat, but the ice-slicked surface beneath her feet quashed that idea. Uhura tried isometric exercises instead, but they didn't seem to keep her much warmer. She finally fell back on swinging her arms back and forth as rapidly as she could. That at least gave her the advantage of counting how many times she had clapped her hands together rather than the ridiculously slow passage of her five allotted minutes.

At clap 173, Uhura thought she saw her hands leave a filmy blue path through the darkness as she swung them in front of her.

Fear propelled her into an unbalanced backward scrabble. She'd forgotten about the icy footing, and when her boots hit a ledge she hadn't been expecting, they skidded out from under her completely. Uhura got her hands down in time to catch her weight and avoid the worst of the jolt, but she was left sprawled and unable to tell which way she had been facing before. She stared fiercely out into the darkness, trying to ignore the melting optical illusions that floated across your vision when you tried too hard to see in the dark. Maybe what she had glimpsed had just been another of those phantom traces of light, coincidentally moving in the same direction as her hands.

"And maybe you're just going nuts," Uhura told herself bracingly. But as soon as she spoke she realized she could see the filigree edges of her misted breath turn blue in the darkness. Her hands shot up, the one with the whistle to her lips, the other to the lumpy carbide light on her helmet. But with her teeth clamped on the small whistle and her fingers poised on the igniter lever, Uhura paused. Now that she had made the decision that would soon bless her with light, she ironically found her nerves steady enough to tolerate another few moments of darkness. And there was something different about this blue light, something she wanted to make sure of before she sparked the carbide's fierce glare and drove it completely out of sight.

Uhura swung her head back and forth, trying to use the more light-sensitive corners of her vision. As soon as she did that, she realized what she was seeing. The bluish glow wasn't hanging in the air—it came through the ice crust that covered the walls of the conduit. Beneath the ice, Uhura could just glimpse a dim and deeper blue-violet radiation shining from the ancient alien walls. It refracted into brighter shafts of blue inside the wall's icy coatings wherever internal cracks and fractures caught and focused it, then sent it slanting out into the cold air. It had been one of those natural crystal mirrors that had illuminated Uhura's hands and breath. If she hadn't been standing in exactly that spot, Uhura realized, she might never have seen the light at all.

She scrambled to her feet, wondering if the sides of this conduit had been glowing all along. If the ice back along their path had been thicker or milkier, neither she nor the two weapons officers might have noticed that near-ultraviolet glimmer. But now that she had seen it, there could be no further doubt. The light was rising off the engraved alien metal that lined this alien passage, and where it was focused into a stronger shaft, it looked exactly the same as the blue phosphorescence that had rippled through the ice cave an hour ago.

That answered two of the questions that had been haunting Uhura while she alternately walked and waited in the dark. Now she knew the force that had swept away Captain Kirk and Ensign Chekov hadn't been an accident, hadn't sprung unplanned from any natural deposit of transperiodic ore minerals. It was a product of some unknown alien technology, still alive and working in this cave despite the millions of years that must have passed since its makers had left or gone extinct. And worse than that—Uhura also knew that their departure from the ice cave hadn't delivered them from the dangers of this ancient alien installation. It had merely put some space between them and the most dangerous part of whatever offensive or defensive force had sprung to life here in the dark.

Far off down the conduit, a whistle blew once, then fell silent. After a pause, it blew again. Martine or Tomlinson, Uhura realized, summoning her up the trail to join them.

Had it really been five minutes that she had sat there, watching the glow of alien light and mulling over all its implications? Uhura shook her head in disbelief and felt ice slide down her neck from the hoarfrost that had settled on her hair. She reignited her carbide lamp, tucked her whistle back into her pocket, then headed up the slippery ice-floored conduit. The back of her neck was prickling, and she knew it wasn't just because of the ice crystals melting their way down to her jumper's collar. Now that she knew these conduits were intrinsically connected to the alien force that had been activated in this underground structure, she couldn't rid herself of the feeling that the darkness she passed through was somehow watching her.

"Lieutenant Uhura?" Martine's carbide glow came partway down the conduit to meet her, not normal for a shift change. "Be careful, the ice is really thick up here. We're back to where the waterfall used to be."

Uhura took a step up toward the other woman and found herself sliding back down the steep, icy slope rather than advancing up it. She accepted Martine's outstretched hand to pull her over the crest of the former plunge pool, which now looked more like an ice-filled fountain permanently frozen in mid-splash.

"Did Mr. Jaeger find the blowhole Survey Team Three used to come down here?"

"He found where he thinks it used to be," Martine said, grimly. "It's completely covered with ice."

Uhura followed her around the frozen torrent of thickly clustered icicles that had once been a waterfall. "Could we break through?"

"Wrong question," said Sanner's voice from somewhere far above her. There was a crunch of metal digging into ice, and a flurry of crushed ice crystals floated down over Uhura's upturned face. Her carbide glow reached up to meet another, ten meters higher and obscured by the jagged edges of the broken conduit ceiling. "The real question is, do we *want* to break through?"

"Zap?" Uhura took a step back, trying to angle her head so she could see the geologist clinging to the icy wall of the fracture. He had set a rope on pitons as he went up that wall, but he was unwinding it just as carefully now that he was on the way down. She watched him rappel down another half meter, his carbide glow swinging wildly as he turned in midair to approach the ice at a different angle. "What's the matter? Is it too slippery for us to climb out?"

"Probably." Sanner kicked up a second shower of ice shavings as he dug his crampons into the ice. His voice sounded unusually flat, especially considering the rush of his rapid descent. "But trust me, Lieutenant, you wouldn't want to come this way, not even if I carved you a spiral staircase out of that waterfall."

Uhura frowned, remembering the dim violet-blue glow of the conduit she had just left behind. "The force field, or whatever it is that we saw in the ice cave," she said. "You saw it on the upper level of the cave?"

"In living color." Sanner unwound the last loop of his rope, levered out the piton it had been lashed to, and did an unbraked slide down the rest of the way to the bottom. Shaved ice clung to his helmet, and glittered on his jumper like diamond dust, an incongruous contrast to his somber dark eyes. "Not just tendrils of it, either—the same kind of solid sheet we saw below. It must go right up through the rock like it wasn't there. Hell, for all I know, it keeps going right up to the surface!"

"How close did you get?" That was Jaeger's slight German accent, echoing from the far side of the frozen plunge pool. Uhura glanced across and saw that the rest of the party had gathered there, making a tight knot for warmth while they waited for Sanner. She couldn't see Davis in the huddle, and assumed Wright had placed the injured crewman in the middle for protection. With the cold this intense and their cave jumpers leaking heat, hypothermia was a danger for everyone, but especially for the disabled members of the party. Uhura glanced at Jaeger as well, and wasn't reassured by the way his bruised cheek and cut lip stood out against a too-pale face.

"Not even a hundred meters," Sanner said. "I had my carbide turned way down, so I could see it from far away. And when I saw it, I just turned right around and headed back. We spent enough hours poking around up there to know that there was only one way in."

"One way at that end of the system," Jaeger agreed. He paused to grit his teeth against a chatter. "But there's still the warm draft we felt through the rubble pile in the upper chamber. One of those cracks must lead to the surface."

"Yeah . . . one of those hundreds of tiny cracks." Despite his words, however, Uhura could see a spark rekindle in Sanner's tired face. Clearly, the thought of squirming through hundreds of tiny cracks appealed to him. "I didn't think you guys would want to go back and start digging there all over again."

"What other choice do we have?" Palamas inquired, sounding almost as dispassionately logical as a Vulcan. Uhura wondered if she did a lot of work with Mr. Spock on the Science Deck. "If we can't go out through either the upper or lower level at this end, and we can't use the transporter, then we have to try the rubble pile again."

"And we'll have lights this time, so it'll be easier to see what we're doing," Yuki Smith said cheerfully. "And a lot harder to fall off."

Uhura nodded. "It's decided, then. We'll go back up to the breakdown cave where we found Team Three, and start digging our way out. Let's head out, same order as before."

Sanner coiled up the last of his rope and stuffed it in his backpack, then headed over to Jaeger. "Come on, Karl," he said, with surprising gentleness. "Let me give you a hand, just over this slippery part here."

The older geologist grunted and let Sanner haul him to his feet. His teeth were definitely chattering now. "Just because you were right about

the light going through to the upper level doesn't mean you know everything about this cave system," Uhura heard him grumble to his fellow scientist. "For instance, those weren't vadose passages back there."

"Oh, yeah? Then what the hell were they?"

"Tension cracks, from the deroofing stress created by the conduit—"

Their voices dwindled up the tunnel, and the other members of the
original survey team and the rescue team trailed after them. Uhura
watched Wright lift Davis to her feet and gesture the quiet D'Amato to
help support her on the other side. The surveyor was barely hanging on to
consciousness now, her eyes narrowed down to pained slits as if even
their carbide lights were too strong for her. Uhura gave Wright a questioning look and got a shake of the head in response that told her wordlessly what she needed to know. Davis wasn't going to be able to take
much more of this cold and constant movement. If they didn't manage to
break through that rubble pile and get the injured surveyor some proper
medical attention soon, they would run the risk of losing her entirely.

Tomlinson and Martine waited with Uhura until the last of the other
team members had left the frozen waterfall. "Which of us gets to play
rear guard first?" Tomlinson asked. He might have been trying to sound
playful, but the words came out just plain weary.

"None of us." Uhura met his surprised gaze with a look she hoped
was stern enough to cut off questions. "We know that curtain is still back
near the entrance—"

"Not really," said Martine. "Zap said he saw it a hundred meters
away, but we don't know exactly where he was when he saw it. We
walked a long way from the entrance to that section where Mr. Chekov
fell through."

Uhura sighed. She'd been hoping she was the only one to have that
disconcerting thought. She could see from the two worried young faces in
front of her, though, that the implications had sunk in on both Tomlinson
and Martine. She chose her words carefully, trying to think about how
Captain Kirk had inspired Chekov to reconstruct his map. "If that force
field is moving, we'll just have to deal with it when it arrives," she said,
although she didn't have the least idea what she meant by "deal with it."
"In the meantime, the important thing is to dig our way out of the rubble
pile quickly."

"And we'll be most effective at doing that if we're not panicking
about when the force field might arrive," Tomlinson guessed, nodding.
"That's a good thought, Lieutenant. We'll keep our mouths shut about it."

"Thanks," Uhura said. "I wasn't sure you'd understand."

Tomlinson glanced down at Martine, then both of them smiled unexpectedly. "When you work in the weapons banks, Lieutenant Uhura, the

first thing you learn is not to listen to the battle reports about what might be coming your way," Martine informed her. "You already know you're the part of the ship that the other guy is aiming at. If you waste all your time worrying about when you're going to blow up, then you probably *will* blow up."

"And you won't have any fun in the meantime." Tomlinson touched the small of Martine's back to urge her up the conduit, and kept his hand there as they began walking. Uhura lifted an eyebrow, then saw that he was surreptitiously helping to support the weight of her heavy pack under the guise of flirtation. She wasn't sure what Kirk would have said about that, but decided that she wasn't going to make an issue of it.

The spiraling path up to the large column-filled upper chamber seemed much harder to climb now than when they'd first walked it. Uhura intellectually knew that was because she was far more tired and downcast than she'd been the first time through, but she couldn't help feeling a little nervous as the conduits twisted, then straightened, then twisted again. Had they lost their way without the benefit of Chekov's map? Had Jaeger in his weariness led Sanner and Smith down the wrong side of those branches they'd gone through? Could they be walking into another ice cave, with another curtain of rippling force waiting for them?

A waft of distinctly warmer air against her cold-chapped face proved that the last of her worries, at least, was unfounded. Uhura glanced up from trudging last along their track, in the place she thought the commander ought to have. Ahead of her, she could see only a sharp turn in the passage, but she could already hear the way the other crew members' voices echoed through a large, hollow space. And the warmth of the air flowing out of that upper chamber wasn't an illusion. When Uhura stepped inside, she could actually feel her cave jumper relax its tight, insulating grip on her as it adjusted to a more reasonable temperature gradient. That must be the draft of surface air Jaeger kept talking about.

The sound of voices seemed unusually loud, even given the echo effect Uhura remembered from their first entrance into this cathedral-like space full of travertine columns. She glanced around, seeing Wright and D'Amato carefully lower Davis back to the makeshift bed they had left here, while Palamas began to pile silver emergency blankets on top of her. Jaeger sat in another huddle of blankets nearby, his hands wrapped around the minuscule warmth of an unmounted carbide light. That wasn't where all the noise was coming from.

Uhura's glance swung around to the giant rubble pile at the back of the cave, where Sanner and Smith had already gone to begin their assault. Tomlinson and Martine were joining them, and all four voices were raised in what sounded more like exhilaration than anything else. Uhura blinked, becoming slowly aware of her own tiredness and resultant stupidity. She couldn't see anything worth getting that excited about over there—no sudden breaks in the roof of the cave, or shafts of sunlight slanting in through the boulders. So what on Earth—?

The knot of crew members split apart, and turned to cross back to Uhura. She blinked again, and scrubbed at her eyes to make sure she wasn't mistaken. Four members of the team had headed across to the rubble pile, but five members were walking away from it now. And the small, dark-haired man in the center, walking slowly but steadily back toward Uhura, was none other than Ensign Chekov.

# Chapter Nine

AT LEAST THE FIRST question Lieutenant Uhura asked him was the easiest one to answer. "Are you all right?"

Chekov nodded stiffly. "Yes, sir." Then he felt compelled to add, "I think so, sir," because he was cold, and confused, and his stomach felt as though it had collapsed into water inside him, and it occurred to him that he might not be the best judge at the moment of whether or not he was functional.

Apparently agreeing with him, Uhura turned to motion Diana Wright forward out of what had become a surprisingly large group of people. The medic took his elbow and led him back through the little crowd, to where another woman in a gold cave suit already lay stretched out with her hand over her eyes. Chekov felt weirdly inappropriate seating himself on a pack near her feet, as if he was impinging on a stranger's bench space in a public spaceport.

It was weirder still to have the others follow him and Wright with such confident familiarity, crowding around the makeshift bed and staring at him expectantly. He stole looks over Wright's shoulder as she examined his skull and shone her light into his eyes, trying to pick out someone he recognized in the jumble of unknown faces.

His eyes found Sanner standing with an older man in science blue who looked like he'd been on the losing end of a fistfight. Suddenly aware of Chekov's attention, Sanner blurted out, "Where's the captain?" as though he'd been holding his breath around the question ever since they'd stumbled upon Chekov.

"I . . ." Of all the comments which could have been on the tip of Sanner's tongue, this was not one Chekov had expected. He blinked, unsure how to respond to such an obviously serious and yet ridiculous question.

"I thought he was up with you," he finally managed, feeling utterly stupid. "The last time I saw him, sir, he was still with the rest of you."

"You both disappeared together." That was Uhura, visible again at the front of the group now that she had pushed her way between a tall blonde woman in blue and a short, stout, smiling woman in security red.

It was their syntax, Chekov realized abruptly, the English language's damned capacity for inaccuracy and misunderstanding. If he could figure out how to clarify what he was saying, they'd realize there was no way he could know where the captain had gone once he himself had hit the water. "I didn't disappear," he said very carefully, trying to speak clearly and choose the right verbs. "I fell."

Uhura's eyes widened in what could only have been surprise, but the scientist at Sanner's elbow shot his hand into the air with a triumphant smile. "Ah ha! I *knew* it!"

Sanner pinned his companion with a curmudgeonly scowl. "Where? I'm telling you, the floor there was completely intact rock." It wasn't clear if he directed those comments at Chekov or the other man, who must have also been a cave geologist.

Before Chekov could figure out how to answer, the taller woman near Uhura asked, "Ensign, how did you end up back here?"

*Who* are *you?* he wanted to exclaim. Out of all this weirdness, that was the part that alarmed him the most—the fact that six people whose faces meant nothing to him had apparently joined their party in the brief span of time when he must have been unconscious. Somehow they all seemed to know him and care about the details of his mishap, and he couldn't recall even the most basic introductions. He understood that they must be the members of Survey Team Three, lost in the cave several hours ahead of the landing party. But when had they become part of the rescue party and no longer just the rescuees?

"I don't know, sir." He directed that initial answer to the scientist who'd specifically asked him, then turned away from Wright's examination to face Uhura squarely. "I mean, I fell when the ledge became icy after we fired our phasers. Sir, I don't know where *this*—" He gestured vaguely around him. "—I don't know where we are now. I . . . I thought there was water below us where I fell, but . . ." But he was obviously dry and undrowned, and the thin skim of hoarfrost that covered the flowstone columns here came nowhere near explaining the icy plunge that was his last coherent memory.

"We're talking about what happened after that." Uhura came a few steps closer, calm despite his growing panic. "A long time after that, Mr. Chekov, when we went into Mr. Jaeger's ice cave—did you fall again there?"

"There *was* nothing after that." He wished he didn't sound so frightened, so desperate. "I'm sorry, sir, but I don't know anyone named Mr. Jaeger, or anything about an ice cave. I only know that I fell down the crevasse we were walking along, and then..." Then came the horrible chill of being swallowed by near-freezing water, the darkness, the realization that he was standing all alone in a vast empty chamber with a carbide lamp too wet to relight and no whistle around his neck. He'd called out once or twice only to have his voice bounce back to him in grotesquely attenuated echoes. It had actually crossed his mind that he was dead, that this was all there was. "And then I was here," he finished lamely.

The *tock-tock* of water dripping and freezing on the cavern's flowstone floor was what had finally saved him. Unless Hell was vastly more damp than predicted (or Heaven vastly more unpleasant), he had realized that he was still inside the caves of Tlaoli 4 somewhere, which meant the others would find him eventually. Chekov had unscrewed his useless lamp from the top of his helmet then, and had used the helmet itself as an uncomfortable perch on which to sit and wait. In the small eternity that had crept by since then, he hadn't even tried to imagine an explanation for how a fall into an underground cave pond had washed him up here. He realized now that this was because he'd known even then that no good explanation existed.

Diana Wright was the first to break the silence. "It could be shock." She shrugged when the others all looked at her. "He doesn't show any signs of having a concussion, or any other physical damage for that matter. But we don't know exactly what that force field did to him."

Chekov twisted around to stare at her, convinced she must be joking. "Force field?" But the medic, unsmiling, only glanced a further question toward Lieutenant Uhura.

"Ensign, I want you to listen to me." Uhura squatted down in front of him, catching him by the arms and making him look her in the eye. Her smooth dark face was remarkably calm and serene, considering how insane she must think he was. "After you fell down the crevasse, Captain Kirk jumped into the water after you and you both broke through a rock ceiling into a lower set of cave passages. That's where we are now. We located Survey Team Three—" She motioned toward the unfamiliar people surrounding them. "—that's Lieutenant Jaeger and his people." The older scientist by Sanner—Jaeger, Chekov realized—sketched a short, polite nod. "They led us to the other end of the cave system, to a chamber a lot like this one, where Mr. Jaeger thought we might be able to find a faster way back to the surface."

"You mapped the whole way," the burly female security guard added. "I helped you." She held up his tape measure as if this somehow proved her claim. Her warm smile made Chekov feel oddly guilty that he couldn't even recall her name.

"Once we got there," Uhura continued, "you and Captain Kirk walked out into the middle of the room..." She trailed off into a shrug, the way people do when the only thing they can think to say is something embarrassing or unpleasant.

Sanner, on the other hand, never seemed at a loss for words. "And you vanished. Poof. Into thin air."

Chekov looked back and forth between them for what seemed a very long time, not even sure how he felt about all this new information, much less how he was supposed to react to it.

"You don't remember anything?" Uhura finally asked.

Chekov shook his head miserably. "I'm sorry, sir."

"What about the captain?" The woman on the pile of supply packs barely moved, her hand still across her eyes and her lips still drawn down into a tense line. Her words sounded thick and blurry. "If that force field sent Ensign Chekov here, maybe it sent the captain here, too."

The other members of the combined parties stirred restlessly. Even Chekov caught himself squinting out into the darkness as though expecting to catch some glimpse of something no one else could see.

"If he's here," Sanner asked, "then why haven't we found him?"

Uhura pushed to her feet. "Maybe he's lost his memory, too. Maybe he doesn't even remember who we are." She turned to the slim young man holding Angela Martine's hand. "Tomlinson, Martine, start searching that side of the cavern. Smith—" This was apparently the broad-shouldered security guard. "—you'll come with me. Mr. D'Amato, I want you to stay just outside the entrance and watch in case that alien field gets any closer."

The quiet male scientist at the back of the group nodded and pulled together his gear. "I'll keep my lamp turned off."

As D'Amato started off, Sanner volunteered, "And I'll start trying to clear out that alternate exit."

"Keep Mr. Jaeger on the ground!" Uhura obviously meant it as a warning, and didn't move her gaze from Sanner until he'd sighed and given her his promise. Then she said to Wright, "Stay with Davis and Chekov."

"Lieutenant!" Chekov only meant to stop Uhura with his call, but Sanner and Jaeger also paused and looked back at him. He reminded himself to be more specific when he addressed his commanders in the future. "Lieutenant Uhura, sir, I want to help." He came forward a step, hands extended, when he saw her open her mouth to contradict him. "I know I don't remember everything, sir, but I feel fine. And I want to do my part. Please, sir."

Uhura glanced a question at Wright. The medic shrugged. "I can't find anything obvious wrong with him."

The lieutenant hesitated only a moment longer, then sighed as though sure she was going to regret her leniency. "All right. But if you start to feel sick or dizzy or—"

Chekov tried to smile reassuringly. "I promise I won't fall down any more cliffs."

From close by in the near darkness, Sanner made a little noise that was half laugh, half snort. "You're about five hours too late on that one, mister."

"*Drake.* Hailing. *Enterprise.*" Sulu clipped each word into its own distinct sentence, knowing they would arrive in a barrage of subspace static. Beneath Tlaoli's drab and timeworn surface, some monstrous force was stirring to life. The planet was spitting out subspace noise on every possible communications frequency now, and interfering with most of the shuttle's sensors as well. Even the *Drake*'s most basic altitude-finding instruments had error readings high into the red. Sulu had learned the hard way not to trust them when he'd nearly plunged the unwieldy cargo shuttle into a saltwater swamp on his first trip down to the surface. On his second trip he'd flown strictly by sight rules, even through the garnet-colored glow of sunset.

"*Enterprise* . . ." After that one word, Lieutenant Palmer's voice disintegrated into another blast of static. Sulu forced himself to wait, his fingers tapping impatiently on the transmit button. If it had been Uhura, he would have replied right away, secure in the knowledge that she wouldn't say more than she needed to on such a static-clogged channel. But just as he'd expected, the junior communications officer was continuing to send unnecessary instructions through the snarl of background noise. "*Drake, please report in.*"

"I'm trying to," Sulu growled, but he was careful not to depress the transmission switch until after he said it. From the narrow passageway that led to the passenger compartment, he heard a stifled snort from one of the geologists. "*Drake* is returning to *Enterprise*. Estimated docking time, twenty forty-five."

"*Acknowledge. Commander Spock* . . ." Whatever else Palmer said was lost in another tidal swell of static.

"Everything okay now?" Geologic Technician Fisher poked his head through the passage in an oddly tentative manner. Although he was technically second-in-command, and therefore had the right to occupy the copilot's seat, Sulu had summarily evicted him during the launch. He'd told Fisher it was for safety reasons, which wasn't entirely untrue.

Scotty's magnetic shielding had kept his engines powered up, but they hadn't protected the *Drake* from the sudden and unexplained changes in course heading that he'd felt back on the *Enterprise*. In the much smaller mass of the shuttle, they felt like buffeting blows of invisible wind rather than gentle diversions of orbit. Sulu had needed all of his concentration and considerable skill as a pilot just to guide the shuttle up through Tlaoli's treacherous gravity well.

"We're past the worst of it." Sulu could see the *Enterprise* emerging around the curve of Tlaoli 4, a shining silver beacon against the utter blackness of deep space. Like a small second moon, the ship was catching sunlight from a star that Sulu could no longer see. Tlaoli's sun had set just as he had loaded the two remaining geologists from the survey team and their precious fossiliferous samples. Below him, the crimson and orange remnants of a glorious dust-filtered sunset made the planet's western horizon look as if it were on fire.

Fisher took another tentative step into the cockpit. He wasn't looking at the *Enterprise* or, to Sulu's relief, at the alarming displays of red light that flashed across the pilot's console. All of his attention was focused on the darkening planet they had just left behind.

"I wonder what the hell is going on down there?" the geologist muttered, sinking into the copilot's seat with a frown. "God, I hope we didn't send Jaeger and his team into some kind of subspace window or wormhole..."

"You couldn't know that it was going to be that dangerous," Sulu told him. "Tlaoli got the highest safety rating a frontier planet can have."

"That was before we found nineteen wrecked starships down here," Fisher said gloomily. "We should have known there might still be something dangerous around. But all we could think of was that we might have found a natural transperiodic ore deposit, and that wouldn't be dangerous to people, only to starships with warp cores..."

"You never found any alien ruins in your survey?"

"No," Fisher admitted. "But Tlaoli's deeply eroded. Anything that was built on the surface has turned to dust or deep-sea mud by now." He craned his head to catch the last glimpse of the planet's dried-blood twilight. "But maybe the aliens who used to live here built something underground for protection, some kind of planetary defensive system that could explain what happened to the *Enterprise*."

"It still wouldn't necessarily threaten people who went near it." Sulu swung the *Drake* around to line her up with the orbital plane of the *Enterprise*.

"No." Fisher heaved a worried sigh. "Unless maybe it thought they were there to attack and disarm it."

As the *Enterprise* approached, Sulu could see the shuttle bay doors roll open along her secondary hull. On his previous trips, the doors had to be manually wrenched open and closed, taking four engineers in spacesuits several minutes to achieve what normally would have taken a few seconds. But Commander Scott must have finally restored full power to the bay, allowing the shuttle to swoop in without even needing to brake. The doors rolled shut behind them and Sulu felt the usual turbulence shiver through the shuttle as air flooded back around it. He held the *Drake* steady until it was done, then dropped onto its landing pad, where empty grav-sleds and full pallets of medical equipment waited side by side.

"Go back and help Kulessa get your samples ready to offload. I want the shuttle emptied as quickly as possible," he told Fisher.

The geologist rose from his seat obediently enough, but paused in the cockpit door to give him a quizzical look. "You're not making another trip back down tonight?"

Sulu forced himself to look back at Fisher without a giveaway glance at the red warning lights on his console. "Why not? The cave team could be out on the surface now."

"But landing on that karst surface, in the dark—" Fisher broke off, shaking his head. "Better you than me, buddy."

Sulu waited until he'd gone, then leaned forward to reboot the shuttle's instrument buffers. They blinked and went dark, then began coming back on one at a time. Some of the gauges still flashed red, warning that even at this distance Tlaoli's subspace racket was interfering with their ability to function, but most came back a solid, reassuring green. The pilot grunted in satisfaction and began running the shuttle through a preflight mechanical safety check. In the background, he could hear the thump and whir of grav-sleds being maneuvered out of the hatch, a straggle of conversation cut short by Fisher's voice, then silence. A few moments later, as he'd expected, a single set of footsteps echoed up the hatch and through the empty passenger compartment.

"Lieutenant Sulu."

Sulu glanced over his shoulder, startled. He'd expected to see Chief Engineer Montgomery Scott, intent on making sure that his makeshift magnetic shielding was still strong enough to protect the shuttle's warp core and engines from Tlaoli's mysterious power fluxes. But the wiry figure in the doorway wore science blue rather than the red of ship's services.

"Dr. McCoy." Sulu glanced from the physician's intent face to the old-fashioned black bag he had slung across one shoulder. "Here to give me another antiviral booster shot?"

"Nope." The doctor came forward to sit in the copilot's chair, dropping his bag beside him. "Although I probably should. Scotty says only a lunatic would think about making a flight down to that damned planet after dark."

Sulu tried to make his face as impassive as possible. "It's not that crazy. I've been down there twice already and I know what to expect..."

McCoy waved him to a stop. "I'm not arguing with you, son. The sooner we get down there, the better I'll like it."

"We?" Sulu said, startled again. Before his first trip to Tlaoli, he and Commander Spock had agreed that it made no sense to risk a second life in a shuttle that had a statistically significant probability of crashing. The probability was now much more than just statistical, but if he pointed that fact out to McCoy, he would risk getting the trip itself cancelled. Sulu searched around for another reason to reject the doctor's company. "Sir, this cargo shuttle is only rated for twelve passengers plus pilot. And there are already twelve people down at that cave site."

"Some of whom may be very badly injured," McCoy reminded him gruffly. "What's the good of getting down there and finding someone too hurt to fly out again?"

"But the shuttle's weight limit—"

"—won't be exceeded, provided we leave all their gear and samples behind." McCoy pulled a data padd out of his bag and punched a file up on it. "Captain Kirk deliberately selected the smallest crewmen he could find for his cave rescue team, and the two of us aren't much bigger than they were. If you add in the survey team—well, Tomlinson's pretty hefty and I'm always amazed by how much Yuki Smith weighs for her size, but those other cave experts are all lightweights, too." He turned the padd to show Sulu his final calculation, and the pilot winced. There was no question that it was several percent less than the shuttle's weight allowance, even taking into account Scott's new magnetic shielding.

"I still think you should stay here, sir," Sulu said. It was one thing to risk his own neck, but he couldn't let another member of the crew come along trusting in a safety margin that wasn't there. He saw McCoy's stubborn headshake and took a deep breath. "Doctor, what I'm trying to tell you is—"

"That if you left now, it would be on a suicide mission," said a deep and completely unexpected voice from behind them.

"*Spock!*" McCoy swung around in his seat, glaring at the Vulcan who stood in the shadows of the cockpit door. "Don't you know better than to sneak up on people when they think they're the only ones on board? You could have given us both a heart attack!"

"As first officer, I have examined the quarterly medical reports for both Lieutenant Sulu and yourself, Doctor." Spock's voice retained the impassive tone that he usually used when verbally sparring with McCoy. "Neither record suggests a susceptibility to myocardial infarction."

"That's not what I meant!"

"Then I fail to understand why you said it." Spock ducked through the cramped passageway to the passenger hold and straightened to his full height in the cockpit. Sulu suppressed an urge to lay his hand across his red-flashing instrument panel as a keen Vulcan gaze swept across it. The motion would have been just as damning as the telltale gauges, and he had the distinct feeling that it didn't matter anyway.

He was right. "Mr. Sulu, may I see the instrument log from your last flight segment?" Spock asked blandly.

"I've already zeroed it out, sir," Sulu confessed. There was no point in continuing to prevaricate when a superior officer had obviously guessed what you were up to. "It was mostly error readings anyway."

"Yes, I know." Spock flickered an eyebrow at Sulu's startled look. "You should have known that Chief Engineer Scott would never install a brand-new device on a shuttle without adding a monitoring circuit to report on how it was functioning, Mr. Sulu. The subspace interference prevented us from making real-time observations during most of the flight, but as soon as the *Drake* came back into secure transmission range, all of her data banks were copied to engineering. Mr. Scott called me when he saw the size of the error readings."

"Well, what about 'em?" McCoy demanded. "You wouldn't expect subspace instruments to work right down on that power-sucking planet, would you?"

"No," Spock agreed. "But when sudden vertical displacements in the shuttle's altitude exceed the error margin of her proximity alarms by a factor of ten to one, it is clearly unsafe to fly at night. Especially in a terrain such as the Tlaoli karstland, where the elevation can change by thousands of meters from one second of flying to the next."

Sulu met the chief medical officer's astounded look with a wry smile. "I tried to tell you that you didn't want to come," he said. "Would you like to give me that antiviral booster now?"

McCoy scowled. "What I'd *like* is to get down to that damned planet as quickly as possible! For all we know, people are dying down there—" He swung around to glare at Spock as if that were somehow the Vulcan's fault. "—and you're telling me we can't even leave until the sun comes back up?"

This time, to Sulu's surprise and delight, Spock's lifted eyebrow had a distinctly ironic slant. "I do not recall making that statement, Doctor."

McCoy looked even more frustrated by that reply, but Sulu had already guessed what the science officer's response meant. "Moonlight!" he said. "Mr. Spock, when does Tlaoli's moon rise? And how full will it be?"

"Gibbous." Spock said it so calmly that Sulu knew he must have weighed this option long before he'd ever arrived in the *Drake*'s cockpit. "It will rise over the horizon of the karst plateau four hours from now." He gave Sulu a considering glance. "At that time, Lieutenant, and no sooner, you will receive my permission to take the *Drake* down to Survey Team Three's relocated base camp. *Not* to the cave itself."

"Aye-aye, sir," said Sulu.

"Huh." McCoy was less intimidated by the severe tone Spock adopted when he was functioning as ship's commander. "And what if something awful happens to them in the meantime?"

Spock let out a slow and measured breath. "There is no higher probability of 'something awful' happening in the next four hours, Doctor, than of it having already happened in the past ten."

"I know," McCoy said, a little grumpily. "That's what I'm worried about."

"Bring me up another marker!"

Sanner shouted his request back to Chekov in the same way he had at all the previous stops—as though he fully expected Chekov to trot up to join him, hand outstretched, a variety of reflective spot markers to choose from. In reality, the passage's fifty-centimeter head clearance made it hard for Chekov to even dig the markers out of his jumper pockets, much less crawl within an arm's length of anything but Sanner's feet.

"Here—" He thumped his hand awkwardly on the sole of Sanner's boot, then tossed two or three markers past the geologist's hip in the hopes one would land within reach. "Sir, perhaps it would be better if you carried the markers."

"Are you nuts? I've barely got room to carry the stuff I've got." Light swung at apparent random across the floor, the low ceiling, into Chekov's eyes as Sanner twisted to grope for the markers in the mud. "Don't worry—I'm getting a really strong breeze up here. We've got to be close to the exit by now."

"I hope you're right, sir." Chekov raised himself up as high as he could on his elbows to stuff the remaining markers deeply enough into his pocket that they wouldn't work themselves out again. Ironically, he banged his helmet against some outcrop or other not in lifting up but on the way back down again. "I'm not sure how we're going to get the others even this far."

He felt Sanner stiffen, almost as though a physical chill had blown through their dark crawlspace. "We're not leaving anybody down here." Sanner's voice was uncharacteristically quiet and grim.

"Of course not, sir." Chekov hadn't meant to imply that they would.

But he couldn't help thinking about how pale and silent Davis had been when he last checked back with the party in the big chamber. Or about how Jaeger, despite his stubborn good humor, had the softness of a scientist about him, and hardly looked capable of making such a cold, arduous crawl even when he hadn't first toppled down a breakdown pile. Chekov knew with every fiber of his heart that they couldn't abandon anyone to this frozen underground. He just honestly had no idea how they were going to avoid it.

Not for the first time, he wished Kirk were still here.

"Come on," Sanner grumbled abruptly, "let's keep moving."

Chekov waited until Sanner had dragged himself a few meters further down the passage, then took a deep breath to steel himself, and started after.

When they'd first dug past the last rubble of the breakdown pile in the big chamber and found the narrow vertical shaft that led up to this level, Sanner and Jaeger had both assured Chekov that the force of the breeze that greeted them meant that a substantial passageway existed beyond the restricted opening. Once or twice along the crawl, it had even looked like that might eventually be true. But every time the passageway seemed as though it might trend toward a little taller, a little wider, a little less muddy or crowded or crooked, it cinched back down again a few meters later and stretched further into what seemed like infinity.

More than once, Chekov had wanted to ask Sanner at what point they gave up. When did a caver admit that a passage went nowhere? That they were just crawling farther and farther away from knowing where they were? The tunnel around them barely looked like a cave anymore. Mud slicked the floor like engine lubricant, and tree roots dangled in irregular clusters from the low ceiling like woody stalactites. During one fifteen-minute delay while Sanner sawed through a particularly thick obstruction with a completely inadequate utility knife (which at least the geologist had thought to bring with him, thank God), Chekov had pushed himself backward out the way they'd come in to reassure the waiting party members that he and Sanner were all right, they hadn't gotten lost in the claustrophobic maze. As it turned out, that thought hadn't even crossed anyone's mind. While they'd been waiting patiently for a report, it had only been less than an hour, nowhere near long enough to worry. It only felt like longer when you were on the inside.

Now, another half-hour further along, he found himself growing numb to the pain in his arms and shoulders, and to the passage of time. There was nothing to look at, nothing to talk about. Even Sanner had run out of appropriate wisecracks what felt like miles ago. Whenever Chekov let himself think about anything besides dragging himself forward, one arm's length at a time, his mind invariably circled back to Kirk, like a ship dragged into an event horizon, unable to tear itself away. Kirk, who was more powerfully built than any of them, even Yuki Smith. Kirk, who was nowhere to be found in the cathedral-like space of the upper chamber, but who could not possibly have passed the party unnoticed on their way back from the "ice cave." Kirk, who could only have exited that upper chamber by squeezing out through this same tiny passage that Chekov and Sanner had been clawing their way through for the past two hours, and who simply could not have done so. *Could* not. Not by any stretch of anyone's imagination.

If Chekov didn't dare suggest that their injured party members couldn't make this crawl, there was no point in drawing anyone's attention to the impossibility of a completely healthy Kirk having done so.

"And thar she blows!"

Ahead of him, Sanner's feet suddenly slithered forward and rolled off to one side. Chekov restrained the first surge of hope that tried to swell up in him—he was too tired to survive another disappointment. But by the time he'd managed to drag himself alongside Sanner, the gentle brightening of the air around them had become more apparent, and the muddy walls had fallen away until there was no mistaking what Sanner lay on his back laughing up toward.

Chekov rolled over and followed his gaze upward. "Daylight."

"The last of it, at least. God, that looks good."

Chekov reached up to dim his helmet light, the better to appreciate the ruddy sweep of clouds just visible through the sinkhole above them. "It also looks far away." He tried to visually estimate the height from where he lay, but found it surprisingly hard to do while on his back.

Sanner reached to sink his fingers into the nearest wall. The opposite wall was more than a man's height away, but looked to be coated in the same slimy, dripping mud they'd just squirmed through. "This crap isn't very climbable, either," Sanner decreed, wiping his hand on the leg of his jumper. Some of his puckish humor returned with a crooked grin. "Wanna try standing on my head?"

Chekov didn't need a better height estimate to know the answer to that. "I don't think we'd be tall enough." He pictured Sanner standing, then multiplied the image two more times. "But more of us might be."

"Look at us! We're in the circus!"

Even though Sanner and Tomlinson differed in height by only a couple of centimeters, Yuki Smith wobbled atop their shoulders with a good bit less stability than Chekov had hoped for. But the top of her head came within two meters of the surface, and there were enough tree roots and vegetation overhanging the lip of the sinkhole to make up for the rest of the distance. They didn't technically have to reach the surface with their pyramid in order to get themselves out.

Sanner grimaced and slewed against Tomlinson as Smith shifted her weight yet again. "I don't think we're gonna make it."

"I'll make it," Chekov told him. He hadn't crawled all the way back to the upper cavern and led Tomlinson and Smith out here just to fail now. He tied another knot in the rope Sanner had looped around his waist. "If you would, Lieutenants..."

Sanner and Tomlinson shifted slightly to make a stirrup with their hands, and Smith whooped delightedly as she teetered. Chekov wasn't sure if he should feel reassured by her fearlessness, or alarmed by her complete lack of concern for the stability of their structure. He decided his nerves would be steadier if he settled on the former. At least Sanner had been smart enough to suggest they all put out their carbide lamps until they were done climbing on each other. They could avoid burning each other in embarrassing places even if they couldn't manage to effect a graceful escape from this cave.

Planting one foot in the stirrup, Chekov stretched his arms up to catch at Smith's hands as he heaved himself upward.

She caught him with surprising strength and ease, and guided him to place his feet atop hers on the other men's shoulders. For one uncomfortable moment, Chekov realized how close they all were to overbalancing and tumbling back down into the bottom of the sinkhole. Smith braced her back against the muddy wall behind her, and Chekov was forced to reach past her shoulders to steady himself when Tomlinson and Sanner staggered under their combined weight. *I'm an idiot!* he thought angrily. *Not only will this stupid idea never work, we're just going to end up with four more injured party members to try and drag out of this cave!* Then Smith's hands closed on his waist, and she hefted him high enough to plant one hand on her head and one knee on her shoulder. From there, he moved as quickly as he could into a standing position and stretched overhead to reach for what looked like the most secure loop of exposed root.

His fingers clawed at the mud five or six centimeters below the handhold. "I can almost..." He willed himself to reach farther, almost lifted up on one foot to extend his length. *I am not going to strand us down here for the sake of a few centimeters!* "Stand on your toes," he ordered abruptly.

Sanner made an explosive noise that might have been a laugh. "Stand on *what?*"

"I'm serious!" He only needed the tiniest bit more height. "Stand on your toes!"

Someone grumbled something Chekov couldn't quite understand from the bottom of their pyramid, then the whole human structure shifted a little aimlessly. Chekov felt himself swayed back away from the wall, and his heart leapt up into his mouth as he grabbed for whatever purchase he could find on the crumbling soil face. The root which had hovered just beyond his reach suddenly seemed to surge up in front of his face. He grabbed it, grabbed at another shorter root less than an arm's length away, and heaved himself up toward the precious surface. "Push!" he shouted down at Smith. "Push me up!"

Her hands clamped onto the bottoms of his boots, shoved—and he was up. The grass at the edge of the sinkhole gave spongily beneath his hands and knees. He crawled another body's length away, pursued by images of collapsing the rim back down on the others and plunging them all back to the floor of the hole. When he reached a distance where the ground felt hard and dry and unyielding, he rolled onto his back with a groan. Beautiful stars, beautiful warm breeze, beautiful dry, clean grass. It was all he could do to keep from stripping out of his cave suit just to feel the balmy flush of dry air across his duty uniform.

"Hey, Ensign? You okay up there?"

Chekov suddenly remembered Smith and the lieutenants still down in the sinkhole, balanced precariously one on top of the other. He rolled to his knees and began working at the knot in the rope around his waist. "Everything's fine!" He hoped Smith could hear him. He didn't want to venture closer to the crumbling lip of the sinkhole if he didn't have to. "I'll tie off the rope."

The roots that had helped him to the surface supported a thick, twisted tree that seemed to grow upright only so it could bow back down and sweep the ground with its crown. Smaller siblings peppered the undulating rocky landscape, their broken-backed shapes recognizable in the dim starlight only because the rocks that crouched alongside them weren't swaying in the night breeze. Chekov leaned his weight into the last pull on the knot, to make sure his handiwork would hold. "The rope's secure!"

That was when he saw the footprints.

Not footprints, really, but mud scars and dents of deliberate disturbance on the opposite side of the sinkhole's mouth. As though someone else had clawed his way to the surface, tearing loose grass and rocks as he labored to drag his body over the edge to freedom. Someone without the support of a human pyramid beneath him. Someone who had performed the miracle of making the horrible slippery climb without help.

Chekov pulled off his helmet and turned up the drip on his carbide lamp. Acetylene hissed with renewed vigor, and the small flame he finally ignited leapt suddenly bright in front of the round reflector. He walked around the sinkhole to train the light more fully on its torn-up edge, then began a careful scan of the ground nearby. He could orienteer, but he was no tracker. What might have been a footprint leading away from the cave exit wasn't always followed by another, and they sometimes seemed to point in contradictory directions. But the splayed, muddy handprint he found on a boulder ten meters away from the edge was unmistakable.

He heard someone tromp up behind him with a confident, unhurried ease he was already learning to recognize.

"Everything okay?" Smith asked, leaning over his shoulder with a friendly intimacy she didn't seem to realize.

Chekov barely noticed her closeness. "I don't know . . ." He nodded toward the handprint still pinned by his helmet light.

Smith grunted in surprise. "Do you think that's the captain?"

Chekov shook his head slowly, then allowed, "It must be," because that was what his stomach had told him from the beginning. He lifted his eyes to the still, moonless darkness beyond the reach of their lights. "But where does he think he's going?"

# Chapter Ten

"Uhura to *Enterprise*. Come in, *Enterprise*."

A roar of static filled the storage tent where Survey Team Three had left their main communicator, wedged between the sample crates and supplies they had hastily dumped into this shelter when they relocated their base camp. As Uhura had cleared a path to it through the mess, she had found a spare photon lamp and now had it jacked up to its highest illumination, as if that could somehow erase the memory of too many dark hours underground. The volume on the communicator was also turned up as far as it could go. Uhura was so tired that she couldn't make her eyes focus on the flickering bars of the frequency monitor, so she was trying to make her ears do the work instead. Unfortunately, even loudly amplified static had a tendency to become tedious after a while. Every time Uhura caught herself drifting off, she jerked upright in the hard metal seat and forced herself to send another hail. She was beginning to doubt the ship could hear her any better than she could hear it, but the activity at least kept her a little more alert.

The tent flap opened with a hiss of parting electrostatic seals, letting in a swirl of Tlaoli's dusty air along with a figure so caked in dried mud that his once salt-and-pepper hair had become a solid, grizzled gray. Deep furrows of weariness added to Zap Sanner's appearance of having prematurely aged, but the cave specialist's eyes still held their usual cheerfulness.

"Hey, Lieutenant," said Sanner. "We've got some soup and coffee going over in the mess tent. Why don't you come get some?" He grinned and jerked a thumb at the communicator. "I bet you'll be able to hear that from there just as easily as you can here."

"Sorry." Uhura dialed the volume down to a normal level, and only then realized that the static roar had given her a headache. She rubbed at her forehead and grimaced as she felt mud crumble and sift down between her fingers. "I assume you finally got Crewman Davis up to the surface?"

"Yeah. Once you've got enough rope and pitons and come-alongs set at the top, you can haul damn near anything out of a cave." Sanner gave her a quick, embarrassed look. "Uh, sorry, sir. I didn't mean—"

Uhura smiled and shook her head at him. She had no trouble believing that the captain had scaled that brutal vertical slope on his own, but she wasn't ashamed of waiting until Sanner had rigged a sling and pulley system to help her scramble up to the top. She knew that physical courage was part of what made Kirk a natural and inspiring leader, but right now, Uhura was willing to settle for just being the highest-ranking officer in the group.

"How is Crewman Davis feeling?"

"She's pretty out of it," Sanner said bluntly. "Wright found a working set of medical instruments here and got the subcranial bleeding stopped, but she says Davis needs microsurgery within a few hours."

"And we have to get her to the *Enterprise* for that." Uhura gave her static-clogged communicator a frustrated look. She still remembered the surge of hope she had felt when they had retraced their rugged hike through the karst to Team Three's relocated base camp, and she'd seen that its power generator was still up and running. She'd thought that with the more powerful base communicator here she might actually have a chance to reestablish contact with the ship, but it looked as if Tlaoli's static interference had expanded to clog the entire subspace spectrum.

"Any luck yet?" Sanner asked, following her gaze to the communicator.

"No. I haven't gotten even a flicker of signal to focus in on, much less a response."

The furrows in his mud-caked face deepened a little more. "You don't think the *Enterprise* left the system, do you?"

Uhura felt her head shaking before she'd consciously decided to do it. "Commander Spock would never leave us stranded down here, knowing we were in trouble."

"Yeah. Especially not with Captain Kirk..." Sanner's voice trailed off uncertainly, and Uhura winced. If and when the *Enterprise* ever responded to her hail, she wasn't sure how she was going to explain what had happened to the captain. *First he disappeared into thin air, then we think he came back with amnesia and ran away from us, and now he's probably out wandering around on a dangerous karst plateau in the middle of the night.* It was almost as if the Psi 2000 virus had chased them back through space and time, creating yet another insane crisis, but this time without the man who'd extricated them from the last one.

"Hey," Sanner said, awkwardly. "Don't worry, Lieutenant, we'll find him as soon as it's light out. In the meantime, you really should get something to eat. Can't you set that thing to hail the ship automatically?"

"I'm afraid they won't be able to separate a normal hail from the subspace interference. I've been using a rolling frequency assignment to find out which bands are penetrating the noise best. Then I'll pulse those manually to send the Starfleet code for 'emergency pickup.' "

"Can't you just set the transmitter to pulse that signal on all bands, all the time?"

"Yes, but..." Uhura's voice trailed off. She was still thinking like a ship's communications officer, she realized, assuming she had to be present at the com in order to elaborate on the simple emergency signal. But the *Enterprise* already knew what the situation was down here on Tlaoli. Even an automated and coded message sent from the location of the base camp would be enough to tell Mr. Spock they had managed to escape the cave. "You're right, Mr. Sanner. Hang on a minute while I program that in."

"No problem," he said, and grinned again. "I told that kid Chekov to guard our share of the food with his life. I'm pretty sure he took me seriously."

Somewhat to her own surprise, Uhura felt laughter bubble up through her exhaustion. "Shame on you, Zap. It's his very first landing party—he's going to take *everything* seriously."

"Well, somebody has to cure him of that." Sanner unsealed the tent seams again and held one wall up for her to pass through. Uhura stepped out and paused, waiting for her eyes to adjust to the profound darkness of night on an uninhabited planet. It didn't take long to notice the light spilling out from the open mess tent, or the tantalizing smell of coffee and bread and vegetable soup that came with it. Uhura was halfway there before she even noticed the dim lemony glow on the opposite horizon.

"Zap, what's that light out there?" she demanded, pulling the cave geologist to a halt. He glanced in the direction she pointed, scrubbed a hand through his beard and muttered under his breath as if he were counting something.

"Moonrise, I think," he said eventually. "Sun won't be up for another three hours or so."

Uhura followed him into the mess tent. "Do you think the moon would give us enough light to look for Captain Kirk?"

Sanner shrugged. "Depends on what phase it's in. We'll have to ask Jaeger about that." He suited his action to his words by raising his voice to a cave-piercing bellow. "Hey, Karl! Will the moon be bright enough for us to start looking for the captain right away?"

Jaeger glanced up from the mess tent table on which he had spread several topographic and geologic maps. "That depends. Do you care if you fall into a sinkhole or two along the way?"

"Never mind." Uhura crossed to the food service unit in the corner, where the quiet, dark-haired ensign was guarding a steaming kettle of soup and half a loaf of rehydrated bread as conscientiously as if they were made of dilithium. The soup had a scorched taste, as if it had been heated up too quickly, and the bread was slightly soggy, the way rehydrated food always was. But after the tense and exhausting hours she'd spent underground, Uhura had no complaint to make about either. Even the coffee, brewed bitingly strong the way security guards always seemed to make it and poured out with an apologetic smile by Yuki Smith, tasted like pure ambrosia—at least, once Uhura had surreptitiously mixed in several teaspoons of sweetened dry cocoa that she found on a lower shelf.

It was a measure of Uhura's hunger that she didn't really notice the level of noise and activity in the mess tent until after she'd spooned up the last of her soup. Then she looked around in some surprise. She was sure she had remembered to issue official permission for her subordinates to get some sleep in the hours before dawn. After the long and arduous journey they'd made through Sanner's umbilical exit from the cave, and then the nerve-racking scramble up the muddy slopes of that final sinkhole, she thought most of them would have been thankful to head for the camp's dormitory tent. But aside from the injured crewman Davis and her attendant medic Wright, not a single member of Survey Team Three or the cave rescue party appeared to have heeded her suggestion. Uhura was so new to the idea of being in command of a mission like this that it took her a moment to realize that it was probably her own example of staying awake and at work that had inspired their behavior.

At one table, Sanner, D'Amato, and Palamas had cabled their scientific tricorders into the base camp's generator and were extracting the data they had gathered before the power failure, arguing vigorously about its internal errors as they did so. At another table, Chekov and Smith had gone to help Jaeger sketch out yet another reconstruction of the alien cave system, this time overlain directly on a topographic map of Tlaoli's surface. And in an empty space near the entrance, Martine and Tomlinson were assembling scaffolding and power supplies into something that looked like a small siege tower. Uhura got up and went to join them.

"What are we building, Lieutenant?" she asked, peering up at the apparatus he was attaching to the top of the structure

"A light flare, sir." Tomlinson showed her the bank of photon lamps he had lashed together. "Angela and I thought if the captain was wandering around at night, not sure where he was, and he saw a really bright light..."

"Good idea," Uhura agreed. "But will it be visible all the way back at the cave exit where we lost him?"

"If we calculated the voltages right, it should be," Martine answered. "We've jacked the power up with a couple of heavy-duty electron accelerators, but these photon lamps are combat-rated and they should be able to handle the load. We'll point them straight up, of course, so nobody gets blinded."

Uhura shot her a quick look, trying to decide if that had been a joke, but both weapons officers gazed back at her gravely. "Very good," she said, for lack of anything more intelligent to say. "Um...is it ready to go?"

"Yes, sir."

"Then let's take it out and set it up."

That at least, seemed to have been the right thing to say. Martine stopped fussing with the wiring and Tomlinson clambered off the scaffold and whistled for Chekov and Smith. The two younger crew members came over as if they'd been half-listening for his signal, and the three of them heaved the small tower up to their shoulders while Martine and Uhura lifted the tent flaps out of their way. A few steps past the tent wall, they plunked the light flare down again.

"It doesn't really matter where we put it, since it's pointing straight up," Tomlinson explained to Uhura. "Now, all we have to do is make sure we don't blow out the main power circuit when we first turn it on."

"I'll turn off the food server, and tell those guys inside to unplug their tricorders," Yuki Smith said and slipped back into the tent. When she came back, the four scientists trailed after her, D'Amato with his unplugged tricorder still clutched in his hands. "Okay, everything's off."

Martine finished connecting the flare's power cables to the main generator feed while Tomlinson climbed up the scaffold again to check the photon lamps. "Ready to go," he reported as he vaulted off. There was a pause, and Uhura realized everyone was looking at her expectantly.

"Power it up, Mr. Martine," she said, with more confidence than she felt. She had never realized before that part of being in command was taking responsibility for the ideas and decisions of your crew as well as your own.

"Aye-aye, sir."

There was an ominous crackle from the midsection of the tower—Uhura hoped that was just the accelerators jacking up the voltage—then a fierce white column leaped high into Tlaoli's night sky. Even at its margins, the glare was strong enough to make Uhura blink and turn away. After a moment, her eyes adjusted well enough to see not only the flood-lit sprawl of the base camp but also the rocky rim of the dry canyon in which it was located. Tlaoli's lemony little moon had just finished lifting over that rocky horizon, but its light paled to dim ivory beside their flare.

"Lieutenant." That was D'Amato's diffident voice, somber and pitched low enough that only Uhura could hear. "I'm not sure this is such a good idea."

"Why not, Mr. D'Amato?"

The geologist held out his tricorder, on which small lights were blinking furiously. Its display panel showed a single blue curve that was dropping, slowly but steadily.

"What's that?" Uhura asked.

"Total power consumption here in the base camp," D'Amato said. "Unless this contraption of Tomlinson's is reducing our generating capacity, which seems unlikely, the curve implies—"

"—that something is draining our power," Uhura guessed. "The alien caves?"

D'Amato nodded. "The power loss isn't very noticeable, this far away. At least, not yet. But apparently we're not really safe even here, sir. We're still not outside the reach of whatever force is coming from inside those caves."

"Will running the flare make our power loss worse?"

D'Amato queried his tricorder, then shook his head and showed her its unhelpful splay of extrapolated curves. "Hard to tell, sir. All this sub-space interference is still messing up the analytical circuits. It might be doing that. And we might lose power at exactly this rate without running it at all."

Uhura frowned and tried to weigh various scenarios of failure against each other. No power meant no more hails to the *Enterprise,* but no light flare meant no chance of bringing Captain Kirk in tonight, before he could stumble back into the clutches of whatever alien weapon or transporter they'd encountered back in that cave. If they were going to lose power anyway, there was no reason not to run the flare, but if they could conserve power by shutting everything down right now . . .

"Sir, I hear something," said a polite Russian voice from behind Uhura. She turned and found Ensign Chekov standing with one ear cocked toward the light-slashed sky. "I think it's a shuttle."

Like any good communications officer, Uhura could make her voice ring like a bell when she needed to. "Quiet, everyone!" she commanded. Silence dropped over the base camp, except for the annoying crackle of the high-voltage accelerators. Uhura was about to order Tomlinson to turn them off, too, but then she heard what Chekov's less distracted ears

had already caught—the distant but unmistakable wail of a shuttle dropping at high speed through a planetary atmosphere. Uhura glanced up at
the sky, then realized how useless it was to look for a shuttle's blinking
lights past the white column of light they had sent fountaining up into
Tlaoli's sky. That thought led to another, more urgent one.

"Tomlinson, Sanner, Chekov, Smith—get this thing out into an open
space!" Uhura ordered. "If the shuttle's using it to home in on us—"

She didn't need to complete that sentence. The four crewmen picked
up the light flare by its makeshift legs and marched in double time out toward the edge of camp, while Martine frantically strung out power cables
behind them. "Almost out of line," she warned as they passed the supply
tent.

"Set it there, on the edge of the open space." Uhura cast a glance back
toward D'Amato. "Is the power holding out?"

He nodded. "It's not dropping any faster than it was before. Or any
slower." D'Amato glanced up at the approaching drone of the shuttle. "I
just hope the same power draining effect doesn't hit the shuttle when it
starts getting close to us."

It certainly didn't seem to. With a confident, roaring swoop that told
Uhura who the pilot was likely to be, a slice of shadow detached itself
from the dark eastern sky and flickered into a big silver cargo shuttle as it
passed through their fountain of light. It swung around and hovered in the
light just long enough for them to read the name *Drake* on its blunt hull,
then settled down in the open space with a thump violent enough to suggest the pilot hadn't been completely sure where the ground was. There
was a pause before the shuttle's hatch swung open to let out a wiry, blinking figure.

"This had better be the new base camp for Survey Team Three," said
Dr. McCoy's familiar caustic voice. "Because I'm not getting back in that
shuttle until there's enough light for Lieutenant Sulu to notice that not a
single damned one of his instruments is working."

It was strange, Sulu thought, how out of place he felt down here. It
wasn't just that his uniform was clean instead of mud-caked, or that his
skin wasn't dark with bruises. He'd been just as clean and healthy at the
first two landings he'd made on Tlaoli, and it hadn't seemed to separate
him from the weather-beaten survey teams he'd picked up there. But
there was something almost claustrophobic in the way the survivors of
the Tlaoli caves moved around in small groups, never alone. There was
some bone-deep terror that haunted them, a shadow that darkened even
their initial shouts of welcome and relief.

None of their halting explanations of the alien technology they'd encountered had really explained that fear to him, either. All Sulu had been able to gather was that some kind of alien transporter system had been activated by draining the power from their instruments. He'd told them about the power loss the *Enterprise* had experienced after trying to transport them, and they agreed that it probably explained why it had gotten so much colder and more dangerous in the caves after that. But Sulu still didn't understand why the alien force had flung only Captain Kirk and one hapless young ensign through space, when it clearly had the power to haul down entire 190-ton starships. Or why Ensign Chekov had lost only a few hours of his memory after that experience, while Kirk might have lost all of his.

The dark-haired young man had been standing quietly at the edge of the group when they'd broken the bad news about Kirk's absence, and Sulu had to clamp his teeth down hard to bite off the comment he otherwise would have made. But he still couldn't erase the uncharitable feeling that it was rotten luck to have lost the ship's captain instead of a brand-new and unknown crewman. He'd wondered at the time, catching a side-long glimpse of the ensign's bleak face, if the young man thought the same thing.

Now he stood next to Uhura and that same silent ensign, watching the rocky western horizon for the first nebulous glow of sunrise. Around them, the base camp bustled with activity despite the predawn darkness: scientists downloading their data onto lightweight cubes so they could leave even their tricorders behind; weapons officers and security guards deactivating the gear they were leaving behind; McCoy and Wright exchanging curt medical comments as they operated in what had been the camp's mess tent. The photon light flare that had led him through the moonlit jumble of the karst plateau to the base camp had been switched off moments after they'd landed, to preserve power for McCoy's emergency surgery. The internal clock that most pilots developed told Sulu it wouldn't be long now until dawn.

Uhura apparently felt the same way. "If Dr. McCoy's not finished operating by the time the sun's up..." she began suddenly, then trailed off as if she was still deciding exactly how to end that statement.

Sulu smiled at her in the darkness. After the months they'd spent working together on the main bridge crew, he already knew what she was thinking. "I can take a quick trip aloft to look for the captain," he finished for her.

"But only if McCoy's not ready to go," Uhura warned him. As the group's commanding officer, she had reluctantly decided that Sulu's first priority after sunrise was to evacuate the wounded and exhausted members of Survey Team Three, and bring down a fresh crew of security guards to conduct a more effective search for the captain. She had impressed Sulu both by ignoring the howls of protest this brought from her junior officers, and never disclosing how painful he knew the decision to delay searching for Kirk must have been for her. But with the hours to sunrise running out fast and no sign that the emergency surgery in the mess tent was close to being finished, he'd been hoping Uhura would allow him to conduct at least a quick and limited search. Apparently, he wasn't the only one with that thought.

"Sir." There was a pause, as if young Ensign Chekov had to gather up his courage to add anything to that monosyllable. "Sir, if Mr. Sulu takes the shuttle up, couldn't we climb one of the karst mounds near here and watch him? In case he spots the captain right away?"

" 'We?' " Uhura gave him a stern look. "Mr. Chekov, Dr. McCoy's medical scan showed enough microscopic scarring in your lungs to prove that you practically drowned when you fell down that waterfall—"

"—but he also said I hadn't suffered any permanent damage, sir," Chekov said stubbornly. "And, sir, Crewman Smith and I are the ones who tracked the captain out of that sinkhole. We know which direction to look for him."

As justifications went, it was pretty feeble, but even Tlaoli's dim moonlight was enough to show them the shadows of guilt and remorse that looked out of the younger man's eyes. Sulu knew how he would feel, if he had been the undeserving survivor of that alien force field. He cleared his throat to catch Uhura's attention.

"If that photon flare managed to draw the captain in close to us last night, Smith and Chekov might not have to travel very far to find him," Sulu said. That wasn't a very strong argument, either, but the speaking look of gratitude he got from the ensign made him add, "There's no point in me spotting him from the air if we don't actually go get him."

"True," said Uhura, frowning. "But we don't have any way to communicate with the shuttle. If you spot the captain, how will you let Mr. Chekov know?"

"Double-dip," Sulu said. He could see the first tinge of sunrise bleeding into Tlaoli's western sky now. "The energy fluxes down here bump me around a lot, but they never throw me the same way twice. If Mr. Chekov sees the shuttle rise and descend two times over some part of the karstland, he'll know I saw Captain Kirk there."

"And we'll only go to get him if it looks like he's within an hour's walking distance," Chekov promised recklessly. "Otherwise, sir, we'll mark his location and come right back to camp."

Uhura sighed. "I know I shouldn't let you two convince me, but..." She glanced over her shoulder at the creeping light of dawn. "Lieutenant

Sulu, go get the shuttle ready. Mr. Chekov, take Smith and Tomlinson, and climb up the nearest karst mound. And I don't want anyone to fall. That's an order!"

"Aye-aye, sir." Chekov answered with such youthful and serious sincerity that Sulu couldn't help exchanging smiles with Uhura before he turned away and headed for the shuttle.

That young Russian would make a reliable crewmate one of these days, the pilot thought as he climbed into the cockpit. Once he lost his rookie nervousness, and got a rudimentary sense of humor, he might even be good enough to end up serving on the bridge.

Chekov didn't envy Lieutenant Sulu the piloting feat he'd volunteered to perform.

"Was that a dip?" Tomlinson asked anxiously. Squinting into the rising sun, he rose up on tiptoe as though the additional centimeters would improve his view.

His own eyes still locked on the shuttle, Chekov shook his head. "No, sir. He's only jockeying for altitude." Even as Chekov spoke, the shuttle executed an elegant swoop along the slope of one towerlike hill, then rode her own velocity a half-kilometer higher in the parchment-yellow sky.

As part of Starfleet Academy's major in Astrogation and Piloting, Chekov had taken a short course in shuttle piloting. The portly craft at their disposal had been old, ill-used models no longer safe for extra-atmospheric flights, and most of the students in the program had secretly suspected they weren't all that noble for local usage, either. The morning winds that swept San Francisco Bay had tossed the clumsy ships about like soccer balls, more than once threatening to deposit one atop Mt. Tam or crash them all into Alcatraz. At the time, the flights had been a little bit scary, but also challenging and fun. Chekov often imagined that this must be what it felt like to ride a starship through an ion storm, or weather the conflicting gravity wells of a trinary star.

Now, as he watched Lieutenant Sulu coax a decidedly unaerody-namic craft to stay aloft with hardly any sensors or flight controls to speak of, Chekov understood why no one else on the *Enterprise* had much hope of becoming chief helmsman anytime soon.

"I hope when he does finally see the captain, it's closer to our hilltop than that one." Yuki Smith trooped up to join them, as good-natured as always despite the rugged climb. As strong as she was when it came to lifting and hauling, she apparently couldn't climb the nearly vertical karst terrain quite as easily as Tomlinson and Chekov. "That's more than an hour away, isn't it?" She seemed to direct the question toward Chekov, if only by virtue of being tight against his shoulder when she asked it. "And if we can't walk there in an hour, we're not allowed to go. Right?"

Chekov tried not to let the worry churning in his stomach sour his tone. "Once we start walking, it won't matter how far away it is. It's not like the ship can stop us by beaming us up or anything." He remembered Sanner's grim promise in the cave passage. *We're not leaving anybody down here.*

The shuttle banked to widen her sweep, and Chekov turned a slow circle so as not to let the ship out of his sight. He nearly bumped into Tomlinson when the weapons officer made no corresponding move. He smiled down at Chekov, but didn't step aside.

"If I were you, Ensign, I'd be careful who I let hear me talk like that." The lieutenant's demeanor was just as friendly and relaxed as it had always been, yet Chekov heard the edge of something more serious than casual conversation. "At best, ignoring Lieutenant Uhura's orders is willful disobedience. At worst, it could be considered mutiny."

Chekov understood how Tomlinson meant it—not as a warning, but as a bit of fraternal advice from someone with more years on a starship to a woefully inexperienced comrade. And he was even fairly certain that Tomlinson understood that he'd said what he did out of loyalty to Kirk, not defiance of Lieutenant Uhura. But neither realization kept the blood from his face or the mortification from his voice. "Yes, sir. I understand, sir." He forced himself to add, a little stiffly, "Thank you, sir," because the tiny part of him that wasn't writhing in humiliation truly did appreciate what Tomlinson had tried to do.

Still smiling, Tomlinson gave him a clap on the shoulder as though they'd only been discussing some unlucky sporting event. "Lighten up," he suggested. "You're gonna be out here a long time."

At first, Chekov had assumed Tomlinson meant out in space, on a starship, serving Starfleet—all of which Chekov did hope to be doing for quite some time yet. But later he wondered if the lieutenant hadn't experienced some sort of unexpected psychic insight, and instead had meant they would all be trapped on Tlaoli for days or weeks or years to come. It was the sort of thing that started to occur to one when unimaginable disasters followed on each other fast enough.

Smith caught their attention with an excited whoop. "I think he's found him!" She jumped up and down a few times, pointing out toward Sulu's shuttle as it cinched around in an ever tightening turn. "Just above that little forest, or stones, or whatever," she rushed on. "I think he dipped!"

Chekov and Tomlinson hurried to flank her at the edge of their knoll. Some distance ahead, still blanketed in shadow from another of the steep hills and blurred by the heavy mist, a broken landscape of some kind of complex shapes lay across the ground like pieces of a three-dimensional jigsaw puzzle that no one had been able to finish. Chekov understood Smith's confusion. He couldn't tell, either, what made up the irregular structures, or even how far away they were. He was willing to guess, however, that it was under an hour's quick hike.

The shuttle's nose dipped downward once, twice, directly over the center of the broken landscape. Smith whooped again, and they all three flailed their arms to let Sulu know they'd seen his signal. The energetic signaling felt both silly and invigorating. Kirk wasn't lost. He was on the planet, only a brisk walk away. Everything was going to be all right after all. Chekov caught himself laughing along with Smith as they started down the slope toward Sulu's signal.

None of them actually saw the shuttle go down. Chekov saw it bank away to the south in a loop that took it far behind them, heading back toward the base camp, he assumed, to let Uhura know that the rescue party was on its way to retrieve the captain. It had occurred to him to wonder if Sulu would be able to return with the others if it turned out the captain needed something like medical assistance from Dr. McCoy, if he could actually put the shuttle down in the terrain toward which they were headed or if they'd have to somehow drag Kirk free of it before counting on any outside help. He turned to voice this concern to Tomlinson just in time to glimpse a strange, brilliant flash of light explode like a halo beyond a row of ragged dark hills. Then a clap like thunder rolled over them and echoed away, passing back and forth across the valleys until it seemed like it would never die.

After a very long moment, Tomlinson was the only one to recover his voice enough to speak. "Oh, God, what now?"

Chekov knew the answer with a sick certainty that frightened him. "I think we just lost the shuttle."

# Chapter Eleven

IN ANY OTHER CIRCUMSTANCES, Uhura thought somberly, Tlaoli's karst-lands would have been beautiful. In one direction, huge monoliths of limestone rose from a mist whose drifting movement gave them the illusion of advancing like waves on a storm-beaten sea. At their feet, the mist had cleared away enough to reveal a rocky gray plateau so broken by crevasses and solution cracks that it resembled a maze, or a jigsaw puzzle scattered on a gigantic scale. Beyond that, an army of smaller rock formations marched off toward the horizon, so hunched and gnarled with erosion that they looked like petrified versions of the weather-beaten trees living in their shadows. Feathery plumes of mist crowned the largest tree-fringed hollows, marking places where the caverns below blew cold, damp breath up into the morning air through sinkholes and solution pipes. It was the kind of landscape that could have taken your breath away.

If you hadn't already been hammered into numbness by repeated blows of shock, disbelief, and despair.

"The last time we saw him was just over that little ridge, the one that looks like a row of teeth." Tomlinson took a careful step forward on the slick stone of their karst mound and pointed the direction out to Uhura. She turned to look that way, measuring the distance with the part of her brain that remained coldly alert and functional despite this latest disaster.

Uhura's first, almost hysterical, impulse had been to deny it, to refuse to believe Chekov when he'd come back to the base camp with the news that the shuttle had gone down. Oddly enough, it had been the stifled edge of fear in the young ensign's voice, the desperate look in his own dark eyes, that had steadied her enough to thrust that impulse aside and acknowledge reality. Sulu had admitted that he was flying the shuttle on a razor-thin safety margin, with unreliable instruments and unpredictable changes in altitude caused by Tlaoli's strange power fluxes. It shouldn't really have come as a surprise that he had crashed, but once again Uhura had let herself be lulled into a treacherous sense of hope.

Dr. McCoy had just come out of the mess tent to report that his emergency operation on Davis had been a success when they had seen the joyful flurry of leaps and arm waving atop the karst mound to the north. Everyone watching from below knew that meant the unseen shuttle had made a find. Even though they had all seen the bright glint that flashed across the sky, their celebratory cheer must have drowned out the distant explosion that followed. Even the sound of running feet hadn't alarmed them—after all, wouldn't one of the crewmen sent to watch the *Drake* come hurrying back to tell them how far away Captain Kirk had been spotted? But even before she saw Chekov's grim face, something about the sound of his labored, almost sobbing breath as he approached warned Uhura that the news would be bad.

Now, after a near-vertical climb up a fractured limestone cliff that had seemed more of an annoyance than the terror it might otherwise have been, Uhura couldn't even decide how bad the news actually was.

"Why isn't there any smoke coming up from the crash site?" she demanded.

Silence fell over the karst mound, profound enough to let Uhura hear the rustle of wind through the bonsai trees many meters below. Tomlinson stared over his shoulder at her as if he'd been stunned by the question, while Smith and Chekov exchanged baffled and forlorn glances, like cadets caught unprepared by a pop quiz. It wasn't until Jaeger hurtled over the edge of the fractured rim-rock with a painful gasp, followed a moment later by the man who had hoisted him up that slope, that anyone even acknowledged Uhura's question.

"Wind couldn't be blowing it away," Sanner said, leaning down to haul Jaeger to his feet. "Look at the mist from those cavern vents down there—straight as a plumb line."

"Maybe the shuttle landed in a pond or something," suggested Smith. "That could explain—"

Her voice hadn't carried much conviction to begin with, but it shriveled away entirely at the explosion of snorts she got from the two cave geologists. "There's no standing water that high on a karst plain," Sanner informed her. "The water table's hundreds of meters below, down at the feet of those big towers over to the east."

"Oh." Smith took an abashed step backward, teetering for a moment on the edge of the mound before Chekov grabbed and steadied her. "Of course."

"I think..." Jaeger unfolded one of his topographic maps, smoothing it down across the rippled gray surface of the karst mound and anchoring it with chunks of rock. A dirt-stained finger traced a path from the round contours of their current perch to the more linear elevation lines that marked Tomlinson's little ridge. "Yes, look. That sinkhole over there—" He stabbed at another set of concentric circles, these marked with slashes like inward-pointing teeth. "—is where we first entered the upper level of the caves. That means the hollow where you saw the shuttle disappear—" His hand swept over another section of the map, where the contour lines spread further apart. "—sits directly over the ice cave where we first lost Captain Kirk."

*"Damn."*

That was Zap Sanner, expressing himself with his usual irreverence. For once, Uhura felt as if the cave specialist spoke for all of them. She cleared her throat, but it still took an effort to put the horrible thought she'd just had into words.

"You think Lieutenant Sulu flew his shuttle into that same alien force field we encountered in the ice cave?"

Jaeger peered up from his map, gray eyes glittering in his bruised and slashed face. "There might be other possible hypotheses," he said dryly. "But have you ever heard of something called Occam's razor, Lieutenant?"

"The simplest explanation is usually the right one," blurted Yuki Smith, as if to atone for her previous mistake.

"Yes," said Jaeger. "Precisely."

Uhura squinted past the jagged ridge rocks, but the rusty glare of Tlaoli's morning sun drowned any hint of blue light that might have rippled in the shadowy hollow beyond. It was no wonder Sulu had flown into the alien force field unwittingly. Uhura just hoped Captain Kirk hadn't stumbled back into it unwittingly, as well.

Although if he had....

"We know Ensign Chekov went from the ice cave to the upper breakdown chamber where the survey team was stuck without lights," Uhura said, abruptly. The conclusion she had just come to was so disquieting that she wanted to make sure she verified each logical step with her subordinates. "And we're pretty sure that's where the captain was sent as well, right?"

"He couldn't have gotten past us if he'd materialized anywhere else," Jaeger agreed.

Sanner nodded. "And it sure looked like someone crawled out of that sinkhole ahead of us."

"Someone did," Chekov said flatly, then added a belated, "Sir."

"Then we have to assume the upper chamber is where the alien force field always sends people." Uhura made the only decision she could, given the evidence they had, although it took all her willpower to actually say it. "We'll have to go back into the cave and look for Sulu there."

Tomlinson let out a sound halfway between a groan and a grunt of surprise. "Lieutenant, you don't think the *shuttle* could possibly have gone down there, do you?"

"I don't know what that alien installation can and cannot do, Mr. Tomlinson," Uhura said. "But that cavern was certainly big enough to hold a shuttle."

"Provided it didn't try to materialize around one of the flowstone columns," Jaeger commented. "Or take enough kinetic energy with it to flatten it against a wall."

Uhura sighed. "I know there's no guarantee we'll find Lieutenant Sulu down there, Mr. Jaeger, much less alive. But if there's even a small chance he was sent there, then he's trapped underground without any caving equipment, and probably without power or lights, either. We *have* to make sure we're not leaving him there like that."

That stark statement left a trail of unhappy silence after it, broken eventually by the youngest member of their group. "Sir," said Chekov. "I'll volunteer to go back underground with you."

Smith glanced over at him, then let out a large, resigned sigh. "Me, too."

Uhura couldn't quite summon a smile, but she at least managed to give them what she hoped was a kindly look. "Actually, I need you two and Mr. Tomlinson to look for Captain Kirk up here, since you were the ones who saw where Lieutenant Sulu signaled that he found him." She lifted her gaze back to the karstlands, where the morning mist was breaking into glittering strings and shreds. "Take Martine or D'Amato with you, and keep a tricorder turned on while you walk out there. If you see it start to lose power, or get a ridiculous error reading, I want you to turn around and come back immediately. I don't want to send anyone else through that alien transporter if we can help it."

"Aye-aye, sir," chorused Chekov and Smith.

Tomlinson, however, had served for longer on the *Enterprise* and had a rank technically equal to Uhura's, even if he was considerably junior to her on the command list. "Who will you take down into the caves with you, sir?" he demanded.

"Mr. Sanner, of course." Uhura glanced over at the cave specialist. She needn't have worried—Sanner was already tugging the topographic map with its superimposed sketch of the various cave levels away from a reluctant Jaeger and muttering something about counting cave reflectors.

"And either Lieutenant Wright or Dr. McCoy, whoever is willing to come and provide medical care, in case…" Uhura trailed off, unwilling to tempt fate by putting her worst case scenario into words. "We shouldn't need any more people than that, as long as we leave the ropes up on the edge of the sinkhole to get us out."

"Getting *us* out won't be the problem," Sanner said. "And if we got Davis out with a fractured skull, I'm pretty sure we can take Mr. Sulu out no matter what's happened to him." The cave geologist surprised Uhura with a snort of wry but genuine laughter. "What I want to know, Lieutenant, is how you think we're going to get the *shuttle* out if it's down there."

"We're not," Uhura said frankly. "But if it is there, Mr. Sanner, we just may use its warp core to take that alien force field out, once and for all."

Tlaoli's sun was not as bright as many, or as hot as some. The polished brass disk that had finally lifted itself above the farthest ridges of exposed rock barely warmed the air, and the tentative fingers it reached between monolithic shoulders of rock were too pale and watered down to burn away the mist that still swirled catlike around their ankles. No wonder the vegetation consisted of nothing more than stunted trees and scrubby grass, Chekov thought. The anemic morning fog looked to be all the moisture the karstlands got, at least during this time of year, and if Chekov understood what Jaeger had said earlier over their reconstructed maps, even that little bit of moisture was sucked beneath the surface into the caves below almost as soon as it touched the ground. It struck him as almost absurd to realize he had nearly drowned only a few dozen meters beneath a veritable desert.

"Careful." Yuki Smith nudged him, none too gently, out of the path of another sinkhole. He'd seen it, just as he'd seen the dozen others she'd felt the need to steer him around, but he thanked her anyway. Apparently, the security guard was convinced no one could monitor their direction on a hand compass and watch where he was going at the same time.

Behind them, Robert Tomlinson and Angela Martine muttered over tricorder readings, running just as much risk of stumbling into a sinkhole as Chekov did, as far as he could see. He spared a glance over his shoulder to make sure they'd navigated themselves safely past that particular obstacle, then turned his attention back to his compass and the bearing he hoped was taking them closer to Captain Kirk.

"I hope their tricorder is as good as you are at finding trouble before we step into it," he commented to Smith. He felt a little awkward making small talk with someone he hardly knew, but Smith insisted that they'd become good friends during the hours of cave travel he no longer remembered, and he *had* climbed on top of her head. It seemed the least he could do.

Apparently, he could have done it more quietly.

"You worry about your end of the hike, Ensign," Tomlinson called forward to him. "We'll worry about ours." Staring fixedly at the tricorder screen, he pulled Martine to a stop before waving at Smith and Chekov. "Hold up."

They halted obediently enough, although Chekov kept himself half-oriented toward the compass heading they'd been following, as if he'd suddenly forget which way they'd been going.

Martine shook her head at the tricorder readings without waiting for Tomlinson to elaborate on why he'd stopped them. "That's not a big enough error," she said. "It's not outside our standard deviation."

"But it's bigger than we've been getting," Tomlinson argued. "And Lieutenant Uhura said we should turn back at the very first sign—"

"She said we should turn back if the error readings became ridiculous." Chekov gritted his teeth against the embarrassment of everyone turning to stare at him, but didn't back down. "I'm sorry, sir, I didn't mean to interrupt." Which wasn't entirely true. "But the possibility that we're close to the alien transporter's range of affect is remote, sir." He held out his compass toward them as though the bobbing needle there would make everything clear. "Mr. Jaeger's maps of the cave system—"

"They're your maps, too," Smith pointed out, but Chekov only nodded absently in acknowledgment.

"—indicate that the alien force field most likely originates south-southwest of the base camp. We're maintaining a strict easterly heading to reach the rock formations where Mr. Sulu saw the captain. While I appreciate that Lieutenant Uhura wants to be careful, we're much more likely to fall down a sinkhole right now than walk into the alien energy field."

"That's assuming the force field hasn't expanded enough to intersect our route," Tomlinson said, a little grimly.

Chekov nodded. "Yes, sir, it does. Because if the field is maintaining a spherical shape the way Mr. Jaeger speculates it is, then by the time it reached us out here it would have already passed over the base camp and everyone else in the party." He felt immediately awkward when his extrapolation flashed alarm across the others' faces. It occurred to him for the very first time that what he viewed as practicality might come across as coldness to others. He wondered if he should do something about his tendency to give that impression, then decided he'd worry about it once they'd located the captain and gotten everyone safely back on board the ship. "It's just, if we're going to assume the worst, then there's no sense going on. If not..."

The lieutenant sighed and pushed the tricorder into Martine's hands as though too frustrated to watch it anymore. "All right, good point." It struck Chekov that being in charge of a party didn't necessarily mean you always knew what to do. "Let's keep going, then. If we get any ridiculous error readings..." He glanced aside at Martine, mirrored her grin despite himself, and sighed again. "We'll ask Mr. Chekov then whether or not we're allowed to worry."

The sun kept them company as they threaded between sinkholes and twisted trees. Chekov tried to keep them on as straight a course as possible, given the landscape, but twice had to back them out of a confusion of collapsing ground and find a way around to solid footing again. When they finally reached the broken forest of stone where Sulu had spotted Kirk, it came upon them suddenly, like a beach giving over to the sea. For some reason, Chekov had assumed they would have to climb down among the standing stones, into the solution cracks like mice between house walls. Instead, the exposed rocks suddenly towered over them like giants at parade rest, and they were on the bottom without even trying.

Tomlinson and Martine drew alongside Chekov and Smith, and Tomlinson shaded his eyes to squint up at the jigsaw of broken plateaus. "So I wonder if the captain took the high road or the low road."

At least with four of them they didn't have to make the same decision. They split along separate fractures, Tomlinson and Martine seeking out the steep trails that would take them to the top of the rocks while Chekov and Smith wound through the lower valleys. They each had a whistle from the cave rescue supplies, but Chekov did what he could to keep everyone in sight, even if only occasionally. No matter how certain he'd sounded about it being safe to continue, even he couldn't shake a sick feeling of dread that one of them would stumble into the alien transport system and disappear without the others realizing.

Stripes of pale sunlight rimmed the tops of the maze-like cracks, painted on almost ruler-straight above the shadows cast by the rocks on every side. Chekov couldn't believe the sun wasn't higher by now. Surely it was at least mid-morning. But the uneven floor that wound and cut its way through the stones was still chilly in its darkness. It was almost like wandering through the caves again, only this time without the warming nanosuit or the reassuring presence of Sanner at his back.

"What are we going to do if we find him?"

Chekov jumped aside, falling back against one of the walls with his heart hammering. Smith drew back from the narrow crack through which she'd spoken, her face almost vanishing into the shadows. "Sorry about that."

Chekov tried to cover his startlement by straightening and clearing his throat. "I just didn't expect the rocks to talk."

She giggled, a discordantly girlish sound, and came forward again to frame her face in the crack. "I'm serious, though. If the captain is running away from us, and he doesn't know who he is... What are we going to say to him? I mean, what's going to make him hang around and listen?"

Chekov didn't know how to answer her. He hadn't gotten that far in his own thoughts. Amnesia or no, he couldn't quite believe that Captain Kirk retained no sense of himself, no rationality or dignity or sense. Even if, for some reason, the captain thought he was being pursued by enemies, surely his first sight of them would tell him that they were friends and he was safe.

If not....

"I don't know," he admitted at last. "We can't very well chase him."

"Actually I'm more worried about catching him. He's a strong guy, you know."

That was something else Chekov had never really thought about, but he was sure Smith was correct. This whole rescue operation was beginning to look more uncertain with each question the security guard posed.

High above them, and some distance ahead, a whistle shrilled in silver-bright alarm. Smith pulled away from her peep hole, out of sight, and Chekov jerked a guilty look back over his shoulder toward where Tomlinson and Martine must have gotten well ahead of them. "They've found something!" The captain. They must have found the captain.

He tried to mark the whistle's direction based on the slant of the sunlight and the rise of the stones, but wasn't entirely certain he could maintain his orientation while jogging through the rock maze in search of a way through. Several twists and turns out of sight to his right, he could hear running footsteps, irregular on the rocky ground. He opened his mouth to warn Smith to be careful about hurrying so fast toward their destination lest she lose her footing and break a leg. Before he could do so much as call her name, though, a running figure plowed around the rocks in front of him and crashed them both into the dirt.

Chekov knew the instant it happened that he hadn't collided with Smith. He had a quick impression of slender youthfulness and ratty civilian clothes just as he and the stranger went tumbling, and while his imagination wasn't quick enough to assign any meaning to this impression, he at least understood that it wasn't Smith. Rolling, Chekov shot out a hand to grab a flailing ankle when the other person tried frantically to kick himself free and get up again. "Stop! I'm not—"

The boy didn't wait to find out what Chekov was or wasn't going to do. Lashing out with his free leg, he kicked the ensign hard twice, once on the wrist and once further up the inside of his arm. But as much as that hurt, it wasn't the boy's blows or even the violence of his cursing that shocked Chekov into releasing him. It was the fierce hazel eyes that burned in the handsome young face, and the unmistakably Kirk-like set of his fourteen-year-old jaw when he finally wrenched himself loose, got up, and ran.

Uhura had thought that going back into the caves of Tlaoli would be one of the hardest things she'd ever had to do. Intellectually, she knew that squirming down through the twisting passage that had led them out through the rubble pile would be physically dangerous and emotionally draining. But when the time came to take that first step down into darkness, all she really felt was numb and exhausted. After nearly twenty hours of constant toil and danger, Uhura's mind no longer seemed able to envision possible disasters, and the jangle of stress hormones in her bloodstream had lost its sharp edge. She followed her own orders as automatically as if they had been given by someone else, setting one foot below another on the swaying cat's cradle of ropes that dangled down into the muddy sinkhole, until she stood beside Sanner at the bottom.

"Heigh ho, heigh ho," said the cave geologist with a crooked smile, while they waited for McCoy to join them.

Uhura tried to find a smile to match his, although she suspected it looked more like a wince. "And just who are you calling a dwarf?"

"Hey, I think I'm pretty bashful." He reached out and adjusted Uhura's water drip until her carbide light glowed a little brighter, then grunted in satisfaction. "You want to make sure you can catch all the reflectors ahead of you. There should be twelve of them."

Uhura blinked at him, startled back into alertness. "I'm going first?"

Sanner nodded. "That passage is too narrow to pull someone through. If Dr. McCoy gets stuck, I'll need to push on him from behind."

"I'm not going to get stuck." A wiry figure in anomalous gold jumped off the last rung of ropes and came sloshing through the mud to join them. Ensign Davis's cave jumper had been the one that fit McCoy best for height, although it stretched a little tightly across his shoulders and sagged in a few other places. "I feel like a greased pig already, with all this mud I'm wearing."

"If you think you're muddy now, just wait until you see the soil zone we're going to crawl through," Sanner said cheerfully. He consulted the folded map he had pulled from his jumper's chest pocket. "All right, it's three hundred meters from here to the edge of the rubble pile. If anyone gets stuck, just yell for the person behind you to come up and push. Ready?"

"Hell, no." Despite his wry words, McCoy had been the one who'd insisted on coming with them, even using his authority as the ship's chief medical officer to overrule Wright's protests that she knew the caves better. He followed them willingly enough down the sinkhole, although he couldn't refrain a snort when he saw the ankle-high wedge of darkness that was their entrance. "I can't believe you got Yuki Smith out through that crack," was all he said, however.

Uhura caught a last glimpse of Sanner's grin as she lowered herself to her hands and knees. "I pushed, Tomlinson pulled," Sanner told McCoy, his voice fading behind her as she squirmed through the jagged opening. "And to tell you the truth, I think that opening might have been just a little wider by the time—"

The passage twisted a meter past the entrance and Uhura lost the sound of the others' voices. The tightly clinging walls of the passage echoed back her own sounds to her with claustrophobic intensity—the scrape of her gloves as she hauled herself around projecting rock corners, the thump of her booted feet pushing off any ledge or wall they could find to propel her forward, the hiss of her strained breath.

It seemed forever until Uhura saw the first glint of a cave reflector, guiding her past a vertical crack that looked far too narrow to represent a viable alternate route. The second reflector warned her away from an even less appealing solution cavity along a bedding plane, but the third one was mounted at a place where the passage widened for a deceptive moment, then split into two halves. Uhura turned her carbide light back and forth several times, but there was no mistaking it. Sanner had posted the cave reflector squarely over the more narrow and sloping of the two passages.

"Hey." A groping hand caught at her ankle, withdrew, and then gave an inquiring rap on one boot sole. "Something wrong?" McCoy asked.

"I'm trying to make sure . . ." Uhura squirmed one outstretched hand back to her face, tugged off the glove with her teeth and licked at the tips of her finger. She stuck her hand forward again and realized at once that she hadn't needed to make her skin wet to feel the sucking indraft of warm outside air being pulled into the cavern below. It blew strongly against her unprotected skin, and to her surprise it pulled into the narrow uphill slant of the fork. "All right," she said, and twisted to her left to fit her shoulders through the crack.

She realized almost at once that had been the wrong decision, since another twist of the passage put her on her back instead of her stomach, without even enough room to spin herself around. By then it was too late to back out—she could hear McCoy bumping and cursing his way through after her. Fortunately, this was the section of cave whose roof was snarled with tree roots, allowing Uhura to pull herself hand-over-hand along it instead of crawling. It would have been the easiest part of the trip so far, if the roots hadn't made the ceiling so soft and crumbly that at every other pull clots of dirt and mud scattered across her eyes or nose or mouth. Somewhere along the way, Uhura lost the glove she had been carrying between her teeth ever since she'd stripped it off to check the draft, but by then she barely cared.

The cave passage angled down again, this time steeply enough to dump her in a slithering rush into a larger, shoulder-height chamber. Uhura barely remembered to pull herself out of the way before McCoy came hurtling through after her, upside down and coughing. A moment later, Sanner's carbide glow descended the slope right-side-up and a lot more sedately. He emerged with a loopy grin that made Uhura want to smack him.

"Boy, you guys make good time!" said the cave geologist. He dug around in his chest pocket, then tossed Uhura her abandoned glove before she could make any of the crushing remarks that came to mind. "I'm going to tell that kid Chekov that he's a slug compared to you."

McCoy paused in wiping mud from his face to give the other man a sour look. "I don't care what you tell Chekov," he said. "Just tell me that we're almost to this big upper chamber of yours."

"About halfway," Sanner estimated. "But there's no more spots quite as tight as that. Want me to go first now, Lieutenant?"

Uhura finished pulling on her glove and opened her mouth to say "Yes," but what came out instead was a decisive, "No." It startled her a little, because it wasn't what she would have expected of herself, but she had to admit that she liked being in the lead. The constant need to look for cave reflectors kept the crawl from becoming too monotonous, and the knowledge that McCoy could easily push her through any spot where she happened to get stuck made the constricted twists and turns of the cave passage seem a lot less claustrophobic. "I don't mind going first," she said, smiling under her mud mask when she realized it was actually true.

"Onward and downward, then." McCoy tightened the strap of his cave helmet under his chin. "Although I'll warn you—if we find Mr. Sulu drinking coffee at the base camp when we get back, I'm going to dump him down this sinkhole just on principle."

The sound of Sanner's guffaw followed Uhura into the next winding section of the cave. The passages here were generally wider, with only occasional places where what looked suspiciously like blocks of broken roof crimped the space down to a few dozen centimeters in height. Uhura wriggled through easily enough, although she tried not to think about how hard it must have been for the sturdier members of the original cave party, Tomlinson and Smith and Wright, to make this trip the first time through.

After the last of the pinches, a final cave reflector glittered over a spot Uhura remembered: a jagged hole in the passage floor that opened like a narrow downspout over the rubble pile below. She crawled over to the edge of it, angling her carbide light into the rush of arctic cold air that came blasting up from the darkness. The drop was at least three meters down to the unstable footing of the breakdown pile that filled the back end of the big cavern. Uhura grimaced, but when she pulled her head back out, her light splashed over the slim length of rope Sanner had left dangling from a couple of pitons at the top. She scuttled around to that side of the hole, tested the rope with a jerk, then swung herself down onto it just as McCoy's carbide light appeared on the far side of the opening.

"What, don't we get to slide down this drainpipe, too?" he asked tartly.

"Not unless you want to start an avalanche when you land," Uhura retorted. McCoy crawled out to the edge and watched her rappel downward, grunting when he saw the size of the breakdown pile below. With the glare of his carbide light added to hers, the immense size of the column-filled cavern below began to reveal itself. Uhura could feel the cold biting harder at the skin of her face and neck as she entered the main chamber, and she fervently hoped that didn't mean the alien force field had grown to envelop this end of the cave system, as well.

It wouldn't make sense for it to do that, Uhura assured herself, as she found her footing on a large boulder and released the rope for McCoy to use. After all, if the purpose of this system was to transport people here, it wouldn't also take them *from* here. Although it made Uhura wonder why, with the sophisticated energy-gathering technology these unknown aliens had apparently been able to construct, they had used their force field simply to send people from one end of an hour-long walk to another. Or had this once been part of a much larger transportation system, similar to the continent-wide transporter systems back on Earth, that had simply eroded through countless millennia down to just this last functioning piece?

Sanner followed McCoy down the rope and added his carbide glow to theirs. The combined illumination lit the cavern all the way to its end, painting long, thin shadows like prison bars on the floor from the cathedral-like columns that supported its arching roof.

"No shuttle," said the geologist, unnecessarily.

"No," Uhura agreed. She lifted her voice to a ringing shout. "Sulu! Lieutenant Sulu, can you hear me?"

Only silence answered her. The cold must have frozen even the water dripping off the columns, which had previously filled the chamber with a sound like tiny aqueous chimes.

"Want to go down and look around?" Sanner asked after a while. His voice sounded distinctly more glum than it had a moment before.

"Not yet." Uhura reached up to twist the control knob on the water reservoir of her carbide lamp. A memory of waiting in the darkness of alien conduits and seeing an indigo-blue light glowing behind its ice-covered walls had sprung unbidden into her mind. "Turn off your lights for a minute."

McCoy gave her a scandalized look. "Lieutenant, are you nuts?"

"You can only see the alien force field if your eyes are adjusted to total darkness," Uhura explained. She heard the last of her acetylene gas hiss into the combustion chamber, then her side of the rubble pile suddenly became a little darker. Sanner was already extinguishing his own carbide light, and, a moment later, McCoy grumbled and reached up to dim his, as well. Their lights went one right after the other, wrapping them in utter, stifling darkness.

With neither sound nor light to orient herself, Uhura felt oddly less sure of her balance on the rubble pile, although she knew for a fact that she'd wedged herself securely between two boulders just a moment before. Only the hard press of rock against her back and the bite of cold air against her skin kept her from feeling as if she'd entered a sensory deprivation tank.

"Over there," said McCoy, in an unnecessary whisper. His hand brushed across Uhura's shoulder as he tried to point in the darkness. "That one big column—is that the light you meant?"

Uhura touched the doctor's hand to see which way it was oriented, then put her own hand against Sanner's shoulder to point the way for him. She kept it there to steady herself as she turned very carefully to look in the direction McCoy had indicated. Her eyes registered light almost immediately, but it took her a moment to actually focus on it. The cloud of golden sparks flitting like fireflies around one of the columnar cave formations was so different from what she'd expected to see that Uhura wondered if she'd have noticed it anywhere near as quickly as McCoy had.

"Actually," she said wryly, "no. That's not what we saw before at all."

"But maybe it makes sense," Sanner said. "The blue light was the part that made you vanish. Maybe the part that makes you appear should be another color."

"Maybe." Uhura dug her teeth into her lip, straining to see what kind of pattern those golden shimmers were making in the darkness. "Dr. McCoy, do you see...?"

"Yes, I do." McCoy began scrabbling with his carbide light in the darkness. "Dammit, how do you get this thing back on?"

"Here, let me—" Sanner reached across Uhura to adjust the water drip and ignite the flame. The glow of McCoy's lamp dazzled Uhura blind for a moment, but her eyes adjusted fast enough to see the questioning look on one man's face and the grimness she'd been afraid of on the other's.

"What's the deal?" the geologist asked, glancing back and forth between them as if their silence had alarmed him. "What the heck did you guys see?"

"A human shape," Uhura said, trying to keep her voice calm and unshaken. "The lights were outlining it, as if it was just starting to appear." McCoy was already scrambling down the rubble pile, and she snapped her own helmet alight, then levered herself out from between her boulders to follow him. "The problem is, it's appearing right in the middle of that rock column."

# Chapter Twelve

THE SWARM OF GOLDEN SPARKS inside the stone column grew brighter, tracing more and more clearly the outline of a human body trapped inside solid rock. Uhura scrambled recklessly down the pile of cave rubble, her boots skidding off one frost-slicked boulder after another. She could see the jerk and bobble of McCoy's carbide lamp become a swift, straight line when he reached the bottom of the breakdown pile, then disappear entirely as he approached the glowing pillar.

A fierce golden-white fire seemed to have ignited inside the rock formation, brilliant enough to illuminate the breakdown cavern all the way up to its sparkling ice-crusted roof. The light also showed Uhura the smooth pavement of water-laid flowstone that surrounded the column, with not a loose stone or broken stalactite in sight. She skidded to a stop at the foot of the breakdown pile, looking for a sharp-edged chunk of rock she could use as a hammering tool.

"Don't bother with that." Sanner vaulted down off a boulder somewhat higher than her head. Uhura glanced up to ask what he meant, and saw that he was already striding across the cavern toward the pile of gear Survey Team Three had stacked into a makeshift bed for the injured Davis. The cave specialist threw off the emergency blankets and dove into the backpacks below like a terrier digging for a rat, tossing out sample bags and surveying markers until he finally emerged with a rock sledge in one hand and a prybar in the other.

"*This* should let us break through that rock formation." Sanner handed the bar to Uhura and hefted the sledge onto one shoulder, grimacing in a way that made her wonder if he'd hurt himself coming down the rubble pile. "And I complained about Jaeger's damned handprints..."

Uhura opened her mouth to ask him what was wrong, but a shout from the heart of the cavern interrupted her. The gold light was bright enough now that, when she turned, Uhura had to squint against it to see McCoy. The doctor had plastered himself up against the rock column and was using some kind of antique medical sensor whose cables ran from his ears to a metal disk that he held pressed against the stone. He paused for a moment to peer out into what must have looked like darkness to his light-blind eyes, then beckoned when he spotted them.

"Hurry up," he yelled. "We've got to get him out of here!"

Uhura leaped to follow Sanner as he ran toward the glowing column. As they got closer, she could see that the light was coming from deep inside the rock, turning the outer layers of flowstone into a translucent alabaster shell. A blurred but familiar face was visible beneath the stone.

"Is Sulu alive?" she asked.

"I can hear him breathing." McCoy moved the metal disk to another part of the flowstone casing. "The transporter must have taken the stone out when it put him in. But he sounds ragged, like he's gasping. There might not be any air in there with him."

"All right, you guys, stand back." Sanner hefted the sledge as they obeyed him. "God dammit, here goes a thousand years of laminar accretion," he said regretfully, and swung.

The first blow rebounded off the stone with a crash that stung Uhura's ears and made her eyes blink shut involuntarily. She saw McCoy wince and yank the cables out of his ears. A network of little cracks appeared on the glowing surface, radiating out like rays from the dent Sanner had made, but nothing broke or fell. The cave geologist stripped off his cave gloves, spitting on his hands despite the bitterly cold air, then hefted the sledge and swung again. A louder crash was followed by a fierce crackling sound. Uhura threw a worried glance at the ceiling, but a moment later a shard of flowstone detached from the face of the rock formation and came clattering down at her feet.

"Pry bar." Sanner held out his hand like a surgeon demanding an operating tool. Uhura handed it to him, then began clearing away the curving fragments of flowstone as he pried them off the column, one by one. Their outer surfaces were ridged and crenulated with layered travertine, she noticed, but their inner surfaces were oddly concave and smooth. Uhura ran her gloved fingers over one and frowned.

"Zap, wait a minute," she said. The geologist levered off one last milky fragment of rock, then stepped back to catch his breath. Uhura took his place beside the column and lifted her hands toward the much clearer figure of Lieutenant Sulu.

A smooth curve of almost invisible transparent metal met her palms inches away from the pilot's face. To her surprise, it wasn't anywhere near as cold as the cavern's bitter air. Even through her insulated gloves, Uhura could feel that it was warm and humming with the vibration of some inner force.

"I don't think this is a rock formation," she said over her shoulder. "I think it's some kind of stasis chamber."

"One that got covered up with travertine in the millions of years since the aliens left?" Sanner glanced around at the other pillars throughout the room, spaced with what now looked to Uhura like suspicious regularity. "Do you think they're all—?"

"Could be." McCoy had plastered himself against the luminous curve of the alien stasis chamber, cables plugged back into his ears. "Sulu's still breathing—in fact, it sounds like he's breathing a little easier."

"He's not awake, is he?" Concern brought Uhura up next to the doctor, slitting her eyes to peer into the fierce alien radiance. The pilot's eyes were serenely closed, but there was something about his face that was beginning to bother Uhura. She studied him closely, noticing a network of lines like fine scars around his eyes, his mouth, between his dark eyebrows. Or were those . . . wrinkles?

"What's that uniform he's wearing?" Sanner peered over her shoulder. "That's not the one he had on back at the base camp."

Uhura craned her head to look down into the remaining shell of stone, and blinked in surprise. She had watched Sulu climb into the *Drake* a few hours ago in a clean gold uniform tunic and regulation trousers. Now, he wore a scuffed and stained combat jacket, camouflaged in an odd combination of violet and green, over a black and gray jumpsuit whose silver piping traced a strange, silhouetted version of the familiar Starfleet insignia on the front of its neck-hugging collar.

"What the hell—" McCoy shouldered both of them aside as he slid himself around the edge of the chamber, staring down at Sulu's right arm. "Look at his hand!"

Uhura scrambled back up on the pile of fallen shards, then gasped as she caught a glimpse of what the doctor was staring at. What had once been Sulu's right hand hung below the blood-stained sleeve of his jacket, but it was barely recognizable now. Blood rilled up and was somehow invisibly wicked away from that awful tangle of shredded tendons and shattered bone. Every few seconds, some part of it was gently moved and pressed against another. Muscles seemed to swell and knit across those joinings, then atrophy away again, allowing the bones to be moved to a different location. Uhura glanced up at the pilot's serene, sleeping face, then back at the ruined hand again, not understanding how both could belong to the same body.

"The chamber's trying to fix him," said Sanner excitedly. "It must have him sedated or something, and now it's trying to put his hand back together. It's not a stasis chamber, Lieutenant! It's a healing device."

"An *alien* healing device." McCoy watched the gentle manipulations of Sulu's wounded hand, then startled Uhura with a curse. "Dammit, that's the second time it put his first metacarpal into the correct CM joint and then took it away again. I don't think it knows what the hell it's doing!"

"It must be programmed to heal according to an alien body plan," Uhura said in dismay. "And it's trying to match Sulu to that."

"But if it can't..." Sanner glanced worriedly at the bloodstain growing darker on the pilot's right sleeve. "And he keeps on bleeding like that..."

"He'll die." The doctor banged a fist on the glowing curve of transparent metal separating them from the injured pilot, cursing again when his blow rebounded harmlessly. "Can we break through this thing?"

"With a phaser, maybe," Sanner said. "Not with a sledge and a prybar."

"*Look!*" Uhura stiffened, feeling the back of her neck prickle with horror even in the bitter cold. "What is it doing to him now?"

The phantom swelling of muscles had stopped, and now, one at a time, the broken bones and hanging tendons looked as if they were melting into mist. Uhura heard McCoy take in a sudden sharp breath, then let it out in a long sigh of regret and resignation.

"I guess it's not such a bad doctor after all," he said gruffly.

"But—" Uhura watched the alien chamber remove the last jagged fragments of bone from the pilot's crushed wrist, but it wasn't until it begin sealing the fractured ends of his radius and ulna that she understood. "It amputated his hand?"

"Yes," McCoy said. The blood had stopped dripping from the edge of Sulu's jacket and new skin crept out from under it, sealing across the severed bones. The doctor sighed again. "Which is exactly what I would have had to do, if I'd been the one to treat him."

"But what happened to him?" Sanner demanded. "If all the alien transporter did was take him out of the shuttle and send him down here, how did he get his hand crushed? How did he get dressed in those clothes?"

Uhura had lifted her gaze to the pilot's sleeping face again, and not only because it was easier to look at than the useless stump of his right arm. "And how," she asked slowly, "did he get to be twenty years older than when he left camp this morning?"

\* \* \*

Chekov hesitated for only an instant—just long enough to think, *I don't understand! We both went through the same alien force field, and* I *don't feel any younger*—then blasted frantically on his whistle and scrambled to his feet.

Tomlinson materialized at the lip of one rock plateau before Chekov had even let the whistle fall from between his teeth. "Did you see him? Did he get past you?" Chekov nodded miserably, but Tomlinson barely paused long enough to notice. "Angela saw him. It isn't the captain, and I don't know how he could have gotten here—"

"It *was* the captain." Chekov interrupted without considering protocol, or even realizing how absurdly sure of himself he would sound. "It was Captain Kirk."

"Did you *see* him?" Tomlinson asked again, more peevishly this time.

"Did *you?*" Chekov countered through his stung pride.

At almost any other time in Chekov's life, he would have been acutely aware of the impropriety of snapping at a senior officer that way. Right now, he only knew a profound annoyance when the lieutenant screwed his face into a scowl and gestured dismissively down at him. "We can argue about this later. Which way?"

Chekov bit off the impolite retort that first boiled up, and instead pointed down the winding passage ahead of him before breaking into a run himself.

He was surprised how familiar the shadowy twists and turns seemed—he hadn't thought he was paying that much attention when he first navigated his way into the karst maze. Maybe it was all the practice tracking and backtracking through the cave system. While Chekov knew they had been on Tlaoli for less than twelve hours (and he had apparently completely forgotten at least three of those), it felt as if he'd been finding his way through some rocky passage or other for days and days. He barely had to glance at the cracks that splintered off to left and right to remember which ones circled back to meet him, which narrowed down to impossibly tight fissures or dead ends.

*What if Kirk slipped through one of those?* The thought brought him to a sudden halt at the mouth of one dark, knife-thin passage. No matter what Tomlinson believed, Chekov knew they were no longer looking for a powerfully built adult male, with all the attendant assumptions about where Kirk could have climbed to and how he could have got there. An athletic young boy on the brink of manhood could slip into some frighteningly small spaces. Chekov realized with a start that this same boy had already sped through the crawlway that had challenged him and Sanner for hours. And the boy had done it without having to remove any of the roots and rocks that Chekov and Sanner had been forced to rearrange in order to fit through the same space. If Kirk—*this* Kirk—decided to dart into one of these tight side passages, there wasn't a one of them on the landing party who could possibly follow him.

Another whistle shrieked far off to his left, this one warped by its passage in and around the twisted mazework. Cursing, Chekov backed out of the narrow dead-end, ducked right to circle one of the pillars, then cut as directly toward the sound as he could manage.

The little path he finally followed brought him closer to the top of the maze than he expected. He came upon Smith from above, sliding down the sharp water-worn rock at the expense of both his trouser seat and his palms.

The security guard spun to face him as he landed, her dark eyes anomalously wide. "You're not going to believe this—"

"He's young," Chekov cut her off. "He's just a boy. And he's frightened."

She nodded fervently. "Can I still get in trouble? I mean, I hit him! I was trying to stop him, and I hit him! Is he still the captain? Are they going to court-martial me?"

The question was more esoteric than Chekov could handle at the moment. "He's still the captain. But if they court-martial you, they'll have to court-martial us all by the time we manage to catch him." He remembered grabbing at the boy's ankle, and how close he'd come to striking out himself. "I think they'll understand that we're only trying to help him. Which way did he go?"

Smith pointed overhead. "Up the way you came down. You didn't pass him?"

He hadn't. And there hadn't been that many options for where the boy could have gone.

"He's up top," Chekov said with sudden certainty. "He's trying to get past us overhead."

Smith leapt to follow when he scrambled back up the incline. "Mr. Tomlinson and Mr. Martine are up there." She gave him a hard push from behind, then reached for a hand up in turn.

"He may not know that." Chekov hauled her as far up as he could, glad that she was able to pull herself up easily enough once she'd secured a handhold. "And he can't know the topography as well as we do. I don't think he realizes how hard it will be to get back off the rocks again." He turned in a quick circle, looking for some sign of the boy's passage.

Smith mimicked his move, but didn't seem to have anymore success. "Where does he think he's going?"

Chekov remembered the terror behind the determination on the boy's face, and tried to imagine what would move a younger version of his captain to feel such desperate fear. "Away from us. Wherever he's going, it won't be back the way he came." He started to whip his compass out of its pocket, then realized he could just glimpse the lumpy tents and ground rover of the survey team's base camp between the misty hillocks. He grabbed Smith's arm. "Come on."

Away. Away from the base camp, away from the caves. Whatever Kirk thought he was running from, he'd awakened in the same big, dark, empty chamber as Chekov, probably with even more fear than Chekov had felt. He'd followed the breeze outside, and had gone to this much effort already to put distance between himself and that place. Chekov had a feeling that was all Kirk knew about where he was going—he was just getting away. He probably wouldn't even think about what to do next until he was far from the danger he'd already faced, and felt a lot more safe.

They found him again about midway across the broken plateau. The cracks had swelled to ridiculous widths, dropping bare rock sides into valleys where so much of the dirt had washed away that you could almost see down into the cave systems below. The boy made a single convulsive move toward the edge when he saw them approaching. Chekov put an arm out to slow Smith, and stopped her when she reached to take hold of her whistle.

"We need to call the others," she whispered. As though they were conspirators and the boy some worrisome kind of spy.

"We need to not frighten him." Chekov hadn't failed to notice the measuring look Kirk cast at the next plateau over. Even Chekov wondered if the boy could clear the gap with a single running leap.

"Please don't try it." Chekov resisted the urge to call him "sir," then felt absurdly disloyal for leaving the honorific silent.

The boy cast a final look over his shoulder before straightening as proudly as any young king. "Why shouldn't I?" His hands worked nervously, unconsciously at his sides.

Chekov risked taking a few careful steps closer. "Because you can't possibly make it. I could land a shuttle in that gap." He felt more than saw Smith move a few steps to his right. A little of the tension in his stomach eased. At least they both understood that they needed to make sure the boy didn't dart past them. Maybe he should have let Smith call the others after all. "I think we have a misunderstanding here. You don't need to be afraid of us."

The last step was apparently too many. The boy flung his hands up in front of him, shouted suddenly, "Stop!"

Chekov did.

"Why do you have to find me?" The boy sounded suddenly pleading, and much younger even than he looked. "Just tell them you didn't find me! I promise, I won't tell anybody. My dad is in Starfleet, everybody will believe me. I'll tell them I hid in the woods, and I never saw anything." His eyes stood out unnaturally dark in his pale face. "Please, I just want to go home."

Chekov wished it were that simple for any of them. "You can't go home, not yet."

Tears welled up in the boy's eyes, as though the last shred of his reserves had abruptly eroded away. He was suddenly shaking too hard to remain standing. Sinking to his knees, he hugged his arms across his chest and lowered his face in what might have been either desperation or shame. "Please..." His voice was so quiet, Chekov could barely make out the words. "Please..." he whispered, almost in prayer. "Please, don't kill me...."

"Something's happening."

Uhura snapped abruptly awake at the sound of McCoy's voice, and only then realized that she had been sleeping. Because there had been nothing else they could do, they'd wrapped themselves in silver emergency blankets and arranged themselves around the glowing alien medical chamber in the upper cavern, waiting for it to release this strangely altered version of Sulu into their custody. Despite the cave's bitter cold, the possible danger, and the shock of what they'd just discovered, the sleepless hours she'd spent on Tlaoli had finally caught up with Uhura. She'd fallen asleep partway through that vigil, so suddenly and unexpectedly that she hadn't even realized it in time to stop herself.

She lifted her head off its lumpy and muddy pillow, then felt that pillow stir beneath her. Uhura grimaced, realizing belatedly that it was Sanner's shoulder she'd been slumped against. Fortunately, the cave geologist must have fallen asleep, too. He woke now, snorting muzzily and blinking out into the darkening glow of the cave. The golden light inside the chamber was slowly glittering away, ebbing down to a last few golden sparks.

"Is he awake?" Uhura asked quietly.

"Not yet." McCoy had shed his blanket and was standing near the column again, using his carbide lamp to peer into its darkening interior. "But it looks like—hey! He's *gone!*"

Uhura scrambled to her feet in a tangle of blankets, hearing Sanner curse and do the same beside her. Two steps brought her up to the pile of shattered travertine that lay around the alien chamber, but even when Sanner added his carbide glow to hers and McCoy's, they saw nothing inside that invisible cylinder of metal now but empty darkness.

"It must transport people out when they're healed," Uhura said, frowning. "That would explain how Chekov and the captain got out into this chamber without breaking through the travertine shell."

Sanner grunted agreement. "I was wondering why we hadn't seen a couple of these columns all cracked apart like Easter Eggs. But where's Mr. Sulu now?"

"Around here somewhere, I bet." Uhura reached up to open the water drip on her carbide lamp to a reckless pour, but the light only spread out a few meters further, leaving the rest of the echoing stone cathedral still bathed in darkness. As far as she could see, however, nothing stirred between the travertine columns that disappeared up into darkness. "Like Chekov and the captain, he might be disoriented, and not really sure what's going on."

McCoy dropped his voice to a murmur. "Uhura, he probably knows you better than any of us. Call for him."

She nodded and cleared her throat to shout, then thought about how tense young Ensign Chekov had been after his journey through the alien transporter system, and lowered her voice to a gentler pitch. "Hikaru, where are you?" Uhura slowly turned, making sure her voice was projected to carry into all the echoing corners and crevices of the cavern. "Don't worry, we're here to help you."

"*Uhura?*"

The voice was completely familiar, deep and resonant with just that slight hint of a native California accent. But the emotion in it was so foreign that it took Uhura a moment to recognize it as not just amazement but utter, bone-deep disbelief.

She took a step toward the darkness where she thought Sulu's voice had come from. "Yes, it's me." She made an urgent shushing gesture at Sanner when it looked as if the geologist was going to open his mouth. McCoy came soft-footed over to join her, nodding approval when Uhura glanced up at him inquiringly.

"Keep him talking," the doctor mouthed, barely loud enough to be heard over the hiss of their acetylene flames. Then he turned his own carbide lamp off completely and stepped away into the darkness. Comprehension crossed Sanner's face, and he extinguished his light, too, vanishing in the opposite direction from McCoy. Uhura hoped the unusual brightness of her own head lamp would keep the unseen pilot from noticing the loss of the other lights.

"Sulu, how do you feel? You were—you were very badly hurt." That seemed safe enough to say. Surely Sulu would have noticed his amputation by now, although he might not have any more understanding of why it had happened than they did.

"I know." The disbelief was still clear in Sulu's reserved voice, although an odd, wry note had been added to it. "I thought I was going to die back there. Too," he added in what sounded like a significant tone.

"Back in the shuttle, you mean?" Uhura ventured, although even as she said it, she knew it couldn't be true. But her eyes had caught a scrap of movement at the flickering edge of her carbide light's halo, and she was pretty sure McCoy and Sanner must have seen it, too.

Sulu's laugh rolled out into the darkness, unexpectedly bittersweet. It was so recognizably the laugh of a man who'd lived a long time and seen a lot of pain that Uhura winced, but there was still a core of genuine humor buried deep inside it. "I always think I'm going to die in that damned Gorn shuttle whenever I let Chekov fly! But Pavel never lets us down." He paused, then spoke again more somberly. "We were the ones who let him down this time, Uhura. We didn't make it, and now we're where—in Hell? Or is this some kind of alien purgatory that we have to wait in before we're allowed to finally be done with it all?"

"Sulu, we're not dead." Uhura began walking toward him, both because the sudden grim note in his voice alarmed her, and to cover the soft sounds Sanner and McCoy made as they crept closer through the darkness. She wasn't sure of much anymore, but she knew they couldn't let this altered Sulu, recently injured and disoriented as he must be, slip past them into the alien conduits and be lost. "We *are* in an alien installation, one with medical chambers that healed you before you could die." Uhura took a deep breath, then bravely continued. "How else could your right hand have been amputated and then healed so fast?"

"You know about that?" A quiet step in the darkness, and Uhura saw the slim figure in the mottled battle jacket separate itself from the shadow of a nearby column. "Did the alien medical chambers here heal you, too? Even after I saw you lying there by the gate with that hole blasted through your heart—"

The pain cracked through the calm shell of his voice so sharply and unexpectedly that Uhura winced at the sound of it, even before she absorbed the shock of his words. Before she could say anything in reply, a flurry of running steps and a thud in the darkness told her that one of the unseen watchers had flung himself at the pilot. There was the sound of a struggle, brief and unexpectedly violent, then a painful groan that sounded suspiciously like Sanner.

"All right, all right, I give up! Hey, I was just trying to make sure you didn't go running off and get lost in these caves."

"I don't know you." Suspicion hardened Sulu's voice until Uhura barely recognized it. "Why should I believe you when I don't even believe it's really Uhura who's talking to me?"

"Steady there, son," said McCoy's voice from the other side of the column. "Don't do anything you'll regret later. All it's going to take is a little light to get this all cleared up—"

"*Doctor McCoy?*" Sulu's voice changed again, this time to a harsh and self-doubting growl. "God, I must be pumped full of torture drugs! I'm hearing people who I know have been dead for years—"

"Let's see if that's the truth," McCoy said calmly and Uhura heard him snap his carbide igniter once or twice. The flame caught and danced to life on the helmet he held in his arms, throwing its pale yellow glow up to splash on the contours of his face. Uhura came forward to join him, pulling her own helmet off and holding it in front of her the same way. It hadn't occurred to her, until she saw what McCoy had done, that the downward glare from her head-lamp must have kept Sulu from seeing who she really was.

"Ouch," Sanner grumped in the darkness, but a rustle of cloth and the sound of footsteps told Uhura that Sulu must have released him. The pilot stepped into the circle of light she and McCoy now made, his strange black and violet camouflage jacket breaking up his slim outline when he moved in a way that proved how effective it was. The network of fine lines around Sulu's eyes and mouth had deepened with his baffled frown, but his gaze was steady and sane as it moved from McCoy to Uhura and back again.

"Either it's really you, from back about twenty years ago," he said to the doctor, "or the Gorn have gotten a lot better at synthesizing torture drugs than the last time they caught me." His glance swung back to Uhura. "You look twenty years younger, too, but I'm not—" Sulu lifted his right hand as if to touch his own face, then stopped and stared at the healed stump that used to be his wrist. Uhura watched him worriedly, but all he did was tug down his empty black uniform sleeve to cover the amputated limb, smoothing the fingers of his left hand awkwardly across the glittering silver slashes embossed there. "I'm the same forty-seven-year-old former starship captain who took our last pulse bomb into Tesseract Fortress and never came out again," he said quietly, almost to himself.

"Because you came here instead." Uhura tried to infuse her voice with equal parts calmness and firmness. It wasn't easy, especially when Sulu pinned her with a gaze so self-controlled and keen that she knew he hadn't lied about having been promoted to starship captain. She went on, feeling her way awkwardly through an explanation that she wasn't quite sure she really understood herself. "I think there's been some kind of time slip, some kind of exchange between different versions of you and your younger self. It's stardate 1704.3, Sulu, and we've triggered an alien force field, some kind of transporter device, on a planet called Tlaoli 4. Do you remember any of that?"

"Tlaoli?" The black-clad older version of Sulu shook his head. "I don't remember any planet by that name. All I remember from around that stardate was getting to that blue planet a day after it exploded, too late to rescue the geological team we were supposed to pick up. What was its name? Psi or Phi something?"

"Psi 2000." Uhura exchanged glances with McCoy and saw the doctor looking as puzzled as she felt. "In the history you remember, we didn't arrive in time to visit that planet? You don't remember catching a viral infection there, or Joe Tormolen dying after he—?"

She stopped, because Sulu was regarding her with what looked like suspicion again. "Joe Tormolen didn't die that early," he said. "It wasn't until after war was declared and the *Enterprise* crew was split up and sent off to the front. He was on board the *Delphi* when the frontier fleet tried to stop the Gorn from invading the Prellant system. I was in command of the *Hotspur* by then, with you as my com officer and half my crew made up of *Enterprise* ensigns and cadets yanked out of the academy for war duty. And you—" He turned to McCoy grimly. "—you were already dead."

"No," Uhura said. "No, that's not—that can't be our timeline. In our timeline, we made it to Psi 2000 before it blew up, but we lost Joe Tormolen to the virus he caught there. And then we had to cold-start the engines, which threw us back in time three days . . ." She trailed off, seeing from the dubious look on the older Sulu's face that he didn't find this alternate history particularly credible or convincing. Uhura took a deep breath and started again. "We came down here on Tlaoli 4 to rescue a survey crew who were trapped in the caves. While we were here, we ran into some kind of force field, one that seemed to be part of some kind of ancient alien transporter system. It made the captain and Chekov vanish, then made them reappear here, in this cavern. As a side effect, it seemed to cause them to lose some of their memory—"

"Chekov is here?" Sulu took an eager step forward, his lined face lighting with the first hint of gladness Uhura had seen there. "Did he come through this alien machine of yours, too? Is he all right?"

Uhura bit her lip, wishing she didn't have to disappoint him. "He's here, yes, but the Chekov I mean is the young ensign who belongs to this timeline. He's always been here, the same way you were always here until just a few hours ago."

Sulu nodded, his face growing still and thoughtful again. "The younger version of me, you mean. A different younger version that I can't remember having been."

"Yes." Uhura glanced at McCoy and got a silent nod of encouragement. Either the doctor still thought she was the best one to deal with this version of Sulu, or he didn't want to upset the former pilot by forcing him to talk to a man he considered long dead. "That younger version of you was still aboard the *Enterprise* when we lost Chekov and the captain. You came down to the planet in a cargo shuttle to take us back to the ship, but the captain was still missing." Uhura swallowed down the bitter taste of the words she had to say next. "I allowed you—I ordered you—to take the shuttle up to look for him. And you got caught by the alien force field yourself. We came down here to this cave because we thought it might send you here, where Chekov and the captain had been sent. We didn't know it would heal you. Or that you wouldn't be the same Sulu that had vanished."

The older man in the battle jacket remained silent after she stopped speaking, but he no longer looked suspicious. His dark eyes crinkled thoughtfully, if he were mulling over the ramifications of what she had just told him. Uhura wondered what kind of life this alternate Sulu had lived that allowed him to accept this bizarre twist of fate with neither denial nor protest, but instead with what looked like stoic resignation.

"Which captain?" he asked at last.

Uhura stared at him through the cavern's shifting shadows, unsure of what he meant. "Which captain of what?"

"Of the *Enterprise*." Sulu gave her another of those sharp, probing gazes that his younger self had not yet developed. "Which captain of the *Enterprise* did you lose in this alien transport device? Pike? Hoffman? I know we only had him for a few months, but I think that was around stardate 1700 or so. Or is it that idiot Mitchell?"

Uhura had opened her mouth to answer, but the reference to the former first officer of the *Enterprise*, who in her timeline had died on an alien planet several months ago, left her speechless. McCoy, on the other hand, was startled out of his tactful silence.

"Gary Mitchell was never the captain of the *Enterprise*," he said bluntly. "And neither was anyone named Hoffman. The captain we're talking about is James Kirk."

Only silence followed his statement. Uhura felt a sudden rush of odd sensations: a strange, hollow shakiness in her arms and legs, a sickening swoop in her stomach, a leaden pounding that began to thrum inside her ears. It took her tired brain a moment to realize that all of these were symptoms of terror, and another moment to grasp that the terror emanated not from any part of the alien caves around her, but from the completely blank look on the face of the Sulu who stood before her. Because she knew, even before he stirred and answered McCoy, exactly what he was going to say.

"I don't know anyone named James Kirk," the older Sulu said. "He may be captain of the *Enterprise* in your timeline, but for all I know, in mine he never even existed."

# THE JANUS GATE

## FUTURE IMPERFECT

# Chapter One

THE CARGO SHUTTLE BUCKED and shuddered, caught in a savage wind gust that had erupted out of a still, clear dawn. Sulu threw a disbelieving look out his cockpit window at Tlaoli's garnet-dusted sky and saw nothing in its sunlit haze to indicate a storm brewing. He could even see plumes of mist, the exhaled breath of hidden caves, rising straight and calm from the splintered landscape of karst and sinkholes below him. But despite the testimony of his eyes, his hands and ears told him that a relentless avalanche of air had the shuttle clenched in its grip. Sulu could feel the little ship falling farther and farther away from the stable, banking turn he'd begun just a moment ago.

He'd been exultantly heading for home then, after locating a shadowy figure moving through the wilderness of fractured rock, a figure that could only be his own lost captain. That unexpected success, made on the one brief reconnaissance flight Sulu had been allowed before evacuating the rest of the stranded landing party from Tlaoli, had buoyed his spirits amazingly. After hours aboard the *Enterprise* fighting Tlaoli's unpredictable gravitational shifts and dangerous power drains, while Captain Kirk and his rescue party struggled to survive the killing cold and darkness of the caverns where the original landing party had been lost, it seemed as if the strange alien force that guarded this ancient planet had finally lost its grasp on them.

Then from nowhere, gale-force winds roared out of a clear morning sky and sent the shuttle *Drake* skidding out of control.

Sulu gave up trying to fight the wind's pull and instead swung the shuttle hard into it, hoping he could break through to calmer air on the other side. But before the roar of the engines had time to deepen in response, before the straining nacelles could even start to shriek in protest, the *Drake* snapped to a stop and hung frozen in midair. Sulu's breath caught in his throat. In all his years of flying, in craft as small as hang gliders and as large as the *Enterprise,* he had never before felt this kind of sudden arrest. This wasn't one of the alien planet's odd gravitational perturbations, or the unstoppable power drain that had made the *Enterprise* nearly crash into its surface only a few hours ago. This was simply—stillness.

Sulu had no idea how long it lasted—a few microseconds? half a minute?—but there was absolutely no doubt about how it ended. The *Drake* was slammed out of its stillness by the unmistakable blow of an atmospheric shock wave. Sulu's inner ears told him the little ship was flipping sideways, but the sudden darkness outside his cockpit window blocked any view of what had exploded down on the planet, or which way he was being thrown by the blast. The deafening noise of detonation caught up with him an instant later, fast enough and loud enough to tell Sulu he'd been near the epicenter of whatever had just blown up.

The only thing that saved him from losing control entirely was the adrenaline spiking in his blood from the wind gusts he'd been fighting a moment before. Sulu found himself responding almost before he was consciously aware of the need to do so, flinging the shuttle across the vector of the blast instead of fighting it, then spiraling its uncontrolled tumble into a gravity-assisted dive that made the metal nacelles scream in protest as he exceeded their strain limit. That sound sharpened into a howl of torn metal as Sulu hauled the *Drake* up out of its dive, praying every second that the blinding smoke around him wouldn't suddenly turn into rocky ground. When he finally got control of the *Drake* again, it was riding the bow wave of the explosion like an awkward surfer. The shuttle's steep, nose-up position told Sulu more clearly than the red-flashing lights on his controls that he'd done some permanent damage to the nacelles. But for now, he was content to hold the *Drake* in whatever position gave it some aerodynamic equilibrium, letting the wave of battered air sweep him ever farther from the epicenter of the explosion.

The smoke began to clear away from his cockpit windows, revealing tantalizing shreds and scraps of ruddy light through its breaks. It didn't look much like the cold rose-quartz dawn Sulu had taken the shuttle up into. In fact, if he didn't know better, he would swear the light had the sullen humid glare of the tropics. Sulu glanced down at his instrument panel, whose gauges still flashed overloads and error readings from the strange subspace interference fields that had made them all useless on Tlaoli. With a sudden and completely unjustified intuition, he swept a hand across the bank of power switches, zeroing them all to black, then watching them as they booted back up again. Each and every gauge came back a steady, reliable green, even the one warning him about the high levels of tension where the shuttle's hull met its damaged nacelles. The subspace interference had vanished.

Wherever he was now, Sulu thought, it was nowhere near the strange alien caves of Tlaoli.

The smoke thinned a little, then, without warning, the shuttle surged away from the spreading wake of the explosion and into clear air as the propulsion of its own engines finally outpaced the weakening atmospheric shock wave it had been swept up in. Sulu saw a looming shadow of hills ahead of him and pulled the *Drake* up as gently as he dared, trying to spare its weakened nacelles now that he was free of the blast wave. He was so intent on crafting a low-stress, minimum-clearance arc over those hills that it took him a long moment to realize they were completely the wrong color.

The one thing the *Enterprise* had known about Tlaoli before it sent survey teams down to study it was that the little planet was ancient and dry and mostly barren of life. The only vegetation Sulu had seen, in his three trips down to the alien planet, consisted of drought-gnarled trees and thorny shrubs the same dry gray-brown as the rocks and dirt around them. But *these* hills looked as if they were made of sodden emerald velvet. Their canopied trees rose in such a lush tangle that Sulu couldn't see any trace of bare ground between them. In fact, the only things that didn't glow a vivid shade of green were the violet-gray strands of mist and ground-fog nestled in the hollows and winding valleys of the forested hills.

Sulu pursed his lips to whistle in amazement, but to his surprise, he found them too dry to allow any noise to come out. That observation led to another—his hands were shaking despite their tight grip on the *Drake*'s helm control, and his pulse was pounding so strongly that he could actually feel it throb beneath the skin of one temple. He would have put the fear down to the aftermath of being engulfed by a mysterious explosion if he hadn't caught his gaze straying again and again to a gauge that he normally paid no attention to. With a start, Sulu focused on it now—and realized that the fundamental constant of planetary gravity to which all of his other shuttle instruments calibrated themselves had shifted up by three percent. The reading confirmed what some subconscious part of Sulu's brain must have already noticed and understood and been horrified by.

The *planet* he was on now was *not* Tlaoli.

Sulu gritted his teeth, fighting the urge to bank the *Drake* around at the speed he'd normally have used in an emergency, as if he could somehow find his way back to Tlaoli and the *Enterprise* just by reversing course. Some rational part of his brain knew that all the maneuver would accomplish would be to finish the job of tearing off the cargo shuttle's nacelles and strand him on this unknown world forever. But it still seemed worthwhile to find out what had exploded upon his arrival here—a wormhole? an antimatter/matter space warp?—so he maneuvered the wounded shuttle into a slow, gentle arc and watched the crushed-velvet hills drift below him.

The verdant palette of chlorophyll-based colors should have warned Sulu that this unknown planet probably wasn't anywhere near as empty of animal life as Tlaoli had been. But it still came as a shock to him when the green mass of forest abruptly ended, towering a surprising height above the black rock walls that succeeded it. Sulu's startled gaze followed those walls up toward the horizon and saw them merge with others, rise in height, then become blunt terraces bristling with spikes—no, not spikes, he realized as the *Drake* came closer, but hollow pipes, pipes that were moving sideways, pointing outward, turning to aim—at him!

Sulu cursed and wrenched the *Drake* into an evasive maneuver, momentarily forgetting the shuttle's torn nacelles. Fortunately, his downward dive kept torque to a minimum, at least until he was forced to pull up out of it. In the meantime, he watched puffs of what looked like smoke emerge from the snouts of the moving weapons and wondered just how primitive this unknown culture was. Clearly, they recognized even a distant flying object as a threat and were prepared to shoot at it . . . but what exactly were they shooting? Nothing seemed to explode near him or on the ground below, even long after the smoke had emerged, so it wasn't some kind of explosive device or torpedo. Projectiles, perhaps, small enough to make no sign when they missed their mark and fell to the ground.

The weapons along the black stone terraces slowly tracked him as Sulu hurtled down toward them, coaxing the shuttle out of its dive by painful fractions of arc, wincing as he heard the occasional shriek of metal ripping just a little further. He could tell that the barrels of the weapons weren't able to keep pace with his headlong dive, although to his surprise they all seemed to be trying. That was a gift he hadn't expected, that the crews who were manning those installations wouldn't realize that what came down must—if it were to survive—head back up again. If even one weapon stopped trying to track along his path and instead paused, waiting to meet him on the way back up again, Sulu was doomed.

But none of them did. He ground out the last nerve-racking curve that lifted the shuttle from descent to ascent again, then began a horizontal turn at an angle he hoped they wouldn't expect. It took him not back toward the rain-forested hills he had come from, but directly toward the cloud of smoke that still hung thick and sullen over the tallest towers of what now looked unmistakably like a fortress.

The shuttle darted into the smoke, and Sulu lost all sight of the weapons following him. He could still hear them, though, a constant pounding thunder that made his head ache and his eyes blink in conditioned response to the blows of sound. Still, nothing more than sound seemed to hit the *Drake* as it fled with excruciating slowness through the lingering remnants of the explosion that had greeted it upon arrival.

Sulu began an upward climb while he was still shrouded in smoke, grimacing as his evasive maneuver carried him so close to one black stone tower that he almost thought he could see a glare of eyes through its narrow slitted windows. Then the smoke cleared again and he found himself high above the central hub of this kilometers-wide installation. The weapons around the fringes no longer seemed to be aiming or firing at him—no puffs of smoke drifted out of their long hollow barrels. By now, however, Sulu was feeling too battered by fate to take that for a good sign. He glanced around the hazy tropical sky, then finally remembered that his long-range scanners would work here and slapped a hand down to activate the vessel-detection screen. It took only one glance to tell him that his pessimistic instincts had been correct. A raft of small yellow lights lay directly astern, already matching the *Drake*'s not-very-impressive velocity. And even as he watched, the scanner showed a flicker around the nose of the foremost ship that indicated some kind of power field had been detected there.

Sulu groaned and straightened the *Drake* out to give its nacelles the most support he could, then jacked the engines up until the tensions measured along the hull flickered between yellow and red. To his surprise, the unseen chase ships only matched his increase in velocity—they didn't try to close the gap between them. Now why, if they could have gone that fast to begin with, Sulu wondered, had they waited for him to increase speed before they did? Was there some minimum firing range they needed for the energy weapons that his scanners showed being fired now from several ships? If so, perhaps they had miscalculated it for a ship as strange to them as his must be. Not a shiver or rattle went through the *Drake* as those power flickers winked on and off the scanner's detection screen.

He left the swath of central towers behind and crossed back over black stone terraces, empty of everything except the turning barrels of weapons that protruded from the edge like fangs. A towering green tsunami of forest appeared beyond the final perimeter wall, rising almost to the shuttle's altitude and promising safety if only he could disappear into its deepest hollows. But the same glance that told Sulu how close he was to shelter also showed him the turning spikes of the weapon barrels, swinging around in unison to intercept his course. He groaned in dismay and self-disgust. After all his years in Starfleet Academy and aboard Starfleet's premier deep-space vessel, he should have known better!

Sulu had made the most basic mistake of space exploration, assuming that the alien strategists who commanded in this fortress would follow the same rules of tactics as known civilizations did. Humans or Vulcans or Klingons never fired antispacecraft weapons if there were more of their own fighters than enemies aloft, because of the risk of being hit by friendly fire. But these fortress fighters were either a more ruthless or more self-sacrificing lot. Sulu began—much too late—to lift the *Drake* up to a less dangerous altitude, and saw the raft of yellow dots behind him on the long-range scanner increase altitude to match his without ever getting closer. That gap suddenly made sense to him. It would give the perimeter weapons a clear interval to fire before they encountered their own ships.

It also gave Sulu an idea.

Praying that the *Drake*'s abused nacelles would take the strain, he began to level the shuttle off at an altitude that still kept him dangerously close to the unknown weapons ahead. Just as he expected, the long-range scanners reported his chasers doing the same thing. Then, just as he crossed over the edge of the black stone terrace and into weapons range, Sulu began a sharp banking turn at the tightest angle he could manage and still keep the nacelles from shearing off. It took the *Drake* into the sudden thundering fire of the ground weapons, and this time Sulu could hear the sickening thuds as projectiles hit and cratered the shuttle's duranium hull without ever breaking through. He winced, but held his course. The *Drake* was a cargo shuttle, never meant for battle, and its shields were designed to ward off particles of space dust and fragments of comets, not armored projectiles. Sulu wasn't sure how many of those impacts it could take without breaking apart at the seams, but he was gambling that it wouldn't be long until the fusillade ceased.

He craned his head to watch the weapons from the side of his cockpit as he swung the shuttle around, and allowed himself a grim smile of satisfaction. These unknown fighters might not be predictable, but they were certainly consistent. Once again, all of the weapons were tracking him in unison, following the *Drake* faithfully around on its 180-degree turn, until they found themselves pointed at their own ships as well as at the intruder. There was a moment of confusion when waves of projectiles slammed into the leading chase ships, bringing several of them down with surprising efficiency before the thunder of the ground weapons rolled into silence and smoke drifted away from their empty barrels.

The phalanx of chase ships was in chaos now. Sulu took advantage of it to thread his way through them and cut sideways, slipping over a different part of the outer stone wall before the ground weapons got a chance to retrain their sights on him. He lifted the *Drake* with a stomach-churning lurch that just cleared the towering wall of green on the other side, then settled down to hug the tops of those monstrous tree canopies as he raced for the hills on the horizon.

It took the remaining chase ships a few moments to regroup, and another minute for Sulu's vessel-detection screen to give him the bad news he'd expected. Now that they were all past the edge of the installation, there was no doubt that those alien ships were faster than the *Drake,* probably faster than it had been even before the powerful explosion back at the towers had half-torn its nacelles off. He jacked the engines back up as high as he dared, but he could still set only a snail's pace compared with the ships behind him. It was only a few moments before they were in visual range again, a half-dozen blunt-nosed attack ships with darkened cockpit windows and parabolic wings. Sulu could see through the side of his cockpit the heat-wave shimmer of the energy weapons that the scanner insisted were being fired from their snouts. Still, the *Drake* flew on without so much as a lurch or twitch of response.

The cargo shuttle's strange imperviousness to their weapons must have been apparent to the attackers, too—one buzzed him overhead, close enough to make the *Drake* shudder and roll in the wake vortex trailing behind it. Sulu dragged the shuttle back to equilibrium with difficulty—the torn nacelles had a tendency to exaggerate every loss of stability into a sideways roll. It wasn't until a second attacker buzzed and flew off, leaving him enveloped in the heat-shimmer of its energy weapon's discharge, that Sulu noticed that all of his control panel gauges were black and powerless.

Sulu's eyebrows shot up as he realized what must be protecting the *Drake.* Chief Engineer Montgomery Scott had insisted on shielding the cargo shuttle's warp core and engines before Sulu took it down into the dangerous power-draining force fields of Tlaoli. Now the unknown aliens on this planet—maybe even the same ones who built that underground installation—were firing some kind of energy-dispersive weapons at him. Those weapons would probably already have sent any normal shuttle plummeting down to the surface in an unpowered swan dive. The *Drake*'s stubborn ability to fly seemed to be making the aliens both impatient and, Sulu suspected, somewhat nervous.

He took a deep breath and slowed the engines again, holding his course as he was buzzed several more times by the flickering shapes of the attackers. There didn't seem to be anything else they could do but fire those heat-shimmer pulses at him, but that didn't make Sulu feel safe. With half-torn nacelles and a pockmarked hull, Sulu didn't want to spend hours being jostled by them or, even worse, drive the aliens to desperate tactics like a suicide ramming. He was equally reluctant to put the shuttle down while they watched and circled overhead like vultures to mark the spot where he landed. What he needed was to convince them they didn't need to worry about him anymore, and for that he was going to have to use a fairly desperate tactic himself.

Sulu inched the *Drake* upward a few hundred meters to give himself a little maneuvering room and a better view of the landscape below. There was rain forest everywhere below him now. The alien fortress had dwindled to a distant smudge of smoke behind a range of hills, and ahead of him the sky was painted with tiger stripes of orange, saffron, and crimson around a setting tropical sun. The forest was vast and featureless, webbed everywhere with streamers of violet-tinted fog as the cooling air drizzled out its moisture. Then, off to one side, Sulu caught a glimpse of what looked like a shattered mirror whose tiger stripes matched the sky. He wasn't sure if it was a lake or an enormous river, but at least it was something to orient himself by in this endless span of green. Sulu took a deep breath, waited for one last attacker to shower him in heat-shimmer, then cut all power to the shuttle's engines.

They made them practice this maneuver in Starfleet simulators, over and over again, but Sulu discovered that it didn't really prepare you for the gut-wrenching feel of fading momentum and dragging gravity, the sidelong plunge that couldn't really be called a roll, the spinning plummet that increased with such shocking speed that by the time he cut the engines in again he was far closer to the forest canopy than he had planned.

The trees closed in around the shuttle while he was still trying to pull it out of its dive, and Sulu heard a rising shriek from the nacelles as their ripped seams tore open further. He made one last effort to lower his speed, but the torque was too much for the hull. With a sound almost like an explosion, one nacelle tore off completely, followed a moment later by the other. The *Drake* plunged downward, still spinning uncontrollably but powered enough to turn its deadly vertical plunge into a dangerous horizontal slide. And the trees themselves helped, their many branches flickering past too fast to see but braking his momentum just the same. The *Drake*'s shields warded off the worst impacts from the larger branches, although Sulu didn't think they would be much help if he hit one of the monstrous trunks that must rise through this greenery somewhere. But as the ship twisted and lurched and skidded slowly downward through the darkening shade of the canopy, the one thing he was sure of was that it must have looked to his pursuers like a real, honest-to-God crash.

He ended up sliding only slightly canted along a humus-littered forest floor, and finally bumping to an almost laughably gentle stop against a fallen log whose diameter matched the shuttle's height. Sulu cut the engines off again with shaking fingers and wondered if he should power-down the warp core in case its shielding had been damaged. He would think about that in a minute, he promised himself, after he caught his breath and wiped the sweat of suddenly humid air off his face. The shuttle's battered hull must have sprung a leak on its way down through the forest. He would know soon enough if there was anything toxic to humans in this planet's atmosphere.

In the meantime, he could finally relax long enough to realize that he was now a hunted man on an alien planet whose name he didn't know and whose location could be almost anywhere in the galaxy.

"Oh . . . this isn't good. . . ." Shaking her head slowly, Yuki Smith did something Pavel Chekov had never dreamed a Starfleet security guard would do—she retreated several steps toward the center of the small karst plateau, as though contemplating running away entirely. "He's *crying!*" she whispered fiercely in Chekov's direction. "They don't train security guards to deal with crying."

Chekov didn't think it worth pointing out that Starfleet Academy didn't exactly offer electives in dealing with crying for Astrogation majors, either. Instead, he just nodded as though her objection made perfect sense, and kept his attention focused on the boy who knelt a few meters in front of them on the edge of the uneven plateau.

The boy wasn't really crying anymore. The tears had lasted only a few wrenching, naked moments, when Chekov and Smith had first cornered him at the edge of the steep drop-off. Now, the only remnant of the boy's tears was a sheen of wetness on his cheeks and a ragged edge to his breathing that made it sound as though he took three quick breaths on every too-deep inhalation. His fear had already begun to mutate into something else—something cunning and more productive. Chekov couldn't precisely identify the emotion glowing in the boy's keen hazel stare, but he'd seen glimpses of it on the face of the adult James Kirk during the last eighteen hours. He suspected it meant that even a very young James Kirk would prove a formidable adversary.

"Listen to me." Chekov struggled to pitch his tone just the right distance between solicitude and belligerence to keep the boy from bristling.

He was close enough to his own teen years to remember how much he hated adults speaking to him as though he were stupid, but just far enough away from them to appreciate how stupid teenaged boys often were. "We're not going to hurt you. You said your father is in Starfleet. Then you know we're here to protect civilians, not to hurt them."

The boy's eyes flicked back and forth between gold uniform and red, touching briefly on sleeves, insignia, and waists. Anticipating the boy's concern, Chekov spread his arms out to either side. "Look—we don't even have weapons."

It seemed to bother the boy a little that this stranger would understand what he was thinking. Sinking back on his heels, he thrust his chin vaguely in Chekov's direction. "What's that?"

It took Chekov a moment to realize he meant the small device still curled in Chekov's left hand. "A compass. For finding our bearings." He held his hand out flat in front of him so the boy could see the imprinted face and the swinging, hair-fine needle. Moving his hand slightly in a more distinct offering, he said, "Here. Take it."

Interest moved across the boy's face, replacing suspicion for the first time since they'd pinned him here. Once again, Chekov was reminded of Kirk's fearless curiosity, and he felt an irrational surge of guilt to be standing on the surface of an alien planet trying to reassure a fifteen-year-old version of his own commander. *Whatever this place did to you,* he found himself promising silently, *we'll fix it.* Because the thought of the *Enterprise* without Kirk in command was simply intolerable.

Stooping slowly, Chekov folded the compass closed and set it on the wind-polished rock at his feet. A nudge with his toe sent it skittering just far enough for the boy to lean forward and pick it up. Chekov watched him open it and turn it this way and that to check the needle's lazy swing, and tried to decide if the boy looked any calmer. Light from the freshly risen sun cut sharply across the boy's left shoulder, hiding half his expression in shadow as he bent over the small device. At least his breathing had steadied to a more regular rise and fall.

"We have a base camp about an hour's walk from here—" Chekov began.

This younger Kirk cut him off with the same impatient brusqueness that would strike fear into the hearts of his subordinates when he was twenty years more refined. "I saw it."

Chekov had to bite back an abashed and automatic, "Yes, sir." Instead, he fought to keep his voice rigorously even. "You should come back to camp with us—"

"No!" No longer some dim reflection of a great starship commander, he was just a boy again, obviously angered by the fear that flew too easily into his protest. His hand closed convulsively around the compass, and he glanced once, briefly, over his shoulder as though considering anew whether he could jump the deep rift between the karst towers. The sun made him squint and look back too quickly.

Chekov nodded, pretending not to notice the boy's vehemence. "Well, we can't stay out here all day."

"You can't, maybe." The boy lifted his chin in a brave defiance that wasn't at all feigned. "I'm not going anywhere."

*You have no idea how true that is.* If they didn't find out what this planet had done to Kirk—not to mention to Lieutenant Sulu, and possibly to Chekov himself—Chekov had a feeling none of them would be going anywhere anytime soon.

"Do you rank her?" The boy asked it suddenly, as though the thought had only just occurred to him.

Chekov glanced aside at Smith, strangely unsure how to respond even though the answer was obvious. He was too used to being the most junior member in any gathering to think of himself as ranking anyone. "Yes. I'm an officer." It was the first time he'd ever said that about himself.

"Then make her leave." The boy clicked the compass shut and folded it into his fist like a talisman. Alert hazel eyes locked on Smith, daring her to move. "She's security," he continued defiantly to Chekov. "You're just some command maven. If anybody can hurt me, it's her." He glanced away from her only long enough to pin Chekov with his stare. "Make her leave."

From ranking Starfleet officer to command maven in just under thirty seconds. A new galactic record, certainly. Still, the boy wasn't wrong, and Chekov had to give him credit for thinking clearly even if he was less than subtle about how he expressed it.

"Go on." He turned pointedly away from the boy, letting Kirk see that he was willing to turn his back while nodding to Smith. "Find Tomlinson and Martine. Tell them everything is all right."

He would have been disappointed if Smith hadn't hesitated at least a little. She glanced unhappily at the boy, then back at Chekov before finally answering his command with a businesslike "Aye, sir," and turning to climb back down the karst summit the way they'd first come up. She disappeared over the edge with an athletic vault that was much more graceful than Chekov suspected he himself would have managed.

"Who are Tomlinson and Martine?"

Chekov turned back to the boy, trying to exude the same easy confidence he had seen in a much older Kirk not so very long ago. "Two of the other officers stranded planetside with us. I don't want them to worry when they see I'm not with Smith."

Something about that made the boy frown slightly and lower his chin. "You're stranded here?" Morning shadows darkened his eyes again.

Chekov nodded. "There are twelve of us. About half are from the planetary survey team we came down here to rescue."

The boy gave a snort and a surprisingly mature, ironic smile. "Some rescue."

Chekov couldn't argue with him about that.

"So . . . where are we, exactly?"

"Tlaoli 4." A look that might have been fear flashed through the boy's eyes, so quickly masked that Chekov would have missed it if he'd glanced away. "A planet in sector alpha nineteen," he explained, still trying to decipher the boy's expression. A thought occurred to him, and he asked, "Where were you . . . before you were here?"

"On vacation. With my family in the Pantazis sector." He fought with himself a moment before admitting, "I don't know how I got here."

"We don't know how you got here, either." That was likely to be the understatement of the day. "Did you . . . find yourself inside the cave?"

The boy straightened, obviously startled by the question. "Yeah."

"How did you find your way out in the dark?"

He shrugged. "It wasn't that dark. I mean, it was nighttime where I was before, so my eyes were already adjusted. The light from the stalactites or stalagmites or whatever was bright enough that I could see the hole in the roof."

Chekov remembered groping for his helmet in the thick darkness, stumbling into a sit, waiting with his heart in his throat while the cave around him whispered under its patina of frost. "There was no light in that cavern." He had never been more certain of anything in his life.

"There was just the one pillar. Gold light, like a transporter beam, only it never came together." The boy shrugged again, settling more comfortably back on his heels. "It was bright enough."

*There was no light.* He was sure of it—more sure than he was about anything else that had happened so far on Tlaoli—and the boy's equal certainty frightened him a little. But before he could ask for more detail about the claim, Kirk announced bluntly, "Now I get to ask a question."

Chekov nodded. "All right."

"What ship did you come in on? A starship?"

He nodded again, but hesitated before saying, "The *U.S.S. Enterprise.*" They had to breach the subject at some point, and sooner was no doubt better than later. Still, he found himself wishing Lieutenant Uhura were here, with her calm demeanor and expert communications skills.

To his surprise, the boy lit up at the mention of the ship's name. "Hey! I know your captain!"

Chekov felt a leaden weight fall into his stomach. "You do?"

"Robert April. He's a friend of my dad's. He came to our house for Christmas last year." Relief was palpable in the boy's smile as he climbed to his feet. He seemed even younger than before, the weight of his own safety suddenly cast off his shoulders and into adult hands that he trusted and loved. Chekov doubted he would ever again see James Kirk so vulnerable and acquiescent. "We can go talk to him. He knows where my dad is stationed—he'll know what to do."

Suddenly sorry he'd allowed the subject to arise, Chekov said carefully, "Captain April isn't here. In fact..." There was nothing to do now but plough headlong into it. "Robert April isn't captain of the *Enterprise* anymore."

"But I don't understand..." The boy frowned, knuckles white around the compass in his young hands as though clinging to that small device would make what he was about to hear less disturbing. "If Robert April's not captain of the *Enterprise*... who is?"

# Chapter Two

Torn between dismay and disbelief, Uhura stared across the flickering shadows of the Tlaoli caverns at the man who'd somehow been exchanged for their vanished shuttle pilot by the same mysterious alien force that had also swept away Captain Kirk and young Ensign Chekov. Could she really trust this older version of Sulu who claimed he'd been a starship captain once, who said that in his future both McCoy and Uhura were dead, and who insisted he'd never heard of Captain Kirk? Did she *really* know him the way her heart said she did, just because he looked and sounded and acted like the friend she had ordered to fly into danger a few hours ago?

"I'm sorry," the older Sulu said, scanning their faces in the uncertain light cast by Uhura and McCoy's carbide lights. His deep voice held a note that hadn't been there before, one so unexpected that it took Uhura a moment to identify it as compassion. "I can see it upsets you, but it's true. In all my time in the service, there was never a Starfleet captain named Kirk, on the *Enterprise* or any other ship."

"But there should have been." It was an unreasoning protest when Uhura said it, but as she heard her own words echo back to her from the walls and healing chambers of this alien cavern, their implications sank in. "There should have been. And maybe there *would* have been, if we hadn't come here to Tlaoli." She turned to glance at McCoy and Sanner. "We thought this was an alien transporter, but what if it's actually a *time* transporter? If it moved Captain Kirk in such a way that he disappeared from our timeline before he became a captain—"

"Then *we* wouldn't remember him, either," Sanner objected.

McCoy grunted. "Maybe this machine is moving people between parallel dimensions where things are just a little different. Whenever we talk about the possibility of time travel, Spock always quotes some many-worlds hypothesis and says there's no such thing as a single timeline anyway."

"The Everett-Wheeler interpretation of quantum mechanics," the older Sulu said, nodding. "Of course, the Vulcans proved that was only partially right back in 2285, when they constructed the first artificial pinpoint singularity—" He broke off, looking rueful. "Um...Maybe I shouldn't be telling you that."

"If Doctor McCoy is right, it might not be our own future you're revealing," Uhura said. "But knowing about the future won't help us figure out what the transporter is doing. What we really need to compare is the past."

"To decide if we're from one shared timeline or two parallel dimensions?" Sulu began absently rolling up the right sleeve of his jacket, as if to get the blood-soaked and clammy fabric away from his skin, then saw what he was doing and pushed it down again. "Sorry about that. I don't suppose there's anything you can do about the temperature in here?"

"We could leave," McCoy suggested.

Uhura opened her mouth to agree with him, but Sanner forestalled her. "I'd like to take a look back down the conduit system before we do that, Lieutenant, to make sure we know just where that force field is sitting now." He saw Uhura's frown and tapped his unlit carbide lamp. "I promise I'll turn it off every couple of minutes to make sure I don't walk into any different time zones. But I've got an idea I want to check out."

"An idea about the development of the caves?"

"No, about the power supply for that alien transporter." Sanner thumbed the lever of his carbide and ignited the gas flame, then began poking through his backpack. "I made one of our spare carbide lamps into a portable stove while we were back at the base camp, just in case we found Lieutenant Sulu hurt and suffering from hypothermia. Now where the heck did it go?" He hauled out several coils of rope and bags of pitons before he excavated one of Scotty's carbide lamps, wearing what looked like an old-fashioned sunbonnet over the side that normally would have been open for illumination. "It's got lots of carbide rocks and water in it, so you can run it pretty hot, but you'll need to keep the heat contained. Maybe you can make a shelter out of the survey team's packs and those emergency blankets we were using before."

Uhura took the primitive heater from him, her frown deepening as she watched him stuff the rest of his gear back into his pack. "Zap, did you *plan* on doing more exploring while we were down here?"

The cave specialist gave her a look that was only half-abashed. "I didn't plan, exactly, I just thought if there was a chance to look around a little more . . . But I swear, Lieutenant, I'm not going caving now. If this power supply idea I've got checks out, we might actually get a handle on how this alien transporter works." He swung around before she could reply, apparently taking her permission for granted. "Lieutenant—uh, I mean, Captain Sulu? Could you tell me where the planet you came from is located?"

Some of his former suspicion crept back into Sulu's slitted eyes. "Why do you need to know?"

"I don't need an exact location, sir," Sanner said hastily. Apparently Uhura wasn't the only one who could feel the air of authority that proved this older version of Sulu really had been a starship captain. "I'm just trying to make a rough estimate of the transporter's power consumption."

Sulu considered that for a moment. "It's near the Omega Orionid cluster, close to the galactic fringe," he said at last. It wasn't a very specific location at all, encompassing many parsecs of space beyond the borders Uhura knew in her time, but it seemed enough to satisfy Sanner. The geologist made a note on the edge of the cave map he and Jaeger had reconstructed, then surprised Uhura with a chortle. "Better than I thought," he said cryptically, and went jingling off through the darkness toward the spiral passageway that led down to the rest of the alien conduit system.

"Our cave specialist," Uhura said to Sulu, hoping that would excuse the scientist's behavior.

"So I gathered." There was an amused note in the older man's voice that sounded familiar. After a moment, Uhura realized it was the way Captain Kirk sounded, too, when he was the one dealing with the dedicated single-mindedness of scientists. "Did you come to explore these caves because you knew there was an alien transporter device down here?"

"Not exactly." Uhura lit the carbide stove Sanner had cobbled together and handed it to Sulu, since he needed its warmth most. He took it awkwardly with his left hand, then brought his right forearm around to steady it with a look of grim determination, as if he'd already come to terms with the need to relearn all the mechanics of motion. "We left survey teams here to explore and catalog this planet—Tlaoli 4—while we went on to Psi 2000. That was the blue planet you remembered self-destructing before you could reach it."

Sulu nodded. "If I recall correctly, we lost the research team that was stationed there."

"So did we." Uhura began looking around the shadowed depths of the cavern for the jumble of equipment they'd left behind when they'd climbed the rubble pile and squirmed out the narrow, winding exit. Had that only been a few hours ago? It seemed like a previous lifetime, now.

"In our timeline, we had enough time to send a landing party down to the planet to try and locate them. The landing party caught the virus that had already killed the researchers. It made them—" She broke off, searching for a word that could encompass both the mischievous antics and maniacal acts that the Psi 2000 virus had made various *Enterprise* crew members perform over the past few days.

"Loony," said Dr. McCoy, coming back with the emergency blankets they'd dropped beside the alien healing chamber. "One of 'em locked himself inside the engine room and shut the warp core down for eighteen hours."

"With the planet about to explode at any minute?" Sulu whistled softly as he followed them toward the piles of stacked crates and packs. "What did you do?"

"Captain Kirk and Mr. Spock figured out how to intermix our stocks of matter and antimatter, and cold-start the engines." Uhura bent down to rummage through one of the open crates, looking for rope. She found some and began stringing it from the rough wall of equipment to a nearby travertine pillar. "That worked, but it accidentally threw the *Enterprise* backward in time. We didn't want to confuse the first version of ourselves by reporting to our next assignment early, so we came here instead to repair the ship's engines and help the survey teams we'd left on Tlaoli finish up their work."

"So how did you find this alien transporter that sends people back and forth through time?"

"By accident." Uhura finished knotting the ropes around the column, then propped them up with a surveying rod to support the weight of the emergency blankets. "The surveyors we left behind here found some ancient wrecks of starships. They suspected there might be a natural deposit of transperiodic elements underground creating a space warp in this area, and they came down here to see if they could find it. Instead, they stumbled across an ancient alien installation that drained all the power from their lights and instruments, and stranded them here in the dark. They'd already been trapped for several hours when the *Enterprise* got back into the system."

"So you brought another group down to rescue them." Sulu gave the heater he held an awkward shake and listened to the rattle of carbide rocks inside it, then sniffed at the odor of acetylene gas. "Using primitive chemical combustion lamps?"

"That's right. The alien devices down here drained all our electromagnetic power sources. We needed something that didn't run on dilithium fuel cells." Uhura draped one of the emergency blankets over the ropes to form a triangular ceiling, then hung the others along the remaining sides. The metallic fabric had an annoying tendency to slither off the ropes until she figured out how to weld it to itself with quick touches from her helmet's hot metal flame reflector. "We found the stranded survey team, but when we tried to beam out, the alien device drained all the power from the *Enterprise*. That seemed to charge up the device enough to actually start moving people around." She held up the last blanket for McCoy and Sulu to step inside the makeshift tent, then picked up some emergency rations she'd found and followed them through. "We thought they were just moving through space."

"But now that you've seen me, you think they were moving through time instead," Sulu said. "Or through alternate dimensions."

"Yes."

Silence followed that exchange, as if its implications were so profound and bewildering that words couldn't immediately grapple with them. In silence, Uhura handed out the ration sticks she'd found while McCoy silently spread the last emergency blanket across the cold travertine cave floor. Sulu settled down cross-legged on it, looking as relaxed as if he were sitting in a padded captain's chair. From the weather-beaten look of his purple and green camouflage jacket, Uhura suspected he'd spent the past few weeks in just this kind of rough accommodation.

"This isn't too bad," McCoy said at last. Uhura knew he must be referring to the quick buildup of warmth inside their silver-walled shelter, since he couldn't possibly mean the desiccated protein stick he held clenched between his teeth like a pipe stem. "Now, exactly what do we need to figure out about our past histories?"

"Point of divergence," Uhura said.

"Overlap," Sulu said.

They glanced at each other for a moment, a distinctly measuring exchange. Back in his own place and time, Uhura recalled, Hikaru Sulu had been the ship's captain and she merely one of his subordinates. But they were in her time here, and until Captain Kirk was reunited with the rest of the landing party, Uhura was officially the officer in charge. Nevertheless, there was no reason to create a command conflict with a man so many years her senior in Starfleet, a man who'd been yanked out of his own time and place through no fault of his own.

"We can keep track of both as we go along," she offered, and saw Sulu smile gently at her, as if she'd been an ensign who'd just answered a tough question correctly. Perhaps after knowing another version of her for twenty years, that was how she seemed to him now. "Um—where should we start?"

"Let's try some major historical milestones," said McCoy around a

mouthful of ration stick. "Did you have a Battle of Cheron in your history, Captain Sulu?"

"When Earth defeated the Romulan Empire back in 2160," Sulu said,
nodding. "A year later, the United Federation of Planets was established.
Was there a Battle at Donatu V in your timeline?"

"Yep. In 2242, about three years before I entered college," McCoy
said. "It was our last major run-in with the Klingons."

"That was true in my timeline, until 2273," Sulu said. "The Klingons
weren't really friendly with us before that, but we weren't at war with
them until after the Gorn invasion."

Uhura was still trying to locate the point at which the older Sulu's
history diverged from hers. "In 2266, you were serving aboard the *Enterprise* with me and Dr. McCoy?"

"Yes. You and I were part of her crew when she left spacedock in
2264, under the command of Captain Marshall Hoffman. Dr. McCoy
joined us a year or so later, when Dr. Piper left for a research position
back on Earth. Does that sound right to you?"

"Everything except for the captain's name." McCoy grimaced and
put down his protein stick half-eaten. "If we *are* from alternate dimensions, then they must be pretty damn parallel."

"And if we're from the same dimension, then the only discrepancy so
far seems to be the absence of Captain Kirk," Uhura said. "At least, until
this Gorn invasion you've been talking about. When did that happen?"

"Stardate 6047.9, Earth year 2269." The older Sulu's voice deepened
a little, as if that date had been etched so deeply into his memory that he
couldn't even say it without emotion. "The *Enterprise* was in spacedock
for refitting by then...not that it would have mattered. The other starships did what they could, but there wasn't much anyone in space could
do." Sulu lifted his right arm as if to rub at his face with fingers he no
longer had. He winced and put it back down into his lap, covering the
healed end with his left hand. "Sorry," he said again.

"Nothing there you need to be sorry about, son," McCoy said, although Uhura suspected he and Sulu were now almost the same age.
"We'll get you fitted with a good mechanical prosthetic just as soon as we
get back aboard the *Enterprise*. But who *are* these Gorn you keep talking
about?"

Sulu blinked at them across the makeshift tent, as if it was a question
he could barely comprehend. Then he shook his head in mild self-disgust.
"That's right, you haven't met them yet. And maybe you never will...but
we did, back in 2267. It was our first contact, both with the Gorn and a
more advanced race called the Metrons. The Gorn were hostile to us from

the start—they decoyed *Enterprise* into sending a landing party down to a planet called Cestus III, where they'd already destroyed a Federation outpost. We fought them there and won, but when we pursued them, they fled through Metron space.

"I don't know if the Gorn were trying to throw us off their trail or get us in trouble with the Metrons, but either way it didn't work. The Metrons caught us both and decided to resolve our conflict with a hand-to-hand battle. Just the Gorn captain against our captain." Sulu's lips quirked, as if his memories of that encounter weren't exactly glorious. "We'd lost Captain Hoffman by then, in a nasty run-in we had with the Romulans that nearly got the *Enterprise* destroyed. There wasn't anyone in the quadrant due for a starship promotion, so Commodore Mendez gave Gary Mitchell a brevet-command and we were stuck with him for the next six months." He glanced up at them. "You said he was already dead in your timeline?"

Uhura nodded. "It was early in our five-year mission. We found an ancient recorder buoy and went to investigate what had happened to the ship that left it there, the *S.S. Valiant*. That didn't happen in your timeline?"

The lines on the older pilot's face deepened in frowning concentration, as if it were an effort to reach so far back into his memory. "I think I remember us finding the recorder buoy," he said at last. "But Captain Hoffman decided it wasn't worth investigating because we were too close to the galactic rim."

"And Captain Kirk decided that it *was* worth investigating." Uhura exchanged thoughtful glances with McCoy. Little by little, the alternate history this version of Sulu remembered was starting to make some sense to her. "So, in your timeline Gary Mitchell was in command of the *Enterprise* and had to fight the Gorn. Did he lose?"

"No, he won." Sulu's voice deepened in distaste. "He buried the Gorn captain alive, throwing rocks down on top of him after he was caught and helpless in a pit trap Mitchell had dug. The Metrons showed us the whole thing—and they showed it to the Gorn ship, too."

"So the Gorn wanted vengeance?" guessed McCoy.

"For one dead captain?" Sulu snorted. "No, that probably seemed like perfectly normal warfare to them. What the Gorn wanted vengeance for was what happened to them after the fight was over. The Metrons told us that whichever race lost the fight would be banned from space forever. We didn't find out until later just how they meant to do it. Apparently, after Mitchell killed the Gorn captain, the Metrons destroyed every Gorn spaceship in existence—along with all their crews. Then they locked the Gorn down on their colonies and home planet, and kept them there with force fields too powerful for anyone to break into or out of."

"Then how were the Gorn able to invade the Federation?" the doctor demanded, incredulous.

"We didn't know that for a very long time," Sulu admitted. "All we knew at first was that the Gorn were taking over our outer colonies without traveling through space to do it. They were coming through some kind of energy portals, a new planet-to-planet transporter system they either invented or discovered—"

"A transporter system like this one?" Uhura asked in dismay. "If they found some other part of this alien device, maybe they were able to figure out—"

She stopped because Sulu was already shaking his head at her. *"Not like this one,"* he said grimly. "I came out of this one healed. No human being who's ever tried going through a Gorn portal has come out alive." He moved his right arm again, this time cradling it in his left so he could rub awkwardly at the amputated wrist. From the compassionate look on McCoy's face, Uhura suspected the former pilot was feeling phantom pain through severed nerve endings. "Going through their portals was the first thing we tried, when we finally realized how the Gorn were moving their armies from planet to planet. We sent platoons of soldiers through after them, but not a single one survived the trip. Only aliens built like the Gorn and the Klingons can go through and survive, and even 10 percent of them die in the process. The fatality rate is 50 percent for aliens like the Vulcans and Orions, and 100 percent for humans."

"I'm starting to see why you've been at war with the Gorn for twenty years," McCoy said, frowning.

Sulu nodded. "We couldn't even begin to fight them until they finally moved back out into space. Before that, we were always sending ships and troops too late to make a difference. By the time we got the distress call, the Gorn would already have hundreds of thousands of troops occupying a planet. It would take years to dislodge them after that, if we could manage it at all." His face tightened, as if what he had to say next was so hard that he couldn't trust himself to get through it without steeling himself. "We lost entire branches of the service, and millions of civilian lives. We lost most of the planets the Gorn attacked. And if nothing changes about the situation, in the next year or two I think we're going to lose the war."

An appalled silence followed his words. It was hard for Uhura, serving at a time when the dangers of space lay only at the far edges of the Federation, to get beyond a stunned feeling that the future this Sulu described was simply impossible. But there was no disbelieving the grief that deepened the creases on his timeworn face. She cast around for something, anything, that might alleviate it.

"Hikaru, if you're not from an alternate dimension, then maybe your timeline shouldn't have been like that. If we can figure out how to put Captain Kirk back where he should have been and fix whatever went wrong in the past, then maybe none of the future you know will have to happen."

"That would be . . . nice." Sulu gave her a crooked, bittersweet smile, so unlike the flashing fearless grin of his younger self that Uhura almost didn't recognize him. "But after what I've seen for the past twenty years, you'll have to forgive me if I don't really believe it will come true. And that means you've got to do more than just figure out how to find this lost captain of yours. You've *got* to get me back to the place you took me from."

McCoy squinted at him through the flickering carbide light. "But when you first saw us—didn't you say you thought you had just died there?"

"Yes," Sulu said. "I still have to go back."

"Even if it means going back to certain death?" Uhura asked.

"Yes." Sulu lifted his amputated wrist for them to see, holding it up without self-consciousness for the first time. "If I had succeeded in detonating that pulse bomb where I wanted to, this would have been the best thing that ever happened to me. But I know I didn't. You have to send me back to Basaraba, so I can try again."

"*Why?*" McCoy demanded.

"Because *my* entire future depends on it," the older man snapped. He paused, eyeing their uncomprehending faces, then took a sharp and rasping breath. "God help me, if I'm in a Gorn torture cell right now and this is all a hallucination, I'm going to wish I really was dead. But if you are from the past, I have to make you understand where I was when this time machine of yours grabbed me. And why you *have* to get me back there again.

"I told you the *Enterprise* was stuck in spacedock when the Gorn invaded. Starfleet Command split up her crew and assigned us to a raft of older battleships and scout ships that they brought back into service, mostly to ferry troops from one invaded planet to the next. You and I and Chekov got a lightweight little frigate called *Hotspur* that was assigned to drop the first advance parties on invaded planets. We were given a crew of academy cadets and brand-new ensigns, and we managed to keep most of them alive, at least until the space battles started up again.

"After the Gorn took over most of our outlying planets, they started trying to close down Federation trade routes, hoping they could starve the better-defended inner planets into submission. We used the *Hotspur* for years to run the blockade, breaking holes in the line for cargo ships to pass through. But after the Klingons attacked us, too, it was all-out war in space from then on. And the whole time, the Gorn were still using their damned portals to grab a planet here, a military station there. Our scientists had been studying them every way they could, trying to find out how they worked and whether we could disrupt them. It was hard even getting close to them, and it took two decades before we finally found out what their Achilles heel was. We did find it, though, at last. *We* found it, Uhura."

The emphasis in Sulu's final statement was unmistakable. Uhura stared at him, feeling her breath catch in her throat even though the Uhura who'd helped achieve that breakthrough was part of a future she hoped she'd never live to see. "What was it?"

"A hub," Sulu said with fierce satisfaction. "A single central hub portal that every Gorn soldier had to go through, every time the portals were used. And all we needed to do, to cripple the entire Gorn invasion, was to destroy it."

For a long time after the shuttle crashed, Sulu just sat in the pilot's seat and listened to the soft pelting of rain against the hull. He told himself he was lying low in case any of this alien planet's guardians had been left behind to watch for survivors. But with a rainy gray-violet dusk settling over the rain forest and hundreds of meters of treetop canopy shielding him overhead, the probability of being seen was quickly approaching zero. Deep inside, Sulu knew he just didn't trust himself to make sensible decisions right now. The months he'd spent on the *Enterprise* had taught him to recognize the little tremors in his hands and the swift frantic way his thoughts were spinning as a result of too much adrenaline in a body already reeling from too much fatigue.

He might not have been so wary of making decisions in this state if he didn't have such vivid memories of the bitterly cold vigil he'd stood on Alfa 117 a month ago while the *Enterprise* repaired her malfunctioning transporters. Sulu distinctly remembered thinking at one point toward the end of the ordeal that it would be a good idea to start walking down to the planet's equator. If his feet hadn't been so numb with cold and frostbite that his very first step landed him flat on his back and knocked some sense into him, he might have actually started the 23,000-kilometer trek and missed getting beamed out with the rest of the landing party.

So right now, Sulu was forcing himself just to sit and watch the darkness settle and rain sluice down the *Drake*'s impact-starred cockpit windows. Pelting hard against the shuttle's duranium-clad nose when the wind drove it and splashing soft as poured milk when it didn't, the sound reminded him so much of wet San Francisco nights spent on his great-

great-grandfather's sailboat that he kept expecting to smell salt air and the delicate tang of the old man's jasmine tea. What he got instead was the pungent odor of an alien rain forest, seeping in through the rents where the nacelles had been torn away from the shuttle's hull.

It was a thick and complicated smell, compounded of wet moss, crushed and stripped tree bark, and some kind of night-blooming flowers whose scent was magnolia-sweet and citrus-sharp at the same time. It was an odor the botany enthusiast in Sulu might have enjoyed under other circumstances, but right now all it did was remind him that he was stranded on a completely unknown planet in a completely unknown part of the galaxy. He had never felt farther away from San Francisco, or, for that matter, from the entire rest of his life.

The smell of the rain forest wasn't the only thing coming into the shuttle. A glittering film of small flying insects gathered over Sulu's control panel, apparently attracted to the feverish blinking of the mechanical failure lights. They didn't seem inclined to bite him, but they did keep getting in his eyes and nose and ears. Sulu put up with them as long as he could, then cursed and fled back into the passenger hold. Its steady emergency lighting didn't seem to attract as many of the gnatlike creatures, and the spill of emergency supplies from the shattered shell of one bulkhead reminded him that there was work he could do here before he had to make any irrevocable decisions about his future.

The *Drake* had been stripped of nonessential equipment before its final trip down to Tlaoli, in preparation for evacuating a landing party that nearly exceeded its cargo weight limit. But Starfleet safety regulations decreed that all shuttles carried in their bulkhead storage an emergency medical kit and enough water and supplies to survive being stranded in space for three days. Since the *Drake* normally carried a crew of four, that meant there were plenty of supplies for Sulu to sort through.

The crash had burst two of the four water containers and drenched one of the food packs, which meant Sulu had to spread the individually wrapped rations out to dry on the shuttle's bare floor. At first, he set aside all the ones that had been crushed or whose plastifoil wrappers had been torn open. After seeing how much of his potential food supply he was losing, however, Sulu forced himself to eat whatever he could extricate from the broken containers. His initial intention was just to make some use of food that would be spoiled by tomorrow, but after a few minutes he realized that the salty cold mush of unheated stew and paper-flavored sticks of dehydrated protein felt remarkably good to his grinding stomach. Several crushed remnants of energy bars later, Sulu's tremors had subsided and he found himself thinking clearly again.

Wherever he had been flung by Tlaoli's strange alien force field, his first duty was to get back to the Federation and to Starfleet. Since the *Drake* was no longer spaceworthy, there was no way Sulu could make the trip back on his own, even if he could somehow figure out where in space he was. But the crashed cargo shuttle still had two useful things left in it: an intact warp core and a subspace communicator. The latter had been so completely useless back on Tlaoli that Sulu had turned it off to free himself of the distracting squawk of subspace interference. In the shock of his arrival and subsequent crash, it hadn't occurred to him to turn it back on again.

Scooping up a last mangled pack of carbohydrate wafers and a cannister of sterile water to wash them down with, Sulu headed back into the swarming fog of insects that filled the cockpit. The shuttle's designers hadn't thought to include an insect-repellent field generator in the emergency cache, probably because when they'd thought of emergencies they'd envisioned the shuttle drifting helplessly in deep space rather than wrecked in a primeval rain forest. But Sulu had armed himself from the first-aid kit with a can of disinfectant spray that had a sharp, unpleasant smell. He used it to blow the film of gnats off the communicator controls, then doused himself thoroughly before he sat back in his seat. The insects crowded back against the windows of the cockpit, a spangled and gauzy veil that almost obscured the outside dark and splattering rain.

Sulu brushed a few drowned gnats off the communicator's display panel, then switched the unit on and watched it power itself up. The frequency monitor ran through a spectrum of subspace channels, spiking several times to indicate it had detected communicator signals at that wavelength. Sulu wondered whether he should be reassured or worried that this planet's inhabitants had subspace technology equivalent to the Federation's. He knew he wasn't in the territory of Starfleet's known enemies—the attack ships that had chased him hadn't looked anything like the Klingons' claw-shaped fighters, or the ramshackle pirate fleets of Orion. But Sulu had no idea what Romulan ships might look like, after the centuries of mutual avoidance that had passed since Earth's last hostile encounter with those mysterious aliens. For all he knew, he could be sitting on one of the Romulans' legendary twin homeworlds right now.

It was that unpleasant thought which inspired Sulu, when the communicator had finished its scan and sat waiting for further instructions, to punch in his security clearance code before he did anything else. Then he painstakingly programmed the communicator to broadcast a coded and anonymous Starfleet distress call at the maximum level of security. It took him several minutes to do what Uhura could probably have done in seconds, but at last he sat back and watched his signal go out on a restricted channel hidden in the shoulder of ionized helium's discharge band. To anyone scanning randomly across the frequency spectrum, that short "officer-in-distress" code would look like nothing more than natural subspace noise. Only a Starfleet base that monitored those restricted frequencies and knew how to decode the seemingly meaningless static on them would understand Sulu's cry for help.

He sighed and immediately wished he hadn't. His eau de disinfectant had faded away, and the air around him once again glittered with tiny translucent bodies. Sulu was reaching for the spray cannister when a loud voice from the communicator jerked him upright in surprise. It wasn't preceded by an official Starfleet hailing tone and its owner didn't even bother to identify himself. All he did was say one incredulous and utterly unexpected word.

*"Sulu?"*

# Chapter Three

"LET ME GUESS," said Dr. McCoy, in the hissing silence of the carbide-lit tent. "You were trying to destroy this central hub and stop the Gorn from invading the Federation when we hauled you out of your timeline and into ours."

"Yes." The glint of triumph faded from Sulu's lined face, and left him looking older and more tired than before. He glanced down at what was left of his right arm. "Trying, but not succeeding. The Gorn hub is probably still there and still working."

"What happened?" Uhura asked.

"We were ferrying troops to a newly invaded Vulcan colony when we ran across a Romulan battleship and attacked it." The former helmsman said those words so offhandedly that Uhura felt almost jolted. She had to keep telling herself that for this Sulu, all-out war had become a way of life. "It ran for refuge to a minor planet near the galactic fringe. When we chased after it, we got attacked by so many Gorn fighters that we knew the planet wasn't one of their normal colony worlds. We pretended to veer off, then circled back and saw the installation they were guarding. It looked like it could be the portal hub, so we hit it with all the anti-invasion troops we were ferrying to Xlamat, in a surprise attack." Sulu's lips tightened to a slash of remembered pain. "They were slaughtered down to a man."

Uhura let a moment of merciful silence pass before she spoke again. "What did you do after that?"

Sulu sighed. "We tried taking the *Hotspur* low into the atmosphere and firing every weapon we had—and by that point in the war, as you can imagine, we had an awful lot of firepower. It never even shook the towers above the fortress, much less the main underground portal. After that, there was only one thing left to do. We sacrificed the *Hotspur* to catch a Gorn shuttle and crash-landed them both, to make them think we all were dead." Sulu glanced up at her with another of those strange, bittersweet smiles, as if the years of war had taught him to find a dark thread of humor even in disaster. "Actually, most of us *were* dead by then. There was only a skeleton bridge crew left—you, me, Chekov. While we repaired the Gorn shuttle, we took turns watching Tesseract Fortress and listening to its communicator chatter. We noticed after a while that there weren't just Gorns showing up around that place—all the races they'd allied with or enslaved were there, too, massing and organizing for some major deployment. Maybe an invasion of Vulcan, we thought, or even of Earth. We waited as long as we could, but we didn't want to let them start sending that army through the portals if we could help it.

"So we salvaged our last pulse bomb from the wreck of the *Hotspur* and infiltrated Tesseract Fortress. We suspected the reason our previous attacks had failed was because the portal was generating a subspace force field so powerful that it actually protected itself from attack. Once we got inside the fortress walls, we were going to take our pulse bomb into the portal and detonate it from inside while Chekov—made a distraction."

Sulu's steady voice didn't falter as he recounted his own suicidal part in that final plan, Uhura noticed, but it did when he tried to gloss over the grim reality of what his subordinate had done. She reminded herself again about all the hellish years of war this man had endured, and said nothing. Dr. McCoy wasn't quite so tactful.

"You let that boy deliberately sacrifice himself?"

"Not such a boy in my time as in yours, Doctor. And by 2296, every officer in Starfleet would have sacrificed themselves if it could save another million civilian lives. I just wish it could have been that simple."

"You never made it into the portal with the pulse bomb?"

"No," Sulu said regretfully. "God knows the Gorn transfer enough weapons through that hub during their invasions, but they must have detectors to pick up activated ones. They slammed their security fields down on us before we even got close to the gate, then raked us with explosive projectile weapons. I saw Uhura get hit—felt the bomb get shot out of my hand and saw it start to ignite—and then I was here."

Sulu stopped speaking, and this time both McCoy and Uhura let the silence stretch out undisturbed until the older pilot himself broke it.

"Now do you understand why I have to go back?" he asked, pinning Uhura with a sharp, direct look that reminded her of Captain Kirk. "If my future really is your future, then the fate of my Federation and yours depends on you getting me back through this damned time transporter of yours."

Sulu reached through a glistening film of insects to activate the *Drake*'s communicator, then paused with his finger just a centimeter away. Was this a trap? Could the aliens who chased him away from the military fortress have somehow learned his name, telepathically or through some exotic technology that he couldn't even begin to comprehend?

"Sulu," the communicator said again, impatiently. "I know you're the only one who could have flown that shuttle, much less sent out that old Starfleet emergency signal. If you're alive out there, say something!"

Sulu eyed the communicator in surprise. The threadlike flash of its frequency monitor told him this signal was coming in on the same restricted and high-security Starfleet channel he'd used to broadcast his coded distress call, but that wasn't what made him take a deep breath and complete his motion toward the activation switch. Maybe he was wrong, but he couldn't imagine any aliens, telepathic or otherwise, who would bother to speak English with a Russian accent.

"Sulu here," he said into the communicator. "Who is this?"

*"Bok spasibo!"* said the thankful voice on the other end of the channel. It didn't sound much like a name, but since Sulu didn't know what else it could be, he decided not to make an issue of it for now. "Where are you now, Captain?"

*Captain?*

"I'm still in the shuttle," Sulu said, cautiously. For all that the man he was talking to seemed to know him, there was still something very odd about this conversation. "I—uh—landed it in the rain forest. Where are you?"

"Flying low over the Serippat Hills, with the cloaking device engaged and no Gorn in sight," the other voice said. "Keep talking and I'll triangulate on your signal. Is . . . is Uhura still with you?"

Sulu paused once again with his finger centimeters from the communicator controls, this time ready to break contact. What stopped him wasn't the familiar name of his *Enterprise* crewmate, but the unmistakable tension in the other man's voice when he asked about her. That couldn't be part of some alien plot to lure him out of hiding . . . even if the aliens could read his mind and know that Uhura had been down on Tlaoli with him just before he disappeared, there was no particular reason for them to pretend to be fearful about her. To the best of Sulu's knowledge, she was still safe and sound.

"No, she's not here," he said. "She's back at the base camp on Tlaoli."

There was a long moment of silence. "What?"

The mixture of bewilderment and suspicion in that reply sounded so exactly like what Sulu was feeling himself that he was almost tempted to laugh. Clearly, whoever he was talking to found this conversation about as confusing as he did...and suddenly, Sulu's overtired mind made a connection between this gruff, Russian-accented voice and the self-conscious young ensign he'd met just before he'd taken off to look for Captain Kirk on Tlaoli.

"Is this Chekov?" he demanded.

"Of course it's Chekov," was the sharp and far from self-conscious reply. "What kind of a stupid question is that? Sulu, are you wounded? Did they spray you with any of their drugs?"

"No," said Sulu. "But something's not right here."

The communicator crackled, but it took Sulu a moment to recognize it as the sound of mirthless laughter. "Nothing's been right for a long time now. Stay where you are. I have your location fixed now, and there's still no sign of Gorn. I'll set down in the nearest clearing and come get you."

Sulu opened his mouth to ask Chekov who the Gorn were, how the young ensign had come to this alien planet, and where he had obtained the craft he was flying. But the thread of light marking the open high-security channel between them died abruptly back to its baseline and left him sitting in the rain and darkness, wondering what to do next.

The most prudent reaction would probably be to evacuate the shuttle, but that would put Sulu out in the darkness of an alien forest with very little equipment and even less idea of what he was supposed to do next. He reminded himself that his goal right now was simply to get back to the Federation, which made the presence of a fellow Starfleet officer on this planet a godsend. While there was something odd and almost anomalous about the way Chekov had talked to him, at the moment that familiar Russian-accented voice was his only tie back to Tlaoli and the *Enterprise.*

But the more he thought about it, the more troubled Sulu found himself by Chekov's presence here. He'd last seen the young ensign heading off into the Tlaoli karstlands in dogged pursuit of their lost captain, just minutes before Sulu had encountered the windstorm that transported him here. Even if Chekov had somehow gotten caught up in that same alien force, how could he have arrived on this planet so far in advance of Sulu that he not only had found a shuttle to fly, but also had learned the names of the aliens and the landforms and acquainted himself with strange technologies Sulu had never heard of? It didn't make any sense. . . .

Until Sulu remembered that Chekov was the one other person, besides Captain Kirk, who had previously been abducted by the strange alien force fields of Tlaoli.

Uhura had said the young Russian had been transported a short distance through the caves, and that nothing more had happened to him. But maybe that wasn't true. Maybe the alien transportation device on Tlaoli sent everyone it caught to this distant alien planet. Or maybe—Sulu had an even worse but chillingly logical thought—maybe the alien transporter just sent *copies* of the people it caught. Sulu had met Chekov after he'd been transported through the caves, after all, and the Russian couldn't have been both here and on Tlaoli at the same time. It was far more likely that he and Sulu had both been scanned and duplicated here, the same way Captain Kirk had been duplicated aboard the *Enterprise* a few months ago when the ship's transporter malfunctioned and split him into two complimentary selves.

If his theory was right, Sulu thought, there should be a duplicate copy of Captain Kirk here as well. He repressed an urge to issue a wide-band call for the captain on his communicator, knowing it would be more likely to attract the attention of hostile aliens—these Gorn Chekov had mentioned—than to make contact with a man who might or might not even be present on the planet. He would mention his duplication theory to Chekov when the young man came to meet him, Sulu thought as he waved a veil of gnats away from his face. Then, if they really did seem to be just copies of their original selves, they could worry together about what to do next.

Sulu should have realized how much the soft pelting of the rain against the shuttle's hull muffled any other sounds from reaching it, but he was so busy thinking about the unpleasant aspects of his duplication theory that the footfall he heard inside the cargo's hold took him completely by surprise. He spun around in his pilot's seat and started to get up, but the unmistakable snout of a metal weapon poked him in the chest before he could take a step. Sulu sank back into his seat, blood running cold as a scarred stranger's face followed the weapon into the cockpit.

"*You,*" said the older man in a murderous-sounding but eerily familiar Russian voice, "are not Captain Sulu."

"No," Sulu said, when he could finally manage to speak. "I'm Lieutenant Hikaru Sulu, helmsman of the *U.S.S. Enterprise.*"

That answer, which he expected to be greeted by either a growl of rage or a snort of disdain, instead got him an impassive and intent stare.

"Helmsman of the *Enterprise*?" the other man asked slowly. "Right now?"

Sulu glanced around the insect-filled shuttle and couldn't restrain a small, wry smile. "Well, not right now. But usually, yes." He glanced back up, trying to see past the gleam of the weapon to its owner's shadowed eyes. "And you?"

"You don't know me?"

There was no discernable emotion in that blunt question, but Sulu still felt a little guilty when he shook his head.

"I'm Commander Pavel Chekov, first officer of the *Hotspur*." The older man lowered the weapon and took another step into the blinking glow of the cockpit's instrument lights. Sulu tried hard to match his face to that of the young ensign he'd just met on Tlaoli, but between the ugly scarring and the gauntness, even the dark eyes barely looked familiar. "You're younger than I remember ever seeing you," Chekov said somberly. "So you probably don't even know me yet. But twenty years ago, I was—or I will be—your navigator on board the *Enterprise*."

"Lieutenant, hey, Lieutenant Uhura!" The distant shout from outside the walls of their shelter broke the strained silence that had fallen after Sulu's final grim words. "Lieutenant, you'll never guess what's going on down in that ice cave!"

Uhura lifted a corner of an emergency blanket and felt a rush of cold cavern air displace the warmth that had built up inside the insulated space. The nano-fibers of her caving suit promptly expanded to compensate for the change in temperature, but she could see Sulu wince and hug his blood-stained camouflage jacket tighter around him with his left hand. Uhura motioned for him and Dr. McCoy to stay inside, then let the blanket fall behind her as she ducked out into the larger, column-filled cavern. It took her a moment to locate the glow of Sanner's carbide lamp. It was dim as a firefly and far across the cavernous darkness, but it skipped and leaped toward her with the cave geologist's typical energy.

"*There* you are! With all those reflective blankets you hung up, I couldn't see anybody's light. . . . I thought maybe you guys had left without me." Sanner condensed from a vague shadow beneath his helmet light into something so formless and white that he looked like a ghostly apparition floating toward her. Uhura peered at him as he got closer and saw that his cave jumper was thickly furred with extruded hoarfrost, as if it had gotten completely drenched and then frozen. His helmet was covered with a glittering rime of ice.

"What happened to you?" she exclaimed.

Sanner's grin flashed in the darkness. "Just what would happen to anyone stupid enough to walk under a waterfall in the dark. I was keeping my light turned off as much as I could—"

"Get inside," Uhura ordered, pulling the emergency blanket up and waving the geologist beneath it. He shed his ice-crusted pack as he went, then hunkered down near the little carbide heater and began stripping off his frozen gloves, talking the entire time.

"—since I figured I'd rather hit a rock, or even a waterfall than run into that alien force field without seeing it. Lieutenant Uhura, did you know there were blue emergency lights in all those alien conduits down there?"

Uhura finished resealing the tent walls behind her and came to join the others, settling down at a safe distance from Sanner and the pool of melt water already forming around him. "I noticed there were lights in the walls," she said, remembering the eerie glow she'd seen during their tense retreat from the ice cave. She'd assumed it was part and parcel of the same mysterious force field that had swept away Captain Kirk and Ensign Chekov. Sanner's more prosaic explanation, that the aliens who built and used this place would have needed to illuminate the dark corridors they made, had never even occurred to her. "Were they bright enough for you to keep your carbide turned off all the time?"

"Not really." Sanner shed his helmet and shook shards of ice off the collar of his uniform. "Obviously. But I left the carbide turned off anyway, so I could spot that force field from as far away as possible."

"Where was it this time?"

"I don't know! I never saw it, because there was too much water running in the corridor to get down that far." Sanner gazed expectantly across the tent toward Uhura, as if what he had just said should have meant something to her. Her face must have shown her blank incomprehension, because the geologist smacked his empty gloves across his knee as if that could pound the significance of his words home to her. What it actually did was splatter him with droplets of melting ice. "*Water,* Lieutenant! Running down the corridors, making a waterfall through the hole in the roof where that kid Chekov and Captain Kirk fell through...."

"Oh!" Uhura's eyes widened as she finally realized what he meant. "The ice is melting! The caves must be getting warmer again."

"*Precisely,* as Mr. Spock would say." With a grimace, Sanner blew on his fingers. His bare hands were now wetter and probably colder than they had been before he'd stripped off his waterproof gloves. "This upper cave is the coldest part of the whole system now, trust me. I was soaking wet for fifteen minutes on the way back, but I didn't start freezing until I was halfway up the spiral that leads here."

"Stick your hands up your sleeves," McCoy suggested. "That'll get 'em dry again."

"Thanks." Sanner wriggled his fingers under the edges of his jumper sleeves, and a sheen of extruded water promptly appeared on the outside of the cloth as it wicked the cold water away from his skin. "The farther down you go toward the ice cave, the warmer it gets," he told Uhura enthusiastically. "You can see by the way the fog's building up down there that it's the walls of the conduits that are getting warmer, not just the air flowing through them."

"So what does that mean?" McCoy asked. "If you're trying to convince us to stay down here and do some more caving, Zap—"

"No, no! This tells us something important about energy consumption." Sanner waved his gloves for emphasis, scattering them all with ice-cold drops of water. "When I first heard how the *Enterprise* lost so much power trying to beam us out of here, I started to wonder what was going on down here, energy-wise. I mean, if this place really did have its own transperiodic energy source, it wouldn't need to drain power from us, would it? It would create *heat* as a by-product, not cold, the same way dilithium crystals do when they generate a warp field. But instead, the temperature dropped every time we lost power down here. And I think that means Tlaoli is exactly as energy depleted as we first thought when we surveyed it. The only way the alien transporter can be activated is by stealing energy from any outside sources it comes into contact with."

"Like the power cells in our tricorders and phasers," Uhura said when Sanner finally had to pause to take a breath.

McCoy grunted. "Or the power storage banks of *Enterprise,* after it made contact with that transporter beam."

"Anything with electrical currents flowing through it," Sanner agreed. "I have no idea how the energy gets taken...maybe through some sophisticated subspace magnetic fields, maybe some other kind of alien physics we don't understand yet. But I'm betting that it takes that machine a long time to build up the energy it needs to activate a transfer. And in the meantime, it has to store its power somewhere."

"That would make sense," Uhura said. "But what does the cold have to do with it?"

"Isn't it obvious?" Sanner said. "The energy storage reaction has to be *endothermic,* Lieutenant. The more energy that gets put into the system, the more heat the system absorbs from the ambient environment."

The cave geologist waved his gloves again, this time up at the shadowy rock ceiling that loomed above their sheltering emergency blankets. "That might have been okay a million years ago when this place was basking in sunshine, but now that it's buried underground, it's not so good. Rock is an *awful* conductor of heat, so nothing flows in to replace what the energy storage reaction takes out. The result is an instant deep freeze whenever the machine starts charging itself up."

Uhura took a deep breath of comprehension. "Then when it starts warming up again ... does that mean the device has taken its energy out of storage and used it?"

"*Bingo!*" Sanner rocked back on his heels, looking enormously pleased with himself. "Energy consumption has to be the machine's limiting factor, Lieutenant! And the fact that it's still getting warmer in the caves right now means—"

"—that the alien transporter used up all of its energy transporting me here," Sulu said. The older man's deep voice sounded composed and thoughtful, as if this scientific puzzle was the only thing he had to worry about right now. Uhura's respect for this future version of Sulu was increasing the longer she knew him, as was her conviction that there must be more to the young helmsman she already knew than an easy smile and an enthusiasm for unusual hobbies. "It *would* need a tremendous amount of power to move someone halfway across the galaxy and backward twenty years in time—"

"—especially since it sent our version of Sulu back the other way!" Sanner finished triumphantly.

Uhura felt her stomach knot up. "We don't know for sure that it did that, Zap. He may have just been transferred to some other part of Tlaoli—"

The scientist started shaking his head before she even finished her sentence. "Not according to my calculations, Lieutenant. I estimated how much power the transporter here could have absorbed from all our dilithium cells and from the *Enterprise*. God only knows how much power it takes to travel through time, but if you assume it's an order of magnitude more than what it would take to go that same distance through space ... well, the equation only balanced out if I assumed it was a two-way transfer and the shuttle got sent, too."

"You're forgetting that the alien transporter already used some of its power transporting Captain Kirk and Ensign Chekov," McCoy pointed out.

"No, I'm not," Sanner said indignantly. "It barely needed any power at all to move that kid Chekov around down here. Especially since if he skipped through time at all, it couldn't have been by much. We've still got pretty much the same Chekov we started out with."

"But probably not the same Kirk," McCoy said. "And we won't know where and when the alien transporter sent him until we find the version that got out of this cave and is wandering around up on the surface somewhere."

"But the important thing," said the older Sulu, "is that the warming of the caves suggests the alien device is no longer charged up or capable of transporting anyone, either to the future or the past. Is that correct?"

"I think so," said Sanner. "I just wish I could have gotten down to the ice cave to make absolutely sure the force field was gone. . . ."

"There's another way we can check on that." Uhura swung around to eye the pile of stacked crates and backpacks she had used as the tent's third wall. One crate in the corner was marked with the Starfleet division symbol she knew better than any other in the service. She wrestled it out from the stack, making the tent sag a little in that corner, then threw open the lid to expose the small, portable communicator inside.

"That won't work," McCoy objected. "If the survey team brought it down with them, its power supply should be drained and dead now."

"It is," Uhura said, seeing the telltale darkness where a status readout should have blinked. She lifted the communicator out from the box anyway. "But we brought the last of Martine's chemical battery packs down here with us. You didn't use them for anything, did you, Zap?"

"Nope." The geologist was already rummaging through his overloaded backpack. "They're in here somewhere, probably all the way at the bottom. There we go."

He handed the old-fashioned chemical battery to Uhura, who had already opened the communicator's cover and pulled out the wires connected to its drained power supply. She twisted them around the terminals of the chemical battery instead, then took a deep breath and slid open the partition that let the old-fashioned chemical reservoirs come into contact and start the flow of electricity. She had no doubt that the alien transporter would soon begin to drain this power supply, just as it had drained all the others they had brought down into these caves. But, in the meantime, they just might have a chance—

"Uhura to *Enterprise*," she said into the communicator, spacing her words for maximum clarity. "Come in, *Enterprise*."

There was a pause whose pure silence seemed almost too good to be true, then Uhura heard the tiny click she was waiting for and began to breathe again.

"*Enterprise* here," said Spock's clear and familiar voice on the other end of the open channel. "A status report would be most welcome, Lieutenant."

Uhura repressed an undignified urge to giggle at the austere hint of reproach coloring the Vulcan's response. "Aye, sir." She gave him a succinct explanation of everything that had happened since her last contact with the ship. "We're still not sure what happened to Captain Kirk," she said at the end. "All we know is that the Sulu we have now never served under him or knew him."

Fear of losing her connection to the ship had made Uhura's explanation so condensed that she wondered if even Spock's superhuman intelligence could grasp all the nuances of it. She waited worriedly, watching the power supply indicator slowly decay on the communicator's status panel, and finally heard McCoy grumble, "Come on, Spock, say something," beneath his breath.

"Report acknowledged, Lieutenant." The Vulcan sounded no different than he had a moment before. "Under the circumstances, it would clearly be too dangerous to beam anyone down to assist you, but we will send another shuttle as soon as possible. What do you estimate the current power supply of the alien transportation device to be?"

"Low, we think, but we haven't been able to make a direct observation." Uhura saw Sanner frantically flapping a piece of paper at her from across the tent and realized it was his topographic map of the overlying karst plateau. "Geologic Specialist Sanner has some information about where the danger levels might be highest."

Sanner scuttled across the tent on his knees and bent over the communicator. "Bearing due south from the highest peak in the southern karst plain—" He rattled off a series of numbers and vectors that made no sense to Uhura. "—keep entirely clear of that area," he concluded. "Have the shuttle approach base camp from the opposite side of the karst plain."

"I believe I can pilot in accordance with those restrictions," Spock said calmly. Uhura opened her mouth, but McCoy was already asking the question she intended to ask, a lot more incredulously than she would have dared.

"Spock, you're not coming down here yourself, are you?"

"Certainly I am, Doctor." That urbane Vulcan voice never expressed any emotion as palpably human as worry, but there was an undertone to it now that was at least reminiscent of that emotion. "There will be an unavoidable delay of approximately thirty minutes while Commander Scott installs magnetic shielding around the warp core and engines of a second cargo shuttle. During that time, you will gather all personnel at the survey team's base camp so that we may begin to analyze and deal with the situation as soon as I arrive. That," he added unnecessarily, "is an order."

"Aye-aye, sir," Uhura said, but McCoy wasn't quite as easily intimidated.

"What's the hurry, Spock?" he demanded. "Is there somewhere else we're supposed to be right now?"

"No, but there is somewhere else that we currently *are*," the science officer replied sharply. "And that *Enterprise*—the one that is supposed to exist at this time and place—has probably already been affected by the disruptions we have created in the timeline." Spock's voice became muffled as the chemical battery began to lose its electrical charge, but Uhura still had no trouble hearing the starkness in his words. "If something we have done has erased Captain Kirk from our own past, then the only reason we can remember him now is because we are floating in a bubble of disconnected time caused by our inadvertent slingshot at Psi 2000. And that bubble is due to rejoin the main timeline approximately fifty-six hours from now."

# Chapter Four

TLAOLI'S LITTLE LEMON SUN cast a clean, surprisingly hard light over the scrubby plains beyond the karst plateau. It reminded Chekov of summers in Siberia, where the sun could blind you even though the air was cool, and every midge and shrew and snow tern took advantage of the brief season. Only here on Tlaoli, the ground under their feet was hard and dry, not half-frozen beneath a blanket of mud, and there were no clouds to feather the edges of shadows and grant some rest to the eye. By the time the base camp lifted into view on the edge of a pale horizon, Chekov's head hurt and the back of his uniform tunic was scratchy and damp with sweat. He envied Kirk his youth and civilian status—the boy had shouldered out of his shirt half an hour ago, walking bare-chested in the spring-like morning with no hint of self-consciousness or impropriety.

"So that's where the rest of them are waiting?"

Kirk had slowed his pace a little, squinting under his shading hand even though the sun was still more behind them than overhead. It was pretense, Chekov knew. An excuse to postpone walking into the camp, where he would only find himself off-balance and outnumbered by adults who knew more about him than he did himself. After three months as the newest kid on an established starship, Chekov understood how he felt. So he let Kirk have the delay. Drawing up alongside, he pretended not to notice Tomlinson's irritation as the rest of the party caught up to them and slowed to a halt.

"They should all be there by now." Although he was really only guessing—he didn't know how long Lieutenant Uhura and Mr. Sanner would be underground. "They'll be relieved that we found you."

The boy nodded, a calm, noncommittal gesture. "Do they know?" he asked. "I mean, do they know about me—that I'm *not*…me?" It was hard enough to think about, let alone try to discuss.

"They know we went out looking for Captain Kirk." Chekov had decided that the easiest way to keep things straight in his own head was to think of them as two distinctly separate people with coincidentally similar names. Remembering his own teen years, he suspected it wasn't that far from the truth. "They don't know yet that we found you instead, but they'll still be glad to see you."

"Why?" The bitterness in young Kirk's tone caught Chekov by surprise. "It's not like I'll be any use on board a starship."

"Don't worry, son." Plastering on one of those stiff, insincere smiles that adults would never tolerate having directed at themselves, Tomlinson reached out to tousle Kirk's hair as he stepped between the boy and Chekov on his way to the front of the group. "We'll make sure you're well taken care of." He cast a disapproving glare at Chekov, just missing Kirk's angry duck out from under his hand as he turned back to his own, more important adult affairs. "Meanwhile, Ensign, we've got a report to make to our commander, so let's get moving, shall we?"

Chekov nodded, but he doubted Tomlinson saw that, either. The lieutenant was already striding toward the base camp, apparently intent on proving that he had a job to do and he knew what it was. The only hint of apology came from Martine as she hurried to follow behind—a quick backward glance and the flash of an embarrassed smile. But she didn't hold up to wait for the others, or say anything to the boy who would one day be her commanding officer.

*If he remembers this twenty years from now, you'll never set foot outside the Weapons Room again,* Chekov thought. He was surprised Tomlinson couldn't feel the laser burn of the boy's glare between his shoulders. Or maybe he did, and he just didn't think a fourteen-year-old's indignation mattered.

Tomlinson had been irritable ever since Chekov and Kirk rejoined him on the floor of the karst maze. Smith must have explained the circumstances surrounding her separation from Chekov, because the lieutenant only asked them awkwardly, "Everything okay?" without bothering to introduce himself to the boy in Chekov's company or ask for the newcomer's name. Upon being assured that everyone was in one piece and mobile, Tomlinson had stated simply, "We've got a long walk back to the base camp," and started them on their way.

At first, Chekov had assumed his senior officer was angry at him for splitting up with Smith, or for usurping (however unintentionally) Tomlinson's leadership role by being the one to first make contact with Kirk. But as the morning wore on, and Tomlinson's behavior morphed inexpertly from gruff commander to patronizing buddy and back again, Chekov realized that the angry glances and sharp comments flung his way were only fallout from a more generalized unhappiness. It wasn't Chekov who had Tomlinson flustered and unhappy—it was Kirk.

As soon as the thought occurred to him, the evidence was everywhere. The lieutenant almost never made eye contact with Kirk, but when he did, a peculiar expression that was half resentment, half condescension made his eyes and smile seem like parts of two unrelated faces. He hadn't called Kirk by name even once, resorting instead to ridiculous diminutives like "son" and "young man." Chekov wondered if it was just the shock of finding a much-too-young James Kirk at the end of their hunt that had Tomlinson so agitated, or if any teenager would have done the trick.

"Look!" Smith's exclamation caught his attention sufficiently to break his reverie, but she felt the need to swat him repeatedly on the shoulder anyway. Chekov felt a little bit like Kirk as he ducked out from under her blows. "Isn't that the shuttle?" She acknowledged his movement by changing her swat to what was probably supposed to be an apologetic pat, but was obviously too excited to take offense or feel embarrassed. "Doesn't that mean Mr. Sulu's okay after all? Maybe they figured out how the alien transporter works, and now they can use it to put everybody back to where they were!"

Kirk didn't look as pleased by the prospect as Chekov might have expected. He pretended not to notice the question Chekov glanced in his direction, and instead made himself very busy with shaking out his shirt and jamming his arms down the sleeves.

"At ease, Crewman." Tomlinson's attempt to sound mature and unruffled instead came out as weary disappointment. "Lieutenant Sulu was flying the *Drake*. The nose cone says that's the *Herschel*. They must have sent another team down."

Which begged the question: Why? All they'd managed to do so far was lose or strand everyone who'd set foot on this planet. Adding a few more to the tally hardly seemed productive.

A flurry of activity at the edges of the camp made it clear that someone had been watching for their return. Chekov found himself moving a few steps closer to Kirk, feeling Smith pull in just behind his right shoulder, and hoped the boy didn't notice their sudden protectiveness. Chekov wasn't sure what to expect from the landing party—he hadn't expected Tomlinson's strangely hostile reaction to finding the young man—but he knew Kirk didn't need a flood of pity and disappointment the moment he set foot inside their camp. He suddenly wished they'd been able to whisk him in under cover of darkness. Then they could have told everyone what to expect while the boy was still asleep, and given the shock a chance to run its course before parading him around in public.

But even in the most bizarre circumstances, the *Enterprise*'s crew maintained its professionalism and calm. They gathered quietly, clearly studying the boy but not pointing or gasping or uttering cries of alarm. Kirk returned their frankly curious stares stoically. He reminded Chekov of a young prince, facing his subjects for the very first time.

Oddly, it was Tomlinson who saved them from any further awkwardness. "Is Lieutenant Uhura back yet?" He aimed the question at no one in particular, but the older geologist near the front of the group answered pleasantly enough.

"Carolyn has gone to get her." Jaeger smiled at Kirk with the sort of paternal kindness that somehow ceased to be insulting once you were in your sixth decade. "Ah, but this young man will complicate things, I think."

A cool, deep voice beyond Jaeger caught everyone's attention; the small crowd swung about and parted, almost unconsciously clearing a lane for the tall, black-haired officer. "James Kirk, I presume."

For some reason, when Chekov had imagined a new shuttle crew bringing the *Herschel* down to join them, he hadn't expected Commander Spock to be among those on board.

Kirk looked the Vulcan over with only the slightest hint of surprise. "You can call me Jim." It occurred to Chekov that this young Kirk might very well have never met a Vulcan before.

Spock dipped his head minutely. "Very well. I am Commander Spock, first officer of the starship *Enterprise.*"

Kirk nodded in return, then, seeming to have come to a sudden decision, he stepped forward and boldly thrust out his hand. "I'm pleased to meet you, sir."

Spock arched one eyebrow, but otherwise didn't move.

Chekov had enjoyed precious little exposure to Vulcans himself, despite four years at Starfleet Academy and three months on board the only human ship in the Fleet with a Vulcan X.O. He'd attended one subspace dynamics lecture by a visiting Vulcan researcher (and followed not a single word of it), and been part of the honor guard that greeted a Vulcan chancellor to San Francisco his freshman year. Other than that, he didn't think he'd even seen Commander Spock in the flesh more than two or three times since setting foot on board the *Enterprise.* Yet despite his admittedly meager experience with the race, there was one thing Chekov understood without question—Vulcans did not like to be touched.

He took a half-step forward to catch the boy's attention, but before he could open his mouth to speak, Spock enfolded the boy's slim hand in his own and delivered a single solemn shake. Eyebrows raised all around the small collection of humans.

"Unfortunately"—the Vulcan released Kirk's hand and took what Chekov suspected was an unconscious step backward—"our time is quite limited, and there are serious matters to which we must attend."

Kirk nodded. "I understand. Ensign Chekov already explained about losing your captain and helmsman."

"I wouldn't say we were lost, exactly." It wasn't the strange black and silver uniform that made Chekov's heart skip a beat, or even the dusting of gray in hair that only a few hours ago had been as black as a midnight sky. It was the easy familiarity with which Sulu smiled at him from where he stood waiting at the back of the group beside Uhura, as though they were both in on some grand joke together and Chekov just didn't realize it yet. "I'd say it's more like we're just seriously misplaced."

Captain Sulu's presence at least explained why no one at the base camp seemed particularly surprised to meet the younger Kirk.

Chekov tried hard not to stare while he and Tomlinson made their brief report on the search through the karst maze and the location of their not-quite captain. It wasn't easy. Even though he never spoke, Sulu exuded a presence infinitely more commanding than Chekov remembered from their brief meeting a few hours before—a few decades before. He stood at the back of the group and seemed to draw in attention the way a black hole drew in light. And every time Chekov let his gaze stray toward the older man, Sulu was watching him. Not staring, necessarily, but just looking at him, or through him, as though seeing someone else there in his stead. The silent attention made Chekov uneasy.

When Spock finally said, "Thank you, gentlemen," Chekov caught Smith's elbow to hurry her away with him. He was ready to be away from this uncomfortable encounter, someplace private where he could ponder the implications of an older Sulu and a younger Kirk without having to worry about what either of them were thinking of him.

Instead, Spock's impassive voice snared him with a simple, "Mr. Chekov, if you would come with us, please."

Smith bared her teeth in a playful grimace. "Uh-oh," she whispered. "What did you do?"

"I have no idea."

Nor did he find out any time soon. Spock led McCoy and Uhura into the tent they'd been using as a mess hall, apparently trusting that Sulu, Kirk, and Chekov would follow behind. Once there, someone dug rations and water out of an already opened box, and they all found seats on the various tables, chairs, and packages crowded into the shelter. Chekov left his dry rations with Kirk after he saw that the boy had already polished off the two packs he'd been given. He could always find something to eat later, and right now all he wanted to do was sit down.

As soon as he was off his feet, fatigue all but ambushed him, leaving him feeling sick and a little dizzy. He calculated quickly that it had been nearly thirty hours since he'd last slept, and more than half that since he'd had anything to eat. He suddenly felt very stupid for having left his food with Kirk. It helped a little to see that the boy had already finished Chekov's share and was starting in on Uhura's. He tried to remember what it was like to have that sort of bottomless appetite.

When Sulu and Spock had finished explaining the dismal details of Sulu's future, Kirk played with an empty ration packet for another minute or two, folding and unfolding it thoughtfully. He looked neither puzzled nor worried, just pensive. "So you don't remember me as your commander because this alien transporter took me out of your timeline before I became a captain." He shifted a questioning frown to Spock. "Doesn't that mean you already know I won't be going back?"

"No." Even though he didn't say "captain," Chekov could almost hear the gap where Spock meant the word to fall. "Captain Sulu's future is but one possible future, selected for by your disappearance. If we return you to your own time, we have every reason to believe that the timeline will correct itself to its original course."

Kirk nodded slowly. Folding. Unfolding. "And that's because we have this...bubble to work inside. This time bubble you guys created when you cold-mixed the engines."

"A bubble," McCoy said, "which apparently bursts on 1707."

"So how do we return me to my own time?"

"By figuring out how you—and me—were brought here in the first place." Sulu steadied himself with his good left hand as he took a seat atop one of the tables and folded his legs to lean on. "What were you doing right before you found yourself here?"

Kirk recoiled a little from the intensity of Sulu's gaze. Not in fear, but in the way young men sometimes did from adults they weren't yet sure they trusted. "Riding a shuttle." But he shrugged with a stiff defiance all out of proportion with the question being asked.

"That's it?" McCoy raised his eyebrows in what might have been surprise, glanced at Spock and Uhura, then back at the boy again. "Just riding a shuttle?"

Again the irritated, uncommunicative shrug. "My dad was stationed at a Federation embassy off-world. We were leaving, on our way home." He wadded the ration pack into a ball and flicked it away from him. "There's nothing else to say."

The doctor settled back in his chair and sighed up at Sulu. "Not a lot of points of similarity there."

Sulu's eyes still hadn't left the boy's face. Whatever he saw there made him shake his head slowly. "There has to be something the transporter system keys onto. It can't just be pulling us out randomly."

"Why not?" Kirk crossed his arms and lifted his chin, daring the captain to contradict him. "It's alien, isn't it? Who knows what it thinks is important. Maybe it's what we had for lunch, or the phases of the moon."

"Perhaps." Spock shut the tricorder in his lap and folded his hands atop it. Chekov couldn't tell if the Vulcan simply chose to ignore Kirk's sarcasm, or if he really didn't hear it. "But before making any such assumptions regarding the device's motives, we should acquire more data."

McCoy gave a distinctly unhappy snort. "How? You want to just send someone else into the cave and see who it spits out in exchange?"

"I do not believe that will be necessary, Doctor." Dark eyes locked on Chekov at the other end of the tent, as emotionless and unyielding as a tractor beam. The young ensign suddenly felt himself jolt completely awake and alert. "Mr. Chekov, you have also passed through the alien transporter device, correct?"

"Yes, sir." He tried to sit up a little straighter, only to discover that the morning's cross-country hike in Starfleet issue boots had left him stiff and inflexible. "But it didn't work, sir," he went on, climbing awkwardly to his feet so that he could at least be standing at attention. "I mean, I'm still me, sir—I didn't go anywhere." It was only then that he realized everyone in the tent was staring at him as though he'd just risen from the grave. A cold little knot of fear wound together in his stomach. "Did I?"

"Hey, look on the bright side. At least you're not an Andorian camel anymore."

Uhura glanced across a supply tent that had been hastily cleared and converted into a medical research laboratory through the addition of a portable medical diagnostic bed and a few strong photon lamps. Spock and McCoy were discussing the best way to recalibrate the doctor's medical tricorder now that its sensors were no longer being disrupted by subspace interference from the underground alien transporter. Between them, a very embarrassed-looking Chekov sat hunched on the equipment crate they'd used as a support for the rolled-out diagnostic bed, shirtless and with old-fashioned patch sensors attached to his bare chest and shoulders. Diana Wright was monitoring the readout on her own medical tricorder, and clearly trying to make the shy young ensign feel a little better about being the center of everyone's attention. Even from across the tent,

Uhura could see how fast and tense the young Russian's heart rate looked on Wright's display screen.

"Why should it think he was any species of camel?" Sulu asked curiously. After their mud-drenched journey back out of the Tlaoli caves, the older man had gladly exchanged his camouflage jacket and black tunic for a regulation uniform from the original survey team's stores. A mild painkiller injected into his amputated wrist and a cup of steaming coffee had erased a surprising number of the creases from his middle-aged face, but there was still an authoritative note in his voice that made it impossible to mistake him for his younger self. Uhura had noticed that most of the younger officers in the base camp had slipped into the habit of referring to him as "Captain Sulu" without even noticing they were doing it. Even Spock tacked on an occasional "sir," when addressing comments to him, although the older man had never made an issue of it.

Diana Wright cleared her throat a little self-consciously. "When we were down in the cave and all our instruments were malfunctioning, that's what my tricorder thought we were. It was just a joke, sir, to try and get Mr. Chekov to relax. I need a good baseline pulse rate to compare with his old medical records."

"Oh." Sulu paused, eyeing the young Russian with a reminiscent smile. "Pavel, relax. This can't be any worse than that hockey game you played in Murmansk your senior year, when the coach sent you to the showers early and you found out after you were wet that you'd entered the women's locker room by mistake."

Chekov cast him a startled glance and the white line on Wright's display leaped upward for a moment before resuming its rapid pulsing.

"That didn't help," said Wright.

"Sorry." The comment seemed addressed as much to Chekov as to the medic. "I keep forgetting it's only 2266 and you don't really know me yet."

"No, sir." The young ensign looked away, then back again with a little more color in his face. "And it was Minsk."

Sulu lifted an eyebrow. "Are you sure? I thought the national hockey play-offs in 2260 were in Murmansk."

"Minsk," Chekov said again, more strongly. "I made the play-offs both years, '59 and '60. And it was the play-offs in Minsk where I sprained my knee and was sent to the showers early."

"Was that the year you played the team from the Kola Peninsula?"

"No, that was '60. I stayed in that game until the end—"

"Got it," said Wright in satisfaction. "All right, Ensign. You can take your beauty patches off now."

Chekov began to peel off the thin-film sensors, but paused to give the older man across the tent another startled glance. "You did that on purpose."

"Did what?" Sulu asked innocently. "You don't expect an old man like me to remember your high school hockey record perfectly, do you?"

The Russian opened his mouth to reply, then suddenly seemed to remember that the man teasing him was a much higher-ranking officer. Another wave of color mounted his cheeks, then ebbed away again. "No, sir," he said stiffly and finished detaching the rest of Wright's sensors. "Can I leave now?" he asked her.

"We're just getting started, son." McCoy came over to the diagnostic bed with his medical tricorder once again emitting its usual quiet hum. "Put your shirt on, then lie down there again. How were his vitals?" he asked Wright.

"Normal, once he calmed down. And a perfect match for the baseline records we downloaded from the ship. No sign of metabolic aging or change."

McCoy grunted. "That just means he's within a few months of the age he was when he stepped into the machine. Let's try a scan of cellular telomere length." He programmed the tricorder with a few expert flicks of his hand, then swept it across Chekov's stiff, supine form. "Hmm. No statistical difference there, either."

Spock craned his head to peer at the results on the doctor's display screen. "If it exists, the time difference must be of less than one day's duration, or you would see at least a degree of genetic decay. I would suggest scanning for carbon 14 isotopic rations. Mr. Chekov, have you eaten since you came out of the Tlaoli caverns, or drunk anything besides water?"

"No, sir." Even from where he lay on his back, Chekov slipped Uhura a quick, apologetic glance. "I know I was supposed to, sir, but I just didn't feel like it. I made sure to stay hydrated, though."

"Excellent," said the Vulcan, without a trace of concern for the long hours which the young officer had gone without eating. "Your carbon isotopic ratio will not be contaminated by anything except minor atmospheric carbon dioxide, which has equilibrated within your lung tissues."

McCoy frowned as he made adjustments to his medical tricorder. "I'm still not sure how much this is going to tell us, Spock. Even if I compare his C-14 and C-12 ratios to his last baseline exam, there are thousands of things that could have affected them between now and then—"

"But we have a much more recent record of Ensign Chekov's isotopic composition than his last physical, Doctor," said Spock imperturbably. "Unlike you, he was transported down to this planet. Since that was approximately twenty hours ago, his records are still stored in the transporter console's transient buffer."

Diana Wright had stepped back beside Uhura and Sulu to clear more room for McCoy and Spock near the diagnostic bed. "Does the transporter really keep track of things like the individual *isotopes* of carbon in our bodies?" Uhura asked the medic softly as McCoy began a slower scan across Chekov's rigid body. Wright shrugged, but Spock's Vulcan ears must have caught the murmured question. He glanced up from consulting his own scientific tricorder.

"The transporter duplicates our bodies atom for atom, Lieutenant. That includes discriminating between the light and heavy isotopes of every element which can be fractionated by the body—"

McCoy snorted. "Next you'll be claiming that it keeps track of the quantum spin states in our electron shells. Or the picowatts of electrical discharge along our nerves. Spock, I just don't believe any computer designed by organic beings can process all that information!"

"Indeed." The Vulcan gazed down at the doctor with a familiar air of patient superiority. "Then the isotopic ratios which I have just transmitted from my tricorder to yours must be figments of both our imaginations."

"Hmmph." McCoy examined his tricorder with a scowl, as if it had somehow betrayed him by accepting the data. "All right, let's see how it compares to what I just collected . . . huh. Well, I'll be a monkey's uncle."

Chekov lifted his head from the diagnostic bed in alarm. "What does it say?"

"Don't worry, there's nothing wrong with you," McCoy assured him. "The isotopic ratios are very close, but they're not identical."

"Nor should they be," pointed out Spock. "Considering the rate at which carbon 14 decays to nitrogen even within human cells. If Doctor McCoy would be kind enough to transfer the isotopic data he has just collected back to my tricorder, I shall extrapolate the decay rate and determine if—" The Vulcan science officer's tricorder beeped and he bent over it immediately. After a moment, he raised his head and gave McCoy a look of reluctant admiration. "I see you have already calibrated your data for decay changes, Doctor. And it appears you are correct. There is indeed a slight discrepancy."

"About five hours, would you say?"

"Five point two five, to be precise."

Chekov pushed himself up to his elbows, his gaze growing more worried as it swung back and forth between the two scientists. "What does that mean?"

"It means," McCoy said, "that you're about five hours younger than you should be."

Silence descended on the supply tent, profound enough that in the distance they could hear the sound of dishes clattering in the mess tent and Sanner's voice from somewhere on one of the nearby karst mounds, calling, "—now dig your crampon into that crack over there to your right—"

"So the alien transporter really did move him through time?" Uhura asked. "Just not as far through time as it moved Captain Kirk and Mr. Sulu?"

"Precisely." Spock stepped back without taking his eyes from the young Russian ensign as McCoy put a hand under Chekov's elbow and helped swing him to his feet. "Now the question we must answer is— why? Ensign, tell me everything you remember about your encounter with the alien force field."

"I can't do that, sir." Chekov met Spock's gaze steadily, although his voice wavered a little with uncertainty. "I don't remember anything about it."

"What do you remember about the time before and after?"

Chekov straightened his shoulders, standing in a posture Uhura recognized as the one you assumed at Starfleet Academy when you were being quizzed at the end of a field exercise. "I remember falling down from the ledge we were walking to get into the cave, sir. The next thing I remember after that is waking up in the dark. After a while, Lieutenant Uhura and the other cave team members came and found me there. They told me that Captain Kirk and I disappeared together, but I don't remember any of it."

"Fascinating." Spock turned his probing gaze from Chekov to Uhura, and she could see the young man's shoulders slump a little in relief. "Lieutenant, after Ensign Chekov fell from that ledge, he remained with your rescue party?"

"Yes, sir." Something was niggling at the back of her mind, but Spock's lifted eyebrows told her he was waiting for additional information. "He came with us from the waterfall where he fell, to the cave where we found the lost survey team. We waited there to see if the ship could beam us out, then we tried to walk out of the cave again. Ensign Chekov was with us the whole time, mapping our path back down the main alien conduit to the ice cave where we encountered the alien force field for the first time. Then he and Captain Kirk vanished together."

Spock nodded. "How many hours would you estimate that took?"

"About three?" Uhura glanced instinctively at Chekov for confirmation and saw him wince. Regretting her own lack of memory, she turned to look at Wright instead. "Did you notice?"

"My chronometer wasn't working, but I'd guess it was closer to three and a half," the medic said.

"That would fit with ship records of your communications from the cave," Spock agreed. "After the ensign vanished, how long did it take until you found him again?"

"About another hour and a half," Uhura said, then belatedly did the math. "Which adds up to five hours."

"Indeed." Spock steepled his fingers and gently rested them against his chin. "If the Ensign Chekov we have here was transported by the alien device through time from the point at which he fell from the ledge to the point at which you found him in the upper cavern of the cave system—"

"The same cavern that you found me being healed in?" Sulu asked shrewdly.

"Yes," Uhura said, and it was more than just an answer to the older man's question. "That would make him five hours younger than he should have been." The memory niggling at the back of her mind suddenly shouldered its way into her consciousness, and she gasped. "When we found Ensign Chekov at the bottom of the waterfall below that ledge— Diana, do you remember how disoriented he seemed? He kept saying that it seemed like things had already happened—"

"And that it seemed as if it had been a long time since he had fallen from the ledge," the medic agreed. "He was fine, physically, except for being wet and hypothermic, but it did seem like it took him a while to get back to normal."

"But I couldn't have gone straight from falling off the ledge to the cave where they found me five hours later," Chekov protested. "If I did, who was with them for the rest of that time?"

"You were," Spock answered calmly. "A version of you taken from another point of time and sent backward to replace yourself."

The young ensign cast Uhura a slightly hunted look, and she stepped forward to stand beside him. "But what point could that version have come from, Mr. Spock?" she asked gently. "He was wearing his caving suit and had all his same tools with him—"

"Except the cave map," Diana Wright reminded her. "We thought he lost that falling down through the water, but maybe he never had it."

"It is likely that he had it the *first* time he fell," Spock said. "If my current hypothesis is correct, that would have been the time when he was drowned by his fall." He held up a hand when Uhura, Wright, and Chekov all tried to speak at once, and they obediently fell silent. "I suspect you managed to revive him on that first time through the events in question. It would therefore have been *that* Mr. Chekov who first encountered the Tlaoli transport device. At the moment the slightly older Mr. Chekov stepped into it, the device sent his healthy body backward in time for you to find beside the waterfall, and sent the younger Mr. Chekov's drowned body forward through time to the cavern with the healing chambers. The same place to which it sent Captain Sulu and young Mr. Kirk when it replaced both of them with their healthier counterparts."

There was another long silence as they absorbed what Spock had said. He glanced around at their startled faces, lifted a quizzical eyebrow, and added, "This is, of course, still merely a hypothesis."

"How can we prove it?" McCoy demanded. "Or disprove it? It's not even a hypothesis, Spock, if there's no way to do that."

The Vulcan science officer gave him an exasperated look. "We will first subject my idea to critical analysis, Doctor. If it remains feasible after that, then we will move on to the next phase of examination."

"Well, I think it makes sense for me to be replaced by a healthier version of myself." Sulu touched the empty right sleeve of his regulation gold tunic. "And if the alien device had no way of knowing that Chekov was going to recover from being drowned, then I suppose it made sense for it to replace him, too. But what about your missing Captain Kirk? That young man I just met looked as fit as a young wolf cub—and about as self-reliant as one, too. Why replace him with an older version?"

"Unless he wasn't telling us the truth about where he came from," McCoy said slowly. "I think I should go talk to him."

The sound of a cleared throat caught everyone's attention, but it took Uhura and the rest of them a minute to realize the unlikely source. Ensign Chekov, who had retreated to the shadows of the supply tent while they discussed the mechanics of the alien time transport system, now stepped back into the fringe of the strong lights. "Sir, if you don't mind, I think maybe I should do that," he suggested tentatively. "I'm not that much older than he is, after all."

Chekov's rationale made Spock look baffled, but McCoy's blue eyes twinkled in comprehension. "That you aren't, son. Why don't you go see what you can do? If young Jim Kirk won't talk to you, just bring him back here and we'll see if I can do any better."

The young Russian nodded and slid out of the supply tent quickly, as if he was afraid they'd drag him back for some last medical test if he delayed. Sulu watched him go with a reminiscent smile. "I'd forgotten what a worrier he was when he was young," he commented to Uhura. "Once you're friends, you need to remind him not to take everything so seriously."

She nodded in agreement, but even as she did, Uhura felt a small shiver of something that was not quite déjà vu and not quite fear. It was unsettling to get these small, slanting glimpses into her own personal future. The larger picture of future wars and galactic disasters that this older Sulu had painted was abstract enough for her to comprehend, even if it was disturbing. It was the tiny, almost unconscious revelations of future friendships and confidences that made the skin prickle on the back of her neck.

"All right, Spock," McCoy was saying. "What else do we need to do to prove whether or not this idea of yours holds water? We have only fifty more hours to get Captain Kirk back, remember."

"Forty-eight point nine hours, to be precise," Spock corrected him. "And once we have resolved the anomalous data point of why the machine would have exchanged our James Kirk for his younger self, the only remaining question is one of intention. We do not know what the aliens who designed this system originally intended it to accomplish. If they meant to permanently replace the individuals whom they exchanged through time, then there may be no way for us to reverse the process. But if they intended the exchange to be temporary, then they must also have designed the transporter to work in both directions. Unfortunately, we cannot know—"

"Maybe we can, Commander," Uhura interrupted. "I didn't have time to tell you before, but we found alien writing down in the system of conduits between the ice cave and the healing chamber. There might be enough there for our translators to decode."

"That would be of great assistance," Spock admitted. "Even so, we will need to go about the next phase of our proceedings with the greatest care and caution."

"Why?" McCoy asked, frowning. "What is this next phase, anyway?"

"The one prescribed by the scientific method for any valid hypothesis," the Vulcan said. "Experimentation."

# Chapter Five

THE DRUMMING OF RAIN against the *Drake*'s hull suddenly sounded twice as loud to Sulu, as if his senses had been intensified by shock. He stared at the older man across the shuttle's cockpit, taking in his battle-scarred face, the green and violet camouflage jacket streaked with rain, and the unfamiliar Starfleet insignia, thin and luminous as silver wire, on his black uniform collar.

"You were my navigator twenty years ago?" Sulu repeated, as if hearing it in his own voice could somehow make it more comprehensible. "Aboard the *Enterprise*?"

The older man who'd said he was Pavel Chekov glanced around the shuttle instead of replying. His frown touched only his forehead; his mouth seemed to be held in an unchanging grim line by the network of old scars around it. "Which *Enterprise* shuttle is this? The *Copernicus*? The *Jocelyn Bell*? I remember we lost the *Hawking* studying a super-nova . . . but that might not have happened yet for you."

"It's the *Edwin Drake*."

"I don't remember that one." Chekov reached out to touch the instrument panel with the kind of nostalgic affection Sulu had once seen Scotty display toward an obsolescent voltmeter he'd found in an emergency tool kit. "What a relic. . . . How the hell did you get here in it?"

"I didn't fly here," Sulu said. "I got transported by some kind of alien force field from Tlaoli 4."

Chekov's gaze came back to Sulu's face and the weather-beaten creases around his eyes deepened, although it was hard to tell if the expression was one of surprise or of suspicion. "I don't remember visiting any planet named Tlaoli, much less losing you there. What year is it for you?"

"It's 2268, stardate 1704.4." Sulu saw the blank look on Chekov's face and tried to think what might have stuck in his memory after twenty years. "Right after I caught the Psi 2000 virus and ran through the ship pretending to be D'Artagnon. You must remember *that*."

"Actually, I don't." Chekov mulled it over, rubbing a hand absently across one shoulder as if it ached. "I was just out of the academy in 2268—I didn't know any of the senior officers. But I would have remembered if we lost a shuttle." He flicked a glance at Sulu's face. "The whole ship talked about it when Mr. Spock was stranded on Taurus II with the *Galileo*. We all expected Captain Mitchell to throw Commissioner Ferris into the brig for ordering us to—"

"Captain *who?*"

"Gary Mitchell. Or maybe he was still the ship's first officer when you—" The older Chekov broke off abruptly, as if something in the quality of Sulu's silence had alerted him. "Mitchell isn't your second-in-command," he stated with a perceptiveness that startled Sulu. Had the young Russian ensign he'd met back on Tlaoli possessed the same shrewdness beneath his awkward uncertainty, Sulu wondered, or had his apparently violent future sharpened his wits? "Who is?"

"Our science officer, Mr. Spock," Sulu said. "We lost Mitchell early in our five-year mission, when Captain Kirk tried to take the ship past the edge of the galaxy."

They stared at each other through a swirling gauze of gnats, until the older man finally cursed and flapped a hand across his face. "This is too complicated to figure out here. And it isn't safe to stay. The Gorn have probably sent out automated surface trackers to home in on your warp core's radiation signature. I'm surprised they're not already crawling all over you."

"The warp core and engines are magnetically shielded," Sulu said. "And I'm not sure—"

Chekov had already swung back toward the shuttle's cargo hold, but he paused to throw a sharp look across his shoulder. "You're not sure you trust me." He made it a statement rather than a question, as if it seemed to him a perfectly sensible way to feel. "What you don't know is that you and I are probably the last two humans left alive on Basaraba. This is a Gorn planet, and you've already found out how they treat anyone they don't know." He swept his weapon's gleaming snout around and Sulu instinctively flinched, but all Chekov did was rap on the communicator's power switch and deaden its displays. "Starfleet can't help us anymore. And there's a chance the Klingons might be able to decode a signal as old as that one."

*Klingons?* Sulu's sense of having fallen into a nightmare dimension deepened abruptly. The feeling was enhanced when Chekov slung his weapon up across his good shoulder and left the cockpit without another word, like a mystical figure in a dream. Whether or not Sulu followed was apparently up to him.

It took Sulu only a few seconds to decide that his best chance of survival in this alien hell lay with someone who had already survived it for a while. And for some reason, he had no doubt that this Pavel Chekov was that person. There was something stubbornly real about the older man, grim and battle-hardened as he was, that defied any attempt to see him as either an alien-induced hallucination or an imposter. With a resolute breath that stirred up swirls of startled gnats, Sulu scrambled to his feet and followed the other man out of the wrecked shuttle.

They paused in the cargo hold long enough to scoop up the emergency food supplies Sulu had packed, but left the water behind. "No shortage of that on Basaraba," Chekov said. "We salvaged a heavy-duty purification unit from the *Hotspur.*"

Sulu hefted his bag of supplies and followed the older man out through the shuttle's half-sprung hatch into the night. To his surprise, the rain was neither as cold nor as driving as he'd expected from the sound of it on the shuttle's hull. Instead, it came down in a way he remembered from an orchid-collecting trip he'd once made to Jamaica, a lukewarm, dripping shower with only an occasional drench as leafy branches far overhead dumped the moisture that had pooled on them. Despite the pleasant warmth and humidity, however, Sulu soon found himself wishing he had on something more waterproof than his uniform tunic. The rain-sodden cloth chafed where the bag of supplies swung back and forth over his shoulder, and plastered so tight to his skin elsewhere that his sweat stayed trapped beneath it.

Despite the rain, or perhaps because of it, the forest was hushed enough for Sulu to hear the rasp of Chekov's breath as he led the way down a vine-draped alley through the trees. "Water buffalo path," the other man said over his shoulder. Then, because it seemed to occur to him that he ought to explain further: "Not really water buffaloes, that's just what we call them. They're about twice as big."

"Dangerous?"

Chekov snorted. "Only if you fall asleep and don't smell them coming. They move about a kilometer an hour, fertilizing the soil all the way."

Now that he had mentioned it, Sulu could smell the musky organic odor stirred up under his feet. He expanded his mental wish list from rain gear to waterproof hiking boots. The buffalo trail angled uphill, and Sulu could tell from the way his own breath began to rasp in his throat that they were either at high altitude, or on a planet with an atmosphere less dense than Earth's. "You mentioned Klingons," he said, to take his mind off his unsatisfied need for oxygen. "In your time, they're at war with the Federation?"

"They're part of the Gorn Hegemony." Chekov paused a moment, as if trying to think back. "Have you met the Gorn yet?"

"No."

"Nasty reptiles with a huge grudge against the Federation. We had a battle with them a few decades ago and got them exiled from space as a result. They never forgave us. A few years later, they found a way to strike back using a new kind of trans-space portal to send their armies directly from planet to planet. They wiped out and enslaved the Romulans in less than a year. The Klingons signed a war powers pact with them not too long after that." Chekov's voice turned a shade more grim. "The Federation has been fighting them for almost seventeen years now."

"And this is one of their planets?"

"This is the hub of their entire trans-space transport system." Chekov fell silent again, perhaps to let Sulu absorb the impact of that. "The *Hotspur* ran across it by accident a few weeks ago. We notified the Federation, but we knew it would take them months to organize an invasion that could reach this deep into Gorn space. So once we saw that the hub was a permanent fortress, not something the Gorn could pack up and move—"

"That stone building with the tall towers?"

"Yes. We decided to attack. It looked like the Gorn were massing a large force here, maybe for an invasion of one of our home planets. We were afraid a few months might be too long to wait for reinforcements."

Sulu nodded, but had to wait a moment to speak. The trail was getting steeper, but despite his own ragged breath, Chekov didn't seem to see any need to moderate his pace. "How did it go, the attack?"

Even in the darkness, he could sense irritation in the glance Chekov threw him, as if the question had been not only pointless but also remarkably stupid. "When I told you we were the last two humans on Basaraba, what did you think that meant?" the older man asked sarcastically. "That everyone else on the *Hotspur* had gone away for a week of R and R?"

"No, I assumed they were all dead," Sulu said as evenly as he could manage between gasps. "But even a suicide attack can be a tactical success."

"Well, ours wasn't." And that was the end of the conversation.

The buffalo trail angled up a forested ridge at a surprising slant for a path carved by such large herbivores. Sulu could feel the muscles in his legs burn as his lungs struggled in vain to pull more oxygen out of the thin air. The towering trees into which he had crashed the *Drake* had been left behind as the rain drifted into a thick and clinging fog. The higher they climbed, the more the trees shrank, until Sulu found himself walking through a shoulder-high cloud forest whose shrubs were webbed with flowering epiphytes and hanging streamers of violet moss.

Along the jagged crest of the ridge, even the shrubs thinned out in places to barren scars of talus and stone. Chekov turned off the buffalo trail and headed for the nearest of those clearings. Sulu followed him, so intent on keeping pace despite his aching lungs that he barely noticed when the other man came to a sudden halt. Chekov threw out a warding hand, but it was too late. Sulu had already run into what felt like a curving wall of solid metal, even though all he saw ahead of him was air.

"I probably should have mentioned that I left the cloaking device on." Although Chekov didn't sound particularly remorseful about his omission.

Sulu stepped back, rubbing at the sore spot on his forehead, which had taken the brunt of the unexpected impact. "It wouldn't have mattered, since I wouldn't know a cloaking device if it hit me. Which," he added dryly, "it apparently just did."

"It didn't hit you, *you* hit it." Chekov was tapping some kind of code into a small hand-held device. "And technically, it wasn't the cloaking device you hit. It was the shuttle."

Sulu opened his mouth to say something in reply, but a sudden metallic ripple in the air above him made him curse and duck away involuntarily. A parabolic wing materialized so close overhead that it seemed as if he should have somehow sensed its presence, followed by a familiar blunt-nosed fuselage with a darkened cockpit window. With an involuntary shudder that made his sweaty uniform tunic feel clammy and cold, Sulu recognized one of the alien fighters that had chased him.

"It's a Gorn ship," Chekov said, once again reading Sulu's silent reaction with unexpected shrewdness. "Equipped with a Romulan-designed cloaking device to make it invisible, just like all the others. We sacrificed the *Hotspur* to bring it down, so we could use it to infiltrate Tesseract Fortress with our last pulse bombs."

Sulu frowned, remembering the violent explosion he had materialized into. "I think maybe I saw that attack."

"I *know* you did," the older man retorted. "It's the only reason I'm still alive. The Gorn assumed your shuttle was the attack ship. If they'd realized it was one of their own cloaked fighters, they could easily have brought me down by cross-firing their energy disruptors." He clambered up onto one wing and levered open the opaque cockpit window, then swung himself down into the interior and promptly vanished. "It tells you everything you need to know about the Gorn that they don't bother to make their own ships immune to their weapons," said his muffled voice from inside. "And that they don't believe in sitting down when they fly. Can you make it in?"

"I think so." Despite his younger muscles, it still took Sulu two tries to haul himself up the slippery polymer surface of the fighter's sleek wing. He finally wriggled up on his belly far enough to clamp his fingers around the edge of the open hatch, then hung gasping there for a moment, peering down inside. The aura of dreamlike unreality that kept washing over him on this planet came flooding in stronger than ever when he saw the Gorn cockpit. Chekov sat on a bare metal floor, strapping blocks of wood to his muddy boots so he could reach the controls, which were arranged in a half-circle high under the translucent cockpit window. There was no rudder, no screens or instrument gauges, only a few rows of switches and several indented hollows that must be hand-activated flight or weapons controls.

"Get in," said the older man. "There's plenty of room—the Gorn are a lot bigger than we are." He stood, balancing himself on his makeshift stilts with surprising ease. "Wedge yourself in or you'll get a close-up view of the warp core when we accelerate. The Gorn also don't bother to insulate their cockpits from their engine compartments."

"How nice." Sulu heaved himself over the rim and dropped several feet down to an unpadded metal floor. "It doesn't look like they bother to soundproof either."

Chekov fished the cockpit cover closed with a long branch, then pulled on a black helmet marked with the same wire-thin Starfleet insignia that he wore on his uniform collar. "There are more of our helmets in back. They generate sound-damping fields, but there's nothing they can do about the subsonic reverb."

Sulu hunted around until he found the helmets Chekov had mentioned, wedged against a strut support near the Gorn shuttle's left wing. One was a little too small for him, but the other fit perfectly—so perfectly, in fact, that it felt as if it were made for him. Sulu was suddenly reminded that when Chekov had first responded to his anonymous distress signal, he had called for him by name. And by title.

"This ship, the *Hotspur,* that you came here on—" he began, but Chekov was already flipping switches. The Gorn shuttle's engines coughed to life behind him, wobbling up to an unbalanced and deafening roar before the helmet's sound-dampening fields threw a muffled veil of artificial silence over the noise. Sulu cleared his throat and was startled to find he couldn't hear that sound, either. He guessed that advanced communicator technology had learned to distinguish voices from other sounds. "Chekov?"

"Yes?" The Russian-accented voice somehow sounded more familiar when it was separated from the older man's scarred presence, as if it could still belong to that diffident young ensign back on Tlaoli.

"The ship you came here on as second-in-command, the *Hotspur*—" Sulu said again. "Who was her captain?"

The silence that followed his question vibrated with more than just the silent subsonic reverberations of the Gorn shuttle's roar. "You were," Chekov said brusquely. "Until you died today in Tesseract Fortress."

"That's it! Just kick off and fall—you've got a good ten meters!"

Sanner's voice drifted cheerfully over the sunny plain, as unaffected and natural as if it were the song of some native bird. Chekov envied his easy nature. The geologist stood at the foot of one of the towering karst erratics with his head tipped back and his weight thrown into the rope he had looped around behind him. Above him, Kirk dangled on the other end of the line, effortlessly rappelling himself down the rock face in long, lazy arcs. They might have been a father and son on vacation, instead of a quirky Starfleet geologist and a temporally displaced civilian boy.

Sanner grinned at Chekov as he drew near. "Hey, Ensign! Want to give it a try?"

Even without the hours underground and the long morning of hiking, the suggestion would have made his stomach curl. "I've already had enough climbing on rocks for this mission, sir." But he added, "Thank you," anyway, so that Sanner wouldn't be offended.

The geologist laughed so heartily that Chekov suspected he'd asked only because he'd thought the reaction would be worth it. Hopping to one side, Sanner made room for Kirk as the boy dropped the last few meters to the ground. "Too bad we didn't have Jim here when we were making that stupid human pyramid." He tossed aside the rope only to catch the pair of gloves Kirk underhanded in his direction. "He's a natural."

"I did a little rock climbing before." Kirk tried to sound casual as he unbuckled the leather harness, but Chekov recognized that faint redness in his cheeks. He felt the same thrill of embarrassed pleasure every time a commanding officer complimented him, however slightly. "Me and my brother went to Yosemite on an Outward Bound trip a couple of years ago."

"Next time you go," Sanner told him, "hit some of the really big South American caves. You'll give all your rock climbing gear a good workout, and get to see some great flowstone to boot."

"Sounds great." Kirk let the harness drop to the ground, then used one foot to kick it up into his hands as though totally unaware of the strength and athleticism involved in the movement. Maybe he was. "Thanks, Zap."

Sanner accepted the gear with a smile. "Pleasure's all mine." Then he cocked a nod toward Chekov as he stooped to begin pulling in the rope. "I'll take care of this stuff. You go on with Mr. Chekov." Another puckish grin made his eyes twinkle. "Next time, I'll take you *under*ground."

Chekov waited until they were out of Sanner's earshot to comment, "I should have come with you. It looks like you had more fun."

Kirk wrinkled his nose as he swiped at the dust on the knees of his pants. "That science stuff can get so boring. I'd rather be doing something." He straightened. "So—did they figure out if you were your own evil twin?"

Chekov nodded. "I was apparently switched for another version of myself, just like you and Mr. Sulu." He couldn't believe he said it so calmly. The chill that had set in when Spock first declared him five hours too young hadn't faded. In fact, he felt like he'd been dunked in frigid water, and wondered if he'd ever be warm again. "It's strange," he said, after what seemed a very long time. "I don't feel any different—I don't feel like I'm not *me*. But I almost drowned yesterday when we first came down to the planet, and now Mr. Spock tells me that I probably *did* drown in some parallel timeline. I wouldn't be here right now if the alien transporter hadn't shifted me by a few hours...." He stole a glance at Kirk, then looked away again when he found the boy's expression self-consciously blank and unreadable. "Maybe it's easier to accept when the gap between then and now is bigger."

Kirk didn't look up from where he kicked a rock ahead of him as they walked. "It isn't." He didn't say anything for a time, then asked, with that same studious neutrality, "Are they going to make you go back?"

The question wasn't what Chekov had expected. "I don't know," he admitted, oddly bothered by the thought. "The device only moved me a few hours, so it's hard to tell how much impact—if any—it had on the timeline."

"But if they found out it had some big impact? Like—" The boy lifted one shoulder in an awkward shrug, his brows knitting with frustration as he struggled to express what he was thinking. "Like some other guy was supposed to get your job after you died, and he went on to be some important admiral who did all kinds of important things. Would they make you go back then?"

"I..." Chekov clenched his jaw on the facile answer that wanted to spring out of him. *No, of course they wouldn't send me back. I'm a part of this crew—I'm allowed to be here.* But if Spock was right, he was really part of some other crew, some other timeline, with no more right to continue than Kirk or Captain Sulu. The fact that he couldn't remember the details of his removal didn't grant him any special dispensation. In the end, all he could say was, "I don't know. I'd like to think that I would do what was right for everyone involved, but I really don't know."

"Even if you knew you were just going back there to die?"

Something in the boy's tone made Chekov pull him to a stop and face him. "No one's going to send you back in time just to die. It's because our timeline says that you lived and became a successful starship commander that we're trying to figure out how to send you back at all."

Kirk lifted stark eyes to the young Russian's face. "Then maybe I didn't come from your timeline."

Chekov let go of his arm, but didn't step away. "What was happening before you came here?" He tried to make the question sound casual, but couldn't ignore the fear stirring behind the boy's fierce expression. Troubled waters beneath a fragile, icy surface.

"I was riding in a shuttle..."

Chekov nodded. "That's what you said before."

"No—" Kirk cut him off impatiently, pressing on as though afraid of what would happen if he stopped. "I mean I was riding in a shuttle full of security commandos." He looked to one side and heaved a deep, steadying breath. This time, Chekov didn't interrupt. "For the last nine months or so, my dad's been stationed at the embassy on Grex." He gave Chekov permission to speak by flicking a glance in his direction. "Do you know about Grex?"

He didn't know if the name referred to a planet or a government or a space station. Whichever it was, Chekov didn't recognize it, so he only shook his head and let Kirk continue.

"They're kind of midrange on the Richter Scale of Cultures." Having something to explain seemed to calm Kirk a little, steady him. *I'd rather be doing something,* he'd told Chekov earlier. "Like they use hydrocarbon fuels and they use radio and stuff, but they never went atomic. Anyway, for a long time they were an Orion slave republic."

"They had extensive unmined dilithium deposits?" Chekov guessed. It wouldn't have been the first time the Orions took advantage of a less advanced civilization. They were thieves more than villains, basically shrugging off whatever primitive defenses the locals could muster as they stripped the planet of any resources they found desirable. Every now and then they would actually interact with the natives and make them into an Orion version of a "republic." More often, though, they left as inexplicably as they had arrived, leaving a barren, shell-shocked population behind them.

"This time it was just their location," Kirk said. "The Orions were using the planet as a waypoint for their pirating fleet. You know—storage, refueling, R and R." He started walking again, but more slowly this time, as though picking his way through dangerous territory. "The Federation wouldn't do anything about it, because Grex isn't a Federation member, and the Orions are their own government, and we can't go sticking our noses into their business all the time." Chekov thought he heard echoes of someone else's voice in the boy's bitter commentary. "So at some point, the Grexxan natives got hold of an Orion subspace transmitter and called the Federation for help." He gave a surprisingly cynical snort. "I guess we can butt into the Orions' business as long as somebody else asks us."

"How did you get there?" Chekov asked.

"My dad was with the peacekeeping force that chased off the Orions. He stayed to run security for the embassy. About a year in, he figured it was safe enough to bring me and my mom and brother out to stay with him for a while."

He fell abruptly silent. Chekov waited while they passed into the shadow of another tall karst column and the dry Tlaoli breeze chased little brush tangles across their path. By then, the silence had stretched too long and hard and painful to endure. "It wasn't safe, though," Chekov finally ventured. "Was it?"

Kirk didn't answer right away, and Chekov thought for a moment that he'd breached the line he'd promised himself he wouldn't cross—he'd treated Kirk like a child, and wrested away control of the conversation like every other impatient adult. But instead of pulling away, the boy only shook his head slowly and sank back to lean on the wall of stone. "One of the native groups got a bunch of weapons out of the stashes the Orions left behind." His voice was steadier now, almost without emotion. "I don't know their names, or what they're fighting about, or any of the political stuff that's going on. But I guess the Orions kept them from fighting with each other for thirty or forty years, and now that the Orions are gone they want to pick up where they left off." His hands, trembling like small, frightened animals, crept into his pockets of their own volition, without his even glancing down. "They started shooting each other in the streets, and shooting the Federation personnel. They had maybe half the city torn up, then they started in on the embassy. My dad and his men were shoving us onto transports just to get us off the ground. There's a ship, the *Eliza Mae,* that's supposed to show up for a supply run in another day or so. We figured we could all stay in orbit, where we ought to be safe, and wait for her." He swallowed hard, like he was swallowing a rock. "I was on a ship with a bunch of the security guys. They shot us down while we were still over the city—I don't know how, they're not supposed to have anything that can do that. But they breached the shuttle as soon as we touched down, and Lieutenant Maione told me to get out and run." The first sparkle of tears pooled in his eyes. "I should have stayed with them."

Chekov didn't have to ask what had happened to the security squad. "You couldn't have done anything."

"I should have stayed with them," he insisted fiercely. "You're not supposed to just leave people who are fighting for you! You're not supposed to leave them behind!"

"It was their job to protect you. They would rather you were away and safe."

"Only I'm not! I wasn't! I didn't know which way to go, and there was so much fighting back toward the embassy. I tried to find my dad, but they caught me! They caught me before I even got ten blocks, and they..."

He dragged the back of his hand across his eyes, but even the sleeves of his neat civilian tunic couldn't catch the tears suddenly spilling over onto his cheeks. He bit his lip to keep from sobbing, then bent almost double to hide his face in his hands.

Chekov recognized that fear only too well, understood how it could strip you naked without warning and leave you feeling weak and helpless even after you were hours and hours away. "They killed you." Just to say it, he had to swallow down the knot of nausea that had suddenly curdled in the pit of his stomach.

The boy dropped his hands away from his face, but didn't straighten. "He had the rifle right in my face. I could see blood on the barrel where he'd shot other people, and it smelled like oil and burned sulfur...." When he finally looked up, the pain on his face was so naked, Chekov had to blink back his own tears of sympathy. "That's where this machine sent your captain." Remorse and fear and confusion braided his voice into an agony. "I know he's great and all, and he's supposed to get the whole universe out of trouble, and I'm sorry I ran away from the shuttle and put everybody in this mess—but I don't see how he could have got out of that. This machine sent him back there and killed him." He reached across and seized Chekov's wrist like a lifeline. "And if you sent me back, it's just going to kill me, too."

# Chapter Six

THE PORTAL YAWNED before them, dim and shadowy with mist. Cold silence seemed to flow out of it, stealing away the small sounds of breath and movement that would normally have accompanied the eight-person research team that stood on its rocky threshold.

"My tricorder detects no trace of subspace activity." Spock's voice sounded deeper and more somber than usual as it broke the hush. It was midafternoon, and Tlaoli's karstlands lay windless and still under the ephemeral heat of its pale sun. "I believe it will be safe to go in through this opening."

"As long as you don't mind coming out somewhere halfway across the galaxy," muttered the irrepressible Zap Sanner to archaeologist Carolyn Palamas, who was shifting nervously beside him. Uhura gave the cave expert a repressive look. Fortunately, Spock was already moving into the shadow of the main cavern entrance and didn't notice Sanner's sarcastic comment. Palamas, however, looked even more anxious than she had before.

Uhura took a deep breath in a vain attempt to quiet her own unease, then followed the Vulcan science officer into the natural cave opening. The half-domed chamber that lay beyond the rock portal looked exactly the same now as it had twenty-four hours ago when she'd followed Captain James T. Kirk into it. Dry limestone walls, a scattering of fallen flowstone shards, a few faint fingers of mist rising from the places where the cave floor had dissolved down through to the cavern's lower level—it all looked very ordinary, as if nothing more dangerous lay beyond this chamber than a few tight cave squeezes and a narrow ledge or two. Uhura tried to recall how she had felt, coming in that very first time, but her memories were too strongly colored by the hours she'd spent after that, trapped in the darkness and cold. She reached up to thumb the igniter on her carbide helmet light, and found its downward wash of light oddly reassuring.

"Subspace activity still below detection limits," announced Spock's imperturbable voice from the darkness ahead of her. He hadn't yet turned on his own helmet lamp, but he moved with surprising confidence toward the nearest misty floor well.

"Watch where you're going, Spock," McCoy called from beside Uhura. "Jaeger said some of those holes go straight down to the cave where they found that alien force field."

"Precisely why I wish to record the subspace emissions coming through them, Doctor." Spock crouched on the lip of one open shaft and swung his bulky tricorder out into its rising plume of mist. Uhura tried to notice if the instrument caught an upward reflection of blue alien light, but all she saw were the spiky shadows she and McCoy threw across the floor as more people entered and lit carbide lights behind them. "Subspace readings appear minimal, consistent with the alien transporter having returned to low-power status."

"It could also be consistent with your tricorder starting to malfunction." Sulu crossed the cave to join the much taller Vulcan. Suited up in a neat cave jumpsuit and helmet, with his carbide light throwing concealing shadows across his lined face, the former starship captain looked remarkably like his younger self. When he spoke, however, the crisp certainty in his voice marked him as an officer long used to being in command. Spock silently acknowledged both the comment and the authority by running a systems check on his instrument.

"Internal readings show very low error levels," he said. "The magnetic shielding that I had Mr. Scott construct for our instruments appears to block out both the power-draining and subspace interference effects, just as it did for our shuttles. I believe we may proceed with caution into the cave's lower level."

Uhura glanced back at the cave entrance, where a handful of glittering carbide lights drowned out the pale glow of Tlaoli sunlight. Of the original survey party that had been trapped down here, only security guard Yuki Smith and archaeologist Carolyn Palamas had been pronounced sufficiently recovered from their ordeal to be included in this third foray into the cavern. Chekov had once again been drafted to help Smith carry their research equipment, and Sulu had insisted on joining the team, as well. Unlike young Kirk—who had been just as eager to come with them—the former starship captain had wielded enough clout to override Spock's reluctance.

"Ready, Mr. Sanner?" Uhura asked.

"Almost." The cave specialist was already stationed beside one of the larger pits in the floor, fishing a knotted rope and pitons from his equipment bag with his usual energy and enthusiasm. "I'm going to turn my carbide off once I climb down there," he said, as he hammered several pitons into the floor and knotted the rope securely around them. "I'd appreciate you guys not shining your lights down to watch me. If that force field is active, I want to have a chance to see it before it sees me."

"The human eye," Spock said, "can detect a single photon of light once it has adapted to the dark. It is one of the few physiological capabilities at which humans excel."

"Uh . . . thanks, Commander." Sanner tugged at the rope to test it, then swung himself out into the open shaft that plunged down through the thick cave floor. The glow of his light descended a few meters, then winked out abruptly. "Well, it sure seems dark down here," said his echoing voice from below.

"Wait a bit to make sure your eyes have adjusted," McCoy advised. There was a long pause, then the rope wriggled against its pitons as Sanner clambered farther down it. "Still pretty dark," he said after another moment. "And a little cold, but nothing like it was the last time we were—ouch!"

Uhura restrained herself with difficulty from leaning over to look for him. "What's the matter, Zap?"

"I climbed down into one of those damned flowstone pillars that formed beneath the solution pits up there. And now the rope's all tangled in it. . . . I'm going to have to burn some carbide after all, or I'll never make it down to the floor." A pause, a series of clicks, then Sanner called in a completely different voice, "Hey! Lieutenant, I think I can see some of that writing you wanted us to look for."

Uhura braced herself at the edge of the open shaft with her own carbide angled down into the mist. "On the pillar?"

"No, on the side of the cave." The rope moved a little more strongly, and she could see the diffuse glow of Sanner's carbide light swing back and forth like a pendulum through the dark. It looked like he was scanning his carbide glow along as much of the cave wall as he could reach. "I don't think this is a cave at all! Now that the ice has melted off, you can see that the walls are made of that same purple metal as the conduits we were in before. And those little ant-track marks are *everywhere.*"

Sulu's intent gaze met Uhura's through the rising plume of mist. Along with Spock and McCoy, he had come to crouch on the verge of the solution pit to watch Sanner below. "It could be an instruction manual for using the time transporter."

Spock lifted an ambivalent eyebrow. "Possibly, Captain. However it is just as likely to be a listing of allowable baggage limits for travelers."

"Or an advertisement for a prehistoric tourist resort," added McCoy dryly.

The rope jerked and shifted a few more times, then abruptly went slack. "Sanner?" Uhura called down the shaft.

"Don't worry, I'm still here, Lieutenant." She could see the glow of his carbide brighten in the swirling fog in the former ice cave as he glanced up toward them. "I'm on the floor now, and I'm going to turn off my carbide again. Tell everyone up there to look away. From *all* the holes," he added emphatically.

Uhura backed away from the opening in the floor, then glanced over her shoulder in time to see Chekov tug Smith away from another of the open solution holes. Sulu, McCoy, and Spock stepped away, too, turning so that their carbide lights were angled back toward the pale glow of daylight outside. There was a long, anxious silence.

"I think I see a little bit of blue force field," Sanner's muffled voice said at last. "But it seems to be confined to the top of one large flowstone mound right in the middle of the cave."

"You think that might be an alien field generator covered in a flowstone shell, like those healing chambers we saw back at the other end of the cave?" McCoy asked.

"Quite possibly, Doctor." Spock swung his shielded tricorder up across one shoulder as he prepared to follow Sanner. "I will give you a more definitive answer once I have measured its subspace emissions. Lieutenant Uhura, you and Lieutenant Palamas may descend and begin translating the alien script as soon as I have established a safety perimeter."

Uhura nodded and saw Carolyn Palamas take a reluctant step forward with her own shielded equipment, a dedicated archaeological translator with visual scanning capabilities. "And the rest of the party?"

Spock glanced across at Smith and Chekov, who had drifted back over to peek curiously down through another open pit. "I believe it will be safer to bring them down with us than to have them fall upon our heads," the Vulcan said, with what appeared to be complete seriousness. The two youngest members of the party slid back from their positions with conscience-stricken looks. "And if Doctor McCoy's surmise about that flowstone mound is correct, we will need all available hands to excavate it."

Sulu glanced down ruefully at the empty right sleeve of his cave suit. "Maybe you should have brought that young captain of yours down here, after all."

"That would have been illogical." Spock swung himself onto the knotted rope and began to descend, his deep voice echoing up through the cavern's walls. "In the event that we find enough information to begin testing the alien time transporter, young James Kirk will be the last person we send through it. However, you, Captain Sulu, may very well be the first."

The Gorn shuttle took off vertically, with a jump so overpowered that it made Sulu's teeth snap together. He barely felt the pain of his bitten lip. The shock of hearing that he was already dead on this planet, in this time, had hit him with unexpected force. It wasn't dismay or disbelief that made Sulu's breath catch in his suddenly dry throat. It was the horror of realizing that the immense explosion he had been flung into was his own funeral pyre, that he had actually witnessed the moment of his other self's death. The first grinding moments of upward acceleration passed in a shuddering blur. It wasn't until the warm metallic tang of blood filled his mouth and forced him to swallow that Sulu was reminded that *he* was still alive. And that his presence here might be something more than just an insane and inexplicable nightmare.

"I died in that explosion," he said, more to himself than to Chekov. "And at that exact instant, I was sent here from another world and time. That has to mean something."

"Not to me," Chekov's blunt voice said from the helmet speaker pressed against his ear. The white hum of sound dampeners had canceled out all other sound, but Sulu could tell from the fuzzy look of the shuttle's inner walls that it was filled with engine noise. The Russian had sunk his hands deep into the sockets that seemed to control the vessel's pitch and speed, bracing his elbows against the bottom rim of the cockpit window to steady himself as his makeshift block stilts vibrated across the bare metal floor.

Sulu wiped a trickle of blood from his chin. "Chekov, listen—the alien transporter that threw me here must have somehow known that the Sulu in this time was about to die. What if it was trying to replace him, by sending me forward in time to that exact point?"

"What if it was?" the older man answered with surprising coldness. "What good did it do for you to come here, when you don't know a damned thing about the situation? If your alien machine had really wanted to help, it would have transported my captain out of the explosion so we could plan a new way to infiltrate and destroy Tesseract Fortress."

"I can help you do that," Sulu said, stung.

There was a pause as the Gorn shuttle switched over from vertical to horizontal motion with a lurch of uncompensated G-forces. "Maybe," Chekov said after he had wrestled the awkward ship into something resembling a level flight path. "But wasting time figuring out what your alien transporter did to you twenty years ago isn't going to destroy that Gorn installation any sooner."

Sulu gritted his teeth hard, both to protect them against the fierce reverberations now shaking the shuttle's bare metal frame and to keep from snapping back at the older man. He reminded himself that this Chekov had lived through a future so ghastly that Sulu could barely imagine it. It was understandable if his priorities didn't include puzzling out the mystery of Sulu's appearance here, much less trying to get him back to his proper place and time.

With a sigh that trickled out between his teeth, the young pilot realized he would have to depend on Uhura and the crew of the *Enterprise* back on Tlaoli to figure out how to return him to his own timeline. If his crewmates had noticed his disappearance, the way they had noticed Captain Kirk's, they might already be trying to discover where he had gone. There was always a chance they would figure out how to haul him back to his own time. Until then, there was nothing Sulu could do, stranded on this hostile alien planet with one hostile fellow human, except help prevent this horrifying future from getting any worse than it already was.

"You're heading back to the Gorn Fortress now?" he asked Chekov as he felt the Gorn shuttle lurch through the minor turbulence that marked an unseen range of hills below them.

"How did you—?" The Russian's suspicious voice broke off, then resumed again with a note of something that might have been amusement if it hadn't sounded so grim at the same time. "The captain always said he lost a lot of his pilot's instincts along with his reflexes after that first time the Gorn tortured him. This must be what he meant."

Sulu repressed a shudder at this glimpse into his own unpleasant future. "What are you planning to do? Bomb the Fortress from the air?"

"We tried that before we decided to infiltrate," Chekov answered impatiently. "We threw almost every weapon the *Hotspur* had at Tesseract after our ground forces were slaughtered. It never even shook them. You—the captain—thought the Gorn's trans-space portal hub must be acting as its own shielding device, generating such a huge energy field that it warded off our attacks."

"So what's left?"

"Not much." There wasn't much left in the older man's voice, either. Even its grim tone had been leached away by sheer determination. "Just us and this shuttle."

Sulu glanced over his shoulder, bracing his feet into the vibrating metal struts of the parabolic wing, and saw the glowing darkness he'd been trying not to think about. God only knew how much subspace radiation was pouring out of that unshielded warp core, but one thing was certain. Without the layers of safety shielding, it wouldn't be hard to sabotage.

"But what about the timing? If it went off before the shuttle crashed—" Sulu wasn't even aware he was muttering out loud, until Chekov's voice answered in his ear.

"—the portal's shields would absorb most of the energy. We have to ride it down and crash just before the implosion."

Sulu craned a look up toward the man at the Gorn shuttle's primitive controls, startled again by the way he seemed able to pick unspoken thoughts out of Sulu's mind. "How did you know I was thinking about imploding the warp core?"

"Because it was what I was thinking about," Chekov said simply. "The captain and I tended to think about things the same way. Probably because I served under him for so many years."

It felt strange to have this older Chekov know him so well, when in his world he and the young Russian had barely met. But if he thought about it, he had to admit that he knew his own starship captain well enough to guess where his thoughts were going, except for those occasions where Kirk made one of his brilliant leaps of intuition that no one else could have either predicted or followed. And, oddly enough, Sulu felt as if he was beginning to know how to read this older version of Chekov in the same way. He hadn't even needed to ask, for instance, whether Chekov had realized that his plan of riding the shuttle down into the Gorn fortress meant they would both be killed in the warp core explosion. Somehow, he knew the older man understood and fully accepted the suicidal nature of his plan. That meant the only objections Sulu could raise to dissuade him would have to be pragmatic ones.

"If we implode the warp core at the same instant that we hit the fortress, you think the portal's shield will fail?"

"No, I think it will probably hold." There was emotion in Chekov's voice now, a note of distinctly Slavic irony and fatalism. "But it doesn't matter. This is the only thing left that I can think to do."

"It might not be the only thing I can think to do," Sulu pointed out.

There was a short pause in which Chekov might have snorted, although if he did the helmet's voice transmitter had edited out the wordless sound. Still, there was no doubt about the skepticism in his voice. "What could you possibly think of now that you couldn't also have thought of when we first landed here? That version of you had twenty years more experience with the Gorn."

Sulu winced, although he tried not to let his uncertainty show in his voice. "How can I know until I really see the Fortress? Maybe I won't think of anything, but all that means is that we'll have waited until sunrise and reconnoitered a little before we decide to crash and burn. Or is there some particular reason that you want to die right now?"

Sulu had meant the question to be sardonic, and he was a little surprised by the pause that followed, as if Chekov were actually mulling it over. His surprise deepened at the note of bitter amusement coloring the Russian's voice when he finally spoke. "I always want to die right now. But there's no particular reason to hurry." He lifted one shoulder in an abbreviated shrug. "I suppose since I've waited this long to do it, another few hours won't kill me."

His last words sounded polished by use, like an old joke that had been repeated so often over the years it had become more of a motto than a punch line. Sulu wondered who had first dissuaded Chekov from committing suicide by tweaking his sense of humor and irony with that phrase. His own older self? It sounded like something he would say, but after seeing what this dismal future of torture and warfare had done to the enthusiastic young ensign he'd met on Tlaoli, Sulu wasn't even sure if he would recognize the captain he had supposedly become in this time and place.

Chekov swung the Gorn shuttle around in a jerky curve that made Sulu's teeth clack together again, this time snapping down on the soft inner skin of one cheek. He reclenched his jaws, this time being careful to speak between them. "Don't the Gorn believe in inertial dampeners?"

"They're from a much higher-gravity planet than Earth."

The shuttle lurched again, then settled into what seemed to be a circular holding pattern. The curving turns were still too fast and uncompensated to be restful, and Sulu carefully levered himself to his feet. "How many hours do we have to wait for sunrise?"

"About three."

Sulu nodded to himself. "That should be enough time," he muttered, this time intending Chekov to overhear. He wondered if the older man would be able to guess at his meaning again, but the Russian glanced down from his stilt-elevated height with a puzzled frown.

"Enough time for what?"

"For you to teach me how to fly this shuttle."

"Last panel, Carolyn," Uhura said. "Are you ready?"

"Ready." The blond archaeologist tapped a command into her translator that made its lights blink amber and red, then let it go so Uhura could begin hauling it up with the rope and pulley system they had fashioned for it. Not all of the purple-black metallic walls of the alien transporter chamber had writing on them, but the ones that did were inscribed from floor to ceiling with rows of ricelike script. In many places, curtains of translucent calcite had built up over the texts, and Sanner had to clamber up and down them wielding his rock hammer to remove the travertine. There was nothing they could do about the dark streaks of oxidation and tension fractures that had cut through other parts of the inscriptions. Uhura just hoped those missing sections didn't contain the most crucial information about Tlaoli's time transporter.

It had taken them over an hour to scan the nine panels of intricate runic script, and during that time Uhura had kept an apprehensive eye on the archaeological translator's power levels. They had brought chemical batteries with them as a backup, but she wasn't sure how many of the scans they would have to redo if they lost the instrument's original dilithium power cell. But so far, the portable magnetic shielding Spock had designed and Chief Engineer Scott had installed on all their instruments seemed to be holding power fluctuations and subspace interference at bay. The dedicated translator's processing unit had been humming away since the first panel was scanned, performing the trillions of cross-correlations it took to decipher a completely unknown alien language.

To Uhura's surprise, it had taken Spock and his work crew far less time to crack off the thick rind of flowstone that had built up around the alien transporter unit through uncounted millennia of being dripped on by runoff from the natural caves overhead. When it was freed from its crystalline chrysalis, the alien device was surprisingly simple to look at: a dozen interlaced and gyroscopically curved ellipses around a hollow inner space. With the travertine coating chipped away, the blue glow Sanner had been able to see only in total darkness settled down into a fierce sapphire flame visible even when all their carbide lights were turned toward it. Despite its increased brightness, the alien light seemed content to remain inside its dark metal cage for now, even when the Vulcan science officer deliberately set a spare dilithium cell next to it and watched its power leach away. The force field's glow intensified a little, but didn't seem to reach any farther toward the metal edges of its generator.

"Do you think it was never supposed to go any farther than this?" McCoy asked, watching the force field from outside the circle Spock had gouged in the lime mud of the cavern floor to mark the safety perimeter. "Maybe all that rock around it distorted the force field into reaching out farther than it was supposed to."

"I do not yet know enough about the device to draw any definite conclusions, Doctor," the Vulcan replied. "The force field has not seemed to change shape since we first removed the travertine from around it, but it is possible that the power required to charge it is so great that a single drained dilithium cell makes no detectable difference. I am loathe to let it drain any more cells before we have obtained more information on exactly what it might be doing."

Uhura lowered the translating device down across the last rows of inscribed letters, then swung it back toward Palamas. "Did it get everything scanned into its graphic memory?"

The archaeologist watched the data scroll across the translator's small screen. "All except for that crack across the top. I'll start the final semantic correlation as soon as these phonemes are done processing." She glanced across at Uhura. "We'll have to make an initial guess at gross linguistic structure to get the analysis started. You're the language expert. . . . What do you think?"

Uhura peered up at the rows of variably slanted rice grains that rose into darkness above them. At first glance, their similarity to primitive hieroglyphics invited her to see pictures in their geometric patterns, but the even spacing between groups warned her that it couldn't be that simple.

"Not pictorial," she said. "I'd guess phonetic, but perhaps based more on varying throat vibrations than lip and mouth sounds."

"All right." Palamas programmed their choice into the translator, then placed it down on the ground between them. "Now, all we can do is wait."

Uhura glanced over her shoulder, hearing a familiar emphatic voice rising from the other side of the cave.

"—first saw the field, it was all the way out to *here*." Sanner stamped on the small rise in the floor where Kirk and Chekov had been standing when they vanished. "And even after that first transport, it kept expanding, Commander. It sure looked to me like the power level was increasing."

"That would have been over an hour after it drained power from the *Enterprise*," Spock observed, "which implies a significant internal delay in the power storage rate."

"But the cave seemed to get colder almost instantaneously when we were firing our phasers in it," Uhura pointed out. "If Mr. Sanner is right about the power storage reaction being endothermic, shouldn't we have seen a delay in the temperature change, as well?"

The Vulcan lifted both eyebrows, a rare sign of appreciation for a particularly cogent point. "Indeed, Lieutenant. Let us assume that both those data points are valid. What does that tell us about the power consumption of this device?"

"That it processes in-phase energy more easily than out-of-phase energy," blurted a Russian voice from the far side of the device. As soon as he said it, Chekov looked as if he had startled even himself with that deduction, and he took a backward step that made him bump into Yuki Smith.

Spock's eyebrows might have gone up just a fraction further, but he acknowledged the young ensign's contribution without any other hint of surprise. "Precisely, Mr. Chekov. The fact that the alien device was able to absorb our transporter beam shows that it is designed to accept large inputs of energy from space. But the rapid processing of your much smaller phaser bursts suggests that its energy receptors are optimized for phase-aligned rather than frequency-distributed energy."

McCoy's carbide light emphasized the downward curve of his scowl, making him look more aggravated than he probably was. "Speak English, Spock. What does that mean for us?"

The Vulcan drummed his fingers on his tricorder, as if he disliked being pushed into making a conclusion on such limited data. After a moment, however, he sighed. "That we can probably control the device's power needs by hitting it with precisely timed phaser bursts from the *Enterprise*."

There was a moment of echoing silence, broken by Sulu's calm voice. "Then are we ready to send the first test subject through this gate?"

"Hardly, Captain," said the Vulcan. "We still have no idea for what ultimate purpose this machine was designed, much less how to control and program it. If you stepped into this force field now, it might send you to a time period in your own past, rather than the future from which you came. We would then add another layer of time paradoxes to the ones which we are currently struggling to undo." He swung around, away from the fiery blue heart of the alien device and toward Uhura and Palamas. "Have we made any progress in translating the texts on these walls, Lieutenants?"

"Yes, sir." Palamas lifted the heavy translator and swung it forward so all of them could see the green status lights blinking to mark the completion of its program. "The bad news is that we only got a sixty-five percent correlation on this first run. We might be able to improve that by refining our linguistic analysis, but it could also be because of the missing parts of the text."

"Understood," said Spock.

Palamas handed the translator over to Uhura. "We requested a summary for each panel," Uhura said, and scrolled down through the output. "Panel one summarizes the geologic and biologic history of this planet, with a lot of emphasis on the fact that its natural resources had to be utterly depleted to cope with continued attacks from a powerful enemy empire. It seems to be almost an ethical defense of this civilization's treatment of their homeworld, in case the universe ever called them to account for it. The second and third panels summarize all the major battles and campaigns of this interstellar war, which lasted for approximately—"

She paused for a moment, frowning at the translator screen in disbelief. "This can't be right. It says the war lasted for seven thousand years!"

"Maybe that was one of the places where you lost some text," McCoy suggested.

"Maybe." Uhura scrolled down to the next translator entry. "The fourth and fifth panel might be ones we need to read in detail. The translator found them hard to summarize, because they contain a lot of numbers and equations and references to quantum subspace magnetism." She glanced curiously up at Spock. "I didn't think magnetic fields existed in subspace."

"According to our latest subspace field theories, they do not," the Vulcan said. "But most subspace physicists would agree that our current theories are neither complete nor entirely correct. What do the other panels deal with?"

Uhura read through the next description once, blinked, then read through it a second time to make sure she hadn't misunderstood. "Panels six and seven seem to be another list of battles, very similar to the ones listed on panels two and three. But the translator seems to think that these battles were somehow fought a second time, in an attempt to alter their original outcome."

McCoy whistled softly. "They discovered time travel," he said. "I bet *that's* what all those subspace magnetic field equations were about. And once they could travel in time, they went back and tried to intervene in their own history."

"They must have been losing the war," Palamas said.

"Or winning in such a way that it wasn't worth the cost," Sulu added in a grim voice.

"Did it work?" asked Yuki Smith. "Did they save their civilization?"

Uhura scrolled down to the next panel, then shook her head. "It doesn't look like it. Panel eight says that their enemies also began crossing through time, striking blows in places where they weren't expected. Then it describes a desperate phase in the war, when the aliens were so low on combatants and stretched across so many fronts in time that they began to recycle their soldiers through time. As each soldier healed up from battle injuries, they were sent back through time to the point where they'd been injured, so they could continue fighting that battle a little longer. The injured version they replaced was brought back here to be healed and sent out again." She glanced up from the translator, frowning. "By the end, it says they had only a few hundreds of soldiers, each one fighting almost alone on a different battlefield in time."

"So they lost the war?" Smith asked mournfully.

"Yes." Uhura scrolled down to the ninth and last panel summary.

"There were still civilians left on this planet, though. The last panel says they used their regular time-traveling devices to escape into the far distant future, setting the machinery to self-destruct behind them so their enemies couldn't track them down. But they left behind this Janus Gate on purpose. The last part of the panel explains that the natives wanted to give this technology to whatever spacefaring race came to the planet after them, in recompense for exhausting all of this world's natural resources."

There was a long silence after she was done. Sulu was the first to break it. "The Janus Gate?" he asked, curiously.

Uhura looked to Carolyn Palamas for help, and the archaeologist sighed. "This translator is programmed to provide mythopoetic equivalents wherever appropriate," she explained. "It's meant to give us a sense of the larger cultural connotations raised when a modern civilization deliberately uses an archaic myth or god as a name for something. In this case, the name of the Roman god of gates and doorways is clearly meant to invoke—"

"The ability to travel forward and backward in time," Spock finished for her. "A bit ethnocentric, Lieutenant, is it not? You could have chosen the name of the ancient Vulcan goddess who presided over the opening and closing of festivals—"

"I don't care if we name it after Woody Woodpecker!" McCoy burst out. "I want to know what we're going to do with it now that we know what it was for."

"Use it, of course." The Vulcan turned his head to regard the older version of Sulu with an unblinking regard. "I presume you are willing to be returned to your battle, now that you have been healed, Captain Sulu?"

"More than willing," Sulu said. "Just as long as you give me something I can use to blow myself up as soon as I get there."

# Chapter Seven

SUNRISE ARRIVED with unexpected violence on Basaraba. The mists that filled the hollows between the planet's cloud-forested ridges curdled up into massive thunderheads just before dawn, and the occasional rain showers Sulu had torn through as he painfully learned how to pilot the Gorn shuttle merged and thickened into a downpour. Lightning flashed across the graying sky, each time leaving it a little brighter than before, as if the sky had to be hacked apart to admit the rising sun. Sulu's sound-dampening helmet drowned out the rolls of thunder that presumably followed, just as it muffled the drumming of rain on the shuttle's uninsulated hull. But he knew the storm was peaking when the Gorn shuttle's parabolic wings began to catch and twist in the churning turbulence. Sulu let the ship flit upward with each gust of wind, then allowed gravity to drift it back into place without ever needing to apply a blast from its overpowered warp engines.

"You already fly this thing better than I do." Chekov's transmitted voice put no more emotion into that praise than he had put into any of the criticisms he'd made when Sulu was first getting the hang of the hand-manipulated flight controls. The Russian hadn't objected to teaching him how to fly the Gorn shuttle, although Sulu wasn't sure if he'd done it for tactical reasons or just because he was bored at the prospect of spending three hours hovering in darkness before immolating himself. "I think I'll let you take it into the Fortress."

"You think crashing it will take a lot of piloting ability?"

His helmet communicator didn't transmit Chekov's snort, but Sulu could feel the gust of air against the back of his neck. The older man had strapped on a second pair of block stilts so he could share the clear cockpit dome that had been designed to fit around one larger Gorn skull. He craned his head past Sulu now, peering through the staccato flash of light-ning toward the Gorn fortress. They could just see its towers and out-spread ramparts emerging in the distance, a darker blotch against the predawn charcoal wash of forest and sky.

"No, I meant right now, when we go in to reconnoiter. You remember what not to do?"

The question was so curt it sounded hostile, but Sulu had grown used to the older man's teaching style by now. "Don't leave a wake trail that one of their shuttles could use to track us," he answered promptly. "I'll go in low enough for our wake to feel like thermal updrafts from the ground."

"What else?"

"No sudden blasts of acceleration that might set off their ion detec-tors. No passes close to open windows where they might feel our draft."

"What else?"

Sulu racked his brain to think of other ways the Gorn shuttle could be detected despite the Romulan-designed cloaking device that Chekov as-sured him couldn't be picked up by sensor or by sight. If all it cloaked was the sound of its own warp engines—

"No breaking the sound barrier?" Sulu guessed.

"Right. And what speed is that on this planet?"

Sulu opened his mouth, then closed it again. There were too many variables of air temperature, density, and composition for him to estimate it. "I don't know."

"I don't, either," Chekov admitted. "But it seems to be a little higher than Mach 1. Stay under the limit you know and you'll be fine."

"Yes, sir," Sulu said and felt another puff of air hit his neck from Chekov's unheard snort. The first time he'd addressed the older man as the superior officer he actually was, Sulu had felt Chekov silently shaking at his back. It had taken him a while to realize that with his face so badly scarred, the Russian couldn't let his laughter out any other way. Even now, after hours of hearing it, the honorific still seemed to amuse his companion. "Should we go now?"

Chekov glanced back at the eastern horizon. The worst of the storm had passed, opening up a slash of silver-blue sky behind it, but rain still splattered down from above them. "Let's wait until the sky clears all the way overhead. I'm not sure how well the visual deception screens can mimic rain when we're flying through it."

Sulu nodded and kept the shuttle in its low-altitude hover until the last of the clouds had scudded past. A golden gleam of sunlight spilled over the encircling ridges and touched the top of the tallest Gorn tower. Its silhouette looked clean and stark against the storm clouds, showing no trace of damage from the explosion that had rocked it the previous day.

"Why do you call it Tesseract Fortress?" Sulu asked Chekov, mostly to break the silence that felt like it was slowly coiling into a tense knot. The Russian didn't seem to notice it as much. When he answered, his voice in Sulu's helmet sounded almost relaxed.

"It was the closest English word Uhura could find to match what the Gorn called it. You know what a tesseract is?"

"A four-dimensional cube."

"Uhura said the Gorn name for this place was ambiguous—one part of it meant 'multiple dimensions,' another part meant either 'enclosure' or 'entrapment.' We needed to call it something, and Tesseract seemed as good a name as any."

Sulu glanced down at the shuttle's minimal control board. All the primitive knobs and levers there controlled the warp engines and the Romulan cloaking device. There was a speaker panel that occasionally startled him with a burst of growled-out Gorn commands but no way to alter the frequency it was set at or to speak back through it. The Gorn apparently saw no need for their fighter pilots to report in, or to know anything more than they chose to tell them. "You listened in on the Gorn's communications?"

"From the *Hotspur.*" Chekov's voice rasped with a faint tinge of what might have been disgust. "Uhura did most of that. Neither Sulu nor I can listen to Gorn for long without throwing up. It's an aftereffect of the drugs they used when they tortured us back in '78." He paused. "I probably shouldn't have told you that."

"Why not?" Sulu asked dryly. "It doesn't look as if I'm going to live long enough to have it happen to me."

"But that can't be right," Chekov said slowly, as if the time paradox had just occurred to him. "If you don't live through this and get back to your own time, how can I remember you being my captain?"

Sulu gritted his teeth against an urge to remind the other man that *he'd* been the one who'd cut off any attempt to discuss this question a few hours ago. "I don't know," Sulu said. "Maybe we're not from the same dimension of reality. You and I remember two completely different captains on the *Enterprise.*"

"True." Chekov paused again. "Do you still want to help me destroy Tesseract Fortress, even if this isn't your own reality?"

"Yes," Sulu said before he could even think about it. A moment later, he realized where that instinctive agreement came from. "I swore an oath when I was commissioned as a Starfleet officer, to protect and defend the Federation. That oath is just as binding here as anywhere else."

"In this reality," Chekov said grimly, *"nothing* would protect the Federation more than destroying Tesseract Fortress."

\*  \*  \*

"Phasers locked on target," said a crackling Scottish voice through Uhura's communicator unit. Magnetic shielding might keep their equipment powered up and operating smoothly, but there was nothing it could do about the interference Tlaoli's strange energy fields injected into the subspace continuum between them and the ship. "Awaiting your order, Commander."

"Fire when ready," said Spock calmly.

Uhura stood on tiptoe in an attempt to see past the Vulcan, but Sulu and McCoy stood shoulder to shoulder behind him, blocking the entrance to the Janus Gate. Just as they had after losing Captain Kirk, the entire caving team had retreated for safety into the alien conduit system that connected this chamber to the other parts of the Tlaoli caves. One previous phaser strike had already turned the air inside the transport chamber colder, making the mist condense back into an icy rind across the walls. The alien light that burned inside the transporter device had deepened to the intense cobalt blue of a photon emission laser, but there was still no sign of the drifting light curtains that had filled the room the first time they had been here.

"Firing," said Chief Engineer Scott. A second later, Uhura felt the ground around her shake with the impact of the ship's powerful weapons. A wave of bitter cold seemed to wash past them without any gust of wind, leaving Uhura almost breathless with the effort it took to breathe the suddenly frigid air. A few moments later, rock fell with a clatter somewhere in the travertine-lined conduit behind her.

"I think we're losing some ceiling integrity back here," called Sanner's muffled voice from farther down the conduit. "You guys better keep your helmets on."

McCoy snorted. "Spock, do you think we could set the phasers to stun those rocks rather than kill them?"

The Vulcan glanced over his shoulder, and Uhura was startled to see that his sharply angled eyebrows had turned white with frost. "So far, we have not even succeeded in expanding the alien force field past its metal containment walls," he said. "The amount of energy required to recharge the transporter may well exceed the structural strength of the overlying rock deposits."

"But, Mr. Spock, it already seems much colder in here than it did when we lost Captain Kirk." The temperature-sensitive nano-fibers in Uhura's caving suit had expanded to their maximum thickness, but she could still feel the cold biting at her skin. "The light from the force field is brighter, too."

Chekov cleared his throat in the shadows behind her. "That could be because we took off its flowstone cover, Lieutenant."

"Or because I'm right and the force field is *supposed* to stay inside the transporter device." McCoy poked Spock in the shoulder, and Uhura saw the tall Vulcan wince. "Come on, Spock, admit I could be right for once."

The Vulcan looked back at the brilliant sapphire fire whose glittering reflections danced off all the chamber's ice-sheathed walls. "Your hypothesis is gaining credibility, Doctor," he admitted. "But according to my calculations, we have so far charged the device with only thirty percent of the energy it was able to drain from the *Enterprise*. Unless we can establish that it was overcharged before, or that its travertine shell deformed its force field in the past, we cannot know what the current status of the Janus Gate device truly represents."

There was a silence, full only of the raspy breathing of eight people trying not to draw in too much of the ice-cold air. Then, from one side, Uhura heard a tentatively cleared throat.

"Commander Spock," said Yuki Smith. "Do you think maybe those blinking lights over there could help us figure that out?"

The Vulcan scanned the entire chamber, his lean face silhouetted by its steady cobalt glow. "I do not observe any blinking lights, Mr. Smith. Where do you perceive them to be?"

"Reflected off that back wall over there." The security guard shouldered past Chekov and Sanner to point the way. Uhura tried to peer in the direction she indicated, but the fiery sapphire glare of the Janus Gate was all she could see reflected in the ice-sheathed wall. Yuki Smith's initial confidence seemed to deflate a little beneath their baffled looks. "Maybe I'm just not seeing things right because I'm color-blind. But it still looks to me like something's blinking—"

Spock gave the security guard a thoughtful look, then lifted his tricorder and angled it in the direction she had pointed. After a moment, he glanced at the screen and gave a single, decisive nod. "Something is indeed blinking back there, Mr. Smith. But it is blinking in a yellow-green wavelength that to our eyes is completely obscured by the cyan emissions of the force field. Thank you for bringing it to my attention."

"You're welcome, sir." Smith fell back beside Chekov, giving him a surreptitious punch as if to say "I win." Uhura had just enough time to see the young Russian grimace in response before her attention was torn away by a sharp protest from McCoy.

"Spock, you're not going in there!"

The Vulcan science officer paused a meter into the ice-walled chamber. "Someone needs to investigate that blinking light, Doctor," he said. "I believe I can read my own tricorder well enough to avoid stepping into a subspace rift."

Uhura took a quick and painfully cold breath, then reached out to take the archaeological translator from Carolyn Palamas. "And I think I can stay close enough behind you to be safe, too." Both McCoy and Sulu swung around to give her disapproving looks, and Uhura held the translator up in front of herself like a shield. "If that light pattern turns out to be some type of communication in the ancient Tlaoli language, we need to know what it's saying."

"I concur," Spock said, before the others could respond. "You may accompany me, Lieutenant, but be prepared to retreat quickly in the event I issue an alert."

"Aye, sir." Uhura was already prepared to retreat—it was being prepared to advance any closer to that eerie alien light that she wasn't so sure about. But by keeping her gaze fixed firmly on the icy cave floor, as if she wanted to make sure of her footing, she managed to follow Spock out into the chamber without any apparent hesitation.

The Vulcan charted a deliberate spiral path around the Janus Gate, watching his tricorder's screen closely as they approached it from behind. Uhura could hear the instrument chattering softly in the silence, and realized Spock must have activated an audible as well as visible record of the subspace instability in the room. That made it a little easier for her to follow him. As they approached the curving metal bulk of the alien transporter, the air grew so bitterly cold that Uhura could feel the inside of her throat begin to ache. She lifted her free hand up to her face and began to breath through the material of her glove.

If Spock noticed the painful chill, he gave no sign. "Subspace readings remain marginal," he said as they began to circle behind the Janus Gate. He spoke loudly enough that Uhura knew the communication was meant as much for their teammates back in the conduit as it was for her. "I am beginning to see the blinking lights that Mr. Smith detected. The source appears to be a panel attached to this side of the alien device."

"A *control* panel?" McCoy demanded, his voice echoing off the icy walls.

"Possibly, Doctor." Spock came to a halt a meter away from the dark metallic structure whose curving elliptical arms enclosed a heart of incandescent fire. He consulted with his tricorder, then glanced over his shoulder at Uhura. "There is an increased probability of subspace rifts on either side of us, Lieutenant," he said in a quiet voice designed not to carry across the chamber. "But there appears to be a safe pathway leading toward that panel. You will need to walk precisely where I do to remain inside it."

"Aye, sir." Uhura swung her bulky translator around and hugged it in front of her, to make sure it wouldn't accidentally touch a subspace rift and be torn away. Spock nodded approval, and did the same thing with his own instrument, tilting it up against his chest so he could continue to watch its subspace readings as he turned and began to approach the Janus Gate. Uhura followed him, careful to place her feet in the dark bar of his shadow. She could no longer catch a glimpse of the tricorder's flashing screen, but she could hear how its gentle chattering had slowed to an almost inaudible hum. "Are the readings getting lower, Mr. Spock?"

"Indeed, they are. I suspect we are approaching a protected station where an operator is meant to stand." Spock came to a halt in front of the panel, whose blinking green-gold lights could be seen easily from this side, and swung his tricorder around in a careful arm's-length arc. Its low hum never varied. "I believe it is safe for you to stand here with me, Lieutenant."

"Spock, are you still out there?" McCoy's voice sounded more exasperated than anxious. "If you are, could you please let us know what the blazes is going on?"

"We have reached the control panel, Doctor, and are proceeding to analyze it." Spock scanned his tricorder across the polished indigo metal with its multiple rows of rice-shaped lights. It looked very different from the dark and roughened surface of the main transporter device behind it. "I do not recall seeing anything like this when we first chipped away the flowstone mound," Spock observed. "This part of the device must have been stored for protection, and released when we began to charge the machine's energy banks."

Uhura's eyes hadn't left the intricately flashing rows of lights with their familiar ricelike shapes. "Mr. Spock, I think those lights are flashing the same kinds of phonemes we saw on the chamber's walls. If I could lift my translator up to scan them—"

Instead of moving out of her way, the Vulcan science officer lifted the bulky translator for her and held it effortlessly at shoulder height while Uhura adjusted the visual scanning rate to adjust for the strobe rate of the blinking lights. English words immediately began scrolling down the translator's main display screen, and Spock angled his head so he could read them along with Uhura.

Status Report: field strength at maximal levels, reserve power buffered at maximal capacity, field integrity optimized for (word unknown) transport. Full transfer mode engaged, viewing mode disengaged, associative transport disengaged, activity buffer (word unknown, word unknown) error in reading file.

"Fascinating," said Spock. "This certainly answers our question about whether the machine requires any more power to be input into it."

"But what do you suppose it means by viewing mode and associative transport?" Uhura asked.

"I do not yet know." Spock put out a tentative hand and touched one of the slightly raised bars on the right side of the panel. As he pressed it, the flashing lights first went dark, then began to pulse again, although this time only one of the rows was lit. Uhura glanced at the translator's display screen. *"Associative transport engaged,"* she read to Spock, whose attention was now on the alien transporter device itself. The fiery glow at its center blossomed suddenly into a paler veil of light that washed out across the entire chamber. Uhura's breath froze in her throat, and she heard a chorus of alarmed shouts from the other side of the chamber. But the blue glow splashed around the control panel as if an invisible seawall held it back, and nothing happened to her and Spock.

"We're all right!" she shouted to the rest of the team, seeing that Spock was too engrossed in his observations to bother reassuring them. "We're testing the machine's controls. Stay where you are."

"How about if we move a little farther away?" McCoy snapped. "That blue light just about nipped off my nose!"

"Undoubtedly because the appendage in question was being put where it should not have been," Spock said almost absently. Fortunately, his voice wasn't loud enough for the doctor to hear. "I believe I now understand the meaning of 'associative transport,' Lieutenant Uhura. In that mode, the subspace rift expands outward so more than just a single person can be sent to the same point in time. That would have been an advantage if the ancient Tlaoli needed to send an entire platoon of soldiers back to a battle from which a single survivor had been plucked."

"I think you're right." Uhura had finally pulled her gaze away from the billowing sea of light, and noticed that the indicator lights had added a second row of words. "The translator says, *'Power insufficient for more than fifteen (word unknown) to be conveyed.'* It can't determine if that Tlaoli measuring unit refers to weight, mass, or just amount."

"Since we do not need to transfer more than a single person back to his rightful place in time, that should not impede us." Spock pressed the second of the raised control bars, and the blue light slowly contracted again, folding itself back into the hollow center of the Janus Gate. Its sapphire glow was no longer steady, however. It had begun to flicker, not as randomly as a candle flame but in a slow visual sine wave that shifted from brighter to darker shades as it repeated itself.

" *'Viewing mode engaged,'* " Uhura read from the alien display. This time she waited to see if the control panel would add a second line to the first. After a moment, it did. *"Time and distance variation enabled."*

"Additional controls are emerging," Spock said, and Uhura glanced over to see two new vertical bars flex up beneath the panel's blue-violet metallic skin. "Viewing mode with time and distance variation . . . Perhaps this function allowed the ancient Tlaoli to select a particular time and place for transport when there were multiple crisis points from which to choose."

"That would make sense," said Sulu's voice. "Why send someone back to a hopeless situation if there was a previous point that might change that entire branch of the timeline?"

"Indeed, I agree—" Spock's voice broke off at the same moment that Uhura swung around, suddenly aware that the resonant voice of their former pilot had been much too clear to be coming from the conduit. She saw Sulu standing just outside the safety perimeter Spock had drawn in the wet lime mud of the floor, now transformed into a gleaming ring of thicker and whiter ice. He had casually slung across his shoulder the spare backpack which Sanner had loaded with all of their emergency rock explosives, and was gazing into the flickering heart of the time transporter with his odd, bittersweet smile.

"You are disregarding orders, Mr. Sulu," said the Vulcan.

"You can't give orders to a superior officer, Mr. Spock," the older man reminded him gently. "And time is running out. Are you ready to try sending me back to Basaraba?"

Spock eyed the other man for a long moment. "Assuming that we have interpreted the Janus Gate correctly and can view the future before we transport you into it . . . yes, Captain. I believe I am ready to make that attempt."

"Good." Sulu glanced around the machine. "When the field expanded a few moments ago, I noticed that there seems to be another clear space on the opposite side of this ellipse. Shall I try standing in it?"

"Yes. Be certain to walk directly in toward it from the perimeter line. You may not be *required* to obey that order," he added dryly, "but if you do not, you may encounter an errant subspace rift that will not respect your rank."

"Spock, are you sure about this?" McCoy demanded from the edge of the conduit. "If we lose this Sulu and can't get our version back again—"

"—then we will have lost only a single crewman from the *Enterprise*," the Vulcan finished bluntly. "It is a risk we must take, Doctor. We need to know how to operate this machine, so that we can return young James Kirk safely to his proper time. We have very little of our own time left in which to do so."

"And the fate of the Federation may be determined by how well we do it." Sulu walked the gleaming line of the safety perimeter until he disappeared from Uhura's view, then reappeared on the far side of the Janus Gate. In its flickering blue glow, Sulu already looked more like a ghost than a person. "Spock, I can see what looks like a set of handgrips on this side of the Gate. Should I take hold of them?"

"I would advise you to," the Vulcan replied. "They are no doubt meant to keep you within a safely protected space."

Sulu stepped forward without hesitation, lifting his left hand to wrap around one of the gleaming metal bars in front of him, then, after a moment's thought, resting his severed right wrist on the other. "It feels like it's vibrating a little," he reported after a moment. "Nothing else seems to be happening."

"That is because I have not yet engaged the controls which vary time and distance." Spock bent over the control panel again. "Lieutenant Uhura, please alert me immediately to any change in the message displays, even before you get a translation for it," he ordered. "Captain Sulu, I would like you to report continuously on what you see and feel. If you suspect at any time that you are about to be pulled into a time and place that is not Basaraba, shout an alarm. The viewing mode we are about to employ seems to be a partially disabled version of the actual Janus Gate transfer mechanism. It should be safe, but I calculate a seventeen point three percent probability that you may be transferred without my changing the settings on the device."

"Understood." Sulu braced himself a little more securely in place, stiffening his shoulders to keep his pack of rock explosives balanced on his back. Despite his rigid posture, the flickering blue light showed his creased face looking neither anxious nor determined, but actually more relaxed than Uhura could remember having seen it before. She tried once again to imagine what kind of life this Hikaru Sulu must have lived to make his final plunge through time to self-destruction a moment of tranquility and comfort, but her mind simply couldn't encompass it. Instead, she tore her gaze away from him and concentrated on watching the translator's screen for the first hint of a new message.

"I am engaging the time controls," Spock said. The force field's glow increased both in brightness and in the frequency of its flicker, and little runnels of cobalt light began to streak across the inside of the elliptical metal cage that held it confined. Uhura squashed an instinctive desire to take a step back from that glowing metal structure. She could see the quicksilver light streaks spiraling to the outside of the Janus Gate now, cutting brighter paths through its crust of oxidized metal as they went. A moment later, the handgrips Sulu held were also netted in strands of light, and the glow did not stop there. It laced itself slowly up Sulu's arms, across his shoulders, and then up like a spiderweb across his face.

"Spock, why have you sent me here?" the older man demanded sharply. "This isn't Basaraba!"

"You have gone nowhere, Captain. Despite what you may see, you are still physically present on Tlaoli."

Sulu turned his blue-netted face around, eyes open but suddenly seeming blind. "I can hear you, but I can't see anything but this ship. What ship is this? It's not the *Hotspur*—oh, God, I know it! It's that Klingon warship, the *Kerzhat,* that we served aboard as a prize crew after the battle at Mirk's World. The Klingons chased after us to destroy it, and if the *Hotspur* hadn't caught up to us again we wouldn't have made it out alive—"

"Message appearing," Uhura said urgently. "The translator says, *'Major crisis point located within five [word unknown] units of time. Question send/not send.' "*

Spock nodded, watching the lacework of blue light pulse around their former helmsman. "If I pushed the third transfer bar now, I believe the light would engulf him and cause him to vanish. I moved the time control only a tiny fraction, assuming that it had many millennia of play built into it. Let me try moving it a little more." Long Vulcan fingers moved on the control panel with intent delicacy, and the blue net of light swirled briefly around Sulu's still figure, then settled into a different braided pattern. "Where are you now, Captain?"

"At the battle of Borsdal Kren," said the older man grimly. "We almost lost the *Hotspur* to a hull breach there."

"The translator says, *'Major crisis point located within twelve [word unknown] units of time. Question send/not send.' "*

"You're getting closer." Sulu seemed a little calmer now, as if he'd realized that he wasn't really where he seemed to be. "Basaraba should be six years further into the future."

"I will attempt to calibrate as best I can." It didn't even seem to Uhura as if Spock's fingers had moved on the controls, but she could see the cobalt glitter as the net of liquid light swirled around Sulu once again. "Are you there yet?"

*"Yes."* Sulu's voice took on a suddenly hard-wrenched note. "I'm in Tesseract Keep, right where I was when they shot us down. I think I see Uhura—"

Uhura took a deep breath as she read the translator's screen. " *'Terminal crisis point located,' "* she said softly, although she wasn't sure why. It wasn't as if Sulu didn't know this was the end of his life. " *'Question send/not send.' "*

Spock's left hand moved slightly on the other control. "I am adjusting the distance controls, Captain Sulu. Where are you now?"

"Inside the corridor that leads to the portal hub!" the older man said. "I must be past the place where they caught us. I can hear shooting in the distance behind me."

"Is this a safe place to send you?" Spock inquired. Uhura gave him a baffled look—given the future Sulu was going back to, there was no such thing as a safe place to be sent—but she heard the older pilot take a deep breath of what sounded like relief as he replied.

"Yes, this is perfect. It looks like I'm beyond the main Gorn checkpoint. Even without weapons, I think I can make it all the way into the portal from here. Send me, Spock."

The Vulcan moved one hand from the vertical bars that controlled distance and time to the horizontal ones that determined whether the person on the other side merely saw a point in their future or were sent rocketing toward it. "Engaging transport mode now," was all he said.

Uhura held her breath as the blue light in the center of the Janus Gate blazed up from its subdued flicker to a phaser-bright glare. The runnels of light wrapped around Sulu suddenly expanded outward and coalesced, wrapping him in a sheath of cobalt flame . . . then abruptly flung themselves off again.

Sulu blinked once, like a man regaining his vision after seeing too bright a light, then focused on them across the steady glow of the alien force field. "I'm still here."

"Indeed," said Mr. Spock. "It appears as if the Janus Gate has decided not to send you back to your future after all."

# Chapter Eight

"How can the machine 'decide' not to send him?" McCoy leaned precariously around the edge of the conduit's mouth, squinting against the icy blue glow still filling the chamber. "Isn't sending people through time what it was built to do?"

Chekov resisted an urge to grab the doctor by the belt and drag him back around the corner to safety. He'd already had his hands slapped once for trying to politely restrain McCoy while Spock first tested the device, and had a feeling he might actually get yelled at this time if he tried to intervene. Instead, he came carefully up alongside McCoy in the entrance, where he might be in position to "accidentally" get in the way if McCoy tried to go any farther into the cavern.

"Spock, maybe you read the instructions wrong."

Uhura looked up from where she and Spock had drawn together over her translator. Chekov wasn't sure if it was anger or frustration that sharpened her normally gentle voice. "If anyone read the instructions wrong, Doctor McCoy, it was me. I was doing the translating."

"But Spock's the one twiddling the knobs."

"I do not believe anyone has made an error." The doctor's criticism made no apparent impact on the first officer. Spock's eyes never shifted from their study of the glowing console, his face beneath the wash of blue light as impassive as ever. "I believe the device functioned precisely as it was designed."

McCoy took a short step forward, turning almost immediately into a tight circle as better sense overrode his instinct to pace into the Vulcan's line of sight. "How can that be? You said it was designed to send soldiers into combat."

"*Healthy* soldiers."

At first, Sulu didn't even look up to acknowledge the attention suddenly cast in the direction of his comment. He stood, barely visible on the opposite curve of the device, with his hand closed around his foreshortened right arm and the pack of rock explosives hanging heavily from his back. For the first time Chekov could remember, the competent, battle-hardened captain from their future looked inexpressibly weary and old.

"Healthy soldiers," Sulu said again, holding up his empty sleeve in silent explanation. "I apparently don't count as a healthy soldier anymore."

Chekov felt an unexpected despair kick him weakly in the stomach. Until that moment, he hadn't realized how much he'd been counting on this transfer to work. How much hope he'd invested in their being able to easily exchange both Sulu and Kirk for their proper counterparts and thus set the world to rights again. It was all he could do to keep from turning away and retreating into the conduit in disappointment.

"But you're the only soldier we've got!" McCoy's objection sounded angry instead of forlorn, but Chekov thought he heard the same desperation in the doctor's words. "Are you saying that there's no time in the future when our Sulu runs into one of your Gorn and needs pulling out? Wouldn't replacing him with a Sulu with no hand be better than not replacing him at all?"

"Apparently," Spock answered calmly, "the device does not think so."

Carolyn Palamas edged a little ways closer to the mouth of the conduit, lifting her soft voice almost apologetically so that it might carry into the cavern beyond. "The original builders must have had some cutoff at which they thought it was no longer to their advantage to keep..." She shrugged, as though unhappy that she couldn't think of a better term. "...recycling a combatant."

"But a *hand...!*"

Sulu interrupted McCoy's protest. "For me it's just a hand, Doctor. A hand I lost because the alien medical equipment couldn't sufficiently recognize it to figure out how to put it back together." The glance he aimed down at the missing limb was more regretful than bitter. "Who knows what the device thinks I've lost?"

Yuki Smith raised her hand tentatively, like a student in class a little afraid of offering something stupid to the discussion. "Does this mean we aren't going to be able to send the captain back?" She tucked her hand in quickly when everyone turned to look at her. "I mean, is the device ever going to think a fourteen-year-old kid is better than the full-grown Captain Kirk?"

Spock seemed to consider the question for a moment. "That is an issue we will confront after we have retrieved Lieutenant Sulu from the future," he said at last.

McCoy snorted. "Which you intend to do how, Spock?"

It was Lieutenant Uhura who volunteered the answer. "By sending someone else." She tipped her tricorder so that Spock could read the screen. "The associative transport function doesn't just take troops with you into battle," she explained aloud to the others while the Vulcan studied her translation, "it also allows you to bring troops *back* for reassignment elsewhere. Which means you should be able to retrieve both me and Lieutenant Sulu from the future, as long as I can find him."

Sulu shook his head. "You can't go."

"I'm the obvious choice," she countered. "You said I was with you... at the end. That means I should arrive close to the same time and place as our Lieutenant Sulu did, which should make it easy for me to locate him. I won't need to be there more than a few minutes."

"You won't *have* a few minutes," Sulu said. "Uhura, we were absolutely surrounded when you and I were killed. The only reason it would work to send me is because I didn't care if it killed me to go. Your Sulu would have been sent back to you, and I would have died, but it would have been *over.* I didn't have to try and reach someone and bring them back intact." He shook his head again, more sadly this time. "Even if he's standing right at your shoulder, Uhura, I don't think you'd be able to retrieve him fast enough."

Uhura met his gaze without flinching, although her voice betrayed her frustration. "But we have to try *something.*"

"I'll go." Chekov didn't realize he'd spoken aloud until everyone turned to stare at him. He fought down a blush, but continued, "You said I wasn't there in the fortress with you—I was in a shuttle up above."

Sulu surprised him with an ironic, lopsided smile. "You were in a shuttle that you were planning to crash into the Fortress as a diversion."

Chekov answered his smile with a shrug. "So Mr. Spock will make sure I transfer in just before that happens, and I won't crash. If Lieutenant Sulu survived being transported into the battle at all, I'll at least have some time to look for him." He looked back and forth from Sulu, to McCoy, to Uhura, surprised and a little angry at the skepticism he saw on all their faces. "I can do this. I want to."

"Do you know how to fly a Gorn shuttle?" Sulu made no effort to hide the sarcasm in his question.

"I can fly a Starfleet shuttle," Chekov countered. "I'm sure you can explain the differences well enough to keep me from crashing if I don't want to."

No one said anything for a long moment, then Sulu laughed softly and rubbed at his eyes as he shook his head. "And I thought the stubbornness came later."

"My mother would disagree."

At the mouth of the conduit, Smith raised her hand again and edged up next to Chekov. "Can't we at least send him with a phaser or something?"

"Good idea. Send us both with phasers." Sulu grinned at Chekov as he boldly stepped away from the console and into the ocean of blue light that could no longer threaten him while he was on his own. "I may not be able to replace myself," he told Chekov, "but I'll bet we can use that associative transport function to send me along as your backup. And you're going to need someone who knows the territory."

Much as he didn't want to admit it, Chekov also knew he'd be relieved to have the company. "All right."

Spock motioned him forward by sketching the path around the edge of the transport field with an economical sweep of his arm. "Then if Mr. Chekov would care to join us at the console"—he centered himself on the device and awoke the strange controls—"I believe the future is waiting."

"It looks like the sky's clear. Let's go."

Sulu balanced himself a little more carefully on his wooden stilts and dug his fingers deeper into the manipulative hollow designed for reptilian claws. The shuttle's warp engines responded with their usual rough surge of power, but he was ready for it now and angled the flaps on the parabolic wings to transform the jerk of upward motion into a smooth forward thrust. The Gorn shuttle sailed out over broad-leaved treetops that sparkled with sunlit pools of rain, heading for the perimeter walls of Tesseract Fortress. It was amazing, considering how short and frenzied his first flight over this alien landscape had been, how indelibly those crenulated walls had carved themselves into his memory. Sulu repressed an urge to slam the shuttle into faster flight, or to take evasive action. As hard as it was for him to believe, he had the evidence of his bruised and aching forehead to assure him that the Romulan cloaking device really did make the shuttle invisible to eyes and sensors. They would only be noticed if he did something stupid, like fly too fast or too close to an open window.

Even knowing that, however, it took all the self-control Sulu possessed to guide the Gorn shuttle into a slow, low-altitude circle above Tesseract Fortress with its outward pointing rows of projectile weapons. He could feel the sweat gathering again under his rain-damp uniform tunic, although this time it was from sheer anxiety and not exertion. *Pretend you're a hawk, soaring on a thermal current,* he told himself. But the ferocious vibration of the overpowered aircraft he was piloting made that illusion hard to maintain.

"The portal hub is located underground, between those two tallest towers," said Chekov's emotionless voice inside his helmet. "When we crash the shuttle, we'll have to take it straight down between them to avoid getting caught up by the wings."

The bleak reminder that Sulu's lifespan in this future reality depended on coming up with an alternate plan for destroying the Gorn fortress suddenly made the shuttle's flight path seem a lot less important. Sulu began peering out through the curved cockpit window at the stone fortress below, letting his subconscious mind worry about balancing thrust and velocity and aerodynamic lift. To his surprise, the shuttle slowed and steadied into an even smoother circle than he'd managed to create when he was concentrating on it. Sulu sent the cloaked aircraft skimming around the first of the towers, staying well clear of open windows and crenulated walls where guards might be stationed. The far side of the fortress held something he didn't remember seeing before—a wide, enclosed courtyard jostling with military vehicles. Each one was surrounded by moving figures whose broad backs glittered green in the morning sun as they loaded pallets stacked high with supplies and piles of gleaming cylinders that must be weapons.

"The invasion forces you were talking about?" Sulu asked Chekov as they glided over the sprawling supply yards.

"Yes." Chekov must have been counting in Russian under his breath. Sulu's helmet speaker picked up only an occasional mutter of "...*chetiresta vocyemnadset, chetiresta dyevyenadset, dyerto...*" before the older man said, "There's almost twice as many vehicles here as there were the day before yesterday. They must be pulling their forces in from all across this quadrant."

"That's good," said Sulu. "When we destroy the gate, more of their forces will be trapped here." For some reason, that comment struck Chekov into an extended silence, just the way Sulu's first use of "sir" had. "What's so funny now?" Sulu asked.

"Nothing," said the emotionless voice in his ear. "It's just that I keep forgetting you really *are* him, only younger. He said exactly the same thing when we first saw this place."

A shiver crawled up Sulu's spine. In his attempt to ignore it, he shoved his hands a little too deeply into the Gorn manipulative hollows and the shuttle surged across the terrace with a burst of speed he hadn't exactly intended to give it. Sulu cursed and pulled it back to a gentle glide, but not before he saw some scaled faces glance upward from their equipment-loading. With any luck, they'd put that puff of breeze down to the last of the sunrise storm.

"Hard aport," Chekov snapped. "Get us out over the forest, as low as you can."

Sulu had served long enough on the *Enterprise* to know when he should obey first and ask questions later. Restraining the urge to hurry, he swung the shuttle across the crenulated edge of the Gorn fortifications and settled it down into the rain-wet fronds of a towering stand of tree ferns, just deep enough to let their visual deception screens blend in with the swaying greenery while leaving them a clear view of the massed Gorn forces. "Do you really think they noticed us?" he asked then, at last.

"No," Chekov said, surprising him. "But even if they shoot up a spray of energy disruptors just for the hell of it, they would knock us right out of the sky. It's not worth the risk." He paused a moment, then added with a thin wisp of something that might almost have been whimsical humor in his voice, "Mr. Sulu, could you turn the shuttle so I can see, too?"

"Sorry, sir." Sulu adjusted the shuttle's position with an ungainly lurch of its engines. It settled back down at ninety degrees to its former position, allowing both him and Chekov to gaze out from the wider side of the cockpit dome.

From here, they couldn't see the equipment loading terrace anymore, but they had a good view of the fortress's outer rim instead. The crenulated wall was almost obscured along this side by a vast tent city that had been erected in the clearing beyond. The tents were arranged with unmistakably military precision, color-coded from practical shades of green to drab grayish-black, then, on the outside the bright clashing reds, oranges, and purples that Sulu recognized as the colors of the great Klingon fighting houses. Knots of massive, green-scaled reptilian bodies clustered near the greenish tents. From their size and the immense sweep of their predatory jaws, Sulu assumed those were the Gorn. The few Klingons he saw among them wore elaborate armor and tied their hair in wilder, more barbaric fashion than the taut Klingon space officers he had met on stations in the Alpha Quadrant. But the distant figures Sulu stared at the longest were the unknown aliens he saw sitting on the ground near the dull black tents. They were the most humanoid of the three, with smooth faces and slender, tall bodies. A squinting look at their pale faces showed Sulu an eerily familiar combination of upward slanting eyebrows and pointed ears.

"Are those Vulcans?" he demanded incredulously.

"What?" Sulu felt their helmets scrape as the older man followed the direction of his gaze. "No, those aren't Vulcans. They're Romulans."

"Really? That's what Romulans look like?" Sulu tried to stand on tiptoe to see better and nearly lost his balance on his ungainly stilts. He steadied himself, then settled the Gorn shuttle back into the tree ferns. "Why do they look so much like Vulcans?"

"Because they're sibling races, originally evolved on the same planet." Chekov's voice had turned very thoughtful. "This is interesting. You don't usually see Romulans in Gorn first-strike battalions."

"Why not?"

"Slave race," the older man said succinctly. "The Gorn crushed the Romulan Empire before they attacked the Federation because they wanted their ships and cloaking technology. The Romulans work for the Gorn at gunpoint, and they're often brought in to help run the bureaucracy on occupied planets. But I've never seen the Gorn trust them to help lead an invasion before."

Sulu frowned, remembering what Chekov had said when he'd first described the situation here. "You said they might be massing for an invasion of one of the major inner planets. If they were planning to invade Vulcan—"

"Then it would make sense to bring Romulans in the first assault wave," Chekov agreed. "Neither the Gorn nor the Klingons can match Vulcans when it comes to strategy and tactics, but Romulans can think the same way as their cousins." He startled Sulu with a sudden smack against his shoulder. "You know, you were right. It *was* worth coming out to reconnoiter the fortress one more time. Take us back."

"Back?" Sulu said blankly, and glanced back over his shoulder at Chekov. "Back where?"

"Back to your wrecked shuttle." Chekov's mouth, held in place by its mask of old scars, never changed expression, but there was an air of fierce anticipation in his squared shoulders and out-thrust chin. His dark eyes gleamed with an expression that caught Sulu by surprise: not just grim amusement, but what looked almost like delight. "We're going to salvage that magnetically shielded warp core of yours and bring it back here. It will do a hundred times more damage than a pulse bomb, especially if we can set it to implode inside of the portal."

"But how are we going to *get* it inside the portal?" Sulu demanded. "Do you know how much a warp core weighs?"

"A lot," the Russian admitted. "Do you know how many Romulan slaves it takes to carry one?"

"No."

"Me, either," Chekov said. "So we're just going to keep on freeing them until we find out."

The transportation alcove on the Janus Gate device looked less like a console and more like a piece of abstract alien sculpture. Chekov stepped gingerly into the curve of its embrace, trying to decide how to orient himself to its incomprehensible features. He could make very little sense in its conflicting lines and contours. Certain surfaces pointed upward, others angled down toward the floor, but he wasn't fooled into thinking this told him anything about what the original architects considered "up" and "down." Even the appendages Sulu had so casually pronounced handgrips looked unsuited to anything Chekov recognized as a hand, much less anything he would have called gripping.

"Place your hands on the device, please."

Chekov nodded and took a deep breath. He'd just promised Smith that the cold in the main chamber wouldn't bother him, that a lifetime of Moscow winters had made him impervious to anything above absolute zero. But he was shivering as he laced his hands around the Janus Gate's contact bars.

A vibration so slight it might have been the racing of a small animal's heart fluttered against his palms. The device wasn't cold like the rest of the chamber—it was blood-warm and yielding, almost like touching his own flesh.

"Using the readings we obtained from Captain Sulu's attempted transport, I shall endeavor to place you in the appropriate time frame." Spock made eye contact with him across the device's blue-flame heart. The weird light painted the Vulcan's face an eerie, dark gray. "However, I would suggest you describe what you see before we complete transport in order to verify the coordinates."

Chekov heard Sulu laugh from somewhere out in the dark chamber behind him. "It wouldn't help much if we both ended up on the *Kerzhat*." He didn't know how the captain could sound so relaxed.

"I understand." Chekov nodded again, swallowing hard in a throat that was suddenly painfully dry. "What happens if I let go?"

Spock lifted a curious eyebrow, apparently considering the possibility for the first time. "Logic suggests that either you will be severed from the device and our contact with your crisis point temporarily lost, or your physical form will be dispersed across the subspace rift into infinity."

Chekov was beginning to suspect that it was best to enter into such heroics with as little information as possible.

"Don't let go," Sulu suggested dryly.

A net of electric blue light swarmed over his hands, and Spock's voice said from a very great distance, "I am engaging the time controls."

Lightning—silent, bright, actinic—seemed to vaporize the frost-blackened chamber around him. In its place, a sky so pale it was almost white, mirrored by an expanse of pristine snow and low, ice-covered houses.

"There's snow . . ." Ghostly sensations distracted him, making it hard to concentrate enough to report on what he saw. The sound of the wind as it cut between the houses. The prickle of snow against his unprotected cheek. "...I hear dogs..." And the syncopated calls of black-headed geese somewhere beyond his view. Chekov couldn't decide if this specific moment was familiar, or just representative of all his accumulated memories of the world he grew up in as a boy.

"That can't be right." Sulu's voice sounded startlingly real and nearby. "We're in a montane forest on Basaraba—we've never been in a snowy environment there. And I've never heard dogs or anything like them."

"Wait..." Chekov felt them rushing up from behind just before they burst into view under him—almost through him. A team of lean, rough-coated dogs towing a sledge, with a driver so young and out of control that he'd already lost one glove and the hood of his gray fur parka. The memory came back to him quite suddenly, and Chekov smiled at his own youthful indiscretion. "No, this is Earth—"

On the other side of the temporal rift, the sled cracked violently against something under the ice, leaped a startling height into the air, then crashed back to ground on its side. Unconcerned with the boy still dragging behind them, the dogs kept running with their tails flailing banner-high over their backs.

"—I'm twelve. I fell from a dogsled and was dragged—" He came nowhere near dying, but it was the first time in his life when he'd been honestly convinced he was about to be killed. If not by the dogs, then by their owner when he found out that Andrei Chekov's precocious son had "borrowed" his team without asking.

"Interesting." Chekov found it hard to believe that Spock found anything intriguing about his misspent youth. The Vulcan proved him right by adding a moment later, "Apparently the time placement controls are more individual than they first appeared."

"It sounds like you're about thirty-seven years off," Sulu volunteered.

Uhura said, "The device says, *'Major crisis point located within fifty-three [word unknown] units of time.'* "

Back in the transport chamber, years away from the boy who finally managed to extricate himself from the sled's rigging and roll to a stop behind the disappearing dogs, Sulu remarked irritably, "It would help to know what 'units of time' the device was using."

"Indeed it would, Mr. Sulu. Unfortunately, we have only limited data with which to work. Mr. Chekov?"

He felt funny answering aloud, as though the distant past version of himself would overhear and turn to look. "Sir?"

"I have located another crisis point. Are you ready?"

"Yes, sir. Go ahead."

The lightning flashed again, erasing the Russian countryside with a cobalt expanse of frigid nothing. He gasped at the sense memory of water flooding into his lungs.

"Mr. Chekov...?"

"It's the cave." He tried not to cough, but found it hard to separate himself from the remembered horror of struggling to find the surface, gasping for air only to flood himself with water so cold it stopped his heart. "*This* cave, earlier, when I...drowned. I'm not directly on top of myself, though. I'm about..." He tried to sense his own presence, vaguely felt the touch of a lifeless limb as it sank toward an unseen bottom. "...about a meter and a half away."

Darkness crashed aside, the faint blue light of the cave suddenly blinding him. Chekov took a deep, grateful breath of the chilly air as across the device from him Uhura reported, " *'Major crisis point located within fifteen [word unknown] units of time.'* "

Spock nodded, but didn't look up from his manipulation of the device. "Thank you, Ensign. Your input is helpful in fine-tuning the device's settings."

Chekov nodded mutely, not trusting himself with words.

The first crisis point had been easy—he'd survived it the first time, he remembered surviving it, and the memory had actually softened into a humorous story with a few years' distance. But the drowning—near-drowning?—left him feeling shaky and sick to his stomach. He barely remembered hitting the water, had no memory at all of being fished out and revived, thanks to the Janus Gate having switched him for a healthier version of himself. So which Chekov had he felt struggling in the dark water beside him? The one who had replaced him an instant before his own death? Himself just before the device switched him out the first time? Some other Chekov, in some other timeline, who didn't earn a second chance because Spock pulled this Chekov back without allowing a transfer?

He scrubbed at his eyes, trying to erase the feeling of cold water against his skin. It was hard enough to think about surviving a brush with death—he didn't like having to worry about whether all the various alternate versions of himself also survived.

"Engaging time controls."

Chekov hurried to wrap his hands around the contact bars. The cerulean flash—then the burnt-orange stain of emergency lighting—the stinging metallic stench of ozone and melted plastic—

Because it seemed important, he said immediately, "I don't recognize where I am." With that admission came a weird, illicit thrill. He was peering into his own future.

Sulu's voice again, unlocatable in the unfamiliar surroundings. "I guess the third time's the charm."

He didn't feel particularly charmed. Something like a hideous reverse déjà vu pushed his heart into the base of his throat. "It looks like I'm on a spaceship...or a station...." Duranium walls, with English writing barely visible in the spastic play of shadow and light.

"Can you see any kind of identifier?" He couldn't tell who asked him that.

His view slewed abruptly, away from the writing, toward a shattered doorway and the smoke-filled corridor beyond it. Chekov realized with a shock that he was almost completely overlaid on himself. A ghost painted into a dream world. Except in his dreams it was usually the sensations which were fierce and vivid, the visuals muddy and hard to recall.

"There was writing on one of the walls...give me a minute...."

He tried to will himself to turn. Instead, his future self glanced down, where an erratic smatter of bloody footprints hinted at a gruesome dance of combat and retreat. He caught a glimpse of his own hand, and a pistol-shaped weapon he didn't recognize.

"...There's been some kind of battle...."

A horrible sensation exploded through him from behind. He gasped, felt himself—one of his selves—arch away from a nerve-flaying anguish that almost rocked him out of his body. Then he was suddenly on his back, pinned to the ground by a force so powerful he swore it had drilled right through him and grabbed hold of his spine—

"Mr. Chekov, please report—"

—then the stinking mouthful of teeth so close to his face he could feel the ivory rasp against his cheek, and he realized the monster was speaking to him—a sibilant hiss that some part of him recognized as words even though he didn't understand. Without willing it, without thinking, he bucked beneath the thing's crushing weight and spat into its iridescent face—

"Mr. Spock, shut it off!"

—and a great clawed thumb curved along the line of his cheekbone and pushed into his eye—

"Shut it off before he lets go of the console!"

Chekov sat down hard on the floor of the Janus chamber, every nerve in his body still singing with the memory of the thing's bulk on top of him, its breath against his face. Curling forward, head between his knees, he clapped one hand over his still-tearing right eye and retched dryly into the other.

McCoy's head appeared around the edge of the conduit entrance. "Everything all right in there?" he called, alarm evident in his tone.

Spock replied with his usual understated calm. "We are all accounted for, Doctor. Please stand by."

"Pavel...?" Sulu slid to his knees beside Chekov. He felt the captain's hands on his shoulders, refusing to let go even when the younger man's first instinct was to scuttle away from the contact. "Pavel, where were you? Tell me what happened."

"...I was..." Chekov forced himself to lift his head and focus on the device looming directly above them. He thought it would help fix him back in this present, but instead it just made everything he was feeling seem more dreamlike and surreal. "...I was captured..." Saying it out loud helped a little. "They talked to me—I don't know what they said, but..."

Sulu's hand tightened painfully on his shoulder, a spastic, involuntary reaction. Chekov turned to look at him, and the captain said, very quietly, "Then you spit on them, and they put out your eye."

He didn't want to think about how Sulu knew the details, so he only nodded.

Sulu twisted to call over his shoulder, "We're still off by about five years."

Spock nodded acknowledgment, reaching to make a series of adjustments to the device's controls.

Sulu turned back to Chekov with an expression so bleak it was painful. "The Gorn took you captive during the evacuation of Starbase Six. I still had sixty-five people to clear out of the lower decks, and it took me more than twelve hours to come back for you." He lifted Chekov's hand gently away from his eye, reassuring them both with that simple gesture that it was intact and still functioning. "We were able to replace the eye. And you never told them a damned thing."

Chekov looked into this stranger's face, and tried to imagine inspiring the loyalty he saw there in anyone, much less this battle-hardened veteran. "You came back for me?"

"I only wish I'd come back sooner."

*But you came back.* He knew what a Gorn was now, and knew that both the Janus Gate and his future self believed at that moment that he was certain to die. Even Chekov wouldn't have faulted Sulu for giving up hope on his friend and not going back to find him. But he'd gone back anyway.

Chekov pushed to his feet, grabbing at Sulu's outstretched arm for support when he found his legs still a little unsteady. "We must be close now." *And I'm not going to leave you abandoned in the future.* If only because of a future debt he hoped would never come into existence, he owed something to this man he barely even knew.

Taking hold of the console, he squared his shoulders and nodded across the device to Spock. "I'm sorry for the delay, sir. I'm ready." The Vulcan took him at his word. "Very well. Engaging time controls...now."

A fierce chill swept over him that he didn't remember from the first near-transfers, then settled on his skin as a sheen of cold sweat. Nerves, Chekov realized. Fear, that was all.

That was all.

He looked up from where he'd fixed his eyes stubbornly on the contact bars, across the device's familiar blue flame and skeletal housing. Uhura and Spock bent so close together over the lieutenant's translation equipment that their heads almost touched, and even the Vulcan's normally unreadable face held an expression Chekov could only interpret as mild surprise.

Uhura glanced up as though suddenly realizing the others would be waiting to find out what happened. "The device isn't identifying any future crisis points."

Chekov frowned, unbelieving. "That was the last dangerous moment in my life?"

Sulu moved up next to him, his expression grim. "We've nearly been killed at least a dozen times in the five years since Chekov was captured by the Gorn. Try again, Spock."

The Vulcan was shaking his head, a brief, regretful motion. "I have already moved the time variation control through a space representing Mr. Chekov's maximum possible lifespan. There may be other possible crisis points before that last one, but there is nothing it can fix on after that."

"Maybe it's not just a moment near dying that the machine locks in on," Uhura said quietly. "Maybe it's the fear that comes from *knowing* you're about to die."

Chekov felt more than heard Sulu's slow sigh. "You could be right. After those twelve hours with the Gorn, it seemed like Chekov never really cared again whether he lived or died." He looked at the young ensign in frank apology. "Maybe if I'd gotten there sooner, I could have saved the whole man and not just the eye."

Disappointment and frustration twisted together in Chekov's heart. "So you can't use me? I can't go?"

"It would appear not," Spock said.

Placing her tricorder beside Spock on the console, Uhura stepped back from the operator's console and squared her shoulders in what she no doubt meant to be a gesture of confidence. But it was determination Chekov saw in her eyes, not necessarily bravery. "Well," she said simply, "I guess it's my turn after all."

# Chapter Nine

"CAN I ASK YOU a question?" Sulu said between gasps. The combination of Basaraba's thin air, rain forest humidity, and his current fierce exertion made his ribs ache with the effort to take deeper breaths than were physically possible. He couldn't see Chekov, but the other man's voice sounded equally labored.

"What?"

"Did the other version of me take your suggestions very often?"

There was a moment of silence, then the Russian's scarred face lifted just far enough over the silver curve of the shielded warp core to glare at him. "Yes, he did. All the time. Why?"

"Because it doesn't seem like you worry a lot about feasibility when you think up ideas like this." Sulu heaved again at the mahogany-tough rain forest branch he was using to try to lever the warp core out of its cradle. The power supply for the wrecked *Edwin Drake* wasn't physically very large, but its dense dilanthanum shell weighed more than an equivalent ball of solid lead. With the added weight of Scotty's magnetically charged cryosteel shielding on top, the core felt as heavy as a chunk of a neutron star. "Why didn't we free some Romulans *before* we came back here to get this?"

That got him a snort and a stronger than usual heave on the other side. "Because they would have stolen our Gorn shuttle out from under us and headed for one of their homeworlds," said the Russian. "I've got a six-centimeter wedge open on this side. I just need another three centimeters to slide the antigrav disk in."

Sulu bent over, trying to recharge his lungs with oxygen for a final attack. He didn't waste any of it talking until after he'd thrown all his weight onto his makeshift pry bar again. The wood creaked ominously, but it made the warp core shift by a noticeable amount. "Is that enough?"

"No." Chekov heaved again on his side of the core. "I just need one more centimeter. Come on, you're twenty years younger than I am!" `

"And used to a lot more oxygen!" Indignation lent Sulu a strength he didn't really have, and he managed a fierce dig under the core that brought it lurching up out of its cradle. He heard Chekov slam the antigrav disk home beneath it, then curse as the silvery sphere began to sink again anyway. Even the powerful antigrav lifter couldn't totally compensate for the core's immense weight. Sulu managed to keep it from settling back into its cradle, but his uneven branch slipped off its smooth surface a moment later and the warp core rattled the shuttle's engine deck with its fall. He heard a gasp that didn't sound like one of exertion, and swung around to the other side of the shuttle.

"Are you all right?"

"Sure." Chekov was nursing one hand inside the other, but there didn't seem to be any particular expression of pain on his scarred face. It wasn't until he reached out to steady the core as it began to slide down the shuttle's tilted deck that Sulu could see the way two of his fingers bent at an unnatural angle.

"No, you're not," he said sharply. "Your fingers are broken!"

The older man grunted, as if that was a trivial detail. "Then it's a good thing I taught you how to fly the Gorn shuttle, isn't it," he said, with one of his mirthless cracks of laughter. "Come on, let's get this thing loaded."

Sulu blinked at him, concern slowly fading into a familiar chill of unreality and horror. This future in which broken bones were barely worth noticing and lives were sacrificed with grim satisfaction rather than sadness was one he suddenly wished he would never have to live through. Perhaps if he died today in Tesseract Fortress, Sulu thought, he could make that wish come true and save himself twenty years of agony and struggle.

In silence, he shouldered his part of the now manageable load of warp core and helped Chekov carry it out to the waiting Gorn shuttle. The smooth surface of the parabolic wing almost defeated them, but the Russian scrambled up into the cockpit and leaned out to lock wrists with Sulu as the younger man braced the weight of the core against his chest and shoulders. With a few fierce heaves that must have made his broken fingers stab with pain, Chekov hauled Sulu and the warp core together up the wing. They rested for a moment with the silver sphere balanced precariously on the cockpit rim, then Sulu swung himself beside the Russian and they lowered it down to the floor together. Not a word was spoken the entire time.

"The weight's too far aft for flight stability," was all Chekov said when he'd finally regained a little of his breath. "You'll have to stand on top of it."

Sulu nodded and slid the warp core as far forward as he could, then tried to balance himself on top of its smooth mag-steel cover. Coated with rotting leaf litter and buffalo dung, his boots slipped off as soon as he released his grip on the cockpit rim and tried to reach for the flight controls. "This isn't going to work."

"Yes," Chekov said flatly, "it is." He hauled himself up out of the Gorn shuttle, then climbed back a few moments later with their rain forest sticks clutched in his good hand. He wedged them between the sides of the Gorn shuttle, jamming the ends into the exposed structural supports of the wings and lashing them together with a length of self-sealing cable. "Try standing on that."

Sulu stepped gingerly up onto the makeshift platform, and felt it bow beneath his weight until it was stopped by the warp core. "It might hold me," he said dubiously. "But if the core slides out from underneath, the whole thing will snap."

"I won't let it slide out." Chekov sat down behind him, pulling on his sound-damping helmet and bracing his own body across the shuttle's hold to box in the core. He took a moment to jerk both fingers into alignment again with a wet *crack!* that made Sulu grimace, then said simply, "Come on, let's go."

Sulu pulled his own helmet on and yanked the cockpit cover closed overhead, then slid his hands into the hollow flight controls. The pressure-sensitive interior felt oddly damp against his skin, although he couldn't be sure if that was because it had collected some of the rain forest's humidity or because of his own clammy sweat. He didn't doubt that Chekov would do his best to keep the *Drake*'s warp core from shifting beneath him, but a lot would depend on how smoothly Sulu managed to fly this overpowered shuttle. With a deep breath, he pressed his fingers down into the right sockets and lifted off with an absolutely vertical surge. He let the shuttle's momentum take it as high as it would go before he added any forward thrust, allowing gravity to smooth the shuttle's transition from vertical to horizontal motion.

They were halfway back to Tesseract Keep before Chekov spoke again. "He modified them sometimes," he said abruptly.

Sulu spared a puzzled glance down at the older man, sitting with his shoulders rigid and braced against the lurching weight of the loose warp core and his broken hand cradled in his lap. "Modified what?"

"My ideas. Captain Sulu usually modified them, to make sure they would work. How close are we to the fortress?"

The abrupt change of subject warned Sulu not to make an issue of Chekov's awkward confession. "About a kilometer."

"Stay outside the perimeter wall," Chekov ordered, then grunted with the effort of keeping the warp core steady as Sulu swung the cloaked shuttle into a tight arc to avoid the Gorn defenses. "Find a place to land as close to the gray tents as you can."

Sulu scanned across the army encampment. "How about right in the middle of them?"

"*What?*" Chekov looked as if he was going to scramble to his feet, but at the last minute remembered that he couldn't leave his position. "How can there be enough room to land there? Those tents were packed in like herring."

"Not anymore." Sulu guided the shuttle in a slow, quiet arc over the encampment. There were almost no Klingons in sight now, and many fewer Romulans. "It looks like they've already started shipping the troops out. About half the Romulan tents are gone."

"*Damn.*" Chekov was silent for a moment, then glanced up toward him with an odd, probing look in his dark eyes. "Were you really serious about landing right in the middle of them?"

"Yes," said Sulu.

"You know we would risk getting caught right away, if there's a Gorn or Klingon in sight when we open the shuttle."

"Yes."

He could see the Russian's lips move as if he had whistled, although his helmet communicator didn't transmit the sound. "You really haven't changed that much," he said. "All right. Take us down, Lieutenant Sulu."

Sulu already had the shuttle hovering near the spot he'd picked—a stretch of open stone near the crenulated wall of the wide mustering terrace, where they could make a quick dive over the edge if their plan failed and they had to escape. He cut the horizontal thrust to zero and let the vertical thrust slowly die away, trying for a graceful landing to match the rest of his smooth flight. The extra weight of the *Drake*'s warp core spoiled that by dragging the shuttle down much harder than he'd predicted. They landed with a rattling thump that must have been audible far across Tesseract Fortress's stone terrace, perhaps even all the way to the guardian towers that now loomed on the horizon.

Sulu didn't waste time apologizing. Even before the roar of the shuttle's engines died away, he threw the cockpit cover open and reached down to haul Chekov up toward the opening. The older man accepted the boost without a qualm, grabbing onto the edge with his good hand, then vaulting over it without hesitation. Sulu followed a second later.

As quickly as they had moved, it still hadn't been quick enough. They landed in the midst of a circle of weapons, and behind each gleaming metallic barrel was a lean, angular face taking aim with unemotional efficiency. Sulu felt a disorienting wave of disbelief—it was like facing an execution squad of multiple Spocks—but he drew himself up and made his expression as austere as he could, to match theirs. After one swift glance around to make sure there weren't any Gorn or Klingon supervisors in sight, Chekov did the same.

So far, the first part of their attack plan had worked. They had found one of the self-governed bands of Romulan slaves who were trusted to work without an overseer. Now, Sulu thought wryly, all they had to do was convince these quasi-independent alien fighters to cast their lot in with two bedraggled humans instead of the entire Gorn empire. He was glad that it was Chekov's job to do the talking.

"Humans," said one Romulan calmly. It didn't seem to be an exclamation of surprise or anger as much as a term of address. "How would you prefer to die?"

"Productively," said Chekov. "By killing as many Gorn as we can and taking their portal hub out with us."

That sent a response rippling through the circle of dark-uniformed Romulans, but it looked to Sulu like a wave of disbelief. Still, they made no move to shoot them or march them along to prison, and no green-scaled figures seemed to be converging on them from either the terrace or the towers. Their absence was explained a moment later when a deep thud echoed across the stone plaza, followed by the growl and clatter of heavy equipment being driven across the stones. The mobilization of the invasion force had saved them—among all the clangs and roars of moving equipment, the thud of their landing shuttle must have only seemed odd to the nearest troop of Romulans, who could see that the noise came from apparently empty air.

"How could you do that?" the leading Romulan asked. Her deep-creased face looked almost cruel with years of hard military service for the Gorn, but her dark eyes glittered eagerly as they bored into Chekov. "All your previous attacks on this place have failed."

"We have a warp core that can be set to implode inside the Gorn transport hub." Chekov scanned their faces, seeing the disbelief deepen, then said, "I know they scan for activated weapons as you enter the portal. But this warp core is shielded."

"How do we know you're telling the truth?" inquired another of the Romulans.

Chekov shrugged. "You can try scanning for yourself," he said. "Or just think back to yesterday, when that strange shuttle flew away from the Fortress after our last attack. The Gorn fired energy disruptors at it all the way from here to the outer ridge, but they never knocked out its warp core or its engines."

"I saw that." The Romulan leader silenced her subordinate with a swift gesture. "You took this shielded warp core from that vessel?"

"Yes." Chekov gestured at the shuttle behind them. "We can carry it, with the help of an antigrav lifter, but we'd never make it past the guards in front of the portal. We need you to take it in for us, disguised as part of your battle gear."

The Romulan leader's slitted eyes looked like chips of dark ice in her expressionless face. "While you stay safely outside?"

"Of course not," Chekov said, just as coldly. "How could we trust you to detonate it and not just turn it over to the Gorn? You'll take us inside with you."

"Disguised as Romulans?" asked the younger soldier.

"No," Chekov said crisply. "Disguised as your prisoners. All you need to do is think of some devious Romulan reason that makes it necessary for you to take us along to Vulcan."

"I think you can rely on us for that." The older female Romulan smiled, revealing a set of artificial titanium teeth. "Your plan is to implode the warp core inside the portal and blast apart the Gorn's transport system from the inside?"

"Yes," said Chekov. "Leaving them open to an attack by the Federation, and coincidentally helpless against any future Romulan uprising."

The Romulans exchanged glances of silent communication, and Sulu gritted his teeth as the agony of waiting for their answer dragged on. He was mentally debating whether their chances of making it back into the shuttle if the Romulans decided to fire were slim or none when the leader finally spoke again.

"This gamble seems worth taking, although the odds do not favor its success. We are willing to wager four lives on it. Agreed?"

"Agreed." Chekov stepped back and rapped his fist on apparently empty air. "I'll even throw in a shielded Gorn shuttle as part of the deal."

After watching Sulu and then young Chekov step up to take hold of the Janus Gate, Uhura had somehow thought it would be easier for her to do it. She was wrong.

It had been easy enough to pass the archaeological translator over to Carolyn Palamas and back away from the alien transporter's control panel. And it hadn't been too difficult to walk the perimeter line around to the other side of the ice-walled chamber, since her blue-tinted reflection seemed to walk along with her. Approaching the actual transport station was a little harder, but it was when she had to step into the strangely angled alcove and find a place for her hands on the alien gripping bars that Uhura found her breath stuck in her throat. Unlike the other two crewmen who had stood here, she had seen this alien blue light sweep out into the chamber and suck people into its time-crossing rifts. Although intellectually she knew she was in no danger right now, the looming possibility that Spock would soon be depressing the transport bar and removing her from this timeline was far more terrifying than Uhura had expected.

"I'm right behind you," Sulu said quietly. He stood where he had for Chekov, in the pool of protection that seemed to extend out from her awkwardly shaped slot. "Just be sure to tell me what you're seeing. I'll let Spock know how much he has to adjust time to get you to Basaraba from there."

Uhura nodded, because right now she didn't trust her tight throat not to strangle any words she tried to say. She tightened her grip on the uncomfortably slanted rods that connected her to the Janus Gate, then forced herself to look straight out into its flickering, dark blue heart. For some reason, seeing Spock gazing back at her with the same imperturbable expression that he usually wore on the deck of the *Enterprise* steadied her nerves and gave her the ability to speak again.

"Ready, Lieutenant?"

"Yes, sir." Uhura concentrated on meeting his gaze and not on watching the liquid streaks of fire climbing the arms of the transporter, then spiraling farther and farther up the bars she was gripping. There was a moment that felt like a strike of unseen lightning, bone-deep but skin-tingling at the same time. She opened her mouth to ask Sulu if this was how it had felt for him, but before she could do that, the ice-sheathed chamber seemed to suddenly leap away from her. It was replaced, after a moment of whirling nothingness, by what looked like the empty interior of a space station. Uhura could see stars glittering through several porthole windows, and what looked like reflected moonlight slanting in from behind her, but there seemed to be no lights other than that. She frowned, glancing around to try to locate something identifiable.

"I'm in a space station. It's dark, maybe unpowered." She tried to take a step forward to get a better view, but she didn't seem able to control her movements in this reality. "That's all I can see."

"Does it look like a Starfleet station?" Sulu asked, seemingly in her ear.

"I think so, but I don't see anything to identify it with."

"I am adjusting the distance control," said Spock's disembodied voice. There was another disorienting whirl, and now Uhura was standing in a dark shuttlebay, looking out through a hull breach at a wrecked starship as it drifted closer. She felt her throat contract instinctively, even though she knew the hard vacuum here couldn't reach her back on Tlaoli. "What do you see?"

"A starship, the *Alexander Jackson,* wrecked and heading for the station."

"That's the Gamma M14 station right before we abandoned it to the Gorn," Sulu said. "Spock, you need to move about eight more years into the future."

"Very well."

Uhura got a brief glimpse of blue light glittering off ice, then everything whirled around her again and condensed into a sandy desert landscape, blasted by a sun much stronger than anything she'd experienced in her time on the *Enterprise.* She told Sulu and heard him sigh. "Almost to Basaraba," he told Spock. "That's Chetay, the planet we were fighting on just before we found the Gorn portal. We nearly died of radiation poisoning there."

"Allow me to make a slight adjustment..."

The desert dissolved and was replaced by a stone-walled courtyard filled with the drifting smoke of a recent explosion. Uhura couldn't be sure, because her other senses seemed so muffled compared to sight, but she thought she could hear the sound of distant weapons fire in the sky. She caught a glimpse of a dark figure sprawled and broken on the stones, and looked away quickly. "I'm in some kind of courtyard, filled with smoke. I think someone's firing at a shuttle overhead, but I can't see because of all the smoke."

*"That's Basaraba!"* Sulu's voice had taken on an urgent sound that made Uhura's own pulse start to pound. "Spock, can you adjust the distance to get her past the Gorn defenses?"

"I believe so." There was another, shorter instant of disorientation, then Uhura found herself standing in the shadow of a stone archway, a tower looming overhead. The dark metal door ahead of her was closed, and she could see barrels of several weapons pointing out of slits in the stone beside it. "How is that?"

"Not good," Uhura said urgently. "The gates are locked and guarded. I think someone might have seen you, Sulu, when you were here before. It looks like they're waiting for us."

"Damn." She couldn't see him, but she could hear the sizzling frustration in his voice. "Is there anything else we can do to get there safely, Spock?"

"Perhaps," said the Vulcan. Uhura's stomach lurched as she felt another spinning moment of transition. Then she was back in the frigid air of Tlaoli's main cavern, staring across the flame of the Janus Gate at the ship's science officer. "I do not believe that varying the distance will provide the margin of safety you will need in order to stay long enough to locate Lieutenant Sulu. But as I become more familiar with these controls, I believe that perhaps we have more ability to vary the time of crisis substitution than I previously believed."

"What does that mean, Spock?" demanded McCoy's voice from the conduit outside the cave. "That you can pick and choose when to send Uhura to the future?"

"Not quite," said Spock. "I am still constrained by the overall timing of the crisis point for which we are aiming. However, since most events can be visualized as a bell curve of probability woven into the fabric of space-time, I can adjust the controls to place Lieutenant Uhura on either temporal cusp of the main crisis point. I may be able to place her in the time stream as much as a day before or after her death."

Uhura heard McCoy make a pained noise at the Vulcan's blunt words. "It wouldn't help her to get there early, before our version of Sulu arrives," the doctor pointed out. "And if she gets there a day late, he may already be gone."

"That would not be logical," Spock said. "Lieutenant Sulu should be able to reason that he must stay near the place where he first appeared, in order to facilitate a rescue from our side."

"And even if he doesn't," Sulu said quietly, "arriving a day late might let me get this pack full of explosives down into the heart of Tesseract Keep."

Spock lifted one eyebrow, as if that was not a major concern for him, but he didn't make an issue of it. "Are you willing to attempt going to Basaraba one more time, Lieutenant?" he asked Uhura.

"Yes," she said firmly. "And while *Captain* Sulu takes his explosives down to the portal hub, I'm still going to see if I can find *Lieutenant* Sulu."

"Very well." Spock bent over his controls, and once again Uhura watched quicksilver fire come streaking out from the Janus Gate toward her. That lightning-sharp shock shivered through her once again, and she found herself back in the original stone-walled courtyard where she'd seen her own limp body such a short while ago. It was empty now and filled with the slant of late-afternoon sunlight. Uhura could see thick rain forest trees overtopping the walls, their branches swaying in the breeze and dumping a glitter of collected raindrops down to the stone walls below. It looked oddly peaceful, after the mayhem of her last visit. Maybe a little too peaceful. Uhura had served in Starfleet long enough to know when something smelled like a trap.

"Spock, I'm not sure you should send us here," she said. "I can't put my finger on it, but there's something—"

There was another shock, a much deeper and more painful one, as if someone had dropped a metal lacework of electrically charged links across Uhura's body. She gasped and almost let go of the alien handgrips under the surge of pain.

"Spock, something's wrong," Sulu said urgently. "She's starting to shake, just like Chekov did... Uhura, don't let go!"

"I won't," she said and tried to see what was going on. Something interfered with her vision on Basaraba now—a shimmer like a heat-wave rose between her and the image of peaceful empty stones. Then, to Uhura's surprise, that image tilted and slid sideways, and slowly vanished behind her.

"Spock, are you changing the distance controls?" she demanded.

"Not at all. In fact," the Vulcan said, "I am attempting to bring you back again from viewing that point in the future. Unsuccessfully."

"*What?*" That was McCoy's indignant voice. "Spock, if this happened because you decided to push the limits on what this transporter could do—"

"I do not believe it is the timing of the transport which is the problem, Doctor," Spock said. "I am beginning to suspect Lieutenant Uhura has encountered some kind of force which is keeping her pinned into that future timeline, even in her half-materialized state."

Uhura took a deep breath, trying to ignore the constant prickle of what felt like small electric shocks across her skin. The sense of movement she felt now wasn't the disorienting whirl of the Janus Gate spinning her into a new time and place—it was the slow and lurching feeling you got when you were being carried by more than one person. With an effort, Uhura managed to slew her gaze around enough to look beneath her and see the bulging, dark-green shoulders of the four reptilian aliens who carried her in what looked like some kind of stretcher or poled support.

"I think Mr. Spock is right, Doctor," she said, wondering if only her teammates on Tlaoli could hear her or if she was making sounds on Basaraba, too. "From what I can see, it looks like I've been caught in some kind of force field. By the Gorn."

Tesseract Keep just felt *wrong.*

Sulu had never thought of himself as a man with a vivid imagination. Piloting a spaceship like the *Enterprise* required steady nerves and quick reflexes, but a talent for envisioning all the possible things that could go wrong would have been a hindrance rather than a help. Sulu's usual restrained demeanor reflected his calm temperament—one of the reasons his wild impersonation of D'Artagnan at Psi 2000 had been so mortifying.

He had expected Tesseract Keep to be intimidating and it was. Hewn of dark stone outside, barely lit inside and swamp-hot with the odor of many reptilian bodies, the Gorn fortress constantly vibrated with a powerful subsonic pulse as its transport hub worked deep underground. What Sulu hadn't counted on was the feeling that swept over him as soon as their Romulan "guards" marched him and Chekov at gunpoint through the stone entrance arch: that there was something so fundamentally flawed about this place that it shouldn't even exist.

"Chekov, what's going on here? Is this place built over some kind of natural dimensional rift?"

The Russian slanted him an unreadable look. "If I knew that," he said, lips barely moving beneath his stiff, scarred cheeks, "I'd know a lot more about how to—"

"*Silence.*" The Romulan behind Sulu dug his weapon deep enough into his ribs to make his breath vanish with a gasp of pain. "Prisoners do not speak."

It was a warning as much as a command, and Sulu tried to look properly discouraged. It wasn't all that difficult. There was still a long line of invasion troops to be cleared ahead of them before they even came close to the portal itself, much less were able to strip off the magnetic shielding of the *Drake*'s warp core and set the powerful antimatter heart to implode. For now, the warp core rode deep inside a Romulan photon-mine battery, concealed among the equally silver hulls of their deactivated weapons. They'd passed through a heavy metallic arch that Sulu suspected was one of the Gorn weapons scanners, but several gates and inspection points still lay ahead of them.

A dark column of Romulans stretched before and behind, stolid as the crates of supplies and weapons into the fortress. Their status as enslaved soldiers was obvious. Unlike the Gorn and Klingons, no large pieces of battle equipment accompanied the Romulans, and none of their arms seemed to be more than standard projectile weapons. Massive reptilian forms prowled along the line, poking at random groups to keep them moving into the shadowy interior of the keep. Sulu had never seen a Gorn except from the air, and he tried to keep himself from staring too openly at the sauroid aliens. But their sheer size, their fierce predatory jaws, and the spurts of mist that drifted from their broad nostrils even in this warm and humid air awoke a sense of unreasoning and instinctive dread. He couldn't imagine fighting these creatures for twenty years; he couldn't imagine taking on one of them in a hand-to-hand fight as Chekov said Gary Mitchell had once done. It was hard enough just to keep shuffling along when one paused to stare at him, craning its enormous head down so close that he could smell the carnivore reek of its breath.

"What is this?"

A deep rumbling sound accompanied that voice, but it took Sulu a moment to realize that it was the actual sound of Gorn speech. The English words came from a translating device the alien held clutched in one of its clawed hands. Sulu kept his head bowed and tried to look oppressed, taking his cue from Chekov's sullen slouch beside him. They left it to the Romulan leader to answer. She had surprised Sulu by being the first Romulan to volunteer for this suicide mission. He just hoped she had thought up a sufficiently convincing story about his and Chekov's presence while they'd been waiting in line.

"Prisoners." She poked Chekov with her weapon, hard enough to elicit a curse. "We caught them trying to infiltrate our camp."

The Gorn swung his massive weapon down toward them, growling. "Human scum. They should be killed."

"Of course," said the Romulan, and Sulu tried to hide his involuntary jerk of surprise by turning it into a cower. "And they will be, once they come through the portal with us. No human ever survives that trip."

"Why bother taking them, then?"

Her dark eyes glittered fearlessly back at her slave master. "Because their dead bodies will have strategic value on the other side."

The Gorn snorted thick mist across them, although Sulu wasn't sure if that was an expression of doubt or frustration. "Explain this strategic value."

Instead of answering, the female Romulan stepped forward and yanked Sulu's head back by the hair, forcing him to slew around with a cry of pain. He found himself staring straight up into the Gorn's sulfur yellow eyes, and fought the impulse to close his own. By now, he had guessed where this was going. "Retinal identification patterns are used to confirm Starfleet security levels," the Romulan said. "We can use theirs to break into the Vulcan's military computers."

"These patterns survive death?"

"As a network of tiny capillary arteries," the Romulan said. "But they must be as fresh as possible. The Vulcan security scanners are undoubtedly programmed to detect postmortem decay."

There was a long, considering pause. Then, without another word, the Gorn swung around and stamped away into the shadows.

"Did we convince him?" Chekov muttered, drawing the words out so they sounded almost like a whimper.

"I do not know." The Romulan leader pushed him forward into the gap that had opened in line while they talked to their guard. "He may be going to consult with his superiors about this—but at least he did not make us step out of line."

"Yes." Chekov glanced sideways, then stumbled a little on the stone pavement and caught himself on Sulu's shoulder. Sulu felt the older man's fingers flex through cloth into skin and muscle, hard enough to make him wince, but he betrayed no sign that a warning had been given. He had already realized that the Romulan leader's explanation of their presence here had been just a little too plausible for comfort. And without words or gestures, he knew what the Russian was now telling him.

If they couldn't get the warp core to implode before the portal began to activate, they were going to have to wrest one of the Romulan's weapons away and make sure their retinal patterns didn't survive one instant longer than they did.

# Chapter Ten

EVER SINCE SHE WAS a child, Uhura had hated to be picked up and carried. It probably had something to do with being the smallest child among many cousins, the one who always got slung onto an aunt's hip or an uncle's shoulder to make sure she wasn't left behind. The inability to prove herself the equal of her older cousins had been frustrating enough to spark a lifelong determination to stand on her own two feet whenever possible. The result was an instinctive surge of irritation rather than fear at the situation she found herself in now—unable to move or control her movements because she really wasn't present in this time stream, unable to retreat back to her actual body because of the force field the Gorn had thrown up around her. Not for the first time, Uhura wished the ancient inhabitants of Tlaoli had never decided to bequeath their time-traveling technology to the races that came behind them.

Except for vision, Uhura's other senses continued to tell her that she hadn't really gone anywhere. She could still feel frigid air bite at her throat when she breathed too deeply, and her hands still ached with the intensity of her grip on the Janus Gate. And she could hear, with perfect clarity, the heated discussion raging in the ice cave about the various ways her teammates might be able to manipulate the time device to bring her safely back where she belonged. But to humans, vision was the supreme sense. Despite all of the evidence to the contrary, Uhura's mind still angrily protested the lurch and swing of her surroundings as the Gorn carried her down a long walled passageway from the courtyard where she'd materialized, out of the slanting sunlight and into the darker shadows of a structure she couldn't really see. The Gorn carried her imprisoning force field in such a way that Uhura could only see out the back of it,

and so couldn't even tell Captain Sulu what part of the Gorn fortress she
was approaching.

"Give me your phaser, Ensign," Sulu ordered Chekov grimly.
"Spock, use the associative transport and send me through the connection
that's holding Uhura fixed at that time—"

"I will endeavor to do so, Captain, as soon as this chamber is
cleared," she heard Spock reply. Then, "Mr. Chekov, take a small party to
the other end of this cave system, where the alien healing chamber is located. If we are successful in retrieving Lieutenant Sulu from the future, I
believe that is where he is most likely to be sent. Contact us by communicator as soon as you observe activity of any kind." There was a pause
while the shadows of the Gorn fortress deepened around Uhura. She wondered if her eyes would adjust to this phantom light change when in reality she was still gazing into the fiery heart of the Janus Gate. "Prepare
yourself, Captain Sulu. I am engaging associative transport now."

Uhura glanced around her limited range of vision, but saw no sign of
Sulu anywhere nearby. "Did the transport succeed?"

"No." There was a biting edge in the older pilot's voice that hadn't
been there before. "What is it this time, Spock? My hand again?"

"I do not believe so." The Vulcan's deep voice sounded more tense
than usual. "I believe the associative transport has failed for the same reason that I cannot reverse Lieutenant Uhura's viewing mode. The force
field which the Gorn are using seems to interfere completely with our
ability to enter and leave the time stream. In fact, I am beginning to suspect it was designed precisely with that purpose in mind."

"The Gorn don't travel through time." It sounded as if Sulu was
frowning. "They only travel through space. Why would they have designed a force field like that?"

"I do not know," Spock said. "I can only speculate based on the effect
it is having on the Janus Gate."

"So what do we do now, Spock?" McCoy demanded.

"Wait," Spock said simply. "And be prepared to take action if the
chance arises. The fact that Lieutenant Uhura is being carried suggests
the Gorn have some purpose in capturing her. If they lower the force field
in an attempt to accomplish it, we should then be able to sever the connection and retrieve her immediately."

Sulu's voice sounded a little clearer, as if he had turned back toward
her. "Can you see where they're taking you, Uhura?"

"No." She had been trying to slew herself around without taking her
hands off the Janus Gate's stabilizing handgrips, but the transporter didn't
seem to translate her physical position into a changed viewpoint on

Basaraba. All she could tell was that dark stone walls were closing in around her, and the passage seemed to be starting to slant downhill. After a while, she started to get glimpses of other figures through the heat-shimmer of her prison. To her surprise, along with squads of armored Klingons and the reptilian giants she assumed were Gorn, long lines of what looked like dark-clad Vulcans filled the halls. She reported that to Sulu.

"Those are Romulans," the older man said. "They must be going along as part of the Gorn invasion force. That means they've probably decided to attack Vulcan. Earth will probably be next."

"We're starting down what looks like some kind of spiral ramp," Uhura reported. "It just keeps going down farther and farther. We keep passing more Kling-ons and more Romulans."

"They must be taking you to the portal!" Sulu said fiercely. "Spock, are you sure you can't send me through? I don't even care if I'm dead when I get there, as long as I can set these explosives to go off without me."

"I would accommodate you if I could, Captain," Spock said somberly. "I am not indifferent to a potential future invasion of Vulcan. But at this point—"

"Sulu!" Uhura heard herself cry out even as she strained to reach across time and space toward a face made pale by its distance. "Sulu, I see you!"

The subsonic pulse of the Gorn portal hub grew louder as they approached the heart of Tesseract Fortress. They had left the entrance level behind long ago, and were now winding their way down a ramp that looked more like the entrance to an enormous pit mine than an architectural element. With the part of his brain that still seemed able to observe and analyze, Sulu found himself wondering if this had originally been nothing more than a mine on an outworld colony until the Gorn had stumbled across some kind of natural dimensional rift that allowed them to create their interstellar transport system. He remembered the discussion of natural subspace anomalies that they'd had back on the bridge of the *Enterprise,* when they first realized that the wrecks of alien spaceships littered the surface of Tlaoli. Had that been only a day or so ago? It felt like another lifetime to Sulu now, one that he would never get to finish living.

"Heads up," Chekov muttered. The lights were so dim down here that they couldn't see much of the ramps above or below them, but a new sound had been added to the constant subsonic rumble of the portal hub. It was the slapping thud of Gorn footsteps, coming down the ramp much faster than the rest of the invasion troops. Sulu felt all the muscles of his back clench with the immense effort it took not to whirl around and betray himself as that rush of feet came closer. Were they about to be exposed as saboteurs, or yanked out of line for further questioning by the Gorn? Sulu felt his breath choke in his throat, arrested by dread and the overpowering muggy heat that rose from the depths of the mine below.

"We can fight our way in from here," growled the Romulan leader, and Sulu heard her release her weapon's safety catch. No alarms appeared to go off when she did, and he wondered if he should tear off the cover of the weapons chest and start stripping the warp core of its shielding now. His gaze met Chekov's in silent query, and the older man gave him back a gruff shake of his head. There was still a chance, a very slight chance, that this downward rush of Gorn had nothing to do with them. It would be unutterably stupid to expose themselves too early if that were the case.

Apparently the Romulan leader thought so, too. She allowed her three subordinates to arm their weapons after she did, but when they began to lift them to their shoulders and sight back along the ramp from which they came, she snapped, "Not yet!" The order came not a moment too soon—the youngest Romulan had just finished slinging his weapon back across his shoulder when the platoon of Gorn came charging along the slope of the ramp toward them. The ones in front carried their normal weapons, their heads out-thrust suspiciously as they ran. Farther back, a group of unarmed Gorn carried what looked like a gold-brocaded sedan chair on their broad shoulders, boxed and curtained as if an ancient Asian emperor was venturing beyond the walls of his palace. As they came closer, however, Sulu could see that the golden curtains around that box were made of crackling sheets of pure energy rather than cloth. It was a portable force field prison, he realized, and it looked more than big enough to accommodate two humans.

"Make way!" roared the foremost Gorn, one clawed hand smashing into the nearest Romulan and hurling him back against the wall. They'd been so involved in anticipating an attack that, unlike the other groups of waiting soldiers, they'd neglected to clear a path through their section of the ramp. Sulu started to reach for the chest holding the warp core, but Chekov grabbed him hard with his unbroken hand and dragged Sulu away before he could betray their nonprisoner status. The Romulan leader single-handedly swung the weapons container out of the Gorn's way while her subordinates ruthlessly swept the two humans toward the wall with the butts of their weapons. Despite the pain, Sulu had to admire the Romulans' quick thinking. Held like clubs now, the weapons could be reversed and used against the Gorn at a moment's notice.

But to Sulu's amazement, that notice never needed to be given. The

Gorn platoon swept past them with only the slightest of scornful looks, obviously intent only on reaching the bottom of the portal ramp as quickly as possible. Sulu dragged in a ragged breath, feeling as if it was the first he'd taken in a while. He let the musky, Gorn-scented air out again in a muffled sigh of relief, and felt the rush of air that meant Chekov was doing the same thing beside him. The last of the Gorn swept past, carrying the glowing force field on their shoulders, and the last of Sulu's breath ripped out of his throat in a cry so strangled he barely heard it himself. He felt more than saw Chekov swing toward him worriedly, but his eyes never left the back wall of that descending prison cell, where a familiar dark-eyed face had for one unmistakable moment peered out and *seen* him.

"What's the matter?" Chekov hissed as the line of troops waiting along the ramp shuffled themselves back into order and began to descend again. "Are you all right?"

"Yes." Sulu could barely force that whisper through his locked-up throat. "I mean, no. Chekov, didn't you see who was *inside* that force field?"

"No," the Russian said. "Who was it?"

"It was Uhura." Sulu met Chekov's disbelieving stare with all the resolution and strength of will he possessed. From this point on, he knew, everything was changed. "*My* timeline's Uhura."

"Uhura, I'm right here."

She heard Sulu's voice close beside her, felt him touch her arm back in the ice caverns on Tlaoli, and shook her head so fiercely she could feel the cold air slashing across her cheeks.

"No, *our* Sulu! He's here! I saw him just behind me, waiting on the ramp."

"Waiting to go through the portal?" Sulu cursed. "He must have somehow gotten in touch with Chekov, and they must be trying to attack the Gorn hub—"

"He seemed to be with some Romulans," Uhura said. "I didn't see anyone else with him." She paused. "I can hear some kind of machine pounding now, it's getting louder as we go downhill. Now we're going through a big metal gate. It looks like it's closing behind us."

"That must be the entrance to the portal hub," Sulu said. "Are they going to try and take you through it? Spock, what would that do to Uhura's connection back to us?"

"I do not know." The Vulcan's voice sounded more taut than Uhura could ever remember having heard it before, which made her own pulse kick with fear. "There is a chance the multiple subspace fields will create enough interference to free her. There is also a chance it will cause the Janus Gate's transport wave to collapse."

Uhura decided she would rather not have known that. "I see a lot more Gorn," she said. "They're looking through the force field at me, and they seem—Mr. Spock, I think they seem scared. Why would they be scared of me?"

"Maybe it's because you're not entirely materialized," Sulu suggested, and Uhura heard McCoy snort in the distance.

"So they're afraid of ghosts?"

"What we *don't* know about the Gorn would take me longer to tell you than what we know," Sulu retorted. "Uhura, do you seem to be moving toward any kind of opening or gate?"

"No, but there's a really bright light shining on the other side of this force field. It seems to be getting stronger—*ouch!*" A painful shock hit her again, stronger and more intense this time, as if she had been thrust through an electrically charged sieve into tiny dissociated fragments. Uhura closed her eyes and concentrated on keeping her hands clenched on the supporting bars of the Janus Gate. She could hear alarmed voices rise around her and feel the cold sting of involuntary tears freezing against her cheeks, but both sensations felt oddly muted, as if her connection back to Tlaoli was fading. That thought frightened Uhura enough to jerk her eyes open again.

At first, all she saw was that the force field around her was gone. Before she could open her mouth to tell Spock, however, she noticed that the heat-shimmer effect had simply expanded outward, multiplying itself to such an extent that it distorted everything beyond it to a crystalline haze. Several dark green smudges—the Gorn?—stood on the other side. On this side, all Uhura saw was the black rock pavement on which she stood, and a completely anomalous upholstered chair. It looked as if it had once been covered in sumptuous gold brocade, but time had faded it to a shredded spiderweb of dull ocher rags over a strange wire frame filled with what looked like electronic circuitry. Uhura took a step closer to examine it, then realized that she had regained control of her perspective in this place, and swung around to see what was happening behind her.

A humanoid figure, so thin-boned and adolescent it was impossible to tell if it was male or female, regarded her muzzily across a stretch of empty stone. It wore a simple Grecian-style robe that might have once been white, but now looked as faded and ragged as the upholstered chair. Dark bruises splotched across the figure's alabaster skin, but its long braided hair gleamed in the bright golden light from the force field surrounding them. Bloodshot eyes the opaque milk green of a tropical swamp peered at Uhura for a long time before the chiseled lips parted to speak.

"How . . . nice. A visitor."

Uhura blinked in surprise. It seemed as if the alien had spoken to her in English, but how could that be? Her universal translator was still back on Tlaoli with the rest of her gear. She didn't think the sounds she heard so faintly here on Basaraba were even being transferred out into the ice cave for her teammates to hear, much less sent back to her in translated form.

"Who are you?" she asked the golden-haired form.

"My name . . ." There was a long pause as the milky green eyes turned oddly vacant and inward. "I don't . . . remember anymore. I had a name once."

Uhura lowered her voice a little, not wanting to stress this fragile, mysterious being. "Do you remember what you're doing here? Are you a prisoner?"

"Uhura." That was older Sulu's voice, quiet as a moth fluttering by her ear. "We can only hear your side of this conversation. Can you phrase your questions to tell us as much as possible about who you're talking to?"

"A *prisoner.*" The alien gifted her with an angelic smile, as if it had been searching for that particular word for a long time and was delighted to have found it. "Yes, I am a prisoner. Of the Gorn."

"I am a prisoner of the Gorn, too," Uhura said. She tried to pack as much information as she could into her next question. "You look like a young adolescent of my species, but you are much taller. What race are you a member of?"

"I am . . ." There was another long and vacant pause, but this time Uhura could see a hint of deeper awareness struggling to bubble up beneath the glassy vagueness of its eyes. "I am . . . a Metron."

"A Metron." The word sounded familiar to Uhura, but it wasn't until she heard Sulu's strangled gasp back on Tlaoli that she remembered where she'd heard it before. This was a member of the powerful alien race that had mediated the original dispute between the humans and the Gorn! The race that had summarily cast the Gorn into exile from space by destroying all their starships along with their crews. "I thought the Gorn used to be *your* prisoners," she said, and heard Sulu's murmur of wordless approval at this line of questioning. "What happened?"

The alien shook its head, slowly, sadly, but it took a long time for it to form words that could express the emotion clouding its thin young face. "I was visiting here to . . . to look, to watch, to see—"

"You came here to monitor the Gorn?" Uhura asked when it seemed to stumble over another word it no longer remembered. The alien beamed at her again, its sadness drifting away like clouds dispersed by a morning sun.

"Yes. I *monitor.*" It pronounced that word the same way it had said "prisoner," like an old friend newly met after a long absence. "I monitor the Gorn. Yes."

Uhura wondered if it had already forgotten her original question. "Then how did the Gorn manage to take you prisoner? I thought the Metrons were a very powerful race."

"Powerful." A wash of pride seemed to clear a little of the mist from the Metron's eyes. "Yes, we are powerful. We exist in more dimensions than most races know. But on this world, the Gorn discovered a ... a substance, an essence, an organic chemical ..."

It was running out of vocabulary again, Uhura guessed. By now, however, she was also beginning to guess what its problem was. "The Gorn discovered some kind of drug, here on Basaraba," she said clearly, so that both Sulu and Spock could hear. "A drug they used to make you helpless while they broke free of their prison."

"A *drug.*" The Metron nodded, as if every new word she gave it added another fragment back to its intellect. "Yes, a drug. They give it to me always since then." A graceful sweep of one bruised hand indicated, for some odd reason, the threadbare chair. "And then this force field keeps most of me in it."

Uhura blinked at it again, wondering if that turn of phrase reflected the alien's drugged mind or some deeper reality. "The force field keeps *most* of you in?" she repeated, to let Sulu and Spock hear the Metron's odd expression, too. "Where is the rest of you?"

"Pulled away." Long slender fingers touched the bruises on its bare arms. "They cut, they separate, they take away ..." The almost violent way it moved its hands suggested to Uhura the word that it might be searching for, although she didn't understand how that word would apply.

"The Gorn *amputate* parts of your body?" she ventured, and got the angelic smile that she now knew meant she had given the Metron not just the word but the entire mental concept for which it had been searching. As far as Uhura could see, nothing seemed to be missing from its humanoid frame, but she remembered what it had said about Metrons existing in more dimensions than other races. "Where do they take the parts of you they amputate?"

It was the Metron's turn to blink at her. "Wherever it is they want to go."

Uhura gasped, so deeply she could feel the frigid air back on Tlaoli drive a spike of pain deep into her chest. When she exhaled again, she tasted an odd tang at the back of her throat, bitter and musky at the same time. *"You* are the Gorn's transport system," she guessed, and heard Sulu's muffled cry of surprise. "They've kept you here, drugged and helpless, for all these years. And they've used you to create their bridges from world to world."

"Yes." The Metron closed its milky green eyes for a moment, then opened them again. They seemed just a little more brilliant when it did, as if a sheen of tears had slid across them. "I try to hurt them," it said, defensive as a child explaining an accident it had caused. "Every time I send them, I try to hurt them. Sometimes I think I kill a lot of them, but usually I don't."

Uhura swallowed past another wave of shock. The taste of bitter musk was growing stronger. "I think some of the ones you've killed were trying to fight the Gorn," she told the Metron, as gently as she could. "You didn't know that?"

"No." The slender alien frowned, and Uhura saw another fragment of intelligence slowly surface from the murk in its mind. "I mean, yes. Sometimes I feel them attack me, those ones who are not Gorn. I wish I could tell them not to. My existence is too strong, it crosses too many dimensions. Any weapon they use will only be turned back on themselves. You will see." Its opaque green eyes met hers, sadly. "You will see, when the ones entering the portal now try to explode the weapon they have brought with them."

Only five Romulan soldiers remained in line ahead of them, now. The powerful heartbeat of the Gorn portal hub had risen to a rhythmic thunder as they descended deeper into the pit below Tesseract Fortress. At the end of the line loomed a massive titanium door which opened just far enough to let in small groups of invasion forces along with their equipment. When it was open, Sulu could see the yellow-white flare of a larger force field beyond it, although he wasn't sure if that marked the edge of the portal itself or was just a protection against last-ditch attacks. He watched as two of their Romulan allies discreetly dug the *Drake*'s warp core out from its covering of photon bombs and left the lid of the weapons chest ajar. A moment later, Chekov eased back to stand beside that opening, slipping his good hand inside to begin loosening the magnetic cover from the warp core's dilanthanum shell. They wouldn't actually take the core itself out until they were sure they were past all of the Gorns' scanners, but this way they would have a head start on activating its implosion sequence once they were actually standing on the verge of the portal.

Time was running out, and Sulu still hadn't decided what to do about Uhura.

She *must* be on the other side of the titanium gate. Sulu had no evidence other than the matching golden color of the two force fields he had seen, but he felt an irrational sureness that he would see her once they had been admitted. *And then what?* he asked himself sharply. If she had been haplessly thrown here by the ancient Tlaoli time transporter, the same way he had been, then they were both at the mercy of the Gorn and nothing could change that. It would make no sense to abort their attack on the Gorn portal hub just to make sure Uhura was all right. Wouldn't the kindest thing he could do be to destroy them both right now in the clean, instantaneous annihilation of a runaway matter/antimatter reaction?

But what if Uhura *hadn't* been sent here haplessly? What if the *Enterprise* crew back on Tlaoli had figured out how these time transfers were happening, and were trying to bring Sulu back to his proper place and time? Would he ruin everything by going along with the original attack plan? Shouldn't he at least try to locate and talk to Uhura before he let Chekov trigger the sequence that would lead to warp core implosion?

The questions tangled in Sulu's mind, hopelessly obscured by the numbing thunder of the hub portal and the freezing awareness that time was running out. The titanium door swung wide again, filling the darkness with the refracted glow of the force field beyond it. Sulu watched the last five Romulans ahead of them haul their sledge full of battle supplies through that gap, then felt a blast of ovenlike heat roll out, along with a musky smell so strong he thought it couldn't just be from the body oils of the portal's Gorn watchmen.

"Chekov," he said, as the door slammed shut and left them staring at it across empty darkness. "As soon as we go in, I'm going to try to find Uhura."

"No." The Russian didn't bother to glare at him, but his voice conveyed his disapproval clearly enough without it. With no one in front to observe them and the tall figures of Romulans shielding them from behind, he had flipped open the lid of the weapons crate and was openly dissembling the warp core inside, although he left the magnetic shielding propped above it to keep any last weapons detectors from going off. "You won't have time. We have to activate the implosion reaction right away."

"But if she's here to help us—"

This time, Chekov did glare at him, a look so hard and ruthless that Sulu almost stepped back from it. "In twenty years, this is the closest we have come to stopping the Gorn invasion," he snarled. "If you screw it up by trying to find someone who is already dead, I will borrow one of these Romulan weapons and shoot you down myself."

It was not a joke, or an idle threat. Chekov meant it. Sulu stood silent for a long moment, holding the older man's stare. None of the Romulans moved or spoke, although Sulu noticed one of the younger ones hitched his weapon a little farther forward on his shoulder, as if to make it easier for the Russian to grab it if he needed to.

"I won't ask you not to start the warp core sequence," he said at last. "But that's *my* shielded warp core you're using to blow up this fortress. You wouldn't be here if it wasn't for me getting thrown out of my rightful place in time. The least you can do before you blow me up is let me find out if Uhura's here because she came for me."

Chekov opened his mouth, but the portal's titanium gate began to swing open before he could reply. The Romulans didn't wait to see if the two humans would resolve their argument—the female leader snapped down the magnetic shielding on the warp core while the other three hefted the crate by its handles and headed for the gate. They moved quickly enough that Chekov and Sulu had to hurl themselves into a dead run to keep up. For all his age and injuries, Chekov still beat Sulu to the opening. Sulu felt the hot metal of the gate slam against the back of his legs as he dove through the last of the gap.

Inside, the yellow-gold glow of the force field was so bright that, at first, Sulu couldn't see past it to the rest of the room. When he finally blinked away the dazzle, he was surprised to discover that the force field was not located at the center. There was a titanium-floored platform there instead, looking surprisingly similar to the main transporter platform of the *Enterprise*. Behind it was what looked like an immense power plant, blasting out a fierce, dry heat along with the thundering roar they had heard all the way down.

It wasn't clear what part the glowing force field played in this unusual transport system, but it was certainly the focus of attention for the Gorn who were present. They were gathered around it, conversing in barely audible and untranslated roars and grumbles. No one seemed to be paying much attention to the empty central platform.

The Romulans paused slightly on the threshold of the room, and Sulu thought he saw a speculative gleam enter the leader's eyes as she glanced back over her shoulder at him. For a chilling moment, he wondered if she was about to betray them to the Gorn for whatever strategic advantage it might gain her, and he cursed himself for arguing with Chekov and placing both of them too far away to grab for one of the Romulans' guns. But although the female's face creased in a remarkably cruel smile, she waved Chekov toward the platform along with the three subordinates who carried the weapons chest. The older man went without a backward glance.

The Romulan turned back toward Sulu, pointing her gun in his direction vaguely enough that he didn't think it was meant to be a threat.

"They aren't watching like they usually do," she said. "But they will notice in a moment that we haven't gone through. Why don't you try to escape now?"

Sulu blinked at her for a moment, uncomprehending. Then he glanced at the others, who'd stopped Chekov before he could step up onto the platform. The Russian knelt beside it instead, stripping off the warp core's magnetic shielding so he could finish activating its implosion sequence. The others closed in around him, blocking the Gorn's view of what he did.

"We need to buy them some time," he guessed. "You want to create a distraction."

"What I want," said the female Romulan implacably, "is for you to escape now."

Sulu glanced around the room, seeing no trace of either Uhura or the portable force field prison in which she'd been confined. No one had come back up the ramp again, so unless they had taken her through the portal itself, Uhura had to be in here somewhere. That meant some of the Gorn peering so intently into the larger force field had to be the ones who had carried her down.

Without warning, Sulu darted past the Romulan officer and toward the force field, trying to let his motion explode in a way that would draw the Gorn's eyes toward him so quickly that they wouldn't spare a glance for Chekov. With a hissing noise, the Romulan leader leaped after him. She let him get just close enough to the force field to see a tantalizing glimpse of shadowy figures inside, then tore him away and threw him down on the ground hard enough to make his breath whoosh out from his chest. Sulu scrambled to his feet, gasping, then hurled himself sharply backward to avoid her threatening advance.

Most of the Gorn still seemed to be engrossed in whatever they were watching, but two or three glanced up to see what was going on. The closest swung his massive weapon around with reflexive and deadly accuracy to aim at Sulu. With an equally fast reaction, the female Romulan vaulted between them and slammed Sulu flat to the ground with the butt of her own weapon. Sulu felt pain strafe up along the side of his ribs, and gritted his teeth against the sudden effort it took to breathe. Broken ribs were a small price to pay for that near-miss. He knew he was lucky not to be dead.

"Human cretin," spat the Romulan. "Either way, you die."

Sulu turned his head against the floor, breathing shallowly to keep his ribs from screaming in pain, and tried to squint past the glare of the force field. All he could detect was that one shadow was much taller and thinner than the other. He couldn't tell if the smaller one was Uhura, but the portable force field cell they had brought her down here in lay tumbled on its side and unheeded next to the larger field's perimeter.

"Shoot him," rumbled the closest Gorn through his crude translating device. "If you take him through the portal, he will die soon anyway."

"Then why waste the energy?" The Romulan reached down and jerked Sulu to his feet, wrenching a groan of pain out of him despite his resolve not to cry out. "He's not worth—"

A shrill warning alarm cut across her voice. It was so familiar, and so reminiscent of his life back on the *Enterprise,* that Sulu felt his stomach lurch with loss instead of shock. A moment later, a computerized voice said in typical calm Starfleet style, "Warning. The antimatter containment field of this reactor has been breached. Evacuate the area immediately. Core implosion imminent."

# Chapter Eleven

EVEN IF SHE HADN'T seen Sulu standing in the long line of Romulans, Uhura would have known immediately that the weapon the Metron spoke of must have been brought in by the last two humans on this planet. She felt her pulse begin to hammer in her throat again, and tried to swallow past the fear. If the Sulu here on Basaraba blew himself up before she could reach him now, she wasn't sure there would be another time to which the Janus Gate could send her where she could save him.

"Spock," she said urgently, not caring now if the Metron wondered who she was talking to, "Sulu and Chekov are bringing some kind of weapon into the portal right now. The Metron says it can't hurt it because it extends across too many dimensions. What should we do?"

She heard the other, older version of Sulu groan at the news, but the crisper voice she was waiting for didn't come. Uhura felt a faint, distant tingle run across her skin and wondered if the Vulcan was attempting to retrieve her through the Janus Gate. She held her breath as the tingle grew stronger, and the bitter musky taste in her mouth almost choked her. Uhura glanced around with sudden understanding, seeing a faint greenish mist coming out from the circuitry at the base of the tattered chair. The drug the Gorns were "always giving" to the Metron must be airborne, and it was coming in through the miniature transporter that had originally been hidden inside that chair! And if she could somehow taste it back on Basaraba, then she was here as more than just a ghostly visual image. There was at least a fractional amount of physical exchange going on.

"Sulu," she said softly, so as not to disturb Spock. "Can you smell anything in the air around me?"

There was a pause, then the older man said just as softly. "A tang, like hair and metal burning. Is that the drug?"

"Yes." Uhura glanced at the chair. "It's coming from a small transporter unit. The Gorn must need to keep it at a consistent level—I think it's been coming in all the time I've been here. If Spock could just take that small transporter unit away—"

"The force field is still interfering with my ability to fully engage the Janus Gate," the Vulcan said, entering the discussion so calmly that Uhura suspected he had heard all of their muttered comments. The ice cave back on Tlaoli must be utterly silent. "But I believe I have enough control to try something else. Lieutenant Uhura, I must ask you to stand as close to the Metron as you possibly can."

Uhura didn't hesitate. Using her will as much as her not-quite-there body, she managed to fling herself across the space between her and the golden-haired alien who was just now parting its lips as if to question her. Even as she went, Uhura felt the tingling sensation grow to an unpleasant needling that made her skin prick into goose bumps of response.

"What are you doing?" The Metron stepped back when she approached, a slow alarm drifting into its opaque eyes. "You shouldn't touch me, it will throw you through the portal..."

Uhura stopped about a half-meter away, seeing that the alien had backed itself almost into the force field. "You have to let me stand close to you," she pleaded. "We're trying to free you."

"We?" The Metron peered around the empty stone floor as if it thought it had somehow missed seeing someone who was in here with them. "Who are *we?*"

"A group of humans from another place and time," Uhura said quickly. She wasn't sure how much time she had left to convince the Metron to trust her. And whatever Spock was planning to do, there was no way of knowing how long it would take for the Gorn's airborne drug to fade from the alien's multidimensional body. "I'm not really here completely... part of me is still back in the place I came from."

"I understand," said the Metron. "That is why they brought you here to me. They must have thought you were another of my race."

"We are going to try to free you," Uhura told it. "But for it to work, I *must* stand as close to you as I can."

The Metron's eyes seemed to grow just a little clearer. "Approach, then," it said, and held its arms out and back, as if holding back something unseen behind it. "I will try to keep from sending you anywhere."

Uhura took a deep breath, her lungs filling with an odd mixture of both frigid and musky air, and moved closer again to the Metron. As she did, the needling sensation across her skin grew even more intense, as if somehow her body was absorbing and reradiating the energy fields in conflict all around her. Uhura steeled herself to bear it, even when it seemed to sink down through her skin into the muscle and bone beneath and deepened from discomfort into actual pain. After a few seconds, she realized that the goose bumps on her skin were still there, however, and a moment later she realized why. The air around her was growing colder, much colder.... Spock was using the Janus Gate's associative transport function to send all he could to Basaraba through her flickering connection. And what he was sending was Tlaoli's glacial but absolutely pure air.

The Metron stiffened and jerked its eyes closed. Uhura thought perhaps it was just trying to hold onto its strength, to hold back the cross-dimensional transfer into which it might involuntarily hurl her. But then the alien's eyes fluttered and opened to stare at her with an expression so intense it was almost awe.

Its eyes were a pure and glittering emerald.

"I am...whole." The Metron glanced down at its alabaster arms and one by one the bruises disappeared. "I am one again." It glanced across the room at the threadbare chair, and that abruptly disappeared as well, making the air crack like thunder as it rushed into the space that had been vacated. "And I *will* be free."

With a roar, the force field exploded outward around them, crumbling into diamond glitter and shrieking fragments of displaced energy. Uhura felt the pain burst away from her as that confining field disappeared. She staggered in the whirling aftermath, and heard Captain Sulu's voice shouting in her ear.

"*Don't let go!* Uhura, don't let go! We're going to try to bring you back!"

"Not yet!" She tightened her phantom, barely felt grip on the Janus Gate and spun around, looking for the Sulu she knew. A massive row of Gorn faced the Metron, their predatory jaws open in what might have been either startled gapes or angry snarls. The golden-haired alien gazed back at them contemptuously. Then, with a flick of its fingers, they were suddenly gone. The Metron turned toward the other figures standing in that chamber, and before Uhura could force words through her cold, dry lips, they vanished, as well.

"Wait!" Uhura cried out, and the Metron glanced across at her. Its emerald eyes were as clear now as a deep-green tropical sea. With the room empty, she could see that there were only two people left: one crouched protectively over what looked like a partially disassembled warp core, one crumpled and gasping with pain on the floor right in front of her. Uhura recognized his stained and sodden Starfleet tunic. "These are my allies! Let me take them back with me—"

"Very well," said the alien, calmly. One gesture swept the two men together and dumped them carelessly at Uhura's feet, then the Metron moved away, floating rather than walking across the chamber to examine the silver object gleaming at the foot of what looked like a huge transporter pad. "Ah...an antimatter power plant. Even better than a weapon...and its confinement shield is just about to breach—"

Uhura knelt down beside the men she had been gifted with, feeling another painful jolt as her not-quite materialized body made contact with them. "Spock, bring us home," she ordered. "Bring us home *now!*"

There was a momentary pause, then the whirling nothingness of time transfer seemed to surge in upon Uhura, this time manifesting itself as a powerful vortex whose core was her. The Gorn portal began to dissolve and spin itself away at the edges of that nothingness, but not before Uhura heard the sound of what must be Metron laughter, light and silvery like fairy bells heard in the distance. Then, distantly but clear as crystal, the sound of the alien's voice.

"What a lovely going-away present for my gracious hosts."

"Here they come!"

Chekov jolted awake with a gasp, snapping his head up off his arms and wondering for one brief, panicked instant where he was and why he was sleeping in the cold.

Then the distinctive smell of the cave's frozen travertine bit at his nostrils, and his eyes locked on the twin columns of swirling gold rapidly brightening out on the main floor. The details of the last two days swept over him like a splash of cold water—including the memory of Spock placing him in command of this little party when the Vulcan sent them up here to wait.

"Let's not get too excited." Zap Sanner's voice sounded closer than Smith's, but still rebounded through the column-filled chamber too wildly to locate. "We might have quite a wait ahead of us before the machine lets them out."

Chekov scrambled to his feet, half-blind in the dark despite the growing brightness of the columns, and called, "Mr. Smith, call Mr. Spock and report that we have activity." He hoped he didn't sound too sleepy or caught off guard.

Smith's answer gave him no clue. "Aye-aye, sir."

Despite the lengthy walk to the upper chamber and the lengthy period of inactivity he'd known was waiting for them there, Chekov had not for one moment considered that he would fall asleep while waiting for his crewmates to materialize. He'd been tense with excitement at his first (albeit tiny) command, and the adrenaline pumped into his system from his own brush with the future still had his stomach fluttering and his mouth too dry. He'd expected to pace back and forth in the dark, monitoring the others' locations around the chamber and keeping his hand close to his communicator in preparation for signaling Spock at the first sign of activity.

Instead, he was groggy from an uneasy sleep that hadn't been at all restful, patting blindly for his helmet among the rocks of the breakdown pile while smothering a fresh yawn against the palm of his hand.

The purring rasp of a carbide ignitor caught his attention, and he looked up just in time to see James Kirk's face appear in the darkness above a freshly lit helmet lamp.

"What are you doing here?"

"Your job, apparently." Kirk passed the lit helmet down to him, then scooped up his own from the rocks nearby and struck its light with a single practiced flick of his thumb. "Don't worry—you didn't miss anything."

Chekov stepped back to give the boy room to hop down to the floor, but didn't make any effort to hide the irritation on his face. Kirk ignored him with what could only be the ease of long practice. Clapping his helmet atop his head, Kirk asked, "Don't any of you guys keep regular hours? Everybody up top is snoozing, too."

Chekov kept his helmet in both hands, remembering what Uhura had said about the lights making it hard to identify faces. "We've all been on emergency status these last few days," he said, starting in the direction of Sanner's and Smith's collected lights. "That has a tendency to disrupt your schedule." *Which isn't an excuse for falling asleep on duty.* But he didn't admit that to his future commander.

Kirk's interest had already been drawn to other things. He waved toward the nearest bright gold column, his mouth tweaked into a grin of triumph. "Told you they glowed."

He had, although Chekov hadn't thought about that particular detail since then. Abruptly, he realized that the glowing Kirk had seen upon his arrival on Tlaoli was someone being healed inside one of these alien medical chambers. Someone who had been plucked from certain death at another point in the timeline and deposited here to be recycled. *Me,* Chekov thought with a little start. *Me, after the drowning. Me, just before I died.* He suddenly didn't feel at all sleepy anymore.

Sanner glanced up as they drew near. His eyebrows flew up almost under his helmet when he caught sight of Kirk. "How did you get down here?"

The boy held out the front of his mud-soaked shirt as though that made the answer obvious. "Through the sinkhole. You left all the ropes."

"I should never have taught you how to rappel," Sanner complained with a sigh.

The geologist's disapproval didn't appear to affect Kirk any more than Chekov's had. "So what is this?" the boy asked, studying the nearest glowing pillar. It had swelled almost too bright to look at directly, the humanoid figure inside blurred beyond recognition beneath layers of ancient flowstone. "Part of your alien transporter?"

"The arrival gate," Sanner said. "The machine puts you through these healing chambers before it lets you out into the room. At least, that's what we're pretty sure it does."

Kirk nodded, his eyes still taking in every detail of the strange device. When he finally glanced aside at Chekov, the ensign wasn't surprised to see an uncertain thoughtfulness hiding there. "This is your pilot coming home?"

Chekov nodded. "That's what we're hoping."

Kirk looked back at the machine. "So who's he bringing with him?"

Before Chekov could decide how to explain the situation they'd left behind in the ice cave, the nearest of the two columns dimmed to darkness and Sanner remarked, rather cheerfully, "It looks like we're about to find out."

Chekov put out one arm as a signal that they all stay together, even though no one had made any particular move to disperse. It just seemed like the sort of thing the party leader should make sure of. "Lieutenant?" Even as he called out, he realized that he didn't know which lieutenant he should be expecting to answer—Sulu or Uhura. After all, Spock must have figured out how to fully transport Uhura into the future long enough for her to retrieve Lieutenant Sulu. If not, how could anyone be arriving now? Suddenly afraid of leaping to an assumption that would only serve to make him look uncertain, he called, "This is Ensign Chekov. Mr. Spock sent us up here to meet you."

Kirk elbowed him silently, and Chekov followed the boy's nod to a dim spot of movement in the pillar-littered darkness. He strained to catch the first spark of reflection off a gold-braided sleeve, or the flash of Sulu's relieved smile as the lieutenant neared the halo of their combined lamplight. Instead, the figure which approached them—unhurried, deliberate—took longer to resolve out of the darkness than a bright Starfleet uniform should have. Then the light finally settled on a heartbreakingly familiar black-and-violet camouflage, and Chekov's heart sank.

Only to freeze at the base of his throat when he saw the newcomer's face.

He didn't look that different. Chekov thought he should probably be pleased about that. No gray hair, no dramatic signs of aging in the smooth, clean-shaven face, just a tiredness so profound that Chekov felt almost guilty for succumbing to his own fatigue only a little while ago. His older counterpart didn't even look particularly surprised. He just rubbed at the side of his face almost absently, then turned away from his younger self and focused his attention on Sanner. "Where's Captain Sulu?"

Chekov clenched his teeth on a surge of annoyance. Bad enough to be summarily dismissed by half the senior officers he worked under, he didn't need to tolerate such behavior from himself. "We left him with Mr. Spock, just down the corridor from here." He stopped short of admitting that they didn't know whether or not Captain Sulu was in fact still there. The answer had the virtue of being true without inviting too many uncomfortable questions. He gestured brusquely toward the other column, already fading toward darkness. "As soon as your traveling companion comes through, we'll rejoin them."

The older man stared at him with an expression that might have been mild amusement or disdain. It bothered Chekov a little that he couldn't tell which. How was it possible that he could grow so far away from himself that he couldn't even interpret his own expressions? A flash memory of a Gorn talon sinking into his eye—and he decided he didn't really want to think too much about the answer to that question.

"Ensign Chekov . . ."

Smith's anxious whisper cut across his thoughts, opening a welcome escape route. He turned away from himself, flushing with discomfort, and let Smith distract him with whatever she had to say.

She held out her communicator when he acknowledged her, its antenna grid still open and her face drawn into a frown of worry. "I'm not getting anything from Mr. Spock's party. I've tried calling twice, but nobody answers."

"It's probably the Gate's subspace interference," Sanner suggested, but Smith shook her head.

"I don't think so, sir."

Chekov took the communicator and ran a quick diagnostic, even though nothing seemed amiss on its small display. The open channel hummed faintly, less clear than a good subspace connection ought to be but nothing like the howling static that had characterized their communication attempts when they'd first come into the caves hours before. A query to Spock's communicator produced the expected chirrup of receipt, but no voice followed in response to the call. Chekov folded the communicator shut and bit his lip as he tried to think of what to do.

Like so much else on this ill-fated mission, the Janus Gate made the decision for him.

"Chekov...?"

He turned at the sound of Sulu's voice, a little surprised, but primarily grateful that the Gate had released its last occupant before he was forced to split the party further to investigate the ice cave's silence. Before he'd even finished his turn, though, he saw that the lieutenant's greeting hadn't been meant for him. It was his older self Sulu approached, and his older self who was on the receiving end of the lieutenant's teasing smile.

"Time travel becomes you."

A look of faint embarrassment crossed the older man's face, and he reached up to rub at his cheek again. "A trivial use of medical technology."

The exchange didn't make any sense to Chekov, and he felt strangely excluded from his own life.

Sulu flashed a glance across the rest of the party, looking for someone in particular and obviously not finding them. "Where's Uhura?" he asked worriedly.

That, at least, was something Chekov knew how to answer. "If you'll come with us, sir, we can all find out together."

The conduits had begun to melt.

"This is a good sign!" Sanner enthused as he led them through gathering curtains of pale, clammy mist. "See, the energy storage system for the Gate makes use of an endothermic reaction...."

Chekov didn't bother trying to follow the geologist's explanation, content to relinquish responsibility for the small party to the newly arrived Sulu and...well, to himself. He didn't have to worry anymore about whether going back to the ice cave was the best course of action, or whether wending their way through the dripping, hissing caverns ran too great a risk of someone getting lost. He only had to obey orders, and trust in the wisdom of those whose ranks let them carry more gold on their sleeves. He didn't know whether to feel relieved or disappointed.

Kirk drew up alongside him and watched Sanner paw through the slushing ice ahead of them in search of the latest spot marker. "It's my turn now, isn't it?" he asked Chekov, calmly and quietly. "To go through the device, I mean."

He meant to sound unconcerned, Chekov knew, but instead his voice came out too rigid, too heavy with inappropriate disinterest. Remembering the fear that had been so naked in the boy's face atop the karst plateau, Chekov let the three officers pull a little ahead of them to minimize any chances of being overheard.

"Whether or not they send you will depend on what Mr. Spock decides we have to do about..." He couldn't think of a comfortable way to refer to the man who was also himself, so settled for, "about our extra visitor," as though they were talking about an unexpected guest at a formal dinner. He turned sideways to avoid being doused by the freshly melted water now tumbling out of the hole Captain Kirk had kicked through the ceiling a whole lifetime ago. "We have a few hours left before we have to make any final decisions."

"But you got your pilot back," Kirk pointed out. "You don't have to worry anymore about losing him when the timeline shifts back to where you think it's supposed to be." He shrugged, looking petulant and angry. "That leaves just me to put back where I came from."

Smith splashed a little closer from behind them. "Mr. Spock's getting really good at controlling what the machine does."

Kirk glanced aside at Chekov, then turned his attention pointedly forward, toward the dark figure most plainly visible through the haze of mist ahead of them. "Oh, yeah," he agreed, with deep irony, "I noticed that."

"He can put you back in your timeline a whole day later than you left," Smith persisted, apparently as immune to Kirk's sarcasm as she was to everyone else's. "He can put you in dozens of meters away from where you came out of. We can even send you back with a weapon, so you can defend yourself."

Chekov tried to summarize what he knew Smith meant to convey. "We'll make sure you go back with every advantage we can give you."

Looking down at his feet, Kirk nodded mutely. Chekov knew the games the boy's mind was playing—offering up visions of all the dangers they couldn't possibly predict in advance, all the ways he could die that none of them could help him avoid. He tried to think of something he could say to reassure the boy, but Kirk deflected the effort by asking instead, "Will I remember any of this? Any of you guys, or what happened here?"

Chekov thought about that very seriously. "I don't know," he admitted at last. "Mr. Spock seems to think that once the timeline is repaired and the bubble we constructed collapses, we'll remember our past as a single unbroken timeline, without these changes and interruptions." He hadn't told anyone that he found that thought just a little disturbing. He didn't like the idea of entire days of his life fluttering out of his memory as though they never existed. Even if they never did.

"But what about me?" Kirk asked. Droplets of mist sparkled where they'd gathered on his eyelashes and hair, making him look ephemeral and oddly fragile. "How can I remember my past as one uninterrupted line? I'm here! You guys might be sending me back with a weapon! How am I supposed to not realize that all that happened?"

Chekov didn't know how to answer him except honestly. "I really don't know. I wish I did."

A startled shout from the front of the group clapped off the mist-shrouded walls. Chekov saw the men in front of them stagger to a hurried, uneven halt, then the mist all around came alive with frantic movement. Metal clattered on freshly exposed stone, *snickting* into softened ice to propel intricate black steel bodies up the walls, across the ceiling. Chekov thrust Kirk behind him, felt Smith close in on the other side, and realized almost immediately how pointless the effort had been.

The little metal creatures were everywhere, pressing in from behind, cutting them off from the front. They dropped from the ceiling like fat mechanical spiders, landing with a lightness all out of proportion with their apparent size. They were each one as big as a human head, but with a confusing combination of limbs and what looked like the world's most intricate sensors. One of them scampered forward with its topmost appendages upraised and waving, aiming itself for Kirk, or Chekov, or both.

Smith thrust herself into the thing's path and kicked at it fiercely. Her foot never even made contact. It leaped onto her leg, then away again, too quickly to see precisely what had happened. But the security guard went down as if poleaxed. Chekov tried to catch her, to protect her from cracking her head against the rocks littering the conduit floor. Instead, they went down together in an undignified tangle.

An arm's length away, the swarm of artificial monsters surged back as a group, as though unwilling to make any further contact with the humans. They reformed into a solid, unmoving line, blocking the corridor leading back toward the breakdown exit and the Janus Gate's arrival columns.

Chekov slid himself awkwardly out from under Smith, trying not to let her drop unsupported to the floor. Kirk caught his arm and helped to pull him upright just as someone else took Smith's head in their hands and rolled her neatly to one side to check for a pulse.

"Is she dead?" Kirk asked. He sounded like a boy again, afraid and unsure.

Chekov's older self twitched the faintest hint of a smile. "No. But it stunned her pretty hard." Standing, he hefted her easily over one shoulder and turned to look at Sulu. "I'd suggest we go where they want."

It was only then that Chekov saw the clear path yawning ahead of them. A staccato line of mechanicals decorated the walls leading toward the Janus Gate control room, but they seemed only interested in watching. When Sulu nodded, saying softly, "Stick close," no one breathed so much as an "Aye, sir" in reply. They simply clustered as tightly together as possible and followed him down the silent rows of machines. The little creatures fell in neatly behind them, bringing up the rear like some perverse mechanical guard.

An odd light from the chamber that held the Janus Gate spilled out into the corridor, polluting the mist and staining it a sickly orange. Chekov knew something was wrong even before they rounded the entrance—the earthy smell of melting ice and wet rock had been almost completely overwritten by a harsh, artificial tang, and the sharp clacks and clatters of mechanical industry filled the silence where the Janus Gate's blue force field had hummed only a few short hours ago. The Gate itself had withdrawn back into its silver metal cage, a blue flame heart pulsing to its own alien rhythm.

The entire chamber had been invaded. Elaborate machines, some of them twice the height of a man, surrounded the Janus Gate's central controls or paced the distant perimeter of the cavern. At first, Chekov thought they were only larger versions of the metal creatures who'd surrounded them in the hallway, then one peeled away from the cluster at the control panel and hurried to gather the smaller machines about it like a hen with her chicks. They disappeared into the body of their larger cousin, becoming new convolutions and appendages as though they'd been there all along.

Reassembled, the mother machine all but enveloped Chekov's small party with two of its long arms and pushed them to join their comrades near the middle of the room.

Spock welcomed their arrival with a minute nod of his head, but the humans clustered behind him gave a collective murmur of relief and jostled forward to make contact. Uhura greeted Sulu with a silent hug, and Captain Sulu joined the older Chekov in settling Smith to the ground with no indication of surprise or alarm at seeing him here. Behind them, McCoy coaxed Carolyn Palamas to look up from her hands and see that the others had returned before shouldering his way through the group to kneel beside Chekov next to the unconscious guard.

"What did we miss?" Sanner asked Spock in a low voice.

Spock didn't answer, absorbed in his study of the aliens. They weren't simply robots, Chekov realized. Along the face of each metal torso, a curving length of window revealed a chamber filled with some type of cloudy fluid or gas. A frail, multilegged creature hardly bigger than a skinned dog floated inside, cushioned by some unseen force that kept it steady while still allowing it to flex and turn as its conveyance moved. When one of the complex machines danced up alongside the guards holding them hostage, it moved with a light, incongruous grace, and crouched to a halt much closer than was comfortable with its large size.

"This is the language."

The words, while cool and easily understandable, would never be mistaken for a human's. Even the *Enterprise*'s main computer had more warmth and inflection in its manufactured voice. They extruded from somewhere unidentifiable on the creature's artificial carapace, a lifeless stitchery of sound that might have been individual notes picked out on a toy piano for all the emotion they contained. It had no recognizable face and precious little movement in its limbs, so it was impossible to tell if it meant the words as a statement or a question.

Spock cocked his head as though he found the attempt at communication fascinating. "Yes, that is the language we understand."

A complex series of movements, too fast and delicate for the eye to follow, produced what Chekov recognized as Uhura's archaeological translator. The alien offered it on the end of one extended appendage. After a moment, Spock reached up to take it, then passed it behind him to Uhura without turning around.

Without warning, the creature whirled away and scuttled back to rejoin its brethren at the Janus Gate console. Blue light glowed warmly on the face of its transparent tank. "This is the language," it announced again in its flat alien voice. "We are Shechenag." As a single gesture, each of the aliens surrounding the Janus Gate pattered complicated hands over the surface of the machine. Looking for something. Reassuring themselves. "This device falls outside your jurisdiction. You will leave now."

A wave of alarm swept through the small group. McCoy started to protest, but Chekov shushed him with a hand on his arm.

"It is not our intention to trespass," Spock said calmly, as though reasoning with grotesquely inhuman aliens were part of his everyday duties. "However, this device has displaced one of our companions—"

"This is understood." An almost panicked spasm of movement flashed among the aliens, then stilled again. "Damage to the timescape cannot be undone through further damage. This device causes damage. This device must not be active."

Something that might have been irritation knit together on Spock's brow, but nothing in his voice or stance betrayed any emotion. "Are you the original architects of this device?"

"We are Shechenag. This device must not be active." The mother hen device hurried toward them again, arms outflung and quivering. The sharp *snick* of metal slashing against metal could only be a threat, no matter how placid the voice of the creature speaking. "You must take your vessel now and leave this space. We give you ten hours to do so."

# THE JANUS GATE

## PAST PROLOGUE

# Chapter One

COLD BIT AT Kirk's cheeks as he followed his youngest crewman deeper into the frozen dark. The glow of the boy's carbide lamp barely disturbed the surface of the blackness, and it didn't soften the hard angles of the fresh ice sheets surrounding them at all. It only pushed the dark ahead of them, one cautious step at a time. Chekov followed the invisible line sketched for him by his compass and Kirk tried not to make the ensign any more nervous than he already was by treading on his heels as he followed.

The maps were good, Kirk thought, flipping through the painstakingly drawn pages and mentally reliving the landing party's passage through each of those chambers and tunnels as he did so. Amazingly good, considering they'd had to be re-created in the midst of everything else the group had gone through to get this far. Now they were close to being out of this subterranean icebox. The exit was only a few tens of meters over their heads—hot showers, full meals, and clean, dry uniforms were just a short vertical climb in their futures, and Kirk was as glad as anyone else to be done with this part of their adventure. At least he could attack the mystery of the starships scattered across Tlaoli's surface from the relative safety of his own bridge, with his crew safe and whole alongside him.

An unexpected bark, popping against the unseen walls of the cavern, yanked Kirk to a halt. He shot a quick look in the direction where the clatter seemed to settle, but, strain as he might, could only see the same opaque blackness that had hidden every other danger since they'd set foot in this cave. Kirk grabbed at Chekov's shoulder to halt him. "Do you hear that?" he asked urgently, releasing the boy to turn and check the party members they'd left near the entrance.

Heat from a sudden fire swarmed up into his face and knocked him to the ground.

Kirk's first instinct was to guard the map—the precious, re-created map that was their best insurance against wandering through these caves forever. He tucked it flat to the belly of his cave jumper and rolled face-down in the frozen mud to shield it from the flames. But just that quickly, the heat and light receded as though sucked out through a blasted airlock, and the ground beneath him was dry and hard and anomalously warm against his frost-reddened cheek.

He reached out one hand to slap at the ground in front of his face. Concrete. He'd fallen down in a cave on the fringes of the frontier, but he'd somehow landed on an expanse of what was unmistakably poured concrete.

Voices and sirens pushed Kirk's senses past what had been the un-seen walls of the cavern, opening up the darkness into an expansive night with five tiny, bloody moons strung diagonally above the tree horizon like a necklace of badly set garnets. Dry leaves skated across the road in fits and starts, leaping spastically into the air where they were startled by hot thermals, then flashing into ash in the dragon's breath of flaming trees and burning buildings. Kirk heard someone cry out in a barking language that he knew wasn't human, but when he rolled to place the sound there was nothing to see but a still unburnt tree line dancing freakishly in the shadows from the fires across the way.

The staccato popping of antique firearms drew his stomach up into his throat even before the more familiar whine of phaser fire sang out in reply. *Starfleet.* Whatever was happening here, there were Starfleet peo-ple involved in it—maybe even his own people. He wasn't going to lie here on the ground and just wait for the battle to find him, not if there was anything he could do to help.

Stuffing the map down the front of his jumper, he scrambled to his feet and turned a circle to give himself a starting point from which to get his bearings. The road on which he stood was unlined and empty—like a logging road that went only one place and didn't need to supply any addi-tional directions to what little traffic used it. An impressive deciduous for-est walled one side, its tattered canopy still scattering the dying leaves of early autumn. Across the road from the forest, a handful of older trees had been left to decorate the edges of a concrete-and-glass city that grew gradually taller as the buildings moved away from the road. It was on this side of the landscape that the fires burned.

Kirk stared toward the stair-step pyramids and cylindrical towers al-ready swathed in robes of flame, until they stood out both bright and dark against the nighttime sky. *I should know this place.* Bits and pieces of memory jostled for attention at the back of his brain, only to be beaten into silence by the horrific scene in front of him. If he knew this town, this planet, it was in some vastly different context. Like a familiar painting, inexpertly re-created from a new and confusing angle. Or tourist streets seen at night when he'd previously only walked them during the day.

That he should know this place seemed terribly important—enough to make his heart pound faintly, like a drum still muffled by distance—but the front of his mind insisted, *No! Go find the others!* before he could spend too long trying to excavate the memory. Blinking hard, Kirk pulled his eyes away from the conflagration, and ducked into the cover of the tree line.

The road arced back toward the heart of the burning city, and the old growth forest followed it only partway. Kirk paused at the edge of the trees and crouched behind a massive trunk to survey the firelit expanse between forest and town. The road itself remained clear, but quick figures darted between buildings and immobile vehicles just inside the edges of the city. Some of them clumped together in terrified, stumbling groups as they scrambled toward perceived safety; others carried what were obviously weapons, although who or what they pursued wasn't always so clear.

Kirk fingered the collar of his gold cave jumper. Movement had cracked off the sheets of mud made brittle by the dry autumn air, leaving him pale and exposed. While his gold command tunic was only marginally darker, at least he had on black trousers and boots beneath the jumper, which would cut his visibility in half. Besides, he had a feeling that the moisture-wicking nano-weave was going to be about the least useful thing he could have brought here with him. He would much rather have had one of Martine's phasers, or at least one of Sanner's climbing ropes.

He stowed the folded jumper in a hollow beneath the tree's hunched up roots, burying it under a few large handfuls of leaf litter and hoping he'd be able to find the spot later if he needed it. He buried Chekov's notebook with its maps and attached mechanical pencil along with the jumper. He couldn't imagine what use he could possibly find for it, but it still somehow seemed ungrateful to just abandon it after forcing the boy to sit on the floor of a frozen cave and re-create the thing from memory.

The weapons fire had thinned, with only a single phaser wailing in futile response to increasingly bold chatters of gunfire. Kirk threaded between shrubbery and buildings, hugging walls as closely as he could so as to present the smallest possible target to anyone trying to shoot down on him from above. *It would help to know who's doing the shooting.* It would tell him what sort of tactics to expect, not to mention what sort of

weapons and what sort of physical capabilities. He didn't like not knowing who the bad guys were.

As if in answer to his thoughts, a pair of gunmen clattered down the
long flight of open-rail steps that wrapped around the building in front of
Kirk. The metallic thunder of their footsteps rang hollowly somewhere in
the back of Kirk's memory, and he suddenly knew the building at his
shoulder was a tall extended-family dwelling without understanding how
he knew that or why it should make the inside of his mouth taste like bile.
When the first man to reach the ground lifted his head at the foot of the
stairs, he looked across the neatly trimmed hedgerow and locked eyes
with Kirk as though he'd known all along the captain would be there. And
even his pale copper-penny eyes looked terrifyingly familiar to Kirk.

Kirk struck out before the man could swing his long weapon into firing position. Twisting to one side, Kirk jammed the muzzle of the rifle
down toward the ground and landed a solid blow on the man's jaw without interrupting his turn. The momentum alone snapped the man's head
aside and wrenched the rifle from his grasp. Still gripping the muzzle,
Kirk stepped neatly over the toppled body and let the rifle's heavy metal
stock finish its swing into the shins of the man above him on the stairs. A
hissing thread of heat tore past very close to Kirk's skull, then the second
man was down atop his partner, and Kirk had knocked him senseless with
the butt of the first man's gun. He rubbed at his temple where the shot had
narrowly missed him, and stared down at the unconscious bodies. He
knew where he was now. He knew *when* he was. He just didn't understand how he had gotten here.

They were both obviously Grexxen—their faces a bronze so extreme
it bordered on greenish, and their hair the same faded copper as their
eyes. A little hair dye and a pair of dark glasses, and either of them could
have passed as human in any metropolitan center on Earth. But they
weren't human—they were Vragax. Even after all these years, thinking
about that militant tribe of Grexxen natives filled Kirk's stomach with
acid and made him want to spit out every foul epithet he'd ever heard. Because even after nineteen years he couldn't forget the helmetlike fall of
Vragax braids, or the smell of their *puhen* oil-based warpaints, or the way
they laughed at how humans died when they shot them down in the
streets.

He shook both men out of their pants with no more care than he'd
have shown a sack full of potatoes. Tying them both to the stairs, he took
their weapons and every power cell and munition they had between them.
One of them also had a string of handheld explosives. The other had a radio that didn't appear to be picking anything up on its open frequency.

Kirk turned it off to keep it silent, then threw it as far away into the bushes as he could.

The streets were familiar now. Eerily undersized, as though he'd expanded them in his memory, and still uncomfortable in that tourist-streets-after-dark way. He remembered abruptly that his father had never let them leave the embassy grounds after nightfall. "It's not a curfew," George Kirk had insisted. "I just won't have any boys of mine showing disrespect for the local authorities with their shenanigans." As though the shenanigans of two human boys could have inspired anything to rival what had finally gone down on this planet.

He checked both the charges and the loads on the gauss rifles as he jogged, almost by memory, back toward the burning Starfleet embassy. They both had several hours' use still in them, and more than sixty shots between them, not counting reloads. He flipped the switch to single shot to save on ammunition. Unlike the Vragax, he had no use for mowing down large swaths of the civilian population with every squeeze of the trigger. Anything he couldn't do one bullet at a time, he wasn't interested in doing at all.

He found the shuttle nose-down in the lawn of a Kozhu-run infant-care facility, half-buried in the dirt it had ploughed up ahead of its long skid, like a dead giant beneath a carelessly thrown shroud. Just like he remembered it. It was easier to see what had killed it, now that he was older and understood better what to look for. A small, exhaust-seeking microbolt had blown away the rear of one nacelle and part of the stern bulkhead. The remaining engine had been just enough to let Ensign Leone put them down in something more like a landing than a crash, but not enough to let either Zeke Leone or his copilot walk away from the attempt. The shuttle had split open on impact, trailing debris and bodies behind it for a hundred meters. The fact that neither the Vragax nor the Kozhu were supposed to have surface-to-air weaponry powerful enough to take down a Starfleet shuttle hadn't saved Leone or the other men who'd gone down on the shuttle with him.

Kirk ducked behind the mound of steaming dirt, just beside where the shattered pilot's seat should have been. Across the shuttle's nose from him, nine men in the red-and-black of Starfleet security littered the torn-up ground like broken dolls. Kirk closed his eyes against the memory of their leader seizing him by the front of his shirt and commanding, *"Go! Get back to the embassy and tell your dad we need backup!"* And, God help him, Kirk had gone. He'd wriggled out the back of the dying shuttle and left them, telling himself it was an order, telling himself he was doing the right thing and that his father would bring back a combat team that would know exactly what to do.

But as fast as he ran, as hard as he tried, he never saw the embassy or Lieutenant Maione's squad again. Until now.

Grabbing the lip of the shuttle's buckled roof, Kirk pulled himself up and over, careful to roll down the other side as swiftly as possible and drop into a crouch in the deep shadows there. He couldn't tell how long it had been since the Vragax natives had finished their slaughter here, but he didn't want to risk being targeted by whoever might still be lurking in the burning darkness that used to be Sogo city. The men around him had been killed by whatever the Vragax had on hand—magnetic propulsion gauss slugs, phasers, the short ceremonial darts from Vragax spear throwers. Kirk knew Maione's men must have taken down a good many Vragax with them, but there were no native bodies mixed in with the carnage. In the midst of their bloody rampage through Sogo, the Vragax still took time to collect their own dead for whatever it was they considered dignified disposal.

Kirk sensed more than saw a furtive movement toward the rear of the shuttle, dark-on-dark, almost silent despite the bits of broken shuttle and restless autumn leaves. Sinking back against the rucked-up earth, Kirk thumbed the primer on one of the gauss rifles and lifted it slowly to his shoulder. The chain of tiny electromagnets lining the inside of its barrel whined almost beyond the pitch of human hearing as they built up the necessary charge.

The shadow creeping up on Kirk along the shuttle's splintered flank halted. "John?" Tension poised the burly silhouette so still it might have been a statue. "Maione, is that you?"

It could have been a recording of Kirk's own voice. *Why did I never notice that before?* he wondered. Swallowing hard, he let the gauss rifle sink to rest across his knees. "Maione's dead." He hoped he sounded confident and in control. He hoped he didn't sound too much like himself. "I'm the only one left."

The other human padded closer, hunkering down on all fours to share Kirk's shadow and the relative protection of the artificial hill. There wasn't enough light to really see him clearly, but Kirk knew even through the darkness that his uniform was Starfleet, his tunic red, and his eyes were the same angry green as the East Coast ocean in winter. He was a commander, he was forty-six years old, and he was the meanest son of a bitch to ever head a security squad. "Name and rank," the man snapped, reaching for the second gauss rifle without asking, much less waiting, for position.

"Forester." Kirk blurted the name without thinking, then was forced to add, "Captain," because he wouldn't be able to hide the braid on his sleeves. "I came in with the last group of replacements."

The other man nodded as though he'd expected as much. "I didn't even get a chance to read you in, sir. My apologies."

Kirk felt an oddly uncomfortable blush push up into his face. "None necessary." *Because I wasn't really here—I shouldn't be here now—* But he made himself ask steadily, "What's your name, soldier?" as though the answer would hardly make any difference, as though he didn't already know.

"Commander George Kirk, sir, interim security chief." He powered up his rifle, then helped himself to one of Kirk's spare clips and shoved it into the half-empty magazine. "And I'm out here, sir, because I'm looking for my son."

For the second time in twenty-four hours, Uhura found herself standing shocked and helpless in the blue glow of Tlaoli's Janus Gate. The first time she had felt this paralyzing fear was when Captain Kirk and Ensign Chekov had disappeared without warning as they tried to evacuate a trapped caving team from these ice-sheathed caverns. Now, with the alien time transporter they had discovered here free of its distorting travertine shell and obediently responding to Spock's commands, the source of her shock was a phalanx of metal-clad aliens who had just banned them from ever using the Janus Gate again.

With all her heart, Uhura wished the time transporter would whip out a glowing blue curtain and make these enigmatic intruders disappear, the same way it had taken their missing captain. But the Janus Gate's power stores were once again exhausted, and the fiery glow at its heart had shrunk back down to a sapphire flicker. Despite the drizzle and mist from the ice melting all around them, Uhura could see that the armored bodies of the cybernetic aliens had linked together to form a solid metal stockade around the Gate.

The aliens who called themselves Shechenag had descended as silently as spiders, gliding down frictionless wires from the solution pits in the ceiling. They had timed their entrance perfectly—the unwary moment when triumph and relief had swept through the *Enterprise* crewmen after they successfully used the Janus Gate to haul Lieutenant Sulu back from the distant future to which he'd been sent. The tense and exhausting hour Uhura had spent as the focus of the alien device had been worth it: Her quest across time had brought back not only their missing helmsman but also the future version of Chekov who'd helped Sulu survive a hellish future where the Gorn ruled the galaxy.

But there had been no time to celebrate. Before they could use the Janus Gate to try to rescue Captain Kirk from his own past, before Sulu and Chekov had even been retrieved from the healing chamber where the

Janus Gate had sent them, a horde of metallic insects had plunged down into their midst, using metallic claws with stinging electrical anodes to herd them all to the edge of the cavern. Any attempt to resist—or even to retain their equipment, as archaeologist Carolyn Palamas had tried to do with her visual translating device—had been met with such swift and ruthless punishment that the victims were either still shaking with residual shock or, like Security Guard Yuki Smith, completely unconscious.

"How is she, Doctor?" Spock asked McCoy quietly while the Shechenag clicked and whistled among themselves, apparently consulting each other on their next move. It was very odd to see the glittering translucent bodies of the actual aliens inside the clear shells of their armored suits, turning back and forth toward one another as the conversation rattled among them.

"I think she's just been knocked unconscious." McCoy looked up from the sprawled body of the security guard, putting his old-fashioned stethoscope back into the chest pocket of his caving suit. The anxious faces of young Ensign Chekov and an even younger James T. Kirk craned past the shoulders of the other members of the party to listen to the doctor's verdict. "If she doesn't wake up pretty soon, though, it might mean something more serious is wrong."

"This one of your species is not injured." The flat machine-generated tone of that voice would have told Uhura it came from among the line of Shechenag even if she hadn't seen Spock turn his head and lift one eyebrow at the speaker. Inside the perfectly still metallic casing, several spindly limbs gesticulated for emphasis. "This one received only mild electron overdose to suppress aggressive behavior."

"Are her symptoms consistent with electrical shock, Doctor?" the Vulcan science officer asked.

McCoy lifted one of Smith's eyelids. "Yes. They're also consistent with giving herself a concussion when she hit the ground." He lowered his voice to a grumble. "Spock, I don't like the idea that those walking tin cans over there are listening to everything we say."

"Indeed," said the Vulcan. "However, lowering your voice is not a logical response to the situation, Doctor. I believe it is safe to assume that their sound detectors are equally as advanced as the rest of their technology."

Uhura wrenched her gaze away from the aliens barricading the Janus Gate, although part of her still desperately wanted to watch to make sure no other insectoid robots detached themselves from those odd metallic bodies. "Mr. Spock, they learned our language from the archaeological translator," she said, in flawless Vulcan. "But it was only programmed for an English translation."

The science officer's slanted eyebrows went up again, this time in appreciation. "A fact which I should have remembered, Lieutenant," he replied in the same language. "Especially since I distinctly recall noting its ethnocentricity in naming the transporter for the human god Janus rather than the Vulcan goddess Yelanna." Spock eyed the Shechenag watching them, then switched abruptly to Andorian. "By using no more than a dozen phonemes from any one language, we should be able to confuse any translating device they might have brought with them."

Uhura glanced at the blank faces around them. "As well as most of our crewmates," she reminded Spock in Andorian, then deliberately turned her back on the Shechenag and gave the rest of their team the Starfleet hand signal that meant, *Covert communication only, enemy is listening.*

What felt like a sharp metallic caliper closed on Uhura's shoulder, tight enough to startle a gasp out of her. There was a flash of black and violet motion between the other bodies, and she suddenly found herself standing between the older versions of both Chekov and Sulu, both of them clearly poised to attack if the Shechenag did anything more threatening. With a hiss of sophisticated gears and tiny bearings, however, the alien merely rotated its limb to bring Uhura around to face it, then released her.

"This one will face us so we can see all of its attachments," the alien said, with no more emphasis or emotion in its voice than before. Inside its clear shell, however, two small stalked eyes swiveled in what looked almost like a glare. "Operations intended to reactivate this device will not be permitted. You have ten hours to leave this system. Departure from this cave should be immediate."

"That sound definite," McCoy said in halting schoolboy French. "We leave?"

Uhura had to bite her lip against a hysterical giggle, since the expression on Spock's lean face would have done credit to the most chauvinistic Frenchman. "We intend to leave," he said in English, answering both the doctor and the alien facing them. "An immediate departure, however, will require a transporter beam to be generated from our ship. With your permission, I will contact them—"

Uhura tried to school her face to look perfectly calm, but she felt her heart leap with excitement as she recognized Spock's ingenious strategy. If the Shechenag didn't know that the transporter beam would repower the Janus Gate rather than take them back to the *Enterprise,* there was a chance they could get the hostile aliens trapped in one of the random subspace warps that floated around the alien device when it was fully charged.

After a moment's pause, however, a burst of chattering from the other Shechenag made the one closest to them step back. A flush of colors passed across the surface of its floating chitinous body, although Uhura couldn't be sure if that represented a flush of strong emotion or just a rapid mental reassessment of the situation. Inside the clear torso tank, its stalked eyes elevated to peer at Spock with what looked like sudden attentiveness.

"Operations intended to reactivate this device will not be permitted." There wasn't the slightest variation in the Shechenag's machine-generated voice, but two of its clawlike appendages flashed upward with violent swiftness. Uhura was abruptly shouldered backward between the older versions of Chekov and Sulu, and had to stand on tiptoe to peer over their shoulders. The cybernetic alien had made no other move toward them. Inside its clear tank, the small floating body was also pointing upward, making it clear that its motion was intended to be directional. "Immediate evacuation can also occur using these ropes," it said. "No disabling has been done to your shuttlecraft. One trip back to your ship will be permitted."

Uhura saw the older version of Sulu glance over his shoulder at his younger counterpart. "Will the shuttle carry all of us in one trip?" he asked in fluent Japanese.

"If we throw out everything including the bulkhead supplies?" the younger pilot replied in the same language. "Maybe."

The older Sulu glanced at the man standing beside him, with the odd bittersweet smile Uhura had seen him use when his sense of amusement was tickled by something other people might think morbid. "We're expendable now, Pavel," Sulu said in rough but understandable Russian. "You want to stay down here and see if we can peel some of these shrimp out of their shells?"

"That may not forward our goals, Captain," Spock informed him in much better Russian, before Chekov could answer. Uhura wasn't sure how the Vulcan managed it, but his voice sounded equally formal and mannered in every language he used. "And there is a distinct probability that you will be needed more for later actions." He switched back to English, turning to meet the translucent gaze of the Shechenag who had issued the evacuation orders. "We will depart in the shuttle when we have transported all members of our party to it. However, we may not be able to leave the system within ten hours, because of the disabled status of our warp engines."

"You are given ten hours to depart the system." Perhaps because of its lack of anything like human emotion, the mechanical voice sounded completely implacable to Uhura. "If you are still within the system after ten hours, you will not be able to depart."

"Are you threatening to attack us?" Spock inquired politely.

The alien's metallic body took an odd, swaying step backward on its multiply jointed legs. "We are Shechenag," it said, just as it had done when it first spoke to them. There was a pause, as if that should have been enough explanation for them. When Spock continued to meet its gaze inquiringly, the alien rattled off something in its native tongue and was answered by a clattering chorus from its comrades. "Shechenag once made war for nine millennia," said the toneless voice. "We make no war now. After ten hours, nothing departs or enters this system for one thousand years. You are warned."

Spock surprised Uhura with a polite inclination of his head toward their captors. "We thank you for the warning," he said, then glanced over his shoulder. In the back of the group, the younger Chekov and Kirk were helping a groaning Yuki Smith to her feet. "Mr. Sanner, please climb up to the cave entrance above us so that we may begin evacuating everyone."

"Spock, you *coq au vin!*" Even in his atrocious French, McCoy's voice sounded recognizably indignant. "We no leave without Jim!"

"*Non,*" the Vulcan said simply. "We shall power up the Janus Gate from space and see if that dismays our enemies."

"Mr. Spock," Uhura said in urgent Vulcan. "If the Shechenag are telling us the truth about fighting a war for nine millennia, maybe *they* are the original inhabitants of Tlaoli. Maybe this Gate belongs to them."

"I have considered that possibility," Spock replied in his native language. "But the ancient Tlaoli people left this Gate for use by anyone who followed them. It would not be logical for them to chase away those successors now, especially if they could simply deactivate the Gate they built." He switched to the more guttural sounds of Tellerite. "I suspect these are not the aliens who built the Gate, but rather the enemies against whom it was once used. That would explain both their fear of using it, and their conviction that it cannot undo the disruptions it causes in the timeline."

The older Chekov cleared his throat. "So you don't think they really know how to deactivate this device?" he asked Spock in slow but passable Tellerite. "All they can do is try to barricade it from us?"

"That is my belief," Spock said.

"And if we cannot destroy their barricade by powering the Janus Gate from space?" asked the older Sulu, also in Tellerite, "What will we do then?"

Spock swept a measuring glance across the Shechenag, with their menacing cybernetic armor and the detachable robots now being arranged in a protective circle around the Janus Gate itself. He paused, then deliberately switched back to English again so all of them could understand his next words. "In that case, we will be forced to *attack* our problem more directly."

# Chapter Two

"YOUR SON ISN'T HERE," Kirk told his father. A flutter of burning cloth, made feather-light by the flames consuming it, drifted down between them to temporarily illuminate George Kirk's hard, determined face. *He's not as tall as I remember.* But he looked exactly as angry.

"He got on board just before you closed up," the elder Kirk insisted. The flames between them guttered down to amber pinpricks in the older man's eyes. "He's fourteen, just a little over a meter and a half, with a smart mouth. You must have seen him."

Kirk didn't try to hide the irritation on his face, although years of practice let him hide the emotion in his voice behind a crisp tone of command. "I didn't say I hadn't seen him, I said he wasn't here." He turned away to flip Maione's body and pat it down in search of weapons he could use if the Vragax returned. Not much to his surprise, none were left. "We sent him back to the embassy after the shuttle went down."

George Kirk had already begun to copy Kirk's weapons check on the other bodies nearby. "And you didn't send anyone with him?"

*Was he always this irreverent with his commanders?* "We didn't exactly have anyone to spare." Although maybe if one of them had come with him, that man would have been spared—would have kept Kirk out of the hands of the Vragax guerrillas—would have gotten them to the embassy in time to make everything different.

*But everything is already different.* The thought froze Kirk with his hand on a dead man's hip. *I'm here this time. I'm delaying my father.* He spun on George, suddenly shaken by the prospect of disrupting his own history. "Did you check the buildings?"

The other man jerked a look at him over one shoulder. "What?"

"The buildings," Kirk insisted, climbing to his feet and hauling up the meager gear he'd been able to salvage. "Between here and the embassy. Did you search any of the buildings?"

George was already jamming an extra phaser and a short string of sonic grenades into his belt. "I was following the shuttle." An awkward pause silenced him only briefly. "I didn't want to be delayed."

*Then when did you find me?* Kirk realized with a sick, almost youthful panic that he wasn't exactly sure how his father had located him that night. He'd always assumed George had noticed some commotion that had led him to the armed Vragax who had cornered his son, or that he had stumbled across the imminent assassination through some stroke of unbelievable luck while on his way from the embassy launch pad to the crash site. He'd also always worried that his father's refusal to go back for Maione and the others had meant he was a self-centered son of a bitch who had found what he came for and couldn't be bothered with anything else. For some reason, it had never occurred to Kirk that his father had actually covered the entire distance to the downed shuttle and searched for him there before turning back toward the embassy. And after ending his blistering tongue-lashing with the words, "Your mother is *never* going to know about *any* of this, you understand?" George Kirk never spoke of that night again. Haunted by the thought of Maione, Leone, and all the others he'd left behind to face the Vragax alone, his son had shamefully followed the father's example.

At least now Kirk knew that no one had abandoned the shuttle's crew. George Kirk had found them, and he'd been just as helpless to save them as his son.

Wrenching his gaze away from the scattered bodies, Kirk motioned his father to join him at the rear of the shuttle. "We sent him back toward the embassy." It somehow made the deception easier when he spoke of himself in the third person. He could function as a captain then, reacting to the situation in front of him and taking the necessary action, and not just as the adult doppelganger of a terrified fourteen-year-old boy. "If you didn't come across him on your way out here, then he either made it back to the embassy—"

"There isn't much of an embassy to go back to."

"—or he's still out there somewhere."

Kirk didn't have to see the look of frustrated disgust on his father's face to know it was there. "I just hope he had enough sense to stay out of sight. The Vragax aren't being too particular about who they shoot right now."

Kirk slung the rifle half-readily across his front and left the shuttle's protective shadow before the urge to backhand his companion drove him to do something he was sure to regret. "He's not stupid," he assured his father without even bothering to waste a glare on him. "And he doesn't want to die any more than you do."

George Kirk fell into step beside him with a skeptical snort. "Sometimes I wonder."

They made better time together than Kirk had alone. Leapfrogging each other down the lengths of empty street, one always keeping watch while the other moved, they tugged on every door they passed, darted furtive looks inside every broken window. Kirk appreciated George's practicality—he didn't waste time kicking in locked doors or investigating intact windows. He might understand little else about his son, but he knew the boy wasn't capable of breaking in anywhere that wasn't already wide open. He just didn't have the strength or the skills.

For himself, Kirk struggled to call up some memory of the streets he'd run down that night, some distinguishing feature of the building where he'd finally been caught. Shouldn't such a seminal event have left indelible images in his brain? He had dreamed about the small, dark room where he'd tried to hide almost nightly for seven months. For years afterward, he could have drawn the pattern of blood and war paint and braids on the Vragax who'd finally cornered him. Yet now that his young life might actually depend on it, he couldn't even remember if the outside of the building was concrete, brick, or wooden shingle.

*Was I even gone this long? Shouldn't my father have found me by now?* That thought had been gnawing at him since they'd left the shuttle crash. What if his presence here had irrevocably altered the timeline? He already knew that no one had been with his father when George Kirk appeared like an avenging angel and killed the four Vragax surrounding his son. No one had come back with them to the embassy, no one had covered the last of their escape. Now that he was here—not only as an adult, but as George Kirk's nominal commander—Kirk wasn't even sure he could stand by and let the security officer shoot down the four natives without at least giving them a chance to surrender. He was just too confident that the two of them together could save the boy without having to resort to that kind of bloodshed.

*But what if you're wrong? What if it's already too late?*

George's urgent hiss knocked Kirk out of his reverie. Jogging up to meet him in an open doorway, Kirk barely caught sight of the older man until he was right on top of him, and then had to drop into an abrupt crouch at his side to avoid tripping over him altogether. George didn't seem to notice. He caught at Kirk's shoulder to direct his attention, then pointed with the muzzle of his rifle as though it were an extension of his own arm, into the blackened interior of the building beyond the doorway. "I hear voices upstairs." He mouthed the words almost directly into

Kirk's ear, passing scarcely enough breath to make them audible. "And somebody's crying."

Kirk couldn't even feel indignant that his father would assume his son was huddled in the dark somewhere weeping. He'd been sobbing when he left Maione and the others at the shuttle that night, and hadn't been able to stop crying until several hours after his father had found him and dragged him back to safety. He was just grateful for the darkness now, so that the embarrassed heat in his face wouldn't give away how ashamed he still was of that weakness.

"I'll go first," George continued. "Keep me in sight, but wait for my signal."

George counted off *one, two, three* with the fingers of one hand, and they swung into the open doorway on *three* as though they'd drilled the maneuver together for months. Kirk blinked hard at the darkness, willing his eyes to adjust, and finally isolated a deeper length of black curving up along one wall. A stairway. George was halfway up it already, silently waving Kirk to follow as he eased around the first landing and peered up toward the second floor. Featureless doors lined the downstairs lobby, each sporting a bright metal plate engraved with Grexxen number pips on the wall immediately next to the doorknobs. An apartment building, then. Or maybe an office complex. Kirk padded up the stairs behind George as silently as possible, listening for the voices his father had followed, and one voice in particular.

The crying was more evident once they rounded the stairwell onto the plushly carpeted second floor. But it was a female, her sobs desperately muffled, and the voice that shushed and tutted to her was neither human nor threatening. "It's not him," Kirk whispered, even as his eyes strayed down the long hallway to the familiar door yawning open at the end. "He wouldn't have gone near them."

He didn't go near them. He hadn't known they were there. He'd simply run as far from the stairwell as he could, passing all the apartments and alcoves and closets, and ducked through that open door into an office whose boxes and equipment he thought would lend him shelter. He'd even tried to lock the door, but was too blind with panic to figure out how.

A terrified scream from inside the nearest apartment made Kirk whirl and snap the rifle up to his shoulder. But instead of a Vragax raiding party, he saw only George Kirk through the opened door, kneeling atop an overturned desk with his gun aimed straight down at whoever had huddled underneath. "Shut up and listen to me," George said, calmly but firmly. "We're looking for a human boy."

"Commander, stand down!"

George spared Kirk only a brief glance out of the corner of his eye, not altering the gun's alignment by so much as a micron. "Begging the captain's pardon, sir, but I've been dealing with the Grexxen for more than a year now. You have only been here a short while."

*You have no idea how true that is.* "I'm still not going to let any officer under me brutalize the natives in the name of familial concern." He stepped up beside George and closed his hand around the barrel of the gauss rifle to make it clear he was prepared to disarm him if the older man forced the issue. "I said stand down."

The hesitation was slight—just enough to rankle Kirk's instincts as a captain, but not so long that he had to respond to the implied insubordination. Kirk found himself smothering a grin as his father climbed down off the desk and stepped grudgingly behind him. As much as George Kirk hadn't appreciated his son's rebellious streak, it wasn't his mother who had given it to him.

Slinging his own rifle onto his back, Kirk turned cautiously to the women huddled behind the big desk and tried to decide if he should squat down on their level or keep a prudent distance. They were both Kozhu, and obviously civilians, but the situation in Sogo city had been so crazy at the end that he wasn't sure if such distinctions meant anything anymore. "Do you speak English?" he finally asked, staying where he was on the other side of the desk.

The older of the two nodded. While her bronze-green face was wet from crying, it was the younger girl who choked volubly on her sobs, hands pressed against her mouth in an effort to keep silent. Kirk's heart thudded painfully with pity.

"We saw the boy." The older woman held the girl against her, and met Kirk's gaze with a dignity that left little room for fear. "Vragax chased him that way—" She jerked her chin toward the end of the hall. Toward the office with its boxes, where the young James Kirk had almost died. "—but when they left again, they left without him."

George was already running in the direction of her nod, calling, "Jimmy! Jim, where are you?" but Kirk stayed with the Kozhu women, going down to one knee after all. The young girl—no older than most of his yeomen—recoiled slightly, and he reached out to touch a reassuring hand to her arm without thinking about how such a gesture would be taken. She stared at him, copper eyes wide and lambent in the darkness, as though she'd just been comforted by a bear.

The older woman frowned gently at him, studying something in his expression or features. "The boy you want—he looks like you. He's your son?"

Kirk laughed softly and rubbed at his eyes. "No, not my son."

"Mine." The growl of anger in George's voice ignited every defensive instinct Kirk had developed over years of having to deal with the man. Turning a glare back at him, he'd just opened his mouth to suggest George Kirk leave his son behind if the boy caused him so much more trouble than he was worth. Then he saw the stark grief on the older man's face, naked and laced with terror in the dim light, and all his youthful defiance sank to the pit of his stomach like a stone.

"He's gone." George's voice betrayed none of the emotion on his face. "He's not there."

Kirk wondered if his father had just never looked like that when in front of his youngest son, or if Kirk had simply been stupid enough to believe only what he could hear in George's voice and not what he could see with his young eyes.

Pushing to his feet, he hauled his captaincy around him like a shield and let his mind race ahead to what came next. *React to the situation.* "What about blood?" If he wasn't in the room, there were limited options as to how he could have left it. "Was there any sign of a struggle?"

George Kirk looked down at his feet, obviously stilling his mind so he could interpret the details of what he'd seen. "Some stuff is knocked around, but there're no windows or equipment broken, no blood."

Then the Vragax hadn't killed him. They'd had the gun in his face, the alien's finger had all but depressed the trigger when George stepped in and brought the party to an ugly end. That little band of Vragax hadn't been working on any kind of larger agenda. They weren't going to drag Kirk somewhere else to do their killing, or take his body with him when they left. He was just one more outlet for whatever rage had boiled over in Sogo that night.

But if his father hadn't arrived in time to rescue him, and the Vragax didn't shoot him... then what? Where was the body, if not the boy?

He looked down at the Kozhu women behind the toppled desk. "You said the Vragax left without the boy. Did they say anything?"

She looked for a moment as though she might actually laugh, but instead she said slowly, as though speaking to a stupid baby, "Not to us. We are Kozhu. We hid from them." Then a certain amount of sympathy must have overweighed her sarcasm, because she added, almost grudgingly, "But they were frightened. One of them was crying and praying to his *beyli.*"

His personal god. Like a guardian angel, some force to protect him from evil spirits and their doings. No fourteen-year-old boy could have made a Vragax soldier so afraid.

George caught at his elbow, drawing him back away from the desk and the natives still hiding behind it. "Captain, sir..." He'd recovered what passed for his composure, looking once again only impatient and vaguely irritated. "We're wasting time here—it must not have been Jimmy they saw."

Kirk shook his head. "It was."

"You can't know that."

He snapped a sharp look at his father. "How many other human boys do you think are out there tonight?"

George didn't have a ready answer.

His anger cooled as quickly as it had flared, Kirk gazed absently down the hall, trying to intuit his own behavior in a set of past events that had never happened. "If he somehow got out of that room, he's headed for the embassy."

"I told you," George said tensely. "The embassy's in pieces."

"But he knows about the auxiliary shuttle pad," Kirk reminded him. "It's outside the embassy walls, and it's the only place that would still have shuttles to get you off-planet." In fact, it was the place from which he and George had fled Grex nineteen years ago, in the very last shuttle to leave the war-torn planet. "There's nowhere else for him to go."

George gusted a grumbling resignation. "A couple of my boys are holding the last transport. But they're not going to wait all night. We'd better hurry."

Yes, they would. But he couldn't help hesitating to glance down at the women, torn between the past he remembered and the future he was still hoping to create.

George followed his gaze only long enough to take his arm again and try to pull him away. "They are part of the native civilian population," the security man reminded Kirk stiffly. "Whatever old scores the Kozhu and the Vragax have between each other, it isn't our problem now."

Variations on a theme. Kirk could have scripted the political argument that would follow, if only they'd had time to indulge in one. Except this time George wouldn't be able to dismiss Kirk's opinions as the delusions of an idealistic little boy. *I'm the captain now. I can do whatever I want to.*

Shaking his arm loose, he pinned the commander with a disapproving glare. "We made it our problem when we agreed to help them rebuild after the Orions were gone. If we turn our backs now, we're no better than the Orions."

"You're worse than the Orions." The woman's tired words shocked Kirk into silence, wounding something more basic in him than a simple political stand. Her weary eyes said she was just as dismayed by his innocence as his father. "They may have called us slaves, but they kept Vragax and Kozhu from killing each other in the streets. It wasn't until Starfleet gave us freedom that the killing began again." She sank back into the shadows, pulling the young girl tighter into her arms and making them both very small against the back of a shattered chair. "Go away now. Go look for your boy. We would rather wait here until the Orions return."

The shuttle flight from Tlaoli up to the *Enterprise* wasn't as bad as Sulu had anticipated.

It was much worse.

The cargo shuttle *Caroline Herschel* which Spock had brought down to the planet was the same class as the *Edwin Drake,* the ship which had been thrown into the future with Sulu at its helm. Both ships had a normal passenger load of ten, but that was when they weren't carrying the heavy magnetic shielding that Scotty had installed to insulate their warp cores from Tlaoli's power-draining subspace fields. In order to evacuate the dozen people left stranded on the planet when the *Enterprise* had lost the use of its transporter, both shuttles had been emptied of all their nonessential equipment. Now they needed to add Spock, McCoy, and the duplicate copies of Chekov and Sulu to the passenger load. Even taking into account the lighter weight of a fourteen-year-old James Kirk, that put them so far over the *Herschel*'s carrying capacity that Sulu didn't even want to think about it.

They spent a frantic half hour under the menacing shadow of the Shechenag ship that had trailed them back from the caverns, emptying the cargo shuttle of everything they could wrench free. Passenger seats, bulk-head covers, even the emergency food and water supplies that they were never supposed to take off without—all of it went flying out the open hatchway. Remembering how he'd flown the Gorn shuttle back on Basaraba standing up, Sulu had even tried to get rid of his pilot's seat, but found that Starfleet's shuttle designers had hidden the control circuits for the inertial dampeners inside it. He settled for ripping away all of the up-holstery and cushioning from its bare metal struts. With the soundproof-ing removed, he made the unpleasant discovery that the dampener's control panel emitted an annoying high-pitched whine, halfway between an unseen mosquito and an overloaded phaser.

Spock paused before settling down in the place where the copilot's seat had once been. "Do you believe you are competent for piloting du-ties, Mr. Sulu?" he asked. "In most circumstances you are a far better pi-lot than I, but if you are suffering from exhaustion or time-dilation effects..."

"I don't think I am, Mr. Spock," Sulu said, honestly enough. "I didn't get much sleep when I was on Basaraba, but whatever that healing cham-ber did to me back in the caves seems to have fixed that along with my ribs." It was true that his ribs were healed, without even an ache or twinge left to mark the place where a brutal blow from a Romulan weapon had broken his bones, and saved his life. But the weariness he'd felt back on Basaraba had been transformed by Tlaoli's alien healing chambers into something more than just a sense of having rested.

What Sulu actually felt right now was a sharp, crackling alertness, the kind that usually meant a spike of adrenaline had just jolted into his bloodstream. He would have chalked it up to trepidation about the upcoming shuttle flight, except that he didn't have the rapid pulse and sweaty palms and hollow feeling in his stomach that too many stress hormones produced. Maybe the ancient Tlaoli didn't just heal their recycled soldiers, he thought. Maybe they also medically enhanced them for the next battle they were going to be sent through time to fight.

Or maybe the alien healing chamber just hadn't known how to repair his body's overstressed fight-or-flight response.

Spock acknowledged Sulu's response simply by handing him a length of lightweight polymer cord. "Your crash webbing was embedded in your seat's upholstery," said the Vulcan. "In case of an emergency, this will have to suffice."

Sulu knotted the cord from one bare metal strut to another, then back again a little farther down his thighs, trying to anchor himself securely enough to the seat that he couldn't be thrown away from the flight controls by unexpected tremors in Tlaoli's gravitational field. Spock took the cord from him when he was done, but since there was nothing left to lash himself to, the Vulcan simply braced himself in the far corner of the cockpit. Outside the shuttle, a wine-colored sunset was slowly staining the eastern side of Tlaoli's rusty sky. Sulu glanced curiously at the shuttle's chronometer and realized with a start that this was still the same day it had been when he'd been hurled into the future. The long rainy night and stressful day he'd spent on Basaraba must not have correlated to the same amount of time back at the *Enterprise*.

"Everyone's roped down in the cargo bay, too?" he asked Spock as he powered up the warp engines. With the bulkhead covers removed to lighten *Herschel*'s weight, the roar of the thrust generators was much louder, too. Sulu didn't envy the fifteen people crowded into the back compartment.

"Yes." The science officer gazed out at the angular Shechenag aircraft that had hovered watchfully over them as they loaded into the shuttle. The alien ship was finally moving away from them, but it didn't disappear. Instead, Sulu noted, it began to systematically destroy the survey team's base camp, not with weapons fire or a bomb but simply by landing its immense weight on the storage tents, one by one. The cybernetic aliens apparently hadn't lied when they said they no longer engaged in war, but that didn't mean they couldn't still be ruthless in their determination to make sure the *Enterprise* crew did no further damage to the timeline here on Tlaoli.

Sulu opened his mouth to say something about that to Spock, then realized he was procrastinating. The shuttle's engines were as warmed up and ready as they would ever be. He took a deep breath, then brought *Herschel*'s vertical thrusters up to full power. The sound of the warp engines rose to an echoing roar in the back of the cargo bay, but the shuttle only managed to lurch a little way off the ground before losing momentum again, like a tethered animal hitting the end of its chain.

"Interesting," said Spock. "As soon as the thrusters lose contact with a hard surface, they no longer have enough power to accelerate us vertically. Perhaps we will need to leave one of the duplicated officers behind after all."

Sulu scanned his readouts, measuring engine output against gravitational pull, then darted a quick glance out through the reddening dusk. "I don't think we'll need to do that, sir," he said, and began to painstakingly work the shuttle around to the right without losing any of its lift.

When Spock had flown the *Herschel* down from the *Enterprise,* he hadn't landed at the base camp itself, the way Sulu had done with the *Drake.* As a pilot, the Vulcan was steady and workmanlike but not particularly talented. Faced with Tlaoli's unreliable gravitational shifts and jagged terrain, he had opted to put the shuttle down on the edge of the windswept karst outside the towers surrounding the base camp. It had been a fortunate decision, leaving plenty of airspace off to starboard for Sulu to now maneuver in. There might be a bump or two along the way, he thought as he aimed the shuttle toward the clearest line of sight, but hopefully nothing bad enough to breach *Herschel*'s hull and make her unspaceworthy.

With another deep breath, Sulu transferred the shuttle's thrust from purely vertical to a slightly more upward-angled vector. With less energy devoted to fighting gravity, more of the engine's energy could be converted into motion. Before it could begin falling back to ground, the *Herschel* began to surge forward, gathering speed as it went. It was still no more than a handspan above the ground, and Sulu could hear the scrape of brittle shrubs and projecting rocks against the shuttle's tough duranium belly. He didn't take his eyes off the speed and altitude gauges, one of which was moving faster than he'd expected, the other of which seemed stubbornly stuck on its original value. Even with the warp engines powered up to their maximum level, he could hear the startled and questioning lift of voices from the back compartment as his passengers endured the brushes and bumps.

"There are several large rock formations ahead of us, at a distance of approximately sixteen thousand meters," Spock informed him in a calm and measured voice. It might have reassured Sulu more to hear the Vulcan science officer sound so normal if he hadn't known that Spock could speak just as calmly even when he was facing certain death. "We will need at least thirty-five meters of additional elevation to provide clearance."

"We'll get it." Sulu had already begun converting their horizontal thrust back to vertical by using the shuttle's own momentum as the catalyst to tip the balance between gravitational pull and upward lift. By slowly nudging *Herschel*'s nose so that it angled up into the darkening Tlaoli sunset, he had managed to raise the shuttle a full ten meters off the ground. If they could just overtop the rocks Spock had noted ahead of them, they'd have nothing but clear air ahead of them and plenty of time to trundle their way up to the *Enterprise*. But the thrust conversion was an excruciatingly slow process, and it wasn't being helped by the frictional drag of the occasional karst moundtops they were still brushing across.

"Thirteen thousand meters," Spock said. Sulu glanced down at his velocity readout and frowned. Their speed had increased to six hundred kilometers per hour, giving them more momentum but also carrying them much faster toward a potentially deadly rendezvous with the karst monoliths whose dark silhouette had begun to obliterate the amethyst glow of sunset. He coaxed the shuttle into a little steeper angle and felt it shudder as it reached the outer envelope of lift that it could sustain. If he tried to angle upward any more steeply, the overloaded craft was going to fall right out of the sky. If that happened, even at the paltry twenty meters of altitude they had managed to gain so far, Sulu suspected not many of his roped-in crewmates would walk away from the crash.

"Nine thousand meters," Spock said calmly.

Sulu swept a glance across his controls, racking his brain for anything else he could do to lighten *Herschel*'s load, or add to its slowly building momentum. As a cargo shuttle, there were no weapons he could fire to create additional push and using the shields to ward away the rocks would only reduce the power output going to the thrusters. He almost wished the shields were already up, so he could turn them off and divert the freed power to their engines . . . and then Sulu suddenly knew what he could do.

"*Hang on!*" he yelled as loudly as he could, hoping the people back in the cargo bay could hear him. He waited until he saw Spock brace himself more securely against the cockpit walls, then reached under his seat and fumbled for the switch that would deactivate *Herschel*'s inertial dampeners.

The reaction was immediate. Uncompensated gravitational forces slammed Sulu back into his metal chair frame and held him pressed there more strongly than any shock webbing could have done. He felt the pull of increasing acceleration in the muscles of his face and throat as he slowly wrenched his head around to read the shuttle's thrust. The difference was small, but crucial: Horizontal thrust had suddenly increased by ten percent. Sulu forced himself to alter the shuttle's angle of ascent slowly, oh so slowly, to keep the uncompensated inertial forces from tearing his passengers—and his copilot—away from their braced holds.

"Five thousand meters." Spock's voice hadn't varied even slightly in its measured tone, despite the fact that Sulu could see the muscles of his chest and shoulders knot as the Vulcan fought to keep from being thrown across the cockpit. Only his superhuman strength kept him in place now. "We still need an additional seven meters of altitude."

"It's coming." Sulu pushed the shuttle up to the brink of its lift envelope again, felt it shudder as it teetered on the ragged edge of staying aloft or plunging back to earth. Its nose wavered, seemed to duck—then one of Tlaoli's random little gravitational shifts suddenly jerked it up and sideways, adding a full three meters to its altitude.

For a long moment, the horizontal part of that jolt threatened to send the shuttle into an uncontrolled sidelong skid. Sulu had to drop the *Herschel*'s nose to keep it from rolling, losing back one of those precious meters to gravity in the process, but the upward jerk had also increased the shuttle's momentum enough to let him push the angle of its climb up another five degrees. He threw a quick glance at the altitude meter and knew with a veteran pilot's certainty that they were going to make it even before Spock said, "One thousand meters to the highest rock formations. It now appears we have sufficient altitude to clear them."

Sulu knew he was right, but he still held his breath as the dark pinnacles of limestone loomed beneath them, far closer than his piloting instincts said any solid object should be to a shuttle now moving at over one thousand kilometers per hour. The *Herschel* passed over them without a bump or scrape of sound, but the wake of air she dragged with her hit the rock formations hard enough to send ripples of turbulence surging out in all directions. Sulu nearly lost his seat as the shuttle bounced through the suddenly choppy air. He grimaced and fought against the continuing unbalanced pull of gravity to lean forward and reactivate the inertial dampeners. It was only after he felt his straining body relax into the stabilized gravitational field that he realized the torque he'd been exposed to had woken up a familiar dull ache in his rib cage. Apparently, the Tlaoli chambers hadn't completely healed the damage there.

"Thank you, Lieutenant," said Spock.

Sulu wasn't sure if the Vulcan science officer was commending him for his piloting or just for turning the inertial dampeners back on again. To be safe, he acknowledged the comment with merely a standard, "Aye, sir."

The *Herschel* continued to lumber upward slowly into the darkening red-violet sky, but now Sulu could ease her back from the precarious edge of her lift envelope and let her ascend as slowly and gracefully as a hawk circling on a thermal draft. The higher they climbed, the less Tlaoli's gravity dragged on them and the more thrust he could devote to rising vertically. The inertial dampeners smoothed out most of the continuing gravitational jolts, allowing Spock to extricate himself from his uncomfortably cramped position in the corner of the cockpit, and move forward to scan the copilot's instruments. Although many of them displayed the warning red that meant Tlaoli's subspace interference had exceeded their maximum error levels, the shuttle's homing transponder still showed a clear vector on its screen.

"Once we reach the edge of the atmosphere, we will need to alter course toward the ecliptic plane in order to rendezvous with the *Enterprise*," Spock informed him. Around them, the sky was darkening with more than the approach of night. The increasingly bright twinkle of stars above the rusty fringe of Tlaoli's horizon told Sulu they were in the upper stratosphere now and would soon reach the point where the air was thin enough to let them safely engage the warp drive. He cut back on the thrusters to keep from overloading them, and began banking the shuttle toward an ecliptic orbit.

"Are you finished torturing your passengers?" asked a Russian-accented voice from the passage connecting the cockpit to the cargo bay. Sulu didn't bother to look around to see which version of Chekov had disobeyed Spock's orders to stay in back until they reached the *Enterprise*. The caustic words were enough to identify him.

"Pavel, you're probably the only one aboard who feels tortured when someone saves your life," said a deeper and much more familiar voice. Despite himself, Sulu felt a small shudder crawl up between his shoulder blades. There had been no time, after the Shechenag captured and herded them through the caverns of Tlaoli, to really absorb the fact that he was not the only version of Sulu in the group. Now that it had time to sink in, Sulu found himself torn between intense curiosity and equally intense shyness, as if there were some point of etiquette that said he shouldn't be allowed to know what he would be like a few decades from now.

He stole a furtive glance at the middle-aged man who had joined the older Chekov in the cockpit door, and was a little startled by how few physical changes he saw, aside from the lines at the corners of his eyes.

The older man had the same trim build, dark hair and dark eyes that Sulu saw in the mirror every day, but there was still something indefinably different about him. Sulu couldn't tell if it was the erect way he carried himself, or perhaps just the confidence that let him smile so wryly at his younger self, but somehow there was no doubting that *this* version of Sulu had earned his promotion to starship captain. Even if they managed to alter the future and avoid the Gorn conquest of space, Sulu thought wistfully as he returned his gaze to his instruments, this was still the man he hoped he would turn into.

The older Sulu leaned over his shoulder and ran a practiced eye across the instrument panel to check their course. "Aren't we going to reconnoiter the Shechenag's main ship before we head back to the *Enterprise*?" he asked, in a voice that somehow managed to imply that it would be a very good idea to do so without actually impinging on Spock's nominal position as commander of the landing party.

"The Janus Gate creates sufficient subspace interference that our instruments here are useless, Captain." Sulu wasn't sure if Spock was deliberately acknowledging the other Sulu's superior rank by using his title, or if it was just a logical way of distinguishing the two different versions of the pilot from each other. "I had planned to conduct a long-range surveillance from the *Enterprise*."

The older man made a noncommittal noise. "The Shechenag might take any approach as a sign we intended to engage them in battle."

"Or at least were disobeying their orders to leave the system," Sulu added tentatively.

"Well, we can at least do a visual inspection." Chekov leaned into the cockpit and jerked a thumb toward the starboard side of the cockpit window. "There's the Shechenag ship, right over there."

It wasn't easy to see at first, but Chekov was right. A shadow of solid black brushed out the star-studded glitter of outer space, on a track that would soon intersect with their own. Sulu cut the *Herschel*'s thrust and mentally cursed his dependence on instruments to orient himself to objects in space. Even though he knew his proximity alerts and sensors were malfunctioning, he hadn't thought to replace them with a thorough visual scan of the sky.

Apparently, the Shechenag didn't feel a need to light their starships from outside for safety the way all Federation vessels were required to be illuminated except in times of war. In fact, there was almost no evidence of light on the ship at all—no windows or portholes or even rings of docking lights to mark the entrances to the shuttlebays it presumably had. If the older Russian hadn't caught sight of it, they might have missed the alien ship entirely despite its massive size and slow movement. Either the cybernetic aliens saw in wavelengths other than the common visual spectrum humanoids tended to use, or they depended on their own instruments even more so than Sulu did. Which made Sulu wonder what would happen to them if they stayed in orbit around Tlaoli for too long.

"What's it doing?" his older counterpart asked after they had watched the ship for a few minutes.

Chekov snorted. "Besides moving through space, not much that I can see."

"No, it's the *way* it's moving." Sulu had noticed it, too, the subtle cycle of deceleration, drift, and acceleration that the Shechenag ship displayed on its slow orbit around Tlaoli. "It looks as if it's slowing down to do something every so often, then moving on again."

"Vulcans cannot see as well in the dark as humans do," Spock said calmly. "Lieutenant Sulu, if you would extinguish the cockpit lights—"

Sulu found the small dial on the *Herschel*'s instrument panel and dimmed both his displays as well as the overhead lights. It took his eyes a moment to adjust to the intense darkness of space, but when they did the pattern of the Shechenag ship suddenly made perfect sense.

"They're dropping satellites!" he blurted.

"Or mines," Chekov said.

A dozen of the tiny objects strung out like dimly glowing pearls behind the main ship, tracing the curve of its orbit around the nightside of Tlaoli and back toward its retreating sunset terminus. The detached objects weren't the only things glowing, either. Strands of light as iridescent as spider silk connected each satellite to the next, stringing them into a necklace that seemed to be held together by electromagnetic force rather than any physical agent.

"It's an integrated network," the older Sulu said quietly. "Once it's installed around the entire planet, it will probably generate some kind of defensive array."

Chekov grunted curt agreement. "If it's anything like the kind we installed around some of our colonies once the Gorn started attacking from space, it won't let ships pass either way once it's been activated. And," he added grimly, "it looks to me like it's being activated as they install it."

# Chapter Three

"HEY, where does this go?"

Chekov automatically detoured the couple of steps necessary to crane a look up the access ladder Kirk had leaped onto and gleefully begun to climb. He immediately felt stupid for having gone through the motions. "Uh..." He barely knew where the main corridors and turbolift shafts led on board this ship, much less all the auxiliary conduits and passageways. Trying to cover his uncertainty, he hauled the boy back down to the deck with a little more force than necessary. "It just goes up to the next deck. It's a maintenance access."

Just in case he hadn't sounded uncertain enough, his older self snorted with unconcealed disdain from where he waited with Sulu on the other side of the corridor. Chekov bit down hard against a flush of embarrassment and tried to act as though he hadn't heard. Bad enough that Spock had given him responsibility for leading their guests to a set of quarters he'd never seen before—it was far worse to have one of them be a man who must know every insecure and self-castigating thought that passed through his head. Waving to Kirk a little impatiently, Chekov said, "It doesn't go anywhere interesting. Come on."

Kirk tossed one last look up the ladder, but followed readily enough when the small group continued down the corridor. Hurrying a little to reclaim his place alongside Chekov, he asked cheerfully, "You have no idea where it goes, do you?"

Chekov didn't look at him. "No."

Kirk nodded as though that confirmed something he'd long suspected. "Do you actually serve on board this ship?"

Chekov darted an irritated glance at the boy, then softened when he saw Kirk's playful grin. Embarrassed all over again, he admitted quietly,

"I'm new," and hoped the Chekov behind them wouldn't have anything to add.

"Does that mean we're gonna get lost?" Kirk actually sounded pleased by that prospect, glancing down the next intersection with an air of boyish adventure. "How many days do you think we can wander the decks without going past the same place twice?"

Judging from Chekov's experience so far, quite a few. "We're not going to get lost." He tried to make the assertion sound confident instead of desperately hopeful. But then the older man behind him muttered something to Sulu that Chekov didn't quite hear, and he felt obliged to add, "It just might take us a few extra minutes to get anywhere we're trying to go."

In retrospect, he probably should have worked harder at making Spock understand his lack of familiarity with the ship's layout when the first officer saddled him with this assignment. But he'd been the last one on an examination bed, in the midst of blowing as hard as he could into the respiratory sensor Nurse Chapel had just handed him, and Spock had lingered in the doorway only long enough to announce, "Ensign Chekov, please see that our guests are settled in these temporary billets," before dropping a padd on the desktop and exiting as brusquely as he'd arrived. At the time, it hadn't seemed appropriate to leap up and chase the first officer out into the hallway just to exclaim, "But I can't even find my *own* quarters half the time! We'll be wandering the ship for hours!"

Now, he was starting to regret that earlier inaction.

"Apparently, in this alternate timeline, crew quarters are no longer on deck six."

The sound of his own voice—but colder, and not as heavily accented—sent an unpleasant shiver up Chekov's spine. It was as if he were hearing his most critical inner demons projected aloud. Halting, he turned back the way they'd just come to find the older version of himself gesturing with mock courtesy down a side corridor that Chekov had just walked blithely past. He recognized it immediately as the route they needed to take to reach the turbolift for the crew's quarters, and wanted to kick himself for not making the realization just a few seconds earlier. The expression of tolerant sympathy on Captain Sulu's face didn't make him feel any better about it, nor did being forced to step in front of both men to resume his lead position as they turned the corner. "Excuse me, sirs..."

Just when he thought the worst of it was over, that cold artifact of his own voice suggested, very close to his ear, *"Vuey mogli vcegda tyanytch nebolshouye karti vashei rukye..."* You could always draw a little map on your hand.

A sharp thump told him that Sulu had cuffed his first officer on the shoulder, apparently with the prosthetic hand McCoy had fitted him with not an hour before. "Pavel, stop harassing the boy."

The elder Chekov didn't seem terribly concerned by his commanding officer's reprimand. "If we left it up to him, we'd be wandering in the desert for forty years."

Sulu snorted. "Do I have to remind you that you *were* him just twenty-five years ago?"

"No," the other man snarled curtly. "It's bad enough that *he* reminds me."

No one said anything after that on the short turbolift ride up to deck six, not even Kirk, who occupied himself by peering into every maintenance panel he had time to flip open during the trip. Inspired perhaps by his own mortification and his willingness to be done with this unpleasant duty, Chekov found the empty billet described in Spock's directions almost as though he actually knew where they were going. He keyed in the access code, then stepped back to clear the entrance as the door slid obediently open.

"I'm afraid nothing's been removed from the previous occupant," he explained, remembering that, too, from the orders spelled out on Spock's padd. "Lieutenant Tormolen died only a few days ago, and with everything that's happened..."

An expression he wasn't sure how to interpret moved wistfully across Sulu's face, as though he'd just been reminded of something he hadn't thought about for many years. "We understand. Thank you."

Chekov stole a glance at his older self's back as the man shouldered past him into the room without bothering to excuse himself or say goodbye. *What did you expect?* Chekov chided himself, feeling embarrassed and angry all over gain. *Some kindly pearls of wisdom about which future girlfriend to watch out for?*

No, of course not... But he wouldn't have minded at least some indication that he could stand to look at himself without being disgusted.

Chekov realized he'd lingered a moment longer than necessary when Sulu smiled at him gently and tossed a nod back over one shoulder. "Don't mind him. He's just sulking because we didn't let him kill himself." A snort from the room behind him was the only indication he'd been overheard. If anything, the captain's smile softened with even greater fondness. "Thank you for everything, Ensign. I'm sure we'll be seeing each other again later." Then he stepped back into the dead crewman's quarters and let the door slide shut behind him.

The moment they were alone, Kirk remarked conversationally, "My future's better than yours."

*My future's just scary.* Chekov turned to look at him, abruptly remembering the instructions McCoy had given him and the other members of the landing party after Spock had left. "We should get some sleep ourselves."

Kirk tossed him a puckish grin. "Can you find your quarters from here?"

Even depressed and half-exhausted, Chekov managed to dignify the boy's remark with a satisfactorily offended glower. "Yes, I can find my quarters. Most of the time."

"Okay." Kirk's grin widened conspiratorially. "Can you find *my* quarters?"

Chekov brought them to a halt in the middle of the corridor. "I am *not* taking you to the captain's cabin."

"Just for a minute!"

"I don't even have the codes to get in."

"I bet I could figure them out." Kirk slid around in front of him, looking smugly pleased with himself and for all the world like the kind of boy who could go anywhere he wanted. "It's probably something stupid, like the birthday of my favorite dog."

Chekov didn't even know that Captain Kirk had owned a favorite dog. "No."

"But it's *my* room," Kirk protested. "Can't I order you or something?"

"Not for another twenty years."

Although he heaved a dramatic sigh of resignation, Kirk's smile remained undimmed, and he fell into step beside Chekov again as though he hadn't really expected a different answer. "Can we at least go see some other part of the ship? I'm hungry—we could go to the mess hall." When Chekov rolled his eyes at the suggestion, Kirk caught at his arm and dragged him to a stop with a little laugh. "Oh, come on! I've barely eaten since I got here, and I can't believe you're not going to show me the whole ship, and besides I'm *way* too excited to sleep."

The mention of food—no matter how fleeting—reminded Chekov's stomach that he hadn't eaten since their arrival at Tlaoli, either, and now the empty cramping was giving his fatigue a run for its money. Since they'd all been ordered by McCoy to get a good meal in addition to as much sleep as possible, he supposed it didn't really matter in what order those events occurred. He motioned Kirk back toward the turbolift with a sigh. "Lucky for you, I know how to find the rec hall."

Heads turned with the usual casual interest when they entered, but a few crew members looked a little longer than Chekov was used to. He found himself wondering how far word had spread about what had happened planetside, and how many of the people staring knew who the boy with him was, and how many others couldn't even guess. They were in the middle of a shift, which meant only a handful of crew were actually present. Still, Chekov tried to hold himself erect and unself-conscious as he led Kirk over to the banks of food slots. Whatever gossip might spring up from this public glimpse of the boy who would be their commander, at least no one could say that Chekov was embarrassed to be saddled with him.

Tapping Kirk's shoulder to retrieve his attention from where it had strayed toward a three-dimensional chess game going on nearby, Chekov explained the food ordering system by keying up his own dinner as an example. Kirk watched the steps keenly, then stepped up to the menu screen with all the delight of a boy given his first 3-D entertainment set. He was still scrolling through the choices when Chekov's food arrived, but seemed to interrupt himself abruptly by pointing to one particular entry and asking, "What's this?"

Chekov glanced at the screen. It was part of the Northern Africa menu, and he couldn't even begin to pronounce the name. "I have no idea."

As though that were precisely the answer he'd hoped for, Kirk promptly punched in that selection and stepped back to wait with a self-satisfied grin on his face. Chekov could only shake his head in wonder. "I cannot believe you're intending to eat something when you have no idea what it is."

"Are you kidding?" Kirk looked honestly surprised at his companion's diffidence. "It'll be fun!"

Whether or not it was fun, it was certainly colorful. A riotous patchwork of bright reds, greens, and yellows decorated a plate that had been draped with what Chekov initially took as a sheet of linen napkin. Closer inspection revealed it to be some sort of pale, clothlike bread. A second piece of the same spongy material had been neatly folded on a smaller plate beside the first. Chekov had to admit that it all smelled very rich and wonderful, but he was still skeptical of anything that didn't come out of the machine in the company of a fork and knife.

"See?" Kirk said as he slid into an empty seat as though already accustomed to doing it every day. "Your food is all just sort of white and sitting there. Mine is interesting and brightly colored."

Chekov took the seat across from him. "Venomous animals are also brightly colored," he pointed out.

Kirk made a disapproving face. "Don't be such a hen. It's on the menu—" He tore off a section of the separate napkin-that-wasn't and used it to scoop up a handful of food. "—so it's not like it can kill me."

Chekov watched the boy dive into his food with a fascination bordering on amazement. It wasn't necessarily the flavor of the food Kirk enjoyed, he realized, it was the experience—the opportunity to do something he'd never done before, even if it was something as simple as eating a North African meal with his hands. He supposed he shouldn't be surprised. After all, if the man who commanded a starship on the very edges of the frontier didn't derive excitement from all things new and different, what was he doing on the frontier at all?

Chekov glanced down at his own considerably less adventuresome meal. *Am I sure I have what it takes to be a starship commander?*

Coughing once, Kirk abruptly dropped his bread-napkin into the center of his plate and clapped both hands to his mouth. Chekov looked up at him in alarm as the boy's eyebrows climbed toward his hairline and his face darkened to an appalling shade of red. "Are you all right?"

Nodding vigorously, Kirk groped for the glass of milk he'd ordered with his dinner, and finally managed to squeak, "Hot!" just before gulping down a series of desperate mouthfuls.

Chekov laughed. "I warned you."

"No, no—it's good!" But even that assurance collapsed into a strangled little cough before it could sound too convincing, and Kirk emptied the rest of his milk in a couple of quick swallows. Still laughing, Chekov pushed his own water across the table and into Kirk's reaching hand.

Finishing only half of the water, Kirk sat back with a loud exhalation of relief, then cocked his head at Chekov as though only just putting a finger on something that had been bothering him for a while. "He never smiles."

"Who?" Chekov asked.

"You." An impatient scowl wrinkled his young face, and he waved his hand in frustration at not having the pronouns to easily discuss what they were all in the midst of. "The other you. Him." He leaned forward to replace the half-empty water glass on Chekov's side of the table. "Even when he says something funny, it's like he knows it's funny, but he doesn't really care."

Chekov felt his own smile evaporate, and struggled not to let it sink into a frown as he toyed with the suddenly unappetizing food on his plate.

"Does it bug you?" Kirk asked, blunt in his youthful sincerity. "Knowing you might end up being..." Words failed him again, and he shrugged. "...somebody you feel like you aren't?"

Chekov returned the shrug. "A little." But that wasn't really true, and he still felt awkward lying to the boy. "A lot," he finally admitted. He dropped his fork onto his plate and pushed it off to one side. "But maybe knowing it's a possibility will help me prevent it from happening." It didn't sound any more convincing now than when he said it to himself.

Kirk gathered another more cautious mouthful of food, and chewed it carefully while he thought. "Maybe it's not good for us to know too much about who we're going to be. I mean, I keep wondering if I'm gonna be *me* for the next twenty years, or if I'm always going to be thinking I ought to be doing this thing or that thing not because I want to, but because it's what a guy who's supposed to be a great starship commander would do."

It hadn't occurred to Chekov until just then that seeing a brilliant future for yourself could be just as intimidating as seeing one you didn't like. "Captain Kirk became a great starship commander without knowing anything about his future. You'll become him just by being who you are."

Kirk looked at him frankly. "So does that mean you have to become Mr. Sunshine?"

"I don't know . . . I don't think so." Chekov said it more because he needed to believe it than because he honestly felt it was true.

"You know what I think?" Down to the bread-napkin lining of his dinner, Kirk began tearing it into individual colorful strips that he could roll up and pop in his mouth. "I think if we can fix the timeline so that the Gorn don't take over the Federation—I think you'll stay a nice guy because the world won't have gotten so crappy."

Chekov studied this young man with all his nascent greatness, and asked, in as neutral a tone as he could muster, "You're not afraid of going back?"

Kirk thought about that long enough to give an honest answer. "A little." Then, with that same quicksilver smile, "A lot. But if I don't go back, there's so much bad stuff that will happen, and so much good stuff that never will." He waved expansively around the now nearly empty rec hall. "I won't get to have this great ship, and you guys won't get to be my minions."

Grinning, Chekov lifted his eyebrow in mock dismay. *"Minions?"*

"Sorry. I meant my brave and loyal crew," Kirk said with patently false sincerity. "I wouldn't want you guys to end up with some other crummy captain like the one who screwed things up with the Gorn. Besides—" He leaned forward on his elbows with a smile so wicked it made his eyes twinkle. "I can't wait to find out how me as a great starship commander is getting along with my dad."

She had actually escaped Tlaoli.

The reality of having finally left the planet where she had spent so many frantic and helpless hours took a long time to sink into Uhura's consciousness. She found herself reaching up to where her helmet carbide used to be whenever she needed to turn on the light in her quarters, and when she put her normal uniform on, the first thing she thought was that it wasn't going to do much good if that alien chill swept through the caves again. Even after two hours of getting cleaned up and debriefed and taking an all-too-brief nap, Uhura found herself wondering what the next crisis in the ice caverns would be.

Her subconscious fear that she hadn't really left the alien planet worried Uhura enough that she mentioned it to Dr. McCoy when she went to get his medical clearance for the early return to duty that Spock had requested. In response, she got a long lecture on the relationship of sleep to residual post-stress tension, as well as a restorative dose of melatonin, time-released glucose, electrolytes, and fluids. Even as he prepared the nutritional supplement, Dr. McCoy grumbled about the order that had woken her early and summoned her back to bridge duty.

"It's those damned Vulcan chromosomes of his," he declared. "Spock thinks because he can go for days without sleep, so can everyone else aboard this ship."

Uhura took the glass the doctor handed her, wrinkling her nose at its chalky look and sterile chemical smell. She refrained from pointing out that McCoy himself hadn't gotten any sleep yet, knowing that would only get her an irritated look and a harumph. Instead, she gulped down as much of her medicine as she could manage in one determined pull, then handed it back to him with a grimace.

"Couldn't you at least put some vanilla flavor into it?"

"I'm a doctor, not a bartender!" McCoy told her tartly. "And you need to finish *all* of that, Lieutenant, or I'm not going to clear you for duty."

"I think coffee would have worked just as well to keep me awake. And tasted a whole lot better." Uhura pinched her fingers on her nose and swallowed the rest of the nutritional supplement. Despite her protests, she could already feel her body responding to McCoy's concoction with a reassuring burst of energy. "Am I allowed to get a real breakfast on my way up to the bridge?"

"Only if you think Spock won't mind waiting another half hour for you to get there." McCoy's lips quirked at the face she made. "That's what I thought. Here."

Uhura took the tray he handed her and discovered it was a portable meal from the sickbay food dispensers, complete with a capped mug of steaming coffee. The fried-egg sandwich wouldn't have been her first choice for breakfast, but unlike Belgian waffles it had the benefit of being able to be consumed inside a turbolift. And after nearly two days of dry emergency rations and meager base camp meals, the chocolate croissant McCoy had added to the tray looked like heavenly ambrosia.

"Bless you, Doctor!" Uhura gave McCoy's cheek a peck as she slid off the examining table. The physician stepped back and muttered something indistinct, a tinge of red creeping up along his cheekbones. "Did you order a breakfast like this for Mr. Spock, too?"

"Spock!" That got her the harumph she'd avoided earlier. "He's just as bad as that grumpy version of Chekov. He wouldn't even let me check to make sure he wasn't exhausted. If he's eaten anything, mark my words... it was probably either an emergency ration bar or some Vulcan version of gruel."

Uhura left sickbay chuckling between hurried bites of biscuit and gulps of coffee. At the last minute, she remembered to make the turbolift stop at the sub-bridge ready deck, so she could dispose of the tray and swipe the crumbs off her red uniform before she reported for duty. The smell of coffee and chocolate must have clung to her strongly enough, though, to earn her a twinkling look from Chief Engineer Montgomery Scott, who was waiting for the turbolift on the back deck of the bridge.

"It's good to see *someone* taking the time to eat around here," Scott said, his voice booming loudly enough to carry back to the captain's chair. Uhura could see Spock standing beside the empty console, as he usually did when he was left in command of the bridge, but the Vulcan didn't appear to have noticed that Scotty's comment was intended for him instead of Uhura. The chief engineer snorted and rolled his eyes at Uhura, then stepped past her into the turbolift and told it, "Engineering."

Uhura paused as the turbolift doors hissed shut behind her, scanning the crewmen at the bridge stations. She recognized some of the faces from the night-shift: Lieutenant Tora Rhada at the helm and Sean DePaul at navigations, Elizabeth Palmer at communications and Richard Washburn at engineering. But the ship's chief astrobiologist, Lieutenant Commander Ann Mulhall, was manning the science station in place of the usual second-shift Science Officer Boma, and the security desk was occupied by the chief of security himself, Antonio Giotto. Unsure of whether Spock wanted her to relieve Palmer in the midst of her shift or carry out some other work detail, Uhura stepped forward and cleared her throat.

"Lieutenant Uhura reporting for duty, sir."

"Indeed," said Spock without turning around, as if he'd been aware of her presence all along. "I appreciate you taking the time to consume a meal before you reported, Lieutenant. It will save you the trouble of being harassed about your dietary requirements by various ranking officers of the ship."

Uhura bit her bottom lip to suppress a giggle. As usual, the Vulcan's comment was perfectly serious. And although Kirk or McCoy might have been able to tease him about that, it wasn't her place as a junior line officer to do so. "Do you want me to man the communications station, Mr. Spock?"

"No." The science officer turned toward her, and she could see now that he held a small mud-splattered instrument in his hands. "Lieutenant Palamas is still being treated in sickbay for the aftereffects of electrical shock. I require your expertise to cross-correlate the records you made down on the planet with Lieutenant Commander Mulhall's database of galactic archaeological artifacts."

Uhura came forward to take the visual translator from him, although she barely recognized the archaeological device now that it had been stripped of its bulky protective cover. "Are the records still intact?"

"Yes. I had Commander Scott remove the magnetic shielding himself, to guarantee nothing was damaged in the process." Spock's face looked a little more gaunt and sharply carved than usual, but nothing else about him betrayed the tense situation they were in. On the main viewscreen, Uhura could see the dark shadow of another spaceship blotting out the stars as it slowly orbited Tlaoli. It trailed a faint line of spider silk in its wake. Uhura realized that must be the Shechenag ship, setting up the network of defensive satellites Captain Sulu had told them about back on board the *Herschel*. She couldn't tell how many of those iridescent strands of force were already in place around Tlaoli, since the dusty garnet glow of its dayside outshone any that might have crossed it, but Uhura suspected there wasn't much time to waste. She glanced back up at Spock.

"Are you looking for any particular information from the Tlaoli records?"

The Vulcan lifted one eyebrow, but his face was otherwise so stolid that Uhura couldn't tell if he was expressing admiration for her efficiency or surprise that she had asked such an obvious question. "I wish to know if the ancient Tlaoli ever encountered a shield such as this when they fought the Shechenag, and, if so, whether they discovered a way to counteract it. Failing that, I wish to know where the Shechenag have come from and why it took them so long to reach Tlaoli after we arrived. Given their insistence on preventing any use of the Janus Gate, they seem to have left it oddly unprotected in an empty quadrant of space."

Uhura nodded and headed over to the science station, where Mulhall greeted her with a preoccupied nod. Uhura didn't hold that against her. All she really knew about the *Enterprise*'s chief astrobiologist was that Mulhall ate, slept, and breathed for her esoteric science specialty. Uhura didn't even try to pry her away from whatever query she was running through her database. Instead, she quietly set the archaeological translator on the science desk beside her and ran its leads into an unused data port, then began downloading its records of the Tlaoli written language into the ship's main computer so they could be translated more thoroughly than she and Palamas had managed down on the planet. Unlike the visual translator, the ship's logic circuits could reconstruct the rice-shaped phonemes that had been obliterated by cracks and tarnish on the walls of the Janus chamber. After a moment, the computer's artificial voice said quietly, "Translation 99.3 percent complete. Continue iterations for additional word discrimination?"

"How long will that take?" Uhura asked it.

"Four hours to achieve 99.9 percent completion."

"We'll go with what we've got." Uhura glanced up at Mulhall inquiringly. "Are you ready to start correlating, sir?"

The astrobiologist nodded again, but this time the full intensity of her pale-gray gaze was focused on Uhura and the translator. It was a little disconcerting. Mulhall was much taller than Uhura, tall enough that she hadn't even needed to adjust the tilt of Spock's display screen in order to use it. Her finely chiseled face held a strength and intelligence that suggested why she had risen to the rank of lieutenant commander, unusually high for a science specialist so young.

"How old do you estimate those written records are?" Mulhall asked, fingers poised over the keyboard to input Uhura's answer.

"We don't know." Uhura felt a flicker of annoyance at the incredulous look Mulhall gave her. "Our instruments weren't working all that well down on Tlaoli. All the geologists could tell was that the alien ruins were older than the caves above them. So they're at least several thousand years old and possibly millions of years older than that."

"Then we won't bother looking for an exact match," Mulhall said crisply. "We'll do a language derivation check. Give me a prioritized list of the ten most common grammatical elements in the language and I'll cross-reference that to every similar structure in our linguistic records."

It was Uhura's turn to look surprised. "Only ten? Wouldn't it be better to use more?"

The astrobiologist shook her head. "Linguistic studies have shown that it only takes six to seven matches to pin down a genetic relationship if it's really there. Once you start using less common language elements, you get too many false positives."

Uhura fed the request into the computer via the visual translator, and saw the flicker of response that immediately crossed Mulhall's display screen. "Will it cause problems if I do some searches on my translation while you run the cross-check?"

"Not until I get a match, and need to refine the linguistic derivation."

"Good." Uhura had been thinking about how she could search the translated Tlaoli writings for the information Spock wanted. Instead of selecting abstract concepts like "defensive shield" or proper names like Shechenag which might have changed through time, she'd decided it would be better to search for the discrete physical objects that would be mentioned if the Tlaoli military records contained any discussion of this type of warfare. She said, "Ship's computer: locate all variants of the following terms in the Tlaoli records: 'satellite,' 'space buoy,' 'orbital platform.'"

"Locating," the computer said, then was silent for a while. "There is only one usage of a term equivalent to any of those words. Translation follows: 'All of the other worlds and satellites we once occupied were lost, one by one, as the war continued for millennia.' Shall I continue?"

"No." Uhura glanced back over her shoulder at the viewscreen. They were now orbiting around Tlaoli's nightside, and the strands of force that marked the growing barricade around the ancient planet glimmered like frostfire in the darkness. They crossed and recrossed at a variety of angles, looking more than ever like a floating spiderweb. "Try locating all variants of the following terms: 'space blockade,' 'space network,' 'space quarantine.'"

"Locating." Another long pause. "There are no parts of the translation that correlate to any of those terms."

Uhura heaved a sigh. "All right. Then see if you can find a proper noun similar to Shechenag. Use a 30 percent differential in pronunciation to locate all possible variants."

"Locating. Word found in two hundred and forty-seven places." Uhura gave herself a mental thump on the head. Sometimes, the thing you thought was too simple to look for was actually the best. "Would you like verbatim translations of all instances where the word is used?"

"Can you compile a summary of those sections of the records, or are the instances scattered around too much to do that?"

"Two hundred and thirteen usages of the word 'Shechenag' are contained within nineteen percent of the text," the computer said. "It will take approximately fifteen minutes to compile a summary of that section. Of the remaining usages, twenty-three are scattered throughout the text and eleven are compressed into a very small passage at the end."

Uhura frowned, remembering the rough translation they had made down on the planet. The largest group of references to the Shechenag probably came from the historical section where the Tlaoli described their millennia-long war. Since the computer had already determined that no references were made in the text to satellites or space blockades, the blow-by-blow details of that ancient conflict might not be all that helpful now. The shorter section was more promising, since it was placed at the end of the text where the Tlaoli granted the use of the Janus Gate to anyone who might find it in the future. If it had occurred to them to add a warning there about their ancient enemies...

"I think I have a partial correlation," Mulhall said, without looking away from Spock's science monitor. "And if I'm right, I've got some intriguing cross-references popping up in a database of Andorian myths and legends. Can I merge your text records into my query now?"

"Give me one more minute," Uhura said. "Computer, mark the longer section of the records for future compilation. Translate the section at the end where the Shechenag are mentioned eleven times."

"Translating." This time, the computer's pause was long enough that Uhura could hear a rumble of voices coming from the security station as Giotto consulted Spock about something. She glanced over her shoulder, but saw nothing particularly alarming on the viewscreen. In fact, the Shechenag ship appeared to have come to a stop, leaving its spidery network less than half complete. "The section can be condensed as follows: 'Use of the Janus Gate should not be undertaken lightly. As we discovered during the war with the Shechenag, some changes made to our benefit in past battles resulted in a poorer future outcome. The likelihood of such inverse results can be predicted, but the Shechenag were never able to do this.

" 'Many unrecoverable disasters were created in the timestream when the Shechenag stole our technology and tried to copy our chronological intervention techniques. In fact, the great interregnum in the war resulted from a Shechenag populist uprising to protest the use of time travel. Ever since that time, the Shechenag sovereignty have tried to exterminate all use of time-slip devices, by themselves or by others.

" 'We do not believe the Shechenag have now or ever will have the technology to destroy this Janus Gate, but the Shechenag sovereignty may attempt to prevent anyone else from using it as we do. Our homeworld lies on the farthest reaches of Shechenag space, in a region where they do not travel due to the risk of encountering other races whose behavior they cannot predict or control. But if the Janus Gate is used, the Shechenag may risk even such encounters in their zeal to protect the timeline. Use of the Janus Gate should therefore be made with adequate precautions against a Shechenag response, and with the understanding that such use may result in a declaration of war upon the user by whatever remains of the Shechenag Empire.' "

"Fascinating." The Vulcan's superior hearing must have let him absorb the computer's report from his position at the security station across the bridge. "That would explain why it took several days for the

Shechenag to arrive and evict us from Tlaoli. However, it still does not answer the question of why they leave the planet undefended in their absence."

"I think I know the answer to that." Mulhall looked up from the science display screen, her strong-boned face alight with the intellectual satisfaction of having solved part of the Shechenag puzzle. "The closest match we've got to the Tlaoli language in our database is an obscure, post-technological civilization out past Andorian space. In trying to find out more about them, I ran across an old Andorian legend that seems to refer to Tlaoli itself."

"Indeed?" Spock turned to give them his full attention, although he didn't leave the security station. Alerted by his presence there, Uhura looked up at the viewscreen more carefully, trying to identify the threat Giotto and Spock must have identified there. "What does this legend say?"

"It's actually very similar to the Irish legends of Brigadoon, a magical town that appears and disappears," Mulhall said with an unexpectedly whimsical smile. "The Andorian storytellers claim there's a whole planet like that, in a quadrant so distant no one remembers its direction anymore. For thousands of years, according to the legend, no one can see or land on this planet, because it's shrouded in some kind of glowing ionic storm. But every so often the ionic storm calms down, and then the planet can be seen and landed on. If you visit the planet at those times, the story goes, you might be killed and eaten by monsters. Or, if you're lucky, you might regain your heart's lost desire." Mulhall made a slightly embarrassed face. "I'm not sure if that last part means much of anything. It's how Andorian storytellers usually like to end a legend."

"Getting your heart's lost desire could refer to the use of the Janus Gate to change an unfortunate decision you made in the past," Uhura pointed out. "And even if it's not monsters, there's certainly something down on Tlaoli that eats spaceships by draining their power supply, and kills them by dragging them out of orbit."

"You are quite correct, Lieutenant." Spock turned back to watch something on one of the security readouts, but his voice continued the conversation just as deftly even without his full attention. "Furthermore, if the glowing ion storm in the story were generated by a defensive barrier similar to the one which the Shechenag are currently erecting around Tlaoli, it may be that they do, indeed, protect the planet for long periods of time, until the Janus Gate manages to bring their barrier down. If the barrier failed shortly before we first arrived here with our landing parties—"

The Vulcan's voice cut off abruptly and Uhura saw his hand move in a blur too fast to distinguish. Milliseconds later, the familiar howl of red-alert sirens echoed through the ship.

"Evasive action, Mr. Rhada!" Spock's voice never sounded desperate, but it could rise to an insistent shout when circumstances seemed to warrant it. It did that now, telling Uhura everything she needed to know about the gravity of the situation. "All shields at full power, but do *not* fire phasers. Do you hear understand, Mr. Giotto?"

"I hear you, Mr. Spock," the security chief said grudgingly. "But if those aliens out there start firing at us—"

"I do not believe they will." Spock's gaze slanted back up toward the viewscreen, and Uhura's followed it. This time, however, she finally understood what she was seeing. The dark shadow of a Shechenag spaceship that appeared to be standing still against the stars—that was an optical illusion, caused by the alien ship's lack of lights and therefore of easy size reference. In actuality, Uhura realized with a start, the Shechenag ship wasn't standing still at all.

It was approaching the *Enterprise* head-on.

# Chapter Four

THE SHRIEK OF THE red-alert siren blasted through the bridge of the *Enterprise,* followed by an urgent cascade of voices as the crew reported in from their stations. It felt odd to Uhura not to be part of that disciplined response, to be merely a bystander on the bridge instead of an integral part of its functioning. All she could do was step back and keep a watchful eye on Ann Mulhall. Science specialists were rarely present on the bridge during times of crisis, and she wanted to make sure Mulhall didn't interfere with the flow of information by asking questions or making irrelevant comments. But the astrobiologist was silent, observing the crew with a fascinated eye as if they were some new species of aliens she had never seen before.

"Evasive maneuvers aren't working." That was Lieutenant DePaul at navigations, watching both his own viewscreen and Rhada's as the pilot concentrated on shifting from one set of random orbital curves to another. The replacement helmsman had steady hands, but she was nowhere near as swift with her course changes as Sulu would have been, Uhura thought as she watched her.

"Shields up." Giotto angled a stubborn look up at Spock. "Main phasers targeted and ready to fire."

"*Wait for my signal.*" There was never emotion in Spock's voice, but the clipped intensity of that particular command told Uhura how much he meant it. "Lieutenant Palmer, are we receiving any communications from the Shechenag ship?"

"I'm not sure, sir." Palmer threw an urgent glance, not at Spock but at Uhura. "There's *something* coming in past the subspace interference, but I've run it through every one of our translating algorithms and it still doesn't turn into language."

"That's because we didn't have working universal translators when the Shechenag spoke to us down on Tlaoli. They translated their language for us." Uhura crossed the bridge toward the communications station without waiting for an order from Spock. As the senior communications officer on the *Enterprise*, it was her prerogative to replace a junior officer in times of crisis. And judging from Palmer's grateful look as she vacated the station, this qualified as one of those times.

Uhura located the channel Palmer had been monitoring, full of the clattering mechanical sounds of Shechenag speech, and routed it to the ship's neuro-linguistic analyzing circuits instead of through the communications station's simpler bank of preprogrammed translation routines. Unfortunately, even the powerful ship's computer would take several minutes to begin breaking down the structure and vocabulary of the alien language, especially if parts of it were actually machine control code as Uhura suspected from the sound. By the time the *Enterprise* crew figured out what the Shechenag were trying to tell them, the two ships might well be engaged in a totally unnecessary battle.

Uhura took a deep breath and adjusted her transmitter to the same frequency the Shechenag were using, then glanced at Spock. "Request permission to reply to the Shechenag, Commander."

"Granted."

Uhura opened a channel back to the alien ship, hoping the muffled sound of machine noise in the background meant that it was being monitored. "This is not the language," she said firmly, trying to replicate as best she could the flat declarative sentence structure of the cybernetic aliens. "We do not intend hostility. We do not understand your orders."

The rattles and whistles on the translator channel stopped abruptly. A moment later, much to Uhura's relief, the shadowy silhouette of the alien ship slowed to a menacing hover on the viewscreen—much too close for comfort, she thought, but at least no longer advancing. She could tell from the almost dazed expressions of relief on the faces of Rhada and De-Paul that there hadn't been much room left to maneuver between the two ships. Uhura suspected that even Kirk, with his steel nerves and fierce determination, might not have been able to watch another ship so nearly collide with his own and not have ordered an attack.

A light flashed on Uhura's board, and she felt her own tension melt a little. "The Shechenag are hailing us in English now, Mr. Spock. They're sending a visual signal as well."

"Put it on the main screen, Lieutenant." If Spock was at all shaken by the near miss they'd just barely avoided, neither his measured voice nor his erect posture showed it. He remained standing by Giotto at the security station, although Uhura couldn't tell if that was because he didn't trust the security chief or because he didn't think a race as alien as the Shechenag would know or care who occupied the captain's chair on the *Enterprise.*

"This is the language." The visual signal from the other ship showed a knot of dark metallic bodies, each with several spidery appendages extended to plug into oddly barren panels around the small bridge of their ship. Uhura couldn't see the torso tanks where the actual aliens were housed, and realized that they must be facing each other at the center of that mechanical huddle. Information from their ship systems and communications must be routed directly to their internal visual displays and control panels, Uhura thought, but apparently they had encountered enough other species to recognize that external viewscreens existed.

"This is the language," she confirmed, seeing Spock nod at her to continue the conversation. "Please repeat previous communications."

"This is not the position."

Only silence followed that enigmatic statement. Uhura wondered if the Shechenag truly thought in such vague and abstract modes, or if their translating technology simply wasn't very good at conveying their true meaning in English. She tapped in a silent query to the ship's computer to see how much progress it had made on decoding the clattering alien speech, but the bar showing its progress had barely crawled a third of the way toward completion.

Spock glanced at her with a lifted eyebrow and Uhura turned her hands up, silently conveying her inability to interpret the Shechenag response. The Vulcan stared at the screen for a moment, then said with just a hint of question in his voice, "The correct position is farther away from the planet."

"Correct position is outside the planetary system." Despite the flat mechanical quality of the Shechenag's translated speech, Uhura had a feeling that statement might have originally held something close to sarcasm. "Eight hours remain allotted for permanent relocation." Several mechanical appendages rose and fell out of the clotted group of Shechenag who seemed to be jointly in command of their ship, as if to emphasize the next point. "Temporary relocation to higher orbital level must be effected immediately. Maintenance of current position will result in irreparable damage."

Spock turned away from the viewscreen's automatic visual pickup, so that all the Shechenag could see was the back of his dark head.

"Lieutenant Uhura, can you degrade our audio signal without actually terminating contact? Lift your hand to your face or turn away from the viewscreen before you answer, please."

Uhura swung around and dropped her gaze to her controls, as if some alarm there had caught her attention. Although she was more used to clearing communication channels than deliberately obscuring them, it took her only a few seconds to broaden the frequency range on their transmission to the Shechenag until it overlapped and included one of Tlaoli's screeching zones of subspace interference. "Done, sir."

"Very good. I wish to know why the Shechenag think our current orbit will cause us damage. Are we experiencing any difficulties in maintaining orbit, Mr. Rhada?"

The pilot coughed, then kept one hand balled at her mouth, as if to stifle further outbursts. "No, sir," she said behind that shield. "No more than the usual instability we've gotten from Tlaoli's gravitational shifts. We're down at the low end of the safe orbital range, but we should be able to maintain here indefinitely."

Spock nodded without turning around. "Mr. Washburn, what about the ship's power supplies? Any sign of problems?"

"No, sir." The engineer's shoulders stiffened, as if he had to actively fight the urge to turn and face his superior officer as he reported. "Mr. Scott says our warp core and engines are fully functioning again, and he's got a backup power supply isolated behind magnetic shielding, in case we suffer another ship-wide power drain."

From the science desk, astrobiologist Ann Mulhall cleared her throat. "Permission to make an observation, Commander?" she asked without turning around to look at the Vulcan.

"Granted, Dr. Mulhall."

"From what I have observed of Shechenag vocal structures, they are not as straightforward as their simple grammar and lack of dependent clauses may make them appear. They actually seem to contain a great deal of deliberate ambiguity, or even tactical misrepresentation."

"You mean the Shechenag are lying to us?" Uhura asked behind the cover of raising her frequency monitor to her ear.

Mulhall shook her head. "Not lying, necessarily, just not telling us a very understandable version of the truth. For instance, the irreparable damage they mention might refer to their ship rather than to ours."

"Or," said Spock with slowly lifting eyebrows, "to the defensive satellite network they are installing around Tlaoli?"

"Quite possibly," agreed the astrobiologist.

"Thank you, Lieutenant Commander, for that insight." The Vulcan's angular face was suddenly very thoughtful. "Mr. Giotto, cancel the red alert. Mr. Rhada, prepare to lay in an orbit at the high end of the stable range, at least another thousand kilometers farther out from the planet. Lieutenant Uhura, slowly fade the interference out of our channel to the Shechenag and re-establish audio contact." The flurry of orders came so quickly that, for a moment, Uhura almost felt as if Captain Kirk were back in command of the *Enterprise*. The impression was deepened by Spock's next words, spoken into the communications panel on the captain's chair. "All senior officers report to the main briefing room. We have a battle plan to construct."

The knock on Sulu's cabin door was so tentative it barely woke him, even from an uneasy and drifting sleep. He lifted his head from his pillow, wondering if he'd heard a thump from some crewman passing in the corridor outside, but after a moment the quiet knocking sounded again.

"Come in." Since he'd lain down in his uniform, all Sulu had to do now was swing his feet off the bed and scrub the remnants of sleep from his face. The catnap hadn't done much to drive away the lingering jitters from his trip through the Janus Gate. Dr. McCoy had spoken soothingly about the natural adrenaline rebound effects after a period of suppressing strong emotions like panic and despair, but Sulu still wondered if the alien healing chamber had done something permanent to him. He had thought about asking the older version of himself if he felt anything similar after he'd come through the Gate, but an unaccountable shyness had walked Sulu past the other man and out of sickbay without making a conscious decision to put off any direct conversation.

The cabin door slid open, and a young gold-clad ensign edged just far enough inside that the door's automatic sensor wouldn't order it to shut again. "You're needed in the main briefing room, sir."

The somber dark eyes would have told Sulu who he was even if the Russian accent hadn't, but the rest of this younger Chekov's face seemed strangely unfamiliar. It wasn't the lack of scarring, Sulu decided, because he'd had time in the alien cavern and the shuttle to get used to the older Chekov's healed face. No, it was something completely different about their expressions, something even more fundamental than the shared line of their eyebrows or curve of their jaw...

Chekov shifted from foot to foot, reddening self-consciously beneath Sulu's intent gaze, but all he did was ask very politely, "Sir, did you hear me?"

"Yes. Sorry." Sulu stamped his feet into his boots and stood, glancing over at the communications console near his room's computer port. No message lights were flashing there. "Why didn't Commander Spock just hail me?"

Chekov gave him a startled look, as if he couldn't believe a senior officer was really asking him for information. "Um...I think he didn't want there to be any confusion, sir. About which version of us was supposed to come to the briefing, I mean."

"So you were summoned, too?" Sulu fell into step beside him as they exited the cabin and headed for the turbolifts. After spending hours on Basaraba with the brusque older version of Chekov, he couldn't resist the chance to find out how different this young Russian was from the man the Gorn invasion had turned him into. "Does that mean we're going back down to the planet?"

"I think so, sir." So far, Chekov seemed a lot like any other brand-new ensign fresh from the Academy—a little shy but not so reserved that he couldn't be drawn into a friendly conversation. "I heard Mr. Sanner and Lieutenant Tomlinson get called to this meeting, too, while I was on my way to get you."

"But not our . . . er . . . other halves?"

Chekov shot him another sidelong look as they stepped into the turbolift. "I guess not," was all he said, but there was a more relaxed tone to his voice now, as if Sulu's tacit admission of discomfort about having an older doppelganger aboard ship had eased a little of his own awkwardness. "Mr. Spock didn't request Captain Kirk's younger self, either. I had to find someone else to keep an eye on him for a while." The Russian blew out an exasperated breath. "He refused to go to sleep as the doctor ordered. I not only had to show him every public area on the ship, I had to haul him out of just about every maintenance shaft, too!"

Chekov sounded so much like an indignant older brother that Sulu couldn't help laughing. "Well, what did you expect? He *is* going to grow up to be the captain. What did you end up doing with him?"

The young ensign flashed him a surprisingly mischievous glance. "I gave him to the captain's yeoman. I told him she might let him see the captain's quarters if he promised to behave himself."

Before Sulu could reply, the turbolift doors slid open on the corridor leading to the ship's main briefing room. Another turbolift opened across the passage and Sulu suddenly felt as if he was gazing into a mirror. The older versions of Sulu and Chekov looked back at them steadily, although there was a twinkle in one pair of dark eyes that wasn't matched in the other.

"Heading for the briefing?" the older Asian man inquired as he stepped out into the hallway.

"Uh . . . yes." Sulu had to push Chekov forward out of the opening so the turbolift doors could close. The young ensign's face had stiffened into selfconsciousness again. "Were you called in, too?" He put as much innocence as he could muster into that question, but his older self apparently knew all the tones of his own voice too well to be deceived. He gave Sulu an ironic glance as they continued down the corridor. The older and younger Russians followed behind in stony silence.

"Not specifically," the older Sulu said. "But seeing that we have about half a century of Starfleet experience between us, we thought we qualified as senior officers."

The briefing room doors slid open to reveal a room already full of crewmen: Scotty, Giotto, McCoy, and Uhura in addition to Commander Spock. Lieutenant Robert Tomlinson and Zap Sanner stood quietly at the back, leaving the last empty chair at the table for an officer with a higher rank than theirs. Sulu tapped the younger Chekov on the shoulder and started around the room to join them, but was stopped by the sound of Spock's austerely cleared throat.

"Did you misunderstand my orders, Ensign Chekov?"

Sulu could see the ensign stiffen into the rigid heads-up posture Starfleet cadets were taught to assume when being disciplined for an infraction of academy rules. "No, sir," was all he said. Sulu opened his mouth to defend him, but his older self stepped forward and motioned him to silence.

"We heard you call a senior officer's briefing to draw up a battle plan, Mr. Spock," said the older Sulu. "It seemed like something we might be able to help with."

"I am not certain Starfleet regulations permit you to take part in this planning session, Captain Sulu. You are not currently a line officer on this ship."

"But visiting captains have consultation privileges," the older man reminded him. "And in my experience, no one objected if they brought their executive officers along. Of course, we had a lot more actual battle planning sessions in our future than you ever had in your past."

The subtle hint didn't change Spock's expression, but Sulu saw Chief Engineer Scott rub thoughtfully at his chin. "You may as well let them be, Mr. Spock," he suggested. "Otherwise, we'll just be explaining the whole thing over again to them when we're done."

The older Chekov stirred and spoke for the first time since emerging from the turbolifts. "If we're going to be part of your battle plan, then we're definitely staying." He took a step over to the empty chair and clenched his hands upon its back, as if to claim it for his superior officer. "So, what do you want us to do?"

A tinge of asperity crept into Spock's voice, although his angular face never changed expression. "The situation is not quite that simple, Commander Chekov. You should be aware that if we succeed in retrieving Captain Kirk from the past and restoring the timeline that he should have created, your own existence—"

"—will pop and disappear like a soap bubble?" The Russian exchanged ironic glances with his captain as he swung the chair around for the older Sulu to sit. "We're aware of that, Mr. Spock."

"Then I presume you understand why I cannot allow you to consult with us now." Spock lifted an eyebrow at the questioning looks the older men gave him. "Logically, neither you nor Captain Sulu may be considered to be allies in any attempt we make to repair the timeline that is keeping you alive."

It was the shoes that reminded him. A stupid little detail that hadn't troubled his mind in nearly nineteen years, the shoes littering the streets around the Federation embassy struck Captain James Kirk now as a poignant indictment of just how helpless they'd all been that night.

"Damned cowards," his father had complained at the time as he hurried his wife and sons past the embassy's public reception area and through the mysterious door stamped STARFLEET PERSONNEL ONLY. Being only fourteen, Kirk had been forced to lever himself up on tiptoe using his brother Sam's shoulder in order to catch a glimpse of what had most recently inspired his father's disgust. Outside the big unbreakable front window, the embassy's native personnel were stripping off their clothes as they ran.

A firm hand had splayed between his shoulder blades, gentle despite the tension Kirk could feel in the press of its fingers, and he let his mother hurry him forward without objecting. Somewhere behind them, he could hear urgent voices conferring over communicator channels, but couldn't quite make out what they were saying.

"They're frightened," his mother said. He knew she was trying to sound collected and brave for him and Sam, but she succeeded in only sounding fearfully close to tears. "They've been working in conjunction with Starfleet, and now they're afraid of what's going to happen to them and their families."

"Fourteen months we've spent working with them," George Kirk agreed bitterly, as usual only hearing the words spoken and not what his wife was trying to say. "Fourteen months, and the minute things go south, they're stripping out of their uniforms and leaving us to cover their retreat."

"George, that's not fair..."

A flutter of cloth blew up against Captain James Kirk's chest now, and he snatched at it with the hand not encumbered by the gauss rifle. What a few hours ago had been a neat blue-and-silver tunic flapped spastically in the breeze, half the buttons now ripped from its placard and the grimy outline of a bare Grexxen foot stamped across its back. Kirk felt a strange whirl of vertigo as he rubbed the soft cloth between his fingers, expecting to find it half-rotted and weather-torn. It didn't feel right to be coming across this fresh evidence of the Federation's failure here. It had all been so long ago . . . but somehow, this long-ago battle had been turned into the reality of here and now.

Up ahead of him, George Kirk lifted a hand to signal *wait* before creeping up the embankment that marked the edge of the wide boulevard the Grexxen called Ith. Roads in Sogo—and elsewhere on Grex, Kirk had always assumed—were evolutionary end products of the organic, looping footpaths Kozhu and Vragax had made over the generations. They had names the way humans named pets, not arbitrary appellations that could be changed with each swing of the political climate. Ith was not Ith Street, or Ith Avenue, it was only Ith and it would remain Ith until the last Grexxen passed away.

A fate the Vragax seemed determined to hasten on this particular evening.

Kirk joined his father on the slope of the embankment when George waved him forward, rolling to his back so he could keep watch behind them while George lifted up to scout ahead. "The fighting's moved farther south," Kirk whispered, taking the moment of stillness to thumb the last of his shells into the gauss rifle and toss the empty magazine away.

George grunted wordlessly in reply.

"That means there's a good chance your son made it back to the embassy all right."

Another grunt, this one carrying a wealth of skepticism. "I just hope he had the sense to head there."

Kirk kept his face turned toward the firelit streets behind them. Part of him wanted to tell his father that he was being unfair to his son, but he knew himself well enough to realize that was just a ghost of adolescent indignation. *You really couldn't blame George Kirk for feeling that way,* he thought, a little surprised by the embarrassment that stirred, ever so faintly, in the pit of his stomach. It wasn't like his younger self hadn't given his father every reason to distrust him this night nineteen years ago—it was just hard to separate where things had started from where they ended up when the excitement was all over.

The last time George Kirk had seen his youngest son on Grex, the boy was wedged into a narrow corridor alongside his mother and older brother, trying very hard not to seem as frightened as he'd become during their hurried evacuation of the staff apartments. He and Sam were the only children, his mother the only woman not clutching an attaché of vital Federation documents or brandishing a phaser.

"Stay with Ensign McCullough." George Kirk held his wife by the shoulders and looked sternly into her eyes, apparently convinced that she wouldn't understand these simple instructions unless she was looking straight at him. "She'll take care of you and the boys until I can join you on the *Eliza Mae.*"

His mother nodded dutifully, but her dark eyes were wide and uncomprehending. "How will we know where to find you? What if the *Eliza Mae* can't pick up everyone? What will happen then?" It bothered Kirk more than he liked to admit, hearing his mother sound so much like a frightened girl.

In one of his rare moments of tenderness, George Kirk reached up to gently sweep her hair aside and cup his hand to the side of her face. "You don't have to find me," he promised softly. "The *Eliza Mae* will have room for everybody, and I'll be coming right behind you, just as soon as all the noncombatants are clear." He kissed her quickly and with an uncharacteristic lack of reserve. "You look after the boys. I can take care of myself." Then he looked a question Kirk didn't understand over her shoulder at the stocky blond security guard, and McCullough nodded once, curtly, in reply. Apparently satisfied with that answer, George stepped back from his wife and summoned the small team of men waiting for him with a wave of his arm. They disappeared down the hall toward the embassy proper without even a backward glance.

"If you'll come with me, Mrs. Kirk." McCullough took her arm before Kirk's mother had a chance to answer, drawing her away from the embassy with resolute politeness. "We'll all be out of here soon, but we have to keep moving."

They had packed in behind the rest of the evacuees, herded down the narrow hallway like sheep through shearing gates. But instead of clever dogs, what pushed them along were the screams that had started up on the streets outside, and the reflections of fires on the walls of the rooms they left behind. Kirk shuffled along with everyone else, clinging to Sam's belt to keep from being separated in all the pushing and confusion. By the time they reached the outside, he was overhot and breathing hard, and the lack of a cool night breeze only made him feel dizzy and sick. Instead of the refreshing autumn bite he'd grown to expect from Grexxen evenings, the air was hot and dry with heat blown over the walls from the fires outside. Flakes of ash drifted down like tiny leaves from monochromatic trees. Kirk watched a small Work Bee vehicle make a swift vertical ascent from the embassy's shuttlepad, its belly painted amber by the burning city streets below it.

His mother combed hair back from her face with one hand and craned her neck to watch the Work Bee disappear. Another small craft almost immediately took its place. "What if they shoot us down before we get out of atmosphere?" she asked McCullough fearfully.

"They can't, ma'am. They've only got projectile weapons and a few phasers, nothing that can hurt the spacecraft once we're airborne." To this day, Kirk didn't know if McCullough honestly believed that was true, or if she'd only said it to comfort the wife of her commander.

They crossed the short expanse of open tarmac at a run, and McCullough sprinted ahead of them to hold the hatch open with her body and push them all in ahead of her. The inside of the tiny maintenance shuttle stank of sweat and panic, crammed almost to bursting with panting bureaucrats and administrators. The seats had been removed, along with all the tools and equipment the shuttle usually carried, and Kirk wondered for one awful moment whether or not this was actually a ship that was supposed to go outside an atmosphere. Thinking back on it now, he realized that this was the moment when he became truly afraid, the point at which he understood that things on Grex had gotten so bad that they would never be fixed and the people crowded into this shuttle alongside him were actually fleeing for their lives.

Just as that realization rocked him, he heard the frantic cry from outside. "Wait!"

The men who had been hauling shut the hatch hesitated, and another young man came running up to shoulder his way inside. His face was flushed, his neat business suit ash-stained and rumpled. But, unlike the other embassy staffers, instead of an overstuffed briefcase he hugged two young children in his arms. The older of the two whimpered fitfully, her face buried against his shoulder as though she couldn't be frightened by what she couldn't see; the younger one stared about the crowded shuttle with huge copper eyes, her round, bronze face angelic with fascination.

Behind Kirk, McCullough announced, not unkindly, "You can't bring them with you, sir."

The young man stared at her. For some reason, Kirk noticed that his eyes were startlingly blue. "You can't expect me to leave them." His British accent seemed perversely civilized and out of place amid all the violence.

"There isn't room, sir—"

"But they're Kozhu!"

"It doesn't matter."

"Their mother gave them to me." He cast pleading eyes around the shuttle. "She was one of the interim adjudicators. The Vragax all know who she is! They'll kill her—they'll kill her family!" He squeezed the children tighter, turning half away from McCullough as though daring her to try and take them. "Please, they're only children…"

McCullough was silent for a long, painful moment, and the Starfleet pilot at the front of the craft called back, "It doesn't matter who or what they are. We're overweight as it is. We might still make it into orbit with you on board, but with you and both the kids…" He shook his head rue-fully. "I'm sorry."

*They're small,* Kirk thought with almost analytical clarity. *They don't even have to stand on the floor.* He ducked under Sam's arm and past the men at the hatch without consciously thinking about what he intended. But by the time his feet hit the tarmac, he was giddy with the rightness of what he was doing.

"Jimmy!" He heard a commotion inside the shuttle that he assumed was his mother lunging forward after him and McCullough and Sam re-straining her. "James Tiberius Kirk, you get back inside this shuttle *this minute!"*

He backed away from the hatchway, just in case she proved able to shrug McCullough off. "Mom, it's okay! I'll take the next transport!" *I'm George Kirk's son—they're not going to leave me behind.* He wasn't so sure about two alien toddlers. "You go on. I'll be fine!"

"We haven't got time for this," the pilot complained from the front of the shuttle, and Kirk yelled back, "Take off without me! I'm okay!" be-fore his mother could order him aboard again.

Just then, a big hand clamped on the back of his neck and pulled him another two steps back from the open hatchway. "I've got him, Rivas." Lieutenant John Maione tucked Kirk against another of the guards behind him with only a token thump of his hand against the boy's chest as a rep-rimand. "Go ahead and lift off. Jimmy can ride out with us. I'll make sure the chief knows." Until that moment, Kirk hadn't realized that he and his mother and brother had been packed aboard the very last shipload of civilians on Grex—if Maione and his commandos were lining up to board the next vehicle, that meant there was no one else left to evacuate. The thought of riding into orbit with the embassy's elite protection troops filled young Kirk with a giddy excitement.

The shuttle's thrusters roared up to power, and brittle leaves skated away from the outtakes just as someone inside leaned out to haul the hatchway closed. "Thanks, John." Rivas's voice only just beat the boom-ing of the shuttle's door. "Take care."

Maione shooed Kirk away from the pad to make room for the next vessel's landing, but the look on his face was wry with amusement, not the anger Kirk expected. "You're dad's gonna kill you." The lieutenant swiped away dry leaves that had clung to the boy's curly hair. "You know, Jim, you might want to save some of that nobility until you're a little older."

Later, when his father railed at him for being self-centered, thought-less, and irresponsible, he clung to the word *nobility* with all the strength of his young heart.

* * *

But both his youthful nobility and its consequences were years in the past now. Or at least several hours. Captain James Kirk realized, as he watched his father click shut a portable IR scanner that he must have found among Maione's men, that he didn't even know what had ever become of the softhearted Englishman and his two young native wards. He remembered that the *Eliza Mae* had arrived only seventeen hours after the evacuation, and that none of the impromptu lifeboats had suffered losses during that time, but he had no idea where anyone who had fled with them ended up after that night. He resolved to seek the young Englishman out just as soon as he was back in his proper time frame.

"All clear." George tucked the IR scanner into his belt and clambered on hands and knees up to the surface of Ith. Even the building fires were dimming by now, their automatic fire suppression systems kicking in despite the chaos running rampant through the streets around them. Kirk and his father covered the last few blocks to the embassy without seeing any sign of the natives they'd be leaving behind. Except for the empty shoes.

The last Federation-owned ship on the planet was an all-but-disposable cargo sloop which had come through the atmosphere when the embassy crew first arrived and really wasn't expected to leave it again. Technically it had boosters enough to put it back into orbit in the event its initial cargo delivery had to be aborted for some reason. Technically. Kirk had never actually heard of anyone attempting such a feat before.

A tall figure, so thin it might have been built entirely of sticks, peeled away from the cargo sloop's shadow and came partway to meet them. "Did you not find him, Chief? Or has he just grown quite a bit from this morning?"

Kirk recognized the melodious voice as belonging to Arran Mutawbe, George Kirk's second-in-command. Even after all these years, he remembered Mutawbe's fierce, ready smile and gentle sense of humor as clearly as he remembered the man's beautiful voice. For some reason, though, he hadn't recalled that Mutawbe stood well over two meters tall. Maybe it was because everyone was taller than he was when he was fourteen, and his young mind hadn't made a distinction based on how much taller they were.

"This is Captain Forester from the last personnel drop." George's voice was as curt and steady as always, but Kirk noticed that he stepped up his pace to the shuttle without waiting to see if Kirk and Mutawbe followed. "Jimmy's not here?"

"No, sir. But we've been hard-pressed to keep a good lookout—the rebels keep circling back to snipe at us. Rory thinks he saw a couple of

Starfleet boys near the tree line a little while ago, but we're not missing anybody and I don't trust the Vragax not to be luring us out into the open." Mutawbe took the gauss rifle when George handed it to him, then the IR scanner and the shock grenades. "Tony took one in the face last time the snipers was past, sir." His voice lowered sadly. "He's not doing so good."

George threw additional equipment off his utility belt into the floor of the sloop, then began reaching in to pull out a fresh phaser and a heavy shoulder bag that Kirk realized with a start was an antique tricorder.

*No, not antique—probably brand new.*

"Then you've got to get Tony out of here," George said without turning around. He tucked the phaser into his belt, then pulled out a communicator and flipped it open to run a check of its circuits.

Mutawbe watched his commander for a moment, then asked carefully, "What about your boy, sir?"

George picked up a handful of extra power supplies for both the phaser and the tricorder, fitting them one by one into his rapidly filling belt. "I'll find him."

"And we'll wait, sir—"

George spun on Mutawbe, his expression in the waning firelight desperate and fierce. "No, you will not wait." He wrestled his tone back under control before continuing. "I will not put any more of my men at risk because my son ran off on some half-cocked adventure. You'll get in this sloop and take Tony and the others into orbit where they'll be safe until *Eliza Mae* arrives. She's three days out, tops. If I can't find Jimmy by then . . ."

He fell silent, but Kirk knew what he was thinking. *If I can't find him by then, he's nowhere here to be found.* The trouble was, Kirk had a feeling that was already true.

# Chapter Five

THE MAIN BRIEFING ROOM on the *Enterprise* froze into silence, the crystalline kind of silence Uhura usually associated with the instant just before a photon bomb went off. Then the older version of Chekov startled her, not by exploding but by wheeling to fix the younger version of Sulu with an unblinking stare.

"*You* saw our future," he said. "How certain are you that I would die to prevent it from happening?"

Sulu looked from the older man to Mr. Spock. "Completely," was all he said, but his voice carried a wealth of conviction. From across the table, McCoy gave Uhura a speaking glance and jerked his head toward the older version of Sulu.

"And we know Captain Sulu would do that, too," Uhura said. "If it weren't for the Janus Gate, he would already have died to stop the Gorn invasion."

"I am aware of that, Lieutenant," Spock said crisply. "But Captain Sulu's loyalty to his own timeline does not imply an equal willingness to sacrifice himself for ours."

The older starship captain smiled. "I had forgotten what a stickler you were for logical certainty, Mr. Spock. I don't know if I can give you any guarantee that Chekov and I are committed to helping you restore the timeline that has your lost Captain Kirk in it. But if we look at this logically...Right now we're floating in an isolated time bubble you created when you cold-started the engines back at Psi 2000. Is that right?"

"That is correct." Spock's voice had taken on an edge it held so rarely that it took Uhura a moment to recognize it as impatience. "We have only twenty-eight hours of that time bubble left before we rejoin the main timestream and once again become the only *Enterprise* in the galaxy. At that point, I calculate a ninety-seven percent probability that we will no longer remember Captain Kirk, and thus will lose all hope of repairing the damage we have done to the past."

Sulu nodded. "And if that happens, if we don't manage to repair the timeline by that point, what will happen to me and Chekov?"

Spock lifted one eyebrow, as if the question was so meaningless it had never occurred to him. Uhura cleared her throat as the silence lengthened.

"If the timeline we rejoin is the one that never had a Captain Kirk in it," she hazarded, "then we might never have found this planet or left any survey teams here to discover the Janus Gate."

"And we definitely wouldn't have gotten thrown back in time," Zap Sanner chimed in. "Because, according to these guys, their *Enterprise* got to Psi 2000 too late to catch the virus that killed the research team there."

The older Sulu nodded, as if they'd confirmed what he was already thinking. "So if we don't repair the timeline and you never find or use the Janus Gate—"

"—then we won't be able to save you or Chekov from Basaraba." McCoy waggled a finger at Spock, looking gleeful at having caught him in a logical lapse. "So much for your worries about them sabotaging our plans! They're going to disappear in twenty-eight hours whether they help us or not."

Uhura took a deep, dismayed breath when she saw where this line of logic was leading. "But if we don't use the Janus Gate, you'll never find out that the Gorn are holding a Metron prisoner in Tesseract Fortress."

"Much less be able to free him and stop the Gorn invasion of Vulcan," the older Sulu agreed. "All in all, I think that gives us several logical reasons to help you get your captain back."

There was a brief silence, broken by several forceful Russian words. Despite her passing knowledge of the language, the phrase wasn't familiar to Uhura, but she saw a startled shade of red touch Ensign Chekov's cheeks as he glanced at his scowling older counterpart.

"*That's* what you can do with your logical reasons," the older Chekov growled, staring steadily across at Spock. "I swore an oath when I was commissioned as a Starfleet officer. Rescuing fellow Starfleet personnel from danger was one of the things I promised to do. It doesn't matter where I am in time, I'm still a Starfleet officer."

The Vulcan gave the two older men a speculative look. "May I assume you would be willing to travel backward in time another twenty years in order to ensure the timeline is repaired?"

"Yes," said the older Sulu and the older Chekov in one voice.

Spock paused a moment, then inclined his head in a grave nod. It was probably as close as he could come to an apology, Uhura thought, and it was certainly all the satisfaction he intended to give a still-grinning McCoy. The first officer resumed their interrupted planning session before the doctor could make any other comments on his logical lapse.

"We are agreed that we will ignore the Shechenag's ultimatum to leave the system," the Vulcan said. "We must send the young James Kirk back to his proper place and time, and to do that we must have access to the Janus Gate. However, I would prefer not to engage an unknown race in battle, as that would be time-consuming at best and catastrophic at worst. Even if the Shechenag have forsworn the practice of war, their technology appears to include enough powerful defensive mechanisms that any confrontation with them could prove deadly."

The older version of Sulu nodded. "So our first priority is to take back control of the Janus Gate in a way that won't put us in direct conflict with its guardians. How do you plan to do that?"

"I have a strategy which I believe will allow us to disable a large enough sector of their defensive shield to get a shuttle through to the planet," Spock said. "If we wait until the Shechenag are occupied with installing the section of network opposite the Janus Gate's location—"

"But they left a guard down in the caverns," the older Chekov said brusquely. "Won't they alert the mother ship when they see us?"

Spock lifted an austere eyebrow at the interruption. "*If* they see us."

"How could they not?" That puzzled question came from the younger version of Sulu, who, like the older Chekov, had entered the caverns only through the Janus Gate, and exited only through the main entrance above the alien time transporter. Uhura opened her mouth to answer him, but to her surprise the younger version of Chekov spoke before she could.

"There's a back entrance to the cave system," he said quietly. "One so small and hard to get through that the Shechenag may not even know it's there."

Geologist Zap Sanner reached over to give the ensign an approving thump on the shoulder. "Finally figured out why they needed *us* on this mission, huh? I hope you still remember the path back from the healing chamber to the Janus Gate. The big meltdown that happened when we brought Lieutenant Sulu back from Basaraba probably took the last of my cave reflectors off the walls."

"It did?" The young Russian looked suddenly uncertain, his gaze shifting from Sulu to Uhura to Spock. "But—but it wasn't *me* who mapped that part of the caves," he blurted at last. "It was the Chekov who went into the Janus Gate and replaced me at the waterfall—"

His older self gave him an incredulous look across the table and Chekov fell silent, an even darker and more mortified blush staining his face. Fortunately, Spock did not appear to notice the ensign's embarrassment.

"I have programmed Lieutenant Jaeger's reconstructed maps into my shielded tricorder," the Vulcan said calmly. "Your knowledge of the caverns will only be required to guide us past the sections Mr. Jaeger and Mr. Sanner could not reconstruct."

Zap Sanner snorted beneath his breath. "That means we're there to carry the equipment again," he muttered to Chekov in a not-very-discreet aside.

"Indeed," said Spock. "It seems only logical to assign that function to crewmen who have the most experience with Tlaoli's caverns. And with the Janus Gate itself," he added, his intelligent glance sweeping back toward Uhura.

She nodded her understanding of that. "What about the Janus device itself, Mr. Spock? Won't the Shechenag still be guarding it, even if they don't see us coming through the back entrance of the cave?"

"That would be a logical assumption," Spock agreed. "However, I did not observe any magnetic shielding on the robotic devices the Shechenag previously used to threaten us. If our plan to deactivate the defensive shield succeeds, much of the power supply will already have been drained from those devices. We should be able to engage the remaining Shechenag in hand-to-hand combat."

"Why not just blast the whole damned cave with phaser fire from the ship, the way we did before?" McCoy demanded. "That would take all the guards out, and charge the gate up at the same time."

Spock's eyebrows lifted in an expression which, in a human, Uhura might almost have called pained. "You may not have been attending to the part of our discussion, Doctor, in which we mentioned our intentions to approach the planet undetected by the Shechenag," he said with crushing formality. "I do not believe blasting our phasers down through their defensive network will accomplish that goal."

McCoy grunted acknowledgment of that. "All right, let's say we get a shuttle down to the planet and manage to take out the Shechenag guards. What do we do then?"

Spock's eyebrows arched a little farther. "Doctor, I believe you are suffering from the same lack of sleep and nutrition that you were so concerned about in the rest of us. Surely you recall our discussion about using the Janus Gate to send our version of Captain Kirk back to his proper place and time—"

"Of course I recall it," McCoy countered, somewhat irritably. *"You're* the one who's forgetting something here, Spock. Didn't we establish with Captain Sulu that the Janus Gate won't exchange a weaker version of someone for a healthier version? Wouldn't that keep us from putting young Kirk into the machine and sending him anywhere unless the adult version of him gets hurt or even killed back in the past?"

"I did not forget that, Doctor," Spock said tartly. "Upon our return to the ship, I scanned the *Enterprise* crew database to determine if anyone else among the crew was stationed on Grex during the brief Starfleet mission there. Out of a crew of three hundred and twenty-six, I calculated that the probability of finding such a crewman was approximately point one five eight, more than high enough—"

"Don't tell me what the odds were, Spock," McCoy interrupted. "Just tell me if you found somebody!"

Security Chief Giotto cleared his throat, a little gruffly. "He found somebody," the older man said. "I served in the embassy protection force on Grex for fourteen months, right up until the natives went on a rampage and threw us off the planet. I was on the very last transport out, but I don't remember much about the evacuation. I got hit in the face by a projectile weapon a few hours before we left, and I didn't wake up until we were back at Starbase Five."

"A life-threatening experience which makes Chief Giotto an ideal candidate for the Janus Gate's viewing mode," Spock said in satisfaction. "If we utilize Lieutenant Commander Giotto to create a connection back to Grex, in the same manner in which we used Lieutenant Uhura to create a connection forward to Basaraba, we can engage the Janus Gate's associative transport and return our young James Kirk to his proper time, if not his proper place in it."

"You're going to throw that boy into the middle of a violent native uprising?" McCoy demanded. "How the hell do you expect him to survive that?"

"By providing him with protection." Spock steepled his fingers meditatively. "It will be necessary to seek volunteers among the crew who would be willing to go back in time to protect young Kirk. However, since we know that the Shechenag will strenuously resist our attempts to use the Janus Gate again, we must presume that our ability to use the device will be limited. It may not be possible to send crewmen to Grex, then wait to make certain they safely deliver the boy to his father before we are driven away from the machine. If it becomes necessary to strand anyone in the past, we would create exactly the overlapping time disruptions about which the Shechenag warned us."

"That's easy enough to fix," said the older version of Sulu. "Instead of *Enterprise* crewmen, you send me and Chekov back with this once-and-future captain of yours. Since we're not going to exist at all once you get your real captain back, it won't hurt the timeline to leave us there."

"That would be the logical solution to our dilemma," Spock agreed calmly. "However, until your existences come to an end when our time bubble collapses, Captain Sulu and Commander Chekov, you remain sapient beings with the right of self-determination. Are you willing to volunteer for this mission?"

"Well, Pavel?" Captain Sulu glanced over his shoulder at his own first officer, his lips curving in an odd, bittersweet smile. "It's a second chance at suicide. What do you say?"

There was no answering smile on his executive officer's rigid face, but something hard and cold seemed to have melted from the older Russian's voice, leaving a thin trickle of amusement behind it. "Sure. When do we leave?"

*This is so wrong,* Kirk thought as he jogged behind his father through the abandoned streets of Sogo. It wasn't the untrafficked roads and half-burned buildings that made his stomach clench, but the fact that he knew he had never seen them this way before—the fact that *nothing* he'd experienced tonight was like what he'd gone through before. *History is different, and I don't know by how much, or why.*

Kirk's memories of the night his family fled from the Grexxen civil war had faded very little over the years. He remembered all too clearly jumping out of the shuttle that would carry his mother and Sam into orbit because of some misguided sense of heroism. He remembered narrowly escaping his father's wrath by immediately reboarding another ship with John Maione and his team of peacekeepers. And he remembered that when the peacekeepers' shuttle had been shot down by the Vragax, Kirk had fled back toward the embassy as fast as he could possibly run, only to be cut off and hunted down in an abandoned office building by a small group of marauding natives. In the past as Kirk remembered it, his father had stormed in and saved him mere moments before he was put to death, then he and George had met Mutawbe and the others back at the auxiliary landing pad where they had successfully escaped into orbit and were rescued by the *Eliza Mae* a mere handful of hours later.

But so many things were already different. Kirk as an adult had not been with his father—those Vragax hadn't lived to leave the office building where they'd cornered their human prey. George Kirk was not left behind on Grex to fend for himself and possibly die.

"God, there's not a native for blocks." George frowned down at the clunky, shoulder-strung tricorder he had balanced against his stomach. Faint gray light from the tricorder's tiny readout illuminated an irritable expression Kirk was beginning to suspect was his father's default when uncertain or under stress.

For some reason, he'd never made that connection as a child. "What about a human?"

George made a little sound of frustration. "I've got something that might be human life-signs this way—" He gestured into the darkness ahead of them and off to the right, then looked in the direction he'd just indicated as if to match what he saw against what the instrument was telling him. "—but it flutters in and out, so I'm not really sure." He turned his fierce glower back down toward the tricorder, and Kirk realized with a strange nudge of affection that his father was embarrassed. "But I could be reading this wrong. I've only used one of these things a couple of times."

The admission unfolded a realization for Kirk that he probably should have made sooner in his life. What his father meant wasn't that tricorders were so new or exotic that he'd never been exposed to them—they were neither—but rather that they'd always been someone else's province. George Kirk had never been one of the breathless command hopefuls who bounced here and there throughout Starfleet ships and installations, learning a little bit about everything on their way up the ranks. He had only ever been a security and weapons expert, and that was all he had wanted to be. The science officers handled the tricorders; George Kirk handled the phasers. When Kirk was a boy, he'd interpreted his father's contentment with his position as a secret indication of cowardice, or at the very least a lack of ambition. He hadn't realized then what it really meant to be a starship commander, or how important it was to have dedicated men like George Kirk in the ranks to assist a commander in doing his job.

"I'm sure you're reading it correctly." Kirk looked around at the buildings and neat lawns surrounding them, already half-recognizing where they were. "It's not like Sogo is crawling with humans anymore. And that's back toward where the Kozhu women said they last saw . . . your boy." He nodded George down a cross street that cut more or less in the direction they needed to go. "If nothing else, that's as good a place as any to start."

By now, Kirk was fairly certain that no matter where they began their search, they weren't going to find the fourteen-year-old James Kirk. In addition to all the other changes the adult Kirk could already identify in the timeline, his mind kept going back to the Kozhu woman's description of the Vragax soldiers who fled the office building where Kirk remembered being rescued by his father nineteen years ago. In the past Kirk remembered, the Vragax didn't live to leave that building; in the version of events he was living through now, they had not only left, they'd fled in terror, praying to their gods for protection. No fourteen-year-old human boy had put that kind of fear in them.

But seeing a human boy vanish into thin air right in front of them might have.

It was the only explanation Kirk could think of that made any kind of sense. Whatever had transported Captain James T. Kirk back to Grex from Tlaoli must have spirited his younger self away at the same time. Which was why George Kirk hadn't been able to find his son to rescue him, and why Arran Mutawbe and the others had left the planet without their boss on board. It was also why Kirk couldn't let George out of his sight, not even for an instant.

The fourteen-year-old Kirk hadn't died on Grex that night, and neither had his father. And if anything happened to George before the younger Kirk was returned, there would be no one on Grex to protect the boy, no one to guarantee he escaped off-planet. Kirk didn't want to think about what that would mean for him personally when he finally got back to his own future.

*Spock, you'd better be working fast.*

George had only voiced a token argument when Kirk insisted upon staying with him to look for his son. Kirk wanted to stay relatively close to where he'd arrived—to maximize his chances of being in the right place at the right time when Spock finally managed to reverse whatever had thrown him here. And his father might be stubborn but he was very far from stupid. Two of them had a much better chance of surviving long enough to find the boy in the first place.

They'd departed the embassy with a tricorder, two communicators, and phasers with fresh power supplies. They'd left the gauss rifles on the landing pad, along with the dead leaves and the blowing ash from the smoldering embassy. Kirk had let his father take the tricorder to disguise the fact that he hadn't a clue how to use the ancient thing. George Kirk's only plan had been to use the tricorder to locate what had to be the only remaining human life-sign on the planet other than their own, and then to keep his son safe and hidden until the *Eliza Mae* made communicator contact when she came into system. Mutawbe hadn't known whether or not the *Eliza Mae* had a ship-to-surface transporter, and Kirk didn't remember the subject having come up nineteen years ago. But even if the only thing they could manage was to send back down one of the evacuation craft after it had been emptied of its refugees, they should still be able to get George and his son off the planet. Assuming, of course, that George and his son and the good Captain Forester managed to stay alive that long.

"You never asked me why."

Kirk shook off his reverie, glad that the darkness would hide the blush tightening his cheeks. *I'm not going to be much help keeping us*

*alive if I don't keep my mind on the present ... or the past ...* "I never had
to ask. He's your son. You can't leave him behind."

George shook his head impatiently, paused, then adjusted his course
to cut through a breezeway between two low-slung cottages. "No, I don't
mean that." He played with the controls on the tricorder, but Kirk sensed
it was only to give himself an excuse not to lift his gaze. "I mean why I
brought them here to begin with. Why I'd drag my family halfway across
the galaxy to some primitive hellhole where the natives still kill each
other because of what gods their ancestors worshiped."

*You're right. I never asked.* Not now, and certainly not when he was a
child. It wasn't that Kirk hadn't noticed that his family seemed to be the
only one condemned to spend Terran summers on whatever ship or station or strange little outpost George Kirk had been sent to that year. Kirk
had always envied all those other unseen children of his father's col-
leagues, the kids who got to hang out and play baseball with their school-
mates during summer vacation—the kids who *got* a summer vacation,
instead of leaving Earth's beautiful spring in time to show up for what
was invariably their destination's midwinter. No matter how much his
mother insisted it was a very small sacrifice they made for their father, all
Kirk ever remembered was the excruciating boredom of three eternal
months confined to the civilian areas of diplomatic posts that hadn't been
designed with teenage boys in mind.

Nineteen years and one unexplained time-jump later, he knew something as a starship captain that he hadn't been able to see as a boy. There
*were* no other families. The men who served with his father were barely
more than boys themselves, still the sons of parents barely older than
George, who wrote letters home to mothers instead of wives. At fourteen,
anyone over the age of twenty had seemed impossibly mature and adult
to Kirk. From the lofty age of thirty-three, he sometimes wondered what
Starfleet was thinking when it sent such young boys out into the dangerous world.

"Don't blame yourself. Command told you it was safe. The Kozhu
and Vragax were both involved in peace negotiations, there hadn't been
ethnic violence in Sogo since before the Orion occupation." It was the
same thing Kirk would have said to any crewman, but it unwound a knot
of old anger he hadn't consciously realized he'd been holding. "Besides,
it was only for the summer."

George stopped abruptly, jerking a sideways look at Kirk that drew
his eyebrows together into a mistrustful glower. "How did you know I'd
only brought them in for three months?"

Alarm clenched a cold fist in the pit of Kirk's stomach, and he stared
at his father without being sure how to respond. Of course Forester

wouldn't know something like that. He'd only just arrived on Grex, as far as George Kirk knew, and he shouldn't have cared one way or the other how one of the security guards here had arranged his family's vacation.

*Should I tell him?* Kirk didn't know why he'd hidden his identity to begin with, except from the vague sense that he should have as little impact on past events as possible. But hadn't the changes already wrought in the last few hours negated any chance he had of extricating himself without leaving evidence he'd been here? He opened his mouth, not entirely sure what he intended to say.

The tricorder in George's hand chirruped sharply. Flipping back the cover, the older man scowled down at the little screen as though irritated that it had interrupted them. Then a look of almost smooth intensity washed all emotion off his face, and he reached to grab Kirk by the arm and drag him through a broken doorway into a building's dark interior.

Kirk followed his father's lead, crouching in the shadows off to one side of the door and squinting out into the nighttime. He heard the band of Vragax before he saw them. They made their way down the middle of the street in no particular hurry, talking and laughing in their native tongue so loudly that they struck cheerful echoes off the buildings around them. There were five of them, three carrying bags that looked like pillowcases stuffed with random items, the other two taking turns balancing a bottle of what was probably the native liquor on the ends of their rifles.

Kirk waited until they'd passed out of sight—but not out of hearing—farther down the street to whisper to his father, "You can apparently read that thing well enough after all."

"The proximity alarms are the easy part." He turned down the device's volume controls, then padded over to a window to watch the Vragax go. "They're not even pretending to keep a watch out for enemies."

Kirk stood and went to join him at the window. "They know Starfleet's gone, and the Kozhu are probably all in hiding by now."

They crept out a rear entrance, making more of an effort now to stay off the main thoroughfares and in the shadows of buildings and bushes. Vragax passed them twice more, raucous and relaxed, and Kirk eventually realized that they were all headed in roughly the same direction. Motioning George to follow, he skirted a row of market stalls and lowered himself into a maze of elaborate landscaping that had somehow escaped the night's violence. Dry branches and spent blossoms crackled under his hands and knees as he crawled to the edge of the planting.

The huge garden followed the edge of a pretty stone quadrangle, raised up to what would be Grexxen eye-level. Lying beneath the tangled planting, Kirk scanned the open area with a sense of growing dread. Tents and campfires and even little circles of tables and chairs littered the blue stone courtyard, augmented by atonal music from a half dozen different electrical devices. Kirk smelled the deliciously spiced roast *dondurma* that was his only fond memory of Grex, and watched a group of Vragax warriors jostling playfully to be first to scoop his share out of the fire. In surreal contrast, a string of Kozhu women were tied one to another around the base of a bubbling fountain that had probably been quite restful before today.

"They're coming from every direction." Kirk risked lifting up on his elbows to watch another loose collection of Vragax wander in between two of the tall office buildings. They were greeted with much hooting and applause. "It's like a gypsy camp... or a bivouac."

Beside him, George angled the tricorder toward the black glass pyramid that crouched just behind the string of captive women. "Whatever it is, those human life-signs we've been following are right in the middle of it."

Reporting to the bridge for the first time since he'd come back to the *Enterprise* felt much stranger than Sulu expected. It wasn't just the fact that he'd crossed so much space and time since he'd last sat at the starship's helm. He'd also never before manned the helm dressed in a form-fitting gold suit made of nano-woven fibers. The caving gear wasn't uncomfortable, since it adjusted its thermal properties to allow for insulation or ventilation as needed for any environment, and he wasn't even the only one wearing it—Giotto and Spock were also dressed for immediate shuttle departure—but it still made Sulu feel conspicuous. Or maybe that feeling came from knowing there was an older version of himself standing on the back deck of the bridge, watching their maneuvers against the Shechenag with a critical forty-seven-year-old eye.

"Are you ready, Mr. Sulu?"

"Not quite, sir." Sulu didn't glance up from the automated course corrections he was inputting to his piloting console, but he could tell from the silence at the other end of the ship's helm that Spock had already finished programming his own station. The first officer had sent Navigations Officer DePaul to man the long-range sensors several minutes after he'd ordered Sulu to relieve Rhada at the helm, but Spock had already finished rerouting the ship's transporter controls from the engineering station to the navigations computer, where he could do the complex calculations that would be required for the maneuvers they were about to attempt. Montgomery Scott had made no protest when the Vulcan informed him he would be the one controlling the transporter beam. No one else had the mental acuity and swift physical reflexes required to handle the duty Spock had assigned to himself.

Sulu's task was simpler but no less challenging: he had to keep the ship hovering in an absolutely true position above the planet while the transporter beam was being used. Any deviation, Spock had warned him, would result in the kind of total power loss that had almost caused the *Enterprise* to crash on Tlaoli thirty-six hours ago. If they'd been in orbit around any other planet, Sulu would have programmed the ship's computer to fire the delicate microbursts of impulse power at precisely the right instant to cancel out the combined vectors of gravity and centrifugal force. But Tlaoli's unpredictable gravitational fluctuations meant that the task of holding several thousand tons of starship perfectly still in space fell to her human pilot. All Sulu could do in advance was input many possible engine firing sequences into the helm computer, so that he could activate any one with a single tap instead of a time-consuming series of keystrokes. He assigned a double-right thrust to his last open control, then glanced up at Spock. "Ready, sir."

Spock acknowledged with a nod but never took his gaze from the main viewscreen ahead. Since they had pulled back to the more distant orbit requested by the Shechenag, the rust-red disk of Tlaoli no longer spilled off the edges of the screen. It shone against the stars like an antique copper coin, the alien defense system a spiderweb of glittering strands across its face. No dark shadow smudged across the stars around it—the Shechenag ship was on the far side of the planet, installing the last satellites for its planetary shield. Spock had used the ship's long-range sensors to make sure of that back in the briefing room, when they had finalized their strategy. Now all they had to do was hope the aliens would remain engaged long enough for them to put their plan into effect.

"Lieutenant DePaul, give me a bearing from the location of the Janus Gate on the planet to the nearest Shechenag satellite."

"Aye, sir." The navigations officer squinted down at the science display screen, which was calibrated for Vulcan eyesight. "Bearing three-four-three-point-eight, two-one-nine-point-two mark eight. Transmitting to your data station now."

"Acknowledged." Spock's thin fingers flew across the navigations board as he calibrated the angle and intensity he would need to give the transporter beam. "Mr. Sulu, are we stabilized above the planet?"

"Aye, sir." Sulu had been carefully adjusting the impulse engines ever since he'd told the first officer he was ready, guessing that Spock would waste no time in commencing the operation. At any moment, the Shechenag might finish installing their satellite network, or circle the planet to check on the side they'd already completed. The *Enterprise* could not be caught doing something as suspicious as transporting absolutely nothing back and forth through the space around Tlaoli.

"Keep us steady," Spock reminded him. "Activating transporter beam now."

Unlike phasers, there was no way to see a transporter beam as it cut through space. For Sulu, that was a blessing. He could ignore the viewscreen above his head and pay attention just to the tiny fluctuations of his piloting curves. So far, all the adjustments he'd had to make had been minor and easy to input by hand. But he knew the pattern of Tlaoli's gravitational jerks and bumps. Any minute now, one should be coming...

A minute flash of blue and yellow appeared on his screen as the *Enterprise* felt the incipient tug of altered gravitational pull and began to drift off-station. Sulu felt one of the preprogrammed controls depress under his fingers before he was even conscious of selecting it, and only knew it was the right one when his orbital curves merged back into a perfect white arc. Maybe he should be grateful for whatever alien adjustments the Tlaoli healing chamber had done to his stress hormones after all, Sulu thought as he gazed in some amazement at his own hands.

"I believe our first attempt at satellite deactivation has been successful," Spock said. He glanced up from the helm toward the viewscreen. "Enlarge sector eighteen to twenty-nine, Mr. Scott."

"Aye, sir." The viewscreen swooped closer and lost most of its resolution as the chief engineer magnified that section of the defensive array. Tlaoli's subspace interference meant that long-range sensors were far more limited in their ability to re-create a distant image here than in other systems, but there was still enough clarity to see the glimmering iridescence of force-lines crisscrossing the planet's murky copper atmosphere. Sulu scanned the screen eagerly, and found the gap he was looking for near the very top. Between two barely visible glints of satellite, there no longer glittered a bright crackling strand of protection. By aiming the ship's transporter beam at the precise angle required to refract it off that energy field and toward the Janus Gate below, Spock had linked the subterranean energy-storage capacity of the ancient time transporter with the satellite's internal power generator. And just as it had done to the *Enterprise* thirty hours previously, the Janus Gate had sucked the satellite dry.

"It doesn't seem to have propagated any further down the network," Scotty commented from his station on the back deck of the bridge.

"Precisely as I suspected," Spock replied. "Each Shechenag satellite is responsible for creating only a single line of force. Therefore, the failure of one will not result in a complete failure of the network." He glanced back across at DePaul. "I am awaiting the vector to the next satellite, Mr. DePaul."

"Sorry, sir." The navigator peered down at his brightly lit display again. "Bearing three-four-five-point-three, two-one-seven-point-zero mark two. Transmitting to your data station now."

"Acknowledged. Steady as she goes, Lieutenant Sulu."

Easier said than done, Sulu thought. Tlaoli's unpredictable gravity field had chosen just that instant to bounce the *Enterprise* through a series of chaotic tremors, each of which had to be counteracted individually. The pilot concentrated on shutting out all extraneous noise from the bridge, all the distracting sounds of voices and machines and even the hum of his own data station. His world condensed down to two things: the position of the *Enterprise* in space on his helm display and the rapid-fire series of impulse engine firings necessary to keep that pristine white spot from splitting itself into unstable blue and amber echoes. His fingers continued to move without conscious thought, sometimes flying across the manual input controls, sometimes stabbing at one of his prepro-grammed firing sequences. It felt like the worst kind of piloting exercise he'd had to endure in his Academy days, the kind where the flight simu-lator kept throwing problems at you faster and faster until it found the point where you failed.

But this time, there could be no failure point. One slip of the trans-porter beam off the energy lines of the Shechenag defensive screen, and the Janus Gate would suck power down from the *Enterprise* just as effi-ciently and ruthlessly as it took it from the alien satellite network. Sulu had to be just as ruthless in his concentration, jettisoning all of his normal attentiveness to the other operations on the bridge. He hunched over his screen, taking full advantage of the hair-trigger reactivity that the Tlaoli healing chamber had given him, accidentally or perhaps on purpose . . .

*"Lieutenant Sulu."*

The intensity of those words finally snapped the pilot's focus away from his helm display. "What's wrong?" he demanded, his gaze skating around the bridge in search of some power loss that he hadn't been able to prevent. All he saw were blinking lights and glowing screens, along with a circle of somewhat startled-looking faces. It took another minute before Sulu realized they were all staring at *him*. "What happened?"

Spock lifted an eyebrow at him from the other end of the ship's helm control. The Vulcan's face looked a little tired, but intellectual curiosity flickered brightly in his eyes. "We have deactivated a sufficient number of Shechenag satellites to create a gap through which the shuttle may pass. You no longer need to keep the ship on station."

"Oh." Sulu glanced down at the helm display and had to forcibly stop himself from punching at another control to drag its slight bluish tinge of drift back to solid white. He closed his eyes for a moment, then carefully tapped in the course parameters that would put the ship back into a normal circling orbit of Tlaoli. "If you would call Mr. Rhada back to the helm, sir."

"I have already done so," Spock said gently. "And she is standing right behind you."

Sulu glanced over his shoulder and saw the second-shift pilot eyeing him with the same awed expression as the rest of the bridge crew. *That wasn't me,* he wanted to cry out as he left the helm and followed Spock and Giotto toward the turbolift. *That was something Tlaoli did to me to make me like its recycled soldiers!*

But when he stumbled a little with an unexpected surge of muscle weakness as he took a step up to the back deck of the bridge, Sulu felt himself caught and steadied by a familiar hand. He glanced up into his own dark eyes, framed with crow's-feet and weathered lines and filled with a wry look of recognition.

"I remember that," the older man said. "It's the aftereffect of piloting through too much of a life-and-death crisis. Don't worry, it goes away after a while."

Sulu paused to let his older self enter the turbolift first while he considered the implications of what the other man had said. If a version of Sulu from a timeline in which he'd never been healed by ancient alien technology knew exactly what he was feeling now—

Captain Sulu gave him an amused look as he stepped into the turbolift in stunned silence. "What's the matter?" he asked, then his eyes narrowed perceptively. "Didn't you already know how good a pilot you were?"

"Not really," Sulu admitted. "I never had to pilot a ship in a situation that critical before."

"I know." His older self met his gaze with a steadiness and resolve that Sulu could only hope to be capable of some day. "And with any luck, if we can rescue your Captain Kirk and put him back where he belongs, you'll never have to do it again."

# Chapter Six

KIRK LOOKED FROM the black glass pyramid to the nearly incomprehensible tricorder readout in his father's hands, then back again. *This is not someplace I ever went to.* Not that such details mattered anymore. They had already strayed so far from events as Kirk remembered them that he was skeptical about whether things could still be set right again.

On the quadrangle below, Vragax moved back and forth between their scattered little camps like sightseers at a bazaar, greeting fellow militants with much laughing and shouting and tossing about of weaponry. Firelight glinted off their tight copper braids, and Kirk thought he could smell the astringent bite of *phak* leaves, which he remembered the natives chewed as a sort of natural amphetamine. He wondered how much of the violence tonight had actually been inspired by a fervent hatred of the Kozhu and how much by the promise of copious amounts of *phak* for all the Vragax left standing afterward.

Tipping the tricorder screen back toward his father, Kirk waited for one of the chattering bands of Vragax to pass out of earshot before whispering, "Are you sure the readings originate inside *that* structure?" There were a half dozen other buildings surrounding the quadrangle, most of them much less inconveniently situated. Even if the Kozhu prisoners hadn't been tethered just outside the pyramid's main entrance, the whole building was set too far into the quadrangle to make a covert approach from the rear possible.

George swung the tricorder in as wide an arc as he could manage beneath their brushy cover, then pursed his lips around an unhappy frown. "It's got to be." He quietly closed the cover and tucked the tricorder behind him. "And the readings are a lot stronger now. There's three in there for sure, maybe four."

"Three?" For some reason, that bit of information made Kirk's heart thump with alarm. "I thought your son was alone."

"That's what I've been assuming." George pushed off with his elbows to wriggle backward out of the bushes, and Kirk ducked his own head out of the tangle of dead foliage to follow. The dry snap and crackle of their retreat seemed dangerously loud to his adrenaline-raw nerves. He held his breath until he'd disentangled himself from the edge of the quadrangle, as though stilling his breathing would somehow make their presence less obvious.

"Jimmy must have hooked up with someone else who couldn't make it back to the embassy in time." Kirk heard his father climb to his feet once the older man had cleared the landscaping, then felt George reach down and grab hold of his foot to guide him out of the last of it as well. "At least he's not out in this all by himself."

Standing, Kirk dragged George away from the garden and the gradually filling quadrangle beyond it. "Who could Jimmy possibly be with?" he hissed, unable to shake his unease. The doorway he snugged them both into was one of the few around them still intact, its sculpted overhang plunging the little alcove into heavy shadow. "What other humans are left on this planet besides you and me?"

He couldn't see George's face through the darkness, but the flicker of distant light in the older man's eyes as he glanced uncomfortably to one side was unmistakable. "Someone must have survived from Maione's team . . ."

"No one survived, Commander. No one." There wasn't much Kirk was still certain of, but that ugly detail hadn't changed.

"There were aid workers," George persisted. "Civilian aid workers."

"And most of them returned to the embassy when the fighting first broke out yesterday. You loaded them onto shuttles yourself, along with the embassy staff."

George's eyes flashed back to Kirk's face with fierce intensity. Kirk could almost imagine the angry glower fueling that stare. "Well, who do you think is in there with him?"

"I don't know," Kirk admitted with a sigh. "That's what bothers me." His eyes had adjusted somewhat to the deeper dark, and he silenced George's protest with an upraised hand. "I'm not saying we shouldn't try and bring them out of there. But don't forget those supposed Starfleet officers Mutawbe's men saw. If the Vragax are trying to lure us into something ugly, this would be how to do it."

The elder Kirk seemed to consider that reasoning, his fingers drumming an impatient rhythm on the case of the tricorder. Just when Kirk thought his father would erupt in frustration, George said, very quietly and evenly, "If there's any chance at all that humans are really trapped inside that building, though, we've got to try and bring them out. Even if my son *isn't* with them."

There was no rational protest he could make to that. Kirk wondered why he'd never noticed before that his father was such an intensely principled man. Maybe it was because the ongoing conflict between dedicated family man and loyal officer so often manifested itself as ill-temper. It occurred to him that all great conflicts between fathers and sons revolved around the fact that you couldn't truly appreciate an adult until you were one.

Kirk stepped away from the doorway only long enough to quickly get his bearings and verify that no Vragax had wandered into their cul-de-sac. "All right..." He motioned George to follow him around the corner of the building, away from the quad. "If we're going in, let's at least try to do it discreetly."

George made a skeptical noise as he paused to check the charge on his phaser. "I don't know how discreet you think we can be with these odds." He counted the power supplies on his belt, picked out the freshest one. "I can take out maybe four at a time with a wide-angle stun, if they're grouped close enough, but there have to be fifty Vragax out there." He flashed Kirk a surprisingly familiar half smile. "How fast can you run?"

"There's not going to be any running." Kirk kicked aside dead leaves and the remnants of what had surely been impressive flower plantings in a former life. His foot thumped against something harder than the rest of the detritus and he stooped to sweep it clean. "At least not if we do this right." Finding a rock too small for his purposes, he straightened and moved on.

"There's a sort of underground marketplace underneath this whole area," he told his father as he carefully kicked his way down the length of the garden. "There are entrances that lead down into it from most of the buildings surrounding that quadrangle. If we can find one of them, we should be able to make our way over to underneath where you're reading those life-signs, then come up from below."

Stuffing his phaser back onto his belt, George hurried forward to help Kirk heft a landscaping rock much larger than the one he'd found before. "How do you know this?" he asked. "I thought you said you'd only just got here."

Kirk stopped himself from saying, *Mom went there once to buy souvenirs,* and instead substituted, "Your son mentioned that his mother came here once. He pointed it out as we flew over." Nodding George back away from the rock, Kirk took the full weight of it in his arms just long enough to swing it like a pendulum toward a ground floor window. He turned his face down toward one shoulder as the window imploded with a magnificent crash.

George came carefully forward from where he'd retreated halfway into the street. "Well," he remarked dryly, "that was certainly in keeping with your suggestion that we be discreet."

Kirk couldn't help but throw his father a boyish grin. "Actually, it is. With all the looting going on tonight, the Vragax are less likely to investigate a breaking window than two men skulking through the landscaping at the edges of their camp."

They broke in the last jagged glass teeth using smaller decorative stones, then braced a branch from one of the flowering trees lengthwise down the window channel so they could lift themselves through the opening without embedding glass shards in their palms. Inside, the rock Kirk had lobbed through the window served as a neat step down to a carpeted office floor and a startling lack of sound. Except for the scattered glass and the incongruous lump of stone, everything else inside sat neatly undisturbed, as though the killing and burning outside were half a galaxy away. A plant with beautiful mottled leaves and a spray of delicate white flowers decorated the edge of an organically curving workspace. It bobbed gently in the night breeze let in through the broken window. Kirk felt weirdly as though he'd just climbed through a portal from hell back into the civilized world.

The hallways beyond the office door stretched out like the dark conduits on Tlaoli, lit only faintly by the starlight filtering through windows at either end. Kirk thought ahead to navigating the underground marketplace without even starlight to see by, and suddenly found himself missing Zap Sanner's carbide lamps.

"Here... What's this?"

The doorway George waved him toward wasn't the same sort as the others lining the hall. Swept into a simple arch, it opened onto a gently sloping path paved in smooth mosaic cobbles. It all looked iron gray in the dim light, but Kirk could imagine the intricate pastel patterns that must be inlaid in the floor and walls. It was the Grexxen eye for delicate color that had first lured his mother down into this native market. Now, on the first night of the alien civil war, Kirk could see just far enough beyond the entrance to tell that the tunnel widened as it wound down into the darkness, but could make out nothing of its beauty.

George put out an arm to block him when Kirk stepped forward to lead the way down. "No, sir. You're the captain, you shouldn't be out front. We don't even know for sure that the Vragax aren't bivouacked down there, too."

For some reason, that simple but earnest objection made Kirk smile. "I appreciate your concern, Commander," he said, pushing George's arm back down to his side. "But if anyone here needs to be protected, it's you. I'm not exactly in a position to take care of a teenage boy without his father around to help me." He drew his own phaser and made sure it was set on stun. "Stay close to the wall, and close to me. If we're going to trip over something in the dark, let's at least not have it be each other."

The wall beneath Kirk's hand felt cool and silky, like enameled wood, and he traced the gradual curve with light fingers as it drifted eternally away from him, trending both around and down. He tried not to force his eyes to focus in the dark, but instead concentrated on keeping his gaze level in an effort to stave off the dizziness he knew was coming as soon as they left the last faint light behind. Even so, he caught himself clinging to the memory of illumination as it fell away behind them. If he wasn't very careful, imagined shadows lured trust away from his hands and feet, and vertigo crashed over him every time the wall led in a direction that felt strange to his eyes or the floor altered slope even slightly. When the cobblestones under his feet finally leveled out, the transition felt abrupt and wrong. His foot clapped loudly as it tried to step down lower than the surface that was there, and he stumbled forward several steps before George caught him by the back of his belt and hauled him vertical again.

Then they stood silent in the heavy blackness and waited for the turbulent shadows to settle.

"What does the tricorder say?" Kirk asked at last. His voice sounded harsh and uncivil in the quiet, but was swallowed too quickly by the dark to be offensive.

Behind him, George cracked the rotating panel that covered the tricorder's face and cued it back to life. The modest light from its readout chased back the worst of the shadows and lifted a little cloud of brightness between them. "There." George turned to follow the reading, like a pointer following his nose. "Down that way, about a hundred meters."

The whole little market seemed less sinister now that a tiny bit of light reached out into it. Darkness still hid the farthest walls and most of the details, but quaintly stained kiosks winked at them as they crept by, and the fresh kiss of jasmine-scented blossoms drifted out from a wheeled cart overflowing with the same flowers Kirk had seen on the desktop upstairs. Who would take care of them now that their merchant had either been chased out of the city or killed? The thought of all those beautiful plants, dead and rotting in the darkness, was just one more tragedy on a list that was already far too long.

Slowing beside a shop front that looked like both it and its charming window boxes should be set up on the streets above, George turned in a slow circle without lifting his eyes from the tricorder screen. Kirk pulled up alongside him, glancing down at the readout from habit, then scowling at his own annoyance when he remembered again that he couldn't read the unfamiliar device. "What have we got?"

"I think we're in range of that building." George craned a look up, then seemed to realize that he couldn't tell anything that way and bent back to his tricorder. "There are a lot of Grexxen life-signs in range, but they're all off that way—" He gestured toward what Kirk hoped was the center of the quad. "The human signs are pretty much directly overhead, except..." His human faith in his own senses betrayed him again, and he glanced back up at the out-of-sight ceiling with a grumble. "We're in the middle of everything down here. There may not be an entrance into that building."

Kirk looked up as well, but what he saw was at least a possibility. "Then I guess we'll just have to make one."

They moved the alien jasmine in armloads, settling the plants as gently as possible around the feet of a potted tree. The wagon itself turned out to be bolted into place. George freed it with two smartly placed shots from his phaser, then swore when Kirk laughed because they had to wait for their eyes to recover from the brilliance. Once under the human life-signs, they braced the wheels with the flower boxes from the little shop, and Kirk climbed unsteadily aboard while George leaned into the wagon to mitigate its rocking.

The ceiling was closer than Kirk expected. He sensed more than felt stone passing close above him, and ducked his head while simultaneously reaching out to orient himself. His hand rapped sharply against what felt like exposed stone. Just that quickly, he found his equilibrium and balanced himself easily with one hand on the ceiling and both feet planted on the rickety little cart.

"Know anything about architecture?" he asked George as he cranked up the charge on his phaser.

The older man snorted so forcefully that Kirk felt it jolt through the cart underneath him. "This is a hell of a time to worry about that."

"Just wondering if we were going to get the whole building falling down on our heads."

George shifted himself to steady the cart a little better, then snorted again. "Like I said, a hell of a time."

Whatever material the Grexxen had used to make the ceiling, it vaporized briskly under the phaser's beam. Kirk started his cut as far out from the cart as he could safely stretch, going by sound and stench to tell when he'd cut through all the levels of stone and timber, and up into open air. When he was only two thirds of the way around a modest circle, a fracture as wide as his hand opened up opposite his cut with a *crack!* like a shot from a Vragax rifle. Kirk recoiled away from the collapsing flap, calling, "Heads up!" a moment too late to serve any real purpose. A startling mass of wires, wood, and concrete crashed down just beyond the nose of the cart, throwing up a choking cloud of pulverized stone and plastic. Kirk covered his mouth and nose with one hand and turned away from the wreckage until the worst of it had settled.

Below him, George Kirk coughed to clear his lungs, but didn't let go of the cart handles. When he could talk again, he commented hoarsely, "Well, the building didn't fall down."

Not so far, at least. Edging up to the end of the cart, Kirk leaned out to hook his hands over the phaser-cut rim of the hole. "Stay out of the way until I tell you it's all clear." It felt ludicrous to worry about the noise now, but he still felt awkward speaking in a normal tone. "And keep your phaser ready in case we have to make a quick retreat."

George held up the weapon in curt acknowledgment, and Kirk pulled himself up through the hole.

The first thing he noticed was the brightness of the atrium, lit from the fires out on the quad. Images of flame danced murkily through layer upon layer of smoky glass panels, peeking into the building without actually rushing inside. Kirk hoped his phaser fire hadn't been as readily visible to the Vragax as their fires were to him. Then, just as he levered himself up onto his knees on the lip of the hole, he noticed the sound of breathing. Not his own breathing. He froze even before he felt the cool touch of a gauss rifle against the back of his skull.

"Don't shoot." He said it remarkably calmly, even to his own ears. It wasn't worth sounding desperate. If it was a Vragax behind him, it wouldn't matter what he said; if it was a human, the sound of another human's voice should be enough to save him.

At least, that's what he thought.

But the gauss rifle against his neck never wavered. "Ah," said a voice that somehow managed to be oddly familiar and yet coldly unrecognizable all at the same time. "So this is the great Captain Kirk."

Sulu didn't remember the caverns on Tlaoli being this *cold* before. The fierce wind that hit them as they descended into the dusky twilight of the sinkhole entrance should have warned him, but although he heard Sanner groan and young Ensign Chekov bite off a dismayed gasp, Sulu didn't connect the strong flow of air to the temperature gradients that must exist underground. It wasn't until the nano-woven fibers of his caving suit expanded to their full insulating thickness before they'd even reached the end of the narrow tube twisting down from the sinkhole floor that Sulu realized this expedition was going to be as physically painful as it was dangerous. By the time they dropped down the final ropes to the massive rubble pile that gave them access to the ancient alien-constructed conduits, the exposed skin on Sulu's face already felt stiff and wind-burned. That tight, raw feeling reminded him of the subarctic night he'd endured back when he'd been stranded by that transporter malfunction on Alfa 117. God, had that been only a few weeks ago? Between the alien virus he'd caught at Psi 2000 and his excursion twenty-five years into his own future at Basaraba, Sulu felt as if that freezing night on Alfa 117 had happened to another person entirely.

And if they didn't get the timeline fixed, that was going to be literally true.

*"Man,* it's cold! Taking out those satellites must have really over-charged the power storage banks down here." The firefly glow of Zap Sanner's carbide lamp traced a startling cascade of skips and bounces through the darkness as he went clattering down the steep ramp of cave rubble. For a startled moment, Sulu thought the geologist had fallen, then Sanner's cheerful voice came booming back up to them. "Come on, you guys! It's not *that* slippery."

"Curb your enthusiasm, Mr. Sanner." Spock's shadowy figure descended the uneven rock surface with smooth, easy strides that got him to the bottom almost as quickly as the cave geologist's reckless scramble. "Please recollect that our mission here is to surprise the Shechenag at the Janus Gate, not to announce our arrival several minutes in advance."

"Sorry, Commander," Sanner said, then added with typical scientific temerity, "You know we're over a kilometer away from them here, don't you?"

"Indeed," answered Spock coldly. "What I do *not* know is the maximum distance at which the Shechenag's cybernetic technology can detect sounds. Do you?"

"Uh, no, sir."

Neither the geologist nor anyone else on their team spoke above a muffled whisper after that, but the frozen cave made noisy conversation for them. The ice that had once been cave runoff cracked and popped against the unyielding template of the limestone walls, and occasionally boomed in the distance as it expanded inside frozen springs and crevices.

Sulu angled the surprisingly small beam of his primitive carbide light down toward the jagged, crevassed rock pile and began to pick his way down the slope. The teenage James Kirk went past him in an agile series of jumps and leaps, although he managed to restrain the enthusiastic whoops that would have doubtless accompanied his downward rush in any other circumstance.

After a moment, a second spot of light crept over to augment Sulu's, closely followed by a third. He glanced up, half-expecting to see the older versions of himself and Chekov, but it was the younger Russian who joined him, followed by the stocky female security guard, Yuki Smith, whose stride seemed to be thrown out of balance by the heavy load of weapons and power-packs she carried. The three of them made better progress by combining the glows of their lights, but they were still the last ones to the bottom. Even Giotto managed to get there before they did despite being burdened with a phaser rifle, and the older Sulu and Chekov were already striding off toward the exit, dimly aglow with Sanner's and Spock's waiting lights.

"Sorry, guys," said Smith ruefully. Most of their pauses had been made to give her better light so she could find secure footing down the slope. "You can go ahead of me now if you want."

"No, thanks." It wasn't easy to see the younger Chekov's face under the steady flame of his carbide lamp, but his voice was dry. "I'd rather talk to you than to myself, if you understand my meaning."

"He is sort of grim and morbid," Smith agreed as they moved onward into the ice-sheathed corridors of the alien conduits. The last time Sulu had walked down this twisting ribbon of passageway, it had been filled with a floating mist of melted ice and he had been filled with relief at having just escaped Tesseract Fortress. Now he winced, remembering a rainy tropical night and a harsh Russian voice informing him that he and Chekov were the last two humans left alive on Basaraba.

"You'd be like that, too, if you'd been through what he has," Sulu said in defense of the man he'd gotten to know in that dark future. "It's only been a few days since every single member of his starship crew was killed trying to stop a Gorn invasion."

He heard Yuki Smith take in an abashed breath, but what he could see of Chekov's face didn't look as impressed. "They were *your* starship crew, too," he pointed out. It was a measure of how much Sulu had adapted to this strange doppelganger existence that he understood which version of himself the young Russian meant. "And you're not anything like him. *You* don't walk around snapping at people and scowling all the time."

This time Sulu heard the emotion below the critical surface of Chekov's voice, an uneasy mixture of embarrassment, regret, and fear. *Is that what I'm going to grow up to be?* was the question he was really asking, whether he knew it or not. *Will I turn out like that no matter what future I end up living through?*

For a moment Sulu wasn't sure what to say, but then an inner twinge of realization gave him the answer. For all of Captain Sulu's calm demeanor and bittersweet smile, there was still an unbridgeable gulf between him and his younger self. And Sulu's inexplicable shyness around the older man had come from his subconscious mind recognizing that fact, even if his intellect did not.

"Actually, I think my older self is *exactly* like yours," he told Chekov in a voice made more intense by the need to keep it down to a murmur. "Mine just knows how to hide what's happened to him a little better than yours does."

"I bet that's because he was the captain," Smith offered with surprising insight. "He's used to hiding what bothers him."

"Is that what it's like to be a starship captain?" The voice from the shadows beside them startled Sulu, and not just because of its unexpected proximity. Young Kirk emerged from behind a shattered fall of ice and rock that the rest of their party had already scrambled past. From Chekov's guilty upward glance, Sulu guessed this was the waterfall he had fallen down to inadvertently discover the alien artifacts that lay beneath the natural Tlaoli caverns. "You have to hide everything bad that happens to you so no one ever knows?"

The young man who would someday be their own starship captain— if their mission here succeeded—didn't sound upset or intimidated by that thought, Sulu noticed. But he did seem a little startled, perhaps by the realization that a captain had to be more than just a brave and brilliant hero.

"Not necessarily." Sulu had spent a fair amount of time, since discovering that at least one future version of himself had made the jump to captaincy, thinking about this question. "You have to do *whatever* needs to be done to make sure your ship carries out her mission. And that means never letting the people below you see that you've given up, even if you have."

The young man stared at him with hazel eyes whose sudden fire reflected more than just the flames of their carbide lamps. "It would be easier to do that if you never *did* give up," Kirk said, then swung away to scramble over the ice blocking the conduit as if embarrassed by his own sincerity.

They followed him down the corridor into a silent world of utter cold. The wind had died away now that they had reached the heart of the cavern's chill, and the crackling conversation of newly formed ice had been left far behind. The still air was as clear and sharp as crystal and almost as painful to breathe. The glow of their carbide lamps seemed to carry a little farther in it, or so Sulu thought until Smith nudged Chekov with an elbow and whispered, "The lights are back on."

Sulu followed her gaze to the side of the cavern and saw the muted glow of alien blue illumination running along the sides of the conduit. That hadn't been there the last time he'd walked these corridors, but then the Janus Gate had been drained of its stored power by the transfer of himself and Chekov from the future. He'd expected the gate itself to be brighter on this trip, since they'd deliberately recharged it by letting it drain the Shechenag satellites in order to deactivate them, but he hadn't expected the entire cave system to come alight with the same blue glow.

"They're brighter this time," Chekov noted. "I wonder if—"

"*Zakritim, durak!*" Whatever those Russian words actually meant, their icy snap struck Sulu and Smith just as silent as the red-faced younger Chekov. "From here on, no sound!"

The rest of their party was waiting for them just around the curve of the conduit. Spock and Giotto were in the lead now, the security chief with his phaser rifle armed and ready beneath one shoulder. A slightly chastened-looking Kirk had been tucked firmly between Captain Sulu and Zap Sanner, several steps behind the leaders. The older version of Chekov motioned them to go on, but lingered toward the back, as if he needed to keep an eye on the last three members of the team. Sulu felt his own face warm and tighten a little, despite the arctic chill of the air. Ensign Chekov no longer even looked embarrassed—his face had taken on a stolid stiffness that probably meant he wished he was anywhere but here. For the first time, he looked startlingly like his older self.

The glow brightened as they continued down the ice-sheathed passage, until the walls and ceiling shone like blue mirrors in its glare. Craning his head to see around the rest of the group, Sulu caught a reflected glimpse of something black and angular on one of those bright walls. He bit down on the warning he badly wanted to shout to Spock and Giotto, and instead grabbed the older Chekov urgently by the shoulder and pointed at the image. The Russian gave him a quick, decisive nod, then vaulted past Kirk and Sanner with surprising speed and force to catch Spock and Giotto before they could round the corner ahead of them.

The young Kirk turned to look eagerly at them. "What is it?" he mouthed without making a sound. Sulu shook his head and Chekov gave him a quelling look, but Yuki Smith put out her hand and wriggled her fingers in a silent imitation of a spider crawling. Kirk nodded and squared his coltish shoulders as he glanced ahead again. When the time came for hand-to-hand combat, Sulu thought, it was going to be hard to make sure that young man kept himself safely out of the way.

Spock had advanced his tricorder around the corner and now drew it back again to check its readings. His eyebrows lifted at what he read, and he turned to give the rest of the team a familiar Starfleet hand signal: *wait until further notice.* Sulu watched him and Giotto disappear around the corner with slow and watchful steps, the security chief with his rifle at the ready. But no shriek of phaser fire or crackle of Shechenag electric weapons echoed back to them. After a long moment, a crunch of footsteps returned, and Giotto reappeared just long enough to give them another silent hand signal: *advance with caution, the way is clear.*

This time, Sulu accompanied Zap Sanner down the passageway. His older counterpart had pushed forward to catch up with young Kirk, who was nearly treading on the older Chekov's heels in his eagerness to see what lay ahead. Sulu was relieved to see that both older officers kept a strategic distance from Giotto to make sure the boy did not plunge headlong into danger. As it turned out, however, their precautions weren't needed. Around the corner, Spock was scanning his magnetically shielded tricorder slowly over a knee-high pile of jointed metal legs and sensors that had once been a Shechenag robot guard. Ice was already starting to accumulate around its crumpled form, and there was no sign of lights or activity anywhere on it.

"Its power supply has been completely drained," the Vulcan science officer reported in a low but audible voice. "Any additional robot guards that lie between us and the Janus Gate are most likely in a similar condition. Follow me."

Their advance this time was considerably less slow and cautious, although it remained scrupulously silent. As they exited the last of the narrow conduit, the alien light rose to a phosphorescent glare that made Sulu shield his eyes with one hand and wish he'd brought some kind of polarizing lenses for protection. He wondered why the team members who'd seen the Tlaoli time transporter in action before hadn't warned the rest of them to expect this. Until he caught the troubled looks on the faces of Sanner and Smith. His gaze slid past them to the younger Chekov, who gave him back a quick shake of his head, as if he had guessed what the pilot was thinking. Sulu read his answer just as easily: This was something none of them had seen before.

The Janus chamber, which Sulu remembered being full of mist and shadows, was seething now with brightness. The illumination glittered off icy walls and made a fiery blue lake of the frozen floor. And it didn't all come just from the blazing heart of the Janus Gate. All around the dark metal device, wisps and shreds of sizzling blue swept the air like billowing shreds of ash blown by an unfelt wind. The chamber looked as if it should be hot as a phaser torch, but the cold emanating from that phosphorescent light was actually so intense that it burned against Sulu's cheeks.

"Fascinating," said Spock as he stared into the glare. From the expression on Giotto's face, Sulu guessed that was not exactly the word the security chief would have chosen to describe what he was seeing. "It appears you were right, Mr. Sanner. The Shechenag satellites must have had larger energy cores than I estimated from their force field output. We have clearly overcharged the power storage systems on the time transporter."

"*And* how," was the geologist's awed response. "Is there any space left to walk around in that mess?"

"I believe so, but it is not great." Spock leaned out a little into the glare and eyed the edges of the cavern. Sulu could see a ring of evenly spaced crumpled robots there, the remnants of a Shechenag perimeter guard. "Mr. Giotto and Mr. Smith, what is the status on your power supplies?"

The security chief glanced at his rifle, then let out a muffled curse. "Down to zero already," he said. "But it was fully charged a few moments ago!"

Yuki Smith went down on one knee behind Sulu, the younger Chekov squatting beside her to help her shed and open her heavy pack. She scrambled among the power supplies she had brought, then gave Spock a troubled glance. "The ones with the magnetic shielding are all right, sir. All the rest are dead."

Spock nodded somberly. "Please attach a shielded power supply to your rifle, Mr. Smith, and station yourself in this archway with it. You will be our lookout."

"Do we *need* a lookout, Commander?" asked Giotto. "If none of the Shechenag's mechanics can survive the power drain in here—"

"We will be safe from attack for as long as the Janus Gate remains charged," Spock agreed. "However, the Shechenag may have retreated only as far from the Janus Gate as the chamber above, which is where they were waiting when we brought Lieutenant Sulu and Commander Chekov back from the future. As soon as we exhaust the gate again by sending James Kirk and his escort to the past, we may find ourselves once again confronting them." His glance swept past the older Sulu and Chekov to rest on their younger counterparts. "At that point, with Mr. Giotto and I locked into the Janus device, it will be up to you to guard us from any interruption. You must prevent that, at any cost. If we are interrupted, there is a strong probability that we will lose all chance of retrieving Captain Kirk from the past. Do you understand?"

"Aye-aye, sir!" Chekov said, the unthinking response of a cadet responding to a drill order. Sulu saw the older Russian give him an odd, rueful look, but he made no comment in either Russian or English.

"Aye, sir," Sulu echoed. "Do you want us here, or stationed around the outside of the chamber?"

"If the Janus Gate continues to absorb power, anywhere you stand inside that chamber might become the site of a subspace rift," Spock replied. He carefully adjusted his bulky tricorder so it lay against the front of his caving suit, then looked past Giotto at the older Captain Sulu. "You remember the protected channel that leads to the viewing slot. It will doubtless be much narrower now than it was before." He widened his address to include the older Chekov and young Kirk, as well as a frowning Giotto. "When you follow Captain Sulu, stay as close to the cavern walls as possible, with your arms held tight to your sides. Any straying into the field of light around the Janus Gate could pull you into a subspace instability without warning. Walk exactly where Captain Sulu walks. Do not cut any corners or take your eyes off the person in front of you. Is that clear?"

"Aye, sir," said Giotto, echoed by the older Chekov and, a little hesitantly, by young James Kirk as well. Then the teenager glanced over his shoulder toward the younger Chekov, obviously trying for a casual, grown-up good-bye.

"Thanks," he said. "For showing me the ship, and everything."

Despite his best efforts, the stress of the moment made his adolescent voice break, shifting it momentarily into a much stronger tenor. It sounded like their own lost captain speaking to them, and for a moment even Spock looked startled. Kirk swallowed and turned back toward the older Chekov and Spock. "Ready when you are," he said bravely. And although his voice had gone back to its usual boyish register, Sulu could still hear the echo of the man he'd someday grow up to be.

The older Sulu nodded and edged his way out into the Janus chamber, brushing the wall with one shoulder and keeping himself angled to stay almost parallel with that metallic surface as he went. Giotto followed, with Kirk and the older Chekov close behind. Spock waited until they were most of the way around the perimeter of the cavern, then began circling the other way. Just as he reached the channel of clear air that Sulu could see glimmering off to the left, the Vulcan made an odd gasping sound and stopped.

"Spock, what's wrong?" the older Sulu demanded from across the chamber. "Sulu, can you see him?"

"It is . . . insignificant." There was a harsh tone to Spock's voice that contradicted his words, but after another moment he continued on his way to the dark alien device in the center of the cavern. Sulu stood on tiptoe, bracing himself against Chekov's shoulder as he peered through the glare, but he couldn't detect any visible wounds or injuries on the Vulcan's tall figure.

"He looks all right," he told his waiting older self. "But he's moving a little slower than before."

"I did not impact any part of the Janus field, if that is what concerns you." The harshness was fading slowly from Spock's voice, replaced by a distinct note of asperity. "Some of the Shechenag robots have mechanical cutting appendages with extremely sharp blades. I happened to encounter one of them."

"Step over that," the older Chekov said to Kirk quietly, and Sulu heard the young man's boots crunch on ice as he obeyed. The older Sulu continued picking his slow and careful way through the shifting billows of blue light, until he stood inside the curving gyroscopic arms of the alien time transporter. He drew Giotto in beside him, then carefully directed Kirk and Chekov to stand as close together as they could in back.

"You have to hold onto these arm-supports," the former starship captain told the security chief. "Don't let go, no matter what you see. It will look like you've beamed somewhere completely different, but you won't really be there. You'll still be able to hear and talk to Spock."

"Understood," the other man said, so shortly that Sulu guessed that the inferno he was facing had unnerved him. "I'm holding on."

Sulu glanced across the central fire to the lone figure on the other side. "We're ready when you are, Mr. Spock."

"One moment. I need to adjust my calculations to take into account the higher power levels we have inadvertently created." Spock's fingers flickered across the alien device's control panel with their usual velocity. "I have located what appears to be a major life-crisis, Mister Giotto. What do you see?"

"It's dark, really dark. And closed in, like a cave or a mine. I can't smell really well, but there seems to be some kind of chemical or acid in the air . . . This isn't Grex, Mr. Spock."

"Very well. I am adjusting the controls." There was a pause. "What do you see now, Mr. Giotto?"

"Fires in the distance. Tall buildings, all dark because there's no power, and streets full of people running . . . yes, *this* is Grex. But I don't remember ever standing in this particular street."

"That is because I have adjusted the controls to send you some distance away from the place where you were injured. I do not want to further complicate the timestream by having your crewmates see two of you," Spock replied. "Does your current location look like a relatively safe location?"

"It's pretty well deserted," Giotto said doubtfully, "But in this city, on *this* night . . . there's really no safe place to send us."

"It's all right, Mr. Giotto." That, surprisingly enough, was young Kirk. "Once we're there, I'll be able to get us to the embassy to meet my dad. I spent all summer wandering Sogo city instead of studying astrophysics like I was supposed to..."

"Then it will be up to you, James Kirk, to get yourself back to your proper place," Spock replied soberly. "I am engaging associative transport now."

Blue-white light flared lightning-sharp inside the Janus chamber, followed by a thundercrack as startled air slammed into the space formerly occupied by bodies. *Four* bodies, Sulu realized in shock and sudden despair. He didn't know whether Chief Giotto had forgotten to hold onto the stabilizing supports, or whether the overcharged Janus Gate had simply malfunctioned. Either way spelled disaster.

Having sent both young Kirk and Chief Giotto into the past, there was now no way at all to bring their own version of Captain Kirk back to the present.

# Chapter Seven

"CHEKOV?" Kirk's brain volunteered the identification so rapidly that even he barely understood what connection he'd heard between the chillingly calm voice and the shy boy Spock had picked out for the landing party earlier that morning. When he turned to look down the barrel of the rifle, though, what he found was a man at least fifteen years older than himself with only a physical resemblance to the boy whose map Kirk had buried at the edge of the forest just a few hours ago. The person behind the dark eyes was clearly someone else entirely.

"Commander Chekov..." Antonio Giotto moved smoothly around into this strange, older Chekov's view, his own gauss rifle primed and humming. "Sir, I'd suggest you put that gun down, or you're not going to see *any* version of the future."

The look Chekov angled at Kirk's security chief suggested he might almost enjoy seeing Giotto try to make good on that threat, but he didn't resist when the third member of their party stepped forward and pushed the muzzle of his rifle to one side.

"You'll have to forgive my first officer, Captain. We've been dodging Grexxen natives for the last couple of hours, and it's made us all a little jumpy."

Kirk thought that he ought to be more startled to find an older Sulu in the company of this older Chekov, but all the other strangeness he'd encountered since leaving Psi 2000 was beginning to make him numb to new surprises. Instead, his attention had locked on the young boy at the very back of their group. Better rested than Kirk was himself, and sealed into a dark gold cave suit not unlike the one Kirk had ditched upon first arriving on Grex. In so many ways, this was the face he still saw in the mirror. It was the face he would see even if he lived to be a hundred years old.

Apparently realizing that they were both staring, the boy tossed off what he no doubt thought was a nonchalant wave. Kirk lifted his own hand in reply.

"Captain Forester?" George Kirk's loud whisper cut across these bizarre introductions. "Captain, is everything all right up there?"

"Forester?" Sulu asked, eyebrows raised. But it was a practical question, not condescending.

Climbing to his feet, Kirk gestured toward the boy they were all obviously protecting. "It didn't seem wise to try and explain who I am." While Sulu nodded his understanding, Kirk leaned over the hole he'd made in the floor and called down quietly, "Everything's fine, Commander. It's just a few of my men." He couldn't help stealing another look back at the boy, and found himself still under his younger self's scrutiny. "And they do have your son." As often tonight as he'd spoken with George Kirk about his son, it hadn't truly felt weird until this moment, when there was actually a physical boy to be both the object of Kirk's search and Kirk himself.

George's voice was sharp with worry and relief. "Jimmy?"

"I'm fine, Dad." The boy drew up alongside Kirk, studiously not making contact with the captain even though he leaned over the same hole to wave down at his father. "These guys took real good care of me."

Shadows drifted past on the fringe of Kirk's sight, blurred and distant through the overlapping panels of glass until they seemed almost like firelit ghosts in the darkness. Vragax on the quad outside, either wandering from place to place or patrolling the edges of the open area they'd adopted as their camp. The immediacy of danger burned away whatever strangeness Kirk still felt at meeting himself and these temporally altered versions of his crew. "Let's move this downstairs before we find ourselves with company."

The boy swung himself down through the hole too quickly for anyone to insist on helping him, followed almost immediately by Chekov and finally Sulu. Kirk listened for the neat thump and slide of each of them using the angled flower cart to catch their weight and guide them to the ground. Outside, Vragax singing swelled giddily in the distance, then receded.

"Mr. Giotto…" Kirk held out his hand to take Giotto's rifle so the chief could climb down.

The security man only shook his head and took a modest step backward, the rifle angled across his chest. "Sorry, sir. You first."

It was so much the answer Kirk would have expected that he had to smile. "Apparently, you, at least, are *my* Mr. Giotto."

"Yessir."

"I'm sure you've got one hell of a report for me."

"Oh, yessir."

By the time he and Giotto had joined the others down below, a cloud of light warmer and stronger than from George's antique tricorder screen pooled around the little group. Kirk recognized the smell of acetylene gas even before he saw the carbide lamps in Sulu's and Chekov's hands, or heard Giotto rasp the wheel on his own lamp. Wherever they'd come from, however they'd gotten here, their cave suits and lamps made it clear that they'd passed through the same caverns on Tlaoli Kirk had. The Tlaoli power drain explained their lack of Starfleet-issue equipment, although not how they'd managed to follow him here, or how they planned to get everyone back. At least the lamps would come in handy in the equally treacherous darkness of Sogo city tonight.

On the other side of the flower cart, a step away from being swallowed by the dark, George Kirk had his son by the arm as though determined to never let the boy out of his grasp again. Kirk couldn't make out the words, but he didn't really have to—even nineteen years later, the memory of that lecture made his face burn with the same angry embarrassment he could see on the boy's face now. No matter what was said in the future, this would be at the heart of every argument between them for the next nineteen years.

"Commander."

His father jerked around at Kirk's summons, his own face stiff with embarrassment even though the darkness hid any evidence of a blush. As though noticing everyone else for the first time, he let go of his son and straightened guiltily.

Kirk didn't get as much satisfaction from his father's discomfort as his fourteen-year-old self would have expected. "We don't have time for that right now. The boy knows he made a mistake." He pinned the boy with his most severe command stare. "Don't you, Mr. Kirk?"

Not yet capable of that kind of steel, the boy only nodded slowly. "Uh . . . Yes, sir."

"Good. Then let's get on with business." He waved everyone away from the hole in the ceiling, just to make sure no one above would suddenly catch sight of the glow from their carbides. When they were safely tucked among a clutter of tables and chairs several meters away, Kirk turned to Giotto. "I'm assuming that when Mr. Spock sent you, he also sent an extraction plan."

His chief of security nodded unhappily. "The plan was for me to maintain contact with . . ." He glanced at Sulu and Chekov as though for assistance, then finished for himself, ". . . our base of operations. Once we located you, I was to return you to Mr. Spock while Mr. Chekov and Mr. Sulu escorted your...Commander Kirk and his son to safety."

Implying that the older men wouldn't be coming back with them. At least not right away. When Kirk looked a silent query toward Sulu, the other man responded without elaborating on that aspect of Giotto's summary. "Unfortunately, we seem to have experienced an equipment malfunction. We lost contact with Mr. Spock almost immediately."

And presumably a simple communicator wouldn't be enough to solve that complication. "So I take it Mr. Spock...isn't here?" He couldn't think of a better way to phrase what he wanted to know without saying too much in front of George Kirk.

Sulu's answer was studiously literal. "Mr. Spock is where you left him."

Which meant Spock was *when* Kirk had left him, and not anywhere Kirk could get to by force of will. Sighing, he gave a curt nod. "Well, he managed to find me once before. We'll have to trust he can do it again. In the meantime, we've got to get these two to safety." He turned to George Kirk and his son. "The *Eliza Mae* won't be arriving for another sixteen hours. Is there anywhere on the planet the Vragax aren't likely to visit before then?"

George frowned thoughtfully even as he shook his head. "I just planned on holing up in one of the more defensible rooms at the embassy," he admitted. "I was hoping *Eliza Mae* would get here early."

"She won't," Kirk and Giotto answered in a single voice.

Their certainty seemed to take George by surprise. "You guys aren't actually the embassy replacement team, are you?" The question had obviously been building in him for a while.

Kirk rubbed at his eyes, not looking forward to constructing a new webwork of lies. "No, we're not."

"Then who *are* you?"

"Special Forces," Chekov said without blinking. He barely looked up from topping off the load in his gauss rifle. "We're here on special assignment. We can't give you the details."

George Kirk nodded slowly, looking back toward Kirk as though this explanation cleared up a lot. "I noticed your uniform was a little different, and I wondered. You could have told me, sir."

"You're right. I should have trusted you." Although it felt strange to be apologizing for a lack of trust just for the sake of strengthening a further lie.

Before George could say anything more, a youthful voice from the center of their group asked modestly, "What about the wind farm?"

It took Kirk a moment to connect the boy's suggestion with Chekov's Special Forces lie, then his mind darted back to their original conversation, and he smiled. *This is why it's good to have a kid around.* He understood the blank looks on George's and Giotto's faces better than they did themselves. Fourteen months on the planet, and none of the adults had bothered to explore beyond the sectors assigned to them by Starfleet. In less than three months, Kirk and his brother Sam had hiked the woods beyond Sogo city so many times they could actually recognize and find individual trees. Only Kirk had been daring enough to climb the long ridge a few kilometers outside town, just to track down the source of a deep, powerful droning he and Sam had noticed a few days before. But he still remembered standing amid a forest of tall white windmills with his hands over his ears and his teeth singing from the bone-rattling hum.

"That's good," Kirk said, nodding approval at the boy. "Even if the Vragax decide to do something about the electrical situation in the city, they aren't going to do it before tomorrow, and the noise alone will keep anyone from using it as a campsite until then." He tried to picture the route up the hill through the trees, and realized it had been overwritten through time by that final image of the windmills against the sky. "Do you remember how to get there?" he asked his younger self.

The boy nodded. "Sure." Kneeling, he plucked a handful of small white flowers from a planting nearby. "The embassy's here." He placed one coin-sized blossom by his right knee. "If we're in under the Kaefen Rae courtyards, we're here." A neat little square of beheaded stems, a little ahead of him and toward his left. "That means the wind farm is this way—" He leaned far forward to tap the ground beyond both props. "—maybe an hour's walk through the trees."

"Northeast," George announced, studying the schematic.

"Will these underground passages take us that far?" Sulu asked.

*That would be too easy.* "I don't think they're that extensive." Kirk looked a question at the boy he knew had memorized the city's layout more recently than he had, and the boy shook his head with a rueful scowl. "But it will get us out from under the courtyard and away from the heavy concentration of Vragax," the captain went on. "Commander Kirk and I came in from the south, but if we head northeast from here, we should be able to find—or make—another way out once we get there."

They tucked George and the boy in the center of their group, with Kirk and Chekov leading, Sulu and Giotto bringing up the rear. It wasn't the most efficient arrangement, considering their only compass was the elder Kirk's tricorder, but even George didn't complain. He wanted to keep his son safe, and he was willing to sacrifice even his valued practicality to guarantee that result. Kirk wondered if he realized how much everyone else here was willing to sacrifice for the very same reason.

As they wound their way through the underground marketplace, individual shops, sculptures, and kiosks unfolded in the pale glow of their carbides like shells lifted out of the sand by a gently rising wave. Kirk watched his reflection ripple past in windows glazed against nonexistent weather, and he thought about the meticulously detailed villages he'd visited in caves back on Earth. What was the humanoid fascination with recreating the surface world underground? He'd thought it a quaint relic from Earth's nineteenth century until he'd visited Grex as a boy, although he hadn't bothered to try and analyze it then. Now he wondered if it was a way to separate from the uncontrollable aspects of the world above, or just an attempt to make the underground world not seem so alien and frightening.

Kirk had a feeling he wasn't going to feel safe underground again for a very long time.

He stole a glance at the man pacing silently next to him, and thought about a very similar younger man who had been walking with him when this all began.

"Ensign Chekov was with me when I was . . . displaced." He tried not to stare too frankly at his companion. "I take it he was sent somewhere else, too?"

The question seemed to take Chekov by surprise. "I wouldn't know about that," he answered gruffly. A discomfitted frown crossed his face, and he seemed to struggle with himself for a moment before finally adding, "But he was fine when we left. He's with Mr. Spock and the others." He looked at Kirk with an interest that was more clinical than curious. "You've been gone from them for more than two days. In my reality, you never existed at all."

"Because my younger self was . . . removed."

"Apparently." Chekov turned his attention forward again. "You mean a great deal to those people. They're risking everything to make sure you're reinstalled in their timeline, just like before." He made no effort to hide the bitterness in his tone. "I hope to hell you're worth it."

A sliver of light, as thin as a hair but blindingly bright, slashed down the edge of Kirk's vision like lightning. He heard George take a sharp breath behind him, but was already bolting aside and waving at the others to follow suit. "Kill the lights! Take cover!"

Whether it was the hours on Grex already spent dodging the enemy or experience from past battles Kirk could only imagine, Chekov and Sulu had responded as quickly and instinctively as Kirk. Carbides went out even as they darted for cover on either side of the cobbled path, and Kirk saw George and his son disappear inside a kiosk full of colored scarves just before the tricorder's face snapped shut and killed its own light.

The darkness didn't last. Light flooded the path they'd just abandoned, spilling from a broad door that hadn't existed even a moment before. Where the wall had split between two empty shops, four huge figures lumbered out into the market with a trio of Vragax trailing solicitously at their heels. Kirk would have recognized the Orions even if he hadn't heard the roar of their voices or seen the flash and clash of their golden ear- and nose-rings. Orion males carried a smell about them as distinctive as their jade-colored skin and dreadlocked beards—the smell of their sulfur-rich homeworld, and too many months crowded into pirate vessels overloaded with spices and ores. Even if they had intended to pass through the marketplace with any kind of stealth, they would have been hard-pressed to reach the surface unnoticed.

By the time the Orions had rounded the bend and their voices had faded into the subterranean distance, the door from which they'd emerged had sealed itself shut as though never having been there at all. Even so, Kirk waited a full five minutes for the smell of their passage to fade before thumping Chekov on the shoulder as a signal to relight his carbide.

"I thought the Orions had been gone from Grex for more than a year." Kirk stared down the path after them, his nerves still insisting they were dangerously close for all that his nose and ears told him otherwise.

Giotto stood from behind a raised garden bed. "So did I."

"And I could have sworn we'd found all the stashes where the Orions hid their pirated contraband." George swung his tricorder back and forth over the now nonexistent door, playing impatiently with the sensitivity controls. "This one must be shielded seven ways from Sunday if even our ship's sensors didn't pick it up."

"Maybe it's not a full-fledged stash," Kirk said. "Maybe it's just the equivalent of an Orion safe house."

George shook his head and turned the tricorder around so Kirk could see its face. "That's no safe house, sir. I may not be picking up anything now that this door is sealed, but the tricorder got a real clear warp core reading for as long as it was open." He hooked a thumb back over his shoulder, his expression tense with excitement. "Captain Forester, there's a spaceship inside that hole."

This was not the first time Uhura had been left in command of the *Enterprise*. As the chief communications officer, she stood fourth in line behind Spock and Mr. Scott as a ranking line officer, and she'd often taken the conn when the senior officers were summoned to sector meetings or other planetary duties. Usually, those were times when the *Enterprise* was stationed in orbit around some stable civilian planet or Federation starbase, not on a desperate deep-space mission with a hostile alien race nearby. But Chief Engineer Montgomery Scott had spent the past two days almost continuously on his feet, first overseeing the repairs to the ship's warp engines, then taking Spock's place on the bridge while the Vulcan joined the planetary team in the search for Captain Kirk. By the time they'd managed to deactivate the Shechenag defense network and send a third expedition to Tlaoli to return young Kirk to his proper time, the tall Scotsman was literally swaying with exhaustion. Dr. McCoy, in one of the periodic visits he tended to make to the bridge during times of crisis, had declared the chief engineer no longer fit for duty and hauled him away for some much-needed sleep. Scott had agreed to go, with one adamant provision.

"If for any reason you can't stay in command of the bridge, lass," he told Uhura blearily, "for God's sake, just don't leave Riley with the conn. After what I've been through the past two days, I don't want to have to cold-start those engines ever again!"

Uhura glanced from the communications station over to the helm, hoping Kevin Riley hadn't heard that jaundiced comment. The young navigator's defensively hunched shoulders told her that he had. It was hard not to feel sorry for him. While other victims of the Psi 2000 virus such as Sulu and Spock had spent the last two days immersed in the urgent quest to recover their missing captain, Kevin Riley had remained cooped up on the *Enterprise,* with nothing to do but mope over his recent all-too-public escapade in the engine room. As soon as this crisis was over, Uhura thought, she would have to invite Riley out to dinner with some friends who could cheer him up. Robert Tomlinson and Angela Martine would be willing to help, she was sure, and perhaps she could ask Ensign Chekov and that young security guard friend of his, Yuki Smith.

Although if the time bubble they were in collapsed before they managed to get Captain Kirk back, there was no guarantee any of them would still be members of this crew. Or even still be alive.

Uhura watched the turbolift doors slide shut behind the departing chief engineer and chief medical officer, then toggled a familiar switch on her communications station. "Lieutenant Hadley to the bridge."

"Aye, sir," said the relief communications officer with surprising promptness. His next words explained why. "I'm on the ready deck now. I'll be there in just a minute."

Uhura set down her portable frequency monitor, wondering wryly if her junior officers had suspected she would soon be needing a replacement. No doubt they considered her a candidate for getting yanked off the bridge, too, after the exhausting day and night she'd spent on Tlaoli. McCoy had indeed scrutinized her very narrowly when he'd first stepped onto the bridge, but he must have had enough faith in the restorative powers of his awful-tasting nutritional supplement to leave her in command.

The turbolift hissed again, and a sandy-haired young man stepped out, still hurriedly adjusting the collar of his uniform. "Lieutenant Hadley reporting to the bridge, sir," he said before he even noticed the empty captain's chair.

"Acknowledged, Lieutenant." Uhura smiled at his startled expression. "You'll handle communications for the remainder of this shift. I'm on the conn until further notice."

"Aye, sir." Hadley waited politely for her to vacate her seat, but Uhura noticed he was already scanning the frequency monitors to see what channels she had open. "Anything special to watch for?"

"Channel three is preset for the emergency communicator Mr. Spock took with him to the planet," Uhura told him. "It's for monitoring purposes only. We're under strict orders not to hail the landing party, so the Shechenag won't suspect we've sent anyone to the planet. Conduct routine scans of all other hailing frequencies and monitor anything that seems like it might be Shechenag transmissions. I've downloaded as much of their language as the main computer could decipher into translator program nine."

"Aye, sir."

Uhura gave her boards one last assessing glance as she stood, but everything was still as it had been when Spock and Sulu had departed for Tlaoli: all subspace frequencies silent except for the natural interference that howled and chattered across the spectrum. If the Shechenag ship had left any of its crew down on the planet to guard the Janus Gate, they apparently saw no need to check in with them. Between the alien silence and Mr. Spock's ban on landing party reports, Uhura had not really had much work to do.

And now she was going to have even less.

Uhura lowered herself into the captain's chair and flexed her fingers on its broad armrests, feeling the living warmth beneath the surface. The entire command console was packed with computer circuits, giving the officer who sat there command and control of the entire starship. Despite all that power humming beneath her fingers, however, Uhura had nothing to do but gaze up at the silent copper planet on the viewscreen and wonder how long it was going to take the Shechenag to work their way back around to this side of the world. When that occurred—if it occurred—her service as substitute captain would really begin. In the meantime, she didn't even have to work at keeping the captain's seat warm.

Uhura had always known that the captain's job was the hardest on the bridge. What she hadn't realized before was that it could also be the most physically excruciating. With no screens to watch or instruments to monitor, the ship's commander had no occupation for those times when tensions were high but absolutely nothing needed to be done. Within just a few moments, Uhura caught herself tapping her fingers restively against the chair's armrests. She bit her lip, forcing her hands to relax and be still. Bored or not, she had to project the image of an alert and attentive commander, or risk losing the confidence of her crew.

Uhura had always thought Captain Kirk's tendency to stride around the bridge and consult his officers at their stations just reflected his own innate energy. Now she was starting to wonder if it was a deliberate strategy for staying watchful and alert.

"Any change in the ship's position, Mr. Riley?" she asked the lieutenant in an attempt to fill the silence.

"Nothing unusual, sir." The navigator's rigid shoulders relaxed a little as he focused on answering her question. "We're exactly on station over the planet's equatorial plane."

"No major gravitational fluctuations?"

"Just the standard bumps and potholes." Relief pilot Lieutenant Alden had clearly filled in for Sulu before, probably while the chief helmsman had been lost on Basaraba. His coffee-colored hands moved confidently over the helm controls, correcting for Tlaoli's unstable gravity fields. "In fact, the perturbations actually seem to be dying out a little."

Uhura studied the glittering force-field lines netting their way around Tlaoli, now almost complete except for the darkened patch Spock and Sulu had deactivated. Was it her imagination, or had a pearly luster begun to shine above the ancient planet's rust-red atmosphere as the Shechenag continued placing satellites on the opposite side of the world? "Maybe part of what the defensive barrier does is keep the planet from dragging any more spaceships down to its surface," she speculated. "That would prevent them from being destroyed by the force field when they were helpless to escape."

Riley gave her a curious look over his shoulder. "I thought the Shechenag were just trying to protect the timestream, sir. Why should they care if ships are destroyed by their force field, as long as nobody makes it to the Janus Gate?"

"I don't know," Uhura admitted. "But we can't assume we really understand them, Lieutenant, when we've barely been able to decode their language. Statements and actions that we've interpreted as hostile may not have been intended that way."

"I think we're about to find out if that's true, sir." A red light flashed at Alden's station. "I've got a proximity alert from the gravitational sensors. Something big is heading straight for us."

Uhura glanced across at Lieutenant Karen Tracey, filling in for Spock at the science panel. "Long-range scanner report."

"I'm not showing anything—wait, yes, I am." The technician adjusted a control at her station, altering the image on the viewscreen to an enlarged quadrant of Tlaoli's rusty disk. A familiar smudge of unlit black could just be seen crossing the dapple of distant stars. "Sorry, Lieutenant. The radiation from the force field lines completely swamped their ion output."

Uhura swung around toward Hadley at communications. "Open a channel to the Shechenag ship, using the same frequency as their previous communications." She saw the young man's hands slide across the controls as he obeyed her. "Engage the partial translator and run my voice through it before transmitting. Tell me when you're ready."

"I'm ready now, sir."

Uhura took a deep breath and turned back to the main viewscreen, in case the Shechenag opened a reply channel. "Four more hours are permitted for our departure from this system," she said, hoping the translator conveyed her attempt to be conciliatory. "We wait to see if our lost crewman returns. No hostility is intended."

There was a pause, then the viewscreen rippled to show the barren interior of the alien spacecraft's bridge. The huddle of cybernetic bodies at the center of that simple space seemed a little smaller, as if some of the controlling aliens had been dispatched on other errands. Of those remaining, two had reared their mechanical suits up on jointed legs to reveal the actual alien bodies inside, agitated as goldfish in a dropped bowl.

"This is all untruthful," said one flat voice, immediately overlapped by a second.

"This is not the native language. You have known our speech always."

"*No.*" Uhura tried to make her own voice just as flat and definitive as theirs. "Our translation device is new and incomplete. We made it to communicate better, to avoid hostility."

"Hostility commenced when you damaged the blocking sphere." The first Shechenag waved several appendages, both real and robotic, to emphasize its point. The gestures seemed almost theatrically fierce in comparison with its toneless machine-generated voice. "We are Shechenag. We do not make war. This planet creates danger for all who come here. We create protection."

"Yes, we know." Uhura swept her own hands out in a placating gesture of her own, although she wasn't sure the aliens would see or understand. She chose every word she spoke with care. "We do not wish your blocking sphere to be destroyed. The satellites which failed were destroyed by the alien machine down on the planet. We watched it drain their power."

That sparked a flurry of twitches and color changes inside several robotic torsos as their translucent occupants erupted into hisses and clatters. None of the comments were turned into English by the Shechenag's translator. Uhura glanced over her shoulder at Hadley, but the junior communications officer shook his head. Their own rough translating device couldn't sort out all the overlapping conversations well enough to decipher them.

The clattering uproar finally died away to a last few cryptic utterances: "Unsure, insecure, observe." "Remove destabilizing force." "Protect. Protect only." The last comment seemed to be the most popular among the joint commanders of the alien ship; several of them lifted and dropped their jointed mechanical arms in a rumble of approval. Their small glimmering bodies turned pale, then clear again, as if they had voiced their emotional reaction to Uhura's words and were now calm.

"Repairs will be made to complete the blocking sphere," the first Shechenag said while others detached various insectoid robots from their bodies and sent them scuttling out of sight, perhaps to communicate their new plan of action to the rest of their crew. "No approach or maneuver will be permitted at this time. Immediate departure from the system is advised."

Uhura took a deep breath, knowing that this was the really risky part. "We prefer to wait for our missing crewman. If he can return through the alien time transporter, he may be able to use a vessel already on the planet to rejoin us."

There was an alarmingly long pause, but no flutter of colorful emotion that she could see inside the translucent tank. There was a stillness to the Shechenag spokesman's cybernetic casing that Uhura thought might indicate either confusion or puzzlement. "No return is possible without intervention in the timestream," the alien said at last. "No intervention is possible without activation of the prohibited device."

"Yeah," Riley said softly, beneath his breath so the translator pickup wouldn't catch the words. "Don't think about that too hard, okay?"

Uhura hushed him with a restraining hand on his shoulder, and only then noticed that she had stood up from the captain's console without thinking and come forward to the helm to confront their opponents, just as Captain Kirk often did. She tried to think the way he would have, too, rapidly assessing and discarding the various excuses they could use to remain in the Tlaoli system without arousing the Shechenag's suspicions. She remembered the comment one of them had made during their own discussion: unsure, insecure, observe. It gave Uhura the rationale she was looking for.

"This is understood," she said. "We will make no maneuvers or approaches to the planet. But if it is permitted, we wish to observe the completion of the blocking sphere to assure our leaders that no further disruptions will occur in the timestream."

There was a brief exchange of clicks among the group crouched around the speaker, then its translucent tank lifted so that the naked swimmer inside could look more directly at Uhura through whatever version of a viewscreen the cybernetic aliens used. "This is logical and permitted," the Shechenag said. "Completion of the shield is estimated in point zero six five planetary rotations."

And with that, the viewscreen blanked out for a moment, then returned to its normal display of space dusted with stars and Tlaoli's sunlit face shining like a polished copper coin in the distance. Uhura frowned up at the ancient planet, but her tired brain just wouldn't do the math computation she needed. She finally turned to Lieutenant Karen Tracey.

"How long is point zero six five rotations in our units?"

The science technician made Uhura jealous by not even glancing at her monitor before she answered. "Given the length of Tlaoli's day, approximately an hour and a half, sir."

Uhura bit her lip again, this time to suppress an exclamation that it wouldn't be dignified to make in front of her crew. She watched the dark smudge of the alien starship cross the stars, then leap into high relief as it passed over Tlaoli's shining surface and headed for the barren spot where ten satellites had been deactivated less than an hour ago. So far, they'd been successful at keeping the presence of their landing party concealed, but that wasn't going to do them the slightest bit of good if the shuttle found itself trapped under a completed force shield.

None of Uhura's options now were appealing. If she allowed the Shechenag to go about their work, the shuttle *might* make it out in the meantime without any intervention on her part. But if they didn't, the *Enterprise* would be forced to blast apart the protective blockade to free their shuttle crew. There was no way to know if they could destroy this unknown alien technology, and even if they did, such an overt act of hostility might gain the Federation a new and dangerous enemy in this sector of space. On the other hand, if Uhura intervened before the blockade was completed, they would probably still make enemies of the Shechenag and possibly endanger their landing party even more. As fearful as the ancient aliens were of time disruptions, she wouldn't be surprised if they tried to seize the shuttle as it left Tlaoli, or even tried to attack the Janus Gate itself.

For one craven moment, Uhura considered asking Hadley to summon Commander Scott to the conn, but she knew the exhausted chief engineer wouldn't be any better than she was at sorting through their limited options. With a sigh, she sank back into the captain's chair and tried to make herself think like Kirk.

"Lieutenant Alden, I don't suppose you observed any of the maneuvers Commander Spock and Lieutenant Sulu used to deactivate those defensive satellites."

The relief pilot threw an almost incredulous look over his shoulder. "Sir, I wouldn't have missed that show for all the dilithium on Vulcan! When the word went out about what they were planning to do, the entire helm section headed for the auxiliary bridge and rigged the viewscreen down there to watch the lieutenant fly that mission."

Uhura gave him a somber look. "Do you think we could carry out that maneuver again if the Shechenag close up the gap in the satellite network?"

Alden didn't even hesitate. "Never," he said. "I didn't even believe the lieutenant could fly that well off instruments until I saw him do it. And no one else on board can handle this ship the way he can. No one."

Kevin Riley swung around from the navigation station to join the discussion. "There also isn't anyone else on board besides Commander Spock who could figure out the transporter angles to that kind of precision. Those satellites are only about the size of an escape pod, and right now we're about ten thousand kilometers away from them. Aiming just to hit them would be hard enough—trying to bounce the beam off them and then down to a precise spot on the planet's surface is statistically impossible."

Uhura frowned up at the viewscreen. A tiny puff of reflected sunlight beside the Shechenag ship marked the launch of a replacement satellite, and a moment later she saw an iridescent strand of light shoot out across the stretch of empty copper sky that marked their landing party's escape route. Impossible or not, she had to make sure the hole in that barrier stayed open at all costs.

Because if it closed, they'd not only lose Captain Kirk and the six crewmen who'd risked their lives to save him, they'd also lose their entire future.

# Chapter Eight

SULU STARED for a long time at the empty space on the far side of the Janus Gate, as if just by staring hard enough he could somehow make Chief Giotto *be* there, crumpled to his knees perhaps, or obscured by the fading blue glow of the alien device. But no matter how long he looked, the space that had just a few minutes ago been occupied by young Kirk, older Chekov and older Sulu—and by the man who was supposed to maintain their link between the past and the present—stood completely and impossibly vacant.

"What the hell happened?" The voice that broke the stunned silence was Sanner's, and it sounded just as shaken as Sulu felt. "Where's Giotto?"

The tall and silent figure on the other side of the Janus Gate finally stirred, glancing down at the alien control board in front of him. "It appears the Janus Gate has displaced him to the past along with the others. The power overload must have thrown it into full transport mode without my instructing it to do so."

Yuki Smith leaned in between Sulu and Chekov, bumping both of them in the back with her phaser rifle. "Does that mean there's another Mr. Giotto back in the cave where we were stuck for so long?" she asked worriedly.

"Possibly. The gate was programmed only for viewing mode...but the power surge may have triggered an actual replacement." The noticeable hesitation in Spock's voice made Sulu wonder if the Vulcan was less sure of his deductions than usual. "Mr. Sanner, you can move more quickly through the caves than anyone else. Check the healing chamber for a light inside one of the columns." There was another, even longer pause, then an audible intake of breath before Spock resumed. "Mr.

Giotto remembered being badly wounded at the time of the native uprising on Grex."

"On my way." The geologist headed off into the darkness with long, loping strides. It took a long time for the clattering sound of his footsteps to fade into the sound of dripping water and uneasy silence. Sulu watched Spock for a long time, then glanced back across the chamber at Chekov and Smith, seeing the same question in their eyes that he was feeling. Why wasn't Spock doing anything, or issuing further orders? It looked for all the world as if the Vulcan had frozen into ice at his station, although, in fact, the Janus chamber was getting warmer and warmer all the time. Had something happened to him, perhaps some side effect of subspace radiation or the last treacherous snap of a rent tearing through space and time?

"Mr. Spock?" Sulu took a cautious step out into the chamber. The curtains of blue light that had billowed around the Janus Gate had at first seemed to be completely gone, but now they looked like they might be coalescing again in the darkness. A damp breath blew on Sulu's frost-burned face, and he stiffened in alarm until he realized what he was feeling was a cascade of mist from melting ice. The nano-woven fibers of his caving suit squirmed against his skin as they condensed down to a thinner and more water-repellent foam. Beads of moisture were already glittering on the suit's outer surface, and runnels dripped off his helmet from a layer of frost he hadn't even known was there.

"Commander Spock, are you all right?" It hadn't seemed odd at first that the Vulcan had stayed at his post beside the Janus Gate, since there was always the chance Giotto would reappear and Spock would need to adjust the controls to bring their version of Kirk back with him. But now that the device had clearly lost most of its stored power, the science officer's continuing stillness was beginning to alarm Sulu.

There was no answer. Sulu took another step out into the mist, then another. Nothing happened, so he edged around the side of the chamber in the same direction Spock had taken.

"Lieutenant Sulu!" The note of concern in that Russian voice stopped Sulu in his tracks. He glanced back over his shoulder at Chekov and Smith, barely visible now except for the misty gleams of their carbide lights. "Watch out for the Shechenag robots, sir. Mr. Spock stepped on one with a cutting blade, remember."

"Thanks, Ensign." Sulu angled his carbide light down toward his feet and saw a crumpled heap of mechanical limbs a half meter in front of him. He stepped over it carefully and continued on his way, as far as he remembered the Vulcan going before he turned to approach the alien time machine along its corridor of safety. Although the Janus Gate was now lit only by the dimmest of flickers at its heart, Sulu paused to scan the ground again and see if he could find any footprints or tracks in the icy crust.

What he saw through the flowing mist made his eyes narrow in dismay. A line of dark smudges ran across the ice, tracing a path from where he stood to the tall, silent figure beside the Janus Gate. When Sulu bent down to touch one of those marks, the frozen slush he brought up on his gloved finger glittered a distinctive green in the glow of his carbide. It was the color of Vulcan blood.

"Mr. Spock?"

Still no reply. Sulu followed the line of bloody footprints toward the first officer, feeling apprehension thud like stones inside his gut. If they lost Spock as well as Giotto, any hope of retrieving Captain Kirk was truly lost . . . but the closer Sulu came, the more apparent it was that Spock had not been pulled into the Gate's time-warp nor made catatonic by some unknown side effect of its use. The Vulcan's eyes were closed and his angular face was deeply intent, as if he were meditating on something profound. Sulu paused an arm's length away, remembering stories he had heard about the nearly mystical ability of Vulcans to survive even severe injuries. Maybe Spock's meditation had something to do with that.

"Is the commander all right?" That was Smith's anxious voice, echoing oddly through the curdled mist.

"I think so," Sulu said. "He looks like he's in some kind of trance right now." Sulu settled himself to wait where he was, not wanting to approach the Janus Gate any closer, yet not feeling right about leaving the Vulcan alone in this defenseless condition. "I'm not going to bother him. It's not like we can do anything but wait and see if another Giotto came out through the Janus Gate."

"What will it mean, if he did?" Chekov asked. "Can we send him back to Grex once he's healed, and then get the captain back along with our version of Mr. Giotto?"

"Maybe . . . but if the younger version of Giotto goes back healed instead of wounded, we'll have changed our timeline again. We'll just have to hope that's not as big a change as taking Captain Kirk out of it completely." Sulu was starting to see why the Shechenag had insisted it was impossible to repair damage to any timeline. Thinking about the cybernetic aliens reminded him abruptly that with all of the Janus Gate's stolen power discharged, the way was once again open for them to invade the caverns. "Don't forget to keep an eye on the ceiling in case the Shechenag decide to drop in on us," he reminded the junior officers.

"We can't see the ceiling through the fog, sir," Chekov pointed out.

Despite the tension, Sulu found himself smiling, just a little, at the young ensign's unfailing earnestness.

"Well, just keep an eye on whatever you can see up there. And let's not talk anymore. If we're quiet, we should be able to hear those robots of theirs clattering against the rocks long before we see them."

The two young *Enterprise* crewmen fell obediently silent, not even whispering to each other in the doorway. Sulu wished he could enforce the same order on the cavern itself. As the temperature climbed, the Janus chamber began to make an entire symphony of sounds: meltwater dripping from a thousand places, then rushing and gurgling its way farther underground, the slow groan and thunderous cracking of ice detaching from the walls. As the minutes passed, the noises echoed back from the rest of the frozen caverns as well, making Sulu wonder how Spock could keep himself tranced amid the din. The only warning he had that Zap Sanner was coming back were the yelps of surprise and dismay that Smith and Chekov made when the geologist came plunging out of the dark conduit behind them.

"Nothing." The word was spit out between tearing gasps as the geologist caught at the edge of the cavern wall to support himself. He must have run at full speed to the breakdown cavern where the alien healing chambers were, Sulu realized, through passages filled with melting ice and mist. For a long time, Sanner didn't manage to make any other sounds but gasps, but then he didn't really need to. The bleakness in that single word had told them everything they needed to know.

"You mean Mr. Giotto wasn't there?" Smith asked anyway.

Sulu could tell Sanner nodded because his carbide glow fell and lifted twice. But it took another few minutes for the geologist to regain enough breath for continuous speech. "There were no lights in any columns...no versions of Giotto hiding anywhere in the cavern. I even checked the ropes up to the exit, but they were all still coated with frost. No one went out that way."

"Then Giotto *wasn't* exchanged with his younger self," Sulu reflected. "I guess that's good, in a way. It means we won't have changed the timeline any further, as long as we can still get Captain Kirk and Mr. Giotto back again from the past."

"But how *are* we going to get them, sir?" Chekov demanded. "We don't have anyone left who has a connection to Captain Kirk's past—"

"Yes." Spock's voice echoed deep and strong as a church bell in the misty darkness. "We do."

Sulu took a step toward the Vulcan, seeing both alertness and pain in his expression. "Are you all right, Commander? Is there any medical treatment we can give you?"

"None that will accomplish more than I have already done," the science officer said calmly. "And it is far more important right now to address Ensign Chekov's question. I believe there is another way for us to contact Captain Kirk and Chief Giotto, but there is one major impediment to our doing so."

Sulu glanced up toward the cavern's ceiling, but saw no robotic intruders swarming down through the billowing fog. "What impediment is that?"

"Power." Spock gestured at the Janus Gate. Inside its gyroscopic arms, the light that had once been too brilliant to look directly at now flickered like a will-o'-the-wisp. "The device has used all the energy we channeled into it from the Shechenag satellites. Unless we find a way to recharge it, we will not be able to retrieve anyone from anywhere."

Between George Kirk and Antonio Giotto, Kirk had nearly fifty years of combined security experience at his disposal. As he watched them tease open the shielded Orion bulkhead using nothing but a phaser's tuning apparatus and George's antique tricorder, Kirk realized that he'd never fully appreciated all the practical skills that came with a good security specialist. Not in his own father, and certainly not in the interchangeable personnel he routinely ordered up as protection forces for his landing parties. These were handy men to have around. He hoped he'd have the opportunity to make better use of them in the future—any future.

A single stony *clunk!* announced the separation of the door's mammoth locking mechanism a mere fifteen minutes after George and Giotto had set to work on it. They backed away from the rapidly brightening entrance along with everyone else, Giotto quickly reassembling his phaser while George worked on realigning his tricorder to scan the freshly opened stash ahead of them.

"Orion locks are so useless," the older man remarked with a mixture of frustration and disgust. "If they didn't use more shielding than God on anything they thought was important, they'd be robbed by their own slave races every ten minutes."

Apparently, that shielding was enough most of the time, though. Kirk doubted that most of the races who had access to an Orion stash possessed the sort of high-end lock-picking equipment George and Giotto had just used. The ruthless practicality that made Orions such formidable enemies in combat probably also kept them from wasting any more resources than necessary, whether it was on locks or lighting or personal hygiene. He was just glad someone in this Orion cabal had seen fit to keep a ship available as an escape route.

Mazelike corridors split in all directions just past the threshold of the hidden door, smooth and modern and drilled out of the surrounding rock with all the sturdy, joisted lack of aesthetics of a crude dilithium mine. Kirk wouldn't have mistaken it for some service access to the underground Grexxen market even if he hadn't seen the effort necessary just to get inside. There was the same faintly sulfurous odor as he'd smelled on the Orions themselves, and the glaringly bright overhead lights pulsed with the disturbing reddish cast of Orion's native sun. Stepping around one of the many piles of crates and grav-sleds littering the corridor, Kirk glanced back at George and his tricorder. "Anything?"

The older man studied the readout for a moment, then shook his head. "I think I've got a pretty clear map of the facility—the shielding's all outside the main perimeter. I'm not getting any life-sign readings except for ours."

"What about the warp core?" Kirk asked.

Another minute adjustment of the device's sensors. "Still there." He used the tricorder to point down one of several possible paths. "A little more than a kilometer, that way."

Giotto stayed close to George, keeping watch for unexpected booby traps or personnel while George led them deeper into the installation using nothing but the tricorder's sensors. They stayed grouped together more closely now, since they no longer had the concealing space of the open marketplace, but they were still careful to keep the boy near the center with the adult men stationed as armed guards all around.

Kirk suspected the Orion tunnels weren't as convoluted as they seemed, but it was hard to tell around the clutter all but blocking their progress. A few steps forward turned almost immediately into an extended wriggle between stacks of equipment and supplies, and it wasn't always clear where they turned a corner or where they left the main conduit for one of its less crowded side branches. Shouldering aside a metal crate that looked almost like an upright coffin, Sulu mused aloud, "I wonder if the Orions are coming or going?"

Giotto leaned back to help him steady the box before it swayed over on top of them all. "They left more than a year ago—I was with the team that tossed the last of them out."

Kirk saw George flick a curious frown over his shoulder at Giotto, and wondered himself which of his father's young subordinates had grown up to be Kirk's chief of security. After nineteen years, Kirk only remembered three or four of George's team from Grex, and those faces were so clouded over by grief and guilt that he seldom thought about them before today. It disturbed him a little to realize how effortlessly the past could shield itself from the present.

Turning back to his tricorder, George seemed to set aside the question of Giotto's identity as yet another Special Forces enigma that he had no right to pursue. "He's right—the last of the Orions supposedly shipped out fourteen months ago. And we've had the whole planet locked down tight as a drum since then, to make sure nobody else tried to raid the contraband stashes the Orions left behind." He shook his head definitively. "There's no way the Orions or anybody else got a ship past us and landed under Sogo city without us knowing about it."

"Then these Orions have been here all along," Chekov said.

Giotto made a face that said he found the possibility unlikely. "But why? What's in it for them to hide out underground on a planet they don't even control anymore?"

The lack of interest in Chekov's shrug couldn't have been more profound. "I'm just telling you the tactical realities, based on what you're saying." He stepped aside to glance down one of the side corridors, obviously more concerned with keeping watch than actually entering into this discussion. "I have no idea what the hell's going on around here."

"No, he's right," George said thoughtfully as he picked his way around several piles of some unidentifiable ore. "If you think about it, it explains a lot. Ever since we got here, there's always been a core of Vragax who refused to cooperate in the rebuilding process, no matter how hard Starfleet tried. They'd be part of negotiations with the Kozhu about how to structure a democratic government right up to the point when they just refused to come back to the table. No explanation given. Or they'd seem to agree to a division of arable land in the southern hemisphere, then instigate nighttime raids on Kozhu settlements there." He motioned for Giotto to help him open a wider path down the middle of the hall. "After fourteen months, we'd made next to no progress in getting this planet back on its feet as a free society, all thanks to them."

Kirk remembered his father's angry tirades about the lack of native cooperation from the first time he'd been on Grex. As a boy, he'd always believed his father reacted with so much anger because he didn't think the Federation should be on Grex to begin with, and so saw every setback in the restructuring process as proof that the Federation's efforts were being wasted. It had never occurred to Kirk that the irritation George had expressed so freely in those days had been because he so badly wanted the mission to succeed and didn't know how to make that happen.

It was his younger self, though, who said with almost adult clarity, "I guess they weren't representing any real Vragax faction. The Orions were putting them up to it all along."

"We should have known the Orions wouldn't give up the planet so easily." It was the first time Kirk could remember hearing his father respond to anything his younger self said as though they were equals.

"Hell, we should have known they'd try and sneak in the back door after we'd locked the front! When the violence broke out tonight, we all assumed the Vragax rebels had found a stash of Orion weapons we'd somehow overlooked. I mean, how else could they get the gauss rifles and the sonic grenades and the microbolt that took down Maione's shuttle? It never occurred to us that there had been Orions here the whole time, stirring up dissent and supplying a handful of troublemakers with weapons to guarantee the rebuilding process never got off the ground."

"I guess a few bad apples can ruin an entire planetary society." Chekov heaved one of the abandoned grav-sleds upright, then caught it with one hand before it could drift any farther down the hall. "This is all very fascinating," he said with a complete lack of sincerity, "but we still need to get you and your son off this planet." He rolled one of the metal crates onto the waiting sled. "Can we save the history lesson until later?"

Kirk nodded Giotto to stay close to George and the boy as they continued down the hall, then stepped forward to hold the sled steady while Chekov heaved another metal-sided crate on top of the first. "What are you doing?"

"Assuming the Orions are going to come back at some point." This time he waved for Kirk to help him lift a particularly heavy piece of strange equipment. "Once we find this ship, we still have to get into it and figure out if we can fly it. I thought slowing the Orions down might be a good idea."

By the time he saw the big bay door at the end of their hike, Kirk thought it might be a good idea, too. This was no flimsy Orion bulkhead, meant only to keep out a few primitive natives with stone knives and wooden spears. This was the same sort of state-of-the-art installation found on the *Enterprise*'s shuttlebay, with all the attendant check systems and safeguards.

"Get to work," he told his father and Giotto. Then he tossed a grin at Chekov and the Russian's sledful of crates and loose metal equipment and supplies. "I can see they must have had Boy Scouts back in Moscow."

He was surprised when he got a wry half smile in return. "Be prepared."

They stacked up a wall waist-high and twice that deep, lining the exterior with the more irregularly shaped pieces of heavy equipment and leaving the relatively smooth, even sides of the metal crates on the inner surface closer to the big bay door. Kirk wasn't sure how much protection the barricade would actually afford them if the Orions returned with anything more powerful than gauss rifles, but it kept them busy and out of the security officers' way.

Sulu helped Chekov wrestle the now-empty grav-sled through the gap they'd left in the barricade for that purpose. "Once we find this ship," he asked Kirk quietly, "are we sure we can actually get it out of here?"

If he'd meant the soft pitch of his voice to keep George or his son from overhearing, he was apparently unsuccessful. "Oh, it'll get out, all right," George said without looking away from his work on the door. "Every one of these stashes has at least one small escape vessel for the head Orion poobah, with a launch tube leading out to the surface."

"How small?" That was one element of their plan Kirk hadn't considered when George first reported a warp core available for hijacking at the end of this tunnel. "Will it be big enough for all of us?"

George still didn't turn around, and Kirk couldn't tell from the pause before his father answered whether George also hadn't thought about that particular detail, or whether he'd simply hoped it would end up not being an issue. "I don't know," the older man finally admitted. "The size of the ships varied in the other stashes. But don't worry—" He looked back at Kirk and the others with grim resolution. "We're not going to leave anyone behind."

Which was a laudable sentiment, Kirk thought, but didn't necessarily mean everyone would be leaving the same way.

Turning to help drag crates across the last narrow opening, Kirk asked Sulu quietly, "What exactly *is* the plan for getting the rest of us out of here?"

The other captain gave him a rueful look. "Just what your security chief said—he was supposed to stay linked with the alien transporter device so that Mr. Spock could use him as a focal point to bring you back through." He nodded across at Chekov, who continued arranging the last level of barricade in grim silence, as though he wasn't even part of their conversation. "Pavel and I were going to stay behind and make sure the boy got out of here to grow up safely."

"But Mr. Giotto lost his link to this transporter, which means Spock lost his link to us. What was Plan B?"

Sulu picked up his gauss rifle and turned it over to check its charge. "We were working with limited resources. There was no Plan B."

"Gentlemen," Kirk said gently, "Mr. Spock *always* has a Plan B."

Chekov turned from dropping the last crate into place, and Kirk thought for an instant that he glimpsed what almost looked like regret or despair in the older man's lean face. Then the tearing whistle of a gauss rifle's projectile crashed through the top edge of the barricade from outside, spraying blood and splintered metal across them all.

She couldn't watch the viewscreen anymore.

Uhura swung the captain's chair away from the ugly metamorphosis

that was taking place on Tlaoli. An hour ago, the ancient planet had
glowed in darkening shades of copper, garnet, and rust as the curving arc
of sunset crept across its dusty sky. Now, what was left of its dayside
looked like a cataract-blinded eye floating in space. The Shechenag must
have completed the rest of their protective satellite barrier before discovering the hole Spock and Sulu had punched through to the Janus Gate.
Now that they were repairing that hole, one satellite at a time, their force
field had brightened and coalesced from spider-silk strands to a thick,
opalescent shroud. The blanched planet reminded Uhura a little too much
of the eerie swirling aura of Psi 2000 just before that doomed planet had
exploded. She knew Tlaoli wasn't going to do anything so drastic, but if
the landing team couldn't escape before the planetary defense shield was
completed, the results would be far more catastrophic than the mere destruction of a planet.

Freeing her gaze from the progress of the Shechenag starship on the
viewscreen also served to free Uhura's mind from the decision-making
quandary that had kept her torn between action and inaction for the past
hour. With only thirty minutes to go before the Shechenag completed
their defensive shield, she could no longer simply wait for the shuttle to
appear. She would have to assume that it wasn't going to get out in time,
and react accordingly.

"Lieutenant Hadley." Uhura could tell from the way the junior communications officer spun around to meet her gaze that he was ready and
waiting for the orders he expected her to give. Her next words made his
reaching hand freeze in midair, however. "Call Lieutenant Kyle to the
bridge at once." Before he had time to do more than look disconcerted,
Uhura added with a smile, "And put the ship on yellow alert."

"Aye, sir." Hadley resumed the gesture he'd interrupted, and an instant later yellow alarm lights began to strobe across the bridge. With his
other hand, he opened the intraship channel that would connect him to the
*Enterprise*'s most skilled transporter technician. "Lieutenant Kyle, report
to the bridge immediately. Repeat, report to the bridge immediately."

There was a way all good communications officers had of packing a
wealth of meaning into the standard ship hails without ever sounding dramatic or unprofessional. Uhura had used those subtle changes in voice,
pitch, and tonality so many times herself that they had become almost
subconscious. Hearing them now in Lieutenant Hadley's unfamiliar male
register made her suddenly aware of why Starfleet still insisted on having
a human communications officer instead of assigning that work to the
ship's main computer.

Hadley swung back around toward Uhura, his gaze slipping past her
and up to the viewscreen, as if Tlaoli's swirling pallor was just too

strange to look away from. Uhura had to clench her hands around the armrests of the captain's console to keep from glancing back herself. "Lieutenant Kyle's on his way," the junior officer said. "Lieutenant, should I hail the landing party now?"

"No," Uhura said flatly. "If Commander Spock hasn't left the planet yet, it's because Captain Kirk isn't back yet. And a communication from us saying that the satellite shield is closing won't make the Janus Gate work any better or any faster. All it will do is warn the Shechenag that someone is using it." Uhura turned toward Karen Tracey at the science station. "What we have to do is make sure that shield *doesn't* close until the shuttle is on its way back to us. And for that, we'll need the best fix on the Janus Gate that your long-range scanners can give us, Lieutenant."

"Aye, sir." The technical officer ducked back over her display screens.

Uhura swiveled back toward the helm, keeping her gaze on the two men there rather than on the ominous pale crescent that hung on the viewscreen above them. "Riley, I need you to keep track of that Shechenag starship on a meter scale if possible. Can you do that?"

"Aye, sir." All of the self-consciousness had left the young navigator's voice as he manipulated his instruments to triangulate on a moving target rather than a distant lodestone star. "Got it, sir."

"Send the coordinates over to helm and engineering. Tracey, your coordinates for the Janus Gate need to go to the same two bridge stations." Uhura suspected Captain Kirk wouldn't have given the crew his directions all helter-skelter like this, but her mind was racing so fast that it was two steps ahead of her voice. She took a deep breath, forcing herself to think through her next series of commands before she gave them. "Lieutenant Alden, I want you to line the ship up with *both* Riley's and Tracey's coordinates."

"Aye, sir." The pilot's reply was confident enough, but the sidelong glance he gave her betrayed a little confusion. Uhura took a deep breath, realizing that this was the point at which she had to share her strategy with the rest of the crew, and see how they reacted to it.

"I don't want to engage the Shechenag ship in battle unless that's our very last resort," she said. "What we're going to do is obstruct their work so they can't finish their defensive network. It won't be anything fancy, like Commander Spock and Lieutenant Sulu did with the satellite network, but if we can place the Shechenag ship exactly in line between us and the Janus Gate, I think we can manage to disable her in a way that won't seem like it's coming from us. Can you keep the *Enterprise* on that station, Lieutenant Alden?"

"If I can't, sir, you better demote me to shuttle pilot," the helmsman replied resolutely, and Uhura felt the *Enterprise*'s impulse engines surge as she came around to her new heading.

The turbolift doors hissed open, and Lieutenant John Kyle strode onto the bridge. His bony face wore its usual deadpan expression, but the shrewd blue eyes were alert. "Lieutenant Kyle reporting to the bridge, sir. Do you need me to relieve the helm officer?"

"No, Lieutenant. I want you at engineering." Now that the critical part of her operation was at hand, Uhura found that she couldn't remain seated in the captain's chair no matter how hard she tried. She scrambled to her feet and went to join Kyle at the bridge's engineering station. Watkins, the on-duty engineer, was already vacating his station and heading for one of the auxiliary bridge monitoring stations so he could continue his work of coordinating bridge control with engine room response. "I want you to route the main transporter controls through here so we can aim and fire them like a weapon. The angle of the beam relative to the *Enterprise* may change, but the vector will always remain oriented toward the same spot on the planet's surface."

The transporter technician glanced down at the spatial coordinates that had been sent to the engineering station by Riley and Tracey. When he looked back up at Uhura, his pale eyebrows had curved into a distinctly dubious arc. "We're aiming the transporters at that Janus Gate area again?"

"Yes."

Kyle cleared his throat gingerly. "Forgive me for asking, Lieutenant, but have you cleared this with the chief? If we're going to risk losing all the ship's power, I think he'd like to know about it in advance."

Uhura frowned at the skeptical tone of Kyle's voice, but she knew better than to reprimand him. As one of the ship's main transporter technicians, he reported directly to Montgomery Scott, and right now he was just doing his duty as an engineer. She said over her shoulder to Hadley, "Contact Lieutenant Commander Scott in his quarters and tell him I need to clear a bridge operation with him." Then she glanced back up at Kyle. Her awareness of how fast time was running out for the landing party put a sharp edge in her voice that even she could hear. "While we wait, Lieutenant Kyle, I suggest you transfer controls and aim the transporter beam. You'll need to make sure it just grazes the edge of this first set of coordinates—" She pointed at the flickering column of spatial data that was Riley's fix on the slowly moving Shechenag starship. "—then hits the Janus Gate as directly as possible."

"Aye-aye, sir." Whatever doubts he may have had, Kyle must have recognized from the intensity of Uhura's voice that there wasn't much leeway for delay. He seated himself at the engineering station and began programming it to take control of the main transporter beam, his long fingers not even hesitating over their work.

"I've got Lieutenant Commander Scott, sir." Lieutenant Hadley offered the frequency monitor to her, as if he'd already guessed that she'd prefer her conversation with Montgomery Scott to be semiprivate. As she crossed the bridge back to her old station, Uhura made a mental note to place a commendation for initiative in the young officer's personnel file. "He wants to know if you need him up on the bridge."

"I don't need you, sir," Uhura said into the transmitter. "I just need to clear a maneuver before I risk it."

"Whisht?" said a sleepy, Scottish voice in her ear. "I mean, what is it that you're wanting to do, lass?"

"The Shechenag are almost ready to place the last satellites in their defensive array. I have the *Enterprise* positioned so they're directly between us and the Janus Gate. I want to aim the main transporters to graze the Shechenag ship, as if we were trying to beam some of its hull down to the Janus Gate."

There was a short—and no longer sleepy—silence on the other end of the channel. "You're trying to get the Janus Gate to latch onto that alien ship and drain its power, the same way it bolluxed us up when we connected to it?"

"Yes, sir. Do I have your permission to try?"

The chief engineer blew out a gusty breath in her ear. "How much longer do we have before the shield closes up completely?"

Uhura glanced up at the planet on the viewscreen. Its opalescent glow was definitely brighter than before. "We're not sure, sir. Probably less than thirty minutes."

"And neither hide nor hair of Mr. Spock's shuttle to be seen?"

"No, sir."

This time, the sigh that echoed through the frequency monitor was much more resigned. "Then we'd better do something, hadn't we? Go ahead and try your maneuver, Lieutenant. You've got Kyle at the transporter controls, don't you?"

"Yes, sir."

"Good." In the distance, Uhura could hear the telltale hiss of a microfoam mattress decompacting as weight was removed from it. "Tell Kyle to shut the beam down at the first sign of a voltage fluctuation on the main access lines," Montgomery Scott ordered. "I'll head down to the engine room and make sure the warp core is shunted off from the ship's power circuits. Just in case the lad's aim with the transporter beam is as bad as his aim with darts," he added dryly. "Scott out."

Uhura handed the frequency monitor back to Hadley, and relayed the chief engineer's instructions to Kyle. He nodded, then added a few more lines of code to his rerouted transporter controls. "Do you want me to wait to make sure Commander Scott has time to get to the engine room?" he asked when he was done.

Uhura could hear the almost inaudible twitch of nervousness that lay beneath Kyle's question, probably because she was so nervous herself. Before she could be tempted to agree, she made herself turn and look up at Tlaoli. The dayside of the shielded planet was now a phosphorescent bone-white, while the nightside shimmered in the darkness of space like a drop of molten pearl.

"No," Uhura said sharply. "Mr. Alden, are we on station?"

"Right on station, sir."

"Mr. Riley, do we still have a precise fix on the Shechenag space-ship?"

"Down to one-tenth of a meter, sir."

Uhura would have liked to have taken a deep breath, but her abdominal muscles had locked so tight with tension that she couldn't manage it. She drew in a short, shallow breath instead, and hoped it didn't sound too much like a gasp. When she spoke, however, her voice didn't shake or quiver in the slightest. Uhura blessed her years of communications duty for that.

"Lieutenant Kyle, engage the transporter beam."

"Aye-aye, sir." The transporter technician's voice cracked with the tension Uhura had managed to hide, but to his credit he didn't hesitate. "Transporter beam engaged."

Unlike the phasers, there was no way to see the transporter beam shoot through space, and the lack of lights on the massive Shechenag starship made it hard to tell if any of its hull had been displaced by the beam. But Uhura knew the instant their beam hit the aliens' defensive shield. A bloom of fiery blue-white light erupted from the impact, then mushroomed across the opalescent surface, dissipating as it spread.

"What just happened, Mr. Kyle?" Uhura snapped.

The transporter technician tapped a query into his station desk. "It looks like the carrier wave never reached the planet, much less made a connection back for us to send anything along it." He threw a stymied look back over his shoulder at her. "Sir, our transporter beam just got completely absorbed by that defense shield out there."

# Chapter Nine

UHURA STARED UP AT Tlaoli on the viewscreen. Beyond the massive sil-houette of the Shechenag starship, there was still a visible smudge of shadow on the fiery white crescent of the planet's dayside, marking the place where Spock and Sulu had blasted through the aliens' defensive ar-ray. But the repairs that had already been done to the satellite network had stitched enough of that hole closed to make it look more like a puckered seam than a puncture. And most of the remaining darkness lay far to star-board of the Shechenag's slow-moving ship.

"There's still enough of a gap left for the shuttle to come through," Uhura said, thinking out loud. "That means there should be enough space for us to shoot a transporter beam through, too."

"But we're not in the right place to make that angle, sir," Kyle pointed out. "We can line up the *Enterprise,* the Shechenag, and the Janus Gate, but that doesn't necessarily mean we'll be shooting through the widest part of—"

"I've got it calculated, sir," Riley broke in abruptly. "We need to be about a hundred kilometers closer to the planet and almost over its north-ern pole to make the shot."

"Then let's get there." Uhura seated herself back into the captain's chair in case the course correction was more than their inertial dampeners could easily handle. "Send those coordinates over to the helm, Mr. Riley. Estimated time of arrival, Mr. Alden?"

"I'm already headed for the general area, sir. It should only take a minute or two to re-establish our station." The pilot checked his screen, then frowned across at his navigator. "Do we really need to be *that* close to the thermosphere?"

"It's an oblique shot," Riley and Kyle said in unison.

Lieutenant Alden nodded, and Uhura felt the *Enterprise* shudder a little as it cut across Tlaoli's gravity well at a less than ideal vector. A moment later, another series of bumps shook through the bridge as they encountered a gravitational anomaly. That was a good sign, Uhura reminded herself as she clenched her fingers tighter around the armrests of the captain's chair. It meant they were approaching the area where the ancient planet's mysterious deviations in gravity hadn't been damped out by the Shechenag defensive shield.

"Estimated time of arrival now, Mr. Alden?" Uhura hoped her voice didn't sound as desperate as she felt. The shadowy gap in the satellite-generated force field was getting smaller even as they approached.

"One point five minutes, sir."

A warning alarm went off somewhere on the back of the bridge, and Uhura heard Watkins swing around at his auxiliary station. "We're scraping the planet's thermosphere, Lieutenant," the engineer warned. "The screens are holding so far, but if we stay here too long, the thermal gradient may cause them to fail."

"Be ready to shoot that transporter beam as soon as we've hit the correct location, Mr. Kyle," Uhura ordered. "Mr. Alden, get us on station *now*."

"Aye, sir."

A minute was such a long time when you were balanced on the perilous edge of success and failure. Time for far too many quick, tense breaths, far too many thoughts of all the things that could go wrong...

"We're on station," Alden said.

"Coordinates of Shechenag ship updated and checked," Riley added in the same instant.

"Transporter beam locked and engaged," Kyle said, his voice overlapping the other two. "Beaming now."

There was another breathless pause, one in which Uhura forced herself not to spin around to watch the transporter technician at work. Instead, she stared at the dark, crawling shadow that was the Shechenag spaceship just below them. Nothing appeared to happen to its unlit hull, but nothing happened on the opalescent curve of the planet, either. Uhura waited as long as she could, then said, "Status report, Mr. Kyle?"

"That transporter beam went *somewhere,* sir," he said. "I got just a hint of return on the carrier wave, then it was gone, like we'd never sent it."

"Any power fluctuations?"

"None that I noticed."

"Sir!" Lieutenant Karen Tracey swung away from her science station. "I think something's happening to the Shechenag ship."

Uhura glanced up, but saw nothing obvious on the viewscreen. "What have you got?"

"My long-range scanners are picking up a lot of ionic discharge around their hull, but it's not contained or directed like an engine discharge would be. It's consistent with the signature of an unshielded ship falling into the planet's thermosphere."

"Or with them hitting their own defensive array?"

Tracey glanced down at her readings, then back up at Uhura with a little smile. "Yes, sir. It's consistent with that, too."

Uhura took a long, deep breath. It felt like her first in quite a while, and she heard it echoed in a soft chorus of relief around the bridge. "Congratulations, gentlemen," she said to her crew. "I think we've managed to stop the Shechenag from installing any more defensive satellites. All we have to do now is keep an eye on them in case they need a friendly lift to get out of their own force field." She looked back up at the silent white planet on the viewscreen, and felt a little of her triumph seep away. Tlaoli's dayside had nearly vanished from view, reminding Uhura that even if they kept an escape route open for their landing team, there were only a few hours left for them to use it. "And pray our shuttle returns while we still have time."

The explosion of light inside the Janus Gate took everyone by surprise. It didn't occur to Sulu until much later that he could easily have become part of that blast rather than merely part of its audience.

Ever since Sanner had returned from his marathon run and Spock had come out of his trance, the five remaining members of the landing party had been trying in vain to recharge the alien time transporter. A phaser blast from the ship had been their obvious first choice, but although the emergency communicator had been magnetically shielded to preserve its power, all it spat out at them when they tried to use it was a fierce crackle of static. Either the Janus Gate had just enough power left to disrupt any subspace transmissions that came near it, or, as Spock surmised, the Shechenag defensive shield around the planet was blocking all communicator frequencies.

After that, they tried powering the gate with whatever tools they had at hand. Yuki Smith discharged all of her phaser power cells by shooting her weapon directly into the device. The blue flame at its heart barely flickered in response. Sulu then suggested throwing their single photon grenade into it. Spock had vetoed that idea at first, but after they'd drained the power from all their other magnetically shielded instruments—including his own tricorder—with no apparent change in the Janus Gate, the Vulcan science officer reluctantly agreed to reconsider.

"We have no other energy reserves left, aside from the shuttle's warp core," Spock said thoughtfully. Although he moved a little more rigidly than usual, his voice had returned to its normal dispassionate tone. "We could allow the shuttle to crash on the surface above this chamber, but I am not certain that would allow for an efficient transfer of power into the Janus Gate. When the device's field strength is this low, its power-draining effects do not seem to extend far beyond this chamber."

Smith looked up from repacking her drained power cells and useless phaser rifle. They would have to resort to hand-to-hand combat if a Shechenag squadron attacked them now, Sulu thought. Of course, it might be worth it if they could toss the robotic aliens' power supplies into the gate when the fight was over.

"Is that why we could tromp around the cave for so long when we first came down here, sir, without noticing any problems in our instruments?" the security guard asked.

"Precisely the data point upon which I based my hypothesis, crewman," Spock said, and left Smith looking as if she wasn't quite sure what the answer to her question had been.

"Maybe that was why the ancient Tlaoli built their time transporter on a planet with gravitational anomalies," Zap Sanner speculated. "Once the planet made those ancient starships crash, then the Janus Gate could suck out their power."

Spock lifted one eyebrow at the cave geologist, but his comment wasn't the skeptical one Sulu expected. "You are assuming that the gravitational anomalies here are natural, Mr. Sanner. I am inclined to believe that the ancient Tlaoli may have actually created the instabilities themselves, perhaps by releasing a small singularity into the planet's metallic core—"

"Sir, the photon grenade," Chekov reminded him, although even as he spoke he looked a little alarmed by his own temerity in cutting through the scientists' discussion. "Do you think we should throw it into the gate?"

Spock paused, then gave the ensign a grave and reluctant nod. "Yes, I do. Endeavor to strike the center of the device, Mr. Chekov. We do not wish to damage the Janus Gate by hitting one of its outer arms—"

"Oh, no, you don't." Sulu intercepted Chekov before he could reach into Smith's pack of weaponry, extending himself with the same smooth lunge he used in fencing. "This was *my* idea. If the explosion gets thrown back from the gate, or makes one of those blue subspace rifts appear outside it, I'm going to be the one standing there, not you."

Chekov's dark eyes met his steadily. "But sir, I'm just—"

"—a member of this crew, like everybody else here," Sulu finished, cutting off whatever the younger man had meant to say. *I'm just an ensign? I'm just a new crewman, and more expendable than you?* Or maybe, *I'm just going to grow up to be someone bitter and hateful and I'd rather not do that?* In any case, it seemed even more important than usual to take the initiative on this particular plan. "Hand over that grenade to me, Mr. Smith."

The security guard paused for a moment, then carefully leaned around Chekov to give the small but powerful weapon to Sulu. "He gave me an order," she explained to the Russian. "And it *was* his idea."

Chekov looked frustrated and just a little rebellious. "At least let me come partway with you as backup," he said to Sulu stubbornly. The helmsman opened his mouth to say no, but saw the younger man's desperate need to be part of this rescue. It was almost as if he still blamed himself for that initial walk across the Janus chamber, when he'd inadvertently guided both Captain Kirk and himself into the time transporter's grasp.

"All right," Sulu said. "But you've got to stay at least a meter behind me."

"Yes, sir."

Sulu took a deep breath of air so warm and misty that it almost felt like he was back on Basaraba. Then he swung around and headed out into the Janus chamber with Chekov treading carefully one meter behind. Sulu glanced over at the curving metal arms of the device, and decided that the best place from which to toss the photon grenade would also be the safest place to stand: directly in front of the control station where Spock had stood to use the machine. That way, even if the grenade powered up the gate enough to create those drifting curtains of blue energy around it, Sulu—and Chekov behind him—would be standing inside the channel of protection the device made for its operator.

Sulu angled his carbide light down toward the ground, hoping to use the trace of Vulcan blood he'd seen before to lead him to the correct spot, but too much ice had melted since then. He had to rely on his memory instead, pausing once or twice to check his orientation against the Janus Gate, until he finally caught sight of the control panel Spock had used, and lined himself up with it. By then, Sulu could barely see the trio of glows that marked Spock, Sanner, and Smith watching them from across the cavern.

"I'm going to arm the grenade for time, not impact," he said over his shoulder to Chekov. "Just in case I miss getting it into the field generator."

"Good idea, sir. If it bounces back toward us, we'll have a chance to scoop it up and disarm it before it goes off."

Sulu snorted. "No, Mr. Chekov, we'll have a chance to run like hell. Are you ready?"

"Yes, sir."

Another deep breath of foggy air, and Sulu dug his fingers into the carefully recessed switch that activated the photon grenade's one minute timer. Then, with the same smooth movement he used to slide a riposte back under a fencing opponent's parry, he tossed the grenade up toward the Janus Gate. It sailed in a lazy arc directly toward the heart of flickering blue fire, erupting into a brilliant flash as soon as it hit the alien force field. Sulu hadn't expected the explosion to come before the timer triggered it—he jerked an arm up to shield his eyes, but it was too late to preserve the night sight he'd built up over hours of peering through the underground dimness. He kept his arm raised, waiting tensely for the shock wave that should have followed that explosion of powerful light, but not even a breath of wind hit his frost-burned face. The Janus Gate must have absorbed the grenade's charge before it could convert its light to thermal and kinetic energy.

"Did it recharge?" Sulu lowered his arm and blinked at the alien device. It looked shadowy and blurred, but, then, so did everything else in his light-dazzled vision. He swung around to squint at the equally murky figure in the darkness behind him. "Mr. Chekov, can you tell if the grenade recharged the gate?"

Instead of answering, the younger man's silhouette took a step closer to Sulu. "Sir, are you all right?"

"I'm just light-blinded. *Did the gate recharge?*"

The pale blur that was Chekov's face shifted from an oval to a crescent as he glanced from Sulu to the alien device behind him. "I don't think—" he began, then sucked in a startled breath. Before Sulu could ask what was wrong, or turn his puzzled squint back toward the Janus Gate, a pair of gloved hands clamped onto his shoulders and yanked him forward with one desperate and violent pull. Chekov threw himself in the same direction, boots scrabbling against the wet cavern floor with such ferocity that even in his blinded state Sulu knew he should keep on going. He hit the cavern wall before he saw it, then staggered back a step and gasped for air. Chekov caught at his shoulder again and shoved him onward along the wall, toward the cave threshold where reaching arms caught him and reeled him into the narrow mouth of the conduit passage.

"What—?" Sulu's question was cut off by the tidal wave of light that crashed over all of them from behind. Unlike the brief, blinding flash of the photon grenade, this light was the blue of hot flame, and it didn't die away. Instead it grew and grew, until the whole passage glowed with arc-discharge intensity. Sulu covered even his already blinded eyes, feeling tears of pain roll out from beneath his tightly closed eyelids as the light burned against them. He could feel the wave of intense cold that came after it, and hear the sudden fierce crackle as meltwater turned abruptly back to ice inside the chamber. The temperature-sensitive fibers of his caving suit swelled so fast he could feel the cloth ripple against his skin.

"Did I do that?" he asked when the fiercest part of the light-storm had passed. The other members of the cave team were all blinking and squinting as badly as he was in the blue radiance that bathed them, but Spock managed to get an eyebrow up in spite of that.

"Unlikely," the Vulcan said. "There was too much elapsed time between your grenade explosion and the Janus Gate's response." He eyed the blue glow, which had subsided now to the same kind of rippling light-waves they'd seen before. "This much power can only have come from the *Enterprise*. She either speculated correctly that we were in need of assistance—or she found it necessary to punch another hole in the Shechenag defensive array."

"Does that mean the Shechenag might have closed up our first exit hole?" Sanner asked. Sulu's vision was returning, and he could see the way Smith's and Chekov's faces both tightened at that suggestion. If Sanner was right, and they didn't get Captain Kirk back soon, they might find themselves trapped forever on this small, dead planet.

"You said you had another way to retrieve the captain," Sulu said to Spock. "Let's do it, now, before anything else happens to interfere."

"Very well," Spock said, and reached for him.

Kirk heard the horrible *smack!* of a high-speed projectile slamming into a human body as he threw himself to the floor, followed almost immediately by George's startled shout of alarm and the muffled thud of someone falling as a dead weight.

*Not the boy! Please, God, don't let them hit the boy!*

But he could hear the boy reassuring someone who'd called to him, in a startlingly calm voice for all that the pitch betrayed his fear. Kirk wedged himself into the corner made by the barricade and the corridor wall, his phaser close across his chest, and took stock of who'd been hit and how badly even as another fusillade of shots pummeled the front of the barricade.

Sulu crouched across the corridor from Kirk, carefully fitting the muzzle of his rifle between the edge of one crate and the wall so he could return fire. Back toward the bay door, George Kirk had his son pinned flat to the floor, shielding the boy with his own body while Chekov scrabbled to overturn the grav-sled between them and the attackers outside. The Russian's right hand left a splayed, bloody print wherever it touched, but whatever injury he'd taken didn't seem to slow him and Kirk couldn't worry about anyone who was still in a position to take care of himself. It was Giotto who had spilled the majority of the blood in the corridor. The security chief lay spread-eagled in the largest puddle, eyes fixed blindly up at the ceiling, not moving.

"Commander Kirk!" Kirk scrambled forward on hands and knees to grab Giotto's belt and drag him to a more protected location. "Keep working on that door! It's our only way out now."

Keeping his son close to his side, George edged back toward the big door a few feet at a time, hauling the grav-sled along behind them as a kind of portable shield. "I'll need his phaser," he called, to no one in particular, and Chekov darted to scoop up Giotto's abandoned weapon and underhand it to George's son on his way to Sulu's side of their beleaguered wall of crates.

The shooting outside paused, and Kirk wondered if their attackers actually had to stop and reload, or if they'd gone in search of more powerful weapons. He hauled Giotto mostly upright by the front of his cave jumper, ignoring the chief's shuddering gasp of pain as he propped him up against the corridor wall. Kirk had heard something once about keeping victims of chest wounds upright to prevent them from drowning in their own blood. He had no idea if this was true, but didn't know what else he could do for the man.

"How is he?"

Kirk spared Chekov only a glance, just long enough to see the look of bleak concern on his face as he submitted to Sulu's businesslike inspection of his own bleeding arm, and that he was in no immediate danger of dying. Still, the raw desperation in his eyes bothered Kirk more than he cared to admit. Kirk turned back to Giotto with a grim shake of his head. "Not good." He was still breathing, but even that sounded tenuous and fluid.

"Believe it or not, Captain, that might actually be a good thing." Sulu finished his examination and wiped both hands on the front of his jumper to clear them of blood. "It passed straight through," he told Chekov, picking up his own rifle again.

Chekov scowled with unconcealed anger. "I know it went through. How do you think Giotto got hit?"

Watching him snap the control on his rifle over to its multishot function, Kirk realized that Chekov was more angry at himself than at their attackers, as though he'd failed in some important duty by not stopping the projectile himself. He'd be a hard subordinate to keep alive for any length of time. Kirk wondered if this was a problem he was bound to face with the young man he'd left back on board the *Enterprise,* too, or if there was something about their unmentioned alternate future to blame.

As Chekov lifted the rifle over the top of the barricade to fire a blind salvo down the hall, Kirk asked Sulu, "Can you see anything from where you are?"

The other captain leaned to put one eye to the small crack he'd managed to insinuate between the crates. "Six gunmen, all natives." He waited through the next round of gunfire. "I don't think they have energy weapons, just projectiles."

That was one advantage. "Either unskilled workers or an advance guard," Kirk guessed. He followed Chekov's example and aimed a single phaser shot over the edge of the barricade on wide-dispersal stun. Native voices shouted in a mixture of anger and alarm, but Kirk heard the clatter of their retreat a few meters farther down the hall. "Now let's hope we can get that door open before one of them thinks to drag in an Orion pulse cannon."

"If we're here that long, we have more problems than just that door." Chekov raised up just high enough to glance over the rim of their barricade, squeezed off a shot at whatever he saw, then dropped back down to floor level again. He turned a furious glare on Sulu. "Where is he?"

The other captain remained calmly attentive to his spy hole. "Give it a minute."

"Why?" Chekov demanded. "They're twenty years in the future, dammit! They could put him in the device *six weeks* after we left, and he should still arrive the moment the man went down!"

Kirk followed the angry gesture thrown in his direction, and realized with a jolt that the "man" Chekov referred to was Giotto. He tightened his hand protectively on the security chief's shoulder. "Is this what you meant when you said Giotto was linked back to the device? That it would somehow replace him if he died?"

"No, that wasn't our plan." Sulu sat back from the barricade with a sigh, rubbing at his right wrist as though it pained him. "But that's something like how the device works. As long as you're healthy, it takes whatever version of you steps into the machine and uses that version to replace a damaged version of you from somewhere else in your timeline."

"Which means the younger version of him we lifted out when we came here should have shown up by now." Chekov's face was drawn with anxiety, and Kirk had a feeling there was more at stake in Giotto's failure to appear than was obvious to him at the moment.

"We're in!"

George's shout rang out just ahead of the bay door's loud exhalation, and the hatch rolled aside with a tremendous rumbling that made their metal crate barricade shiver and spread at the seams. Kirk lunged forward to steady the segment closest to him, and saw two of the Vragax outside break from their own cover to flee down the corridor back the way they'd come. He had a feeling that the Orions and whatever heavy weapons they still had at their disposal wouldn't be long in coming.

Shouldering up beside Chekov, Kirk slapped Sulu on the shoulder and motioned toward Giotto. "Get him inside the bay and loaded on board our transport. Chekov and I will cover you."

The older captain nodded, but it was a boy's voice that said, dismally, "There's only one seat."

Kirk twisted a look back over his shoulder, meeting his own eyes in the doorway even as a projectile burned past his ear so close that he heard the buzz of its passage. The boy was on his knees, as protected as possible, craning around the edge of the bulkhead with his eyes wide and hollow with despair. "It's a personal escape craft." Kirk knew he was trying to sound adult and brave, but he was too close to tears to be convincing. "There's only one seat. My dad says I can fit under the panel while he flies, but—"

"Go!" Kirk told him. Nothing else the boy had to say mattered.

"I'm not leaving you!"

*This isn't the shuttle!* Kirk wanted to shout at him. *I'm not Maione!* But he knew the boy wouldn't understand, not for another nineteen years.

Instead, it was Chekov who said, "Don't worry about us. We have our own escape route."

It occurred to Kirk that his young ensign was going to evolve into a rather accomplished liar.

"But I heard you," the boy protested, his hands clenching and unclenching on the bloodied floor. "Mr. Giotto isn't coming."

Chekov cracked open his rifle to expel a jammed projectile from the barrel. "Mr. Giotto was Plan A." He sounded much calmer than before, but his face was still grim and pale. "We still have Plan B."

The boy said nothing for a moment, and Kirk heard his father call, "Jimmy! We have to go, son!" from somewhere farther back in the shuttlebay. Instead of answering that shout, the boy asked, very quietly, "You really have a Plan B? You're not just lying to me."

For the first time, Chekov turned to look at him, and the sincerity in his expression made Kirk both angry and glad. "I wouldn't lie to you," the older man said, taking advantage of the strange, earnest trust in the boy's eyes in a way that made clear to Kirk he hadn't been the one to earn it in the first place. "We have a Plan B. Now go with your father."

The boy hesitated for another long, painful moment. Then, just before Kirk would have broken from the others to drag his younger self into the bay, the boy backed away from the doorway and let it roll shut behind him with a boom like distant thunder. As though that final sound were some sort of signal only he could understand, Chekov turned stonily back to the barricade, and away from their last chance of escaping Grex alive.

Kirk watched him reassemble his rifle and switch it back to single rate-of-fire. "I don't suppose we have something more than a good lie to fall back on."

The shuttle's launch roared through the corridor, toppling metal crates both across their barricade and around their Vragax attackers down the hall. "I didn't lie," Chekov said, charging the gauss rifle's barrel until the whole gun began to hum. "We really do have a Plan B." He looked up at Sulu, and Kirk saw the silent communication that passed between them even though he didn't know the language.

But he recognized the shocked disbelief on the other captain's face an instant before Chekov swung the rifle toward Sulu—and fired.

For a moment, Sulu thought the Vulcan was intending to use him as a support because he no longer had enough strength to walk back out to the Janus Gate by himself. But when Spock's fingers tightened around his shoulder like a vise and steered him toward the blue-lit chamber with ir-resistible Vulcan strength, Sulu realized he was going to be used for something more than just a crutch. A jolt of shock went through him when he realized Spock was guiding him toward the far side of the time transporter, where Giotto had stood—and then vanished—just a short while before.

"You don't need to push me, Commander," Sulu said. The words were prosaic enough, but he hoped they would convey his determination to carry out whatever obligation his duty as a Starfleet officer required. "I can see well enough to walk out on my own."

The Vulcan science officer relaxed the intensity of his grip, but did not let go of Sulu's shoulder. "You have never approached this part of the device, Lieutenant," he replied calmly. "With the amount of power in the Janus Gate now, the protected area leading to it has undoubtedly nar-rowed."

Sulu blinked and swung his head back and forth so he could use the more light-sensitive edges of his vision. "I see it." Ribbons of intense blue fire twisted and burned on either side of the chamber, but a channel of clear air kept them from meeting each other. "I can get there from here, Commander."

His voice must have carried his willingness clearly enough for even a Vulcan to comprehend. Spock removed his hand from Sulu's shoulder. "I believe I will be able to send you directly to Captain Kirk on our first at-tempt, but if you see Basaraba instead, tell me immediately. And what-ever happens, Mr. Sulu, do not release those supports."

Sulu followed his gaze to the oddly curved attachments projecting out from this side of the alien time transporter and felt his fingers curl in-voluntarily, as if to memorize the muscle motion he would need to keep himself linked to Tlaoli and the present. "Aye, sir," he said, and started down the evanescent path toward the roiling blue fireball that was the Janus Gate.

Despite his stiffness, Spock moved back around the edge of the chamber quickly enough that he was already in place by the time Sulu had summoned up the will to place his hands on the black metal supports. Runnels of liquid blue light already crawled along the arms that enclosed the gate's subspace field generator, only a few centimeters away from his fingers. Sulu forced himself to stand still as those streaks of light spiraled toward him.

"I have set the machine for viewing mode," Spock said calmly. Sulu nodded, trying not to think of what had happened the last time they had tried to use the Janus Gate to peer into the past. It didn't seem as if the room was quite as bright now as it had been then, but there was no guarantee the *Enterprise* wouldn't send another phaser shot or transporter beam down at any moment, adding more energy to the alien power storage system. "This should take you directly to—"

Sulu gasped, then nearly choked on the intense bite of cold air inside his unwary throat. There had been no warning, just an instant of disorientation and a sense of sudden jarring—then he was standing somewhere completely different. An echoing space like a corridor or a shuttlebay, brightly lit by red-tinged photon lamps and echoing with the *spang* and *whirr* of projectile fire. Sulu glanced around, finding himself just barely able to swing his head and completely unable to move aside from that.

"This definitely isn't Basaraba," he informed a Spock he could no longer see, and saw an abrupt jerk of motion off to one side, as if someone else had heard and recognized his voice.

"*Sulu!* Here!"

He knew that harsh Russian-accented voice, although it grated now in a painful way it had never done before, even in their most desperate moments together on Basaraba. Sulu clenched his hands around the cold metal supports he could still feel back on Tlaoli, and with an enormous effort slewed himself around to look in that direction. He could see two faces swing up to stare at him from behind what looked like a tumble of battered metal crates. Gunfire still blazed out across the room behind them, but neither man was shooting back at their attackers. Instead, it looked as if they were huddled over two fallen comrades—one propped awkwardly against the corridor wall, the other cradled inside Chekov's bloodstained arms.

"*Go!*" the older Russian said, his voice cutting like a ragged knife through the clatter of weapons fire. "Take Giotto and *go!*"

The other crouching man rocked back on his heels. "You knew he'd come," he said, in a voice Sulu recognized even when it sounded as shocked and exhausted as this. "It's because of the way the time machine works—"

"That you're going to be able to get back to where you should be, and erase everything that has happened in my lifetime!" Chekov reached out with a long black rifle, but all he did with it was shove Kirk farther away from him. "Now *go!*"

The captain scrambled to his feet and turned to heave Giotto upright, in preparation for hefting him in a fireman's carry. Sulu heard the security chief groan in pain, and with another surge of sheer willpower managed to pull himself closer to both men.

"Mr. Spock, I have them! I have Captain Kirk and Commander Giotto." Sulu almost reached out with his real hands, but caught himself just before his fingers slipped off the cold metal arms of the Janus Gate. This required a mental effort, not a physical one. He felt his teeth dig into his lip, felt blood drip and then freeze against his face as he forced himself to stretch the disembodied shadows of what would have been arms if he had really been present in this timeline. Something as sharp and unpleasant as an electric shock jolted through him. A flash of eerie blue light leaped out from where Sulu seemed to stand and connected with Giotto. An instant later, the security chief was gone.

Sulu heard a distant sound of startled shrieks and wails of fear, and the gunfire stopped abruptly. In the ringing silence that followed, he could hear Chekov whispering, over and over again, "...I'm sorry...I'm so sorry..."

Kirk threw one last glance over his shoulder, and in the blue light that Sulu realized must be coming from himself, he saw compassion blossom on the captain's face. "He knew—" he said softly. But before he could complete the sentence, another electric jolt shuddered through Sulu, and Kirk disappeared as well.

But something still connected Sulu himself to this past he'd never lived through. He squinted through the sterile glare of reddish light, not at Chekov, but at the slumped figure in his protective grasp. There was no way to see the dead man's face, turned as it was into his first officer's bloodstained shoulder, but Sulu recognized that wiry build. He saw it in the mirror every day.

"You shot him." It wasn't an accusation so much as a belated realization, an understanding of how Spock had managed to send him to a place he'd never been. The glare Chekov gave him scorched his face with embarrassment. Sulu suddenly knew what Kirk had been trying to tell the older Russian. "I know you only did it to get me here. He must have known, too—"

"He didn't know anything." The older man's voice had thickened to a barely recognizable mutter. "Except that he was going to die—"

"To keep the Gorn invasion from happening," Sulu insisted. "And you know he would have wanted—"

He broke off, because it was clear his words weren't needed anymore. Chekov had lifted his head, an odd, arrested expression chasing the pain out of his eyes for the first time Sulu could remember. "Do you hear that?" he asked softly.

But before Sulu could reply, the Russian officer's crouched figure, and that of his crumpled captain, rippled once as if a wind had blown through them, then faded into darkness and were gone.

# Chapter Ten

ONE MILKY THREAD at a time, the alien ship spun its slow cocoon around the blurry red disk that was Tlaoli. Kirk had started out counting each of the tiny satellites as the big ship placed them, but soon lost track as the white cataract they constructed grew too bright and dense. Now, the black surface of the ship stood in stark silhouette against that glowing backdrop. Soon, the alien protection sphere would be complete, and not even a hint of the planet's russet surface would be visible then. Only the Shechenag knew what would happen after that.

*Enterprise* had towed the big ship out of the planet's thermosphere the moment the shuttle cleared the satellite field. They'd deposited the Shechenag safely beyond the range of the Janus Gate's power-draining effect, even though Spock believed the device was too low on power now to reach beyond its own atmosphere in search of more. Kirk tried to explain the concept "Better safe than sorry," but only earned himself a stoic Vulcan lecture on the illogic of making decisions based on statistically unlikely outcomes.

It took the Shechenag less than four hours to reinstate power and return to their self-appointed task. They'd answered no hails in that time, and sent out no signals that Uhura could detect. They might have been any other soulless force of nature for all that they seemed interested in discussing their mission with the humans or finding out how the final activation of the Janus Gate had been resolved. Maybe they already knew. Kirk felt a strange guilt at having caused such vast upset and disruption for another race, like a child whose innocent game of catch inadvertently destroyed a priceless stained glass window. He caught himself wishing he could somehow go back and prevent any of it from happening.

*But that's how we got here in the first place.*

"You sent for me, Captain."

Kirk drew his attention away from Tlaoli's slowly accreting shroud, back to this dark observation deck and the officer who'd just entered it behind him. Spock's reflection in the transparent aluminum window gazed back at him with the same cool patience Kirk had been trying to get used to ever since promoting the Vulcan after Gary Mitchell's death. He remembered the pain he'd seen on that face only a few days before, when the Psi 2000 virus uncovered a cache of buried emotion so raw it would humiliate even the sternest Vulcan. And he wondered which Spock was the one he'd begun to let into his confidence—the one who admitted to loving his human mother, or the one he was afraid stood behind him now.

He turned his focus back outward toward the Shechenag ship. "Yes, Mr. Spock, I did." Two more satellites drifted neatly into place while he struggled with how to approach what was bothering him. "I've been thinking about the events leading up to my . . . retrieval from the past," he said at last.

Spock nodded as he stepped closer to the long window and joined Kirk in studying the alien construction. "And certain—" He paused to choose his words, and the unexpected show of consideration irritated Kirk. "—emotionally charged aspects of the events disturb you."

"You knew." He hadn't wanted to sound accusatory, but found he couldn't hide his anger and disappointment despite his best intentions. "After Giotto was accidentally transported, there was no way to reestablish a link to Grex without using someone who was already there." He looked at the Vulcan bluntly. "You knew Chekov was going to kill Sulu to make that link available."

"Indeed." Kirk knew it was irrational to expect remorse in the Vulcan's tone, but he still found himself wanting something more than mere logical acceptance of what had happened. When Spock gave it to him, however, it was in a very different form than he'd imagined. "Commander Chekov informed me of his intentions before the transfer was attempted."

Kirk swallowed around the sudden unpleasant lurch in his stomach. He thought he'd been prepared for where this conversation would take them—into the unsavory reality of his alien first officer convincing a subordinate human to do something unthinkably merciless. It had never occurred to him that the human involved had actually volunteered for the task.

"When we returned to the Janus Gate against the Shechenag's wishes," Spock continued, "I calculated a significant probability that they would endeavor to regain control over the gate and, in so doing, interrupt Mr. Giotto's contact with the device. If that occurred and Mr. Giotto was rendered unconscious or even killed, there would have been no other way to reestablish our link to Grex. It was an unfortunate weakness in our plan, and one which Commander Chekov identified without input from me." He seemed to consider for a moment whether or not to go on. "Unfortunately, we had already determined that certain aspects of Commander Chekov's personality made it impossible to use him as a focal point for the device. Our only recourse was to utilize Captain Sulu in that capacity. And in order for the device to work properly, Captain Sulu could not be informed of that in advance."

Kirk didn't know which part of the solution seemed most cruel, being the man who didn't know how his life was going to end, or being the man who knew he was going to end it.

"You must understand," Spock said, with a gentleness Kirk didn't think he'd ever heard in that voice before. "Captain Sulu and Commander Chekov were fully aware that your retrieval would result in the negation of the timeline representing the world they knew. Rescuing you from the past meant the end of their existence, regardless of how it was accomplished." When Kirk said nothing in response, the Vulcan reached out and touched him lightly on the sleeve. "Jim, it was a future they would have done anything to prevent."

*And one of them did.*

"But what if this wasn't enough?" He looked up at his first officer, his hands curling tight around the rail at his waist. "What if *I'm* not enough? Spock, a man killed his best friend because he believed I could change the world. Is any one person really that important?"

One of the things he valued most about Spock was that he earnestly considered any question you asked him, no matter how unanswerable. "One person," the Vulcan said at last, "perhaps not. But one event can change the course of history. And in the future they remembered, it was a single encounter with the Gorn which laid the foundation for the Federation's destruction." He met Kirk's gaze without flinching. "As captain of the *Enterprise,* you will be the man who determines the outcome of that encounter."

Kirk wasn't sure he found that reassuring. He tried to imagine Gary Mitchell as a starship commander—straightforward, hotheaded Gary Mitchell. He'd been a good man at heart, but Kirk also knew that Gary hadn't been the sort of man to think about things too deeply. He didn't doubt for a moment that Gary would kill an alien starship commander if he believed it was the only way to save his crew. But would Kirk really do anything so very different? Short of sacrificing his own ship and crew, what other choices would he have?

Kirk stared out at the Shechenag and their nearly completed array, although they weren't the aliens he was thinking about. "So when we meet the Gorn at this planet called Cestus Three, all I have to do is figure out how not to irritate the Metrons—or, failing that, how to keep the Gorn commander alive when he's doing his best to kill me." He angled a wry grin up at Spock. "And I'll have to do it all with no memory of anything we found out here, won't I? With no idea what it means to the Federation if I fail."

The Vulcan actually seemed a little flustered by the question. "I cannot answer that with any certainty."

No data, of course. No other starship had been flung backward in time, then had to wait for the timeline to heal itself just to find out what they would or wouldn't remember. Or maybe they had, and the lack of evidence only served to prove Kirk's suspicions.

"Maybe it's better if we don't remember," he said aloud, letting his science officer off the hook both in relation to his question and the horrible events that had returned him to the *Enterprise*. "Maybe it isn't good to know too much about the consequences of the decisions we make." He tried on a resigned smile that probably looked as inauthentic as it felt. "Thank you, Mr. Spock. You're dismissed."

Spock merely lifted one eyebrow and dipped his own head in return. "You are welcome, Captain." Then he backed gracefully to the door, and let himself out.

Kirk watched him leave, wondering if humans were as incomprehensible to Vulcans as Vulcans sometimes seemed to him. And wondering if Vulcans valued the friendships possible in such combinations, or merely viewed them as the unavoidable by-product of close association.

*I have to be fair to the Gorn.* He watched the Shechenag place the last link in their network, saw the gleaming cataract obscuring Tlaoli swell brighter and brighter. *If I remember nothing else about these three days, I have to somehow remember that.* He didn't know who the Gorn were, or what they looked like, or how he could possibly alter the course of a future so terrible that men would kill people they loved in an effort to avoid it. But as the brilliant shell around Tlaoli spilled over into complete invisibility, he realized that there would be nothing here to see or find, nothing outside himself to remind him. It really would all come down to him, and how he responded to a single alien commander when he thought all other choices were gone.

*I have to be fair to the Gorn. No matter what happens, I have to be fair—*

It was odd, Uhura reflected, but it felt as if it had been a long time since she'd been able to go to the rec room and eat a normal, leisurely meal.

She took her time at the menu panel, finally selecting a type of Basque seafood crepe that she had never tried before and a chocolate-hazelnut croissant for dessert. Then she spent almost as long deciding which kind of tea would best complement her dinner. It felt like a luxury just to be able to think about things as trivial as food, although if Uhura really cast her mind back, she couldn't remember anything much more important happening during the past few days. Still, there was no telling what urgent mission the *Enterprise* might be sent on now that their three-day jaunt into the past had come to an end and they were resuming normal Starfleet duties. She decided to just enjoy the sense of tranquility while it lasted and not worry about the future.

As she paused to stir honey into her pot of silver-thread tea, Uhura noticed a young security guard fidgeting indecisively at the edge of the eating area, her own supper tray tucked under one arm. The young woman's frank and cheerful face sparked a vague memory of having met her on some past landing party or other, and as she came up beside her, Uhura gave her a friendly nod of greeting.

"Waiting for a table to open?" she asked, conversationally.

"Uh...no, Lieutenant. Not exactly." The security guard looked a little abashed, but only a little. "There's a guy sitting all by himself over there," she confided. "I was thinking I'd go sit with him, because I'm really sure I met him once, but I can't remember his name."

Uhura followed the direction of her glance to where a dark-haired young command ensign sat alone at the end of one table, gazing rather disconsolately down at his plate. "Oh, I know him," she said. "Come on. I'll pretend to introduce you and then if it turns out that he already knows you, we can all laugh about it."

"All right." The young woman followed her readily enough through the maze of tables. "My name's Yuki Smith, sir. Just in case you weren't sure."

Uhura tossed a smile back over her shoulder. "I think I knew that...but it never hurts to remind a senior officer who you are when you're new on board."

"That's for sure," Smith agreed. "I could have sworn Chief Giotto had me slated for the next landing party that went out, but he must have mixed me up with someone else, because the roster came out today and I'm on ship duty for the next three missions."

The dark-haired ensign looked up in surprise when they halted beside him, pushing his chair back and starting to rise despite the fact that it looked as if he'd barely touched his dinner. "Do you need this table, sir? I can move—"

"But then we'd just have to follow you," Uhura replied, then laughed as his surprised look turned into something closer to alarm. "I came over to introduce you to someone I thought you'd like to meet. Yuki Smith, this is—"

She hadn't realized, right up to the very second that she was about to say his name, that she didn't actually know it. Of course, she knew it. For some reason it had just slipped off the tip of her tongue, the way words could do when you were very tired and sleepy. Although after three uneventful days of rest and recuperation from the Psi 2000 virus, right now Uhura didn't even have that excuse to justify her inexplicable lapse.

Her training as a professional communications officer stood her in good stead, however. "I'm sorry," she said to the young man, as gracefully as she would have apologized if she'd mistakenly used an Orion frequency to hail an Andorian vessel. "I know I should remember your name, but I just—forgot it."

"It's Chekov, sir. Pavel Chekov." His Russian accent seemed familiar, and he returned Yuki Smith's nod of greeting as if she were someone he already knew, but he eyed Uhura with real puzzlement. "I'm not sure why you should remember me, sir. I'm new on board, and I haven't done a turn at communications duty."

"Yet," Uhura said, seating herself at the table with her supper. The more she thought about it, the less able she was to pin down why she'd been so sure she knew this young man. But even if she didn't, it never hurt to let junior officers think that their seniors were keeping track of them at all times.

A smiling Yuki Smith took the chair opposite Chekov and pointed at his dinner. "What's that you're eating? It looks interesting."

"I'm not sure." The young Russian glanced down at the spongy round of pan bread with its colorful heaps of pureed legumes and stewed meats. "It seemed like something I should try . . . but now I'm not sure what parts of it are safe to eat."

"Northern African stews can be pretty spicy," Uhura agreed, as she dug into her seafood crepe. "I'd watch out for the red ones, if I were you. The yellow ones are probably milder."

"How *much* milder?" he asked worriedly.

"Here, I can taste it for you and let you know if it's okay." Smith stuck the tip of her fork into one of the yellow stews and lifted a morsel to her lips. A moment later, her cheerful face turned bright red and she reached abruptly for her water glass. "*Wow.* If that's mild, I'd hate to taste the hot ones."

"Yes." Chekov regarded his meal gloomily. "That's what I was afraid of."

A fourth chair squeaked against the decking, and Uhura glanced up to see Sulu plunk himself next to Chekov with all the familiarity of an old friend. "Hey," the pilot said. "What's good for dinner?"

"*Not* the North African platter," Yuki Smith advised him. "Unless you're really mad at the roof of your mouth. Sir," the security guard added belatedly, as if she'd just noticed his rank.

Sulu glanced from her to Chekov, then across the table at Uhura. She saw the same sudden lack of certainty in his dark eyes that she'd felt a moment before and took pity on him. "Lieutenant Sulu, I think you know Pavel Chekov and Yuki Smith."

"I think so, too." Was it Uhura's imagination, or did Sulu sound just the slightest bit puzzled by that fact. "Aren't you going to eat any of that food, Chekov?"

"No, sir." An unexpected glint of humor flashed in the younger man's eyes. "I'm just trying to decide whether to take it to the food disposal chute or a hazardous waste port."

"Here, give it to me." Sulu ripped off an edge of the spongy bread and scooped up some of the darkest red stew, making both Chekov and Smith wince in anticipation. But the pilot's complexion never changed as he ate it. "So," he said to Uhura around another mouthful. "I hear you're having a dinner party for Riley?"

She nodded. "To make him feel a little better, after what happened back at Psi 2000."

"I assume I'm invited since I made an idiot of myself back there, too. Who else is coming?"

Uhura glanced across the mess hall to where the ordinance and weapons officers had gathered for their meal. Two of them sat a small but significant space apart from the others. "Well, I *was* going to invite Angela Martine and Robbie Tomlinson, but apparently they have other plans."

Sulu followed her gaze, his eyebrows lifting. "Huh. Since when have those two been an item?"

"I'm not sure," Uhura admitted. "I hope they don't get in trouble for dating within the same department . . . but they do make a cute couple." Her eyes fell on a closer couple, one of whom was shyly offering the other half of her sandwich. "Are you two free for dinner tomorrow night?"

Chekov choked on his first bite, and Sulu had to lean over to thump the ensign between the shoulder blades before he could answer. While she was waiting, Uhura heard the scientific discussion at the table next to theirs rise to a heated pitch.

"—theoretically possible, Zap, but why are you even worrying about it?" said an exasperated Germanic voice. "I've never heard of any caves with those kinds of thermal gradients."

"Well, geez, Jaeger, we're on a five-year, deep-space mission here. You don't think we might run into *some* kind of cave we've never seen before while we're out here?"

"I'm sure we will. But I'm not going to waste *my* time trying to balance a thermodynamic equation for something that might not even exist. And even if it did, this ridiculous notion of endothermic energy storage—"

"I don't know if I *can* come to your dinner party, sir," Chekov said, when he'd finally regained his breath. "I mean...I think I'm scheduled for a second-shift turn in astrophysics."

"I know Lieutenant Boma pretty well," Uhura assured him. "I think I can arrange a change in shift for you. Can you come, too, Yuki?"

"I sure can. Thanks, Lieutenant." The security guard caught sight of the wall chronometer and made a dismayed noise. "Speaking of shifts, I'm going to be late for mine in another minute. You can have the rest of my fries, too, Pavel. See you guys tomorrow!"

They waved her good-bye, then finished their meals in an oddly companionable silence. "I'm headed down for the gym," Sulu said, as he rolled up the last rag of bread and popped it into his mouth. "You want to come along, Chekov?"

The Russian gave him a worried look. "You're not going to practice fencing, are you, sir?"

"Not for a long time," Sulu assured him emphatically. "I was just going to use the weights and punching bags." He rose to his feet and gave the younger man a friendly tap on the shoulder. "Who knows, you might get lucky and have Captain Kirk ask you to be his sparring partner. It's always good to catch the captain's eye when you're one of the new scuts on board. Otherwise you'll never get picked for a landing party."

"Knocking me down might make the captain remember me," Chekov agreed, following Sulu toward the door. "But I don't think it will get me any closer to a landing party. In fact, if I was the captain—"

Uhura finished the rest of her croissant in quiet and happy tranquility. The best part about serving on the *Enterprise,* she thought, was having so many good crewmates to work with that you were always meeting new ones even years into the mission. And wasn't it interesting how it sometimes seemed as if you had known them all along...

"I'm glad someone's happy around here," said McCoy's amused voice behind her, and Uhura realized with a little start of embarrassment that she had been humming one of her favorite songs beneath her breath.

"If you listened to Spock, you'd think the entire galaxy was coming to an end."

Uhura scooted aside politely to let the ship's doctor and chief science officer sit down with their own dinners. It was typical of them, she thought, to share a meal even as they argued through one of their philosophical disagreements.

"I made no such statement, Doctor," said the Vulcan, calmly. "I merely pointed out that we have no logical way of knowing if our three-day journey into the past had any permanent effects on our future."

"Well, I don't feel any different than I did before we left Psi 2000," McCoy retorted. "Do you, Lieutenant?"

Uhura considered that question for a moment. "A little more tired," she decided, and saw the concerned look Dr. McCoy gave her. "I know, report to sickbay for a checkup," she said before he could. "I will, sir, but I think it's just the work we've all been doing. The last three days went past in such a blur..."

"My point, precisely," said Spock. "No one on the crew seems to have very clear memories of what we spent the last three days doing. I can only conclude that we have somehow merged with or been overlain by the versions of ourselves which already existed in the timeline before we returned to it, whose memories do not include the duplicated period of time."

"That doesn't sound very logical to me," McCoy retorted. "That other version of the *Enterprise* went to Psi 2000 and then got thrown back in time. It didn't stick around to merge with us."

"Not in our original timeline," Spock agreed. "But if we created changes in the timeline while we were duplicating ourselves, it is possible that we altered our own future enough to slide into a parallel timestream where we did not go to Psi 2000—"

"Not according to my medical records, which still show that I had to give viral antitoxin to about two hundred crewmen infected with the Psi 2000 virus!" The doctor pointed across the table with his fork. "Face it, Spock. This is all just wishful thinking, because you want to have been right about the dangers of going back in time."

The science officer arched a disdainful eyebrow. "Unlike you, Doctor, I do not attach emotional desires to my scientific hypotheses. I am merely attempting to explain certain anomalies that I have observed in the memories of the crew since we have returned to our proper place in time."

"I don't have any logical rationale for saying this, Mr. Spock," Uhura said quietly. "But if we *did* alter the timeline when we were back in the past... I have a feeling that we did it for the better."

"Me, too." McCoy waved his fork as if it were a triumphal flag. "That's two votes to your one, Spock. We win."

The Vulcan looked pained. "That is the most illogical way of confirming a hypothesis that I have ever heard you use, Doctor. And I have heard you use quite a few completely illogical thought processes..."

"It's just as logical as saying that we've slipped into some different timestream that nobody knows is different. What about that favorite saying of yours, Spock: a difference that makes no difference is no difference? Doesn't that apply here?"

"Indeed, Doctor, but you have not yet convinced me that there is no difference. If you had taken the time to examine the evidence before you made up your mind, rather than afterward—"

Uhura slid out of her seat and headed for the rec room door, smiling as she heard the familiar debate roll on without her. Mr. Spock might have been right about the unknowable impact of their three-day journey into the past, she thought. But it was reassuring to see that some things never changed.

**Look for STAR TREK fiction from Pocket Books**

**Star Trek®**

*Enterprise: The First Adventure* • Vonda N. McIntyre
*Strangers From the Sky* • Margaret Wander Bonanno
*Final Frontier* • Diane Carey
*Spock's World* • Diane Duane
*The Lost Years* • J.M. Dillard
*Prime Directive* • Judith and Garfield Reeves-Stevens
*Probe* • Margaret Wander Bonanno
*Best Destiny* • Diane Carey
*Shadows on the Sun* • Michael Jan Friedman
*Sarek* • A.C. Crispin
*Federation* • Judith and Garfield Reeves-Stevens
*Vulcan's Forge* • Josepha Sherman & Susan Shwartz
*Mission to Horatius* • Mack Reynolds
*Vulcan's Heart* • Josepha Sherman & Susan Shwartz
*The Eugenics Wars: The Rise and Fall of Khan Noonien Singh,*
    *Books One* and *Two* • Greg Cox
*The Last Round-Up* • Christie Golden
Novelizations
*Star Trek: The Motion Picture* • Gene Roddenberry
*Star Trek II: The Wrath of Khan* • Vonda N. McIntyre
*Star Trek III: The Search for Spock* • Vonda N. McIntyre
*Star Trek IV: The Voyage Home* • Vonda N. McIntyre
*Star Trek V: The Final Frontier* • J.M. Dillard
*Star Trek VI: The Undiscovered Country* • J.M. Dillard
*Star Trek Generations* • J.M. Dillard
*Starfleet Academy* • Diane Carey
Star Trek books by William Shatner with Judith and Garfield Reeves-Stevens
*The Ashes of Eden*
*The Return*
*Avenger*
*Star Trek: Odyssey* (contains *The Ashes of Eden*, *The Return*, and *Avenger*)
*Spectre*
*Dark Victory*
*Preserver*

#1 • *Star Trek: The Motion Picture* • Gene Roddenberry
#2 • *The Entropy Effect* • Vonda N. McIntyre
#3 • *The Klingon Gambit* • Robert E. Vardeman
#4 • *The Covenant of the Crown* • Howard Weinstein
#5 • *The Prometheus Design* • Sondra Marshak & Myrna Culbreath
#6 • *The Abode of Life* • Lee Correy
#7 • *Star Trek II: The Wrath of Khan* • Vonda N. McIntyre
#8 • *Black Fire* • Sonni Cooper
#9 • *Triangle* • Sondra Marshak & Myrna Culbreath
#10 • *Web of the Romulans* • M.S. Murdock
#11 • *Yesterday's Son* • A.C. Crispin
#12 • *Mutiny on the Enterprise* • Robert E. Vardeman
#13 • *The Wounded Sky* • Diane Duane
#14 • *The Trellisane Confrontation* • David Dvorkin
#15 • *Corona* • Greg Bear

#72 • *The Better Man* • Howard Weinstein
#73 • *Recovery* • J.M. Dillard
#74 • *The Fearful Summons* • Denny Martin Flinn
#75 • *First Frontier* • Diane Carey & Dr. James I. Kirkland
#76 • *The Captain's Daughter* • Peter David
#77 • *Twilight's End* • Jerry Oltion
#78 • *The Rings of Tautee* • Dean Wesley Smith & Kristine Kathryn Rusch
#79 • *Invasion!* #1: *First Strike* • Diane Carey
#80 • *The Joy Machine* • James Gunn
#81 • *Mudd in Your Eye* • Jerry Oltion
#82 • *Mind Meld* • John Vornholt
#83 • *Heart of the Sun* • Pamela Sargent & George Zebrowski
#84 • *Assignment: Eternity* • Greg Cox
#85-87 • *My Brother's Keeper* • Michael Jan Friedman
    #85 • *Republic*
    #86 • *Constitution*
    #87 • *Enterprise*
#88 • *Across the Universe* • Pamela Sargent & George Zebrowski
#89-94 • *New Earth*
    #89 • *Wagon Train to the Stars* • Diane Carey
    #90 • *Belle Terre* • Dean Wesley Smith with Diane Carey
    #91 • *Rough Trails* • L.A. Graf
    #92 • *The Flaming Arrow* • Kathy and Jerry Oltion
    #93 • *Thin Air* • Kristine Kathryn Rusch & Dean Wesley Smith
    #94 • *Challenger* • Diane Carey
#95-96 • *Rihannsu* • Diane Duane
    #95 • *Swordhunt*
    #96 • *Honor Blade*
#97 • *In the Name of Honor* • Dayton Ward

**Star Trek®: The Original Series**

*The Janus Gate* • L.A. Graf
    #1 • *Present Tense*
    #2 • *Future Imperfect*
    #3 • *Past Prologue*
*Errand of Vengeance* • Kevin Ryan
    #1 • *The Edge of the Sword*

**Star Trek: The Next Generation®**

    *Metamorphosis* • Jean Lorrah
    *Vendetta* • Peter David
    *Reunion* • Michael Jan Friedman
    *Imzadi* • Peter David
    *The Devil's Heart* • Carmen Carter
    *Dark Mirror* • Diane Duane
    *Q-Squared* • Peter David
    *Crossover* • Michael Jan Friedman
    *Kahless* • Michael Jan Friedman
    *Ship of the Line* • Diane Carey
    *The Best and the Brightest* • Susan Wright
    *Planet X* • Michael Jan Friedman
    *Imzadi II: Triangle* • Peter David
    *I, Q* • John de Lancie & Peter David
    *The Valiant* • Michael Jan Friedman
    *The Genesis Wave, Books One, Two,* and *Three* • John Vornholt

*Immortal Coil* • Jeffrey Lang
*A Hard Rain* • Dean Wesley Smith
*The Battle of Betazed* • Charlotte Douglas & Susan Kearney
Novelizations
*Encounter at Farpoint* • David Gerrold
*Unification* • Jeri Taylor
*Relics* • Michael Jan Friedman
*Descent* • Diane Carey
*All Good Things...* • Michael Jan Friedman
*Star Trek: Klingon* • Dean Wesley Smith & Kristine Kathryn Rusch
*Star Trek Generations* • J.M. Dillard
*Star Trek: First Contact* • J.M. Dillard
*Star Trek: Insurrection* • J.M. Dillard

#1 • *Ghost Ship* • Diane Carey
#2 • *The Peacekeepers* • Gene DeWeese
#3 • *The Children of Hamlin* • Carmen Carter
#4 • *Survivors* • Jean Lorrah
#5 • *Strike Zone* • Peter David
#6 • *Power Hungry* • Howard Weinstein
#7 • *Masks* • John Vornholt
#8 • *The Captain's Honor* • David & Daniel Dvorkin
#9 • *A Call to Darkness* • Michael Jan Friedman
#10 • *A Rock and a Hard Place* • Peter David
#11 • *Gulliver's Fugitives* • Keith Sharee
#12 • *Doomsday World* • Carter, David, Friedman & Greenberger
#13 • *The Eyes of the Beholders* • A.C. Crispin
#14 • *Exiles* • Howard Weinstein
#15 • *Fortune's Light* • Michael Jan Friedman
#16 • *Contamination* • John Vornholt
#17 • *Boogeymen* • Mel Gilden
#18 • *Q-in-Law* • Peter David
#19 • *Perchance to Dream* • Howard Weinstein
#20 • *Spartacus* • T.L. Mancour
#21 • *Chains of Command* • W.A. McCay & E.L. Flood
#22 • *Imbalance* • V.E. Mitchell
#23 • *War Drums* • John Vornholt
#24 • *Nightshade* • Laurell K. Hamilton
#25 • *Grounded* • David Bischoff
#26 • *The Romulan Prize* • Simon Hawke
#27 • *Guises of the Mind* • Rebecca Neason
#28 • *Here There Be Dragons* • John Peel
#29 • *Sins of Commission* • Susan Wright
#30 • *Debtor's Planet* • W.R. Thompson
#31 • *Foreign Foes* • Dave Galanter & Greg Brodeur
#32 • *Requiem* • Michael Jan Friedman & Kevin Ryan
#33 • *Balance of Power* • Dafydd ab Hugh
#34 • *Blaze of Glory* • Simon Hawke
#35 • *The Romulan Stratagem* • Robert Greenberger
#36 • *Into the Nebula* • Gene DeWeese
#37 • *The Last Stand* • Brad Ferguson
#38 • *Dragon's Honor* • Kij Johnson & Greg Cox
#39 • *Rogue Saucer* • John Vornholt
#40 • *Possession* • J.M. Dillard & Kathleen O'Malley
#41 • *Invasion! #2: The Soldiers of Fear* • Dean Wesley Smith & Kristine Kathryn Rusch
#42 • *Infiltrator* • W.R. Thompson

#43 • *A Fury Scorned* • Pamela Sargent & George Zebrowski
#44 • *The Death of Princes* • John Peel
#45 • *Intellivore* • Diane Duane
#46 • *To Storm Heaven* • Esther Friesner
#47-49 • *The Q Continuum* • Greg Cox
    #47 • *Q-Space*
    #48 • *Q-Zone*
    #49 • *Q-Strike*
#50 • *Dyson Sphere* • Charles Pellegrino & George Zebrowski
#51-56 • *Double Helix*
    #51 • *Infection* • John Gregory Betancourt
    #52 • *Vectors* • Dean Wesley Smith & Kristine Kathryn Rusch
    #53 • *Red Sector* • Diane Carey
    #54 • *Quarantine* • John Vornholt
    #55 • *Double or Nothing* • Peter David
    #56 • *The First Virtue* • Michael Jan Friedman & Christie Golden
#57 • *The Forgotten War* • William R. Forstchen
#58-59 • *Gemworld* • John Vornholt
    #58 • *Gemworld #1*
    #59 • *Gemworld #2*
#60 • *Tooth and Claw* • Doranna Durgin
#61 • *Diplomatic Implausibility* • Keith R.A. DeCandido
#62-63 • *Maximum Warp* • Dave Galanter & Greg Brodeur
    #62 • *Dead Zone*
    #63 • *Forever Dark*

**Star Trek: Deep Space Nine®**

    *Warped* • K.W. Jeter
    *Legends of the Ferengi* • Ira Steven Behr & Robert Hewitt Wolfe
Novelizations
    *Emissary* • J.M. Dillard
    *The Search* • Diane Carey
    *The Way of the Warrior* • Diane Carey
    *Star Trek: Klingon* • Dean Wesley Smith & Kristine Kathryn Rusch
    *Trials and Tribble-ations* • Diane Carey
    *Far Beyond the Stars* • Steve Barnes
    *What You Leave Behind* • Diane Carey

#1 • *Emissary* • J.M. Dillard
#2 • *The Siege* • Peter David
#3 • *Bloodletter* • K.W. Jeter
#4 • *The Big Game* • Sandy Schofield
#5 • *Fallen Heroes* • Dafydd ab Hugh
#6 • *Betrayal* • Lois Tilton
#7 • *Warchild* • Esther Friesner
#8 • *Antimatter* • John Vornholt
#9 • *Proud Helios* • Melissa Scott
#10 • *Valhalla* • Nathan Archer
#11 • *Devil in the Sky* • Greg Cox & John Gregory Betancourt
#12 • *The Laertian Gamble* • Robert Sheckley
#13 • *Station Rage* • Diane Carey
#14 • *The Long Night* • Dean Wesley Smith & Kristine Kathryn Rusch
#15 • *Objective: Bajor* • John Peel
#16 • *Invasion! #3: Time's Enemy* • L.A. Graf
#17 • *The Heart of the Warrior* • John Gregory Betancourt

#18 • *Saratoga* • Michael Jan Friedman
#19 • *The Tempest* • Susan Wright
#20 • *Wrath of the Prophets* • David, Friedman & Greenberger
#21 • *Trial by Error* • Mark Garland
#22 • *Vengeance* • Dafydd ab Hugh
#23 • *The 34th Rule* • Armin Shimerman & David R. George III
#24-26 • *Rebels* • Dafydd ab Hugh
    #24 • *The Conquered*
    #25 • *The Courageous*
    #26 • *The Liberated*

Books set after the series
    *The Lives of Dax* • Marco Palmieri, ed.
    *Millennium* • Judith and Garfield Reeves-Stevens
        #1 • *The Fall of Terok Nor*
        #2 • *The War of the Prophets*
        #3 • *Inferno*
    *A Stitch in Time* • Andrew J. Robinson
    *Avatar, Book One* • S.D. Perry
    *Avatar, Book Two* • S.D. Perry
    *Section 31: Abyss:* • David Weddle & Jeffrey Lang
    *Gateways #4: Demons of Air and Darkness* • Keith R.A. DeCandido
    *Gateways #7: What Lay Beyond:* "Horn and Ivory" • Keith R.A. DeCandido

**Star Trek: Voyager®**

    *Mosaic* • Jeri Taylor
    *Pathways* • Jeri Taylor
    *Captain Proton: Defender of the Earth* • D.W. "Prof" Smith
Novelizations
    *Caretaker* • L.A. Graf
    *Flashback* • Diane Carey
    *Day of Honor* • Michael Jan Friedman
    *Equinox* • Diane Carey
    *Endgame* • Diane Carey & Christie Golden

#1 • *Caretaker* • L.A. Graf
#2 • *The Escape* • Dean Wesley Smith & Kristine Kathryn Rusch
#3 • *Ragnarok* • Nathan Archer
#4 • *Violations* • Susan Wright
#5 • *Incident at Arbuk* • John Gregory Betancourt
#6 • *The Murdered Sun* • Christie Golden
#7 • *Ghost of a Chance* • Mark A. Garland & Charles G. McGraw
#8 • *Cybersong* • S.N. Lewitt
#9 • *Invasion! #4: The Final Fury* • Dafydd ab Hugh
#10 • *Bless the Beasts* • Karen Haber
#11 • *The Garden* • Melissa Scott
#12 • *Chrysalis* • David Niall Wilson
#13 • *The Black Shore* • Greg Cox
#14 • *Marooned* • Christie Golden
#15 • *Echoes* • Dean Wesley Smith, Kristine Kathryn Rusch & Nina Kiriki Hoffman
#16 • *Seven of Nine* • Christie Golden
#17 • *Death of a Neutron Star* • Eric Kotani
#18 • *Battle Lines* • Dave Galanter & Greg Brodeur
#19-21 • *Dark Matters* • Christie Golden
    #19 • *Cloak and Dagger*

#20 • *Ghost Dance*
#21 • *Shadow of Heaven*

## Enterprise®

*Broken Bow* • Diane Carey
*By the Book* • Dean Wesley Smith & Kristine Kathryn Rusch

## Star Trek®: New Frontier

*New Frontier* #1-4 Collector's Edition • Peter David
  #1 • *House of Cards*
  #2 • *Into the Void*
  #3 • *The Two-Front War*
  #4 • *End Game*
#5 • *Martyr* • Peter David
#6 • *Fire on High* • Peter David
*The Captain's Table* #5 • *Once Burned* • Peter David
*Double Helix* #5 • *Double or Nothing* • Peter David
#7 • *The Quiet Place* • Peter David
#8 • *Dark Allies* • Peter David
#9-11 • *Excalibur* • Peter David
   #9 • *Requiem*
  #10 • *Renaissance*
  #11 • *Restoration*
*Gateways* #6: *Cold Wars* • Peter David
*Gateways* #7: *What Lay Beyond:* "Death After Life" • Peter David
#12 • *Being Human* • Peter David

## Star Trek®: Stargazer

*The Valiant* • Michael Jan Friedman
*Double Helix* #6: *The First Virtue* • Michael Jan Friedman and Christie Golden
*Gauntlet* • Michael Jan Friedman
*Progenitor* • Michael Jan Friedman

## Star Trek®: Starfleet Corps of Engineers (eBooks)

*Have Tech, Will Travel* (paperback) • various
  #1 • *The Belly of the Beast* • Dean Wesley Smith
  #2 • *Fatal Error* • Keith R.A. DeCandido
  #3 • *Hard Crash* • Christie Golden
  #4 • *Interphase, Book One* • Dayton Ward & Kevin Dilmore
*Miracle Workers* (paperback) • various
  #5 • *Interphase, Book Two* • Dayton Ward & Kevin Dilmore
  #6 • *Cold Fusion* • Keith R.A. DeCandido
  #7 • *Invincible, Book One* • Keith R.A. DeCandido & David Mack
  #8 • *Invincible, Book Two* • Keith R.A. DeCandido & David Mack
  #9 • *The Riddled Post* • Aaron Rosenberg
#10 • *Gateways Epilogue: Here There Be Monsters* • Keith R.A. DeCandido
#11 • *Ambush* • Dave Galanter & Greg Brodeur
#12 • *Some Assembly Required* • Scott Ciencin & Dan Jolley
#13 • *No Surrender* • Jeff Mariotte
#14 • *Caveat Emptor* • Ian Edginton
#15 • *Past Life* • Robert Greenberger
#16 • *Oaths* • Glenn Hauman
#17 • *Foundations, Book One* • Dayton Ward & Kevin Dilmore

**Star Trek®: Invasion!**

#1 • *First Strike* • Diane Carey
#2 • *The Soldiers of Fear* • Dean Wesley Smith & Kristine Kathryn Rusch
#3 • *Time's Enemy* • L.A. Graf
#4 • *The Final Fury* • Dafydd ab Hugh
*Invasion! Omnibus* • various

**Star Trek®: Day of Honor**

#1 • *Ancient Blood* • Diane Carey
#2 • *Armageddon Sky* • L.A. Graf
#3 • *Her Klingon Soul* • Michael Jan Friedman
#4 • *Treaty's Law* • Dean Wesley Smith & Kristine Kathryn Rusch
*The Television Episode* • Michael Jan Friedman
*Day of Honor Omnibus* • various

**Star Trek®: The Captain's Table**

#1 • *War Dragons* • L.A. Graf
#2 • *Dujonian's Hoard* • Michael Jan Friedman
#3 • *The Mist* • Dean Wesley Smith & Kristine Kathryn Rusch
#4 • *Fire Ship* • Diane Carey
#5 • *Once Burned* • Peter David
#6 • *Where Sea Meets Sky* • Jerry Oltion
*The Captain's Table Omnibus* • various

**Star Trek®: The Dominion War**

#1 • *Behind Enemy Lines* • John Vornholt
#2 • *Call to Arms...* • Diane Carey
#3 • *Tunnel Through the Stars* • John Vornholt
#4 • *...Sacrifice of Angels* • Diane Carey

**Star Trek®: Section 31™**

*Rogue* • Andy Mangels & Michael A. Martin
*Shadow* • Dean Wesley Smith & Kristine Kathryn Rusch
*Cloak* • S.D. Perry
*Abyss* • Dean Weddle & Jeffrey Lang

**Star Trek®: Gateways**

#1 • *One Small Step* • Susan Wright
#2 • *Chainmail* • Diane Carey
#3 • *Doors Into Chaos* • Robert Greenberger
#4 • *Demons of Air and Darkness* • Keith R.A. DeCandido
#5 • *No Man's Land* • Christie Golden
#6 • *Cold Wars* • Peter David
#7 • *What Lay Beyond* • various
*Epilogue: Here There Be Monsters* • Keith R.A. DeCandido

**Star Trek®: The Badlands**

#1 • Susan Wright
#2 • Susan Wright

**Star Trek®: Dark Passions**

#1 • Susan Wright
#2 • Susan Wright

**Star Trek® Omnibus Editions**

*Invasion! Omnibus* • various
*Day of Honor Omnibus* • various
*The Captain's Table Omnibus* • various
*Star Trek: Odyssey* • William Shatner with Judith and Garfield Reeves-Stevens
*Millennium Omnibus* • Judith and Garfield Reeves-Stevens
*Starfleet: Year One* • Michael Jan Friedman

**Other Star Trek® Fiction**

*Legends of the Ferengi* • Ira Steven Behr & Robert Hewitt Wolfe
*Strange New Worlds*, vol. I, II, III, IV, and V • Dean Wesley Smith, ed.
*Adventures in Time and Space* • Mary P. Taylor, ed.
*Captain Proton: Defender of the Earth* • D.W. "Prof" Smith
*New Worlds, New Civilizations* • Michael Jan Friedman
*The Lives of Dax* • Marco Palmieri, ed.
*The Klingon Hamlet* • Wil'yam Shex'pir
*Enterprise Logs* • Carol Greenburg, ed.